Chasing Shadows

By Ashley Townsend

Ink Smith Publishing
www.ink-smith.com

ISBN: 978-1-939156-57-0

Ink Smith Publishing
710 S. Mrytle Ave Suite 209
Monrovia, CA, 91016

Dedications:

To Pinterest, Rock Band, and my awesome friend Watson for providing distractions when I had writer's block, and to Joe-Bear for making my first caramel macchiato and for fueling my caffeine addiction since—to coffee and chocolate, for loving me as much as I love them. Also, thank you to the Ink Smith team for letting me hold this story in my hands (I *never* thought that would happen), and to Roan Carter for designing a cover that I constantly drool over.

And to my first fan, who loves these characters like I do and encouraged me every step of the way. Sarah B., this is all for you, and never forget what amazing adventures God has in store for your future ... and, if you're like my Sarah, your past.

Chasing Shadows

~Chapter 1~

"The king is dead. You have to come back."

Sarah repeated the words over and over in her head, trying to make sense of them. She stared at the redhead standing on her doorstep in jeans and a T-shirt, struck speechless by her sudden appearance. A million thoughts flew through her head as she looked at Karen's expectant face, awaiting her reaction to the news. Karen didn't speak; she just waited, shifting nervously under Sarah's stupefied gaze.

It was impossible—she had to be seeing things. The stress of preparing for college had finally gotten to her, and her muddled brain was tricking her into thinking that Karen was standing in front of her house—in Oklahoma of all places!

But did apparitions speak? Because this one certainly had a moment ago.

Sarah swallowed. She had worked so hard to forget about the past, telling herself that she'd imagined everything—taking a side-trip to the twelfth century, running from a masked murderer, nearly being burned alive with the mysterious blacksmith who had stolen her heart. And then when those vivid memories became impossible to explain away, Sarah convinced herself that maybe if she kept the remembrances hidden for long enough, then she would forget about everything and everyone. She kept those memories tucked away deep inside her, in the place where she saved all the truths she wanted to pretend didn't exist in order to preserve her heart.

Deep down, though, she knew it was all true. There would always be those secret memories that she'd tried so hard to hide gnawing at her conscience, reminding her of those she left behind. Karen's unexpected presence at her door only served to confirm the fact that Sarah hadn't imagined a thing. It also forced her to face the guilt she'd managed to overlook with excuses she knew were worthless.

1

Sarah shook her head at the irony of it all. Not ten minutes before she opened the door, she had almost managed to convince herself that she had moved on and left former days where they belonged—in the *past*. She had a sickening feeling that all of that was about to change.

"Are you all right?" Her friend's quiet question broke the bonds holding her tongue, and her mind cleared enough for her to come up with a semi-intelligent response.

"Seriously?" Sarah asked, her tone dripping with incredulous sarcasm. To relieve nervous energy, she mindlessly rubbed her thumb over the jagged scar on the back of her hand, forcing aside the memory of Will's relief when she fought against the poisonous wound and had at last opened her eyes to find him watching over her.

Red hair swished as Karen risked a quick glance over her shoulder. She turned back to Sarah, her green eyes reluctant. "Is there somewhere private where we could discuss this?" She seemed to have calmed slightly since Sarah had opened the door, though her pale face was still strained with obvious trepidation.

"What, you think someone followed you from the twelfth century?" Sarah's astonishment over the situation had not diminished her sense of humor, or the lilt of sarcasm her words carried.

"You can never be too careful," was Karen's response. Sarah noticed that she truly looked worried about whatever danger was after her, real or otherwise.

Sighing, Sarah inclined her head toward the front door of her house. "We can talk in my room."

"Is anyone else inside?"

Sarah looked at her in confusion. "Well, my mom's here, but no one else."

Karen bit her lower lip in indecision, and Sarah could almost see the wheels in her head turning. "I guess we could sneak in through the back."

Sarah's mouth hung open. "You can't be serious. Come on, just follow my lead." She turned the knob and motioned for Karen to follow her inside. She did so, though her reluctance was almost humorous; one would think she was headed for the execution stand rather than the Matthews' entryway.

Karen stopped in the doorway to the kitchen and remained frozen there. When she refused to budge, Sarah sighed and turned to her mom, who was bent over the granite countertops with her back to them, humming lightly as she kneaded a ball of dough.

"Mom?"

She continued to knead the dough into submission, keeping her eyes on her work. "Mmm?"

"Um, this is my friend, Karen Ashmore." She knew the introduction would get her mom's attention.

Dana Matthews straightened suddenly and dusted her hands off on the front of her yellow- and blue-checkered apron as she turned around to greet the newcomer. The smile she gave Karen was genuine and warm.

"Hi, Karen. It's nice to meet you." Her mom's slight Alabama accent was always more pronounced at times when she was demonstrating some of that famous southern hospitality, like she was now. Even after spending all her married life in Oklahoma, her drawl still managed to sneak into her speech, and that accent combined with her sweet smile immediately endeared her to most.

Although her mom adored their state of residence, Sarah had never really felt like she belonged in Oklahoma. She couldn't shake the feeling that there was something bigger out there for her than a simple life in a simple town. As a kid, she'd fantasized that there was some life-changing adventure awaiting her in the future, which was why she had agreed to assist Karen in her quest to stop the king's murderer.

Sarah's grin turned to a grimace as Karen's words came back to mind, reminding her that they hadn't stopped King Josiah's killer, after all. But she was only one girl. What more could she do?

"Would you like to stay for dinner, Karen?" Her mom's words caused Sarah's mind to settle on the present. "I'm making chili and corn bread. Cinnamon rolls for dessert," she sing-songed enticingly.

"No, I don't think I can. Thank you, though." Karen spoke quietly and actually appeared shy, an emotion that Sarah had never before seen on her candid friend.

"We're going to hang out in my room for a while, 'kay, Mom?"

Dana frowned, and a deep wrinkle appeared over the bridge of her nose. It was the only one on her youthful face that Sarah took proud ownership of, sure it was the product of countless discussions about cleaning her room. Her mom raised an eyebrow in question. "Are you sure that's safe as far as health codes go?"

Sarah laughed at the way her mom said it, though she was being completely serious.

"We'll be fine," she said, turning toward the doorway where Karen waited. "And if anything tries to eat us, we'll be sure to scream." She could hear her mom chuckle behind them as they made their way down the hallway.

"We don't have much time," Karen whispered the instant they were out of earshot.

"We have a few minutes for you to give me some answers," Sarah replied firmly, pretending like she was in control. After the near-fiasco they'd previously experienced, she wanted to have all the facts before jumping with both feet into whatever plan Karen had in mind.

Karen was silent for a moment, though she appeared compliant.

"Where's Lilly?" she asked suddenly, referring to Sarah's younger sister.

"Oh, um, she's sleeping over at a friend's house tonight." Her stomach knotted guiltily when she remembered that it was her fault Lilly didn't know Karen existed. She had done what she assumed was best for her sister by allowing Lilly to believe that their trip to Serimone had been a dream. It was bad enough that one of them had to live with the reminder of another life; she didn't want her little sister to get hung up on the past, too.

They made their way slowly down the hall, the walls of which were lined with a myriad of family pictures. Karen passed them slowly, seeming to absorb the details and stories behind each photograph. She stopped before a large collage frame on the right wall and stared at the one of Sarah dressed in her cap and gown with her dad's parents at her high school graduation. She held her diploma in one hand and hugged her grandma's side with the other. She was smiling victoriously, and her grandparents both looked as proud as her parents had that day.

Below that were two photos situated side by side, and Sarah watched, curious, as her friend's gaze took in each photo. The first was a picture taken last January. Lilly and Sarah stood on either side of their dad in the front yard, knee-deep in fluffy white snow. They all had pink cheeks from the cold, but it hadn't bothered them in the least as they lined up for the picture. Their mom had snapped the photo just as their dad, ever the prankster, had smashed large fistfuls of snow onto his surprised daughters' heads. Sarah smiled as she always did when she looked at the photograph and remembered both her and Lilly's excitement over the first snow day that year.

Karen's unreadable gaze drifted to the next photo of the two Matthews sisters sitting Indian-style in Sarah's bedroom on her plush purple rug. Sarah, fifteen at the time, sat behind her sister and held a clump of the girl's brown hair as she coerced it into a braid. The sweet moment had turned into a humorous candid shot when Sarah crossed her eyes and stuck her tongue out of the side of her mouth, and with Lilly making a not-so-attractive fish-face at the camera.

"How long ago was this taken?" Karen asked quietly, never taking her eyes from the photo.

"Three years," Sarah answered. Her friend straightened and smiled slightly, though there seemed to be sadness in her eyes.

"Which one is your room?" she asked suddenly. Sarah decided not to probe Karen about her interest in the photos or the expression on her face when she looked at them. When she was ready to talk, she would.

Sarah led the way past her dad's closed study door and stepped into her doorway. Karen poked her head inside. Her surprise melted into a grin of amusement as she took in the mess.

"Why am I not surprised?" she asked, looking around at the dirty

4

clothes strewn about the floor, the empty and half-full boxes that littered the carpet and the unmade bed, and the piles of nick-knacks that took up whatever walking space remained. Sarah grimaced. It definitely wouldn't have hurt if she had picked up a little this morning.

Karen cocked her head to the side. "Not that I could find it in this disaster zone, anyway, but where did the purple rug go? The one in the picture, I mean."

Hooking her fingers through the belt loops on her shorts in a self-satisfied way, Sarah gave a wistful sigh. "Ah, yes. The great chocolate pudding incident of 2012. Good times." She frowned suddenly and added in self-defense, "And I was packing."

Karen started slightly, all amusement gone. "What for?"

"College," Sarah mumbled distractedly, looking over the catastrophe that was her room. "Maybe we should go to the backyard."

Karen shrugged. She seemed to be more at ease now, though Sarah could tell that her nonchalance was forced. They walked back down the hallway, and Sarah thought she caught Karen glancing at the pictures again as they passed.

Her mom must have heard them coming, because she called out to them from the kitchen, "Everyone still alive?"

"It's not that bad," Sarah muttered, then louder, "No hasmet team necessary. Just don't try and clean up while we're outside; I have everything organized." She didn't have to see her mom to know that she was rolling her eyes.

Sarah opened the sliding glass door leading to the backyard, and the two stepped out onto the cement patio. She led Karen past the wooden picnic table—littered with Lilly's unfinished summer project of partially constructed birdhouses—onto the lush grass, and to the cherry red swing set. Her dad owned a hardware store in town, and he had built and painted the wooden set when his girls were young. His workmanship had lasted through the years of weather and use, and Sarah still came out here when she needed a place to think or clear her head, which was more often than not, as of late.

Sitting down on one of the swings, she watched Karen take the seat next to her, and they used their feet to push themselves back and forth in silence. Sarah had learned to respect her friend's thoughtful nature and knew better than to force information from her; Karen would volunteer her thoughts when she was ready and not a moment sooner.

"You have a wonderful family." Her soft voice broke the quiet sounds of birds chattering in the trees.

Sarah smiled, wiggling her toes in the grass. "Yeah, they're pretty great." She glanced over at the other girl, stopping her swing when she saw the pensive look on her face. Karen allowed her swing to creak to a stop as well, though she didn't look at her.

"I guess it just made me realize that I missed out on all that stuff families do together," she admitted slowly, as though just coming to the conclusion herself. "I had never really thought that much about it before, but after my parents died, it was just me and the professor. I love Charles like a father, but it's not the same: there were no camping trips, no elaborate graduation ceremony, and I never got to braid my little sister's hair or get into a snowball fight because we were too busy working in dark basements on quantum physics and wormhole theories."

"What about the Joneses?" Sarah asked, trying to lighten her friend's mood with what she thought was an encouraging reminder. "Don't you consider them family?"

Karen stared at the back of the house, but didn't appear to really see it. She looked a thousand miles away. Or maybe it was a thousand years that gave her that distant look. "I do consider them family, in a way. But I still feel like . . . I don't know. I know that they love me, and I love them too, but it's just that we'll never really be a family. You know what I mean?"

Sarah did. Sort of. A sudden thought occurred to her. "Karen?" she asked slowly. "Do you think that if you and Seth got married, then they might seem more like an actual family?" Judging by the pained and slightly wistful look that crossed Karen's features, her query had merit.

"I can't honestly say that I haven't thought about it," she admitted, her green eyes once again focused on the grass under her feet. "Then it wouldn't just *feel* like we're a family, but we would actually be one. Legally, I mean."

"But isn't that what family's all about? Heart, not technicalities?"

Karen's smile was genuine as she looked into Sarah's eyes. "You know, you always seem to have the right words to say."

"Me?" Sarah stroked her chin thoughtfully. "I've never really considered myself much of a philosopher, but maybe I should change my major."

"Well, you sure made me feel better, and you see things differently than most people do." Karen grinned. "In a good way, of course. "

"Thanks," Sarah said quietly. The yard was silent except for the rustling of leaves in the light breeze as the girls set their swings in motion again, and Sarah had to bite her lip to keep from asking the one question that was burning her mind. She didn't have to wait long before the silence was shattered by the words she'd been hoping for.

"I know you're dying to ask me, so go ahead," Karen said without looking up, though there was a grin in her voice.

Sarah expelled the breath she hadn't realized she'd been holding, relieved to have an opening. "You know I'm glad to see you, but what exactly are you doing here?"

~Chapter 2~

"I already told you why I'm here."

Sarah's shoulders sank. "So the king is really dead?" She felt shocked that the king was actually gone. He was terribly sick when she'd left, but somehow she had expected him to survive the illness. It just seemed so surreal, especially since she hadn't been there when it happened.

"Three days ago," Karen answered solemnly. "Queen Meredith and the prince are really grieving over his passing, especially since they weren't allowed to see him in his last days—you know, because they weren't sure if it was contagious. I heard the physician declared that it was the illness that took him, but I still think it was foul play."

Sarah hesitated. "You mean you still believe his brother Cadius poisoned him?"

"I *know* he's responsible for his death, but I don't know how to prove it. That's why I need your help."

Sarah shook her head at the ridiculous idea. "What on earth can I possibly do to help you from here? I was useless last time, remember?"

Karen remained silent for a long time, her expression pained and regretful. "You know I wouldn't ask this of you if there were anyone else."

Sarah stood abruptly, setting the swing in motion. "You're seriously asking me to come back?" The words were whispered in disbelief. Emotions raged within her; excitement, surprise, fear, guilt. When Karen had appeared on her doorstep and said she needed to come back, Sarah had been too surprised to take her seriously. But now that the request was presented to her again, she knew Karen was dead-set on having her help.

Karen's eyes pleaded for her to understand. "I told you, if there was anyone else—"

"But what about Seth?" she asked desperately. "He has to be a better choice than me. He can help you."

Karen shook her head. "I don't want him to get involved."

"But you don't mind me risking my life?"

"No, of course I do." Karen heaved a gusty sigh of frustration, lifting her bangs off her forehead. "It's just that you're already involved in all of this, so I didn't want to include anyone else. Seth doesn't know half of what

I've done. He doesn't even know my theory about the king being poisoned, and I would like to keep it that way."

This caused Sarah to pause. Karen's reasoning made sense, and she also felt a responsibility to her friend to see this through.

Sarah shook her head and mimicked Karen's heavy sigh. "How did you even get here?" She had thought that the time watch was broken, or faulty at best.

"It gained enough energy to get me back to the lab so I could fix it."

Sarah stared at her for a long moment and then her gaze drifted to her wrist. The sleek, numberless black face of the watch contrasted against Karen's fair skin. Sarah wondered how she had missed it before. "So it's really fixed?"

Karen nodded her head. She stood, reached into the front pocket of her jeans, and held something out to her. Sarah took it in her hand, taken aback, and slid her thumb over the smooth silver band of the watch.

"This one is yours," Karen said, suddenly sounding unsure of herself. "I made some improvements to the watch that the professor and I had planned on before everything went south. This new model is waterproof, so we won't be having any accidental trips to the past," she added with a grin. "It also has a larger storage capacity for GPS memory, too."

"So that's how you found out where I live?" There always seemed to be a surprise around each corner. Sarah suddenly felt like she was back at the loft in the Joneses' barn that first night, remembering Karen's explanation of the inner workings of the watch and how she had inadvertently pulled them back in time. Sarah recalled that night with perfect clarity, and with that memory came others. She didn't want to dwell on those thoughts for too long and instead focused her attention back on Karen.

"Do you remember when we sent Lilly back that last time without her wearing a watch?" Sarah nodded slowly, wondering what she was getting at. "Well, I used coordinates to send her back, since we couldn't give her our only watch to take back with her. It was kind of wishful thinking on my part, since the watch *technically* never worked like that with such minimal power."

Her eyes brightened like it always did when she spoke of the invention, and she went on. "It uses up a lot of battery power to transfer a person using GPS coordinates, so it can be . . . dangerous if handled improperly." Sarah's eyes widened, and Karen hurried to explain. "I was cautious, I promise. She either would have been wholly sent back, or nothing would have happened—no getting stuck in the in-between, I swear."

Sarah exhaled. "Okay, go on."

"Well, it should have occurred to me sooner, but the watch never had the capability to throw coordinates before it took a swim. After you left the same way Lilly did, I realized the implications of what must have occurred in the infrastructure of the watch when water permeated the mechanism that allows us to travel between times."

Sarah held up her hand, sensing that the other girl was about to go into one of her scientific rants that would undoubtedly lose her completely. She couldn't help but grin, though, at her friend's enthusiasm over dropping the watch in a *puddle*. "You're going to have to slow it down with the wormholes and scientific theories stuff." She jerked her thumb toward her chest. "Barely made it through high school science."

Karen actually laughed at this, causing Sarah to smile. It felt good to have a more light-hearted topic.

"Okay," Karen conceded, a slight grin still on her face. "Basically, I realized that the watch was able to store and focus GPS coordinates—sort of like throwing them across the room at a specific object or person. When the watch got waterlogged last time and brought you and Lilly back, it registered only the last coordinates that it pulled someone from. I just followed the trail back to you, and then it gave me the idea to alter the storing process on the sort of 'motherboard' for the watches. Thus, here I am."

Slowly, her smile faded. "I wouldn't have come for you unless I truly needed your help, but there's no one else I can trust to help me stop Cadius from becoming king. And we have to go back before too much time passes there."

Sarah bit her lip, still having difficulty believing that any of this was happening. A part of her wanted to go with Karen without a backward glance and have another adventure, regardless of the consequences. But the more logical side of her held her back from throwing caution to the wind. She shook her head. "But won't Prince Adrian become king now? I mean, isn't that how it works?"

Karen was silent for almost a full minute before she spoke. "That's part of what I'm afraid of. If Cadius was able to so easily kill his own brother for the throne, I don't think he will have much of a problem dealing with the next obstacle in his way. It's becoming harder for me to sneak around unnoticed, since some people believe I'm a witch who escaped a deserved fate." She cringed. "Not that many people were there when Dunlivey arrested me, but it's starting to get more risky for me to go into town if someone recognizes me. That's why I need your help."

"What about the Shadow?" Sarah asked anxiously, though the words were hard to say. Part of the reason she had such a hard time complying with Karen's request was because of the way she had left, but more specifically, who she had left behind.

Karen shrugged. "He disappeared almost four months ago. No one has been able to find him, and believe me, they've tried. Both to kill him *and* to get his help."

Sarah's blue eyes jerked up, staring at Karen as though she were crazy. Four months? That wasn't possible.

"But he saved you from the dungeons a few weeks ago," she said, finding her voice. "I remember you telling me the story. And I saw him just before I left, so there's no possible way he's been missing for that long. I've only been back a few weeks!"

Karen appeared surprised and then her eyes softened in sympathy. "Technically, you left Serimone a little over four months ago. I told you a while ago that when you travel back and forth, the continuity between time in the real world and wherever we disappear to isn't consistent; they aren't parallel to each other or linear, like time zones, and it's impossible to say how time passes in one world while we're in another."

Sarah remembered a conversation like that, but vaguely. How could it have been such a short time for her and so long for the others? Then she recalled Karen's words about the Shadow's lengthy absence and gnawed on her lower lip. Gone for several months? She couldn't believe that anything would prevent Will from his self-appointed duties as the elusive protector of Serimone.

Her breathing stilled for a fleeting moment of alarm. Had something happened to Will? She almost shook her head at the absurd thought. Though Karen didn't know Will's secret, she did know how Sarah felt about him and would have told her if he were in danger. Wouldn't she?

Karen was motioning with her hand to the watch Sarah clung to absentmindedly. "I still have no idea how exactly the lapse in time between our world adjusts, but when I modified the watch, somehow it seems to have slowed the rate of time in your world."

Sarah wrinkled her brow, trying to follow as she pulled her thoughts to the present. "So time in the other place has always moved faster?"

Karen lifted her shoulders in a shrug. "I don't know, exactly. I'm not a scientist, but it seems like use of the time watches affects how time flows between worlds." She began to use her hands animatedly as she tried to convey her ideas to Sarah. "Maybe using them speeds things up when we go to the past, or maybe when we travel back to the present, we get dumped close to the same instant we left. It's just a theory, though."

"Or it could be like moving through molasses when we jump a thousand years," Sarah added absentmindedly. "Like it slows us down when we're trapped in the in-between world or space-time continuum, or something."

Karen's hand stilled mid-motion, and she was grinning. "Who's the scientist now?"

Rolling her eyes to disguise her own grin, Sarah retorted, "Well, I read a lot of sci-fi, so my ideas are mostly based in fiction."

"Then come back with me and decide for yourself," Karen urged, suddenly serious again. "You know I would never ask this of you if there were someone else. Please, Sarah, I really need your help." Karen's earnest plea hit its mark, though Sarah was still hesitant to agree.

"But what can two teenage girls do about a medieval tyrant?"

"Two teenage girls that can travel through time," Karen amended, eyes twinkling as she waved her wrist in the air.

Sarah smiled reluctantly. "Yeah, how could I forget?" She sucked in a deep breath, staring at her legs as she spoke. "Is there a guarantee that I can get back?"

She could hear the surprise and relief in Karen's voice. "So long as we keep our watches with us."

"How long would we be gone for?"

When Karen didn't answer, she glanced over at her. Karen pressed her lips into a thin white line. "Like I said, I can't say for certain. I know it's a lot to ask of you. You probably thought that you would never have to come back, and you don't—the choice is up to you."

Sarah let her eyes wander the backyard for several long moments, wondering what she should do. Though she was still intimidated by the prospect of facing whatever, and *whoever,* awaited her, she still felt this crazy, desperate need to flee from the stress of real life for a time. Maybe she was being impulsive, since most normal girls would just go to the mall for an afternoon reprieve, but this seemed like as good an excuse as any to escape. Besides, Sarah had never fallen into the "normal" category.

Karen, seeming to sense that she needed time to process everything, remained silent while Sarah weighed the pros and cons in her head. What better way to forget about real life than to immerse herself in a life of the past?

"Fine," she said at last.

Karen started. "Fine?"

"Fine, I'll go back with you."

Karen visibly brightened. "Really?"

"Yes, but I can't give you any guarantees. If things are really bad or we get into trouble, I think we should just abandon ship, regardless of whether or not the real killer is put away. That's my one condition, but it's a deal breaker."

Karen hesitated briefly, and then nodded her head in acquiescence. "Okay. I can live with that. Then we will have tried our best."

Sarah nodded. "I guess we should go, then, huh?"

Karen watched her intently for a moment, looking like she was trying to read the feelings she was hiding. "You don't have to do this, you know. You have a choice."

Sarah nodded her head, suddenly reminded of a conversation she'd had with Will about choices. She wasn't sure if she was making the right one, though she tried not to dwell on that for too long as she fastened the sleek watch around her wrist.

"No, I've made my decision. Now let's go before I change my mind and start to question my sanity."

Karen actually smiled slightly as they left the swings and stepped onto the patio. "What are you going to tell your mom?" she whispered.

Sarah shrugged, sounding more certain of herself than she felt. "I'll just tell her that I'm staying over at your house, which *technically* I will be." She took a deep breath and pulled the door open, making her way into the kitchen and sending up a silent prayer that all would go as planned.

Her mom was just shutting the oven door when they entered the kitchen. Sarah took an appreciative sniff of the sweet aroma that permeated the room before clearing her throat to get her mom's attention. She glanced over her shoulder at them and smiled.

"Hey, girls. If you don't mind waiting, I'll have some treats coming out of the oven for you to taste in a little bit."

"Um, no, that's okay," Sarah began. "I mean, they smell great, but I was wondering if I could spend the night at Karen's house? You know, one last *hoorah* before school starts."

"Oh." Sarah tried to not feel guilty over the dismal look that crossed her mom's features. She knew her mom wanted to spend every last second Sarah had left at home together, especially since it was just the two of them tonight.

"I mean, we could camp out in my room." Sarah spoke with calculated slowness.

Her mom made an obvious effort to paste on a brave smile. "Honey, it would be a crime to sleep in a room that the W.H.O. wouldn't go into, even if they could find some new species of bacteria to study."

Sarah rolled her eyes, but was unable to contain her grin. "Ha-ha. Very funny."

Her mom's smile was more genuine now, though a hint of nostalgia still hung in her blue eyes. "Of course you can go. Have fun."

"Thanks." Sarah hugged her mom for longer than a typical goodbye required. She pulled away reluctantly and saw the tears that pooled in her mom's eyes, though she quickly blinked them away.

"It was nice meeting you, Mrs. Matthews," Karen said, speaking for the first time since they had reentered the house.

Sarah's mom smiled. "You are welcome here anytime, sweetie. Give me a call if you girls need anything."

"We will, Mom." Sarah sent a small wave over her shoulder as they walked to the front door. She hoped her mom wouldn't notice that she didn't bring an overnight bag.

The two girls stood just outside the front door. "So, what exactly are we supposed to do now?" Sarah asked, shoving her hands into the pockets of her shorts and rocking back on her heels. She let her gaze wander the yard and stiffened.

Her sister Lilly stood frozen in open-mouthed shock on the pathway leading up to the house, pointing with a trembling hand. Her wide eyes were fixed on Karen. "But you—how—"

"Hi, Lilly!" Karen greeted brightly, looking like nothing were amiss.

Oh no, Sarah inwardly moaned. This had seriously come back to bite her in the seat meat. Walking forward slowly, she held up her hands as if she were moving toward a startled kitten. "Don't freak out, Lil."

Lilly's swallow was audible, and she stuttered unintelligibly until she at last managed to shriek, "Holy cow!" Then she skipped excitedly past Sarah and started doing that hunched-shoulders dance she did whenever she was positively giddy, fingers jabbing the air to punctuate her excitement. "It was all true! Holy smokes, this is awesome!"

She stopped suddenly, oblivious to Sarah's grimace and the way Karen balked at the gleeful girl. "I have to tell someone. This kind of stuff doesn't happen everyday. *I traveled through time!*" Lilly giggled, seemingly on cloud nine. So much for the heavy guilt Sarah had been harboring for weeks.

"Whoah, hold up there." Sarah gripped her sister's shoulders to still her jittering, needing her full attention. "Lil, you can't tell anyone about this."

The younger girl laughed, as though the idea were absurd. Then she gaped at her sibling's grave expression. "You can't be serious."

"Dead serious. Nobody can know about this."

Lilly's excited gaze darted between the two girls. "You're going back, aren't you? Can I come? I just walked back for my toothbrush. Give me two seconds." She made a move for the house, but Sarah held her back.

She cringed, knowing her sister wouldn't like what she had to say. "You can't come with this time."

Crestfallen, Lilly whined, "But why not? I can sleep over at Kacey's another night." She threw her arms wide and practically yelled, "We're defying gravity! Or whatever!"

Sighing, Sarah wiped her sweaty palms against her shorts. She would *not* miss the heat, that's for sure. "You just can't." She held up her hands in self-defense at Lilly's suspicious glare. "I know that's a lame excuse, but it's too dangerous to bring you along again if I don't have to. Hopefully, I'll be back before anyone has a chance to miss me, but just *promise* me you won't make a peep to mom or anyone else." Lilly chewed on her lip, and Sarah narrowed her eyes. Her sister wasn't exactly known for sealed lips.

"I'm serious."

Lilly's shoulders sagged. She kicked a pebble and watched it skitter down the path. "Okay, fine," she huffed dejectedly. "But it really stinks to be left behind. Nothing exciting ever happens here."

Pulling her in for a hug, Sarah exhaled. "I know, Kiddo. I know. But I promise to bring back stories."

"Can I at least write about it in my diary?"

Sarah leaned back to shoot her a look, and Lilly backed toward the door. "Fine, but I expect really great stories if I have to keep my mouth shut. And tell Leah I say 'hi.'"

Sarah smiled. "Deal." She suddenly wondered how long it would be until she saw her baby sister again and swallowed. "I love you, Kiddo."

Brow furrowing nervously, Lilly said, "But you'll be back soon, right? You promised."

"Yeah." Sarah nodded her head decisively. "I'll always come back." Her sister looked relieved by the oath, but realization twisted Sarah's insides. She was forever destined to live in Bethany, Oklahoma—maybe as a wife, or she might someday manage the pet store in the small town. But she would always return to her normal life and leave the extraordinary behind.

Karen, who had relaxed after the surprise of seeing Lilly's reaction, was grinning as she waved to the young girl and stepped off the porch. She motioned for Sarah to follow and leaned in close as they walked briskly along the sidewalk.

"Is there anywhere that is kind of secluded around here?" she whispered.

Sarah thought for a minute. "Well, there's a park just around the corner. It has a lot of trees and overgrowth, but it's not exactly 'secluded.'"

Karen seemed to be considering it. "Does it have any public restrooms?"

Sarah squinted an eye, and the left side of her face scrunched in uncertainty. "Well, yeah, but . . ." Her voice trailed off as she took in Karen's hopeful expression. "Oh, no."

~Chapter 3~

"This is disgusting," Sarah mumbled, trying to hold her breath in the small room. She sidestepped a piece of toilet paper soaking in a small pool of water on the floor. At least, she hoped it was water.

Karen shrugged, seemingly unaffected by the smell and cramped quarters of the one room stall. Living in the twelfth century had seriously diminished her sense of smell. "I didn't want to use the watches in broad daylight. This seemed like our best option."

"I still think we could have done it in my room," Sarah replied stubbornly.

"*If* we could have gotten in, your mom would have known something was up. You remember what happened last time you came, don't you?"

Recalling the lightning and Richter scale quaking of her room, Sarah sucked in a breath. She immediately threw a hand over her mouth as the stench assailed her senses.

"Just hurry up before I gag." Her voice came out sounding nasal as she pinched the opening of her nose to ward off the smell. Karen grinned, pressed a button on the watch she wore, and grabbed Sarah's free hand.

The room suddenly flooded with white light, temporarily blinding them both. The metal toilet seat made a clanking noise as it jiggled from side to side as the room began to tremor. The slight shaking quickly increased to a dull rumble, and then the room began to quake dangerously.

Sarah didn't want to grab onto anything that she couldn't see in the restroom, so she planted her feet spread apart and held onto Karen's hand for dear life. The earth beneath them seemed to groan in protest as the floor continued to tremble, and Sarah's toes began to tingle, the sensation creeping over her body until it flooded every limb. Seconds seemed to stretch into minutes for the occupants of the cramped stall before the quaking lessened. The ground let out one last big shake that sent them both to their knees before everything stilled.

Sarah pulled her palms from the floor with an "*Ew!*" of disgust and scrambled up on shaky legs—God only knew what was on that floor. The bright light had disappeared, and she blinked rapidly until her eyes adjusted to their new surroundings. She blinked again, though nothing was wrong with her vision. Dry leaves crunched beneath her feet as she took a step back in astonishment.

They were in the forest again.

"It gets less shocking after a while," Karen said. Sarah turned and watched the redhead rise gracefully to her feet. She pulled a dried leaf out of her hair and smiled brightly, spreading her arms wide. "Welcome back."

Sarah looked around at the sparse woods and the trails littered with fallen leaves. All was quiet except for the wind as it rustled the highest branches of the trees.

"I can't believe it," Sarah breathed, completely in awe of what had just happened. She didn't care how many times she did that: time travel would never cease to amaze her.

She blinked up at the fading sun, shrouded by a canopy of gold, red, and brown, and wrapped her arms around her middle against the cool wind. "We just traveled back in time a thousand years. Again," she added in disbelief.

Karen laughed at her slack-jawed expression—now that they were back in her world, she seemed more at ease. She stepped lightly in front of Sarah and started down a long, narrow trail that wound around the trees, obviously expecting her to follow. Sarah jogged after her to catch up. "Where are we going?" she asked, still having a difficult time taking it all in, even though she had been through this before. Her eyes darted about the woods, soaking in every detail of the winter trees and cloudy sky.

"We have to go to the Joneses' to get changed into something more appropriate."

Sarah glanced down at her shorts and T-shirt. She shivered as a cool wind lifted her hair off her shoulders and blew it about her face. Changing was probably a wise idea.

"It all feels so surreal," she said, sure her voice expressed the wonder she felt over reappearing in the same forest that she and Lilly had emerged from a few weeks ago.

"What do you mean?" Karen asked, skipping over a thick branch in her path. She tilted her head to get a better look at Sarah as they walked.

She shrugged and let her gaze wander over their surroundings. "I don't know. It just seems strange. I thought I'd never have to come back here again, or even *get* to come back. I assumed the whole time traveling episode was just a one-time thing, and I expected the king to live through his illness, not be defeated by it. And I never imagined I'd get to see you again." She smiled fondly at her friend. "Although I am glad that happened. I was actually starting to miss you, as crazy as it sounds."

Karen laughed lightly, and the trees seemed to mimic the sound as it

16

echoed through the forest. "Gee, thanks. But I'm really the one who suffered. You'll recall I had to go a bit longer without your presence to brighten my days."

Sarah smiled contentedly. The light banter between friends felt good, and they lapsed into a companionable silence, playfully nudging one another with their shoulders. All Sarah's fears seemed to have melted away once the decision was made, and she traipsed through the forest with lighter steps.

The two young women eventually came to the end of the trail, and Sarah sucked in a breath as she stared at the modest two-story wood home. The sight of the house instantly flooded her with reminders of the laughter, tears, and every promise made during those days. One face in particular came to the forefront of her mind and caused the other images and memories to fade away, flooding her with warmth.

She shook her head to rid her mind of Will's memory before she became lost in fantasies of not so long ago.

Karen stepped in front of her and motioned with a hand for her to follow. Sarah trailed behind as they tromped through the tall golden grass and made a wide arc around the house, the dry brush making a *wisp*ing sound against her exposed legs.

"Is there a reason that we're sneaking around?" she asked quietly.

Karen glanced over her shoulder at her briefly. "I don't want them to see us before we change."

Sarah nodded in understanding, though Karen couldn't see her. They crept around the backside of the barn, and Karen peered around the corner, signaling that the coast was clear. They moved forward silently, and Karen pulled the large door opened. She glanced over her shoulder one last time before closing it behind them. Sarah welcomed the warmth of the building, glad for shelter from the cool temperature outside.

"You should think about joining a special ops group of the CIA," Sarah said, trying to lighten her friend's serious look. She received a grin for her effort.

"Let's see if we can find something to wear." Karen looked more relaxed than she had during their stealthy trek through the fields. Months of hiding out in this very barn seemed to have made her wary of being exposed on the other side of that door.

"I still can't believe how many dresses you have in here," Sarah remarked, tucking a wavy strand of auburn hair behind her ear as she leaned over the open trunk in the corner. She heard Karen laugh beside her.

"Go ahead and pick one," she urged.

Sarah looked through the jumble of dresses, taking in the array of colors and fabrics inside. One in particular caught her eye, and she snatched the visible corner of the dress and pulled it out to better examine it. The pale blue velvet was stunning, and Sarah sucked in an appreciative breath as she took in the intricate white detailing, scooped neckline, and white sash emphasizing the waist. The sleeves were fitted but flared around each wrist, which were adorned with the same white lace that decorated the neckline.

"You will look fantastic in that," Karen commented.

Sarah turned to look at her, unsure. "You really think so?"

Karen nodded her head enthusiastically before snatching a brown wool dress from the stack. "I'm gonna change. If that's the one, then go ahead and use any of the empty pens to put it on." Sarah nodded, and Karen made her way down the center aisle between the stalls, ducking into one and closing the door behind her.

Sarah stared at the dress for a moment longer before following the trail Karen had made across the hay-strewn floor and entering one of the empty stalls next to the goats. Not even bothering to remove her tennis shoes, she peeled her clothes off and shivered as the cool air hit her exposed skin. The pendant tapped against her chest when she moved, and she glanced down at it in surprise, having forgotten she'd hurriedly put it on when Karen rang her doorbell. What would Will think when he saw that she had kept it all this time?

Just let it go, Sarah reprimanded herself, shaking her head over how easily her thoughts turned to him. Forcing back whatever thoughts or memories might surface, she quickly pulled the dress over her head and let it fall gracefully to the floor. She made sure that the sleeves covered her watch before gathering her clothes in her arms and exiting the stall. The dress fit her slender curves and five-foot eight-inch frame perfectly. She couldn't help but wonder if Karen, who was a few inches shorter than her, had purchased this dress with her in mind.

She found Karen leaning over the trunk and sifting through the mass of clothing, her brown cloak swishing about her heels. Sarah walked up beside her and dropped her own clothing inside the trunk. Karen hardly seemed to notice as she continued her search.

"Aha!" she cried suddenly, startling Sarah. She pulled something out from the mass of dresses and proudly held before her a cape of the same blue as Sarah's dress.

"You'll need this to keep warm," she said, tossing it in Sarah's direction so she could close the trunk's lid with both hands. Sarah caught the cape and fingered the soft fabric for a moment, then draped it over her shoulders with a flourish. She wrapped the looped ends of the cape around the gold, button-shaped ornaments just below her collarbone on either side of the dress. Swaying back and forth, she smiled as the fabric swished from side to side. Her tennis shoes peeked out beneath the hem when she did so, but she didn't think anyone would really notice.

"If you're ready, then we can go." Sarah started and glanced up at

18

Karen, who was standing beside the barn door, her hand poised on the wood.

"What do you mean?" Sarah asked, her heart picking up a beat at her friend's words.

Karen stared at her oddly, as though the answer to her question were obvious. "To town, of course."

"Why do we need to go there?" Sarah asked casually, trying to hide her anxiety. She felt a confusing mixture of excitement and fear over the possibility that she might meet the one person whom she had neglected to say farewell to. She wanted so badly to see Will, but she also dreaded the anger that would most likely be directed at her over her abrupt departure. She just hoped that he hadn't lost his faith in her completely during her absence. But like they said, absence makes the heart grow fonder. . . .

Sarah shook her head to dispel the wishful thought. Maybe he hadn't even noticed she was gone.

"We can't exactly do any investigative work from the Joneses' barn," Karen said, forcing Sarah's mind back to the present conversation. Karen opened the door a crack and peered outside.

"We're good," she said quietly, pulling the door open just enough for them to slip through. She closed it and crouched low. Sarah mimicked her stance and awkwardly dashed to the edge of the woods. Though she felt ridiculous, she didn't dare question her friend's methods, since Karen had mastered the art of sneaking around undetected. An escaped "witch" could hardly run about town with a target painted on her back without picking up a few tricks along the way.

Once they entered the tree line, they both straightened and began walking briskly through the thicket. Sarah's legs were longer than Karen's, so she had no trouble keeping up with her clipped pace.

Sarah pushed a branch out of her way and was caught off-guard as it swung back to smack her in the face. She hastily swatted it away, accidentally slapping herself in the process. She loudly blew away a wad of dried leaves that had collected on her lips and watched Karen's retreating form, none the wiser. Feeling terribly awkward compared to Karen's graceful movements, she was grateful that her friend was unaware of her embarrassing gaffe. Sarah collected herself and silently pulled once-dry leaves from her mouth as she moved past the offending branch, giving it plenty of space.

"Isn't it a long way to town?" she asked, deciding to duck under the next branch rather than risk personal injury in her attempt to move it from her path.

Karen looked over at her and grinned, her green eyes sparkling. "I told Seth that I needed to go into town and had him hitch the wagon for me earlier. I left it somewhere around here. Pretty crafty, huh?"

19

"Then I guess you were really betting on me coming back with you."

Karen shrugged. "I was certainly hoping that was the case, but I would have understood if you couldn't. This isn't real life for you, and it's not your responsibility."

"I feel like it is," Sarah quietly replied. She spotted the wagon through the trees, pointing it out to her friend, and they stepped into the small clearing. The horses seemed agitated at being left alone for so long and pawed eagerly at the ground.

Climbing into the wagon seat beside her friend, Sarah inhaled a steadying breath, taking in the scent of pine and forest with it. She had forgotten how good the air smelled here. "I promised I'd help, and I will." She squared her shoulders. "Plus, I believe in you and know you're right about Cadius. I'm not quitting this time . . . unless, of course, our lives are in imminent peril," she was sure to add.

Karen's small smile was filled with gratitude. "But I would understand."

The corner of Sarah's mouth tipped. "I know you would."

With a nod of her head, Karen picked up the reins and urged the horses onto the road.

~Chapter 4~

Sarah was glad she'd thought to wear the cape; the air was crisp as they drove along the narrow road, and she resisted the urge to shiver against the freezing cold seat. They neared the edge of town, and she tried to keep her growing trepidation hidden. Karen would certainly ask her what was bothering her, and she didn't want to go into detail about the questions she didn't have answers for.

Maybe he won't even be in town, she told herself, trying to find comfort in the dismal words. How could she feel so conflicted about something that shouldn't have mattered in the first place?

Karen pulled the horses to a stop just outside of town, and Sarah's heart lurched anxiously at the sudden interruption. But Karen just slipped the oversized hood up to cover her striking red hair, tugging it down to shield her eyes. She seemed to move in painfully slow motion as she ensured her disguise was secure, taking her sweet time to tuck a few silken strands beneath the hood. Right knee bouncing and knuckles turning white as she clutched the edge of the bench seat, Sarah told her pulse to slow even as her anxiety mounted at the delay. She was desperate to keep moving and just get this afternoon *over* with.

Just as Sarah was getting ready to throw herself out of the wagon and run the rest of the way into town, Karen finally seemed content with her disguise and picked up the reins, urging the horses through the town gates. Letting out a pent-up breath, Sarah wriggled in her seat and told herself not to stress over events that might not even take place. But she couldn't keep herself from wondering what his reaction would be when they saw each other for the first time in months, though it had only been mere weeks for her. He might yell at her and question why she had left their friendship behind like she had. Or maybe he would be overjoyed that she was back and take her in his arms . . .

Sarah sucked in a breath and tried to keep her thoughts from running away with her. Karen tended to keep to the shadows when she was in town, anyway, so she really had no reason to fear a surprise encounter.

The wagon stopped suddenly, and she glanced up. Catching sight of the sign for the livery, her heartbeat resumed its erratic pace. "Seriously?" she muttered dryly.

"Don't you want to see him?" At the incredulity in her friend's voice, she turned to look at Karen and caught the confusion in her eyes. Sarah swallowed hard.

"It's just, um, we didn't exactly part on the best of terms." Well, that wasn't entirely true. The last time she had seen him, Will had practically spelled out his feelings for her by giving her the necklace she now had tucked into her dress. But she was unsure what the time apart had done to his opinion of her and was afraid to find out.

Karen's face registered understanding. Her eyes softened. "I had forgotten that you didn't tell him that you were leaving. But maybe that won't matter to him because he will be so happy to see you and fall madly in love with you all over again."

Sarah rolled her eyes, though she grinned at her friend's attempt to encourage her. "I told you, we're just friends."

"Yeah, right. Or maybe you're the Seth in his life and are completely unaware of the love burning inside of him."

Though she said it lightheartedly, Sarah could sense her discouragement.

"Well," Sarah began, sorry for the forlorn look on her friend's face, "if he never comes around to see what a gem he has in you, then who needs him? And then we can put glue in his shampoo or burn his house down."

Karen laughed outright at that. "That took an extreme turn."

With an innocent shrug, Sarah said, "I saw it in a music video once."

Smiling, Karen wrapped an arm around Sarah's shoulders and squeezed her in an appreciative hug. "Thanks for that weirdly supportive pep-talk." She pulled back and stared into Sarah's face, her expression playfully stern. "And you, missy, need to take your own advice and march in there with your head held high. You'll never know what's going to happen unless you get out of this wagon."

"But where are you going?"

Karen's arm fell from her shoulders. She sighed heavily and hopped down from the wagon, coming around to Sarah's side and waiting for her to step down before answering. "I'm going to see if I can spot the professor from the castle gate or near the back entrance. He might be able to give us some information that we can use."

"Isn't it dangerous for you to be wandering around outside the castle?" Sarah asked. She was sure her eyes reflected the concern she felt.

But Karen was already shaking her head. "My only real threat is Gabriel Dunlivey, but he had to step down from his position as captain of the guard now that Captain Quinn is back; no one has seen Dunlivey for a while, so hopefully he's too far under the radar to notice me." Karen tugged on her hood reassuringly. "And these days there's too much fear going around for people to look a stranger in the eyes for too long. I'll try to keep a low profile, though, just to be safe. When I find out anything, I'll come and get you and the horses. Maybe you can ask Will if he's heard anything?"

Sarah nodded, knowing that it was time for them to go their separate ways. Sucking in a breath, she walked toward the front door of the large building, silently humming the death march. Karen called her name, and she glanced over her shoulder.

"I dare him to stay mad with you looking like an ice princess," Karen said mischievously. Sarah smiled halfheartedly for her friend's sake.

"Let's just hope he doesn't think I'm made of ice," she said under her breath as she walked into the livery, pausing in the doorway as she took in the large, L-shaped room. No one appeared to be inside, and she took a hesitant step forward, and then another as she scanned her surroundings. Except for the horses that stared curiously at her from their stalls at the opposite end, life seemed to be nonexistent.

Sarah sighed, though she wasn't sure if it was in relief or disappointment.

She walked slowly through the building, letting her eyes drift over the ancient tools hanging on walls and resting on benches. A worn saddle with cracking leather had been slung over a wooden post that was anchored into the floor, and above it hung horseshoes and bridles. Blacksmith's tools—hammers, pliers, and also a shooing hook for the horses—littered the long table near the fire, which was situated under the chimney in the left corner of the room. She stepped past these things in the large room and passed by the many pens boarding horses at the back, unaware of her destination until she rounded the corner of the stalls and stood before a single one at the back of the livery.

The coal-black stallion stared at her from within, and she could see in its eyes a keen intelligence as she stared back. She didn't reach out to touch the large animal, feeling a little bit uneasy around it without anyone else nearby. The horse walked slowly up to the gate and stood just behind it, watching her. Sarah glanced around, at the line of occupied stalls behind her, wondering why no one was there to watch the horses. Had he hired someone else after what happened to Allan?

Despite the warmth of the building, a small shiver snaked up her spine at the sudden thought of Will's former assistant. She grimaced as her scar began to itch madly, and she scratched at the back of her hand. But the phantom sensation was nothing like the pain she'd felt when Allan dragged the blade across her skin, leaking the poison into her body that had burned like fire as it made its way through her veins, nearly killing her.

Just before that, Allan had trapped the two of them inside an abandoned shack in the forest and attempted to burn them alive—the poison had only been an insurance policy in the event she survived. He would have succeeded had it not been for Will's quick thinking, both in escaping the fire and getting Sarah to his uncle's house for medical help. Though the scar on Sarah's hand reminded her of the horrors of that day, and the venom-induced sleep in the days that followed, it also served as a reminder of how lucky they had been; they'd escaped an awful fate, and Sarah had fought against and survived poison that should have claimed her life in mere hours.

The only one who died that day had been Allan, shot from a distance by whoever hired him to silence Sarah and the Shadow.

It took great effort to stave off the memory of Allan lying in the grass, an arrow lodged between his shoulder blades, rain pooling in his eye sockets as his unseeing gaze watched her. While there were instances from that day that didn't cause her pain—like Will's heroism and her discovery that he was Serimone's elusive vigilante—the vision of Allan's broken body and blank stare served no purpose in Sarah's memory, except to cause her great sadness for someone she wanted to hate. She'd rather forget him altogether.

She had been inside for a quarter of an hour and was growing restless. She considered sitting down and making herself comfortable until Karen came for her, but she didn't want to give the impression that she was waiting for the proprietor to return. Not wanting to seem overeager in case he came back, she left the penned horses and stepped into the doorway. A form moved into her line of vision, and she started, lurching back a step to avoid colliding with the man.

"Whoah, there." He swiped a hand through his mop of blond hair and smiled, showcasing rows of perfect white teeth. Adjusting the bridle on his shoulder, he asked, "Something I can help you with, miss?"

Sarah pulled her head back in surprise. "You work here?"

He nodded and stuck out his free hand, steadying the bridle with the other. She shook it hesitantly and then quickly freed her own hand, though he seemed unaffected by her aversion to him. "My name is Robert, Mr. Taylor's assistant. Can I help you search for something?" His face was open, and his crystal-clear blue eyes were friendly as he fiddled with the gold chain hanging from his pocket. He seemed nice enough, though she was still wary of blacksmiths' assistants after Allan tried to burn her and Will alive.

She shifted around him and backed up a step. "Uh, no, that's okay. I was just looking for someone, but I should really go now."

Robert looked puzzled by her behavior. "All right, then," he said slowly. "Have a pleasant evening." He moved inside with a glance over his shoulder at her, probably wondering if she had robbed them and was trying to make a quick break for it.

Neck heating, Sarah ducked her head and quickly moved down the street. The wind immediately whipped her hair around her face, preventing her from seeing anything. The temperature had dropped several degrees, and she gathered her tangled tresses together and held them back from her eyes as she peered around the corner of the livery. She was able to see the castle gate from her hiding place, but there was no sign of Karen out front. Frowning, Sarah debated her next move. Should she go back inside and wait? But that would mean being alone with that assistant, Robert, and that seemed rather awkward after the way she acted.

She looked around her. Hardly any townsfolk remained in the street, most already having sought out shelter from the biting wind. Sarah had been unable to explore the town the last time she'd come and wondered if now would be a good time to give herself a tour. Karen had recommended that she keep a low profile while they were here, and since there was a serious lack of townsfolk in the square, Sarah figured that there was no better time than the present and jogged down a narrow side street. The wind skipped over the opening between the stretch of buildings, providing the shelter she sought.

Sarah pulled the hood on her cape over her head, hoping that the occasional passerby would assume that she merely wanted to keep warm and not disguise her appearance. She made her way leisurely through the empty street, glad that she could let her guard down for a few minutes. Most of the shops had dark shades drawn from inside, preventing anyone on the street from seeing into the buildings; they didn't have signs hanging over the street boasting the wares that they were selling. Sarah wondered if she was strolling down a neighborhood before she saw the signs nailed to the front of some of the buildings. A few of them had writing on them that she couldn't decipher, but most had painted symbols that looked a lot like graffiti to her.

She moved past a narrow one-story and thought one of the shutters might have cracked open an inch, giving her the feeling that she was being watched. Sarah began to feel uneasy and wished that a friendly face would suddenly appear in the street. Her feet moved a little faster as her eyes roamed nervously over the seemingly lifeless buildings.

Two guards suddenly appeared at the opposite end of the street and began walking toward her, though neither one seemed to have spotted her yet. Though she had no reason to hide, Sarah dashed into the nearest doorway on instinct and pressed herself against the frame, heart pounding against her ribcage.

"If Cadius continues to scare away maids," one of them was saying,

25

"then he's going to put us to work cleaning out ash from the fireplace and cooking in the kitchen."

The other one laughed heartily. "Can you imagine us, covered in flour? No, we'll have to convince the staff to keep on the lookout for new maids to take over at the castle, but they'll have to make due with what we've got until then. And this new lot will have to not scare easily—the last three obviously had no backbone."

They came into view then, and Sarah pressed herself against the wood in an attempt to make herself as invisible as possible. She needn't have worried, though. The guards paid no attention to her as they passed. She slowly emerged from her hiding place and was relieved to see the street empty once more.

She walked quickly past the buildings, hoping that she could get out of there before she encountered anyone else. A noise like that of an opening door sounded behind her, and she spun around to face it, heart beating erratically. The door suddenly slammed closed before she could catch sight of anyone. Whoever was inside must have spotted her and decided to remain indoors.

Calm down, Matthews, she chided herself, adjusting her hood. *You're being ridiculous.* She turned around and began to jog down the narrow street toward the main square, glancing over her shoulder as she moved to ensure she wasn't being followed.

With her attention diverted from where she was headed, Sarah ran straight into something hard, gasping at the impact. Hands gripped her upper arms to keep her from toppling backward and pulled her close, over-compensating for her lost balance. She leaned back to look up at the man who held her, and the action caused her hood to fall back from her face. Her breath caught in her throat as she looked into Will's startled blue eyes.

~*Chapter 5*~

Will. The name was spoken in her mind like a soft breath of wind. She felt a profound sense of exhilaration and apprehension at her unexpected first glimpse of William Taylor in weeks. His large hands on her shoulders kept her firmly planted against his chest, obviously too startled to release her after helping her regain her balance. They stared at each other for several breaths, and both seemed to be at a loss for words—she was overjoyed to see he was alive and well, while he looked completely speechless over her sudden appearance.

Sarah had no idea if she should apologize first or pretend like nothing was wrong between them, so she remained silent in her indecision, waiting for him to speak. His startled eyes, an even darker blue than she remembered, stared back at her; she could read the unspoken questions in his gaze.

"What are you doing here?" Will asked. There was no anger in his words, only astonishment and confusion.

All of her carefully planned answers fled as she looked down at the hand he had on her shoulder. Her eyes returned to his face, and she struggled for words that made sense.

"I'm, uh, visiting," she replied lamely. His powerful presence and the strong grip he still had on her shoulders seemed to have robbed her of speech.

Will looked like he wanted to say more, but a door nearby opened suddenly, startling them both. He dropped his hold on her, and they turned in time to see a woman emerge from inside. She stood on the doorstep and flicked her waist-length dark hair over one shoulder when they looked her way. Her dress was cut dangerously low and hung off her slender, olive-toned shoulders.

"I thought I heard voices," she said, her voice sounding smooth and cultured. She smiled at them, but Sarah didn't find anything welcoming in the woman's gaze, except, of course, when she looked at Will. Her expression was vaguely amused as she smiled at him, and her gaze was a little too bold and possessive for Sarah's liking.

"I didn't expect to see you knocking on my door today, William," she said, her smile almost catlike.

Will's expression remained blank. "I'd hoped you would never expect me to knock on your door, Jade." His voice was not impolite, but Sarah thought she detected an edge to his words.

The woman he'd called Jade laughed lightly, though it sounded more like a practiced sound than an expression of genuine pleasure.

"One day soon," she said mysteriously. She eyed Sarah openly, who felt extremely uncomfortable beneath her scrutiny. "I can see why you aren't coming to see me today, though I believe I am far more entertaining. Pray, what is your name, pet?"

Sarah stared back at the rude woman, silently refusing to give her name, and received a patronizing smile in response. When she remained silent, Will placed his hands on her shoulders. "We really have to be going," he said, not unkindly, as he pushed Sarah past the dilapidated house. Sarah was so startled by the sudden action that she could do nothing but stumble ahead and try to keep sure footing as he pushed her along with his firm hold. She felt a little deflated with the knowledge that Will and Jade knew each other, and he hadn't bothered to introduce Sarah. Maybe she wasn't as important to him as she had hoped.

She glanced over her shoulder to see the woman watching their departure from her crooked doorstep. She caught Jade's eye and quickly turned her face forward, not liking what she saw in the woman's tight expression.

Will let his grip on her shoulders fall away, though he kept a hand at her back to keep her moving. Though he did his best to shield her body with his own against the brutal wind, Sarah still gasped as the cold wind rammed into her, nearly knocking her off her feet. They hurried through town, and he released her to struggle with the livery door. Sarah fought to keep her feet on the ground as her dress and cape whipped madly about her legs.

He managed to open the door and motioned her in first. She ducked inside, and he quickly followed, pulling the horses and wagon into the building. He allowed the wind to blow the door closed behind him with a bang as he untied the animals from the wagon. The horses danced around nervously, and Will let them to trot toward the back of the building, where they couldn't do any harm.

"It wasn't that bad when we left," Sarah said, still trying to catch her breath from their fight against the weather outside. She combed her fingers through her hair to lessen the snarls the wind had created. Robert must have left, because the building was soundless except for the horses' quiet shuffling in their stalls in the back.

"A storm is coming in," Will replied dully, raking a hand back through his own tousled waves. His dark eyes searched her face for a moment, and then he shook his head. "You shouldn't have been down there."

"What? You mean that street?" She shrugged nonchalantly, as if the whole episode were no big deal. However, the eerily silent street and the encounter with Jade had disquieted her. She had actually been greatly relieved when Will came to her rescue.

He moved away from the door and took a step toward her, his face serious and stern, square jaw set. Sarah recognized that look and knew he was about to tell her not to do something. She automatically stiffened in response to the warning that was about to come.

"I don't ever want you going down there. It isn't safe for you to be wandering there alone."

Sarah raised a brow in question. "Why is that?"

The muscle in his jaw twitched and he glanced at the floor. "That woman we met—Jade—well, she isn't exactly involved in an occupation that most would deem credible or . . . moral."

She stared at him in obvious confusion. "And . . ."

Will shifted on his feet and averted his gaze again. She couldn't remember him ever looking so uncomfortable. "She entertains men for money," he mumbled rapidly, seeming relieved to have it out.

"So she's a dancer?" Sarah asked slowly. His eyes widened at her naïveté, causing her own eyes to grow as the full meaning of his words sank in. "Oh," was all she said, feeling dumb.

Will nodded, the tips of his ears reddening. "Most of the women on that street have similar occupations. It's a rough neighborhood that boasts a variety of services, largely revolving around gambling and drinking during the night hours for repugnant men with foul appetites. You were fortunate to have stumbled down there in daylight."

A thought occurred to her, and she stared at him intently. "Why were you down there?" Her attempt to sound casual failed.

He seemed to stand a little straighter. "I was trying to escape the weather and took a short cut. But I can take care of myself."

"And I can't?" she asked, her eyes daring him to say so. He folded his arms across his broad chest and remained silent at her raised brow.

Sarah knew he was just looking after her well-being, but she severely disliked being told what to do, and the fact that he was doing just that after only a few minutes into their reunion grated on her nerves. She felt like reminding him that he wasn't her father and had no right telling her what to do, but she managed to bite her tongue a split second before the words escaped her lips. She inhaled a shaky breath and exhaled slowly, letting her anger out with the air. This was not how she had imagined their first meeting going, and she had spent quite a few hours fantasizing over their reunion.

Swallowing her pride and softening her tone—just barely—she managed, "Thank you for caring enough to be concerned."

His eyes registered surprise as they stared intently into hers. Sarah began to feel uncomfortable and was the first to look away from his intense gaze, though she could still feel his eyes on her. The silence unnerved her, and she wondered if he enjoyed watching her squirm beneath his gaze or if he simply didn't realize what he was doing.

"Why did you come back?" His question caught her off-guard, though she should have expected it. She turned her face to him again, trying to come up with a reasonable answer. The only thing that came to mind was the truth.

"The king is dead. Karen and I are trying to stop him before he succeeds in claiming the throne."

Will's look remained impassive, though that muscle in his jaw trembled as he clenched his teeth together. Judging by the way he kept his emotions hidden beneath an expressionless facade, he had gone back to the habit of blocking people out. It hurt Sarah to see him doing it to her, and it was especially painful to realize that her leaving had destroyed any progress they had made in their friendship. Over the months she was gone, his trust in her had waned and maybe even died out completely. She just prayed that she would be able to earn it back someday.

"You should not be involved in this," Will said.

Sarah quirked a brow, surprised at the command. "And why is that? It seems that the Shadow is nowhere to be found, so who else is going to figure out what happened?"

The words slipped out before she could stop them. He narrowed his eyes, and she could see that her unintentional barb had hit its mark. She sighed and her anger vanished like a vapor in the wind with the realization that she had just stirred his ire.

"I'm sorry, Will. I shouldn't have said that." She stared at the ground, her accursed pride keeping her from meeting his gaze lest he see the remorse written across her face. Would there ever come a day when she could hold her tongue and not bring about someone's anger with her own careless words? Sometimes she envied the way he could hide his feelings behind an uncaring mask and pretend that things didn't affect him. But even when he was pretending, she knew he cared about more than he let on, and she hoped the same was true about his feelings for her.

"I'm sorry I didn't say goodbye," she whispered, risking a glance at him through her lashes. He kept his arms crossed and shrugged his shoulders indifferently, as though it didn't matter in the least. Even though she knew he was only trying to protect himself, it still hurt her to see him so closed-off. Her defenses rose to cover her hurt.

"Fine, play that game. But don't expect me to—"

She was interrupted by the sound of the livery door opening. Karen entered and the wind slammed the door behind her. "Agh! It's stormy like a—" She froze in place, hand stilling on her head as she tried to fix her hair. She looked between the two of them, quickly assessing the tense atmosphere in the room.

"Hi, Will," she greeted awkwardly. Turning to Sarah she said, "Umm, sorry to interrupt."

"It's fine," Sarah and Will replied in unison, both sounding a little sharp.

Green eyes darted between the two of them. "Okay," she said slowly, then to Sarah, "I was just wondering if you had anything."

Sarah was getting ready to shake her head when she recalled the conversation she'd overheard between the guards in the street. She smiled slowly at Karen.

"As a matter of fact, I did."

Karen brightened. "Really? What did you find out?"

"Well," Sarah said, enjoying the suspicious look on Will's face as she leaned toward her friend conspiratorially. If anger was the only emotion she could elicit from him . . . She knew it was childish, but she couldn't stand seeing him so expressionless. "It appears that Cadius has been scaring off some of the help since he's become the prince's advisor. I overheard some guards talking, and they said that the castle is looking to fill some positions."

Karen chewed on her lower lip thoughtfully. "That might honestly work."

Will took a step forward, his eyes narrowed in that familiar way as he looked between the two girls. "What might work?"

Sarah smiled innocently up at him. "I am going to get a job at the castle."

~Chapter 6~

Will's eyes darkened as he stared at her, though his face revealed nothing. Sarah felt slightly triumphant over getting him to show some emotion, even if it was frustration directed at her. She knew it sounded twisted, but seeing any expression on his face gave her hope that he wasn't completely lost to her.

"You can't be thinking about working there," he said in that quiet, even tone that he used when he was trying to mask his frustration.

Karen's eyes darted between the two of them as they stared each other down. "You know, I don't think I've ever looked around this place. Why don't I do that now?" Before either could object, she quickly skirted off toward the back of the building that was farthest away from the brewing storm.

Sarah watched her round the corner and then turned to face Will. "And why shouldn't I?" She maintained her calm as she spoke, knowing that would irritate him more than matching his anger with her own boiling just beneath the surface.

Will unfolded his arms and let them fall to his side. Balling his hands into tight fists, he said through clenched teeth, "Because it is completely foolish to put yourself in that position. If anyone discovered that you were there to spy on the royal family, you could be beheaded."

She shrugged, though the thought turned her stomach. "I don't plan on getting found out." Too late she realized that she had repeated the exact words he had spoken to her long ago, and she had contradicted them at the time.

Will leaned forward slightly, looking into her eyes as he tried to make her understand. "Someone once told me that things happen that we don't plan on." He cocked his head to the side, and that rebellious wave of ebony hair fell across his broad forehead. "Do you realize how dangerous this scheme is?"

She saw that he had lowered his defenses long enough to show what his anger truly was: concern for her. Lowering her voice so Karen didn't overhear her, she said, "I'll be careful. Although it might be easier if I had a little help from a certain someone." She had hoped that the hint might lead to an explanation of the Shadow's absence, but she could tell he took it as a criticism by the way he pulled himself up to his full height, all six-foot-four of him.

Her sigh sounded more like a groan to her own ears. They hadn't even been together for a full thirty minutes, and she had already let her anger override her calm several times, and now her quick mouth made it seem like she thought less of him. "I'm sorry, Will. That's not what I meant." She rolled her eyes at her own foolishness. "I need to learn to hold my tongue more."

"You apologize too much," he said with a shrug.

She let a small laugh escape. "That's just because too often my tongue gets me into trouble." She paused, deciding to just come right out and ask. Lowering her voice until it was just above a whisper, she said, "Why did you quit being, you know, the Shadow?" She watched his face intently in case he let his armor fall long enough for her to see his true feelings. But his shield remained in place.

"No one needed me anymore." His voice was devoid of any emotion, but she imagined that his words held a double meaning.

Feeling that she was the one to blame, Sarah stepped over to him and placed a gentle hand on his arm. She stared up at him, all pretense and pride gone from her face. "People still need you, Will. Some need you more than you'll ever know," she added quietly, sincerely, wanting to encourage him and restore whatever ground she had destroyed by leaving. His eyes flickered briefly with some secret emotion, and then the light went out. She sighed again, her blue eyes searching his darker ones. "I lost you when I left, didn't I?" She hadn't meant to say it out loud, but it was almost a relief to have the words out between them, no longer an un-voiced question rattling around in her head.

Karen suddenly came toward them, leading their horses. Her approach halted any reply Will might have had to her comment. The redhead stopped abruptly when she noticed how close they were standing. Sarah removed her hand from his arm, feeling embarrassed and slightly disappointed at being interrupted.

"Are you ready to go?" she asked her friend.

Karen glanced between the two of them again. She looked nervous and uncomfortable to have intruded. "Uh, I can wait, if you'd like."

Sarah shook her head, suddenly wanting very much to leave. She had forgotten how exhausting it had been in the beginning before Will opened up and let her see who he really was, dark secrets and all. It was a constant battle to decipher his deeper meaning and read his expressionless face like the wordless pages of a book.

"No, I think it's best if we leave."

The wind howled outside. Sarah wasn't sure if the horses would get spooked as Will hitched them to the wagon again, but Karen didn't seem to think so as she jumped up into the seat and grabbed the reins eagerly.

Sarah placed her foot on the step, half expecting Will to help her the rest of the way like he always did. But he didn't offer to take her hand or even make a move toward her, though the muscle in his jaw spasmed. She plopped her backside down and stared straight ahead as he held the large door open for them. Karen got the horses moving, and as they passed, Sarah risked a quick glance in his direction.

She saw a painful vulnerability in his gaze when he caught her eye, and something else that was indiscernible. Will didn't break eye contact, and she quickly ducked her head so that her hair hid her face.

Karen guided the horses onto the street. As soon as they entered the open air, the wind immediately assaulted them and made it impossible to keep their hair from flapping wildly around their faces.

"That could have gone better," Karen said, glancing at Sarah apologetically. "Sorry."

Sarah shrugged. "It's not your fault," she said loudly to be heard over the wind. She gave up on trying to keep her hair out of her face and let it flow freely in the harsh wind. What was the point anyway? It wasn't like she had anyone to impress. She didn't dare look behind her as they rode along, fearing that he would be standing just inside the doorway, watching her. Her careless words had made enough of a fool of her; she didn't need him thinking that she was pining after him.

Karen struggled to keep the horses calm and moving along the dirt road, but the wind was far less severe once they entered the thicket of trees just beyond the edge of town, and the animals no longer resisted her guidance.

God, why can't Will stop resisting? she asked silently. *You, me, life . . . He's trying to pull away from it all, and I keep messing it up. What am I supposed to do?*

The only answering noise was the rustling of the wind in the trees and the sound of the horses *clip-clopping* along the dirt path.

No still, small Voice spoke. Sarah felt the silence like a thick blanket, smothering her. When all was silent, she had time to think and reflect, and that was never a good thing.

****

Sarah collapsed gratefully onto the straw bed and sighed dreamily.

"Don't get too comfortable," Karen said, tossing a quilt down beside her. "We have to go up to the house in a couple of minutes for supper."

Sarah groaned dramatically. "Do we have to eat dinner? I mean, what does food really do for us anyway?"

Karen tossed a straw pillow at her face playfully. "Other than sustain life? Come on, I told them I would be back for the evening meal. You probably want to get this reunion over with." She offered a hand, and Sarah took it and rose to her feet.

"Fine. But as soon as we get back, I want to hear everything that went on while you were over by the castle."

Karen's green eyes sparkled with mischief as she grinned. "All right, though there isn't as much to tell as what all went on between you and Will before I arrived."

Sarah winced. She had tried to forget about that entire situation and the words exchanged between them, spoken and otherwise. She had actually managed to put it out of her mind for a brief moment, but the reminder that things had not gone exactly as she had planned caused her face to fall. Karen must have sensed the change in her mood because her eyes softened and lost their teasing.

"I am sorry, Sarah. You don't have to tell me anything if you don't want to. I was only teasing."

Sarah shrugged one shoulder limply and mustered a small smile for her friend. "Maybe when I figure out what it was all about, I'll tell you."

Karen nodded, as if that were enough of an answer for her. They left the barn and ran across the grass to the house, trying to get out of the bullying wind as quickly as possible. Sarah was surprised at the stinging sensation of snowflakes whipping against her face. They burst gratefully into the warm house, and Karen closed the door quickly behind them to keep the warmth inside.

Sarah felt a sudden stirring of nervous anticipation as she glanced around the unoccupied living room. A roaring fire provided heat to the room and cast a warm glow over the space and furnishings. A high-backed wood chair had been placed beside the fireplace, and a book lay open with its pages down on the seat. Sarah smiled with fond remembrance of Leah's love of reading beside the fire.

As if just thinking about her could cause her to appear, the youngest Jones walked through the doorway from the kitchen and stepped into the main room. She started when she looked up and saw them standing before her, then her expression of surprise turned to one of delight as she ran to embrace her. Sarah laughed and wrapped her arms around the girl in a tight hug. Leah pulled back and did an excited dance in place that was entirely reminiscent of Lilly's earlier jig.

"Mama will be so happy," Leah said, her copper curls bouncing as she talked. "Karen said that she might bring you to dinner tonight, and I have just been beside myself. We don't have nearly enough girls around here, but with you around, Seth and Josh will be outnumbered when it comes to choosing games, so long as Mama is on our side."

Sarah laughed at the girl's rapid talk. She had forgotten how animated Leah could be and suddenly realized just how much she had missed her. Though she was taller, the girl reminded Sarah so much of Lilly that her fondness only grew for her.

The front door opened behind them, and Sarah turned around to see the men enter. Seth strode in first and paused in the doorway, looking eagerly around the room before his eyes caught hers. She smiled hesitantly. Before she left, they had clearly laid out their feelings for each other, deciding there would be no secrets between them. And though Seth's romantic feelings did not mirror hers, he had respected her wish that they remain friends and nothing more. But Sarah still felt strange around him with the knowledge of how he felt for her, and at the time she had been too embarrassed about his feelings to even tell Karen—a secret she was now glad she'd kept.

But maybe he doesn't feel that way anymore, she thought hopefully. She would never betray Karen like that and prayed Seth wouldn't, either.

Joshua elbowed his brother in the side good-naturedly to get him to move out of the doorway. He grinned at Sarah.

"Welcome back," he said. "Mother and Leah have been beside themselves—"

"I already told her that," Leah interjected, looking pleased to be the first one to deliver the news to Sarah.

Mr. Jones appeared behind his sons, his tall frame filling the doorway. He placed a hand on either of their shoulders and urged them forward slightly so he could close the door. He turned around, his expression stern.

"It seems that you have caused quite a bit of chaos in this house once again, Miss Matthews." Sarah would have taken offense at his words if she hadn't seen the sparkle of good humor in the gentle giant's eyes.

She managed to keep a straight face and nodded her head once. "I'll try to keep from doing it again, sir."

He laughed at that, a deep, joyful sound that came from deep inside his chest. "Well, now that I have your word on it, we must go in and eat. I'm half-starved from fighting against this winter."

The large group entered the kitchen. Sarah came in last and saw the small, round woman bustling about the room, grinning as she waited for the older woman to spot her. When she glanced up from her work, Ruth Jones's flushed face lit up with joy. Without a word, she walked over to Sarah and wrapped her in a smothering hug. She held Sarah's arms and took a step back, her smile huge. Motherly affection glowed in her eyes, and Sarah felt her throat clog with emotion.

"Welcome back, dear," Mrs. Jones said quietly.

Sarah just smiled, not trusting her voice. The older woman seemed to sense her struggle with the emotional reunion and motioned for everyone to sit.

"Now that we're all here, let's eat."

~Chapter 7~

Sarah stared up at the rafters, her arms pillowed behind her head. It was completely dark in the still barn, not that she could have focused, anyway—she could hardly see past the images that occupied her mind and kept her from falling asleep.

She thought about how welcoming the Jones family had been and how at ease she had felt talking and laughing with them over dinner; it was as though she hadn't been absent for months as she fit right in with their family dynamic. Even Seth appeared comfortable during the meal and when they parted ways that night, and Sarah couldn't help but wonder if he was over his silly crush on her.

Her mind suddenly brought before her eyes the picture of her and Will standing in the street together as he held her close, and she tried to hold onto the memory of that moment, that brief instant where she assumed everything would go perfectly, before it slipped away and was replaced with reality. It was their first time seeing each other in a long time, and she had imagined it so differently. She was embarrassed to admit that she'd even daydreamed about what it would be like to see him again—a few scenarios to keep the romantic side of her mind occupied during long summer afternoons. Sarah hadn't thought it would do any harm, since she would never see him again, but now those imaginings of tender gazes and cheesy professions of love mocked her, gloating that she would never have any of that with anyone.

She squeezed her eyes closed to block out the images that played on the dark ceiling, wanting to block out the regret and questions circling around in her head. There had been so many things she had wanted to ask Will: Why had he deserted his quest to help others as the Shadow? Was it because of what she'd said to him about it being just a quest for vengeance against his parents' killer?

But her pride and anger had gotten in the way, and instead of seeking answers, she had only managed to stir his own temper and poke at his pride to soothe her own. His words spoken to her long ago on a trail came to mind, and she remembered his grin as he spoke.

You and I are not so very different, Sarah.

She was beginning to think he might have been right.

****

Sarah and Karen ate breakfast with the rest of the family—an affair that was just as noisy and conversation-oriented as dinner—before asking Seth to hitch the wagon. With a roll of his eyes that was offset by his crooked grin, he did just that.

"You know, I should really learn how to do it myself sometime." The snowfall the night before had created a hush over the forest, and Karen's words as they rode along the narrow trail were the only sound to disrupt the silence.

"Do what?" Sarah asked absentmindedly.

Karen glanced at her oddly. "Hitching the horses to the wagon. What were you thinking about?"

"Why does it matter?" Sarah asked, side-stepping the question.

Karen grinned good-naturedly. "You know, for an open person, you sure can be cryptic sometimes."

"I wouldn't say I was being cryptic," she defended.

"You're right. Locked-up tight is more appropriate."

She grimaced. "Sorry."

Karen seemed to shrug it off. "Don't be. I didn't take it personally."

They lapsed into silence as they approached town, and Sarah felt a stirring of anxiety in her stomach. Since Karen's afternoon of eavesdropping outside the castle the day before had proved fruitless, they agreed that their best opportunity to discover anything was for Sarah to get hired as a maid and work from within the castle.

She clasped and unclasped her hands in her lap nervously, her mind working too furiously for her to grab hold of any single thought. "You think I can pull this off?"

"You are going to do just fine," Karen replied, obviously guessing at her doubt. She glanced at Sarah before turning her eyes back to the street. "Were you ever involved in a production at your school?"

The question took Sarah by surprise. "Yeah, small roles," she answered slowly, not comprehending.

"Were you any good?"

She shrugged her shoulders and answered modestly, "I was okay, I guess."

Karen looked at her again and that quick grin appeared. "You're lying."

Sarah gave a small laugh. "Okay, so I got a couple of lead parts. But it was a small town and there wasn't much competition for the role of Dorothy." Her expression turned serious. "But that was years ago, Karen, and I just had to play a wide-eyed girl. This is real life; there are no practice runs or rehearsals. I'm not sure I can do this."

Karen reached over and gave her hand a reassuring squeeze. "I *know* you can do this. I have faith in you, just like you believe in me. I'm sure you learned how to get into character for whatever role you were playing. Just do that and you'll be fine."

Sarah nodded and took a deep breath. Get into character—she could do that. Mrs. Moss, the head of the theater department at her old middle school, had always told the kids participating in her plays that the best way to get into character was to ask themselves questions. Simple ones, like what is the name of the character they're portraying, where are they from, what is their background? Sarah found it ironic that she had rolled her eyes every time she heard those words and was now preparing to put that advice to the test.

Who is my character? she asked herself.

She turned to Karen. "Am I supposed to use my real name?"

The redhead worried her lower lip. "Maybe just your first. Whoever sent Allan after you and Will might be on the lookout for a Sarah Matthews, so it's easier to blend in by giving as little information as possible."

"Should I use a false identity?" Sarah asked, only half-joking.

"No. You don't want to find yourself in a situation where you bump into someone you know and they use your real name."

Sarah nodded, mentally filing that advice away to be used later. "Right, okay. Anything else?"

Karen thought for a moment as she directed the horses toward the castle, ducking her head beneath her hood out of habit. "Remember, you're a servant, so don't be outspoken." She grinned as if that was impossible, and Sarah rolled her eyes. "Only speak when spoken to, and don't challenge anyone of higher rank. We don't want you getting flogged on your first day." Though she said it like a joke, her words carried warning.

Sarah swallowed hard as Karen pulled the wagon to a stop in front of the castle gates. They turned in their seats to face each other. Karen's face was serious and held a note of worry, though Sarah could tell she was trying not to show her fear.

"If it gets too sticky in there, just get out. Don't hesitate to pull yourself away from there if you feel you've been compromised."

Sarah wiggled her eyebrows teasingly, though her insides had turned to jelly. "I feel like a secret agent."

Karen leaned forward, her expression grim and insistent. "I am not

40

kidding, Sarah. I don't care how close you feel you are. This isn't T.V. where the good guy gets away unscathed. Nothing's so important that you should risk your life over it."

"Some things are," Sarah said quietly.

"*But not this.*" Karen emphasized each word to drive her point home. "Getting justice for the king is our goal, but it won't bring him back."

Sarah eyed the sharp spikes at the top of the heavily-guarded gate and swallowed the sudden lump in her throat.

"Don't worry about me," she said with more confidence than she felt. "I'll be fine. Now get out of here before someone spots you."

Karen nodded solemnly as Sarah jumped out of the wagon. Taking a deep breath for courage, she signaled her friend to leave with a wave of her hand. She watched Karen reluctantly drive away and turned to face the intimidating vastness of the castle, suddenly feeling completely alone. Then she remembered that she was never alone.

Lord, help me not to mess this up. Let us be successful and bring whatever evil has been going on here to light.

She advanced toward the open gate slowly, trying to look like she was confident and knew what she was doing. But would a servant really appear self-assured in such an intimidating situation? She allowed herself to reveal a small amount of the genuine trepidation she felt as she approached the men guarding the gate. She kept her head low and tried to pass by them without notice.

One of the guards grabbed her arm and spun her around to face him.

"Where do you think you're goin', missy?" he asked, his stare as hard as the grip he had on her. "We got strict orders not to let anyone pass."

Her heart felt ready to burst out of her chest in surprise, but her frustration over having been caught so quickly overshadowed her fear. "Then why not shut the gate so nobody can get in?" she ground out between clenched teeth.

The man didn't answer her but pulled her with him and released her several feet from the entrance. Wordlessly, he walked back to his post and scanned the perimeter, though he tactfully avoided her fiery gaze.

Sarah had to fight against the urge to try and outrun the guards. But common sense overruled the desire when she realized that having them chase after her as she tried to apply for a position in the castle might not be an incentive to hire her.

"Fine," she muttered under her breath. "I'll find my own way, then."

She walked along the outside of the gate, examining the fortress for any other entrances. There were none. She rounded the far side and was about to give up hope when she spotted the servants' entrance at the back of the gate.

"Bingo." She smiled to herself and started in that direction.

Someone grabbed her arm, and she spun around in fright, assuming that one of the guards had caught up with her. She expelled a gusty breath when she looked up and caught Will's stern expression.

"What are you doing?" she whispered, glancing around to make sure no one had spotted them. There were a few of the townsfolk on the backside of the castle, but none of them paid attention to them. "Were you trying to give me a heart attack?"

"What are *you* doing?" he said, in his quiet way. His hand fell from her arm.

"I asked you first," she shot back, staring up at him.

"Keeping you out of trouble." He adjusted the sack slung over his shoulder, drawing her attention to it.

"What is that?"

"You're evading my previous question."

Sarah cringed. How did he always know what she was thinking? It was very inconvenient when she was trying to distract him.

Giving up on her ruse, she straightened her shoulders and mustered all the confidence she was far from feeling. "I'm applying for a position in the castle."

His eyes narrowed, but she didn't shrink back. "I thought I made it clear how dangerous this will be."

"You did. But I can make my own decisions." She waited for him to tell her otherwise and prepared to argue over the subject with him.

He expelled a sigh and shook his head at her wordlessly. Taking her elbow, he guided her toward the servants' entrance.

"What are you doing?" she whispered, looking around nervously. He kept his eyes straight ahead.

"I am not letting you go in there alone."

Sarah's surprise melted into a small smile. So he did still care. If he had been in a better mood, she might have teased him a little about this fact.

Her smile faded as they neared the tall gate. She felt suddenly insignificant and unsure and moved a little closer to Will. He must have sensed her hesitancy, because his pace slowed and he caught her eye. "Do you still wish to do this?"

She nodded, though she was sure her face still conveyed some of her unease. "I need to do this."

He didn't question her further as they stepped through the unguarded gate and up to the door. He removed his hand from her arm and knocked.

A servant answered. Her face was pale and narrow, and she wore an old apron speckled with flour over her ratty clothes. Her collarbone was pronounced above the neckline of the gray dress, and Sarah was sure that the girl didn't eat properly.

"Yes?" she asked in a small voice. The girl couldn't have been more than fourteen.

Sarah swallowed hard, stomach twisting in a nervous knot.

Will's expression softened as he looked at the girl. "Would you please tell Terrance that Mr. Taylor is here?"

The girl nodded and skirted away like a frightened rabbit, leaving the door open. Sarah no longer had to pretend to be an intimidated servant seeking out employment; she was downright scared with the thought that everyone who worked in the castle was as frightened as that girl.

"Sarah?"

She looked up at Will with wide eyes. His own softened, and he leaned down, looking concerned, and that only caused her heart to beat more erratically.

"We can still leave." His voice was quiet with understanding. Sarah inhaled a shuddering breath and grabbed his arm with both her hands, drawing strength from his nearness.

"Please don't ask me that again," she replied in a tight voice. "I might be tempted to take you up on your offer."

Will looked hesitant to respect her decision, but he nodded, straightening just as a man appeared in the doorway. He seemed surprised to find them standing there together and turned his attention to Will.

"I didn't expect you until next week," the man, whom Sarah assumed was Terrance, remarked.

"It took less time than I estimated," Will answered. Sarah didn't miss the way his expression shifted from warm to businesslike in the man's presence.

Terrance's gaze became suspicious as he stared at Sarah. "And who is this?"

She gripped Will's arm tighter and resisted the urge to hide behind him. The question wasn't directed at her, so she remained silent. Appearing subservient wasn't hard to do with her tongue stuck to the roof of her mouth.

Will's face was blank as he nodded his head in her direction. "This is Sarah," he answered, though he offered nothing more. She breathed a sigh of relief that he understood her need for some anonymity with these people.

The man eyed her up and down, and she blushed beneath his scrutiny. "She working at your place?" His question held a sardonic lilt.

Will gave a slight shake of his head and shifted his load again, grunting under the weight. "Actually, I thought she might find employment here."

Sarah's fingers dug into Will's forearm as they waited for an answer. Terrance hesitated briefly before motioning them in and closing the door behind them. Sarah felt her breath catch in her throat at the sound of the door sealing shut with finality.

"This way," he said, leading them through the kitchen and past the curious stares of the staff. Sarah released her hold on Will and kept her head down to avoid their probing gazes. Balling her hands into tights fists at her sides, she focused on the feel of her nails biting into the tender part of her palms, striving for calm.

Terrance brought them into a small sitting room and asked them to wait, and then he abruptly left them alone. The tiny room was sparsely furnished and very dark. Sarah felt too agitated to sit on the worn sofa, so she remained standing. Will dropped his sack to the floor. The sound startled Sarah, and she looked up at him, catching his concerned expression.

"How did you know I was over here, anyway?" she asked, hoping to take her mind off the present circumstance with the sound of his deep, smooth voice.

"I saw you get tossed out when you tried to go in through the front," he explained. Her cheeks heated as she realized that others had probably seen what he had. "I had just finished the order when I saw you go around the back. In all honesty, I thought it might be a good excuse to make sure you were all right."

Overwhelmed with gratitude, she surprised them both by wrapping her arms around his middle and hugging him tightly.

"I'm glad you did," she said softly. It was supposed to be a brief embrace, but she felt so secure in his arms that she held on, leaning her head against his strong chest and squeezing her eyes closed. She felt him tense up, but then he slowly relaxed and his arms came around to circle her shoulders.

"Please don't leave yet," Sarah whispered against his chest. She couldn't remember ever feeling so unsure over something that she had been determined to do a few minutes before.

His arms tightened protectively around her. "I'm here."

Those were the words she needed to hear most, and Sarah relaxed against him for a brief moment before she heard footsteps coming back down the hall. Will slowly pulled away from her, and she could read the unspoken words in his eyes.

"I'll not ask again," he assured her, and Sarah felt her appreciation for him grow. After the way she had treated him yesterday, he was still her friend and respected her wishes, and that gave her hope for their tenuous relationship.

Sarah took a step back from him as Terrance entered the sitting room.

"Can you cook or clean?" he asked, surprising her with his directness.

"Y-yes, sir," she stammered, surprised.

He nodded his head. "It won't be easy work, and it's a mere stipend for the labor, but you will be provided with food and lodging. Unless, of course, you're renting a room in town?"

Sarah's glance flickered uncertainly to Will and then back to the man. Though it would give her more opportunity to explore the castle, the prospect of staying in this foreign place with people she didn't know was more intimidating than she cared to admit. She opened her mouth to say that she already had a place to stay, but the words wouldn't come out. Something held her back, and for some unexplainable reason, she suddenly felt sure that this was where she was supposed to be.

Swallowing hard, she answered in a small voice, "I'll stay here."

Will looked at her, and she could read the surprise in his expression.

Terrance nodded his head again and clapped his hands together, appearing pleased. It was a very different look than his previous expression of suspicion, and Sarah couldn't help but wonder if he had been testing her. "It's settled then. We'll start you off cleaning the east wing, since we have plenty of kitchen staff at the moment. I'll get Edith to oversee your work."

Sarah was so shocked that she was unable to speak. Her mouth worked silently as she looked from one man to the other. Will appeared just as speechless.

Terrance smiled, causing wrinkles to appear around his eyes and mouth as he directed his focus to the younger man. "Now, what do you have for me, Will?"

Will cleared his throat and quickly covered his surprise. "All the bridles and shoes you requested." He picked up the sack and handed it to the older man. Terrance dropped the bundle to the floor with a clatter, opened the top, and peered inside. Nodding his head, he closed the opening.

"Excellent." The gray-haired man pulled a small pouch from his belt and tossed it to Will. He caught it mechanically, but Sarah could tell that he was still dazed. She imagined her face looked the same.

"I'll fetch Edith so she can start you on your training." Without waiting for either of them to speak, Terrance quickly left the room.

Sarah turned astonished eyes toward her companion. Will looked down at her, and she couldn't ever remember seeing the look of surprise and alarm that he wore now.

"Why did you say that you would live here?" he whispered, his voice sounding urgent.

Sarah wondered for a moment if she had misinterpreted her gut feeling, but she quickly dismissed her doubt. No, she was supposed to remain here, she was sure of it.

"I can't explain it," she said softly. "I just know that for right now, this is where I belong." Her eyes sought his, wanting him to understand when she didn't fully comprehend what she was getting herself into. "I can't help but feel that this is the only way we're going to finish this, once and for all. Don't lose faith in me just yet, Will—don't give up on me."

His eyes were intense. He placed his hands on her shoulders and leaned down so that their faces were only inches apart. "I won't leave you in here for long. We will work through this together."

A slight smile curled her lips. "Are you saying that you're going to help, Mr. Taylor?"

"Yes," he said seriously. "If I am working from the outside and you within, then hopefully we can get you out of here as quickly as possible."

A servant entered the room, and Will straightened slowly. Sarah turned to face the woman in her mid-thirties. She wiped her hands on the front of her plain black dress and smiled at Sarah. The gesture looked genuine and unforced.

"You must be my new charge," she said. Sarah released the breath she had been holding, feeling relieved that the woman seemed pleasant enough.

"Yes."

The woman stepped up to her and held out her hand. Sarah shook it automatically, feeling overwhelmed at the speed at which she had been hired.

The maid's large brown eyes were kind and seemed to convey an understanding of what Sarah was feeling. "My name is Edith." She smiled politely at Will before turning her attention back to the new help. "Come. I cannot be kept away from my duties for too long, and I must show you how things are run around here."

Sarah nodded in response, though she felt a confusing mixture of fright and detachment from the situation. She began to follow Edith out of the room, but stopped when she felt Will's hand on her arm. She looked up into his dark, worried eyes.

"Try to draw as little attention to yourself as possible," he advised quietly.

She nodded bleakly. "If you see Karen, tell her where I am. I'll get word to her if something goes wrong."

"But how?" he asked.

She sighed heavily. "I'll figure out a way. Goodbye, Will." She turned around and slipped from his grasp, running down the hallway after her guide without a backward glance. It was too difficult to look behind her and see her uncertainty mirrored in Will's eyes.

Edith must not have realized that she was missing because she was going on about the workings of the castle when Sarah sidled up next to her, nodding and pretending like she had been listening all along. She tried normalizing her breathing after her sprint down the hall and did her best to take in all that was being said.

"The fireplaces are done every Monday and Friday," Edith explained. "Usually we have servants assigned to that task, but sometimes we have to help them out. The wing that I work in most is on the east side, so I'll keep you with me over there. The dusting in the east wings are done every other

46

day, and we wash the windows on Sundays."

"Always on Sunday. Right." Sarah made a mental note and prayed that she could remember all of the instructions.

"Now," Edith continued, rounding a corner, "since you are new, I will tell you when we must clean the rugs and tapestries. Sometimes it's every week, other instances we need only do them twice a month. I will show you what floors need to be cleaned." She greeted a young servant girl carrying a stack of linens as they passed. Edith grinned conspiratorially at Sarah and lowered her voice. "But I like you, so I won't force you into laundry duty."

Sarah smiled back in relief. "I'd appreciate that."

Edith inhaled a deep breath and let it out quickly. "That about does it. That is the typical schedule, except for when a ball is being held. Speaking of which, preparations are already underway for the annual winter masque at the beginning of the coming week. Everything changes when we have to prepare for an event." She laughed at the look of dismay on Sarah's face. "But you needn't worry about that; I'll be with you every step of the way. You came at the perfect time, though. We're rather short-staffed, which does mean more work for us, but you'll be getting your own room in the servants' quarters."

Sarah nodded and tried to look pleased at this bit of news, but that small consolation did nothing to calm her fears.

~Chapter 8~

Sarah collapsed onto the low mattress in exhaustion, not even bothering to remove her worn shoes. It wasn't nearly as comfortable as her straw bed back at the Joneses', nothing but a lumpy mattress set on a low wooden box, but she was so relieved to be off her feet that it didn't matter. She wasn't used to such hard work and decided that her mom was grossly under-appreciated for keeping the house so clean all the time.

Edith had been kind and helpful when Sarah needed assistance or had a question as they worked side by side, but the woman made sure that she earned her place at the castle. Under Edith's watchful eye and guidance, Sarah had beaten rugs—sneezing all the way—scrubbed the floors so long her knees still throbbed, and dusted until her arms felt like they would fall off.

She had imagined working at the castle differently. Somehow it had seemed exciting, maybe even glamorous, and she had thought there would be plenty of time for snooping.

Sarah gave a small, mirthless laugh in the tiny room. There had barely been enough time in the day for her and Edith to grab a meager lunch and later a small supper in the kitchen before rushing back to their duties.

"Tomorrow is Friday, and things always slow down for the weekend," Edith had assured her when she caught the exhausted look on her face.

"T.G.I. Friday," Sarah mumbled sleepily, closing her eyes. Nearly a full minute passed before she heard the sound of little feet scurrying across the cold stone floor. Her lids flew open and her heart immediately began hammering against her chest.

She lay there, hardly daring to breathe as she listened for the sound again. Maybe it had just been her imagination. Her bed was supported by planks that kept her half a foot off the ground, so she really didn't need to worry about any vermin crawling into bed with her . . . She didn't think.

For the next ten minutes, she lay deathly still, listening intently to

48

every sound as her eyes darted about the small room. She wondered if the shadows she saw were really moving or if she was just being paranoid. After what felt like an eternity of straining her ears to pick up the slightest sound of movement, her body began to relax and her heartbeat returned to its normal pace. Edith had given her a candle to find her way to her room in the dark corridor, and Sarah had neglected to extinguish the stumpy flame when she fell into bed, knowing that it would burn itself out soon. It offered little light, but now she was too worked up to gather the nerve to blow it out, so she left the reassuring light burning on the wooden crate beside her bed.

She could feel her tired body drifting again and was more than willing to succumb to the blackness. She had almost lost total consciousness when a creaking noise coming from the hallway registered in the back of her tired mind. Her eyes opened in a flash and her heart beat wildly against her ribcage as she came fully awake.

Her door creaked open slowly. Sarah held her breath and pulled the wool blanket up to her nose, as though the simple covering could shield her from whatever was creeping her way.

She watched, paralyzed, as a dark form stealthily entered her room. The intruder crept noiselessly over to her bed, and she pressed herself deeper into the mattress. She imagined her eyes must have been huge, though she hoped he couldn't spot the whites of her eyes in the dim light as she watched his every move.

Her intruder came closer, and her shriek was muffled as he pressed his hand over her mouth. She struggled to put distance between them, but the man was strong and managed to hold her down.

"Sarah, it's me," he whispered close to her ear. Her wild thrashing ceased, and the man removed his hands slowly, as if he were afraid she might try to escape again.

Sarah placed a hand over her heart, trying to keep it inside her chest. "Holy cow, Will!" she whispered hoarsely, pulling herself into a sitting position with quivering arms. She leaned her back against the wall and held the blanket protectively against her chest. "How did you find me?"

Will crouched down on the floor. She squinted at his profile, trying to make out his face in the candlelight. "It wasn't too difficult," he said quietly, "though I did enter several wrong quarters before I found yours."

Sarah's eyes widened. "Does anyone know you're here?"

She caught the faint shake of his head. "No, the occupants in those rooms slept through my intrusion. It's a miracle, really, since it was difficult for me to make out their faces if they were turned away, so . . ."

Sarah was still out of breath, but she had not lost her sense of humor in the scare. She stifled a giggle. "You didn't."

"I did." She heard the amusement in his voice. "But I managed to roll

49

them over without them waking, though one lonely woman did make a grab for me in her sleep." She caught the way his dark eyes danced in the light and felt a strange sense of déjà vu as she remembered another instance where the two of them had talked over candlelight. Will had been leaning toward her, like he was now, and she could almost hear his voice and remember the look in his eyes as he told her about his parents' tragic deaths that led him to invent the Shadow.

She shook her head slightly to dispel the memory and focused her attention on the man kneeling beside her. "What are you doing here, anyway?"

Will rubbed the back of his neck with his hand, something Sarah had come to find that he did when he was nervous or stalling until he could find a way to redirect the conversation. She managed to hide her grin.

"I'm waiting," she said when he remained silent.

He cleared his throat softly. "I was coming to make sure that you were all right and, well, perhaps steal you away from here." He spoke tentatively and posed his words almost like a question. He seemed to be trying to judge her reaction to his words.

Her shoulders sagged. "Will, you know I have to stay here and figure this out. I can't just leave. Not yet."

"I was not suggesting a permanent release," he quickly amended, one hand outstretched to stop her from making any further argument. "My only concern is for your wellbeing; the lack of natural air you're subject to in the castle can weaken your spirits. You must get out for a time—for your health. Then I can bring you right back after you get some fresh air."

Sarah could hide her grin no longer. "You mean you want to spring me out of this joint and then put me right back?"

His face clouded in confusion. "I am not sure, but I believe that's my idea."

She had to cover her mouth to squelch a sudden giggle that tried to escape her lips. She had forgotten how her "modern" lingo confused him, but it was fairly enjoyable to watch his face as he searched for her meaning.

Her mirth dissipated as she chewed on her lower lip and debated whether or not it was wise to go with him. Although she had been ready to collapse earlier, his surprise visit had given her a rush of adrenaline that left her feeling wide-awake and alert. There was no way she could fall back to sleep now. But still . . .

"I don't know," she said slowly, but it was obvious she was weakening.

"Please. For my peace of mind." His eyes held a look of pleading hope.

She could feel herself relenting as she watched the candlelight flicker across his face. She shook her head at herself, knowing that she would be exhausted when she performed her duties tomorrow, but the adventure of escaping with Will tonight was too much a temptation to pass up.

"Fine," she said. Sarah thought she caught a slight smile on his lips and realized how much she had missed it. "But I really can't stay out for a long time."

"Of course." He blew out the candle and stood, offering his hand. She took it and pulled herself to her feet, glad that she had kept her shoes on. Holding her hand in his large calloused one, Will pulled her along behind him as they crept noiselessly down the dark passageway. Sarah felt her heart beating in anticipation and unease. If they were caught sneaking out at night, what would they do to her? Fire her? She suppressed a shudder at the thought that they might do worse to a disobedient servant.

Pushing those disquieting thoughts aside, she followed Will silently as he guided her through a series of unlit hallways and stairs leading downward. The air was filled with silence; his mind was occupied with the task of selecting each corridor and guiding her safely to the next bend, and Sarah was busy watching her steps as they carefully picked their way along in the darkness. After several long minutes—during which her initial excitement had begun to fade in her intense concentration—Will guided her down a long, dank hall that ended at a reinforced door built a foot off the stones.

He released her hand and produced a set of keys from his belt, hardly glancing at the twelve or so keys on the ring before selecting one. It was obvious that he'd used this door many times in the past as he placed the thick key in the heavy iron lock and gave it a smooth, familiar turn. The grating sound of metal on metal was soft in the silence, but it caused Sarah to grimace.

He drew the key from the lock and quickly returned the ring to his belt, and Sarah wondered which of the guards had let his attention slip long enough for Will to snag the keys . . . and how many times he had done so in the past.

Grabbing the metal rung in the center of the door, Will pulled it open, the hinges screeching noisily from disuse, to reveal a narrow tunnel behind it. It was long and dark enough that Sarah couldn't see its end.

Will reached back for her hand, and she gripped his a little tighter than necessary, ducking as he helped her step over the inconvenient doorframe and into the elevated passage. She straightened once inside and blinked rapidly. It was darker here than the rest of the castle had been, and she couldn't make anything out in the total blackness before her. She was relieved when Will ducked his head and stepped into the tunnel behind her, brushing past her in the narrow space. He picked up her hand again and began to lead the way up the gentle incline.

His broad shoulders nearly touched the sides of the passageway, and he had to keep his head low so it didn't graze the ceiling. Sarah felt like asking him if he knew where he was going, but reminded herself that if anyone knew their way around the castle in the dark, it was Will.

The passage widened slightly, and the barest hint of light brightened the oppressive darkness. Sarah's shoulder brushed the ivy threaded along the walls. It grew together, thickening until she and Will were walking under an arched mass of tangled vines, tree limbs, and pale lavender flowers. She marveled at the barest shards of silver light breaking through the cracks in the short tunnel of flora. It was enchanting.

Will lifted a hand to push something aside in front of him, flooding the passage with pale moonlight. He flattened his back against the green wall to make room as he held the curtain back, gently guiding Sarah around him and into the night. She hadn't been able to see past him in the narrow tunnel, but she wasn't surprised when she found herself in the forest.

The wind had calmed as night came in, and it was only a gentle breeze that caused the ends of Sarah's hair to dance softly behind her. A haze of clouds hung low in the sky, and a few of the brightest stars peeked through the trees to light the ground. Though it was cold, the snow was not very deep on the earth here—the thick covering of trees had taken the brunt of the storm and suspended most of the white fluff overhead on bowed branches.

Will released her hand, and she glanced over her shoulder to see that the tunnel they had just come through had been built into the side of a small hill. Moss was growing in the dirt and had trailed up the hill in places, and a thick bunch of it hung low over the entrance. She could barely make out the short, tunnel-shaped mass of vegetation just past it.

"So that's how you got in," she said, half to herself.

Will nodded. "Not many people know of this tunnel. I am not even sure that Cadius or the prince knows. It has been a heavily guarded secret for many years."

Sarah grinned and asked wryly, "Then how do you know about it?"

His eyes sparkled mischievously in the twilight. "If you hadn't yet noticed, I am very good at sneaking around."

Sarah took on a serious expression and wagged a finger playfully at him. "Yeah, well, if we get caught, I'm going to sing like a canary."

His chuckle was genuine but soft and came from deep within his chest. She loved it when he laughed, though that didn't happen very often, and was glad that he had let his guard down some with her. That was progress where she was concerned.

"Would you like to walk or sit for a spell?" he asked.

"Let's sit. I don't want to get too tired for tomorrow's work."

Will looked down at her, his eyes conveying sudden concern. "Oh, Sarah. I did not think about—"

52

She waved a hand in the air to stop his apology. "Nuh-uh. No apologies. I'd much rather be out here with you." Her face heated as soon as the words left her lips. "Uh, I mean, you know. I'd rather be in the fresh air." She winced at her attempt to save face.

He leaned down to better see her eyes, and she couldn't have looked away if she wanted to. "I once told you that I found the way you speak your mind to be refreshing. I still admire you for it." He let his gaze wander over the thickness of trees. "That was part of the reason why I didn't want you working at the castle, other than the danger of the situation; I did not want you to lose your spirit and your boldness. It's what makes you who you are."

He placed a hand to her elbow before she could respond and guided her along the powder-white earth. Sarah thought she heard the faint sound of rushing water but couldn't remember ever seeing a lake or stream during her adventures in the forest.

The temperature dropped the further they walked into the thicket, and she couldn't contain her shivering any longer. Will must have noticed her shaking and assured her that they were close. The sound of flowing water was perfectly clear now, and after a few more moments, he guided Sarah to the edge of a small brook that cut a line between the trees.

Sarah caught her breath at the beautiful sight. The brook had frozen thinly in places, and the rushing water beneath the ice bubbled over the broken patches. Water flowed gracefully over the icy rocks, creating small, cascading waterfalls in its attempt to escape downhill. The clearing allowed moonlight to spill in between the trees on either side, causing the surface of the frozen brook to shine like glass. The light reflected in the narrow clearing, not more than thirty feet wide, and illuminated its surroundings. It was absolutely breathtaking.

Will stepped away from her, and she shivered in his absence. Her eyes followed his movements and she recognized the dark outline of his horse as he guided it toward her, stopping a few feet away to allow the animal to nibble at the small tuffs of grass poking out from beneath the snow. Will removed two bundles from the stallion's back, and then his long strides made quick work of the distance between them. He came up behind her and draped a heavy wool cloak about her shoulders.

Surprised speechless at the thoughtful gesture, she could only grab the collar and hold it tight under her chin. The warm cloak immediately staved off the chill coming from the brook, and her shivering lessened.

She watched in silence as Will laid a thick blanket down on one of the driest patches of earth at the base of a large willow tree. Obviously, he had thoroughly planned this out.

He motioned for her to sit and, ever the gentleman, waited until she took her spot before sitting down beside her. Sarah leaned against the thick trunk, smiling softly at his praise of her a moment ago. Even after all this time of her opening her big mouth, he still appreciated her spirit and audacity. Sure, he hadn't said he loved that about her, but she knew that having his admiration was not something to be taken lightly.

Gaze wandering the horizon, she asked curiously, "What's over there?" Will followed her finger to the sloping hill in the distance.

"Technically, the other side of that hill is Glendale Forest. My house is just over that rise."

They were silent for a long time, both content to listen to the owls and crickets call out night's symphony. Sarah fiddled idly with the white sash tied around the waist of her black servant's dress, which Edith had provided earlier, explaining that the kitchen staff wore gray, while castle maids and female servants wore variations of Sarah's uniform. It felt strange to disturb the calm silence by voicing her thoughts aloud, but there was so much she wanted to say and so many questions she had to ask. Sarah wasn't sure if she would get another opportunity like this again, even if it did mean shattering this perfect moment of contentment in his presence.

"You know," she began softly without looking at him, "I never did get a chance to thank you for saving Karen. I still can't believe you did that."

"I promised I would," he replied. She could feel his gaze resting on her and turned her head. The moon was behind him, and she could only make out his profile in the pale light coming through the trees.

"Why didn't you tell me you were leaving the last time we spoke?" he surprised her by asking.

Though she had been expecting it, his innocent question still caught her off-guard. Her shoulders sagged, and she stared at her hands clasped in her lap. The scar on her hand, courtesy of Allan's knife, appeared translucent in the silvery light. "I didn't know I was leaving until after you brought me back that day."

"Did you really leave so suddenly?"

Sarah knew what he was asking and closed her eyes. "It *was* sudden, but there was enough time to tell you I was going." Angling her head, she looked up at him and admitted softly, "I just couldn't do it. I couldn't say goodbye to you because it seemed too final. It was selfish of me, I know, and I'm sorry."

She turned her gaze ahead and hoped he wouldn't see the tears of guilt pooling in her eyes. She hated it when she cried, so she tried to quickly blink the tears away, but her vision still blurred. She rubbed the corner of her eye as subtly as possible.

"You know," Will began thoughtfully. She didn't turn to look at him but kept her eyes focused on some water trickling over an especially fascinating rock. "At first I thought something had happened when I didn't see you for days. Then Karen came by the shop and told me that you had

54

left for home and wasn't sure if you would return." He paused, and Sarah clenched her hands so fiercely that her nails almost drew blood. She ducked her head and allowed her hair to fall in front of her face to hide her shame.

"I chose not to believe that it was true, that you left without telling me," Will went on, his voice tight. Sarah didn't dare look up at his face for fear of what she might find there.

He cleared his throat before he spoke again, his tone softer than before. "I was so sure you would be coming back someday, so I waited patiently for your return. The first month passed, and then another. I admit that I was hurt and angry at first, but then I simply felt . . . I'm not quite sure. Resigned or empty, I suppose. You had begun to break down my armor, and that left me feeling exposed and vulnerable when you left. I had put up these walls and kept others out for so long that when I finally let you in and you departed . . . I felt that I had to be more vigilant about who I allowed to see inside of me. That was why I was so reticent when you returned; I did not want to open myself up to more hurt."

She couldn't recall him every speaking so much at once, and never with as much feeling expressed in his words, even if it did sound like they were difficult to say. Will used his index finger to turn her head around and lifted her chin. He waited until she looked up at him, and when she did, she couldn't turn away.

"But, Sarah, I was wrong for trying to keep you out like that. *I was wrong*," he said, and she knew the words must have cost him. "I realize that now. I think I knew it as soon as I saw you standing inside the castle, shaking from head to foot, yet still determined to do what you knew was right. In that moment, I knew that I did not want to push you away and lose you forever. I could tell it hurt you when I held you at arm's length all those times, and I am sorry for being too stubborn to relent sooner."

Sarah stared up at him silently, completely taken aback by his apology. She hadn't thought that she'd ever begrudged the fact that he kept his distance emotionally from her at times. But now she realized that she had unwittingly held onto the offense she had felt each time he held back from her.

"I really shouldn't have taken it so personally," she admitted, shrugging her shoulders. "I knew it was just your defense mechanism. But if you need my forgiveness, you have it."

His body seemed to relax. "Thank you," he breathed.

Sarah turned her eyes away for a moment to formulate her thoughts, though his finger still held her chin. "Can I ask you a question, Will?"

He nodded his head. "Of course."

She hesitated for a brief second before diving ahead. "Whatever happened to the Shadow?"

~Chapter 9~

Will let his hand fall from her face, unconsciously withdrawing from her. "I already told you what happened."

She shook her head slightly, causing soft auburn waves to bounce around her face. "I know. You said that you weren't needed anymore. But obviously that isn't true, since the whole reason I'm here is because Cadius might be bent on killing someone else."

Will raked a hand back through his hair and sucked in a breath, holding it for a long moment, striving for calm. He should have known that she would want more of an explanation than he had already given to her; she was too smart to be so easily distracted. He felt a reluctant smile tug at the corner of his lips as he realized that he would have been disappointed if she had been so easily mollified by his vague response.

He allowed himself a moment to study her face, grateful for the darkness that prevented her from seeing his close observation of her features. The sprinkle of freckles across her upturned nose made her tanned, heart-shaped face young and girlish and terribly endearing. In the cover of darkness, he found himself lost in the depth of her clear blue eyes. The first thing he had noticed about her in the forest that day several months past was her piercing gaze; her eyes were like a window into her soul that conveyed every emotion she was feeling and each thought that flitted across her mind. He had always had a difficult time looking away from them and was glad he needn't do so now.

"You can't seriously believe that you aren't needed." The sound of her voice shattered the quiet that had settled over them, effectively putting an end to the haze that was clouding his mind. Her wounded tone and the pained look in her eyes pierced his heart.

He let out his breath slowly. "I'm sorry, Sarah. I did not mean to—" He stopped mid-sentence. What had he meant to do, exactly? When he first realized that she had left without bothering to tell him of her departure, he once again withdrew into the protective armor that had guarded his heart before she had entered his life.

During that time, he had hardly spoken to anyone, and the townsfolk and his customers had eventually stopped trying to engage him in polite conversation, simply coming to do business in uncomfortable silence and then leaving as soon as they were able. Will's uncle had even come to make sure that he was all right after he hadn't seen or heard from him in nearly a month. Will had said he was fine, and though it was obvious that his uncle didn't believe his curt response in the least, the man was wise enough to leave it alone.

Will had spent his days filling the orders that were placed during the busy autumn months. Over time, his anger and sullen attitude over her abrupt departure had begun to ebb away and then disappeared altogether. But the questions and pain remained. He gazed into her sad, beseeching eyes and felt regret over the careless way he had abandoned the responsibilities he had taken on as the Shadow. Had he not sworn to avenge his parents and protect those who couldn't do so for themselves?

"Sarah," he began, heaving a heavy sigh. He could see he had her full attention and decided to just come out with it. "Do you remember when you pointed out that I had created my alter-ego because I simply sought revenge for my parents' deaths?"

Her eyes widened in alarm and her face paled slightly. "Oh, no, Will! I said that in anger, but I never meant for you to abandon your quest to help people."

Will held up a hand to silence her before she placed the blame for his actions upon herself. "It is not your fault. I simply got to thinking about what you said, and I realized that you were right. Part of the reason why I went around helping people was because I thought it might send a message to those I sought to defeat—that there was at least one man willing to fight against them for what is right."

Sarah shifted and leaned her side against the tree so her body faced him. "But I never should have discouraged you from helping people. It was wrong of me to say that."

He shrugged. It was no longer important to him—he realized that now. "Don't apologize. Besides, it is not the only reason that I no longer masquerade as the Shadow."

"Well, then, what is it?"

Will glanced away and stared off into the trees. "I am ashamed to admit that I simply ceased caring. I hardened myself against what was happening around me and managed to convince myself that it no longer mattered." He looked back at her and was sure the shame he felt was written all over his face. "Things are worse than ever, and I chose to ignore that fact."

Sarah's eyes softened, and he could see the compassion in her gaze as she reached out and placed a comforting hand on his arm. "I'm sorry that you felt that way, but do you care now?"

"Of course," he replied earnestly.

She nodded her head once and added, "Then it's never too late."

The thin, silvery line on the back of her hand shifted as she gave his arm a reassuring squeeze, reminding him of how he had almost lost her to Allan's scheme. Now that he had her back, he had no intention of squandering this opportunity.

Will smiled down at her, filled with emotions he was sure he could no longer hide, that he *chose* not to keep secret. "I suppose not."

****

Soon after they tied up the loose ends in their friendship, Will took her back to her room and waited outside the door like a gentleman. Then again, he *had* broken into her room in the first place, Sarah thought wryly.

She turned around to face him. His large frame fairly towered over her, though his height and breadth didn't intimidate her as it once had. Underneath that hardened façade she had encountered when they first met, there was a man with an incredibly warm and tender heart. She suddenly recalled the way he had the cloak and blanket waiting for her and couldn't help but grin.

"You know," she whispered so as to not wake the other servants, "you must have been pretty confident in your skills of persuasion to have all that stuff ready for us out there. You were that sure you could get me to come?"

Will smiled down at her, causing the corners of his eyes to crinkle in a way that Sarah found terribly charming. "I'd hoped I might convince you."

Sarah swallowed over the emotions he stirred in her with the tender note of his voice. Remembering that she was still wearing his cloak, she began to shrug off its bulk, but Will put a strong hand on her shoulder to stop her movement. She looked up at him.

"Keep it," he said. "It becomes rather drafty in these old rooms."

Sarah thanked him, feeling overwhelmed. One minute they were at each other's throats, and the next they were sharing a conversation in the most enchanting setting imaginable, and now he was offering her his cloak. Sarah knew he was probably just being considerate, but she couldn't help but feel the gesture was very intimate.

They said their goodnights, and Sarah crawled into bed gratefully. She hugged the collar of Will's cloak close to her face, breathing deeply the comforting scents of the wool. The smell of pine and the sweet aroma of rich earth mingled with Will's own musky scent. These fragrances lulled her into a blissful sleep that she wished would never end.

But her sweet slumber was interrupted when Edith woke her only a few short hours later so they could get a start on their morning chores. It was in the morning when Sarah awoke that the memory of last night felt like no more than a dream. A perfect, wonderful dream. But in her experience, dreams were a wonderful fantasy during sleep that very seldom came true. She hoped this time it would be different.

Now Sarah followed Edith around like a loyal dog, taking directions and trying to act like she wasn't ready to fall asleep on her feet, though she didn't regret last night in the least.

"I must run and check on preparations for the midday feast," Edith was saying. Sarah tried not to groan; it wasn't even noon yet and already she wanted to crawl back into bed and sleep for days.

It seemed they had spent hours in one of the formal sitting rooms on the second floor, polishing the silver tea set and candlesticks that were permanent fixtures in the room. How were the servants able to endure this *every* day? She had gotten to know Edith a little in the past twenty-four hours, discovering that she had a son named Rennault. How did the woman manage to be a wife and mother *and* work this hard all the time?

"Do you think you can manage while I see to the kitchen staff?" Edith asked. Sarah nodded, straightening her back to cover her exhaustion. Her mentor gave a quick nod before exiting the room through the large open doorway that led to the hall.

Sarah watched her go, waiting until the sound of her hurried footsteps could no longer be heard echoing down the hall before allowing her limp body to sag down onto the soft fur before the fireplace. She wasn't sure she could keep this up for much longer, but she might have to if she couldn't find any incriminating evidence against Cadius soon.

And how was she supposed to do that, anyway? The one meal she'd had with the kitchen staff, they'd all seemed so reserved that Sarah knew they weren't going to come right out and offer to help her take down Cadius, and she'd hardly had any contact with the other servants or nobles staying at the castle to learn anything new. She was getting nowhere. Slowly.

Sarah took her vexation out on the short teapot in her hand, rubbing the surface vigorously with the cloth, but the blasted thing refused to shine. Tears of frustration brought on by sheer exhaustion pooled in her eyes and slipped down her cheeks unhindered. She felt like she couldn't do anything right: The king's murderer was running free, though she was unable to prove that. The prince was safe for now, but his potential killer was on the loose, something else that she couldn't be certain of because of Problem #1. So far, she had nothing but a few crazy hunches and her intuition to go on, and it didn't seem to be getting her anywhere.

"God," she murmured, staring at the fur beneath her as she set the pot down. "I could sure use Your help right now. Give me some kind of sign if I'm supposed to give up or go on." She felt like her efforts here were wasted as she spent her time cleaning and doing nothing that she thought to be productive. Was she just wasting her time here?

Sarah heard the sound of low male voices coming from the other room, sending her nervous heart into overdrive. She lurched to her aching feet and began dusting the top of the mantle to look busy; if they came in, she didn't want them to think she had been shirking her duties. But the voices and their owners remained in the adjoining room.

In her curiosity, Sarah moved a little closer to the doorway leading from the large sitting area to the smaller room, absentmindedly dusting a small round table as she listened. Judging by their strained, hushed tones, the two men were having some kind of disagreement. She felt a flutter of excitement at the idea that this might be her first opportunity to do some real snooping.

Casting a furtive glance over her shoulder to make sure that Edith hadn't returned, Sarah abandoned any pretense that she was working and dropped the rag on a table nearby. Stealthily, she crept over to the doorway leading to the more intimate sitting room situated in the east corner of the upper floor. The door was cracked open an inch, and she leaned forward to peer through the opening, straining to hear.

"What do you mean I'm being dismissed?" hissed one of the men lowly. Sarah couldn't see his face because it was hidden behind the door, though his raspy voice sounded vaguely familiar to her ears, grating on an old nerve she couldn't place.

"Just that: *He is dismissing you.*" The other man's voice was calm and smooth and diplomatic as he enunciated each word. He sounded younger than his companion, and Sarah adjusted her position to better see him through the narrow slit in the door.

From her small vantage point of his profile, Sarah could see that the man was lean and tall, and his skin was naturally olive-toned. The pale coloring of everyone else inside the castle walls, and outside as well, caused her to wonder if he was as foreign as she. Well, maybe not *as* foreign, but she thought she detected an accent.

"It would seem that he is going in a different direction," the polished man informed calmly, giving a faintly sympathetic look to the other occupant of the room. "He appreciates the insight you have offered into the matter, but your services are no longer necessary."

The unseen man sputtered before managing to get out, "But I have served him faithfully." His voice lowered to a furious whisper. "I have *killed* for him, and now I am to be cast aside?"

Sarah's heart picked up a beat, drowning out the man's patient response. Who were they talking about? Cadius? She pressed in a little

60

closer to the door and strained to hear.

"You have served your purpose and your contract has been terminated," the cultured man went on, voice lacking inflection; he appeared entirely bored with the discussion, as though he fired people everyday. He raised a dark brow in challenge, almost appearing amused. "Are you questioning the master's wisdom in letting you go? Cadius will not be pleased."

Sarah's breath quickened, and she hoped they couldn't hear it in the lengthening silence. Clamping her hands over her mouth, she breathed quietly between her fingers and waited.

The first man broke the silence, his raspy voice strained and intense. "You will have to drag my cold, dead body out of here before I resign from my position."

Sarah watched as the other man smiled a slow, condescending smile. "I don't believe you wish for that to be arranged."

"And how will you prevent me from exposing her, hmm? What is to keep me from remaining silent? She is the key to this idiotic plan of his."

The smooth man's cocky façade cracked. "How did you—?"

"Cadius is hardly the only one with spies," the man said with a hissing chuckle. "Or should I expose both of them? Women are hardly worth causing a war, wouldn't you agree?"

Surprise melting into anger, the man took a step forward. "How dare you."

"The master wished to keep me ignorant, but I know what she is; I was careful to learn everything I could. Does he think he is the only one with a contingency plan?" It was the mystery man's turn to sound amused, as though he had the upper hand. "I have known his nature too well to be without an escape route."

Something like a faint hiss sounded in the room, and the man's eyes lowered briefly, registering alarm at whatever the other man held. "Have you gone mad?" He took a step forward out of Sarah's line of vision.

She could hear the men scuffling in the room and desperately wanted to see what was happening, but was too afraid to reveal herself. One of the men cried out suddenly, and Sarah distinctly heard a heavy *thump* and a gasp. It was a long moment before she thought she heard a creaking sound. Then all went still.

Footsteps were coming down the hallway, though she ignored them as she leaned in just a little further to see what had happened. But she wasn't minding her balance in her eagerness to see inside, and she pitched forward just enough that her shoulder bumped the door. With a gasp, she managed to catch herself before she stumbled into the room, but was unable to stop the door from swinging open. She felt paralyzed as she watched, almost in slow motion, as the door opened into the room.

~Chapter 10~

The polished man had his back to her as he rested his forearm on a large, solid bench below the window, panting hard. He glanced toward the hall door, and his eyes widened. Sarah cringed as the door she had leaned into at last finished its wide arc and bumped quietly into the wall. The man whipped his head around to gape at her, face strained, and Sarah's eyes widened guiltily. Suddenly, Edith was there, brushing past her in her haste to enter the room, and the man quickly straightened and took a step away from the bench.

"What is going on in here?" Edith panted, eyes wide. "I heard someone scream all the way from the kitchen." She gasped and pointed. "My lord, your arm."

Several other servants and two guards filtered into the room to see what the commotion was about. The man glanced down at his right bicep in surprise, paling when he saw the sickly patch of torn flesh through the chunk of his coat that had been gouged out. Everyone's gazes seemed to drift in unison to the bloody dagger on the carpet near his feet. He glanced up, his eyes going to the doorway as he gripped his arm and hunched over, an expression of barely restrained agony masking his features.

"The physician attacked me." He used his left hand to point toward the other doorway. He winced with the movement and then cradled his injured arm.

Sarah leaned into the room to get a better view and caught sight of a short, skinny man gripping the door handle. His wide eyes stared back at his accuser in disbelief, his mouth working silently.

Edith shook her head. "But, Sir Lisandro, I cannot believe that the physician—"

"What more proof do you need?" the man called Lisandro groaned, motioning to the dagger on the floor. The guards moved forward as one, each grabbing hold of one of the physician's arm. The small man shook his head adamantly from side to side, though he was still unable to plead his case. Whatever anger he had felt before in the heat of their disagreement, it didn't appear that he'd meant to harm the other man. Sarah absorbed the scene silently, eyes huge, hoping that no one asked her to leave as a few more bodies entered the shrinking space.

"What would you like for us to do with him, my lord?" one of the guards asked, his face inscrutable.

"Imprison him," he ordered quietly, furrowing his brow in pain. It struck Sarah as odd that he looked vaguely reluctant to give the command against the man who had attacked him. Perhaps he had a conscience.

The guards turned around and guided the slight man into the hallway. The murmuring crowd began to disperse as they went back to their duties, though a few servants remained to check on the wounded man.

Edith moved further into the room and encouraged Sir Lisandro to rest on one of the wooden chairs on the rug. When he collapsed into it—somehow making the *plop* appear dignified—she took charge of the situation and ushered the rest of the servants from the room, saying that they had duties to tend to. She then ordered the man to remove his outer garment so she could better see the wound. He grimaced in pain as he shrugged out of his ruined coat and shirt, revealing a purple sleeveless under-shirt and the open wound on his bicep. Sarah felt a little queasy at the sight of so much blood dribbling down his arm.

Edith made a *tsk*ing sound against her teeth as she examined the gash, then turned to Sarah and motioned her over. That girl came reluctantly, feeling nervous as the man turned his brown eyes toward her.

"I must run downstairs for some more clean linens," Edith explained as she handed Sarah one of the freshly washed rags she hadn't yet used for mopping. "Press this on the wound until I return."

"You're leaving me?" Sarah squeaked, feeling the color drain from her face.

Edith nodded, and her look was matter-of-fact. "The other women have been known to faint at the slightest drop of blood, and I feel like you have a heartier constitution."

Sarah didn't even register the compliment as she clenched the clean linen anxiously in her hand. The woman might have a different opinion if her charge passed out or lost her breakfast on the rug. "But what about the doctor? Let's send for him."

She received a look that said the answer to that was obvious. "You will do fine if you don't let him bleed out," Edith instructed. Then she took the younger girl's hand and placed it firmly over Lisandro's wound. In a decisive tone that brooked no argument, she said, "I will be back in a few minutes." Then she left them alone.

Sarah gaped at the back of Edith's retreating form until she disappeared through the doorway. She turned reluctantly to the wounded man and encountered his penetrating stare. She quickly averted her eyes. It was silent for one agonizingly long minute as Sarah's gaze darted about the room in an attempt to evade his unwavering stare.

"Looks pretty deep," she remarked, a poor attempt at conversation considering she had yet to get a good look at the wound.

"You seem nervous," Lisandro observed softly. Sarah started at the sound of his voice, husky with pain, and glanced at him in her surprise. The tanned skin between his dark brows was furrowed, whether in pain or his intense appraisal of her, she wasn't sure. Maybe it was a little of both.

"Uh, no, no. Not nervous," she replied quickly. A convulsive swallow followed her statement, and the hand pressed against his arm twitched. He didn't look to be in as much pain as before, and Sarah wondered briefly if maybe shock was kicking in. Oh, Lord, was he going to die on her?

Lisandro nodded his head toward the ottoman in front of the small sitting couch. "You should sit down."

Sarah eagerly bobbed her head in agreement. She retreated a step, and Lisandro's hand came up to cover hers and keep the cloth in place. Though she knew he didn't mean anything by it, the feel of his warm, smooth hand over hers made Sarah uncomfortable.

Quickly, she slipped her hand out from beneath his and pulled the dark-colored ottoman a safe distance in front of him. Sitting down, she had to lean forward awkwardly to reach the wound and gingerly pressed her fingertips to the linen, careful not to touch his hand again as he released the cloth and let his arm fall limply back to his side.

Sarah frowned. The blood had already begun to seep through the thin cloth, and she didn't have a replacement. Pressing down firmly on the wound, she prayed that Edith would hurry with more supplies. Her initial queasiness and fear began to ebb away as she set her mind to the task at hand: Not letting the man bleed to death. Sarah suddenly wished she had paid more attention in her biology class. Maybe then she could recall how many quarts of blood were in the human body and how much someone could lose before they stopped functioning. Not that she could do anything about that now.

She glanced up at the man's face and realized that he was still looking at her. She carefully avoided his eyes and noted that his face had gained back some of its color, and he did not look to be in severe pain anymore. Was that just his body shutting down?

"Can you feel the wound anymore?" She probed gently with her free hand around the wound and then forced herself to meet his steady gaze to gauge his reaction.

He shrugged his good shoulder indifferently, hardly any signs of pain in his dark, distinguished features. Sarah was caught off-guard by his teasing smile. "It still feels as though I was stabbed, if that's what you're asking." There was that accent again.

Sarah eyed him warily, wondering if the color in his face would drain away before he passed out from blood loss. "You don't look like you're in agony," she pointed out, as much for his benefit as for hers.

Lisandro glanced down at his injury beneath Sarah's hand. "I learned to withstand pain from a young age," he said in way of explanation. She furrowed her brow at the offhand comment, wondering what he meant. His gaze drifted back to her face, making her increasingly uncomfortable. "I don't believe I caught your name."

She hadn't given it, but she decided not to correct him after all he had been through. "Sarah," she mumbled. "My name's Sarah." Almost against her will, she looked up at him. His soft smile caused her stomach to jump.

"A beautiful name for a princess." Sarah wondered if he was teasing her. Surely he knew that she was just the help in her drab garment, not castle royalty. But there was no mockery in his expression, only an open curiosity and friendliness that drew her in.

Thankfully, Edith bustled into the room before she had a chance to reply, carrying a small stack of white linens against her side. Sarah felt awash in relief at the timely interruption and gladly stood up so the older woman could take over, hoping that Edith didn't question why her face was so flushed. Sarah silently reprimanded herself. One unexpected remark from a dark stranger and she blushed. Will's face came to mind, and she found herself wishing that he were there with his comforting presence.

Without dropping her load, Edith tapped the ottoman closer to the chair Lisandro occupied and plopped down on the seat Sarah had just vacated. Holding the stack of linens steady on the edge of the ottoman with one hand, Edith carefully removed the bloodstained cloth from Lisandro's arm. He grimaced, and Sarah instinctively cringed along with him, knowing that some of the blood had dried and fused the cloth to his skin.

Without the scab of dried blood struggling to seal the injury or the pressure of the cloth to stanch the flow of blood, the wound began to bubble again, and small rivulets of sticky red liquid ran down his forearm. Though Sarah felt some of her previous color ebb from her face, Edith ignored the blood and examined the deep gash with a critical eye. She straightened abruptly and stood with a shake of her head.

"I will have to fetch a needle and thread," she explained to her patient as she wiped her bloody hands on one of the cloths. Edith spoke in a professional, no nonsense tone that let everyone know she was in control. "The dagger went deep, and I have to close the wound to prevent infection." Lisandro nodded his head in understanding and waited for her to go on. The older woman's all-business manner softened slightly as she searched his face, though Sarah wasn't sure what she was looking for.

"I thought I should inform you," she continued. The blunt edge her words had previously carried softened noticeably, though her voice was still as matter-of-fact. Obviously, she was not going to keep anything from this man. "Since there is no fire lit in this room, I will also have someone follow me back with a brazier and an iron so I can seal the wound closed completely—sewing it shut does not always keep out infection."

"It must be done," Lisandro said with another nod. Sarah had blanched at the idea that Edith was going to burn his wound closed, but the man who was going to receive such rough treatment appeared calm and resigned.

Though she didn't smile, Edith looked relieved at his compliance. "Very well, then." She thrust the linens into Sarah's arms, and she clutched them tightly to her chest. "Keep pressure on the wound and try as best you can to keep the skin pinched together." At Sarah's mechanical nod, Edith hastened from the room, leaving the two alone in the sitting room once more.

Turning back to her patient, Sarah felt his gaze on her again as she sat stiffly and tended to his wound. Did Lisandro realize that he had been staring this whole time? The man and his audacity began to grate on Sarah's nerves. Her previous tension melted away, and she felt more perturbed by the minute beneath his unwavering gaze.

"It's rude to stare," she warned. There was no way he missed the irritation lacing her words, and if he did, the glare she gave him should have cleared things up.

Lisandro actually smiled at her reprimand, flashing his white teeth, which only annoyed Sarah further.

"You must forgive my stare, my lady," he amended, though he appeared more delighted that she had noticed than guilty over his boldness. "But I couldn't help but observe that you are nearly as sunned as I. Everyone in this place is so fair that I was surprised, is all." He dipped his head slightly in a gesture of subservience, and his smile was appealing now. "I meant no disrespect, my lady. You must forgive me for acting like such an imbecile."

My, he was suave. Sarah's spine stiffened instinctively, and she knew this was a man that would make her work to keep her guard up. Her friend Janice back home would have fallen fast and hard for his smooth personality and dark, handsome features. The two friends had similar tastes in men, though Sarah was usually more careful when it came to falling.

She sat up a little straighter and lifted her chin, throwing him a cheeky smile. "Well, if you didn't stare as much, then you wouldn't have to apologize." Her tone was sickly sweet. She knew she sounded rude, but this man put her defenses on-edge, and he seemed to be enjoying it.

Though he turned his head away from her, Lisandro's self-satisfied grin widened, expressing his pleasure at having gotten her to spar with him.

With his eyes on the bench beneath the window, he said, "You speak your mind. Are you sure you belong here?"

Sarah's heart skipped a beat at his question. Now that his gaze was averted, she openly gaped at him. There was no way he had already figured her out, was there? She schooled her features as best she could in case he turned to look at her again. "I don't know what you mean," she replied smoothly, but her voice hitched at the end.

Lisandro's amused look remained in place, though he carefully evaded her eyes. "In some ways you seem as alien as I." Though he spoke directly to her, he looked everywhere around the room but at her. His studied avoidance was actually comical, and Sarah felt the side of her mouth twitch. He chose that moment to glance at her, and she did her best to hide her smile. He seemed to sense her amusement anyway and inclined his head to the side in a gesture of innocent appraisal. Janice would have found the action adorably endearing.

"Do you find something amusing, my lady?" His look of boyish innocence caused a reluctant smile to pull at the corners of Sarah's mouth. He was charming, she'd give him that.

"So, where is it that you're from? What's your background?" she asked, avoiding his question. She didn't want to partake in his teasing game and decided that this was the safest way to turn the conversation, and if it kept his mind off his wound . . .

His smile let her know she hadn't fooled him, but he graciously followed her lead. "I was born in Cadiz and moved into the country with my father and mother when I was nine. I was named for my father, Romeo Lisandro." His smooth voice made the words sound enticing, and his Spanish accent was so perfectly distinguishable as he said the name that Sarah wondered how she hadn't picked up on it before.

"Your name's Romeo?" she said wryly, pronouncing his name like he was a character in Shakespeare's play . . . and he certainly appeared as suave as Romeo. It had sounded far better when he said the name with that accent, but for whatever reason, she didn't want to give him the satisfaction of hearing his name spoken properly.

Lisandro shook his head. "No, my full name is Damien Romeo Lisandro."

"Oh," was all she said. Of course he wouldn't understand her derisive response to his name, since Shakespeare wouldn't write his play of love and tragedy for a few more centuries. She looked at the man across from her and sensed he was waiting for her to divulge information about herself. When she remained silent, his ever-present, slightly cocky grin widened.

"Well, my lady," he said smoothly, still appearing comfortable and unaffected by her silence. "Now it's your turn."

Sarah eyed him warily, hand twitching over his wound. "My turn for what?"

Damien leaned forward and lowered his voice, eyes gleaming with mischief. "It is your turn to tell me who you really are."

~*Chapter 11*~

Sarah's grip on the bloody cloth loosened in her surprise, and the soiled rag dropped to the floor with a *plop*. The sound pulled her from her shock-induced paralysis, and she abruptly broke eye contact with Damien as he moved to retrieve the cloth. She quickly bent down to snatch the rag from the ground before he could, glad for the excuse to hide her colorless face from his scrutiny while she composed herself. When she glanced down at the blood on her shaking hands, she instantly felt queasy.

He knows, Sarah thought, dismayed at having been found out so soon.

She straightened slowly with the stained cloth in her hand, taking her time to calm herself. Being careful to keep her hair in front of her face, she slowly wrapped a fresh linen around the soiled one and placed it precisely on the rug stain; she and Edith would have to clean the mark, and Sarah didn't want to add any more stains for them to scrub later.

Tactfully keeping her face hidden from Damien's probing gaze as she unfolded a new linen, she spoke with a surprisingly nonchalant tone, "I'm not sure I catch your meaning." Sarah leaned forward and quickly pressed the cloth to his wound to catch the rivulet of sticky blood that ran down his lean muscles. She glanced up at his face almost against her will. He cocked his head to the side, and dark brown hair fell over his high forehead as he studied her.

"You look like a fish out of water," he observed with that persistent, self-satisfied grin; it seemed to be a permanent fixture on his handsome face. "You speak your mind too much to have been born into servitude."

"Well, I wasn't born into it," she answered honestly. "This is kind of a . . . *temporary* situation."

Any comment Damien may have had died on his lips as Edith preceded two male servants into the room, both men struggling to carry a brazier between them. They set the lit brazier a few feet from where Sarah and Damien sat and quietly left the room at Edith's dismissing nod. She then thrust the metal rod she was holding into the heat of the coals and glanced over at the two younger occupants of the room.

"Did everything go all right while I was out?" she asked, addressing Sarah directly.

Sarah's gaze flickered briefly to Damien and then back to her. She nodded, thankful for the interruption. It didn't bode well that the man wanted to probe so deeply when she was attempting to be elusive in her quest. But it was a ridiculously large castle, and maybe their paths would never cross under the same roof as long as Sarah remained there. Though the thought was meant to assure her that her cover was momentarily intact, the idea that she may not see Damien after this incident gave her a pang of regret, and that greatly concerned her.

Sarah frowned. Why did she feel so drawn to this man, as though something inside of him pulled at her? She hadn't felt this way since she first met Will, and the sudden thought caused her to feel immense guilt. But why should she? It wasn't as though she was doing something wrong. She wasn't truly interested in Damien; it was only her insatiable curiosity twisting her thoughts.

To be fair, he *was* charming and refined—and he was also intriguingly handsome, with his accent and cheeky smile. Besides, she and Will weren't even an item, so what did it matter if she did find someone attractive? *Not that I do,* she was quick to amend.

Sarah cleaned the blood from her hands in the washing bowl on the table at the wall, and then stood beside Damien with dripping hands, shifting impatiently as Edith continued to warm the rod over the brazier. How long could it take to heat? The growing silence, which both Damien and Edith appeared to be content with, was beginning to twist Sarah's already frayed nerves.

At last, Edith pulled the rod from the fire when the tip had taken on a bright orange glow and walked carefully over to Damien. Sarah suddenly realized that Edith had never brought up her sewing equipment.

"I thought you had to sew the wound closed first," she remarked, eying the glowing rod. Cauterizing the wound would certainly get the job done faster, freeing Sarah for her other duties. It would also prevent infection in the wound, as Edith had said earlier. But still. . . .

Edith shook her head as she came to stand beside them, the hot bar a safe distance in front of her. She huffed in vexation. "I was going to, but that ninnyhammer of a cook borrowed my needle to lace up this evening's stuffed goose." Her look suggestion the cook was one of the most incompetent people in the world. "The lord is losing too much blood to wait for my sewing equipment to be properly cleaned. I think it may be best if we seal the wound as quickly as possible." She motioned with her head for Sarah to move and then took her place when she did so.

Sarah clutched the bloody cloth in her hand, eyes fixated on the

70

glowing rod as it moved toward the wound. It was the best they could do, considering the circumstances and lack of medical care, since the physician had been taken away, but it was also horrifically primitive to Sarah. She suddenly realized that the rod had frozen mid-air and glanced up sharply at Edith's face, catching her look of hesitancy.

"It might be wise if you turn the other way," she advised. Sarah did not need to be told twice and obediently turned her head to the side. A moment later, Sarah heard the sound of sizzling flesh, though Damien did not gasp or cry out. The room was large, but all of its windows were closed to keep the cold outdoors, and the putrid stench of burning flesh quickly permeated the space.

Sarah squeezed her eyes closed against the wave of nausea as the sickening scent assailed her senses. She breathed through her mouth slowly. Losing her breakfast in front of Edith, who appeared to have the situation under control, would not be the brightest move on Sarah's part if she wanted to prove herself capable.

No sound came from the other occupants of the room, and Sarah glanced up cautiously, wondering if it was over. She pressed a hand to her churning stomach and turned away from the sight of Edith rolling the cooling rod gently over the wound to ensure that it closed completely.

"It's the best I can do under the circumstances," Edith said, addressing her patient. Sarah exhaled in relief that it was over, and then winced when she saw how the skin around the sealed wound had swollen bright red from the heat. It looked terribly painful.

Sarah's gaze lifted from Damien's wound to his face, which had paled considerably and was beaded with perspiration. As if sensing her disquiet and concern for him, he caught her eye and smiled reassuringly, though the action didn't remove the deep crease between his brows.

"I believe it will suffice, though," Edith continued, evaluating her work. "I am having an herb poultice brought up, and the dressings will need to be changed twice or three times daily. Sarah will assist you in cleaning and redressing the wound."

Damien had absorbed these instructions with a slightly detached expression, though it brightened some with this last bit of information. His gaze flickered briefly to Sarah before returning to the older woman. While Damien listened to the remainder of Edith's instructions with rapt attention, the words landed on deaf ears where Sarah was concerned.

She was supposed to be his *nurse*? A moment ago, she had thought they would part ways and never meet again after this episode was over, and now she would be at his beck and call. Would Damien truly want her to ignore all her other duties and have her perform the simple task of changing his bandages? Though he could be a little roguish at times, he didn't seem to be the kind of man who would demand her attention like that. Then again, she had only spent an hour with him, at most, so who was Sarah to judge his true character?

She started at the sound of her name and focused on Edith, who was eying her curiously. "Sorry, what did you say?"

Edith stood, holding the cooled piece of steel in her hand. Her brown eyes searched Sarah's face with a mother's intuition. "I need you to run an errand for me," she announced abruptly and without preamble. "You could use the fresh air, and I can apply the poultice myself this instance."

Sarah must have looked more frazzled than she realized to receive such a quick dismissal. She nodded eagerly, though, grateful for the chance to get away from the smell and escape from under Damien's penetrating gaze. Edith gave her instructions for the errand, and Sarah bolted from the sitting room with as much ladylike grace as possible.

Even in the heat of her desire to escape the castle walls, which had suddenly become very confining, Sarah had just enough sense of mind to run to her quarters for Will's cloak, since her task would take her outdoors. She hastily threw the warm garment about her shoulders and didn't pause for breath as she hurried down the stairs, snatching a woven basket from the kitchen and then quickly ducking out the door in order to escape the inquisitive gazes she was receiving from a pair of servant girls. Only once she had emerged into the midday light and heard the crunch of snow beneath her slipper-clad feet did she dare to breathe deeply again.

Standing just outside the servants' entrance, she filled her lungs with the crisp air, savoring the welcome aroma of freshly fallen snow after suffering the stuffy, moldy scent some of the unused castle rooms carried. The sun was at its highest point in the sky, setting the perfectly white snow on fire with a sparkling brilliance that had begun to melt the crystal-clear icicles above the back entrance, though it had yet to thaw the growing layers of winter's mark on the ground.

With the calming winter scene around her and the warmth of the sun kissing the top of her head, Sarah felt nearly herself after a moment outside the confines of the castle walls, which had slowly begun to close in on her over the last two days.

She nearly laughed aloud when she realized that she had yet to make it through her full second day.

Though the sun shone brightly, a chilly breeze played with the hem of her dress and tucked it around her legs. Sarah worked the laces on the long wool cloak and stuffed her hands in the pockets to warm them.

As she walked along the outer gate toward the center of town, she wondered to herself how servants managed to remain sane when they were faced with the same mundane tasks day after day. And all the while, they had to keep up a blank façade. Sarah was shocked at how well the castle servants could conceal their emotions while they dealt with constant demands in an unfriendly environment.

Sarah searched the carts and storefronts in the town square for the produce vendor Edith and instructed her to find. She spotted the hanging sign she was looking for above an open-air cart overflowing with fruits and vegetables. It formed a square shape with the three other produce carts surrounding it, creating a sort of barrier for the covered barrels inside the area. Sarah ambled over to the carts, feeling no need to rush back to the castle just yet and taking her time to admire the wares other shops boasted along the way.

Nearing the four-corner shop, she smiled uncertainly at the waiflike man standing beneath the sign. His salt-and-pepper hair had been cut short, and his skin gave evidence to many years spent in the sun. Gray-blue eyes and a crooked smile greeted her from behind his small collection table as she approached. He looked like the man Edith had described, and Sarah scrambled to remember his name as she stood before him.

She stared into the man's expectant face and, unable to recall his name, fought for safe ground. "Edith from the castle sent me," she said tentatively, hoping he would know what to do with that.

His weathered face brightened, and he stepped between the carts to take her hand in his smaller one, shaking it with more force than Sarah expected from so small a man.

"You must be the new help," he remarked as he pumped her arm up and down, appearing genuinely delighted to meet her. Sarah forced a smile as he released his firm grip, and she had to resist the urge to flex her injured hand. "Sarah, is it?" Her smile faltered at his familiarity with her name. She'd hoped to remain under the radar as long as possible and was dismayed to find that word of the newcomer had traveled so quickly.

She managed a nod and tried to redirect the conversation. Suddenly, she didn't feel as safe and carefree as she had a moment ago. "Edith mentioned that we need to place an order with you."

The gray-haired man nodded and motioned toward his large carts heavy-laden with varying produce. "I just received a barrel each of fresh carrots and dried apples, there are also some especially large heads of cabbage that you might be interested in, and some spicy peppers that I received all the way from Spain. Did Edith happen to mention what the kitchen needs this week?"

Sarah tried to remember what Edith had said to pick up and, much like she had with the kind man's name, managed to draw a blank. She had been in such a hurry earlier that she hadn't paid much attention to Edith's instructions and was now regretting her rush.

The vender must have noticed the clueless expression on her face because he gave her a sympathetic smile. "Why don't I just wrap up a few of the things the kitchen always needs?"

Sarah was sure her relief was obvious. "Thank you." She handed the basket to the man, who went about collecting several items without her assistance.

Left standing idle, Sarah allowed her gaze to drift over the rows of shops and was surprised when she recognized one of the uniformed castle guards as he made his way through the town square. Guards patrolled the area outside the castle all the time, so there was nothing out of the ordinary about his appearance. Disinterested, Sarah was about to turn away when she spotted the young guard stop before the entrance to the street she had stumbled down the day before. He glanced suspiciously over both shoulders before quickly slipping into the shadows and disappearing down the street.

Something about his shifty behavior didn't sit right with Sarah. Curious over what business he might have in that neighborhood, she mumbled a quick apology to the vender and asked him if he wouldn't mind packing the goods up for her while she ran another errand.

"Will do, miss," he replied cheerily. "It will be ready when you get back."

Eyes on the spot where the guard had stood a moment before, Sarah nodded distractedly to the man and stepped away from his cart. Her heart picked up a beat in anticipation as she watched the last traces of the guard's long shadow begin to recede into the side street. The moist wind fought against Sarah with each hurried step through the square, and she gripped her collar closer to her throat as she followed her intuition and the man's retreating shadow as it vanished into the recesses of the darkened street.

~Chapter 12~

Sarah stopped at the edge of the street and eased her head around the corner, watching the strange guard's progress along the rough stones. Satisfied that his back was to her, she pushed Will's warning from her head and moved stealthily along the right wall, keeping her body low. She was pleased that there was only a light dusting of snow in patches on the ground, thanks to the many dilapidated awnings lining the narrow street— maneuvering her feet around loosened stones would cause less noise than crunching over freshly packed snow.

With her eyes locked on the man's back as he moved down the vacant neighborhood, Sarah tried to remember the proper distance for tailing someone as she slowly eased herself around a jagged stoop. She was occupied and didn't notice how the hem of her dress had snagged on the edge of the bottom step. Losing her balance as the dress caught and held on the sharp stone, she pitched forward to the sound of ripping fabric. The fall was too abrupt and her reflexes too slow for her to get her hands up in time to lessen the impact, and she only managed to trap her hands beneath her stomach as she landed prostrate on the street.

Her breath came out in a rush as the ground forced her hands against her diaphragm, and she flopped around awkwardly to free the squished and scraped appendages from under her body and relieve the pressure on her lungs. She glanced up sharply, fully expecting to be discovered by the guard and then promptly fired from her duties. However, the howling wind over the lip of the street had blessedly muffled her gaffe, and the guard continued down the street without a backward glance.

Greatly relieved that her cover was still intact, she let out a shaky breath and used her scraped palms to straighten her skirt. She stood on quivering legs with a muffled groan, wishing she had landed on a patch of snow instead of the dry ground she had been praising a moment ago.

Wary of making the same mistake twice, Sarah was careful to lift her skirts to keep her ripped hem from catching again as she continued to shadow the man. She followed stealthily behind him down the deserted street. Though he was still acting agitated, there was nothing that led her to believe he was involved in anything that might prove useful to Sarah's investigation. She bit her lip, wondering if she was chasing shadows, wasting her time when answers lay elsewhere.

The man slowed and then stopped before one of the smaller buildings, and Sarah quickly dove behind a rough-hewn porch before he spotted her. It didn't fully cover her, but she had left enough distance between them that she hoped he wouldn't notice her crouched against the wall or the tell-tell clouds of warm air leaving her parted lips.

She poked her head up carefully and watched as the man took the steps and the stoop in one large stride, rapping twice on the door. After several long moments, during which Sarah wondered if the man's knock would go unanswered, the door opened and a woman emerged from the darkened building. Sarah shifted slightly to have a better vantage point from her hiding place, removing her slipper from a small puddle of melted snow as she did so. The dark-haired woman turned toward her at that moment, and Sarah ducked her head to avoid being spotted by those familiar eyes.

Jade.

What business did a guard have with her? Sarah mused. She couldn't help but feel—*hope*—that there was more to this visit than the obvious and peered over the porch again.

The young man was speaking in low tones that Sarah couldn't hear, though he appeared a little flustered in her presence. Jade watched him disinterestedly, choosing to remain silent as he filled in the quiet for them both. After having floundered with his words long enough, he at last reached into his coat pocket and produced a letter that he held out for her to take.

Sarah stared at the missive, devoid of any markings except for a large blob of red wax that held it closed. Jade took the envelope with long fingers and glanced at it before nodding curtly to the man and shutting the door in his face.

He appeared as surprised as Sarah at such an abrupt dismissal. He blinked, recovering quickly, and hopped back down the steps, moving toward her hiding spot. Sarah pressed her back against the corner of the porch and crouched as low as possible, though her thighs shook in her awkward position.

As the young man's shadow moved closer, she instinctively forced her body against the wall and watched with wide eyes as he came into her line of vision, moving past the porch. His pace was clipped and he didn't glance around him as he hastened out of the street, completely ignorant of Sarah's cramped body tucked into her hiding place.

She remained in that uncomfortable position, watching his back until she lost sight of him in the crowd before standing slowly. Her legs felt numb, and she tried stepping from foot to foot to regain feeling. She would make a very poor stalker or P.I., since she couldn't stay in one position for five minutes, but her quick thinking *had* kept her from being discovered, and she felt a small sense of satisfaction in that knowledge. Her spirits deflated when she remembered that she hadn't *actually* discovered anything except that Jade was receiving personal notes from the castle. . . .

The envelope!

Sarah suddenly recalled the wax on the front of the missive. As she worked, she had seen the royal crest woven into tapestries and ingrained in pieces of wood around the castle enough times that she could draw it from memory: A warriors sword with an intricately woven, ornamental handle hovered vertically over the center of the royal crown, reaching from top to bottom of the crest. The small figure of a lion, crouched in the attack position, teeth bared in a roar, was set just to the right of the scene. Although she hadn't gotten a good look at the design in the wax of Jade's letter, she had seen enough to bet her soggy left shoe that there were similarities.

Excitement and anticipation moved through her veins, though it took her feet a full minute of awkward hopping to regain enough feeling for her to sneak down the empty street up to Jade's stoop. It was hardly likely that she would discover anything—the guard hadn't dropped any clues when he was there—but Sarah couldn't possibly let the opportunity to snoop pass.

She scanned the snow for any sign of a clue or anything out of the ordinary, and when that proved fruitless, she used her bare hands to sift through the white powder. She was so intent on her task and the deranged hope that she might actually find something that she didn't hear the door above her open.

"May I help you with something?"

Sarah jumped at the note of amusement in the woman's voice. She straightened and saw Jade smiling at her, almost condescendingly, and then watched as the woman's face took on a look of recognition.

"You were with William the other day."

The statement caught Sarah off-guard. Their encounter had been so brief, with Jade pointedly ignoring her throughout the entire thing, and Sarah hadn't expected to be recognized so easily. Then again, from her tone of voice it sounded like Sarah's presence that day wasn't as important as the fact that she had been with Will. Though Jade's eyes didn't move, Sarah felt like she was being assessed and dismissed in one brief glance, and her defenses rose in response.

"I was." Sarah's tone was casual but guarded. She didn't volunteer any more information and simply returned the steady gaze directed at her.

Jade arched one of her perfectly manicured brows at the unspoken challenge, and her painted lips spread into a supercilious smile. It was the same one she had given Sarah the other day, and she wondered briefly if Jade reserved the expression specifically for her to make her feel insignificant, or if she was just fortunate enough to be around when the woman felt the need to belittle someone.

"You must forgive my lack of manners that day," Jade said, sounding cavalier as she flicked her thin fingers in the air as if to dismiss the entire event. "I was simply surprised to see the two of you standing together. You see, I am so used to him coming alone." Sarah could tell her apology was insincere and had been about to excuse herself from the woman's presence until she caught those last words. Though she knew they were carefully chosen to do the most damage, she couldn't help the defensive anger for Will that rose up in her chest.

Sarah tried to maintain her calm, but she couldn't keep her eyes from narrowing at the dark-haired woman. "I seriously doubt that. Will's too honorable and too much of a gentleman." Praising Will's character helped to alleviate those unwelcome doubts that had crept into her mind at Jade's words. Sarah squared her shoulders, speaking with more confidence this time. "He would never."

Jade tipped her head to the side and studied her, her expression almost pitying, as though she disliked being the bearer of bad news. "Wouldn't he, pet? Do you really know your friend so well?"

For some reason, Jade's immediate assumption that they were only friends rubbed Sarah the wrong way. She knew everything that the older woman said was an intentional stab meant to inflict damage, but Sarah still chaffed at the insinuation that she and Will could never be more than friends, and that he and Jade had been something . . . *more.*

The jab hit its mark and stirred up old doubts that Sarah thought were long ago buried. And the fact that Jade could make her question Will's honor with a few carefully selected words sickened her.

Sarah raised her chin defiantly. She resisted the urge to remove the pendant that was neatly tucked inside her dress and shove it in the arrogant woman's face as proof of her and Will's bond. But she wouldn't give this woman the satisfaction of thinking that she had rattled her—more than she had. "I think I know him better than almost anyone."

Jade's dark eyes sparkled wickedly like a cat that had just cornered its prey. "You just might. After all, you were the one who spent so much time with him this past summer." She tapped her chin thoughtfully with a perfectly rounded nail. "Or perhaps that was another child."

Sarah couldn't keep the surprise from her face, too shocked to register the insult to her age. "How do you know about that?"

A laugh emerged from Jade's lips. "Oh, pet. You would be shocked at the things I am privy to through my customers. But I would have to be deaf not to have known the stir you two caused when he carried you into his livery during that storm, and then you didn't emerge until late in the day." She clicked her tongue. "Well, people began to speculate, my dear."

Sarah hated that complete strangers were questioning both her and Will's character, and she felt ill over the fact that he had been forced to live with the disapproving looks and whispered rumors, while she had been complaining about packing for her dorm. She hadn't realized it was so bad when she left.

Jade was watching her face closely. Her deceptively gentle expression couldn't hide the satisfied gleam in her eyes. "And then you left him broken-hearted soon after, did you not? Men do strange things when they feel abandoned." The comment hit hard.

"That's ridiculous." Sarah tried to muster as much assurance in her expression and voice as possible, but the uncertainty and guilt were surely written on her face.

"If you don't believe me, why don't you simply ask him?" Her gaze swept over the cloak Sarah wore. Did she recognize it as the one Will had been wearing yesterday? Then her dark brown eyes lowered to the torn hem of Sarah's black dress, and she clicked her tongue in compassion. "You should fix that before you see him. Keep in mind, pet, he's still a man, and looks are important." She dipped her head cordially, a small smile on her full red lips. Then she stepped backwards over the threshold into the shadows of her home and closed the door in Sarah's face with one final, meaningful look.

~Chapter 13~

Sarah stared at the peeling wood, feeling every last one of the unpleasant woman's words sink in. None of it was true; she knew that.

She staggered backward and then took off down the street, completely ignorant to her surroundings. She couldn't stop the doubt and fear that coiled around her like a malignant disease, clouding her vision until all she could see were her own questions and worries as she stumbled blindly out into the open, fists clenched in anger at Jade and over her own easily swayed faith.

She felt ridiculous for doubting Will's character, since he would never question her morals. In reality they had only spent a week together, yet she felt like she knew his character better than anyone. Jade's comment about that being true sent her mind racing almost against her will. People who had known Will for most of his life were quick to judge him when he had simply been helping a stranger out of the rain. Was there a foundation for their immediate condemnation, a reason for them to doubt his motives?

Their opinions and Jade's carefully selected words shouldn't have mattered to her. She told herself they didn't, and her mind worked furiously to make her believe this and remove the niggling doubt.

Standing at the edge of the rundown street, Sarah's eyes grazed over the busy square, unseeing, as she tried to process the lies she had just been fed. Jade was obviously in love with Will, or at the very least marking her territory and letting Sarah know he was off-limits. The lies were just a pathetic attempt to scare Sarah away. Well, it wasn't going to work.

Unmoving, Sarah glanced at those milling about. It appeared most of the townsfolk had come out of their homes to wander the square today. Were these some of the faces who were spreading rumors and joining in the gossip? She wondered if any of them recognized her as the girl with whom Will presumably had a secret rendezvous, but no one stopped and stared or even turned their head to look at her. Sometimes being invisible had its benefits.

Taking a deep breath, she moved out into the traffic of the square, trying to blend in with the people around her and disappear into the crowd. She kept her face to the snowy ground as she walked across the street, her thoughts dominating her focus. Nervously, she toyed with the short end of the white sash that was tied around her bicep, causing each sleeve on her plain black dress to flare at her elbows.

Someone jostled her from behind as they pushed their way through the sea of bodies. Sarah gasped and stumbled sideways into the path of a large horse and rider. The horse reared back at her sudden appearance, and she stared, wide-eyed, at the flailing hooves of the massive creature as it shrieked in protest. The rider tried to calm his frightened animal and then proceeded to shout obscenities at her. Sarah gaped at him, too startled to move, and felt rough hands grab her arm and pull her out of the man's path.

She looked up sharply to see a strange man pulling her alongside him. "Just keep moving," he said lowly, jaw clenched.

"Stupid wench!" the rider spat at her retreating form. Sarah gaped at him over her shoulder. It hadn't even been her fault!

She let the man guide her across the street with a firm grip on her elbow. "Never been called that before," she said, trying to make light of the situation, but her voice quavered and her laugh sounded breathless to her own ears. The encounter had left her hands shaking.

He brought her over to the produce vender's space, and the gray-haired man hurried around his cart, wide-eyed. "I saw what happened. Are you all right, miss?"

Her heartbeat began to return to normal, and Sarah nodded as her protector released her. "Thanks to him, that is."

"It was my honor to remove you from such profanity," he replied.

The vender clapped the frowning young man on the shoulder. "That was quick thinking, Richard."

"You should have heard the obscene things he said to her." The man—Richard—looked appalled at the rider's actions, glaring at the man's retreating form.

"Richard—"

"Insolence like that is the reason why these people suffer," he went on, as though no one had spoken. "Is a man supposed to stand by and watch such intolerant behavior? Dagwood, I am telling you, only a son of a whore would speak to a lady in such a manner. And in so public a place!" He clenched his fists. "Such slime should hardly be allowed to wander the street."

"Really, boy." The vender looked meaningfully at Sarah, appearing embarrassed at the younger man's vehemence.

Richard swallowed, ceasing his tirade, and gave her an apologetic

81

look. Sarah quickly snapped her mouth closed. "Forgive me. I have proven myself to be no better than that cad."

She had been surprised by the rider's insults, but Richard seemed to have taken it personally. Her shock melted into a grin of amusement over his gallantry and obvious abhorrence of the rider's behavior. "I appreciate your concern, but you don't have to worry about me. I've heard worse. Not directed *at* me before, but still." Pointedly hooking a thumb over her shoulder, she added, "Had a bit of a potty mouth, didn't he?"

Both men looked surprised, then the lines on old Dagwood's weathered face stretched as he laughed. "You're a resilient one, aren't you?"

Sarah glanced at Richard. His red-brown hair had been tousled in the wind, resting in short, tangled strands that he raked back from his broad forehead. Somewhere in his twenties, the deep furrow between his brows seemed out of place, and she was glad to see it lessen as his serious expression eased.

"Thanks for the hand back there," she said, her warring thoughts from earlier falling to the back of her mind.

His golden-brown eyes softened, shoulders relaxing. "You looked like you had seen a ghost."

"Just not all that fond of horses," Sarah admitted wryly.

Richard's frown returned. "Or obscene gentlemen. Despicable," he spat.

Sarah's grin widened at his expression of consternation. "I think the boys where I come from could learn a thing or two from you."

Salt-and-pepper eyebrows rose on Dagwood's forehead, and his jovial manner returned. His eyes lit with a spark of mischief as he leaned in closer to her and lowered his voice. "You just tell us when, and Richard and I can whip those lads into shape."

She couldn't help the laugh that bubbled up in her chest and escaped her lips. He grinned back, and even Richard smiled a little, although he looked surprised at their easy banter.

Dagwood moved into the enclosure his carts created to finish filling her basket, saying over his shoulder, "I didn't expect you back so soon."

"The butcher was out," Richard replied. He toyed absentmindedly with the long chain around his neck, and Sarah could make out the faint outline of words on the back of the wooden pendant. "I'll place your order later."

Dagwood shot a look behind him, his expression wry. "You appeared a tad worked up when you returned. Is everything all right?"

Heaving a sigh, Richard subtly shot Sarah a look out of the corner of his eye. "Simply tired of the injustice around here." He dropped the wooden pendant against his chest, and Sarah caught sight of the intricately pressed shape of an animal; it might have been an eagle or a lion—she couldn't say for certain. But whatever it was, he had talent.

Dagwood nodded as if he understood and turned back to his work. "Did you do that?" She waved a finger at the wooden figure.

Richard looked down, almost appearing surprised to see it lying over his heart. His lips tipped fondly. "Ah, no. My mother had it made for me."

"Well, it's beautiful."

Dagwood spun around, looking pleased as he held out the basket that overflowed with sumptuous fruits. "Richard will deliver the rest to the kitchen later today." Sarah's stomach sank when she took in all the food.

"Oh. I didn't think to bring any money with me," she said quietly, embarrassed by her blunder. The man shook his head, appearing unfazed.

"We can put it on the ledger—Edie always does."

Sarah smiled her gratitude and accepted the heavy-laden basket. She held it in front of her, signed her first name only in the book he held out, and thanked the man again.

"No trouble at all, miss." Dagwood smiled. "You tell Edie that ol' Dagwood thinks she's found herself a good girl to help, one with her own mind. And a sense of humor!" He feigned a look of shock as he pressed a hand to his heart, and Sarah grinned at his animated expression.

"Yeah, well, I should probably leave out the part about having a mind of my own, but the rest I will happily relay." He winked at her like her grandpa always did when they shared a secret. Then he grinned at Richard.

"We must do our best to make our girl here feel welcome in town."

Richard appeared surprised as he looked at her. "Are you not from Serimone?"

Shaking her head, Sarah replied wryly, "No. I traveled quite a ways to get here."

Scrubbing a hand over a strong, cleanly shaven jaw, he said with a sheepish smile, "I hope we haven't made too poor an impression."

Sarah shook her head, feeling lighter after their conversation. "Not at all. You two are some of the nicest people I've encountered here."

"*And* now that you have met me and my boy," Dagwood announced gaily, clapping Richard on the shoulder, "you've consequently met the last interesting people in the country."

Sarah smiled. She couldn't help wondering why Richard called his "father" by his first name or why the two men appeared as different as night and day, but she decided not to pry.

Knowing she had to get back, Sarah thanked Richard again for his help, waving goodbye to the older man as she headed back toward the castle, more conscious this time of where she stepped. As she walked, she smiled to herself over her encounter with the kind Dagwood and his gallant son. No one else had even stopped to see if she was all right as she was pushed into the street, and he had run all the way across the square to save her from the horse and its rider's shouted insults. It made her wish that her world could have maintained a bit of the valiance of this time.

When she glanced up at the building before her and caught sight of the sign hanging above the door, she stopped abruptly. The commotion in the street and Dagwood's gentle humor had caused her to forget about Jade and her own doubts, and Sarah was surprised that she had ended up *here* of all places, though she wondered if she had been unconsciously heading this way the whole time.

She hesitated just outside the open door, feeling the warmth radiating from inside. Gripping the handle a little tighter, she stepped inside with no purpose in mind. Maybe just seeing his familiar face would alleviate her unreasonable doubt.

The heat of the building was heaven after the cool air outside, and as the chill left her body, her anxiety began to fade. The sound of metal-on-metal echoed through the shop, and Sarah followed it around the corner. She found Will bent over an anvil near the fire, skillfully flattening out the tip of an iron rod with a large hammer while Robert shoed a horse at the back of the room.

Neither man was aware of her presence, so Sarah allowed herself a moment to watch Will. It wasn't as if she had never seen him at work before. On one rainy afternoon, he had shown her how to work the metal, but she had rarely been allowed to observe *him*; he was usually the one equipped with the intense stares that bore straight into a person's soul, determining their character with a single glance. So, she stood there silently and stole a rare moment to watch him unobserved.

His back was to her as he pounded away, raising the hammer to his shoulder before striking the iron with expert blows. Sarah watched his large, calloused hands rotate the rod after each carefully placed hit—the same hands that had guided her through the castle last night and into the woods.

As he worked, the muscles in his back moved beneath his shirt, and he had rolled the sleeves up to his elbows, revealing corded muscles on his forearms. The sight made Sarah think of that moment when he had carried her through the forest, though she had been unconscious at the time. She used to get embarrassed when she thought of him being burdened with her weight as he ran all the way to his uncle's house, but now the memory caused her to smile. She had found herself a real hero.

Her smile faded, and she was beginning to feel that she had been staring too long. She was about to clear her throat to alert them of her presence when she glanced over and encountered Robert's gaze. Her face warmed at being caught, and she forced a friendly smile. Sarah wondered at the slow grin that pulled at the side of Robert's mouth and caused his eyes to crinkle at the corners. He gave her a chin-up gesture before directing his gaze at Will.

"Boss," he said loudly to be heard over the noise in the room. Sarah jumped at the booming noise, nerves a little on-edge. "I think you've got company."

The hammer stilled against the iron, and Will glanced over his shoulder at her. She lifted a hand in silent greeting and received a smile before he turned back to his work and brought the hammer down on the rod one final time. Will tossed the hammer on a nearby table and used a pair of tongs to place the rod into a bucket of water. The hot metal hissed the instant it connected with the surface of the water, and Will left it there to cool.

Pushing his left sleeve further up his arm, he gave her the faintest, heart-stopping smile of pleasure she'd ever seen him wear. It only grew as he walked toward her.

"Hi," she whispered, forgetting her apprehension over Robert's presence.

Will's smile widened, revealing straight teeth she rarely saw. "This is a pleasant surprise."

They heard someone clear their throat and glanced over at Robert as he stood, dusting off his pants. He smiled at the two of them. "Why don't I go see if Roland is open today, boss? I need to stretch my legs a little and get out of this heat."

Will nodded. "Thank you, Robert." The two seemed to share a look before the blond man edged past them and out into the cold. When Sarah turned back to him, she found Will's gaze on the cloak she wore. His eyes found hers again, that soft smile in place.

She quickly glanced down at the fabric, feeling a little awkward with his intense gaze trained on her. He never seemed to realize when he was staring, or maybe it just didn't matter to him. "Um, yeah. It was really cold last night, so it was nice to have. Thanks." Her gaze flickered up to meet his, then lowered to the floor.

Sarah racked her brain for her purpose here but was having difficulty with him staring at her like that. She knew exactly how to react to his anger—in kind—but it always threw her off-balance when he let his defenses down long enough for her to really see what he was thinking. And right now his face told her that last night had meant as much to him as it had to her. She hadn't had enough experience to know how to react to the affection she saw in his eyes and tried to remember why she had come. There *had* been a reason, and when she remembered, the feelings of blissful romance deflated.

Will's smile faded at her expression. "Is something wrong? You look upset."

Sometimes it was annoying that he could be so perceptive. "Oh. I had a little run-in with a horseman on my way over. I'm still a little shaken up." She said it casually, waving her hand in the air to dismiss his worry. It had been the perfect opportunity to broach the subject of her conversation with Jade, but when it came down to it, she couldn't do it.

His dark eyes immediately filled with concern. He touched her arm lightly, and his gaze skirted quickly over her body, as though an injury might materialize. "An accident? Were you hurt?"

Sarah's mouth turned up at the worry on his face. This was the Will she knew, *her* Will—strong, dependable, caring. Not the one Jade's lies had made her imagine. Any remaining anxiety faded.

"I'm fine," she answered. Will nodded slowly and let his hand fall back to his side. She could tell that he wanted to say more on the subject, so she was grateful when he remained silent. She always appreciated his concern, but it made her feel raw and fragile, and she was used to taking care of herself. Granted, she'd gotten stuck in several scrapes that he'd rescued her from, but she didn't mind playing the part of the fallen damsel so much as she disliked feeling like a completely helpless girl.

"So," Will said a little too brightly, obviously sensing her need for independence. "Did you have business around town, or are you just here to see me?"

Sarah grinned at his teasing tone. "Actually, I was in the neighborhood, but," she added, almost begrudgingly, "I don't necessarily *mind* seeing you."

This received a chuckle. It was good to see him in such high spirits. "I feel quite special now. What was your business in town?"

One of her shoulders lifted in a shrug. "I had to run an errand, and I met Dagwood, the produce man, and his son Richard. He's the one who saved me from becoming a pancake on the road." She said the words lightly, but still caught the faint wince that crossed Will's features. She tried to distract him quickly. "I also saw a guard in the square today."

He raised his brows at that. "A most unusual occurrence."

Sarah laughed. "Well, it wasn't that strange, but I was following a hunch, okay?"

He folded his arms across his broad chest, looking completely relaxed as he leaned a hip against the table. "All right. What did you find?"

She suddenly realized what she had said and hesitated to go on. Will had told her to stay away from Jade, and the neighborhood entirely. But she couldn't very well expect him to be honest with her when she wasn't willing to tell him everything. "I, um, I sort of followed him to Jade's house."

Will's expression remained the same. Actually, it looked frozen in place as he stared at her. Then his mirth ebbed, slowly. "What were you doing down there? I thought we talked about this."

86

She told herself to remain calm and explain the situation to him. "I know, and I'm sorry. But I was just following the guy, and I didn't think there was time to get you, and it was daylight," she added weakly, then sighed. "I was being foolish, I know. And if it makes you feel any better, I totally regret it after talking with Jade. But I don't plan to—"

"You *spoke* to Jade?" He actually looked startled. "What did she say?"

Sarah studied his face for a moment, sensing what she understood to be worry. "She was just trying to get me riled. It was stupid—forget about it."

Will wrapped his fingers around her arm and bent down so he was at eye level with her. His face looked angry, but she knew it wasn't directed at her. "Did she say something to insult you?"

She shook her head, though Jade's words had been very offensive at the time. "I told you, it doesn't matter. She was being petty." His eyes stayed locked on her, waiting, and she rolled her eyes at the absurdity of her conversation with the older woman, almost too embarrassed to voice it aloud. "She was just jealous because she saw us together the other day. And she said"—Sarah looked at the ground, feeling a little ridiculous—"she said that you and her, *you know*—that I drove you into her arms, which is totally a lie," she added quickly, daring to look up, hoping for a chuckle to ease the tension she felt building between them. But his expression registered surprise and then hurt—surprise that she had found out and hurt that Jade had betrayed his trust? Sarah swallowed.

"It *is* a lie. Isn't it?" He straightened and averted his gaze, shaking his head at the ground. The movement was so slight that Sarah almost didn't catch it, but when she did, her apprehension grew.

"I can't believe she would . . ." Will's voice faded, and he shook his head again. When he looked at her, she was sure he saw the growing doubt on her face, or at least heard the tremor in her voice.

"She *was* lying, right?" A knot of dread was coiling tightly in her stomach, making it hard to breathe. Her fingers tightened around the basket handle, and she was sure her knuckles had turned white.

He pulled back a fraction of an inch, as if slapped. He remained silent and folded his arms, jaw tight as he stared back at her. Why didn't he just tell her Jade was lying and relieve her doubts? She waited for him to deny it—she *prayed* he would deny it.

But he just stared at her, expressionless, though his brows drew together ever so slightly. The sight broke Sarah's heart almost as much as the truth beneath his emotionless façade: He couldn't deny it because he had promised her long ago that he would never lie to her, so apparently he was deciding not to say anything at all.

Sarah backed up a step. The action wasn't intentional, but the realization was too staggering to stand still, and she saw a brief flicker of hurt cross Will's brow.

"Oh, God," Sarah whispered. "You didn't. . . ." The words hung in the air between them, and her eyes filled with unwanted tears as the silence lengthened. This seemed to break Will's stony façade, and his eyes registered alarm at her tears.

"Oh, Sarah," he said, looking distressed as she hastily wiped her eyes with the back of her hand. He reached out to touch her arm. "I'm sorry. Please don't—"

Something akin to a strangled whimper was released through Sarah's closed lips as she jerked away from his fingers. "No," she said quietly, though it sounded more like a groan of denial in her throat. "Just don't." She choked back her tears. She didn't want him to see her like this, like some pathetically broken creature, and she couldn't stand to look at the distress and pain in those same eyes she had drowned in so many times before.

She shook her head, though the action felt half-hearted. "No, I can't believe you would . . ." She couldn't even say it. A part of her still wanted desperately to cling to the illusion of the perfect romance with the perfect man, however brief it may have been.

Feeling sick, her eyes narrowed accusingly to cover her welling hurt, though some of the effect was lost with the tears blurring her vision. "I told her you weren't that guy—that you would never use a woman that way. I stood up for you. God help me, I had *faith* in you." She tried to cover her distress by retreating into defensive anger, but the anguish and betrayal she felt were obvious in her broken words.

Will's expression had become increasingly stricken with each word she spoke, and he quickly closed the small distance between them, holding her arms with hands as gentle as his eyes. She so desperately wanted him to deny it, so she didn't shrink back at his touch but stared up at him expectantly. She was sure her face mirrored the torment brewing in his as she gripped the basket like a lifeline between them. "Sarah, you have to believe me when I say I am truly sorry. There's no excuse for my actions. I never should have—"

His apology was the final straw. Sarah wrenched free of his grasp, ignoring his wounded look. She bit her lip to keep from crying and fled for the exit to the sound of Will calling her name. Her vision blurred, and she plowed straight into Robert as he came in through the door.

"Hold up, now," he said as he steadied her. He pulled back and all amusement drained from his face when he saw the tears threatening to spill over. "What happened?"

She could hear Will's feet pounding against the floor just behind her as he called her name again, sounding as close to panic as she had ever heard him. She pushed against Robert weakly, feeling all the fight leave her body. He released her, though his gaze moved between her and Will as he ran up behind them. She took off down the street, knowing if she looked back and saw the truth in his face, her heart would break all over again.

****

Will stopped in the doorway to his shop and called her name one last time as he watched her disappear into the crowd, catching brief glimpses of her every now and then as she dodged carts and passerby as she fled. From him.

She never looked back—not once.

Will swallowed hard and rubbed the stubble on his jaw in frustration. It started to mingle with the fresh anguish coursing through his veins, making his blood feel thick and heavy. He felt as though his veins were moving leaden molasses, weighing him down and pressing him into the earth.

What had he done? Why had he remained silent? He could have spoken—a lie, the truth, fabricated a story to alleviate her doubts; it didn't matter. But he should have said *something*. Her eyes told him that the words weren't important, and she had only needed for him to tell her it was untrue and that he was there for her. It would have been so simple to ease her mind, but his pride had kept him from speaking, and his silence had only confirmed her doubts.

"What happened?" He turned to look at his worker, whose eyes were wide.

Will shook his head, his throat too tight to speak. This was his worst fear come true, why he had told Sarah to stay away from Jade and her jealous moods. He had watched her beautiful, tan face change slowly as her doubt grew. The idea of a tryst between himself and Jade had seemed so absurd to her at first, and then he had watched the fear and hurt cloud her features and knew he had made a mistake in not speaking up. He had lost her trust, perhaps forever.

"You okay, boss?" Robert asked hesitantly. He looked worried.

Will gave the slightest of nods, though he knew it was too weak to appear genuine. "I'm fine," he murmured. But he wasn't—not in the least. He had seen how her eyes clouded with distrust when he remained silent. Oh, God, her eyes! He squeezed his own closed against the image of her face, though the action didn't stave off the realization that he had just broken the heart of the only woman he would ever love.

~Chapter 14~

Sarah moved through the square with her eyes downcast; she didn't want anyone to ask why her face was a mixture of anger and sadness, didn't want to stop for even a second as she hastened toward the castle. Her eyes stared, unseeing, at the street beneath her as her frozen, slipper-clad feet slipped quickly over the stones.

There was no hurry, really—she knew Edith wouldn't need her back from her errand for a while longer—but she moved hastily through the crowds, anyway, trying to escape the sting of fresh betrayal. Maybe if she could just put enough distance between her and the shop and Will's silence that had spoken volumes, then this whole thing would disappear, and she wouldn't have to question his loyalty.

She bumped into several people while she wasn't looking, and she barely heard their gasps or shouted curses and reprimands. The fact that she was being constantly jostled by passerby and bumping into people herself was nearly lost on her. Actually, it was almost comforting for her to feel as though, for a moment, she could get lost in the sea of people coming and going, living their lives like always.

A cold blast of air broke through a gap in the throng and hit her full in the face. Sarah sucked in a breath at the startlingly cold, wet air, grateful for the way it cleared the numbness spreading over her mind.

Her sister Lilly said that for someone with so much wild imagination, she could be far too logical sometimes. But Sarah was good with logic; it was real and comforting and *logical*. It made sense of things that seemed scary, turning the monsters into mice and disproving the impossible. When she thought logically, things became manageable, something she could deal with. And right now it reminded her that whatever had happened between Will and . . . Jade—Sarah nearly choked on the name—occurred when she wasn't around. She hadn't even been in the same century!

On top of that, it wasn't like she had the right to feel that Will had been disloyal, because they had never been a couple, never defined what they were. Sarah cringed when she realized how true that was. Sure, he had held her hand and shot her that little boy smile and stared into her heart with those soulful eyes. But there were no promises made, no verbalization of anyone's feelings, no kisses shared. Even as she willed herself to be realistic about it, Sarah couldn't shake the feeling of disappointment, though she knew there was no one to blame but herself for placing Will on such a high pedestal: It only made it a longer drop to the ground.

Her eyes burned guiltily, and she clenched her fists, sniffing back her tears. She had no right to cry.

A moment before, she had been grateful for the large number of people surrounding her, enveloping and hiding her. But now the growing throng seemed to press closer as the height of the midday haggling drew near, suffocating her. The air around her suddenly seemed stifling with the mass of bodies, and each breath was harder to take than the last. She had to get out of here.

Wringing her hands together to warm them, Sarah looked around her, searching frantically for an escape before she realized that the castle gate was so close. Rudely forcing her way past a woman, she kept her eyes on the spires as she moved, doing her best to push aside her nagging thoughts in her desperation for air. When she was able to move without running into anyone, she broke into a jog, never having thought she would be so relieved to see the castle gate looming above her, or the servants' entrance, which suddenly seemed very safe and welcoming.

Sarah didn't pause at the door, but thrust it open, barely breaking stride. She grimaced at the noise her entrance made, but no one rushed out to the hall to see what the commotion was about. Being more careful this time, she slowly closed the door, hearing the satisfactory *click* of the latch.

She leaned her back against the door, still gripping the handle behind her, taking a moment to catch her breath. The heat coming from the kitchen fires brushed against her face, though the frigid temperature outside seeped through the door and worked its way through her layers of fabric, numbing her back. That was how she felt: warm on the outside but cold and numb where it counted.

She listened to the sounds around her, willing her mind to focus on them as her pulse slowed. The kitchen was abuzz with activity as the cooks prepared for the evening meal—a wooden plate clattered to the ground and skittered across the floor; a male voice loudly reprimanded the mishap and shouted out an order that Sarah didn't quite catch; large knives repeatedly came down hard and fast on the makings of supper.

Sarah concentrated on the sounds coming from within and felt a little more composed after a few minutes. She knew she wouldn't have the entryway to herself for much longer, and, not wanting to be caught idle, she took a deep breath and moved toward the back stairwell. Like in the street, she kept her eyes trained on her shoes as they shuffled forward, disappearing and reappearing beneath her torn hem. She frowned, knowing she would have to ask Edith to help her mend it later.

She sidestepped just in time to avoid colliding with the pail of water set in front of the bottom step and glanced up sharply. The same young maids she had seen just before she left the castle were on their hands and knees in the foyer, scrubbing the stones that had been beneath the rug they'd rolled and set aside. Sarah had thought she was alone, but they had obviously noticed her as they paused in their tasks and stared openly with their hands frozen, mid-scrub, on their brushes.

Sarah was acutely aware of the way their looks of practiced detachment turned into expressions of animosity when they saw her. Their eyes narrowed in unison, and Sarah was surprised at the cold gazes she received—one looked like she was hoping to set Sarah on fire with her stare. She glanced over her shoulder to see if she had left a trail behind her, but most of the snow on her shoes had come off on the rug in the entryway.

Unable to help the question in her eyes as she shot them one last look, she quickly ducked her head and jogged up the stairs, forgoing any ladylike grace as she took the steps two at a time. She was sure she could feel the maids' eyes following her and reflexively tightened her grip on the basket as she raced up the staircase toward her room, the only place left where she could be truly alone and away from prying eyes. Right now the dingy, cramped quarters waiting at the end of the hall seemed like a haven to Sarah, and she couldn't get there fast enough.

Ignoring the few servants working at the top of the stairs, Sarah turned and went in the direction of the servants' quarters, focusing her eyes on the end of the hall. Her chest rose and fell quickly, her flight up the stairs having taxed her, though she knew that part of her erratic breathing was from trying to suppress the tumultuous emotions that raged just below the surface.

The walls became progressively dingy the further she went, and the absence of wall hangings and decorations was almost a welcome sight. Her breath quickened when she saw her door. Throwing it wide open, a gasp stuck in her throat.

The room was completely empty. What few possessions she'd had before were now gone, and the bed had been stripped down to the straw mattress. The nub of a candle had been removed from the table beside the bed, and even the extra threadbare blankets she had neatly folded at the end of the mattress were gone.

Sarah glanced down the hallway, wondering if perhaps she had broken into the wrong room, but she was sure this was—*had been*—her room only just this morning.

She dropped to her knees before the small trunk that had contained a spare servant's dress and the clothes she had worn to the castle, plunking the basket down beside her. An apple rolled across the floor unnoticed as she ripped the lid open, her eyes frantically searching the empty chest for some sort of explanation—even her sneakers were gone! She felt suddenly deflated, realizing that someone had either stolen everything, or this was no longer her room, no longer a place of solace to scream into her pillow.

"There you are!" Sarah jerked her head around and caught Edith's gaze as she stood in the doorway. The older woman looked greatly relieved to see her, then her expression turned apologetic as she took in Sarah's confusion. "I was hoping to catch you before you came in so I might explain."

Sarah's shoulders sagged and she released the lid, which banged loudly against the body of the trunk, letting her hands fall limply into her lap. She gave Edith an imploring look. "So I'm fired. You're kicking me out—just like that?"

Edith's brows drew together. "Heavens, no!" She came into the room and pulled Sarah to her feet, snatching the basket and the forgotten fruit from the floor. Wrapping her fingers around Sarah's arm, she guided her down the hallway. Her voice softened, the same way it did when someone was about to deliver bad news. "Dear, your room has been moved."

"Huh?" Sarah asked, not comprehending.

Edith leaned in as she maneuvered them around a buxom maid dusting the stair railing. She eyed the servant warily and lowered her voice. "It was requested that we move you to more comfortable lodgings."

A laugh of sweet relief bubbled its way past Sarah's lips. "Is that all? I thought I had been canned."

Edith looked startled at her reaction. "We would never just turn you out like that. You're invaluable to me, Sarah, what with the chaos of preparing for the ball." Her expression turned stern. "They would be hard-pressed to take such an important staff member from me, especially one who actually has an ear for instruction." Edith patted her arm reassuringly. "No, put such thoughts from your mind. You're safe with me."

For the first time since arriving back at the castle, Sarah felt herself smiling. She would have to be careful to follow orders now to keep on her mentor's good graces.

They passed another stone staircase, this one blanketed with a deep maroon carpet that cascaded over the steps. Sarah was baffled when she realized that she was being guided toward the west wing of the castle. On her first day, Edith had told her that a portion of this wing was reserved for important guests and ambassadors when they came to stay or conduct business, though Sarah hadn't been allowed to see it until now. But she knew immediately upon noting the growing opulence around her that they were headed into the heart of the extravagant guest wing. She felt a thrill of excitement over getting to discover a new part of the castle, but she couldn't ignore the niggling apprehension that stirred in her gut.

The passageway opened into a large room on the right that led to another flight of stairs spiraling downward. Edith kept to the wall on their left, and Sarah followed her like an obedient dog to the other side of the room where it split into three passageways. She trailed her guide down the long, wide passageway in the middle.

The transformation during their walk was noticeable, but now the difference was staggering. It was as though these corridors were dripping with opulence: Thick, ornately embroidered tapestries hung from the walls, some decorated with the royal crest, while others depicted nature scenes in rich tones. Sarah's old room had connected to a hall that was dingy and cramped, with completely unadorned walls or cheery decorations of any sort. The passageway was too narrow to mount and safely burn torches, so the walls turned inky-black in the night, save for the occasional tiny circle of flickering light cast by a servant's candle as they made their way to their room.

The walls of the passageway they now walked, which housed a ridiculous number of doors leading to who-knew-where, were covered with some extravagant ornament or another, and unlit torches were interspersed throughout the opulence, mounted and awaiting an aristocrat's next whim for light as they made their temporary residence in these halls. Sarah had never felt so insignificant or intimidated.

"I thought you were going to show me my new room," she whispered to her companion, trying not to draw the attention of any of the occupants that loomed just behind these closed doors.

Eyes focused at the end of the hall, Sarah eyed the rectangular table with the overly large flower display atop it as they drew nearer with every step, making Sarah feel like they were edging closer to a dead end.

She tried again, voice low, "If they've moved all my stuff, we should go back. Or do we have something to do before you show me which room is mine?" She knew she was rambling in her nervousness, and she shot Edith a questioning glance, noticing for the first time her pinched expression. She had bustled into the passage before, but now Edith's footsteps were slower and closer together, hinting at reluctance that Sarah had not noticed before. The look on the older woman's face only increased Sarah's apprehension. There was something she wasn't sharing.

"That is what I'm doing," Edith explained calmly, though her voice sounded strained. She released Sarah's arm as they stopped before the final hulking door at the end of the passage on the right. She pushed it open and took a step back. "This one is your room." She suddenly looked more like a servant and less like the mentor and friend Sarah had come to know her as.

Shooting her a quizzical glance, Sarah got no further than the threshold before she froze in place.

She had never truly felt the gap between classes back home, but there was no denying the vast difference in this place. Her sad quarters in the servants' wing couldn't hold a candle to this room, bedecked in such startling elegance that it caused her to temporarily forget her earlier distress.

Draped over the large four-poster bed was a canopy of thick red velvet detailed with an embroidered pattern of gold leaves and stems, entwining to create an intricate pattern on the fabric. The material was wrapped around each of the four pillars and tied with golden chords, pooling on the ground at each corner of the bed.

Her eyes moved over the mahogany night table that had been placed beside the head of the mattress, the legs of which had been artfully carved with the same leaf pattern on the canopy. The burgundy bedcoverings had been pulled up underneath the pillows and tucked tightly on all sides, creating a crease-free surface that Sarah was sure she could bounce a quarter off of.

A large fur rug was positioned in the center of the enormous room, and Sarah gaped at it before her eyes wandered to the writing desk pressed against the side of the room nearest her. The paper screens had been pulled back, and the light coming through the windows on either side of the bed reflected off the silver inkwell positioned next to the wax seal on the desk.

It was not the gaudy opulence she had been expecting from her view of the guest wing, and Sarah realized she was taking everything in with wide-eyed shock. The room screamed of a breathtaking and simple beauty, and she was never more aware of the fact that she didn't belong here.

She remembered to snap her mouth closed before she turned to look over her shoulder at Edith, though she couldn't manage to blink her saucer-sized eyes. Edith gave her the faintest of smiles and motioned with her head for her to go into the room. Sarah walked in tentatively, feeling like she was intruding at the same time she felt drawn into the room by an invisible pull. This wasn't hers; it couldn't be.

"Are you sure we're in the right place?" she asked, her voice smaller than she would have liked.

"Yes, miss," came the response behind her. Sarah could tell from the sound of it that Edith hadn't followed her inside.

Her eyes roved over the walls and the furnishings again as she wandered aimlessly. Lightly dragging her fingertips across the surface of the rich mahogany desk, she felt a disbelieving smile touch her lips. This was her room now.

Her eyes wandered to the small stack of lambskin papers that had been neatly placed in the center of the desk, waiting for her to touch the tip of her ink-dipped quill to their surface, filling them with secrets and promises before sealing each one.

Lips parted slightly in surprise, Sarah gingerly touched the single rose in full bloom that had been placed on top of the stack. She stared at the flower, and the contrast of the tan page it lay in the middle of caused the petals to look blood red.

~Chapter 15~

Sarah pulled her hand back from the rose, as if pricked by an invisible thorn. Something was gnawing at her insides as she remembered what Edith had told her earlier. She turned to find her standing in the doorway, looking uncomfortable.

"You said that someone requested I be moved. Who was it?"

There was a brief hesitation before Edith answered quietly, "Lord Lisandro. He wished for you to be moved nearer his quarters for the duration of your service."

Sarah's left eye narrowed, and she shook her head from side to side. "But it isn't an issue coming from my room to change his bandages."

Something in her mentor's expression caused a lump of apprehension to form in Sarah's throat, choking her as the silence lengthened. "Edith," she managed at last, her voice strained. "Where is his room? And *why* would he want me so close to him?"

She watched Edith's eyes fill with sympathy and . . . worry? "He requested that you be as close as possible; his quarters are just across the hall from this room."

"But that makes it look like—" Sarah's words died on her lips when Edith didn't dissuade her train of thought. The lump of dread turned into a rock of horror that lodged in her throat, making it nearly impossible to breathe. She prayed she was reading more into the situation than there was, though all doubt over Damien's intentions was removed when she recalled the expressions on the faces of the servant girls downstairs. She had recognized the pure hatred but hadn't remembered the underlying jealousy until now: They thought she didn't deserve to be his *mistress.*

Just thinking the word made Sarah sick.

A look akin to that of a protective mother bear came across Edith's features as she hurried into the room and gathered both of Sarah's hands in her own. "Whatever his exact intentions for moving you over here, I will *not* let him harm you." she said firmly. "No matter what, my lady."

"Stop it, Edith. I'm nobody's lady."

"You are now."

Sarah's head snapped up to meet her friend's troubled gaze. "What are you talking about?"

A heavy sigh left Edith's lips. "When Lord Lisandro requested that you have this room, he also demanded that you be made a lady in the eye of society. You are no longer a servant—you are *free*."

Sarah gaped at her in bafflement, shaking her head. "But he just met me. He can't *make* me a lady! Can he? Can't you take me back to my other room?"

"He has great influence, and I cannot disobey a direct order," she answered softly, looking distressed. Sarah had never seen the sturdy woman so close to tears. "Oh, Sarah, you must forgive me! I should never have left the two of you unchaperoned, but I never imagined that he would be so possessive after only knowing you for so short a time."

Sarah felt her body shaking in both fear and anger, all directed at Damien. "Edith," she said firmly, relieved when her voice didn't betray her inner turmoil, "whatever ideas he thinks he has for me have nothing to do with you. You've been nothing but kind to me ever since I got here." Her grip tightened. "And he can drop dead if he thinks he's going to touch me; he's got a whole other thing coming to him if that's what he has in mind."

The shocked look on Edith's face melted into an amused smile, though the anxiety still clung to the corners of her eyes. "I believe he should have though twice before inviting you to live so close. I don't believe he will sleep peacefully with you nearby."

Sarah shot her a half-hearted grin. "You know it! He'd better sleep with one eye open and not run into me in any dark alleys, or I'll go all ninja on him." She received a chuckle, and Sarah squared her shoulders, willing determination into her every fiber. "I can take care of myself. And, hey, maybe he just took pity on me and I'm his charity case for the week while I'm his nurse. I'll be back working by your side within a few days once he gets better."

Edith's smile became strained. "Perhaps." She didn't sound convinced. She squeezed Sarah's hands before releasing them and walking backward toward the door. "I must go now, but I'll stay close by. If you need anything, my lady, just send for me." Sarah nodded, and the door closed behind her friend, the sound echoing one final note against the stone walls.

The room suddenly felt very empty and cold in Edith's absence, and she picked up the rose and clutched it to her chest, the only other living thing in the room besides her. In the silence, the overwhelming jumble of emotions Sarah had been battling washed over her in earnest. In an instant, she was made aware of the implications of this beautiful room—this gift and the man across the hall who expected something in return. But maybe she was reading everything wrong.

She was dully aware that she would be getting out of her duties for a while, but that also meant she would no longer have Edith's constant company. And the previous excitement she had felt over discovering her new living quarters had quickly faded to a gnawing terror, and without Edith's calming presence to distract her, Sarah remembered anew Will's betrayal.

Alone, frightened, and more confused than ever, Sarah threw herself face-first onto the bed, clutching the rose like a lifeline when she could no longer keep the tears at bay.

****

Will went back to his work, venting his frustration upon the cooling piece of iron with the weighty hammer. He could feel wary eyes on the back of his neck and knew Robert was watching him as he warped the rod until it was unrecognizable. He glared at the wrecked piece of metal, and, glancing up, directed his steady gaze at his hired hand. "Don't you have a task to do?"

Robert's look was full of pity. He didn't move. "Pardon me for meddling, Taylor, but—"

"Then don't," Will said, more exasperated than angry as he swiped a wrist over his sweating brow.

"—I was thinking," the blond man went on, as though he hadn't heard. "You should go after her, if you're so torn up about it."

Will stopped his work, laying the hammer aside. Leaning his hip against the workbench, he folded his arms and gave the other man a blank stare. Robert was an excellent worker, but he certainly expressed his opinions a little too freely for someone in the employ of a lowly blacksmith. "What caused you to think I am upset?" Will ground out crossly.

"Doesn't take a genius to see what I did when she came in." Robert flashed his pearly-white teeth. "She wasn't bad to look at, if you don't mind me saying." Would it matter if he *had* minded?

Noting Will's stony expression, Robert's tone gentled when he spoke. "You're in love with her, but something obviously went terribly wrong in the five minutes I was out. Want to talk about it?"

Will's folded arms rose and fell as his chest expanded with a heavy breath. "I seem to be cursed when it comes to relationships."

"Why do you say that?"

"Because I've damned every last one that comes my way," he exploded, vexed beyond control. "Either by what I say and do, or by what I

99

don't."

Robert grinned lazily. "I guess it's a good thing that this is strictly a business relationship, otherwise I might have to worry about anvils dropping from the sky."

Will's laugh sounded more like a huff, though the sudden release felt good.

"Not that I have much experience with women," Robert continued, "but I know enough to tell you that you should go after her before she gets too far."

Will was already shaking his head before he finished. "No, she wants to be alone. I need to give her time."

"Wrong move." At Will's skeptical glance, Robert held up his hands before he completely dismissed his advice. "Like I said, I know I'm no expert, but it's my understanding that when a woman runs away, she expects you to follow."

"Like a test?"

"Of your undying love, I guess." He shrugged. "It makes sense, in a way. Think of it like the way you might train a horse." At Will's quirked brow, Robert hurriedly continued. "I'm not comparing them to animals, just using an analogy you'll understand. But you spend time training a wild mare—or stallion, in her case—trying to get it to trust you, but you can't tell how strong the bond is until you walk away. If the animal follows, you know."

"I suppose *I'm* the wild stallion." Will let that sink in and realized it wasn't too far off. He drew his gaze from a bale of hay in the corner and gave Robert an appreciative glance. "I had never thought of it like that," he admitted reluctantly.

Robert grinned. "Well, my mother raised me never to think of women in terms of animals or livestock, but I thought it might get your attention."

Nodding, Will headed for the door, throwing on his cloak, a man with a purpose. He knew she would be too far gone to be found among the traders and consumers milling about, but his gaze still wandered the street as he moved outside. When his eyes locked on Jade's dark ones, nearly black from this distance, he stopped in his tracks, anger immediately rising to the surface. Their friendship had ended years ago, but how could she have betrayed him in such a way?

She smiled coyly at him, and his spine stiffened. Jade turned away and moved through the crowd with her chin high. Men glanced at her as she passed, while others, presumably customers, avoided her gaze at all costs, some even cutting a wide birth around her. Jade cocked her head slightly, and though he could not catch her expression, Will assumed that she either smiled or blew a kiss to a man close by, judging by the way the woman walking beside him slapped his arm and then hurriedly pulled him along.

A good head taller than most of the townsfolk about, Will easily kept track of Jade's slender form as she sashayed down the Dark District, her unrestrained hair swaying back and forth as she moved, drawing most of the male eyes present when they thought no one was looking. Jade did like to cause a stir wherever she went.

Will ducked down her street, resisting the desire to look about him and see if anyone noticed his path. Jade was already out of sight—safely behind closed doors, no doubt—and Will hastened down the typically deserted street with purposeful strides. What was he expecting? An apology? He doubted he could get a woman as stubborn and prideful as Jade to get on her knees, though he was loathe to admit that he would never ask her to do such a thing, tempting as that might be.

Clenching his fist, he pounded on the door with a single hard rap, which took more self-control than it should have. Jade could have beaten him down the road by no more than a minute, but he waited longer than that on her stoop with no sound from within.

Vexed, he ground his teeth and barked in a loud voice, "Jade, open up! I want my money back!" She loved to be the center of attention, but he knew she hated when people made a stir outside her door: Unhappy customers were bad for business.

As expected, Jade ripped the door open before he got out the last word. Though he could see in her eyes that she was frazzled, she pasted on the fake smile that she used to practice on him. His blood boiled at the seductive gleam in her eyes, but it was anger, not desire, that caused his body to heat. Her jealousy had ruined one of the few relationships that meant anything to him.

"Oh, William! What a *delectable* surprise." The innuendo was like a barb—intended, he was sure. "And to what do I owe the pleasure of this visit?"

"You know why I'm here." Will had to force his jaw to unclench to get the words out.

"Ah, of course. Would you care to come in?" Jade asked, dark eyes filled with enticement. She leaned against the doorframe in a practiced move meant to allure. "We would be far more comfortable inside while we discuss your . . . predicament?"

Will took a step back. The action was an obvious decline to her proposal—he wasn't fooled in the least or even tempted to accept her offer. Her open invitation would certainly be difficult for many men to refuse, but Will was wise enough to know that she offered temporary pleasure that would only take a piece of him, not give anything of worth. Besides, there was only one woman he could ever want now. Anyone else would just be a poor imitation.

"Why did you tell Sarah that we had been together?" he demanded.

Not that it would mend the wrong done, but something in him was itching for a good fight after months of being cooped up.

Some of Jade's composure was slipping, and she rolled her eyes, a piece of the spunky girl he once knew revealing itself. "I can't fathom why it was an issue—"

"*Why?*" He hadn't meant to shout, but he was at his wits' end and wanted a straight answer from her. For once.

Jade didn't even flinch, perhaps because she was used to men speaking loudly at her. "I was making things simple for everyone." Will opened his mouth to tell her that she had *complicated* things for everyone, but she surprised him by asking, "Did you deny it?" At his hesitation, her look became knowing.

He blinked. "Well, no, I—"

"You see? I simply saved her the pain of discovery before she became too attached." Jade's eyes darkened and flashed, though her voice remained even. "I allowed her to see the simple fact that all men are the same: prideful, disloyal, and believe that a woman's only purpose is to gratify their whims." She cocked her head, her professional side regaining control as she grinned at him, toying. "Now she knows how incapable of love your sex truly is." She sighed dramatically. "A pity, considering the two of you made a handsome couple, though her skin *is* a little dark," she threw in, almost as an afterthought. She examined her nails as though they were far more interesting than this conversation.

Will glared at her. How had they ever been friends? "You ruined everything, you know. She was the one, and you may have destroyed whatever was holding us together." He invaded her personal space, his face close to hers. Some of her triumph faded, and her throat worked in a swallow, though her face showed almost nothing.

Lowering his voice to a low, taunting growl, he asked, "Does it make you feel good to know that you may have run off the only woman besides my own mother that I've ever cared for?" He intentionally excluded her. It was a low blow, and he knew it in the way she flinched at his words. But he was too wound-up to stop. "Will you sleep better at night knowing that I will be alone for the rest of my days? If you can't have me, then no one can, is that it?"

"She doesn't deserve you," Jade whispered, voice wavering. He had hoped to intimidate her, but he felt no triumph in it as he glimpsed in her face the child he had once known. She placed her hand over his heart. Her fingers seemed to have a mind of their own as they slid up and around his neck, trying to pull him closer. Her eyes gleamed possessively once more, desperation apparent in their fathomless depths. "I was doing what's best for you. For us—"

He'd had enough.

102

Growling in frustration, Will whipped around, breaking her hold, and jogged down the steps. He was halfway down the block before he heard her quietly latch the door. How could she still be clinging to that fantasy, or was it all a pride issue? She had always needed to win at everything.

He swore under his breath when he realized how much time he had lost in such a worthless conversation. Jade had probably planned on them meeting in the square, and like the fool he was, he had played right into her hands.

Well, his own pride could go to Hades. Robert was right: He needed to fix this and go after Sarah before it was too late.

~Chapter 16~

A soft knock sounded on her bedroom door only a few minutes into her pity party. Sarah jerked her head off of the soft burgundy bedspread, heart hammering in her chest in anticipation and dread as she waited to see if the noise had come from one of the other rooms. The knock sounded again, and this time there was no doubt someone was tapping on her door.

Peeling herself off the bed, she hastily swiped a palm across her reddened cheeks, realizing that she was still holding the rose. She placed it gently on the rumpled covers, being careful of its delicate petals. She felt ridiculous over her tumultuous emotions and told herself—again—that what Will did in his free time wasn't her concern. And what did it matter that some guy had moved her next door?

Sarah felt sick.

"Who is it?" she called out, her voice cracking. She prayed it wasn't Damien.

"It is Damien Lisandro, my lady."

Sarah could have sworn. She hadn't expected him so soon. Clenching her fists at her sides, she tried to think of something to buy her time—to find a weapon, climb out through the window, scale down the wall to the snowy earth—she didn't know.

"Give me a minute!" She hoped he couldn't hear the edge to the words.

She reached for her naked wrist, suddenly remembering the watch Karen had given her. She had removed it this morning so she didn't lose it, but where had she put it? She closed her eyes, and a desperate groan escaped her lips when she pictured it safely nestled at the bottom of the trunk in her old room. The trunk that was now empty.

Her eyes snapped open. Edith had said they'd moved her things to this room, and she prayed they hadn't confiscated it or tossed it out.

Oh, God. Oh, God, oh, God, please, Sarah prayed over and over, no

104

other words coming in her desperation. She ran to the wardrobe on the right wall and flung the doors open wide, sifting through the folds of variously colored fabrics, the details of which—and also the fact that it was stocked full of gowns—were completely lost on her as she shoved the dresses aside and scanned the wooden bottom of the small closet. Nothing.

Sarah didn't bother to close the door as she dashed to the desk, her eyes widening as she took in the four small drawers on each side of the oversized desk: nine in total, including the one in the middle. *Oh, for the love of—!* She started on the left side and ripped the top drawer open, then the next one down, and the next. She finished with that side before moving onto the long, flat drawer in the center of the desk, jerking it open and slamming it closed. She placed her hand on the knob of the next drawer before she registered a muted scrape as the contents of the previous one slid about.

With a startled gasp, she pulled the middle drawer out again and expelled a breath of relief when she saw the watch lying safely inside. Picking it up as though the sturdy mechanism were made of porcelain, Sarah secured it around her wrist. Some of the tension left her body as the light pressure of the watch against her skin served to remind her that she had a means of escape, if it came to that.

Mustering whatever courage she had left, Sarah tipped her chin up as she opened the door, determined that he would never see her broken.

Damien seemed to have been waiting patiently outside, appearing completely at ease as he smiled at her, though it quickly faded to a look of concern as his eyes roved her features. "My lady, have you been crying? Are you ill?"

She felt her face heat, feeling embarrassed that he had so quickly seen the marks of her tears. "I'm fine," she answered, hating the way her voice became so quiet; it only made her sound weaker.

He tipped his head to the side, assessing her. Sarah would have thought the action looked cocky had it not been for the look of warmth and concern in his eyes. "I'm a fairly good listener."

She shook her head, feeling uncomfortable that she felt so, well, *comfortable* in his presence. "No thanks."

Damien smiled softly when she didn't offer up any further information. She was surprised at the genuine look on his face, but she still wasn't sure if she could trust him . . . or herself.

"Would you like me to leave?" he asked.

Sarah was taken aback that he would let her so easily dismiss him. She told herself not to be fooled by his kindness and respect for her privacy, or the way eyes the color of gold-flecked espresso watched her, and she definitely was not going to be fooled by his handsome features. She was smarter than that.

105

Folding her arms tightly across her chest like body armor, she asked, "What are you doing here, Damien? Better yet, why am *I* here?"

He seemed pleased that she had used his name, and Sarah silently reprimanded herself for giving her captor any satisfaction. "I was hoping that we might get to know one another better."

It sounded innocent enough the way he said it, but Sarah knew better. Righteous anger flared up at what he was implying.

She took a step closer to him, though she was still tempted to run away with her tail between her legs. Straightening her body to reach her full height, she unfolded her arms and clenched her hands into fists at her sides. "If you actually think that by throwing out a few compliments and playing the role of gentleman, I'm just going to roll over and play along, well"—she jabbed a finger into his chest and managed not to wince as her appendage bent against lean muscle—"then you better think twice about messing with me, pal." She tried to look tough, though she knew her eyes were too wide and her voice quavered too much for her to appear threatening.

Damien looked completely shocked at her outburst. "You couldn't possibly believe that I—" His face relaxed, and his sudden chuckle threw her. He reached for the hand that was still poking him in the chest and then released it without a fight when she tried to wriggle free. "Oh, my lady, I'm so terribly sorry. What you must think of me!" He shook his head and pulled at his collar as if he were suddenly very warm. "It's simply that with my injury and you being my caretaker—that is to say, I felt very at ease in your presence and requested that you be moved nearby to help me improve. To save us both time. That is *all*."

Sarah was sure she couldn't look more confused. "Wait, so you didn't move me up here for . . ." She couldn't even finish the sentence. To Damien's credit, he looked embarrassed as his eyes shifted around the room, though she was sure it was nothing compared to her mortification. What a complete idiot she had been! But though she felt like a total fool, she couldn't have been more relieved.

A giggle of relief bubbled up from her stomach, and Damien's eyes snapped up when she couldn't contain her laughter any longer. "That's great to hear!"

The surprise and embarrassment ebbed from his features as his face relaxed once more, and he even chuckled a little. "You looked like a fierce kitten ready to paw me to death if I touched you."

"Hey, I'm tougher than I look." She glared at him and received a laugh for her look of death. Grinning, she shrugged. "It usually works better on yarn balls and bowls of milk."

Damien gave her a slow, heart-melting smile that Janice would have swooned over. His dark brows rose on his forehead. "Who knew you had the ability to jest? I thought you could only glower at me."

Sarah laughed, feeling a little euphoric in her relief. "Yeah, well, I've got a temper too, so you might want to think twice about crossing me."

That smile was still in place, and his dark eyes gazed into her own with a familiarity that he didn't possess, but somehow it was so sincere that Sarah wondered if maybe he understood her better than she thought. "You have a beautiful laugh, my lady."

She swallowed and shuffled her feet, feeling suddenly self-conscious. His expression was so genuine that Sarah couldn't tell if it was a line or not. "I'm nobody's lady," she murmured, repeating the words she had spoken to Edith. Trying to steer the conversation into safer territory, she said, "Speaking of which, why did you ask them to lay me off? I mean, I could just stay here and be a servant at the same time."

Damien appeared younger as he fidgeted awkwardly, looking shy and very boyish for someone in his early-twenties. "In all honesty, I wanted to know you better, and this was the best way I could think of to do it. I know it was presumptuous of me to think that you would prefer a . . . higher life, but I felt that—" He looked so confused and nervous that Sarah felt herself softening as she waited for the rest of his explanation.

Expelling a heavy sigh, he looked at the ground as he spoke. "I can't honestly say why I felt the need to release you from servitude after only having just met you, but"—his gaze found hers, and she swallowed at what she saw there—"I saw you like an angel come to save me right after I had been stabbed, and you tended to my wound and were so kind. I have not seen compassion like that in many years." Sarah cringed as she recalled how she had slapped the cloth to his gash when he aggravated her.

"You don't belong in servitude, scrubbing floors and pounding rugs," he continued, his expression sincere and magnetizing. "Forgive me for saying so, but you appear like you belong here as much as I do. We are both fish out of the lake, you might say, and I desired to set you free. You were made for more; I felt this when I first saw you." Damien shrugged shyly. "I know how strange it must seem, but I admit my hope was that we might become . . . friends."

So she wasn't the only one who felt the odd connection between them. Sarah made a conscious effort to keep her mouth closed. His honesty was far too disarming for her comfort level, though that *was* one of the sweetest things anyone had ever said and done for her. She glanced over at the rose on the bed and grinned at him to cover the soft smile caused by the fluttering in her stomach. "Do you give all your friends flowers?"

He returned her grin, going along with the change in mood. "Only the most special ones who can withstand the sight of open wounds and blood."

"Well, I *did* have to leave the room," she reminded him, "but I'll still accept the rose." They smiled at each other, the watch on her wrist completely forgotten. Sarah could deal with playful and sarcastic, but it was odd to think that a near stranger would do so much for her. It was also incredibly flattering, and she wondered at him having so quickly disarmed her.

"Ah!" Damien exclaimed suddenly. "I nearly forgot my purpose for calling. I wanted to see how you are settling in."

"Well, I've been here for about twenty minutes, so things are good so far." She quirked a brow. "Anything else?"

He motioned to his injured arm, crooked safely against his side. "I am also in need of some new dressings, and I believe I still require your assistance with that."

Sarah's blue eyes widened. "Oh, Damien. You should have told me sooner. What do you need me to get you?"

He gasped, feigning a look of shock as he pressed a hand to his chest. "You sound as though you care about my health, my lady."

She balked at him and then rolled her eyes, contemplating giving him a playful shove, but she felt uncomfortable touching him so soon in their new "friendship."

"As your nurse I'm required to care, so tell me what I need to do."

Damien grinned, and she found that his face was even more handsome when he smiled. *But barely*, she amended. "Do you have any new dressings and the poultice?" he asked.

"I'm not sure," she said slowly, glancing over the room.

He nodded. How did he manage to look amused and carefree all the time? "I had them put some pieces of fresh cloth in your trunk for this purpose, but I'm afraid I didn't ask them to make the poultice beforehand."

Sarah frowned. "Oh. Do you happen to know what's in it?"

Shaking his head, Damien answered, "I'm afraid I do not. Would you like me to ask someone?"

She considered it for a moment before waving her hand in the air. "You're the invalid, I'm the nurse. I'll go find out."

She bustled past him like a woman on a mission and then paused just outside the doorway. Turning back around, she caught Damien's grin and shot him an embarrassed grimace. "Um, where would I go to do that, exactly?"

She was grateful that he didn't tease her about the out-of-place girl trying to play the role of the independent, self-assured woman. "You will have to find the alchemist for the proper herbs," he said.

Sarah sighed. "Super." Heading down the hall, she muttered sarcastically, "I guess I'm off to see the wizard."

****

Sarah shivered as she descended the cold stone staircase, her apprehension as much to blame for her shaking as the cold itself. She clenched her jaw as she crept downward, mindful of where she stepped in the near darkness, as if a wrong move or noise could disturb the dead from their slumber.

Her fear was unwarranted, but the only time she had been this far underground was to visit the dungeons, and that experience had not been a pleasant one. This time Sarah felt none of the curiosity she'd experienced when she and Will had slipped into the dungeons to see Karen. Sarah remembered her face—tear-streaked and dirty, but eyes bright with hope when she saw the two of them—and cringed at the memory of Karen's imprisonment. How many days had she been trapped down there? Five? Six? Sarah's stomach knotted at the very thought, and in the end, she hadn't even been able to save her friend.

But the Shadow had.

She was honest with herself and acknowledged that descending into the depths of the labyrinthine halls below was so daunting because she was completely alone this time. Will had been with her that day—he always seemed to be there when she needed him most—so strong and reassuring as he guided her to her friend, and his compassion for her that night in the midst of her distress had cemented him in Sarah's heart.

Will's concern for her had never been fabricated. It was never more obvious to her than when she'd realized that he had stayed by her side for days after she'd been poisoned. Her stomach warmed at the memory, and she knew that if Will were with her at that moment—regardless of the unresolved feelings between them—he would hold her hand to guide her. She longed for that comfort now.

The stairs ended, and she stopped where the hallway curved to the left. She held her candle high, the light bouncing off the cold walls and casting shadows across the dark path until they faded into the blackness.

"Follow the path around to the left." Hoping to break the stony silence around her and keep her mind from making the darkness more sinister than it truly was, Sarah whispered aloud the instructions from the servant she'd met at the top of the stairs—the same man who had also kindly provided her with the small candle. The hallways and turns had easily confused Sarah, and he had been the third servant she'd asked directions from, not to mention the guard who'd seemed none too happy to be interrupted from his important duty of standing in front of a door. She had decided to steer clear of any guards for the rest of her stay at the castle.

"Do not veer off to the right too soon," she whispered, her breath causing the flame to flicker and nearly go out. Sarah froze and sucked in a lungful of stale air, terrified at the possibility of being left in complete darkness. She hardly dared to breathe even after the flame came back to life.

With one hand cupped protectively behind her only source of light,

Sarah moved slowly through the passageway, her eyes flickering to the dancing flame every now and then as she mentally went over the directions—*Third arch, go right. Follow the stairs down . . . take the left tunnel.*

Making her way down yet another flight of stairs, she walked forward slowly, stopping, almost against her will, in the middle of the floor where the four passageways connected. Her spine tingled in apprehension an instant before she realized where she was. She told her feet to move down the tunnel leading to the alchemist's lab so she could abandon her wandering in the creepy tunnels. But still, she found she couldn't move.

These passages all looked impossibly similar, but the tightening in her stomach told her that if she continued on through the tunnel just ahead, she would end up in the dungeons. She wasn't sure if it was out of morbid curiosity or nostalgia for that night nearly a millennia ago, but Sarah found herself straining to hear any sound coming from the tunnel as she stared into the darkness ahead.

She was so focused on listening for noises coming from the dungeon that she didn't hear the rat until it climbed over her foot. Her shriek echoed off the stones as she jumped away from the vermin, though it had already scampered down another corridor, squeaking in fright. Sarah lost her grip on the candleholder, futilely grappling for it in the air. The small flame was extinguished by the wind her flailing hands stirred, and she lost sight of it before it clattered to the ground.

Frozen in terror, her heart beat erratically against her chest. The candle was useless to her now since she had no way of lighting it, so she didn't bother searching for it in the dark. She stood there, body rigid, staring at the lighted tunnel but too afraid to move an inch.

In the total darkness that enveloped her, she waited for the grating noise of dragging chains and the sound of life wasting away to start up suddenly, or the blood-curdling screams of torture and whimpering children and prisoners who had given up hope. At the very least Sarah expected to be able to hear a guard or two shuffling around in the passage as they moved from cell to cell, checking on the neglected inmates.

Nothing.

The absence of noise was somehow more ominous than the ones Sarah had braced herself for. She shivered as a cold wind whistled softly in the tunnel on its way to her, curling through her hair and touching her body with icy fingers as it brushed past her. A whip suddenly snapped somewhere down the way. She jerked in surprise, and her breath caught when she made out the faint sound of the lifeless, almost inhuman moan that rode on the breeze coming from what she imagined must be the torture chamber.

Sarah's bones chilled at the hollow, wavering sound of someone too

110

weak to cry out, and she stood there another moment in wide-eyed horror, feeling helpless to do anything. Could she help whoever was being beaten? Did they deserve punishment? Maybe she could steal a guard's key and release the prisoners, then whisk them off to the forest where they could build a village of their own.

Her shoulders sagged in defeat when reality struck and she regained her senses: She was no Robin Hood—she was nobody's hero. With no weapons and even less common sense if she followed through with her tomfool plan, she would never be able to overpower the guards, carry the wounded prisoners to safety, and even though her dad owned a hardware store, she had absolutely no idea how to build anything if it didn't come with instructions, let alone an entire town from scratch. She was powerless to do anything, and she knew some of them belonged in there, anyway.

The reminder was like a bucket of ice water over her head, and she quickly ducked into the safety of the tunnel on the left, though she felt like a coward for doing so. But there was nothing she could do to help them, and her interference would only make things worse when she failed.

Even escaping into the warmth of the lit tunnel wasn't enough to abate the remaining chill from the cold wind and the hollow moan it had carried with it. Rubbing her arms to warm them, Sarah stood close to one of the mounted torches, relishing its warmth as she looked for the open doorway belonging to the alchemist. Spotting the wide, door-less entrance a ways down the long corridor, Sarah nearly skipped to the entrance in her haste. A drawer slammed shut from inside the room just as she stepped into the doorway, rattling the vials and tubes on the table at the center of the room.

The only person in the small space—a slight, wiry man—was hastily trying to right the instruments he had overturned on the two shelves stacked at the back of the table. He looked frazzled at her sudden appearance, though Sarah was fairly certain she had made enough of a racket to alert him of her presence as she ran like a frightened mouse through the corridor.

"I'm sorry, I didn't mean to startle you." She stood in the doorway, unsure if she would be of more use helping him clean up or staying out of his way. Before she could make up her mind, he had put all the empty vials back in their places and straightened the contents of the table. He looked up and shot her a nervous smile through the menagerie of vials, his right eye magnified through one of the shakers filled with a clear green liquid, giving him the look of a mad scientist.

Through the gap between the bottom shelf and the table, she could see him ball his shaking hands into fists. "Not at all!" His voice sounded constricted and overly bright, and he cleared his throat. "You must tell the prince's advisor that it is not quite ready yet. I will alert him the moment of its completion."

Sarah blinked. "Oh, I'm not here because of the prince or Cadius."

The older man rubbed a twitching finger beneath his straight nose, and she noticed that there was a small pink mark on either side, like he had been pinching it earlier. He narrowed his eyes at her, like he was squinting to see better in the brightly lit room. "Oh? I assumed you came to summon me on behalf of the prince. Is there something else for which my assistance is required?"

His apprehension was palpable. Sarah stepped into the room and stood on the other side of the desk. She leaned down to better see him through the shelves and smiled, putting on a calm and open expression to alleviate his nervousness. "I'm supposed to collect some herbs for a poultice. Damien Lisandro sent me."

"The lord?" He appeared surprised, raising his nutmeg-colored eyebrows until they nearly touched the smattering of gray at his temples. "Was someone injured?"

Now it was Sarah's turn to look surprised. Stories seemed to circulate quickly among the staff, and she'd assumed that everyone had heard about the encounter between Damien and the doctor by now. How far removed from the world was this man? "Well, the lord was stabbed, actually. By the doctor."

His eyes widened as they searched her face for the truth, revealing irises that matched the patches of darker hair on his head. The candlelight played off the gray flecks speckling the brown of his eyes, making his surprise and disbelief even more apparent. "The physician? I can scarcely believe such an account."

"I saw it happen myself." Well, that wasn't entirely true, since she hadn't *actually* seen the doctor stab Damien, but she had heard them arguing, which was practically the same thing. "Were you friends with the doc"—Sarah corrected herself—"the physician?"

"I would not go so far as to say that. We were more . . . colleagues," he answered slowly, sounding guarded. "But Malcolm hardly seems the type to attack anyone, let alone a lord. It just seems so unlikely."

He was around the desk and mere inches from her before Sarah was fully aware of his movements. His look was a mix of urgency and curiosity and . . . excitement? How starved was this man for news from upstairs? "You said you saw the event?"

"I didn't technically *see* it happen," Sarah admitted. "But I did hear the two of them arguing about something, and it was pretty obvious what the physician had done."

The gray in the man's eyes sparkled in the light. "Ah, so you did not see it with your own eyes." He paused. "Are you quite sure they were having a disagreement?"

Sarah thought back. Had it been only just this morning? "I didn't catch all of it. But the physician sounded peeved about something, and they were

112

definitely arguing."

Stroking his beard thoughtfully, he asked, "Is it possible that someone put him up to it?"

Sarah thought about that and then shrugged her shoulders, wondering what he was implying. "I didn't see anyone else, if that's what you mean."

"The eyes can be deceptive," he murmured. For whatever reason, the corner of his mouth tipped, as if he were holding a secret.

"Your name, child?"

"Sarah. I'm one of the—" She halted, remembering that she was no longer a maid. "I'm staying at the castle."

He smiled with pleasure that wasn't fabricated. "The honor is mine." He dipped his head. "Charles Ashmore, at your disposal."

~Chapter 17~

Sarah gaped at him, mentally slapping herself on the forehead for her stupidity. "Professor?" she whispered when she found her voice.

Charles started, appearing alarmed at the use of his adopted daughter's name for him. "Where on earth did you hear that?"

Automatically glancing at the door to make sure they were alone, Sarah suddenly wondered when she'd become so paranoid. Was this what it was like for Karen, constantly looking over her shoulder and wondering if the next person she encountered would turn her in?

And Will. He must live with the same kind of anxiety that someone might uncover his secret. Sarah began to understand the closed-off, stony-faced Will she originally met. But he had to know it was inevitable—someone would eventually discover who he was, and Sarah was fearful that even with all the good he had done, there were those who would see him hanged without a second thought.

Sarah realized that the professor was gripping her shoulders. "Child, where did you hear that name?"

She blinked at his intensity and underlying excitement. "You are the professor, aren't you?"

Even in the silence, the look on his face was enough of an answer. Sarah could hardly believe she had found him and that she might have walked away without ever realizing who he was. Though Charles Ashmore and Karen were not related by blood, somehow she had expected them to resemble each other. But the only similarity between the two was their slight figures and penchant for science, though even that was far more extreme on the professor's part.

Inclining her head toward him, she held up the hand with the watch on it and whispered, "I'm a friend of Karen's. You know, a *friend* of Karen's."

The light in the professor's eyes seemed to brighten as he examined the watch, though he was careful to keep his expression even. She could tell he was practically bursting with excitement, but his voice was controlled as he hedged, "Are you saying that you are from . . .?"

He let the question hang, and Sarah grinned at the game he was playing, though she couldn't fault his caution. "I'm from Oklahoma, in the twenty-first century," she whispered.

Charles let out a hearty laugh that startled her. "I knew there was something strange about you! How on earth did my dear girl manage such a feat? Were you in the lab with her? Have you come to this country before? Are you showing any side affects yet? Come, come—sit down and tell me everything!"

Sarah felt a little overwhelmed with all of his questions as he guided her to a stool behind the table. She watched the man open the only drawer built into the table, quickly pulling her knees up as he jerked the compartment open. Charles hardly seemed to notice her, nor did he appear to realize that she hadn't answered a single one of his questions.

His eyes were almost feverish in light of this possible "discovery," and Sarah could almost see the wheels in his scientifically inclined mind spinning wildly. Now that he was no longer in character, she was able to see the eccentricities that Karen had alluded to before, and the fact that the professor had neglected to ask after Karen's welfare wasn't lost on her, either.

Charles produced a pair of wire-rimmed glasses from the drawer and slid them on. "There, now!" he exclaimed, sounding surprised. "Aren't you a young thing?"

Sarah couldn't tell if that was a compliment or an insult. "I'm eighteen, Mr. Ashmore—just a little younger than Karen." The hint fell flat, and she sighed. Pointing at the glasses with a lone finger, she asked, "Why did you stash those before I came in?"

He smiled at her. "You are astute, aren't you? My dear girl has found herself a like-minded ally, I see." Waving to his glasses, he replied, "I hid these because I assumed you were one of the guards, and we don't want to introduce spectacles into society too early now, do we?" His English accent became more apparent as he spoke, and Sarah vaguely recalled Karen mentioning that he taught at Oxford for a time.

His eyes drifted to the open doorway, and he frowned deeply, muttering, "Now I have to be especially careful of guards walking in on me unannounced, since Cadius ordered the door removed. I would hate for my research to be interrupted by a trip to the gallows for witchcraft if they saw my spectacles as a threat. Though I am nearly blind without them," he continued unhappily, adjusting the glasses on the bridge of his nose.

"That's kind of why I've been helping Karen out," Sarah baited.

He blinked. "So I won't be sent to the gallows?"

Sarah resisted an exasperated sigh. Charles might be intelligent enough to unearth a notch in time, but he was completely oblivious when it came to human subtly. "*Nooo.* I tried to help *Karen* when *she* was in prison on the charge of being a witch."

She was rewarded with a flash of worry lines across his forehead. She wouldn't normally put so much effort into drawing a negative response from someone, but Sarah felt that her friend deserved some concern for all she had been through, especially from the man who had raised her after her parents died.

"Is she all right?" he asked. His eyes flickered to the doorway, and Sarah could almost see his mind going to the dungeons. "Is she still here?"

"No, the Shadow saved her just before she was supposed to hang."

The professor's head whipped around to face her. "The legend? He's real? Have you seen him yourself?"

This time she sighed aloud. Charles's attention span was like that of a four-year-old. "Yes, he's real. He and I are sort of friends," she answered honestly. At least, she hoped they were still friends after today.

"Fascinating," Charles murmured, stroking his bearded-chin. "I so wish I could observe him, but without my eyeglasses . . ."

"Why don't you just wear your glasses so you can see him for yourself?" Sarah asked, a little more curtly than she had intended. He didn't seem to notice her sharp tone, but she softened it anyway. "It doesn't really matter if someone sees them or not. It's not like it can affect the future, or anything."

His hand fell away from his chin. "Oh, child, we can't be certain of that. There are far too many variables to take into account." Now the hand was waving in the air to exaggerate his point, and he motioned to the vials, tubes, and pouches littering the table and shelves. "That is why I am doing so much research here, and also around the castle when I am permitted—to see if I can find any correlation between the future where we live, the past we know from there, and *this* time where we currently abide. Then perhaps . . ." His voice faded as his eyes drifted to the shelves lining the walls around the small room. Sarah could tell his mind was already working around the complications.

"But I could help you escape," she volunteered, surprising herself. But now that the option was out there, it made more sense than Charles remaining here as Cadius' puppet. "Wouldn't it be easier to do your research from *outside* the castle?"

She watched him shake his graying head. "I must stay here and find out all that I can."

Sarah stared at him dubiously. "Don't you want to be free and see Karen again?"

"I must finish my studies here," he replied firmly, lifting his sleeve to expose a time watch of his own. "I can leave anytime; I *choose* to stay.

Karen knows of my devotion to my creations, my discoveries. She understands why I must remain here."

Karen had once explained that the professor wanted to remain at the castle with his research, rather than be free with her, though Sarah had assumed that the situation was only temporary. But after meeting Charles for herself, she realized why her friend had longed to be a part of a tight-knit family like the Joneses. The eccentric professor might love Karen and be her last surviving relation, but Sarah could imagine why it had never felt like *home* with Charles Ashmore.

"It's quite the little ruse you have going on here." Sarah swirled her index finger in the air to indicate the room.

Charles smiled as if they shared some great secret. "I was quite fortunate to have been caught when I was. Look at me!" She tried to return his enthusiasm, but her smile was weak. He didn't appear to notice, anyway. "And the master Cadius takes such fascination in my work and has readily financed all of my studies, even providing tests for me to conduct. It is so refreshing to be appreciated for my talents."

"I'd imagine so," Sarah murmured, though she wasn't sure a response was necessary.

"So!" He clapped his hands together, startling her. She was having a difficult time keeping up with him. Sarah watched as he rubbed his palms together eagerly, staring at her like she was an appetizing dish that he was preparing to dive into. "You never did say how you came to be here."

With a sigh, she told him about the watch being damaged and the storm at her house that had pulled her and Lilly back in time, and then she relayed how Karen had found them.

"And you say it deposited you at Karen's exact location?" the professor interrupted.

Sarah thought back. "Yeah, I would say we were pretty close to each other."

"Fascinating." Charles went back to stroking his short beard, and she could tell he was no longer talking to her as he mused, "Obviously, the damage done to the timepiece did not disable the GPS, or they would not have arrived in such close proximity to the watch." He motioned for her to continue. "What happened after that?"

Surprised to be addressed again, Sarah blinked and then continued with her story, watching his eyes widen enthusiastically when she talked about encountering Gabriel Dunlivey and the Shadow in the forest, but he managed not to interrupt this time. "Then Karen said that the watch had enough energy to transport, so I sent my sister back."

"So it *did* lose power when it was damaged?" he clarified.

"Yeah. Karen mentioned that something similar happened before."

Charles nodded. His expression turned suddenly grave "Yes. After the

117

disloyalty of a colleague of mine, I brought into our confidence one of my students, a rather young man with a brilliant mind for science and history. We experienced a similar event, though he recovered enough power to return." He swallowed thickly. "After nearly losing him, we managed to protect most of the system from multiple types of destruction—water damage, heat exposure, etcetera—but we never discovered how to maintain the energy store once it had been damaged, without returning to the lab for modifications, that is."

Sarah didn't waste her breath telling him that he could go home and work on the issue. The professor seemed lost to his own thoughts and didn't pose any more questions, but now her own curiosity was longing to be satisfied.

"Mr. Ashmore?"

He blinked as if coming out of a trance. "Yes, child? Is there more?"

She cleared her throat quietly. "Well, I really haven't talked to Karen that much about this whole thing—you know, wormholes and continuums, and all—but earlier you asked me if I was showing any side affects. What did you mean by that?"

The man appeared baffled. "You mean Karen did not discuss it with you?" Sarah shook her head, and he mimicked the movement. "Just after we replaced the machine with the more convenient watches, we three were able to travel quite frequently and with great ease, so we never bothered to stay in one place and time for very long. But then we began to notice . . . changes," he answered carefully.

Sarah narrowed an eye. "What kind of changes?"

He seemed hesitant to answer, and Sarah felt her trepidation return. "You must understand that time travel is no simple feat. Your body is solid mass and does not simply reside somewhere one moment and then— *poof*!—appear in another the next instant. It must first be broken down, every molecule disintegrated and altered into transferable atoms that can . . . float through time and space, so to speak."

He held his hands in front of him, palms-up, the expression on his face almost apologetic. "For a few brief moments, you cease to exist. It's the only possible way to move through the fabric of time—to be broken down on a molecular level. But the alteration of the genome is so severe that sometimes it cannot be properly reformed when a jumper is dropped and pieced together again." The professor smiled slightly at a memory. "That is what my student called us—jumpers."

With a blink that pulled him from his spell, his hands started moving again as he became more animated in his explanation. "The alterations and degeneration of atoms is a highly extreme process—fragmentation of ones very genetic makeup is hardly natural." Charles laughed as thought he'd made a joke. Sarah blinked, and he went on, straight-faced once more.

"Thus they are unnaturally reformed, sometimes erroneously and haphazardly when ones organs become exhausted from scrambling to piece together a human being."

She snapped her mouth closed. "So, you're saying that I could grow an extra toe, or something?"

Charles actually laughed at this, though she was being completely serious. "An additional appendage—what an idea! I would very much like to see that." Sarah gaped at him, but he didn't appear to notice as he resumed waving his hands expressively before him. "I suppose it's possible, if given enough time. Eventually, the genome alterations would be irreversible, though we have yet to experience so extreme a change."

Yet. Sarah grimaced.

"But my girl and I took trips less frequently when we noticed highly unique changes such as this"—he pointed to his gray-specked eyes—"that appeared a little over a year ago. Some cases were more or less severe, regardless of whether the subject had traveled five times or fifty. Even inanimate objects were affected over time."

The last part really caught her attention and managed to distract her from the image of an extra eye in the center of her forehead. "Other subjects? Like the guinea pig?" She felt her stomach coil. "Or your assistant and Karen?"

Through the scruff on his neck, Sarah caught the subtle movement of his Adam's apple as he swallowed. Nervousness. "I've taken up enough of your time, and the lord will be in need of his poultice by now, I believe."

He stood, snatched an empty wooden bowl from the table, and walked away from her to sift through the vials and other containers on the shelves before Sarah could voice her objections. She watched as he collected herbs and tossed them into the bowl, adding liquids and powders to the mix.

Charles brought the bowl back to the table and ground everything together until it resembled a thick paste. Pouring the contents into a leather pouch, he said, "Apply a *very* thin layer of this to the wound. Make sure your hands are properly washed before doing so, and let the poultice air-dry a few moments before wrapping the wound with a fresh bandage. It will need to be changed twice a day, in the morning and in the evening, to keep the wound clean. You must also gently wash the wound each time before reapplying the poultice. This will last you until it is no longer needed." He cinched the top of the pouch and handed it to her, along with a stack of fresh bandages from one of the shelves. She didn't attempt to tell him that she had bandages back in her room.

Holding another small pouch out to her, he explained, "A salve of my own invention that should prevent scarring. Two days with the poultice to pack the wound and seal it, and then a fortnight with the salve. Do you understand my instructions?"

119

"I think so," Sarah answered with a nod, trying to recall everything he'd said.

With a curt nod of approval, Charles reached for a tall candle on the table and lit the wick by the flame of one of the stumpy candles littering the surface. Offering her a smile and a bob of his head, he held the slender stick of wax out to her. "Best wishes, and it was delightful to meet you, Sarah."

She readjusted her armload to accept the proffered item, feeling the ridges of dried wax trails along the sides. "You too," she answered absently, watching the candle to make sure she didn't drip any wax on herself. She turned and walked toward the hallway, gripping the stack of bandages that she didn't really need a little tighter and leaning back when her load tipped precariously.

"Sarah?"

She turned around in the doorway. Charles hesitated, wringing his hands and looking uncomfortable. "Tell Karen . . . Tell her to take care."

A small smile tipped her lips. "I will, Professor."

Then she turned and went back the way she'd come, treading the hall slowly, hoping that with two different sets of instructions running through her head, she would be able to find her way out of this maze. But when that same chilling wind caressed her skin in the outer passageway, her only thought was to find the quickest route out of there. She bolted for the closest staircase, scampering across the stones like the mouse she had frightened earlier, not pausing for a moment to see if she could find the candle she had lost.

~Chapter 18~

Sarah juggled the stack of bandages as she made her way up the stairs, focusing on the top of the pile where the leather pouches were sliding back and forth with each motion. She received a few odd stares from the staff as she shuffled down the passageway leading to her room, panting from her sprint up several flights of stairs.

Shifting her load, she gripped the cold candle in one hand—having endured the hot, dripping wax only until she reached the lighted tunnels—and took a moment to find her balance on one foot so she could kick the door open without toppling over. She hastened into the room to escape the curious and accusatory stares she was receiving, catching the side of the door with her hip and awkwardly thrusting the thick piece of wood closed, satisfied when the lock clicked into place.

"Sarah?"

She screeched and jumped, sending the carefully stacked layers of bandages flying. One pouch fell to the ground with a squishy *thump*, while the other gracefully arced through the air toward the open window beside her bed. It landed near Will's feet, where he stood half hidden behind the drapes, a startled look on his face.

Sarah had the candle in a death grip and hurled it at his figure reflexively. "Stop *doing* that!" she fairly shrieked, still on-edge after her race from the darkened dungeons.

Will leaped from his hiding place in time to dodge the flying object. The candle split in two when it hit the wall, the curtains causing the impact to make a solid *thwump* before it dropped to the floor.

He walked toward her, hands outstretched in surrender, but he halted a safe distance away. "Stop doing what?"

"You always sneak up on me," she said as her heart rate slowed, though it wasn't beating normally just yet. "I could have killed you, you know."

Will glanced pointedly at the candle lying broken on the floor and almost looked like he wanted to grin. Almost. "Yes, I can see that. If I were made of wax, I might be dead."

Sarah gaped at him, and any traces of mirth drained from his countenance. "Sorry," he apologized. "I should have informed you of my coming."

"How did you even get in?" she asked, not yet recovered from the shock of seeing him in her room. She still wasn't sure how to act around him after their . . . *disagreement* earlier. She found herself struggling to look at him without picturing Jade's triumphant face in her mind, and Sarah wondered if he felt uncomfortable around her after her embarrassing breakdown in his shop.

He shrugged. "The unlocked door, the open window, a secret tunnel— you choose." His dark eyes took in the elegance of the room in one deft glance. "I had a difficult time finding you, though, until I overheard someone mention that the new servant had been 'promoted.'" One broad shoulder lifted in a shrug.

"So . . .?" she asked slowly, honestly curious about how he had managed to sneak in. Will's lips stretched into a ghost of a smile at her unspoken question.

"The open window," he answered.

Sarah's eyes went wide, and she brushed past him to lean over the windowsill, getting a nice view of the snowy cobblestones below the slick stone wall. Hands spread on the sill, she glanced over her shoulder at Will, who was watching her with a blank expression. She didn't like it when she couldn't read him. "You came through *this* window?" she questioned doubtfully.

"It was not the first time I've scaled the castle walls." She couldn't keep the awe and shock from her face, and Will looked away, stooping to gather the bandages strewn about the room. A flicker of embarrassment had crossed his features before he turned away, though his jaw was set in a tense line that let her know something was eating at him other than her unintentional flattery.

Picking up the discarded pouch nearest her and giving a quick tug on the straps to ensure that it was still closed, Sarah tossed it onto her bed next to the forgotten rose. She watched Will for a moment as he knelt on the floor, cleaning up the mess without being asked. Some of it was nervous energy, she could tell, but she also knew that it was his way of making up for scaring her. And possibly make amends for something else.

Her heart clenched.

She leaned down next to him to help collect the strips of fabric, his body nearly twice as tall as hers in their crouched positions. He glanced down sharply at her when she placed a bandage in his arms. His eyes probed her face, and his brows puckered, stretching that half-moon scar and reminding Sarah that they both bore marks from Allan's treachery. Before she could ask herself what he was searching for in her features, he stood abruptly and walked over to the bed, dropping the bandages in a haphazard pile on the quilt. He frowned at the mess, looking unsure about what the next step should be.

Bachelors, Sarah thought wryly. *No idea how to fold laundry.*

She walked up next to him and touched his arm lightly. She felt him start and knew he was more frazzled than his composed features let on. When his eyes finally met hers, she gave him a faint smile.

"Sorry about freaking out earlier," she said, though just thinking about the immediate pain of her discovery turned the smile on her face into a grimace.

Will shook his head, sending that wayward lock of hair onto his forehead. He placed his hands on her shoulders and leaned down, his eyes intense and tormented. She hated seeing him like that, but she had no idea how to make it better. "You have nothing to apologize for. I am the one who wishes I had handled the situation differently."

Sarah wasn't sure if he meant his cold demeanor in the livery earlier or the "situation" with Jade. Then she realized she didn't really want to know, so she kept quiet.

He expelled a heavy breath. "Is it all right if we discuss this now? I cannot let it go unresolved."

She wasn't sure if things between them *could* be fixed or if there was even anything to be resolved, though she so wished to forget everything that had happened in the last day—she was so confused and torn. But he had been a friend first, and it wasn't his fault that she had fallen for him.

Both needing and dreading to hear him out, Sarah nodded reluctantly, and then immediately shook her head. He looked hurt at her refusal, and she spoke quickly. "I mean, I do think we need to talk about everything, but I forgot that someone's coming over any minute now."

Will's eyes drifted to the rose lying on the bed amongst the bandages. A lone brow lifted, which was never a good sign.

"It isn't like that," she said quickly, knowing where his train of thought was headed. She huffed, frustrated that there wasn't enough time to resolve their situation. "I just can't do this right now."

"Chores?"

She averted her eyes for a second too long. "Someone asked for my position to change."

His gaze roamed the room again, and he appeared to glimpse it with new eyes. "Ah, I see." He turned back to her, a mixture of hurt, fear, and trepidation in his gaze. His jaw tightened. "Why, precisely, were you moved *here*? This wing is reserved for nobles and dignitaries." But from his tone, he'd already formed his own reasons.

"Look, Will, you don't have to worry about me. Damien's a nice guy."

His lower lip dipped almost imperceptibly in surprise, face flooding with concern. "The new lord? Had you even met him before he *changed* your position?"

Oops. Sarah grimaced at how much she'd revealed. "Well, I met him earlier today, and he seems really nice. And at any rate, it isn't like that— what you're thinking. I'm just here to be his nurse."

Will eyed the flower, the muscle in his jaw twitching. "I can see that. What is ailing him, I wonder?"

She balked at him. "Come on! You can't honestly believe—"

"Where are his quarters?"

Sarah hesitated. "Across the hall." She could have kicked herself for speaking.

That single brow rose slowly on his forehead, and his eyes flashed, making Sarah wince at the barely concealed anger she saw there.

Someone rapped on her door twice, then Damien's voice called through the wood, "My lady?"

Sarah's eyes widened at his horrific timing, looking back and forth between the door and Will, who was glowering in the direction the voice had come. It wouldn't look good if she were caught with a guy in her room, especially one who had snuck in. "Just a minute," she called out, her voice nearly squeaking out her reply.

Shoving Will toward the window, she whispered, "You have got to go. We can talk later."

He fixed his gaze on the door as she pushed him across the room, her hands planted firmly on his chest. His eyes had darkened to the color of the ocean depths that scuba divers didn't dare navigate. "Actually, I have yet to meet this lord that has set the town abuzz."

"Don't do this to me," she groaned. "Damien doesn't deserve your distrust; he's a nice guy."

Will looked baffled. "Why do you defend him? How can you be sure he is deserving of your faith?"

Sarah had begun to wonder the same thing, but she felt completely at ease around Damien and had already made a fool of herself when she jumped to conclusions. Maybe she was making up for things in her own way, but she was answering honestly when she said, "I can't say why, but he is."

His eyes blazed as he took her wrists. "If he lays a hand on you—"

For whatever reason, his words made her previous doubts resurface, and she did her best to push away the niggling uncertainty. "Ever the big brother," she muttered, taking her hands from his grasp, though she felt her cheeks blazing at what he'd implied.

Will looked surprised at her reaction, but she was too flustered to make amends. He could spend "time" with Jade while she was away, but a kind man took pity on her and saved her from servitude, and suddenly *she* was the one whose virtue was being questioned? She hiked her chin. "I can take care of myself."

"I know." Sarah was taken aback at the sincerity in his words and the reluctant acceptance on his face.

"Sarah?" Damien called from behind the door, sounding uncertain.

"Hold on!" she called out, praying he didn't barge in on this scene. She gave Will an imploring look. "Please, I need you to go now. We'll discuss this later." She didn't wait for his answer but spun back around and bolted for the door, stumbling over the rug in her haste. Gripping the handle, she took a moment to compose herself and glanced over her shoulder. Will was gone, the window wide open.

Taking a deep breath, she opened the door and did her best to smile brightly at Damien. "Come on in."

The handsome Spaniard glanced inside her room but did not enter. "Did I come at a poor time? I thought I heard voices."

Sarah shook her head quickly. "It's just me." She motioned him inside and closed the door behind him. "How is the arm?"

"It still feels as though I've been stabbed, so I suppose all is as it should be."

Sarah smiled sympathetically. "Yeah, I'm afraid so."

Damien's gaze perused the room and landed on the wardrobe she had left open in her haste to find the watch. "Did you not like the dresses I had brought in? There is a red one that I believe will look particularly lovely on you."

Sarah realized she was still wearing her black uniform and hoped he didn't think her ungrateful for his kindness. "Actually, I haven't really looked at them yet. But I'm sure they're all beautiful," she was quick to add.

"I wanted you to feel as comfortable as possible, though I wasn't sure of your tastes." His look was uncertain.

It was genuine when she thanked him. "We should probably check out that wound, though, before it sits for too long." Glancing around the room for a place that he could sit, she motioned Damien over to the chest at the end of her bed and went about gathering the poultice and bandages in her arms. Sarah dropped the pile on one side of the chest and then snagged the water pitcher from beside her bed, leaning down to place it on the floor where they would be working. She straightened and nearly jumped when she turned around to see Damien just behind her, holding the back of her desk chair with his good hand.

"Uh, thank you," she said, taken aback at the gesture. He didn't seat himself until she had taken her place on the chair, and Sarah bit back a smile at his impeccable manners.

She untied the pouch and leaned her head down to stare at the goopy contents. "It looks weird, but at least it doesn't smell too—" The words died on her lips.

Damien had removed his shirt—in record time, it seemed—though he was no longer wearing the undershirt he'd had on earlier. Sarah tried not to stare at the hard, lean muscles on his arms and stomach.

Oh, good Lord, she inwardly grumbled. She trained her eyes on the blistered skin like it might worsen if she removed her gaze. Briefly, she considered asking him if she could just cut the sleeves off his shirt, but that could make the situation more awkward than it already was. Risking a glance at his face, Sarah saw that he was completely at ease as he watched her. The man was either hot with fever from his earlier ordeal and wanted as few clothing layers as possible, or he was just very confident about all of . . . *that.*

As he should be. The wry thought slipped out before she could stop it, and she grimaced, as though he might hear her wandering thoughts.

Blinking hard several times, Sarah focused her attention on her fingers as they reached for a strip of cloth and then disappeared into the pitcher, avoiding his gaze. "I have to clean the wound first." She tried to sound confident, though her hands shook as they wrung out the excess liquid from the cloth. Gently, she dabbed at the bubbled and gashed skin. It looked pink and distorted where the hot iron had been, and dried blood still clung to his skin.

Damien inhaled sharply, the air hissing through his clenched teeth. Sarah winced at the sound and the way every muscle in his body stiffened at her touch.

"I'm sorry," she murmured, forcing her apologetic gaze to meet his brown eyes. "I wish I had something to dull the pain."

"You're doing fine," he assured her, but his voice sounded strained.

Forcing lightness into her voice, she lifted a brow and asked, "How come you're always trying to comfort me when I'm the one torturing *you*?"

Damien gave a strained chuckle. "Because it seems to cause you more pain than it does me."

She knew that wasn't true, but she didn't bother to correct him and went back to work. It may have been some macho show, but there was something in the way he said it that told her the words were for her benefit alone. The gesture was thoughtful; he seemed to be full of kindness toward her. The only problem was that it made her like him more.

It was silent for a long moment as Sarah dabbed at the wound, carefully avoiding eye contact with him. But his muscles were so strained and tense that she knew she had to say something to get his mind off his discomfort, if only a little. "You mentioned your family before. Why don't you tell me about them?"

Damien was quiet for so long that she wondered if he had heard her. When she looked up at him in question, she saw that he was gazing across the room intently. "There really isn't much to tell," he said slowly. Sarah focused her eyes back on her task. She wasn't going to push him if he didn't want to talk.

"My mother was a wonderfully kind woman." His voice was soft and thoughtful, and Sarah was surprised that he had spoken at all in the lengthening silence. When she glanced at him, she could tell his mind was far away, and his lips had softened into a smile. "She doted constantly, always causing me to smile and laugh. She was a bright, shining star amidst the shadows."

He lapsed into silence again, grimacing when Sarah dragged the cloth carefully over the length of the wound to wipe away the caked-on blood. She was working as fast as she could without tearing the newly sealed flesh, so she tried to keep him talking. His voice was also steering her mind away from what she was doing. "What about your dad? Wasn't he around?"

Damien cocked his head to watch her hands while she worked. She was going to tell him to look away, but he didn't appear upset watching her clean the wound, so she let it be. His face had paled, and it seemed good for him to have something to focus on. "On occasion. My father was a wealthy tradesman, you see, and it kept him occupied out of town most days."

Sarah shot him a look that conveyed how sorry she was to hear that. "That must have been hard to grow up with your dad gone so much."

He shook his head, but still his eyes remained glued to her hands as she washed them in the pitcher, as though they held the memories he was calling upon. "His absences were a reprieve for us all, my mother especially."

Sarah paused in drying her hands on a fresh cloth. "Your parents weren't happy together?"

Dark hair rustled as he shook his head again. "My mother loved my father, but life was trying for her. Father was—how do you say . . .?"

"Sick?" she volunteered.

Damien shook his head. "No. Well, yes—that, too, I suppose. But I believe the term is *abusive*." The word seemed difficult to say, and Sarah didn't think it was just his accent that caused his hesitation. His voice soft and tinged with something mirroring confusion, Damien added solemnly, "He beat my mother to death one night."

Sarah gripped the forgotten cloth in her hands and stared at him. "Oh, Damien, I'm so sorry."

His lips curved into a sardonic smile, though the haunted look never left his eyes, and he appeared embarrassed that he had revealed so much. "It was a drunken accident. Still, I never forgave him for what he stole from us."

"Us?"

"Yes, my sister Isabella and I." Some of the darkness ebbed from his gaze at the mention of his sister. "We came from a rich estate back in España, a beautiful world that was all our own. When Father was absent," he added drolly. "We did everything together, and even in our father's cruelty, we knew that we had each other. She was the only thing that kept me grounded there all those years. But when Mother died . . . Well, that was the final motivation that was needed, and we left shortly thereafter."

"Did your mom, umm, pass away recently?" Sarah couldn't help asking. Talking seemed to be the only thing keeping his mind off his raw wound.

Damien stared at the ceiling, looking like he was counting back in time. "I was twelve," he said slowly, "so it has been over a decade since her death. We left shortly after."

Sarah snapped her mouth closed but couldn't keep her brows from rising in shock. It seemed impossible to image herself and Lilly out on their own five or six years ago; she wasn't sure they would have made it in the world alone. Their parents weren't perfect, but suddenly Sarah ached for them and Lilly, to be home away from the responsibility and expectations resting on her shoulders.

It felt strange to long after two completely different worlds—one where her family waited, along with the sameness that had driven her away, and this other world that didn't exist but gave her all the excitement and adventure that she had craved back in her small town. She felt like she was playing house, living her life at home and then coming here to *experience* life.

She suddenly remembered what the professor had told her in his lab about there being repercussions to traveling through time, and Sarah knew that someday she would have to decide. Her heart could never belong to two different worlds.

It dawned on her that Damien had done what she had yet to do: Choose.

Dropping the damp towel in her lap, she asked quietly, "Weren't you scared when you ran away? I mean, how did you ever decide that you couldn't stay in one place any longer?"

Damien's face suddenly became drawn. "Yes, we were both terrified to leave the only home we had ever known at so young an age—Isabella was only eight at the time—but I knew it would have been a worse fate for us to remain with that man."

His chest swelled as he inhaled a large breath, holding it for a moment

128

before exhaling, and Sarah realized that she had been holding her own breath. He shrugged, trying to appear cavalier about the whole affair, though his eyes were far away. "We moved around quite a bit, going wherever we could find work. I performed whatever jobs I could obtain, and Isabella apprenticed seamstresses in every town; she showed great promise, too. It was difficult, but we had each other, and that was all we needed. Eventually, we saved enough to barter passage out of España to Ridlan."

"What happened after that?" Sarah asked softly, completely engrossed in the story. It couldn't end there, because that would mean his sister would be here in the castle, and no one had mentioned that Damien had any relations staying there.

He pressed his lips together, and a muscle in his jaw shuddered. "Isabella died."

Sarah's shoulders sank, saddened that their story had not ended happily. "You had a rough life," she observed quietly.

The sigh that came from him was one of resignation, and she could tell that he had given up any unfeeling pretense. His eyes found hers, and the saddest smile she had ever seen touched his lips. "Sometimes it seems that I cannot see the sun's light for the shadows that chase me." Expression becoming suddenly earnest, Damien leaned toward her. She was so caught up in his intense espresso gaze that she didn't pull back when he moved into her personal space. "But I know the light is there, waiting for me to lay hold of it. Does that make sense?"

Sarah saw within him an aching vulnerability that she wasn't sure he'd meant to reveal. Several heartbeats passed before she cleared her throat and broke eye contact with him to reach for the pouch. For a moment, she'd imagined that the air between them had crackled with electricity, but she quickly shook off the ridiculous notion and focused her attention on his words.

Dipping two fingers into the small leather satchel, she gingerly smeared the thick paste onto his skin, her brow drawn thoughtfully. "Whenever my sister, Lilly, and I are down, my dad has this saying that always perks us up." She took a deep breath, calling upon the memory of her father's voice and smiling when she heard it crystal-clear. "'When you're facing the sunshine, you can't see the shadows.' It's just a reminder to focus on the bright things in our lives and not the dark bits."

She glanced up at him through the veil of her hair. Damien had been watching her, and he smiled warmly when she met his gaze. "Your father sounds very wise."

"He is." She went back to massaging the poultice into the wound, and his body relaxed a little under her gentle touch. Closing his eyes, he groaned softly as the cool substance soothed his scorched flesh.

"Your friend was a little heavy-handed with her tools, I'm afraid."

Sarah shot him a saccharine smile, and her voice turned teasing. "I guess it's a good thing she didn't find her sewing needle, then." He chuckled, and his grin stayed in place while she carefully wrapped his bicep with the gauze.

They lapsed into silence again, and Sarah worried her lower lip as she questioned how thoroughly she needed to wrap the wound. She was busy counting the number of times she had gone around his arm when he spoke up, startling her.

"I should have thought to give you a flagon for that."

Her head shot up. "A what?"

"An urn or jug of water to preserve it." She followed Damien's gaze to the blood-red rose on her mattress.

"Oh," she said, suddenly feeling awkward. "Don't worry about it." She did *not* add that she had contemplated drying the flower between some paper and saving it—a memento to take home with her. No one had ever given her flowers before, and she couldn't help but feel flattered. It was silly, she knew, but her first rose was special.

Sarah held the loose ends of the bandage in indecision for a long moment, trying to decide how to tie it off. She hoped that Damien hadn't noticed her hesitation and said quickly to distract him, "Do you pamper all of your guests like that?"

"Oh, no." He actually looked self-conscious as he rubbed the palm of his good hand against his thigh. "Forgive me if it was rather untoward, but I meant no disrespect. The rose is a sign of beauty and purity, and in the village that I came from, it was often used in marriage ceremonies to represent such qualities."

Sarah cocked her head in the direction of her bed, still clutching the useless bandage ends. "Was that a proposal, then?" she asked with a teasing brow. He laughed, causing her to grin. Her smile faded when she remembered that she had said something similar to Will just a few weeks ago. The pendant seemed to cool as her skin heated in shame. Why did she feel guilty innocently talking and joking with Damien when Will had done far more after she'd left?

In that moment, Sarah made the decision that regardless if Will returned her feelings or not—and it was looking more like the latter from where she sat—she would not stop living her life. She would *not* be the girl who waited around for the wrong guy forever. Though at the core of her being, she knew that there would always be a little piece of Will that followed her around like a bit of deadly shrapnel lodged in her heart, causing it to bleed a little every time it beat.

Swallowing the lump in her throat, Sarah ducked her head and gingerly tucked the loose pieces of gauze under the wrapped bandages.

"That should stay." She tried to sound certain.

Damien lifted his bandaged arm to survey the damage, putting in just a little too much effort into scrutinizing her work. Sarah eyed it herself, frowning in displeasure at the bulging dressings and the rivulet of medicine oozing from beneath a loose patch.

"It seems I have the best attendant in the country!" he exclaimed suddenly, his jovial manner returning in full force—to compensate for her lack of good work, she was sure. Sarah laughed anyway, and his own face relaxed into that sly grin of his, a dimple in his right cheek revealing itself.

"I'll do better next time," she assured him. It was a welcome reprieve to be around someone that she could be herself with, or as much of herself as this century would allow. It felt good to laugh again, too, without worrying about shadows lurking around the corner. Both literally and figuratively.

Sarah stood as he replaced his shirt, for which she was immensely glad. She didn't want to stoke the rumors by having him leave her room half-clothed. Being careful of her shoddy work, though he didn't seem to mind that she wasn't a pro, Damien eased the garment over his head. The upper portion of the shirt was loosely laced, dipping low enough that it was difficult for Sarah not to appreciate his smooth, tan chest.

She quickly averted her gaze.

Holding his wounded arm bent and close to his side, Damien followed her to the door, smiling down at her with an almost sheepish expression. "Thank you for listening, my lady. It is a relief to know that I have a friend in this dreary place."

Sarah's lips stretched into a smile as she opened the door. "Anytime." He turned to leave. "And, Damien?" His eyes met hers, and she knew that her friend Janice would have melted into their depths. "No more of that 'my lady' stuff. It's just Sarah to my friends."

His face changed. Gone was the swaggering Spaniard she had first met, replaced with a lost boy who had just found a companion. Sarah had a heart for strays, and it twisted in her chest at the way his face lit up with surprise and pleasure at the word "friends." She decided right there to take him under her wing.

With a simple nod and a quick "I'll do my utmost," Damien strode across the hall to his own room, closing the door silently behind him.

Sarah shook her head as she latched her own door, wondering if there wasn't a whole family left in all of Serimone. Will's parents had been murdered, the king had been killed by—well, she was *supposed* to be working on that—Karen's parents died in a car accident, and she and the professor barely saw each other. From what she gathered, Edith and her husband were estranged and she rarely saw her little boy, and now Sarah discovered that Damien had experienced so much pain and loss in his childhood. It was no wonder Karen longed for a normal life with the Joneses; they seemed to be the only complete family in the country!

"He was rather forward, wasn't he?"

She whipped around at the sound of Will's voice and watched him emerge from behind the drapes once more. She gaped at him. Had he been there the *whole* time? Her neck warmed, again contrasting against the cool metal of her necklace, a constant reminder pressing against her heart.

"What are you doing in here?" she gasped. "I thought I told you to go!"

"There was a guard below, and he might have seen me scaling the wall." Will raised a brow, his expression sardonic. "I would have jumped down the three stories, risking bodily harm, if I had known you were in such a hurry to be rid of me."

Sarah stood there, dumbfounded. Had he just made a *joke*? And a very sarcastic one at that. His buttons were definitely pushed, but she was too exhausted to rise to the challenge and ask him if the guard had been below the window the *entire* time.

"No, I don't want you to plunge to your death. But you should have given me a signal or something, and I could have distracted Damien long enough for you to escape."

Some of his fire seemed to have evaporated, but he still looked upset. That muscle in his jaw feathered out across his cheek. "You were distracting him enough already." The words came out sounding regretful.

Sarah sighed, knowing his overprotective nature was jumping to conclusions. And despite everything, she still cared what he thought about her. "I don't know what you think you heard, but Damien and I are just friends. Didn't you catch that part?"

"Sarah," he said under his breath, shaking his head. When Will's eyes met hers, his dark blue gaze appeared troubled. "A man only gives a woman flowers if she means something to him, something more than a simple friend."

Why did his words always hit her doubts right on the head? Yes, at first she had suspected that Damien might have been interested in her romantically, but her romance-radar had always been a little off, so she wasn't going to jump to conclusions. But when she saw the look on his face as he left her room, she knew that what he needed most right now *was* friendship. And that much she could give him.

"A guy and a girl can sometimes be just friends," Sarah said quietly. "I mean, look at us." She watched his eyes—the only place where she knew she could find the truth—closely as she spoke, hoping for some sort of denial, a declaration of his feelings.

But Will ducked his head, a few locks of dark hair falling over his eyes as he backed toward the window before she could find whatever

132

answers were there.

"I see." His voice was guarded. He placed a hand on the ledge of the window, looking ready to vault over the sill. But he hesitated at the last moment, his knuckles paling as he tightened his grip on the stone, knees still bent. The stance made him look like he was fighting against himself and the desire to leave, but something seemed to be keeping him there.

That familiar muscle in his jaw flickered as he slowly straightened and raised his head to meet her eyes. "Is that what you want? For us to be . . . friends?"

This time Sarah was the one to pause beneath his penetrating gaze, trying to read whatever hidden message was there. The truth was that she did want them to be friends, but she also wanted their relationship to be so much more.

And if he doesn't feel the same way? Sarah's heart skipped a solid beat at the thought. There would be no turning back, no reversing the words that pressed against her ribs and threatened to choke her if she didn't say what was on her heart.

But could she really risk baring her heart to him, only to have it crushed when he didn't feel the same way? It would destroy their fragile friendship, one that already hung by a single fraying thread, and she wasn't sure how she could cut him out of her life completely if he didn't reciprocate her feelings.

In her moment of weakness, a darker voice reminded her that honesty hadn't done them much good lately; she was honest about where she'd been, and it had broken her heart when Will was honest about where *he* had been. Now their relationship was in limbo because of it, because of the truth.

Swallowing the desire to express her confused feelings, Sarah said, "I want us to be friends," relieved when she didn't stammer over the words.

Will's chest swelled with air, and his lips parted as it escaped his mouth in a shaky breath. His nod was almost imperceptible. "As you wish." Then he launched himself over the ledge.

Sarah's eyes widened in alarm, and she ran to the window to peer down at him as he quickly scaled the wall to the ground.

With shaking fingers, she closed the window screen to keep out the cold that seemed to have found its way into her bones. Now she was alone in her new home with her few possessions, the necklace and the single rose, and left to ponder what either one meant. Her breathing was the only sound in the room—that and three words that played themselves loudly in her head:

As you wish.

~Chapter 19~

Sarah still had not changed into one of the beautiful dresses that Damien had supplied for her when he arrived that evening to have his dressings swapped out, though he made no comment about her servant's uniform. For some strange reason, she was hesitant to let it go.

Taking advantage of his knowledge of the castle and his association with the royals, she asked Damien—as covertly as possible—about his opinion of the royal family while she cleaned his skin, which was already looking less scorched after only a few hours. She knew this was all thanks to the miracle poultice the professor had concocted and had nothing to do with her poor ministrations as nurse.

Even though Sarah could focus her full attention on Damien's responses now that he had discovered his undershirt, her inquiries got her nowhere: His answers about the family were either too vague to satisfy her or completely unhelpful in cluing her into who might be the phantom assassin, as Sarah had come to fondly call the king's unidentified killer. After a few attempts to pry some information from him, she let the matter drop before he became suspicious of her intentions.

Sarah lay in her soft bed that night, sinking into the mattress, dressed in a nightgown that rested against her body like satin. Every sensation around her seemed off, and yet also wonderful and alluring—the sound of the wind gently brushing against the closed screens, the dying embers in the fireplace, the feel of her feet rubbing against the luxurious bedcovers, the soft scent of the rose on her bedside table.

Her abnormal surroundings and the problems that weighed heavy on her heart should have caused her unrest, but she was too exhausted to fight sleep when it came. She snuggled further into the covers and closed her lids with a contented sigh, thinking that she could get used to the high life.

****

She awoke feeling refreshed, luxuriating in the warmth of the bedcovers as she stretched her arms overhead into the frigid air. Hiking the blankets up to cover her cold nose, she lazed in bed a while longer and watched dust particles float lazily in the shaft of light coming through a gap in one of the window screens. It was so perfectly peaceful that she was surprised when the quiet was shattered by a hushed disagreement just outside her door.

Sarah ignored the argument and resumed her delay of the inevitable moment when she would have to leave the warmth of her bed. She was busy enjoying the first-class accommodations when her ears pricked at the sound of a voice outside. Was that Edith's voice? The intense whisperings were too quiet for Sarah to make out, but she was almost positive that her friend was on the other side of that door.

The low discussion ended abruptly, and her suspicions were confirmed when Edith bustled into the room without so much as a knock, looking bright-eyed and flushed as she kicked the door closed behind her. Sarah made a mental note to lock her door later, though she knew that it wouldn't keep *some* people out.

The covers fell from her shoulders as she sat up in bed, and the cold air immediately clung to her bare arms. Edith's frown softened when she caught her wide-eyed stare.

"Good, you're awake. I've brought your morning meal." Edith carried over the heavy-laden wood tray and placed it on the bedside table. Releasing a satisfied breath, she turned her attention to Sarah.

"Don't look quite so shocked," she reprimanded, all at once caring and firm. "I said I would keep an eye on you, did I not?" Sarah smiled, thinking it ironic that she had thought her mentor to be abrasive her first day, and now her motherly sternness provided comfort.

Sarah folded her legs beneath her and shifted into a sitting position, relaxing into the stack of pillows. "I wasn't sure when I would get to see you again, since we aren't working together anymore."

"I would have been here sooner but was prevented from bringing supper to your room." Disgruntled, Edith huffed, muttering under her breath, "Impudent fools."

Startled, Sarah asked, "Am I not allowed to have visitors?"

"What? Of course you may." Edith shook her head. "No, they simply prefer to station younger, more attractive servants in the guest wing and keep the seasoned staff at their usual posts. I nearly had to strangle the maid who was supposed to bring that to you." She motioned with her head to the tray, her chest puffing victoriously. "She was new and rather young, but quite the persistent thing."

"But I'm guessing you won the argument, anyway." Sarah shot her a knowing grin and received a conspiratorial look.

"What do you think?"

"Right. So she resigned?" Edith laughed, the sound a mixture of pleasure and relief, and Sarah knew she was reassured to see her in good spirits.

Edith's smile faded as quickly as it had come, and she looked suddenly awkward. "Have you seen the lord recently?" The words were spoken casually—almost amusingly so—but the underlying question was laced with uncertainty. Obviously, it wasn't enough for her to simply see that Sarah was unscathed.

"Not since I changed his bandages yesterday afternoon. I'm *fine*," Sarah added, sensing that she needed to hear the words. "We were so far off base, Edith. Honestly. I'm his nurse that he took pity on, so there's nothing to worry about. He just wants a friend here."

Alone in her room last night, she had been left with Will's assumptions lingering in the air, stirring her doubt and uncertainty until they rang in the silence. But now in the clarity of daylight, Sarah knew how unfair it was to pin unfounded accusations on Damien. She wouldn't be stupid, but she was definitely going to give him the benefit of the doubt. He deserved that much.

Edith's eyes shifted to the untouched food, and she encouraged her to eat. She refused to join her when asked, but Sarah eventually convinced her to sit on the bed and keep her company. Edith seemed uncomfortable sitting idle, but she soon unwound and was laughing and smiling right along with her.

One hour and an empty tray later, Edith excused herself for a few minutes so Sarah could use the chamber pot, which was as embarrassing as it was tricky, before returning to help Sarah get dressed. They riffled through the wardrobe, and Sarah was shocked at the number of dresses that Damien had supplied her with; it was especially surprising when she realized that she liked every one of them.

She and Edith selected an elegant white hooded dress. Sarah felt strange about having her friend dress her, but Edith put her at ease, chatting as she helped slip the garment over the thin white gown Sarah already wore. The low square neckline revealed the silver pendant, and Edith nodded to it as she adjusted the dress on her shoulders.

"Lovely." She caught her eye. "Is it from someone special?"

Sarah didn't bother to mask her sigh. "I thought so at first, but now I'm not so sure."

Edith nodded but didn't press her. She helped her into the black floor-length coat, with thin white scroll and leaf detailing on the fabric, and pulled the embroidered dress sleeves through the arms of the coat. Then she set about lacing the sides of the coat together with black leather strings to tighten the fabric around Sarah's midsection.

Edith helped her into a pair of elegant black lace-up boots and stood back, surveying Sarah's appearance and tapping her own lip in uncertainty.

"What?" Sarah asked. "Should we put my hair up? More jewelry?"

"No, you have lovely hair." She grinned. "But I should probably brush it before I let you go."

Sarah chuckled good-humoredly, knowing how true that must be. She hadn't seen a mirror in days and wondered how badly tangled her curls had become. "Thanks, but I can just run my fingers through it later."

With a nod of consent, Edith walked over to the window, pulling the screen back to let in the fresh air and morning light. "Well, then! I believe you are presentable," she declared, smiling at her. "But I must get back to my duties before I'm missed."

Sarah watched as she scooped up the empty tray and headed toward the door. Impulsively, she said, "Thank you for being my friend, Edith." That woman stopped in her tracks and tilted her head to the side, her face serious again.

"It is good to know who your true companions are," she said, her lips curving with fondness. "And the next time you need me, I will fight my way back up here, if I must."

Sarah grinned at her tenacity. "Okay." Then Edith breezed through the door, closing it firmly behind her.

****

Life at the castle was not as exciting as she had expected.

Sarah killed some of the morning running her fingers through her messy waves as she looked through the wardrobe after Edith left, even though the two of them had inspected every item earlier. Then she wandered aimlessly around her room just for something to do, wishing she had thought to ask for a book as she ran her hands over the blank pieces of parchment on the writing desk.

She picked up the heavy wood handle of the seal and tipped it upside down, rubbing her thumb over the risen swirls and shapes that had been pressed into the bronze. On closer inspection, Sarah realized that it was different from the royal seal she had expected.

Obviously, she chided herself. They would never give a guest—a prior *servant*—a seal with the royal family's crest on it. This design depicted a valley with stars dotting the horizon, an eagle set in its center, and was completely devoid of any lions or crowns.

When she had rifled through every empty drawer and had run out of things to keep her occupied inside, she leaned out the window and watched the sun play hide-and-seek behind thick gray clouds, reflecting off the freshly fallen snow. It was too cold to leave the window open, but the brisk air was refreshing and smelled of winter.

Sarah strained her eyes to watch the dark little spots that were the townsfolk move through the square beyond the castle gate, which was presently closed. Once, she had imagined that the spiked tips had been fashioned to keep something or *someone* inside the castle walls. She was suddenly very aware of those walls, ones that seemed built to give the illusion of freedom while keeping its occupants prisoners in their own minds.

It was a welcome distraction when the expected knock on her door came two hours later. Hopping off the wide ledge of the window where she had been memorizing the patterns of the guards' movements in the courtyard below, Sarah hurried to the door, pulling her fingers through her hair as she went. Her stomach fluttered—at the blessed possibility of distraction, she told herself.

Flinging the door open, she was not at all surprised to find Damien standing there. She shot him a welcoming smile before motioning him inside. Closing the door, she quickly wiped her slick palms on her dress before he could turn around. It still felt odd to have a man in her room for any reason, though she was dying for distraction, enough so that she found herself looking forward to cleaning his wound.

The corners of Damien's eyes crinkled in a slow smile when he took in her appearance. "That was one of my favorites."

"Oh," she said slowly, confused. Was he complimenting her on the dress or applauding his own taste? She could tell by his face that he hadn't meant anything by the comment, and she was coming to realize that the man had no filter. It could have been his attempt at small talk. Maybe he felt as awkward as she did—even after their "bonding" experience yesterday—and was just better at masking it. At a loss, Sarah simply said, "Well, it's beautiful. Thank you."

Damien nodded and ran his good hand back through his wet hair. He must have just showered, Sarah mused. Or taken a bath, as was more likely in this era. She couldn't help sniffing appreciatively. He certainly smelled nice.

Sarah's ears tingled in embarrassment when she realized what she was doing. Why was she even thinking about his hygiene at all?

Damien was smiling at her, and she felt a moment of panic that he had read her thoughts. "I used to dote on Isabella and loved to see her face light up, so it felt good to do something nice for someone else for a change."

A breath left Sarah's lips. He thought of her like a sister? That, she could deal with. Offering him a genuine smile of gratitude, she said, "Well, I appreciate being thought of, but don't think that you have to keep giving me gifts. You've done enough for me already."

"I told you, it is my pleasure." He looked so sincere that she didn't force the issue, though she wasn't sure she would ever be comfortable accepting such lavish offerings from him all the time.

Folding her arms across her chest, Sarah suppressed a sudden shiver. She should have had Edith show her how to make a fire when she was here earlier.

"Are you cold, my lady?"

Her eyes went heavenward as she chafed her arms. "Damien, we talked about this. No 'my lady' anymore." She smirked. "Friends don't have to be so formal, you know."

He smiled good-naturedly. It seemed so easy for him, and Sarah envied his constant joy in spite of his rough upbringing.

Abruptly, Damien turned and walked across the room, removing his coat and draping it over the desk chair in one fluid movement. He crouched before the fireplace and used one hand to stack a few logs of firewood inside without being asked.

"You shouldn't be doing that with your injury," Sarah said, alarmed, as she caught the way he held his right arm bent and close to his side. She would be the worst nurse in history if she allowed her wounded patient to make her a fire. "It really isn't that bad in here," she lied, curling and uncurling her toes inside her boots to warm them. "I can have someone help me make one later."

"A lady should never have to make her own fire."

Sarah moved to stand beside him. "Come on. I'm supposed to be helping you recuperate, not putting you to work. You're going to hurt yourself."

He grinned up at her, and that cheeky playfulness had returned. "One doesn't need both arms in perfect working order to produce an adequate flame. And besides, what better recuperation than to help a young lady and receive her joyous admiration?"

Sarah ignored his waggling brows and huffed. Why was she so annoyed? When she looked back down, Damien's face had turned sober.

"Does this truly upset you?" Eyes that had been teasing a moment before were now earnest and searching. How could the man be so brazen and comical one moment, and then look so caring and sincere the next? The way he studied her with his lips pursed and his head tilted to the side reminded Sarah of a child—how they didn't quite know how to sort their emotions but instead expressed each one as it came.

His openness threw her, but she found that it was refreshing to know that she could count on him to be honest. She was always second-guessing herself with Will, so it was nice to have it all out on the table for a change.

"It really is not strenuous in the least." Damien motioned to the logs on the floor of the fireplace. "And you have my word that I won't do anything to tax myself."

His innocent expression and the fact that he would be cautious of his health to ease *her* mind prevented Sarah from staying mad at him.

Her frustration melted away as she shook her head, smiling. Did he really have to be so darn endearing? "Sorry, I shouldn't have jumped on you like that. I just didn't want you to hurt yourself. But, hey"—she held her hands up in surrender—"I would probably burn the castle down, so if you think it's okay, who am I stop man from making fire?"

She wondered if the caveman reference might be lost on him, but he still grinned, sensing the joke.

"Would you like for me to show you how?" Damien shifted to the side to make room for her.

She hesitated, then knelt beside him. "But I thought a lady wasn't supposed to touch firewood with her fingers, only with her eyes." She batted her lashes innocently.

Damien chuckled. "Something tells me that you would do it anyway, so I might as well teach you to do it right. I would be forced to save you if you set your room aflame, and that *would* be a strain."

Sarah grinned, glad for the easy camaraderie between them. She paid close attention as he rearranged the firewood, staggering the pieces so that they looked like a teepee. He began to gingerly hike up his shirtsleeve, but flexing his bad arm seemed to pain him, and Sarah could see him getting frustrated with the simple task. She placed a hand on his shoulder, and he looked down at her and nodded once.

"Thank you."

Sarah began folding his sleeve, and she could feel him staring into the fireplace. "Does that help?" she asked, nodding to the odd configuration of firewood to distract him, hoping to keep his pride from smarting over the fact that he had to have a girl assist him with his own clothes.

"Yes, it helps the air to circulate between the gaps; space keeps the fire alive."

Sarah frowned. *Huh.*

When the sleeve was past his elbow, Damien grabbed a good handful of kindling and stuffed it under the logs and in the cracks, explaining as he went. The mechanical movements seemed to relax him, and the lines in his forehead eased. Sarah found that she was watching his face as much as his hands, wondering at the tranquility she saw there.

Striking the flint, he bent low to light the fire, and Sarah paid close attention to where he placed the flame. Damien rested his good hand on the floor, bracing himself as he leaned his head down close to the kindling. He blew gently on the weak flame and continued to breathe life into it. Sarah watched, mesmerized as he deftly encouraged the sputtering flame with gentle breaths until it caught and grew, sustaining itself. She smiled and clapped encouragingly.

Still bent low, Damien turned his head to smile at her, the growing fire casting a warm glow over his features. "Voilà," he said softly.

"Show off." She lightly nudged him with her shoulder. Damien didn't seem in any hurry to have his dressings changed, and she was enjoying the feel of the of the fresh winter air at her back and the heat of the fire washing over her face. They sat there for several minutes, warming themselves by the fire and listening to the faint sounds coming in through her window.

"Hey, Damien?"

"Hmm?" he murmured, looking contentedly at the flames.

"Am I allowed to leave?"

He started and looked at her. "What do you mean?"

Sarah tapped her shoe on a red-yellow ember that jumped from the fire onto the stones. "Well, I wasn't sure if my staying inside the castle at all times was some sort of stipulation as long as I'm your nurse."

When she looked back at him, Damien's expression was . . . guarded? He looked away, and the fire played off the gold flecks in his eyes. "You are not being held here against your will, if that is what you are implying. I explained that you are my guest, and you will remain that way for as long as you wish, regardless of my health. It is your choice to stay or leave; not I nor anyone else can keep you here."

Sarah detected resignation in his voice and smiled softly. Apparently, he had as few friends here as she did and was wary of losing a single one of them. "Good. Because I think you and I should bust out of here for the afternoon."

His mouth dipped in surprise, and she laughed. "An outing?" he asked slowly, as if the very idea were outrageous.

"Yes." Sarah nodded her head firmly. "I'm going crazy trapped inside, and you could use some fresh air. Come on. Let's live in the moment. So, waddaya say, pal?"

His smile had grown with each word she spoke, and he laughed at the moniker, the sound deep in his throat. Jumping to his feet, he held out a hand. "Shall we, then?"

She accepted the proffered hand and stood, dusting her backside off. "We can't go now, though. I have to swap out your bandages."

"*Sarah*." He stressed her name with an exasperated lilt, dipping his chin as if he were addressing a child. "I thought we were 'living the minute,' as you said." He tapped the vertically sculpted line of scruff on his clefted chin, as if pondering something very deep. "Now how can we do that if we wait until another minute? And honestly, would you rather scrape my wound or breathe in the fresh air?"

Sarah mock-grimaced. "When you put it like *that*." She gripped his good arm and began pushing him toward the door, grabbing his coat from the chair as they passed. Damien's laugh prevented her from hiding her smile any longer.

"But you will need gloves, my dear," he said, still chuckling. "And I shall need to fetch my cloak."

"Oh, where's the fun in that?" Sarah said. But she ran back to the wardrobe, anyway, snatching a black pair of gloves. Wagging the gloves in front of him, she said, "*Now* we can break out of here." She was feeling giddier by the minute and had to resist the urge to hum the *Mission: Impossible* theme song and creep stealthily down the hall.

Damien held the door open for her. "You know," she said over her shoulder as she skipped past, "I think this is the beginning of a beautiful friendship."

He sighed dramatically. "What have I gotten myself into?"

~Chapter 20~

"So what should we do now that we're past the fuzz?" Sarah made a show of glancing up and down the street as she skirted alongside the wall of the building, peering around the corner before ducking into the deserted alley. Peeking out, she motioned for Damien to follow her.

He looked amused at her antics as he jogged to catch up. "Pardon?" The word escaped his lips in a frosty cloud.

"You know, the feds, the po-po, 'The Man.'" She eyed the street suspiciously and glanced back at him. Her shoulders slumped when he merely grinned incredulously. "The guards, Damien. Keep up!"

He laughed, and Sarah was glad to see him in such good spirits. It made her want to act like an outrageous fool more often.

Damien placed his hands on her shoulders and leaned forward so that he could see around the corner. "We appear to have outsmarted the buzzards, as you called them."

Sarah laughed at his confusion, feeling lighter than she had in a long while. "Fuzz, Damien. Buzzards are birds."

A lone brow shot upward. "Oh, really?" He leaned his face down so that theirs were inches apart, grinning impishly. He reached his good arm above her, and Sarah's heart rate picked up when she was pinned between him and the wall. Startled, her eyes followed the movement, and she glanced up just as he tipped the snowcapped sign above them.

With a shriek, she ducked her head into his chest, hoping to avoid some of the raining powder as a good six inches of snow fell on their heads. She felt Damien's chuckle build in his chest before it left his lips.

She leaned back slowly, still clinging to the front of his cloak, and blinked away a few wandering snowflakes that drifted through the air. Damien's wet cheeks were flushed with pleasure, and she could see that he had taken the brunt of the avalanche: Snow clung to his dark lashes and lay in piles on his shoulders, and the white, cone-shaped mound on the top of his head was a stark contrast to his tan skin.

Sarah doubled over laughing. "You looked ridiculous," she gasped, clutching her aching middle. She could feel snow melting in her hair and dripping down her face, and she wiped her cheeks with the back of a gloved hand. Clearly pleased with himself, Damien gave her an oversized smile as he brushed the light dusting of snow off her shoulders. "You know I have to retaliate, don't you?" she asked.

"It was purely coincidental that it fell at that moment," he said hurriedly, taking a step back with his hands raised in surrender. That haunted look no longer clouded his eyes, which glinted mischievously even as he feigned an expression of innocence.

"Uh-huh. Yeah, sure." She slapped the last of the white fluff from her sleeve and then started laughing again when Damien shook his head like a dog, sending a fresh spray of snow over her. "And was that purely 'coincidental'?" she asked, giggling.

He paused almost thoughtfully. "I should watch where I step now, shouldn't I?"

"Definitely."

They grinned at each other. Damien held out his arm to her, his shoulders still covered in melting snow. In that moment he resembled a bright-eyed kid so much that Sarah wondered how many years it had been since he'd had fun and been able to just enjoy his youth.

All work and no play, Sarah thought as she took hold of his arm. He didn't seem to care about his appearance as they moved out into the open, and his lack of insecurity made her feel more confident and uncaring of how odd they must look sauntering through the streets, snow-covered and arm-in-arm.

"I have to do a few things while we're in town," Damien said regretfully as they came upon the square. He helped her around a muddy snow pile that carried the marks of countless wagon wheels and footsteps.

"I guess I can't make you forgo all of your responsibilities." Sarah shrugged good-naturedly. She didn't care what errands they had to run; she was simply glad to be away from the castle and outside of its suffocating walls.

"Good." He guided her across the street, and Sarah's back stiffened when she saw the livery sign waving in the light breeze. She knew she couldn't avoid Will forever—that would never resolve anything if she intended to keep their friendship alive—but trepidation still snaked up her spine, despite her best efforts to calm herself.

"Are you all right?" Damien's soft voice cut into her musings. Was she that transparent? How was she supposed to face the man inside and pretend that everything was copasetic when she couldn't manage a poker face good enough to fool someone who'd known her a day? Will knew her

144

too well, and he would see right through it.

She forced a weak nod, but her steps halted before they reached the door. "Umm, I think I'll wait out here."

"But it's freezing." Damien shivered for emphasis. "I heard that the owner always keeps a fire going inside. You should warm yourself while we conduct business."

She managed a smile. "Fresh air's good for you, and I've been cooped up for so long that I hate to go inside so soon." That much was true.

He nodded, though he looked reluctant to leave her. "I'll be just a moment."

Sarah watched his back until he was nearly inside and then quickly ducked around the corner of the building. Resting the back of her head against the siding, she released a heavy sigh. She felt guilty about abandoning Damien, but she knew if she went inside and saw Will . . . Well, she wasn't sure *what* would happen, but it was sure to be awkward, and the last thing she wanted to do was spoil her and Damien's morning together.

The sky was gray and overcast, and the sun no longer poked through the clouds. Sarah tried to remember the last time she had prayed. She'd made plenty of requests and had thrown out complaints the past few days, but how long had it been since she had *talked* with God? A day? Two?

I've just been so busy at the castle, taking care of Damien and getting situated in my new room. She knew her excuses were weak. It wasn't as though she had to take the time to prostrate herself on the ground and sing a humble dirge first. Who was she fooling, anyway?

Sarah squeezed her eyes closed for a moment, trying to clear her head. Releasing a breath, she looked back up at the sky. "I guess this is a little overdue, huh?" she whispered. No one noticed her tucked into the space between buildings, so she wasn't concerned with someone overhearing what appeared to be a one-sided conversation.

"I know I'm being a coward, but what am I supposed to do about all of this? You can't possibly have it in Your plan to have this . . . *thing* between me and Will work out. I know it's impossible, so I could use a little help to not fall for him anymore if we get our friendship back on track." *Or if it's easier for both of us to just leave it alone, since I have to go back soon . . .* Her thoughts drifted off, hoping for Him to fill in the blank with some advice or insight. She watched the heavens for a sign of some kind.

Anything will do, she encouraged silently. *A lone white dove in a ray of light, lightning, a shooting star, a unicorn dancing on a cloud. Heck, I'll even take a glimpse of the sun, if you don't want to be quite so showy in public.*

She waited.

Nothing.

145

And no dancing unicorn.

Her shoulders sagged in disappointment. "Guess I have to make my own decision on this one," she murmured, taking the ensuing silence as a yes.

"Sarah?"

She whipped her head toward the backside of the building, surprised by the familiar voice. Will stood at the lip of the alley, arms loaded with firewood. He looked hesitant and unsure, and he seemed to clutch the mound of wood a little tighter when she caught his eye.

Sarah pushed off the wall and straightened. "Hi," she offered meekly, feeling awkward at being caught loitering outside of his business like a crazy ex.

"How are you?" he asked after a long pause.

"Fine." She nodded before remembering to ask him the same thing.

"I am well, thank you." Now that the pleasantries were over, an awkward silence took over.

Sarah's eyes darted around the gap between buildings, looking for something that might spark some conversation. Her lips parted, twitching with the desire to either excuse herself or say something to delay the inevitable moment when they would part ways, but her mind had gone into sleep mode.

"It's good to see you outside the castle again."

Her eyes met his, and Will looked just as desperate to say something of worth in the heavy silence. But they were still stuck on clumsy small talk. He shifted his load, muscles straining with the weight of it, but he remained where he stood.

Tension seemed to crackle in the air between them like static electricity.

"Were you taking that inside?" She directed the tentative question to his armload when the silence between them became too uncomfortable to endure any longer.

"Hmm?" Will glanced down at the firewood and seemed surprised that he was still holding it. "Oh. Yes." But he didn't move. His gaze flickered over her face, to his feet, the hem of her dress, back up to her eyes again.

Sarah couldn't stand the silence; it left her too much time to think and wonder what he was thinking. "Can I help you carry that?"

"Thank you, but I have it. I wouldn't want you to get your dress dirty."

It didn't sound like an accusation, but something in the way he said it let her know he begrudged the person who gave it to her.

"I really don't mind," she said, feeling suddenly small. A soft smile played at the corner of his mouth.

"It's no trouble, but thank you." He hesitated. "It is beautiful, by the

146

way. Your dress."

Sarah didn't know what to say to that, so she remained silent, their last conversation weighing heavy on her.

Will took a tentative step into the narrow passage, and then another. "I need to . . ." He balanced his load so he could point a finger down the alley.

He wanted to get past. Of course. For one silly, girlish moment, Sarah had thought that maybe he just wanted to be closer to her. She tried not to let her disappointment show even as her cheeks heated.

"Oh. Yeah, of course," she stammered, pressing herself into the side of the building to make space for him.

He kept his eyes down, dark hair falling across his forehead, as he moved in front of her and then stopped abruptly, his feet suddenly rooted in the snow. Will slanted her a look, as if something had just occurred to him. He angled his head to the side so the wayward lock of black hair that always tempted Sarah's fingers fell down over his eye. "Did you come to see me?"

To Sarah, the question spoke volumes, though she could tell he tried to hide his eagerness.

"Actually, I was waiting for someone."

Will's brow furrowed briefly before his expression cleared. "Lisandro?"

She rubbed her palms together anxiously. "We both needed to get some fresh air, and he had some business." Sarah waved her hand back at the livery wall she leaned against, as if that explained everything.

"Oh. Of course." He didn't seem angry about the situation, and Sarah wondered if he regretted their parting as much as she did. He lowered his head until they were at eye level. His concerned gaze bore into hers, rooting her to the spot, not that she wanted to move. Or could. "And you are well?"

Sarah knew what he was asking. She unconsciously reached up to fiddle with the pendant in nervous energy. He didn't seem to have noticed it yet, and she held it in her fist, strangely wary of him spotting his gift to her. "I already told you that nothing is going on. Damien just needs a friend at the castle as much as I do. It isn't anything like what you're thinking."

Will's lids drooped slightly, and his lips tipped in a sad smile that Sarah didn't quite understand. "It never is," he murmured.

She heard Damien call her name, silencing any reply she might have come up with. Her nervous gaze flickered to the opening of their little cocoon.

"Be sure that he treats you well." His quiet words hung in the frigid air between them. Sarah nodded robotically, feeling confused and dazed as she returned his stare. His words rang out like a farewell, but was it her imagination, or had Will leaned in a little closer?

He blinked once, and the momentary break in eye contact seemed to sever whatever invisible string had been pulling him toward her. As if coming out of a trance, he straightened slowly, sincere eyes searching hers. "And if you are ever in need of a friend"—he took a steadying breath—"I am always here for you. Always."

His gaze was intense and probing, urging her to say something, and it suddenly looked like he wished his arms weren't occupied as he gripped his load a little tighter. But Sarah had no idea what he wanted to hear, so she simply whispered, "Thank you, Will," and watched a brief emotion flicker over his face, but it was too quick for her to interpret the fleeting expression.

He nodded, a single movement, as he backed away. "He's searching for you. I should go."

Sarah was about to contradict him but realized meeting Damien was probably the last thing he wanted to do right now. For his sake, she let him go. "Okay. 'Bye."

She watched as Will hurried down the path. He glanced back just before he exited into the open, and his steps seemed to slow as he shot her one final, unreadable look. Lowering his head, he moved quickly, brushing past Damien just as the Spaniard rounded the corner and spotted her.

"There you are!" He looked relieved at the sight of her and hurried over. "I lost track of the time and wasn't sure where you had gotten off to. Why are you back here?"

Sarah's heart was still pounding from his and Will's near encounter, though Damien didn't appear to have even noticed his presence.

She swallowed. "I was enjoying the quiet."

"Is my constant chatter grating on your nerves already?" he asked dryly.

She rolled her eyes, the tension in her body lessening with his easy manner. It was nice to have an uncomplicated relationship, one that she didn't have to fight for—or against—constantly. "Has anyone ever told you you're incorrigible?"

He grinned roguishly. "All the time." She smiled, which only caused his grin to widen.

Eying his empty arms, she asked, "Didn't you get anything?"

He shook his head. "Not today." Rubbing his hands together conspiratorially, he said, "Now should we continue on our errands before some gossip spots us here and we elicit a *scandal*?" He shivered at the thought and lifted his elbow.

Sarah felt herself smiling, though her conversation with Will still weighed on her. Taking his arm, she forced cheer into her voice for Damien's benefit; she didn't want to be the reason this excursion ended on a poor note. "Oh, let's!"

A wicked grin tipped his mouth and lit his eyes. "Are you saying that we should move along, or that we should give them something to gossip

148

about?"

The quivering lip hinting at her grin undermined the reproachful look she shot him. Tugging him forward, she said, "I meant let's *go*, Romeo. Focus."

He didn't resist, but she could feel him chuckling silently beside her as they left their little alcove. She resisted the urge to look back, imagining Will standing in the livery entrance, watching them stroll off together. She stiffened at the thought and gently disentangled her arm from Damien's, pretending she needed her hand to rub an itch from her cold nose. He didn't seem to notice that she didn't take his arm again.

"I have one more errand to run, outside of town."

Sarah glanced up, surprised at the sudden declaration. "Okay."

"Is there anywhere you would like to go while I finish up? A place where you need to be?"

She immediately envisioned a quaint little home with a girl reading on the porch, wildflowers decorating the landscape in the summer, and siblings playing soccer in the field behind the barn, where a good friend waited.

Suddenly, she knew exactly where she needed to be.

****

Eyes focused straight ahead, Sarah tapped an impatient rhythm on the bottom of the wagon with her foot. She had convinced Damien to rent the cart from the butcher, instead of going back to the livery. Will hadn't met the newest lord in Serimone yet, and she intended to keep it that way.

"That's not going to get us there any faster."

She gripped the edge of the seat to still her jittery movements and gave a breathy laugh. "Sorry. I'm just so excited. It seems like forever since I've seen my friends."

Angling his head to the side, Damien shot her an amused look. "I was not criticizing your enthusiasm. Actually, I think it wonderful that you are looking forward to this visit so much. I was concerned you would have nothing to occupy you while I completed my last errand and that it might dampen our spirits." His eyes flickered to the road for a brief moment before he returned his gaze to her, the corners of his eyes crinkling. "But it appears your anticipation is contagious, and I am giddy with delight."

Sarah laughed at his theatrics but didn't take offense. However silly he was being, she could tell he was enjoying their time together. And though her delight in Damien's company was genuine, she also welcomed the distraction from her encounter with Will.

Smile widening at her laughter, Damien steered the horses around a bend in the road to keep them on the snow-covered path. "You have a beautiful laugh."

She might have read into the words if they had come from anyone else, but his tone was direct and observational, not flirtatious. It was odd how natural his remark seemed, and she didn't miss a beat. "Well, I happen to find you quite amusing, so you'll get used to it."

That self-satisfied grin returned. "It's nice to be able to bring someone else joy for once." They lapsed into an easy quiet, and Sarah smiled to herself, watching the snowcapped trees blur together, washing the landscape in white. Everything about this friendship was easy.

But is it fair to bring him into this and then leave? The thought came out of nowhere and was quickly followed by hollow guilt. Sarah had already become connected to a few people in this place and knew it would be difficult to leave them soon. Was she being selfish by allowing this relationship to blossom, only to abandon Damien when she went home? The result of her abrupt departure last time had nearly undone one fragile relationship. Could she really risk another?

She watched him out of the corner of her eye. Damien was bent over the reins, elbows resting comfortably on his knees. His eyes were forward, but then his gaze began to wander over the trees, to the edge of the woods, the hazy sky. The scenery seemed to mesmerize him, drawing his attention every few moments. He looked happy and at ease, his lips were even tipped in a small, contented smile, and Sarah knew that however long this relationship lasted, it was what they both needed right now.

The thought of friendship reminded her of how much she wanted—*needed*—to talk with Karen. Her stomach fluttered in anticipation at seeing her friend, and she was suddenly aware of how Karen had become her steadfast companion throughout all the madness they had encountered together. She felt closer to that girl than she did most of the friends she had known all her life. Karen had turned into this ever-constant mark that made her feel safe and rooted to reality. When they were together, Sarah was reminded of home.

Damien glanced her way at that moment and caught her eye. She hadn't realized she was still watching him, and her cheeks reddened at the amused look in his eyes when he saw her staring. Or maybe that was pleasure that set those fascinating gold flecks dancing. "What is on your mind?"

Reality abruptly came crashing down on her head. Sarah realized that she had spent three days in the castle and was coming back to Karen empty-handed. She hadn't tried very hard to find anything recently, but now she wished she had put in a little more effort. She was the mole in the castle, after all.

"Something troubles you," Damien prodded softly when she failed to answer.

Sarah slanted him a look, watching as he observed the emotions on her face. "How do you know?"

He shrugged. "Call it intuition from a fellow troubled soul." His expression was open, gentle. "Anything I may assist you with?"

She hesitated. Had Damien been at the castle when the king died? She wasn't sure, but he'd been there for a few months and might know something more than what she'd discovered, which was a grand total of *nada*. Their relationship was still in the infant stage, but she felt that she could be candid with him.

Folding her hands in her lap, Sarah hedged, "It's just that—I mean, I know I'm new at the castle and all, but I just thought the king's death seemed a bit strange." She lowered her voice and leaned in, as though the sleeping trees might share their secret. "Don't you?"

Damien's brows knit together, and he shot her a speculative look before turning back to the road. "Not particularly, no."

"But you were here when it happened?" she prodded, hoping her eagerness wasn't too apparent.

"I was," he said slowly, obviously wondering where she was headed with this.

Where am *I headed?* Sarah chewed on the inside of her cheek, thinking. She asked the first thing that came to mind to get the conversation moving. "Doesn't it seem a little strange that a healthy man would get ill so fast? And he held on for so long. . . ." Her voice drifted off, and she hoped he would fill in the blank.

"Are you implying foul play?"

Sarah knew it was reckless to come right out and say it, especially to a stranger, but her instincts were telling her that she could trust Damien. Nodding, she said, "I have my suspicions that someone may have plotted against him." It felt odd to say it aloud, but it was also a relief to finally have someone else to share it with.

"That's absurd." Damien shook his head, dark hair tumbling in front of his eyes. But she had clearly hit a nerve of interest.

"Think back, Damien," she urged softly. "Did the king seem off somehow, was anyone acting strange around the castle?"

He angled his head toward her, a look of apology in his espresso eyes. "I arrived after the king became ill, so I would not know the difference."

"But you have to be a little suspicious. It's obvious that foul play was involved." Sarah wasn't thinking logically and would have backed down any other time, but there was something about the way Damien's back stiffened that set her mind into detective mode. "Think about who would have the most to gain from his death."

Damien's eyes widened in alarm, and he stammered, "You cannot possibly suspect the prince would have anything to do with this."

"What? No." She honestly hadn't even considered him on the list of potential murderers.

His shoulders stooped a little in relief, though he was clearly uneasy. "Then who do you suspect?" His voice was guarded, a tone she'd never heard the blunt Spaniard use.

She squirmed in her seat, wondering if she should give up her last piece of information. What would Karen do? Sarah suspected her friend would do whatever it took to avenge the king's death and find his killer. If Damien knew something, she had to find out what it was.

"Cadius seems a likely candidate," she said nonchalantly. "He takes care of the king, the prince, and then takes the throne for himself. Just a thought."

Damien's laugh came out sounding choked. "You can't possible believe that. And the prince is still alive."

Sarah dismissed that with a wave of her hand. "A minor detail I'm sure he'll take care of easy enough."

"You cannot possibly believe something so . . . irrational." It was obvious he was grasping at straws, and that only sparked Sarah's curiosity further.

"Do you know something?"

He looked away. "Have you discussed this with anyone else?" His attempt to sound casual was mediocre, at best.

She watched him, her suspicion rising. "Not yet. But I'm going to figure this out. The king's killer deserves to be brought to justice."

Damien's face changed then, and his eyes snapped to hers. He looked all at once concerned and frightened. Pulling the horses to a stop in the middle of the path, he took hold of her hand, face earnest. "I must ask you to leave this alone. Can you do that for me?"

"So you think something is amiss, too?" A surge of excitement coursed through her, and she didn't even think to pull her hand from his.

Damien shook his head and straightened, dropping his hold as he turned his gaze away. His body looked stiff. "Of course not."

"Then why can't I pursue this?"

"Are you always this obstinate?"

"Yes," she answered without hesitation.

Shoulders rising and falling in a sigh of resignation, he smiled grimly at her. "Then I must ask you to take care who you bring your assumptions to. This is a serious accusation, whether founded on truth or falsehoods, and it will not be dealt with lightly. You may find yourself in a greater mess than you intended if you discuss this with the wrong people."

"Even if it's true?" she asked quietly.

"Yes," he conceded, but he didn't look convinced of there being truth to her theory. "But where is your *proof*? You must understand the gravity of what you're implying. You only have suspicions as a foundation for this

152

accusation, and that is not reason enough to destroy a man's life. Or yours." Their eyes met, and his were full of concern. For her welfare, she realized.

"Why are you so worried about me?"

Damien rubbed the back of his neck and then steered the horses down a narrow lane, the thick blanket of snow stretching out before them left undisturbed on the deserted path.

"It is dangerous to make such a serious charge against someone with so much power"—he shot her a conciliatory look—"even if it does have merit. But a rumor such as this would spark suspicion in the people, and a man who wishes to keep his power will do anything to preserve it." Golden-brown eyes locked on hers, entreating. "If you put your hand in the fire, you *will* get burned. Can't you understand that?"

A chill that had nothing to do with the frigid air snaked down Sarah's spine. Had she really expected to simply waltz around town with immunity, making accusations against the prince's advisor that would get him imprisoned? And Cadius and the men who worked for him were just supposed to roll over, while she walked away unscathed?

Sarah felt a spark of shame when she realized that that was precisely what she had hoped for. Being discovered and silenced had been Karen's greatest fear, and Sarah had conveniently forgotten about the danger as she played the part of the king's avenger. However much she wanted to pretend that this was all a fantasy, it was also very real. And the fear of danger she saw reflected in Damien's face reminded her of this.

"You must stop this."

"I can't," she said regretfully, knowing he was only speaking out of concern. But she would not abandon her friend to a solo chase after a potential killer. And Sarah had to admit that she had her own selfish reasons for staying: This quest had become as important to her as it was to Karen and the Kingdom of Serimone, and she had come too far to turn back. "I have to see this through, Damien. I hope you can understand that."

A sigh escaped his tight lips, and his voice wavered when she spoke. "Then please, for my sake, take care and stay in the shadows."

~Chapter 21~

They did not speak for the rest of the ride, but Sarah could feel his gaze on her every few minutes. She asked Damien to stop when they reached the end of the road where the trees thinned and opened up to the Joneses' land.

Damien halted the horses at the tree line and told her that he would be gone no more than two hours. He looked reluctant to leave, even for such a short time, and Sarah got the feeling that he was still worried about her safety.

Hopping down from the wagon, she threw him a grin to ease his apprehension over her absence. "Don't worry. I doubt there are any spies in the forest." His smile was forced and weak at best, causing her to wonder if there *were* spies lurking in the trees.

Sarah jogged out into the field toward the house, feeling his watchful gaze on her to make sure she arrived safely. The moment she heard the wagon rolling back along the trail, she busted into a run, veering toward the barn in a lurching crouch. If she only had a few hours, she didn't want anyone delaying her and Karen's private conversation.

She ducked behind the corner of the barn just beyond sight of the house. Breathing heavily from her covert dash from the trees, she leaned against the wood siding and ran a hand down the front of her dress. That was when she remembered the black detailing on the gown, which made her stick out against the layers of white snow like a skunk in a flower shop.

Super, she thought. Now she really hoped no one had spotted the well-dressed blur jumping invisible hurtles in the snow.

Squinting at the far edge of the Joneses' land where the whitewashed hills crested and disappeared on the other side into the forest, she noticed the framework for a small cabin tucked into the side of one of the hills. It was still in the early stages and would not be completed for a while, Sarah suspected, but the Jones family would have some new neighbors before too

154

long.

She drew her attention away from the potential home and peered around the corner of the barn to scout out the front of the house, her rapid breaths surrounding her lips with clouds of moisture. All looked silent, and no one appeared to have spotted her, which was a great relief. Not that she had a shining reputation to uphold, but she did not enjoy looking like a complete idiot . . . if there wasn't a good reason for it.

Mustering whatever dignity she could, Sarah slid her way to the barn door and pressed an ear to the wood, listening for any sound within. Nothing.

Satisfied, she pulled the door open by the steel rung, grunting as it resisted her. Her boot lost traction on the snow, and she nearly landed on her backside before she used the rung to pull herself upright. But her movements were jerky and she overcompensated, which ended with her jerking her shoulder into the side of the building with a resounding *smack*.

So much for covert.

Blowing a stray auburn curl off her forehead, she leaned back, pulling on the heavy wood with her full weight until it budged enough for her to slip inside. Sarah struggled to close it and then straightened her skirt, wondering how Karen, with her slight frame, managed to open the massive door everyday and look graceful doing it.

Meandering down the row of stalls that contained a menagerie of animals, she tried to pick up any sound other than the nickering of the horses or the shuffling of the goats nearby. She thought she caught a human voice echoing off the barn walls, but it was so faint she couldn't be sure.

She slowed her steps, listening intently until she heard the sound again. Now she was positive that was Karen's voice. But was someone with her? Curious, Sarah moved through the rows of pens, following the sound of her friend's voice.

". . . not as difficult as you think," Karen was saying.

Passing the only open enclosure in the barn, Sarah jerked to a stop in the middle of the isle, too surprised at what she was seeing to move or turn away.

Karen sat cross-legged on the layer of fresh hay that covered the floor inside the stall, her fingers working to entwine a wreath of straw together by the soft lantern light. Seth sat beside her—*close* beside her—one arm resting behind Karen's back so he could lean over her shoulder to better see what she was doing. But he wasn't watching her hands. Instead, his eyes were fixed on her face, taking in her features with rapt attention, and it was clear every word she said was lost on him.

Karen glanced over at him, fingers still moving over the straw. "Did that last part make sense?"

Seth nodded encouragingly, and she went back to work, though his eyes never strayed from her profile, roving over the lines of her face as if seeing her for the first time. Sarah had never seen him so enraptured. He was gazing at her in awe, like she was food to a starving man or sight to a blind one. Sarah felt a smile growing on her own face.

Karen's concentration had caused a crease to form on her forehead, and she appeared totally oblivious to his attention as she focused on the wreath she was making. Whether she was aware of it or not, the entire scene was very intimate and the start of something special, judging by the captivated fascination Sarah saw written over every inch of Seth's features.

Swallowing against the sudden lump in her throat, Sarah backed up slowly before she interrupted their . . . whatever she had walked in on. She kept her eyes trained on them as she retreated out of the mellow circle of light. Seth pressed his shoulder against Karen's, and she leaned innocently into him, holding the wreath a little higher for her tutorial.

In a spastic moment, Sarah's own feet became entangled for no reason at all, causing her to fall backward into the door of the stall behind her. She ricocheted noisily off the wood and landed in a mangled heap on the floor.

All conversation ceased in the barn. With a pained grunt, Sarah looked up through her tangled mass of hair and the bits of straw that clung to it, catching the shocked expressions on their faces. Trying to smooth things over as neatly as possible, she brushed her hair out of the way and propped herself up on her elbows, trying to look casual to cover her embarrassment. "Hey, guys."

Seth already looked on the verge of laughter, but Karen still appeared shocked by her sudden appearance. Her hands were poised mid-air, though she had dropped her craft on the floor in her surprise. "Sarah, what are you *doing* here?"

Resting her chin on her entwined knuckles, Sarah kicked her legs back and forth like a child. She was going for nonchalance, but by Seth's amused expression over her compromising position, she wasn't pulling it off. "Oh, you know. I was in the neighborhood—thought I'd stop by."

Karen gawked at her, and the mirth Seth had been containing escaped in a hysterical burst of laughter. He didn't appear upset that she had interrupted their romantic interlude as he clutched his stomach, and Sarah felt her own lips slanting upward in amusement.

"Glad to lighten the mood," she said, stumbling awkwardly to her feet and rolling her sore shoulder.

"Are you all right?" Seth asked, barely containing a chuckle as he helped Karen stand. She started to grin as the shock wore off.

"Nothing's broken, so that's a plus." Sarah stopped flexing her arm to look more convincing. "I thought my dismount was pretty graceful, though."

Shaking her head, Karen snatched the straw wreath off the ground and

156

released a soft laugh. "Only you could make such a spectacular entrance look so natural and poised," she joked.

Sarah shrugged. "Don't hate me because I'm gifted in the art of klutzing." She hiked her thumbs into an invisible belt in a self-satisfied way. "I don't like to gloat, but I'm kind of a black belt at it."

Karen really laughed then, and Sarah felt that easy camaraderie she had experienced from the start. It was nice to be reunited, and although it had only been a few brief days, Sarah felt that there was so much to tell her.

Seth was grinning from ear to ear, clearly enjoying their banter as his gaze flickered between the two of them, though it strayed to Karen's face more often than not.

"More of a purple belt at gracefulness, though," Karen teased. Sarah shrugged unrepentantly; it was safer for the world if she stuck with awkward and clumsy and left the poise to Karen. "Come on, let's get you cleaned up. Can you stay for a while?"

"Actually, I only have a little bit and was hoping we could talk, if you're not busy." Sarah's gaze traveled meaningfully between them, and Karen's face heated in a tell-tell way.

"I was just showing him how to braid," she hurried to clarify.

Sarah directed her attention to the broad-shouldered man and did her best to hide her knowing grin. "I think that crown will look very masculine on you. Nice choice."

Seth grinned unashamedly. "I thought it might be a useful skill in the spring, when the flowers come up and I can make you beautiful angels the halos you deserve."

Karen rolled her emerald eyes heavenward. "Be still my heart," she said dryly.

The always-smiling farm boy bowed gallantly. "And now I shall take my cue and leave you to converse. You know, Mother misses having her adopted daughter around," he said to Sarah. "Anything I can do to convince you to stay?"

Sarah shook her head regretfully, wanting more time with the family who had taken her in without a second thought. "I wish I could, but I have to get back pretty soon. Thanks for the offer, though. I miss your mom's home cooking."

He winked at her. "Well, then, it was nice of you to . . . *drop* by?"

"Oh, ha-ha." Sarah shot him a grin before he disappeared through the back door. She looked back to Karen, who didn't appear to realize that her little work of art had slipped from her fingers and fallen to her feet again. "Soooo, what was that about?"

Karen peeled her eyes away from the closed door, looking baffled and a little dazed. "I don't know what you mean."

"Oh, come *on*. It's me. I've seen a thousand romantic comedies."

157

Plopping down on a soft pile of hay in the empty stall, Karen gave a confused huff, eyes fixed on the discarded wreath. "I have absolutely no idea. He's been acting so odd lately—especially nice and attentive. I can't make heads or tails of what's gotten into him."

Sarah sat beside her. "Looks to me like he got bit by the *love* bug."

Karen shook her head, though a wistful expression briefly flashed across her delicate features. "There's no way. We've known each other too long."

"And you fell head over heels, goo-goo eyes in love with him on day one?"

"Well, no," she said thoughtfully. "It was gradual. But I can't allow myself to hope for something like that if his feelings don't exist, especially after our track record of being 'just friends.'" She turned imploring eyes on her. "Can you understand why I'm a little skeptical?"

"I honestly can," Sarah admitted, forcing back a sigh. "But if you had seen the look on his face that I saw when I walked in, you wouldn't have any doubt over how he feels about you."

Karen looked hesitant to believe her. "And what did you see, exactly?"

Sarah's smile was slow and brought about by the hopeless romantic in her. "A man who just realized how madly in love he is. He was staring at you like he had been trapped in the dark his whole life and you were his first glimpse of the sun." She clutched her heart and gave a dreamy sigh.

Karen's eyes did a disbelieving loop-de-loop at that suggestion. "Oh, please."

"I'm serious!" Sarah cried, then lowered her voice. "I admit it sounds cheesy, but you didn't see his face. When I walked in, he wasn't even paying attention to your little straw-hat thing. He was too busy studying your face, and I mean *studying*—like he was seeing you for the first time." She bumped Karen's shoulder with her own. "Call me a sap, but it was just about the cutest thing I have ever seen. Kind of made me want to adopt the poor puppy."

Karen was staring at the floor, looking torn over whether to believe Sarah's words or protect her heart. Sarah had never seen her confident, take-charge friend so uncertain. *Ah, young love.*

"But why hasn't he said anything?" Karen asked quietly after a long silence.

"Maybe he doesn't know you have feelings for him."

Karen's eyes went wide. "But I've been in love with him for so long that there's no way he could have missed it."

"Think about it, Karen," she urged softly. "You once said that you didn't want to ruin your friendship if he didn't feel the same way, so you kept your feelings hidden. You're so good at playing the friends bit that I think you act the same with him as always. And you're so comfortable

158

around each other that I never would have guessed how you felt about him if you hadn't told me. And I'm a girl—guys are slower," she joked. "You might have to help the poor fella along. And you said yourself that he's been acting differently."

Karen bit her lip. "Well, a few times I wondered if something might be there, but I dismissed it as wishful thinking. I just don't know anymore."

Sarah held up a hand before she could completely dismiss the notion. "Just think about it. And pay attention. That guy is giving off flashing neon signs like Vegas."

A reluctant grin emerged. "I'll keep that in mind." Releasing a breath and seemingly exhaling the conversation with it, she gave Sarah her full attention. "Now, what did you want to talk to me about?"

"I don't really have much to report," she said regretfully. "I've mostly been cooped up inside the castle." Except for a romantic, moonlit outing beside the brook, but she didn't want to share that. It had been a few perfect moments between her and Will, and if that was the last pleasant memory she had of him, then she wanted to hold onto it, untainted, in her mind. "But I did meet the professor," she added after a pause, forcing her thoughts back to the present.

"You did?" Karen sounded surprised.

"Yeah. He was very nice and . . . scientific," she answered carefully. She was relieved when Karen grinned.

"That he is."

"You know," Sarah began slowly, "I thought you mentioned that he led you to the Lord, but from what I gathered, science kind of sounds like a religion to him."

Smiling sadly, Karen said, "He did lead me to the Lord. I was very lonely after my parents died and wasn't used to being on my own most of the time, especially after the professor uprooted me from Maine to live with him in Oxford for a year. I ran away one night and broke into the church near our home to hide out." Her expression turned dry. "Though what I didn't know was that it was unlocked because a youth group was going on."

Sarah grinned. "Of all the luck."

Laughing, Karen nodded. "There was an older boy there—handsome, blond, entirely adorable—who later became the professor's protégé. When he asked me to stay, I did, and it was the first place where I felt I belonged after my parents' deaths. The rest is history."

Sarah stared at her. There was a small pause before she said, "I think now I understand a little better why my and my mom's relationship was a little foreign to you. I'm sorry you missed out on that."

Karen shrugged one slender shoulder and plucked at a loose piece of hay in her wreath. "Don't be. It might not be conventional, but I have someone who really does love me, even if the professor has trouble showing affection."

Sarah poked her companion's side with her elbow. "You have more than *one* person who loves you." Karen smiled at the ground. "And the professor *did* want me to tell you to take care." She tried not to wince at how callous the words sounded coming from her mouth.

Nodding, Karen asked, "Did you tell him who you were?"

"Yeah, but it only clarified what he was thinking. Apparently I seem 'off' to people out here."

Karen grinned. "You do kind of have twenty-first century"—she waved her jazz hands in the air—"written all over you. They would have to be blind not to realize that you're special."

She'd meant it as a compliment, but Sarah felt a little putout, since she was doing her best to blend. "But I've *tried* to fit in with these people. What am I doing wrong?"

Looking entirely amused, Karen answered, "For starters you're tan, which I am a little jealous of. But it also has to do with the fact that you speak your mind freely for a girl in this era—they're expected to be subservient and meek." She chuckled. "And you have a mind of your own."

Sarah threw her arms up in exasperation. "Great, so it's my lack of filter that makes me stick out like a sore thumb."

Karen draped a reassuring arm around her shoulders. "No, it's the way that you're so open and honest about everything. You call the world like you see it, no pretense. That approachability is rarely seen around here with all the expectations of convention. I think the fact that you're an open book throws people who are wary to show their true selves."

She squeezed Sarah's shoulders gently. "But it's not a bad thing to be different around here, and I think most people actually find your candidness refreshing. I know I really admire that about you. And Will certainly seems to like your open personality," she added coyly.

The smile that had been growing on Sarah's face vanished at those words. She played with the cord hanging from the front of her coat. After a prolonged silence, the arm resting on her shoulder tightened protectively.

"What's that face?" Karen asked cautiously.

Sarah avoided her gaze and continued to wrap and unwrap the string around her finger. "We sort of had a falling out yesterday."

When she didn't volunteer any further information, Karen pulled her arm back and twisted around to face her. "What happened?"

Sarah's sigh was heavy. "I found out something about him that kind of threw me."

A thin red brow arched. "Such as?"

Sarah went back to playing with the tassel. It seemed easier to talk about it when she didn't have to look anyone in the eye. "Something that he regrets and that shouldn't even affect me, because it's not like we're an

160

item."

"But it still hurt," Karen added gently.

Sarah gave a sheepish smile, and it all came spilling out in a jumbled rush. "Yes. And it's not like it really has anything to do with me—I have no claim to him—but then I blew it out of proportion, and I said some things, and he said some things. And then I think he might have tried to patch it up, but I didn't pick up on it, and it's possible he thought I was just blowing him off." Sarah buried her face in her hands and murmured, "He asked me if I wanted us to stay friends."

"And you said yes," Karen filled in quietly.

Sarah groaned. She spoke through her fingers. "I thought he was saying that it was our only option. But now that I think about the look on his face—" She turned distressed eyes to her friend. "He might have been asking if there was the possibility of more. And I blew it." Plopping her chin on the palm of her hand, she sighed. "Now I have no idea where we stand."

There was a pause, and Sarah knew Karen was processing. She said at last, "Wow. I'm really sorry, but it can't possibly be over. I've seen how he looks at you whenever you're around. I mean, come on." She nudged her playfully. "You two had a steamy rumor circulating the first day you spent time together. Obviously, the townsfolk saw something, too." She hesitated, and Sarah could almost feel her joviality fading. "Is what he did really so bad that you can't get past it?"

"No." Sarah sighed. She seemed to be doing that a lot lately. "I don't know. It was just really surprising and disappointing."

They lapsed into silence then, each consumed with their own thoughts. "Do you want to change the subject?" Karen asked outright.

Sarah nodded her gratitude.

"Okay, then. So how did you run into the professor?"

It was a relief to leave her troubling thoughts behind for a moment. Sarah answered, "I needed some medicine and was sent to find him. It was a complete shock when I realized who he was."

Karen's eyes lit with concern. "Medicine? Were you sick?"

"Oh, no, it wasn't for me. Damien Lisandro is a lord staying at the castle, and he was stabbed the other day. I'm kind of nursing him back to health right now."

"Oh." A pause. "The Spanish lord? You're his nurse?"

"I know it sounds weird." Sarah held up her hands to prevent any remarks. "But I was there when he was attacked, so I was sort of forced into it. It's actually a lot cushier than my maid duties, so no complaints from me."

Karen looked curious, but instead she asked, "So, how are settling into your room in the servants' quarters?" She cringed. "I hope it isn't too bad."

Sarah rubbed her thumb idly over the dress pattern on her lap. "Oh, um, I'm not there anymore."

Karen pulled back to better see her face. "What?"

"Basically, Damien has to have a full-time caretaker, so he asked for my dismissal and had me moved into a better room."

"Where?"

"In the guest wing, across from his room." Sarah wished she had omitted the last part. "I have to change out his bandages a couple times a day, so it makes things a lot easier."

Karen's look could only be described as deeply troubled. "And that's all he's asked of you?"

Sarah rolled her eyes. "*Yes!* It isn't like that at all." How many times had she said that the past day? "He's the one who drove me out here today; he wanted me to be able to get out and see you. Damien's sweet, and funny too. You'd like him, Karen."

"Sounds like you already do." It wasn't an accusation, but the quiet observation rubbed Sarah the wrong way.

"Of course I do. He's a great guy."

Karen's face was full of concern and understanding. Gently, she said, "I'm just saying that you haven't known him very long and should be careful where you place your trust. I've noticed that you have a sort of 'stray dog' syndrome and tend to put your whole heart into what you're doing. I don't want you to confuse compassion for sentiment. Especially so soon after this misunderstanding with Will."

"We're just friends, so there's nothing to worry about." Sarah hesitated, biting her lip, and then admitted softly, "I'm myself with him— no games or trying to discern a hidden meaning in everything he says. It's uncomplicated. Sometimes it's nice to have a relationship that isn't a constant battle, you know?"

Karen smiled slowly, her face full of wisdom that Sarah had yet to comprehend. "I do. But I've also learned that the only relationships that really matter are the ones you're willing to fight for. If it's worth the effort, then that's the test of a worthwhile relationship."

Sarah fixed her gaze on the ground, letting Karen's words sink in. Could that be true? If so, then what was she really fighting for?

"I guess I need to figure out what's important to me," she said thoughtfully.

"Just keep it in mind," Karen encouraged.

Sarah nodded. "I will." A sudden thought occurred to her. "Hey, when I was talking to the professor yesterday, he said that the discoloration in his eyes is a consequence from using the time watches so much, and he mentioned that you had experienced a side-effect too and said that I should ask you about it. Do you have a weird birthmark, or something? A third eye that I should know about?"

"Oh." Karen withdrew, and Sarah started to wonder if she had been too prying and should have just left it alone. "It's just that with how much I traveled, it affected me more than the rest and made it so I can't have children."

Her sudden admission startled Sarah, and her head whipped up in surprise. "What?"

Karen shrugged casually, but Sarah could tell she was more torn up about it than she let on. "Jumping through time so much messes with your body; we aren't made to split into particles like that and reassemble properly. I knew something was wrong—the doctor just confirmed it." Tears had formed in her eyes, and Sarah squeezed her hand. Karen seemed to cling to it for strength. "That was part of the reason why I've never considered anything with Seth. He deserves a family; I can't rob him of that."

Sarah suddenly recalled a conversation around the Jones table her first day back. Seth had made some off-hand remark about having loads of children to help him work the land someday. At first, Sarah had wondered at the pain that had flitted across Karen's features at his seemingly innocent comment, but now she understood. "Don't you think you should leave that up to him?" she asked gently.

Karen's lips tipped almost imperceptibly as she met her gaze. "You know, you're wiser than you give yourself credit for, Sarah Matthews."

She tried to look superior. "I just hate to intimidate people with my vast knowledge."

Karen choked out a laugh past her tears. Wiping a hand across her cheek to collect the moisture, she said, "And you don't have to worry about something that extreme happening to you. It only occurred because I took so many trips before the machine was stabilized. It's much safer now. No threat of becoming sterile," she joked lamely. Sarah didn't smile.

"I'm not worried about me. I'm just—I'm sorry that this happened to you." She wished she could say something to make it right, but she knew Karen didn't expect that from her.

"Not everyone is supposed to have kids," she said softly.

"I guess not," Sarah said thoughtfully. "But, Karen, when you and Seth get married—" She held a defensive hand in front of her face when she received a reproachful look. "Okay, when you marry some random guy whom we've never met"—Karen grinned at her flippant remark—"and you two want to have kids, then maybe you will."

"But the doctor said—"

"Oh, who cares about his opinion?!" Sarah burst out, louder than she'd intended. Lowering her voice, she said, "I believe in miracles, and if God has in mind for you a future with a husband and a van, er, *wagon* full of kids, then what's one human's opinion?"

Karen's eyes had filled again, this time with appreciative tears. Her smile was wobbly and genuine. "You always know how to make me feel better."

Returning her smile, Sarah said, "I meant it, too. I believe in the miracles and fairy tales and happy endings that I read about all the time. Why should your story be any different?"

A lone tear spilled over Karen's lid, but her smile was dazzling.

The atmosphere in the barn lightened after that, and the two friends lapsed into easy and light-hearted conversation for a while before Sarah remembered that Damien would be heading back soon, if he wasn't already on his way.

"I should be going." Sarah stood, slapping stray pieces of hay from her skirt.

Karen rose, as well, albeit more gracefully than her companion. Enveloping Sarah in a warm hug, she murmured into her hair, "Thanks for coming. I really needed this."

Sarah felt her throat tighten. "Me too," she whispered.

She didn't allow herself to dwell on the fact that when she went home to her century, Karen would have been dead for nearly a millennia. Where Sarah came from, her friend hadn't existed for centuries and wasn't available for midnight chats or heart-to-hearts like this. The time they had together was borrowed and precious, Sarah knew, and she wouldn't take a moment of it for granted. Karen seemed to feel the same way as she held on, sniffing back her tears. Who knew how much time they had left together? But they had right now, and that would have to be enough.

They held each other for a moment longer before pulling back and smiling at one another. Karen walked with her to the back door and hefted it open.

"Let me know if you find anything else out."

"I will," Sarah promised, hesitating in the doorway. Cold air blasted through the opening and played with their skirts. The skies looked like they were getting ready to drop another powdery layer at any moment.

"You know," she added thoughtfully. "The strange thing is that I mentioned it to Damien, and it really seemed to ruffle his feathers. He was pretty concerned for my safety when I brought it up, which made me think that your suspicions aren't too far off. Something's definitely up; we just have to figure out what it is."

Karen nodded, though a shadow seemed to pass over her features. "I'll work from my end too, but be careful, Sarah. If Damien knows something, then his concerns are probably well-founded."

Sarah nodded. "You do the same." She turned around, and her eyes caught on the partially built house. She pointed it out to Karen. "Do you know who your new neighbors are?"

Karen squinted off into the distance. "Oh, no, Seth is building that. He told his parents he wants to be independent and bought that portion of land from them until he can find his own." Her vision clouded, and she smiled sadly. "He's moving out soon. Guess I better work quickly."

Sarah tipped her head to the side, studying her friend's face. "You move at the speed you're comfortable with. And remember what I said about Seth. Don't let your fears get in the way."

Karen grinned playfully. "I won't if you don't."

"Okay, I'm going now." She smiled at Karen to let her know there were no hard feelings before dashing across the frozen lawn. She threw a final wave over her shoulder, which Karen returned. She closed the door behind her and then ran in the direction of the house. To go find Seth, Sarah hoped.

Focusing her eyes on the tree line, Sarah picked her way through the snow, tamping down the stirrings of jealous despondency that was trying to take root. She couldn't be happier for her friends and was ecstatic that Karen was going to get her fairy tale ending, her happily ever after with the man she had given her heart to years ago. It was the perfect romance.

But no matter how excited she was for them, it was all a little hard to swallow when Sarah remembered that she would return home soon, giving up hope of any relationship between her and the only man with whom she'd ever pictured a future.

****

She had just made it to the trees when she heard the wagon coming down the path. The road was rarely traveled, since it led only to the Joneses' property and to the dense woods skirting along their land. She released a breath, relieved that she had beaten Damien to the trees before he got anxious and came looking for her. *That* would be an interesting exchange after her conversation with Karen, one that she didn't intend to witness anytime soon.

Rounding the bend where the density of trees and low-hanging branches forced the road to curve sharply to the left, Sarah spotted the wagon rolling along a ways off, the horses being urged a little faster than was necessary. Clearly, Damien was in a hurry to see if she had been abducted while he was away.

Sarah began jogging toward him, and he glanced up at the sudden movement, doing a double-take when he spotted a girl running his way. Damien narrowed his eyes to see through the cold haze, and his face lit with a smile when he realized who it was.

The trees became a blur as she ran, and Sarah forced herself to slow her pace—she didn't want Damien to see how anxious she had been about him coming to search for her—but it was difficult to look composed when she was gasping for air and had to grip the side of the wagon to keep from doubling over.

Damien jerked back on the reins to halt the wagon before it took her arm with it. Scooting across the seat, he jumped down on her side, concern evident in his features. "What happened? Is something the matter?"

Sarah shook her head, fighting for breath. Each gasp of frozen air burned her parched lungs, and she gave a wheezing cough, which seemed to heighten Damien's worry. Swallowing thickly, she shook her head. "I just didn't want to keep you waiting."

His shoulders visibly relaxed. "I thought perhaps something was wrong."

Sarah managed a reassuring smile. *Nothing except for how out of shape I am.* And the high altitude didn't help matters.

He helped her onto the seat, and she sank gratefully onto the thick wool blanket that covered the wood. Damien ran around and hopped up beside her, arranging another blanket around her shoulders. He started to pull the other end around himself and froze. Looking up at her, his eyes went a little wider than normal. It looked like their situation had just dawned on him.

"Oh, er . . ." Damien began to remove the warmth from around him as subtly as possible.

Sarah tried not to grin at his sense of propriety, but the self-conscious embarrassment on his face was endearing. And it was too cold out for him to have the wind on him while she had all the warmth to herself.

Holding one end open, she said, "We can share. I don't mind."

Damien looked reluctant, but he nodded his gratitude and wrapped the blanket around himself again. Sarah was glad that the wrap was large enough that she could maintain a safe distance from her driver. Snuggling up together under the blanket, in the snow, in a horse-drawn "carriage" would be just a little too intimate for her comfort.

"Did you have a pleasant visit?" he asked as he got the horses turned around on the path.

Sarah smiled, though she was confused over the way her heart felt both lighter and heavier after having talked with Karen. "It was great. So what did you have to do, anyway?"

Shrugging, Damien guided the horses around an uprooted tree partially blocking the road. "Nothing of great import." He shot her a smile, and that dimple appeared in his cheek. "It wasn't nearly as entertaining as your visit, I am sure."

Sarah could tell he was evading her question, trying to pacify her and return the conversation to her outing. She tried not to be bothered by it; she

166

knew it wasn't customary for men in this era to discuss business in the presence of a woman. Damien had been brought up with this ingrained into his thinking, and she couldn't fault him for that, however much it irked her to be kept out of the loop.

They returned the wagon and horses to its owner in town, with the welcome addition of a heavy coin pouch from Damien as payment, and then walked back to the castle in silence—Damien's gaze was thoughtful, and Sarah didn't feel like engaging anyone in conversation.

She hugged the coat around her as the twosome passed through the gates, feeling the oppressive heaviness of her confinement wash over her the moment they stepped inside the walls. It sounded fanciful even as she admitted it to herself, but there was something dark that lurked within the confines of the castle, and she felt it every time she stepped inside.

Damien escorted her up the flights of stairs and walked her to her room. Holding the door open for her, he smiled sheepishly. "I realize that I was not very good company on our return trip."

"That's all right. You looked like you had a lot on your mind."

His smile relaxed. "Thank you for your company. It made hardly tolerable errands quite enjoyable."

Sarah's lips pulled into a smile. "I had fun, too. Thanks for sneaking out with me."

Damien placed a finger to his lips and scanned the empty hallway in mock-nervousness. "We mustn't let our delinquency be revealed."

She pretended to seal her lips and then proceeded to toss the invisible key over her shoulder. Her eyes moved to her empty room, and she paused as an idea occurred to her. "Can I make I request?"

"I am at your beck and call."

Sarah grinned. So theatrical and sarcastic, this one. "Well, I was hoping that I could have a maid brought up to take care of me personally."

His brows drew together. "Is there an issue with the woman selected for you?"

She hurried on before she got the girl dismissed. "Not at all. It's just that the maid who stitched you up earlier is a friend of mine. Her name's Edith." Sarah realized that she didn't even know her last name and felt a quick stab of regret over that fact. To seal the deal for Damien, she threw out, "I would be so much more at home here if I could have her with me."

He appeared surprised, but he nodded quickly. "Of course. You should have said something sooner. I will make the request that she be your permanent maid, if it will make you more comfortable."

"It will," she replied eagerly, her face splitting into a smile. "Thanks, Damien."

Those two words looked like they were all he needed. Taking her hand, he pressed his lips to her knuckles. Sarah dismissed the tingle of pleasure that shot up her arm. Still bent over her hand, Damien smiled up at her through a veil of thick lashes, and the torchlight danced across the gold-flecks in his eyes.

"My pleasure." His voice was smooth like honey. Sarah couldn't ignore the way her breath momentarily hitched in her chest, and she was sure he saw her surprised and dumbfounded expression before she found her head.

Pulling her hand free, she backed into her room. "Okay, well, thanks again for the favor. And for this afternoon. It was super." *Super?* Her hip bumped into the door as she retreated into the safety of her room. "We should probably change your bandages later, but I'm beat right now." She considered stretching her arms over her head and feigning a yawn, but thought that might be overkill.

Straightening, Damien shot her one of his trademark grins, but this one was different—*knowing.* "Until then, my lady." He gave a quick bow before walking across the hall to his own room.

Sarah slowly closed the door until the latch caught and then pressed her back against the wood. She closed her eyes and let her head bang against the door. What was wrong with her that she went weak at the knees when a man kissed her hand? She felt humiliated for behaving like those giggly, starry-eyed girls she wished would have some pride. It was painful to watch them get tongue-tied over the slightest sign of affection.

Shame washed over her as she realized that she had nearly succumbed to such an idiotic display. She was stronger than that. What had happened to her resolve?

Suddenly remembering the warm look in Will's gaze as they stood in the alley, she squeezed her eyes closed, trying to hold on to that brief moment and pretend that everything was right with the world. The picture of Damien's face, cast in warm light, as he kissed her hand unexpectedly overcame the image of Will. As reluctant as she was to admit it, Sarah was fairly certain she had seen awareness in his brown eyes, and that scared her more than she cared to admit.

Her heart sped up, traitorous thing that it was, and her eyes snapped open to dispel the image of Damien's slow, knowing smile laced with . . . affection? That couldn't be right, though. But all the arguments she tried to line up in her head appeared useless in the face of what she knew she had seen.

Sinking to the ground, Sarah dragged her back down the door and rested on the balls of her feet. Affection? That was no good.

Surveying the lifeless room, she was once again overcome with sadness. Was her heart so unfaithful that one moment it could melt at the thought of Will and race madly in Damien's magnetic presence the next?

The joy from her outing with Damien and her talk with Karen fell to the stones in a noiseless heap. It was easy to be happy outside the castle when she was distracted, but far harder to find happiness in the silence where her dark thoughts multiplied.

It looked like the barely blossoming start of her tortured excuse of a love life was beginning to wither at the same time that Karen's was blooming into something beautiful. Her lifeless quarters offered Sarah some clarity into the jealousy she had tried to ignore.

Yes, she was incredibly happy for her friend's budding romance and couldn't be more excited for Karen. But in the total silence enveloping her, Sarah realized that it was Seth she envied. With her other relationships falling apart around her, it felt like a tragedy that Seth should steal away one of her closest friends, leaving her with no one in this place.

As it should be.

~Chapter 22~

A nap didn't help to improve her mood. Sarah was too alert and moody to sleep, and she lay awake for over an hour, forcing her eyes shut only to have them open a moment later to stare blankly at the tapestries above.

With her thoughts loudly crashing together in her head, Sarah knew it was useless to try and rest. She sat up with a huff. Throwing the covers aside, she padded across the room in her stocking-clad feet, shivering as the floor's cold seeped through the thin fabric and immediately chilled her toes. She really needed to make a fire, since the fruits of Damien's labor had turned to ash and barely glowing embers in their absence.

Adjusting the rumpled coat she had been too lazy to unlace before her sleepless nap, she pulled out the desk chair and plopped down in the seat, folding her feet beneath her to warm them. Sarah reached for a blank piece of parchment, determined to keep her mind occupied with letter writing.

But to whom could she send it? She didn't have anything new to report to Karen, other than a quick "Hi, I'm depressed and confused— please help me." She could send an apology note to Will, but her mind drew a blank on what she could possibly say to right things. And Damien was around all the time, so she didn't need to write *him* a letter.

She stared at the empty page, feeling herself sinking deeper into her current forlorn state as she became fully aware that these were her only options.

Sarah put her head in her hands and leaned her elbows on the desk, suddenly filled with an aching desire for home. Tears burned the back of her throat and pressed against her palms, but she didn't care, nor did she try to stop them. *You can't have the best of both worlds*, she chastised herself, even as her heart warred within her to have her family close by as she fought beside Karen for justice here.

Knuckles rapped gently against her door, startling her. Sarah's hands

170

fell away from her face as she snapped upright. The sudden release of pressure on her eyes caused a few half-hearted tears to slip down her cheeks. Hastily swiping a thumb under each eye, she brushed her hands on the sides of her dress and hoped that she looked presentable. Maybe it was Edith coming to make a fire. The thought sent a jolt of hope through her, and she flung the door open in anticipation. Her face fell.

Damien's expression melted into one of concern when he saw her bedraggled appearance. "Whatever's the matter?"

"Nothing. I'm just tired." That much was true: Her heart was weary in ways she hadn't thought possible.

He looked hesitant to take her word for it, though he nodded slowly. A moment of silence passed before he asked, "Would you like me to return later?"

Sarah shook her head. "No, we've waited long enough to take care of your arm." She motioned him inside. "Have a seat."

He entered reluctantly, his eyes flickering watchfully to her face every few seconds. Sarah grabbed a stack of fresh bandages and the pouch of salve from the trunk before having him sit down on it. She dragged the chair over to him in silence, feeling his eyes on her. She made a conscious effort to avoid his gaze.

Feeling awkward and reticent in his presence in light of what she thought she'd discovered about his affection for her, Sarah wasn't sure if she could ever feel completely comfortable with him again.

"I requested that your friend be assigned to your room," Damien supplied when she sat down.

She met his eyes for the first time since he'd entered her room. "Thank you."

His head dipped to the side, his expression earnest. "Would you like to tell me what plagues you?"

Considering her current problems concerned him, she decided to keep it to herself. It was sweet of him to ask, though, and it only made her like him more. Sighing, Sarah shook her head. "No, but thanks for the offer."

Damien nodded, pausing thoughtfully. "Do you wish me to leave?" he asked again. This time he looked reluctant.

Sarah found she couldn't lie to him. "No, I'd like you to stay."

****

As she cleaned his wound—which she concentrated very, very hard on to avoid looking at his well-toned arms—Damien regaled her with happier tales from his childhood, of he and Isabella's silly adventures in Spain. Sarah was immensely grateful for the distraction and already felt her mood lifting in his presence. He seemed to subdue her sullenness, and she was able to put her troubling thoughts aside for the time being.

Damien suddenly smacked his thigh with the palm of his hand, eyes bright. "I have a wonderful idea to get your mind off your morose state."

Morose? "Okay," she said slowly. "What is this brilliant epiphany?"

He stood, slipping his shirt over his head. Sarah averted her gaze until the fabric slipped down to cover the lean muscles on his stomach that his undershirt had hiked up to reveal. Damien grinned, and she wasn't sure if it was in light of his grand idea or because he'd caught her flustered aversion of his bare skin.

"Ah, that shall remain my secret." He placed his hands in front of him to get her to stay in her seat when she began to rise. "I will be back in five minutes." And then he breezed through the doorway.

Sarah waited, her curiosity eating at her, but it was also keeping her mind off of the darker thoughts she had been entertaining before he arrived.

As promised, he returned a few minutes later dressed in a heavy black coat, his expression schooled into a gentlemanly mask as he offered her his hand. "Shall we?"

Sarah glared at him suspiciously as she accepted his help. "We aren't going to rob a bank, are we?"

Chuckling, Damien led her from the room, though he never answered her question. They meandered through the castle, down to the ground floor, and then he guided her through a series of corridors leading to the west-facing end of the castle that bordered the forest.

A guard was positioned before the door at the end of the hall Damien led her down. He nodded to the guard as they approached. That man dipped his head in response, promptly turning a key in the lock and opening the door for them. With a smile, Damien motioned her out first.

Sarah stepped out into the crisp air, eyes roving her surroundings suspiciously as she wondered what he had planned. The large open space between the castle walls and the edge of the woods was covered in a perfectly undisturbed blanket of snow. There was nothing there but two horses tethered to a wooden post near the wall.

"What's going on?" she asked, voice quavering slightly as she gaped at the large, well-muscled animals.

She knew the answer to her question before Damien replied, in a self-satisfied voice, "I am going to teach you to ride."

Sarah straightened her shoulders defensively and steadied her voice. "What makes you think I don't already know how?"

He slanted her a shrewd smile. "Earlier, you gave the horses a wide enough birth to give me some idea. And if that was not enough evidence of your aversion, your reaction just now leaves no doubt. But riding has always been a favorite winter pastime of mine. So." He released her arm and walked backwards the rest of the way to the gigantic, four-legged beasts, grinning in challenge. "Are you ready for your lesson?"

She consciously closed her mouth and swallowed the nervous lump in her throat. He was giving her the chance to overcome her fear of riding. It had been almost a decade since the accident, since her left leg had nearly been snapped in two, and she was tired of living with the constant shadow of fear trailing behind her. Sarah made the decision in that moment that it was time to move forward with her life.

But her feet refused to respond. Regardless of the messages her brain sent to her lower half urging her feet to shuffle forward, she remained rooted to the spot. What was wrong with her? An image came to mind of her hand gliding gently over a mare's nose, the stars a bright canopy overhead as a strong, silent presence encouraged Sarah from behind.

Then she realized that she *was* ready to overcome and let go of the chain of worry that she had foolishly been clinging to. The only problem with this scenario was the matter of *who* was standing by her side when she at last moved past her fear of falling.

It felt like a betrayal to move on without Will when he had been the one to help her overcome her original fear, if even for a moment, getting her on a horse for the first time in years. Sarah remembered his comforting strength against her back as they rode. She had been scared at first, but when that melted away, all that remained was the pure joy of riding without fear—just like it used to be.

Damien's face fell when she didn't budge. "You look ill," he observed.

She opened her mouth to reassure him, but her mind had gone blank. It was upsetting that she couldn't even move toward the animals without feeling guilty or wishing that it were Will who were offering to teach her to ride.

Damien noticed her resistance and said with some surprise, "You truly are afraid. I'm so sorry, I did not realize how serious it was. Forgive me."

Sarah shook her head and finally convinced her feet to shuffle forward a step. "I'm the one who's sorry. This was really thoughtful. I don't want to seem ungrateful, but I just—I can't right now. I had an accident a while ago and haven't completely gotten over it." Her eyes were entreating. "I hope you can understand."

"Of course, but why should you remain fearful of them?"

Sighing, she revealed the memory that still made her cringe. "I loved riding growing up, and the summer I turned ten, I convinced my parents to buy me a horse. Every day after school, I walked to the stable where we boarded her and would ride for hours. That horse got me through some hard times." She shuffled her shoe in the snow until she spotted dirt beneath. Damien was silent, waiting for her to go on.

Swallowing, she said softly, voice filled with pained remembrance, "I guess a rabid coyote found its way onto the property and killed a bunch of chickens, and then it got into the stable before one of the workers captured it. They didn't think the coyote had infected any of the other animals, but just in case, my parents told me to stay away for a few days until the owner could check the horses out, but I had to see if she was okay."

"Was your horse ill?" Damien asked gently.

Sarah grimaced, nodding. She recalled with startling clarity the frightened, wild look in its eyes. "I wasn't going to ride her, just make sure she was all right. But when I came into her stall, she panicked and reared back. I was in her way, and she knocked me over to get past and came down hard on my leg." She could still hear the sound of shattering bone and her own scream as it rent the stale air of the stable.

In a voice lacking inflection, Sarah added, "She broke free and got out into the field. They had to shoot her before she could spread the disease to the other animals."

Blinking to pull herself from the memory, she looked up at Damien. Though the reference to the rifle should have been lost on him, his brows were drawn together in empathy, sensing by her tone that the horse had been killed. "Were you badly hurt?" he asked.

"It took me six months before I could walk again, and another year before I was able to do it on my own. I know it's stupid, but it was traumatic, and I've been scared to ride ever since." She looked down, embarrassed. The scars on her left knee had diminished over the years and were invisible beneath the layers of fabric, but she knew they were there; her defects had been fodder for the bullies at school following the surgery and the loss of her "friend." Although the scars had faded, some wounds went more than skin-deep, and she was sure she would have to carry them with her forever.

Damien moved to take her hands in his own. They were strong and smooth as they closed over her fingers. "It is *not* foolish," he said firmly, and Sarah was surprised at the fierceness burning in his eyes. "Everyone fears something, and you should not be ashamed of that."

"What are you afraid of?" she asked, slightly breathless from his sudden nearness.

A shadow passed over Damien's features, and he released her hands with a pained look. "Becoming my father."

Sarah shook her head. "You're nothing like him."

His smile closer resembled a wince. "I pray not." He moved nearer to the forest's edge, turning his back to her, seeming to require a moment to collect his thoughts.

The sadness in his eyes had caused Sarah's fingertips to tingle with the desire to reach out to him. Watching him now, she was filled with immense sympathy for his internal battle against a dark past, and she swallowed back

174

the urge to envelope him in a comforting hug.

I don't want you to confuse compassion for sentiment. Karen's words echoed through her mind, and Sarah was starting to see the wisdom in them. She couldn't allow her mind to go there. She *would not* fall for him, for both of their sakes.

But though she told herself to guard her mind, it was difficult to convince her heart to do the same when it only wanted to take away his sorrow.

Sarah's hands itched to do something. Naturally, she bent down, packed together a hefty ball of snow, and nailed Damien between the shoulders.

He spun around, looking perfectly shocked. Sarah folded her hands in front of her innocently—though incriminating droplets of melted snow ran off her fingertips—and painted on her most angelic smile. "Something wrong?"

Damien was still stunned into silence, and she couldn't contain her giggles anymore, biting her lip as a few slipped past. Her laughter caused Damien's face to relax, and his own grin appeared.

"Did you just assault me?"

She beamed in a self-satisfied way. "This is *my* favorite winter pastime."

"Bludgeoning unsuspecting aristocrats from behind?"

Sarah shot him a look of mock exasperation. "Well, I certainly couldn't sneak attack them from the front, now could I? That's no way to win. And I didn't bludgeon you; killing my opponent in a snowball war isn't very sportsmanlike." She leaned over and snatched up a quick handful of snow that she tossed his way, showering him with powder. He laughed and shook his head, but he didn't retaliate. "Come on, Damien. It's too cold outside to stand still, and you have to get me back—that's part of the game."

He took a few steps toward her, his grin dark with intent. "So it's a game now, is it?" Eyes trained on her, he bent down with deliberate slowness and scooped his hand beneath a layer of snow. He straightened as he packed it into a ball, watching her the whole time.

"Oh, stop building up the tension and launch that sucker!"

Damien's laugh echoed through the silent clearing. "But you don't even have one of your own to strike me back."

Sarah shuffled from foot to foot, partly to keep warm and also because she was feeling more eager by the minute at the childlike excitement she saw creeping into his eyes. Jumping back several steps to put some distance between them, she called, "I appreciate the chivalry, but you won't win if you're a gentleman. All's fair in love and war."

Grinning, he called back, "So is this to be in the way of an execution?"

175

Sarah thought about that. "I'll give you one for free, and then I'm on the move."

Damien chuckled as he wound up, and she stood patiently. The snowball splattered lamely a few feet in front of her. She laughed. "What was *that*?"

"I'm not certain I can hit a lady."

She hadn't thought about that obstacle before him. "Just pretend I'm not a girl." Even from this distance she caught his raised brow as his eyes drifted pointedly over her dress, and she knew she was going to have to help him along.

Setting off at a run, she did circles around him, scooping up snow as she went. She launched a hard-packed ball at his backside, and he jumped, obviously surprised at her brazenness. Sarah only laughed.

He hesitated a moment longer before his face split into a playful grin. He launched a half-hearted attempt at her back as she breezed past him, and she dodged the lazy ball with ease. Apparently, he still had qualms about hitting a girl. Sarah goaded him into not holding back by sending another one flying, where it exploded against his chest.

Damien appeared surprised at her good aim and froze. Then he took off after her, laughing and tossing snowballs at her back as he got into the spirit of the game, slipping and sliding as he went. She dodged most of them, though he was getting the hang of it and caught her in the arm on his last throw, knocking the ball she was forming out of her hands. It crumbled to the ground just as she ducked to avoid another spiraling bomb that *puffed* into a shower of white powder when it hit her shoulder. He needed to learn to pack them tighter, but then again, maybe he was going easy on her. Judging by the way his aim was improving with each toss, maybe that was a good thing.

He was pretty spry for a wounded guy.

"Is that all you got?" Sarah called over her shoulder. She laughingly avoided his attempt to grab her around the waist, though it was apparent by the way he hung back that he was enjoying the chase too much to end it. She cut to the right and blindly tossed an armful of powder over her head to distract him. Spinning around, she scooped up snow as she moved and quickly packed the mound into a perfect projectile. She stood her ground, ready to face-off Western style.

Damien shook the wayward flakes from his hair as he jogged through the cascade of snow settling to the ground. The brightness in his eyes told her he was not going to slow down.

With a squeal, Sarah skipped to the side just out of reach and instinctively threw the snowball into his bad arm. She gasped, knowing how hard she had packed the thing. Damien brushed off the snow as she ran over to make her apologies.

176

"I am so sorry." Her hand hovered in front of the wet spot on his coat. She grimaced as she met his eyes, and her stomach roiled a little in sympathy at the thought of the hard snow slamming into his tender flesh. She rushed on. "I wasn't thinking at all. I feel so bad—that was horrible. Are you okay?"

Damien blinked a few times as if dazed, and she grabbed his good arm to steady him in case he passed out from the pain. His eyes cleared, focusing on her. Snaking an arm around her waist, his grip surprisingly strong after being stabbed just yesterday, he pulled her closer, dipping his head down so their noses nearly touched.

"Just fine," he replied. Sarah's heart sped up. He was so close that she imagined his whiskers grazed her own skin, and she felt rather than saw the grin that spread over his lips. "But I will give you a head start."

She blinked. "What?"

Damien's eyes narrowed wickedly, and the gold flecks were visible even in the gray light as he murmured, "I wouldn't be much of a gentleman if I didn't allow the chase to go on."

It took a moment for his words to sink in, and when they did, she grinned in relief, thankful he was only teasing her and trying to divert her attention from the game.

Easing back until he had no choice but to drop his hold from around her waist, she folded her arms across her middle and eyed him. "Just a head start, huh?"

He mimicked her stance, though his came off relaxed rather than challenging. "I can't let you have all the fun, can I?"

Sarah bit her lower lip to keep from laughing, but he caught the action, his eyes lowering to her mouth. His own tipped, and he leaned forward as he met her gaze. "You had better start running, my lady."

She opened her mouth in mock protest and then surprised him by dashing to the opposite side of the clearing. He hesitated only a moment before taking off after her.

She smiled, the wind stinging her cheeks as they ran in sync, Damien always just a few paces behind her as his laughter carried over the crisp air. Sarah had never felt so free or alive, and she knew that he felt it, too.

~Chapter 23~

Will dropped the pile of wood carelessly beside the fireplace, and the pieces landed in a haphazard heap. He didn't bother to stack it into its usual tidy pyramid but stared at it intently, arms folded across his chest. His eyes remained on that spot, focusing until he was staring blindly and all thoughts unrelated to the hunks of wood began to fall away. It calmed him some to repeat the ritual that freed his mind and had allowed him to push aside the pain after his parents' murders. Without it, he was sure he would not have been able to function under the weight of the emotions that might have destroyed him at the time.

But he could feel his mind rebelling against his restraint, and he allowed a single image to slip through. Sarah smiled up at him, hair fanning out against the pillow to frame her beautiful face. The candlelight reflected off her blue eyes, softening their warmth as they silently conveyed to him that he was good and *worth* something. Will had been taken aback the first time he saw that expression in her eyes so long ago. He had longed to reach out and touch his hand to her cheek in his uncle's cabin that morning.

In his mind's eye, his hand moved out to do just that. But when he blinked, the thumb that he envisioned stroking the curve of her throat belonged to Lisandro. The Spaniard leaned in, and Sarah whispered the man's name as he neared.

Will slammed his fist into the wall to dispel the image. The tranquility of his mind was shattered, replaced by a yawning emptiness and frustration that he could not overcome. Where was his calm? His *control*? He was certainly losing his mind if this was how he spent his days, trapped in disquieting imaginings, which were also untrue, if the complete honesty and innocence on Sarah's face were any indication. She certainly believed nothing was occurring between her and Lisandro.

Will, however, was not so easily convinced of the lord's good intentions. Sarah might trust the man implicitly, but Will wasn't fool enough to completely absolve Lisandro before he did a little digging into his character. He had yet to find trust for the man—the fact that they had never met face-to-face aside—and couldn't be sure that he and Lisandro hadn't experienced the same unsettling vision of a moment ago, though it was, perhaps, far pleasanter for the Spaniard.

The idea of the stranger having *any* thoughts concerning Sarah made him ill.

"You okay, Taylor?" The uncertainty in his employee's voice brought his mind to the present. Will became aware of his scowl and the way his hands were planted against the wall, as though he were trying to push right through to the other side.

Straightening, he squared his shoulders and resumed his usual emotionless mask, but it was becoming increasingly difficult to keep up. Life was wearing on him.

Robert stood with one foot planted inside the building, more than likely having halted when he witnessed his employer attempting to smash a hole in the wall. "You look a little sick." He paused before asking hesitantly, "Is something the matter, sir?"

"I'll live," was the curt response.

Robert nodded and entered cautiously. He stooped to right Will's mess, neatly piling the wood against the wall.

"Saw your friend leave earlier," he remarked as he stacked the pieces. "The lady left with some guy. Wasn't sure if you got to say hello." Will caught the inquiry in his gaze.

Exhaling, he shook his head, and some of the pretense chipped away. "Yes, I spoke with her."

"And the guy?"

Will folded his arms across his chest. "Is none of my concern, nor yours."

Robert seemed to shrug it off, rising to his feet. They had been working together long enough that he appeared used to his employer's dark moods and didn't take offense. "You seem a little agitated, is all, and I wondered if it was connected." He eyed Will, who returned his stare with a disinterested glare. Robert shuffled his feet and seemed suddenly reluctant to make eye contact. "My Nonie used to say that baggage carried by two people is a lighter load. Do you, uh, want to talk about it?"

Will blinked, surprised. Inquiring after his employer's feelings had caused Robert some discomfort, but he had asked nonetheless. Will's Adam's apple bobbed as he swallowed, moved by his concern and willingness to listen. Besides his uncle and Sarah, he hadn't another soul in whom he could confide—certainly not someone who was willing to "share the load" with him, as Robert had put it. For the first time, Will's eyes were opened to his self-imposed isolation, and he realized how lonely he had become.

Scrubbing a hand over his face, he growled into his palm, "It's complicated."

"Relationships generally are." Was that amusement in his voice?

Will moved his hand to the back of his neck and rubbed madly at the knot there. "It isn't—it's not—" He stared blankly at the floor. "As I said, it is rather complicated."

"But you love her, right?" Robert sounded certain of the fact, so Will declined to answer. He slanted a look at the younger man, whose lips were beginning to quirk in a sympathetic, knowing way. "When she was here the other day, a blind turtle could have seen the way you looked at her. Pardon me for saying so, but when she left, you looked like a puppy that had been kicked in the sternum. Kind of like you do now, though maybe a little angrier. And jealousy isn't a great look for you."

He received a steady glare, and Robert held up his hands. "Sorry, poor choice of words. What I'm trying to get at is that your defense mechanism is to shut down, but I guarantee if you do that now, you'll practically be shoving her into the arms of that guy."

However oddly worded, the man made some sense. Will forced himself to lower his shoulders and relax. Releasing a strangled breath, he asked, "So what is it that I should be doing? I've tried everything to no avail." He shoved a frustrated hand back through his hair. Was he truly seeking council from his worker?

Robert scratched his ear, thinking. "Well, have you told her how you feel?"

Will paused, his fingers caught on a few snarled waves. Lowering his arm with precise calm, he answered evenly, "Perhaps there is one thing I have yet to attempt."

Robert shot him an incredulous look. "Okay," he said slowly. "Well, why don't you do that? Or if you can't say it, then show her how you feel. Maybe give her a token of your affection. Girls love that stuff."

The wheels in his head were already beginning to turn, but still he was reluctant to bare his heart. "I'm not sure. . . ."

A shrug. "You can take my advice or leave it. All I'm saying is that I wouldn't let some slick poser like that"—he hiked his thumb toward the door—"steal her away from me. If you don't act now, you'll lose her for sure. And trust me, lost love sticks with you forever."

The man clearly spoke from experience as his face clouded, but Will could tell it was a closed subject.

Trepidation, excitement, and acute fear collided in his veins, but he was not turning back this time. Will nodded slowly, a determined gesture. He clapped his employee on the shoulder, grateful for the man's advice, however unorthodox it might have been. "Thank you, Robert."

The blond man grinned before turning his gaze to the fireplace. They watched the flames dance for a solid minute when Will felt eyes on him. He turned and caught Robert's amused gaze.

"I was thinking now, sir."

"Oh, yes. Yes, of course." Will moved in the direction of the door.

"And, Taylor?"

He glanced over his shoulder. Robert nodded once, and the gesture was full of confidence. "You'll get the girl. The good guy always does."

Will sucked in a breath, hoping to muster the assurance that the other man seemed to possess, but he was far less confident in the outcome.

****

He replayed his speech in his head as he walked, but his mind went blank the closer he came to the castle walls. His palms were beginning to sweat despite the chill in the air, and he swiped a hand hastily down the side of his trousers. He was behaving like a nervous youth coming to court a princess, but he was unable to shake his apprehension. Now or never, had been Robert's meaning. One opportunity to make things right.

He was going to be ill.

Hesitating for a brief moment outside the castle gate, Will ducked his head and went around the long way. Not wanting to vilify Sarah's reputation by coming in through the front gate, he decided to make his way along the outer wall that bordered the forest. It would be easy enough to slip inside via one of the concealed entrances he had discovered as a child.

He moved close to the stones to keep from being spotted by the guards patrolling the parapet walk atop the wall. His anticipation and apprehension increasing with each hurried step, Will lengthened his strides, desperate to put an end to this wait yet also wary of an unsatisfactory outcome.

As he neared the west end of the castle, the lively and incessant sounds coming from the square ebbed until he could pick up the faint sound of a woman's unintelligible shout ahead of him. Pulse quickening, Will paused out of habit, listening intently as he tried to discern the location of the noise. His uncle Thomas had taught him quite a few things about hunting and scouting when Will was a boy, and the older man had frequently stressed the importance of patience and precision, saying that they could mean the difference between hunting and being hunted.

Though he'd loathed hunting as a youth, Will was later grateful for his uncle's instruction: remaining unseen had been necessary in his past endeavors as the Shadow, and, though not as essential, he was grateful for that skill now.

However, when muted laughter came from the same direction, Will dismissed the noises for the moment, heart rate returning to normal, as he focused on the sound of footsteps above. He closed his eyes, lips moving silently as he counted each footfall. Even Will admitted to himself that his actions were a bit extreme, but instinct and past experience had taught him to rely on the shadows, and he preferred to remain unseen. Satisfied that the guard had passed overhead, Will dashed into the trees before the next sentry spotted him and asked why he was snooping around the castle.

Keeping near the forest's edge, Will picked his way through the trees, his ears constantly attune to his surroundings. The noises coming from the heart of town were all but extinct, and the only accompanying sounds were that of the snow crunching beneath his boots and the throaty laugh of a man that carried over the crisp air to Will's ears. Now he was sure there were two of them.

It would be easy enough to outwait the couple, though he wasn't sure if his patience could hold out that long as his eagerness to see Sarah grew with each agitated footfall. He watched the outer wall disappear at the back and knew he had only a little further to go before the forest expanded to his right to curve around the small clearing behind the castle. Will's eyes scanned the open area, searching for the jovial couple, if they were still there. The clearing appeared devoid of life, so he stepped carefully from the covering of the woods, gaze constantly shifting as he moved further into the open. He froze in his tracks when he spotted the man and woman in what appeared to be a lover's embrace.

In a flash, Will retreated to move behind the corner of the wall and flattened himself against it. The gentleman's voice was an indiscernible murmur, and he didn't appear to have spotted the man that lurked in the shadows. Instead of simply approaching the couple like a traditional human being, Will eyed the trees longingly, counting the number of paces to the forest's edge. In a few brief seconds, he could be enveloped in the cover of the trees, and they would be none the wiser.

He had just pushed off the wall when the woman spoke. Will's eyes snapped to the couple as she pulled back from the man, though his arms remained around her waist. Will was some distance from them, but the auburn hair that framed her tan features were so familiar that it left little room to question.

Sarah folded her arms across her chest, and from this distance, it appeared to him that she was being held against her will. The man leaned his face down so their noses nearly touched. Will's muscles tensed as his blood turned to fire. Clenching his fists at his side, he took three steps forward, ready to fight. But then Sarah's face broke into a grin, and she took off at a run, laughing as she went. If he wasn't certain of her identity before, the familiar sound that floated back to his hiding place left no doubt.

Will jerked to a halt, frozen in surprise at her sudden gaiety. The fellow, who he assumed was the infamous Lord Lisandro, chuckled as he

182

ran after her. Will was sickened to realize that the scoundrel kept up the chase for longer than necessary as they tossed snow at one another. He was contemplating bursting in on their little game before the Spaniard got any ideas into his head when Lisandro caught her around the waist, which caused him to lose his balance. Sarah shrieked as they tumbled to the snow, with her landing on the man's chest.

Will's fist balled again, and he felt the delicate stem snap in his grasp. He slowly uncurled his fingers to stare at the offended flower that he had searched so hard to find in the snow. He felt a moment's sadness that he had ruined such a perfect specimen and glanced up at its intended recipient, almost expecting her to have noticed that he'd ruined the gift.

But, no. Sarah had propped herself up on the Spaniard's chest, and his arms tightened around her. Will could not see her face from his vantage point, but the man beneath her was grinning broadly as he lifted his head. Will understood the look on the Spaniard's face; he didn't like it one bit.

His first instinct was a quick-boiling rage that filled him with the desire to rip the man out from under her and slam him against the wall until he could no longer remember his own ridiculous name—a thought that momentarily delighted Will. He had even advanced an unconscious step during their spill, preparing to reveal himself and invoke serious harm on the man if Sarah showed even the minutest sign of struggle.

But the longer it took her to pull away from Lisandro, the more the fight drained out of him. Robert's words came to mind about moving quickly, and Will was struck with the painful realization that he was staring at the result of his own lack of haste. Sarah's previous laughter echoed through his head, and he was forced to acknowledge the possibility that she would be better off with the Spaniard.

As much as Will wanted to spend the remainder of his days with her, what right did he have to impose his meager life upon her? She deserved a man with Lisandro's position, someone she could be proud of and a man of influence who could give her all that she desired—wealth, standing . . . love.

He just hoped the Spaniard would someday be worthy of her.

Will looked again at the broken flower. It had seemed so lovely and pure when he had found it before, but now it looked small and plain and perfectly broken compared to the vibrant rose Damien had given her. When considered side-by-side, there was no contest between the two. The gifts of a lowly blacksmith could never compare, nor could the man, who had nothing of true worth to give except the love in his heart.

But it would never be enough.

His eyes drifted toward them again, willing them to separate, longing for her to look his way. But Lisandro's arms were still tight around her middle, that obnoxious grin stretching across his too-brown face. Sarah didn't appear to be struggling for freedom.

Quickly averting his gaze, Will squared his jaw at the forest, as though it were personally challenging him to let go of the one thing he had been desperately clinging to. His mind made up to do one truly selfless thing with his life, he slowly tipped his hand, and the daisy—the emblem of a fruitless hope—slipped from his grasp and floated softly to the snow. His throat burned, and he loathed the ironic symbolism of the flower as it lay there, its petals pristine but its stem bent at an awkward angle where his fingers had crushed it. It too closely resembled the broken relationship between Sarah and himself to offer him comfort. But it was just as well that the flower was ruined.

He wouldn't be needing it, after all.

Inhaling deeply, he allowed one final glance at what would never be before quickly dragging his gaze, lest he cause himself more undue harm. And then he did the one thing he had sworn he'd never do again after she came back to him that day.

He walked away and did not look back.

****

Sarah pulled back from Damien, laughing at their clumsiness. He chuckled and leaned his head up to grin at her.

"Well, that was delightful," he said, arms tightening about her waist when she tried to pull back. "Shall we play again?"

"Damien," she admonished, a little breathless. From their fall, of course. "You can let me go now."

He grinned unrepentantly, though he tried to look innocent. "Oh, I'm quite comfortable as I am, if you don't mind."

"And if I do mind?" she asked dryly.

His chest rose and fell with a regretful sigh. "Well, then I suppose I would have to be a gentleman and relinquish my comfort for yours."

Sarah waited. He watched her in silence. "Uh, I'd *like* for you to let me go."

Damien's brows shot up. "Oh! You meant *this* instant. Of course!" He helped her stand while Sarah rolled her eyes at him—the man was ridiculous! But she could never seem to hide her smile when she was around him, however absurd his actions.

Rustling sounded near the forest's edge. She squinted to make out the tiny shadow hopping along the ground away from them. "Was that a rabbit?" she asked curiously, though it was too far away to tell.

Damien grinned. "Shall we investigate?"

Slipping her arm through his, she nodded eagerly.

They wandered the yard, edging closer to the trees. Sarah's gaze scanned the ground, searching for tracks. Her eyes landed on a white print in the snow, and she broke away from Damien and jogged over to it, expecting to find an animal's trail veering off into the forest. But as she neared, the yellow and white colors of the flower became more distinct. Damien came up behind her as she stooped to collect it from the snow. The daisy bowed over as she held it up.

"Oh, it's broken." She frowned, showing Damien the severed stem. It was still beautiful, but it flopped around uselessly without support. "Where did it come from?" she asked him, rubbing her thumb over one of the pristine petals.

Damien shrugged. "It must be wild."

"Hmm." It was damaged, but Sarah was somewhat reluctant to toss it away. It seemed a shame to leave it behind, but it wasn't like she had need of a broken flower. She placed it gingerly on the ground, exactly where it had been, and dusted off her hands.

"So!" Damien exclaimed as they walked back toward the castle. "What say you to supper?"

She looked up at him incredulously. "It's the middle of the afternoon, if you hadn't noticed."

He took her hand and placed it in the crook of his arm, rubbing his palm over it gently to generate warmth. The gesture wasn't lost on her, and she felt heat spread through her chest that she was sure had nothing to do with their exertions.

Damien smiled down at her, and the corners of his eyes crinkled in pleasure. "Ah, ever the witty beauty. Actually, I was referring to this evening. I dine with the family every Saturday, or more often if I am able, and would like you to come as my guest."

Sarah swallowed nervously. "Your family?" She hadn't thought he had any left, except for his estranged father.

He looked surprised. "No, the royals. The nobles join them for the evening meal, a chance for all present to bow and flatter the egos of those of higher rank and standing. It is extremely tedious and dull, but it is expected." He sounded bored just talking about it, but Sarah had already zoned out.

"Will the entire royal family be there?"

Damien's eyes narrowed in thought. "Yes, they all generally attend." He met her gaze, and he looked suddenly unsure of himself. "So, would you accompany me?"

A thrill of nervous excitement drove through her veins, and she suppressed a shiver of anticipation and fear at the possibility of coming face-to-face with the king's murderer. "Yes, I'd love to come."

His expressive eyes brightened. "Wonderful! With your company, this evening will be most interesting."

185

He had no idea.

~Chapter 24~

"When is he coming for you?" Edith asked as she rifled through the wardrobe for a proper gown to attend supper in.

Sarah reflexively glanced outside to check the evening sun, but it was already dark; not having a watch left her at a serious disadvantage. "Um, I think din—*supper*—is in an hour, and he said he'd get me a few minutes before. Don't worry," she assured, misunderstanding Edith's fidgety movements. "We have plenty of time to get ready."

Edith emerged from the wardrobe with an elegant purple gown draped over her outstretched arms. Sarah turned back to the foggy looking glass that had been brought in earlier and was practicing piling her hair on top of her head when Edith muttered, "I care not for his patience." The intensity in her words caused Sarah to drop her hair and spin around to face the older woman. Her expression was troubled, and a line had appeared between her knit brows.

Edith's movements were stiff as she placed the gown on the edge of the bed and smoothed it out to prevent it from wrinkling. She turned around and caught Sarah's mouth agape before she snapped it closed.

Expelling a heavy breath, Edith came up behind her and motioned for Sarah to face the mirror again. Deft fingers combed through her waves and mechanically arranged them at the back of her head. Sarah remained silent as she stared at her hands clasped tightly in her lap. From Edith's strong reaction, something heavy burned her mind; she wasn't one to overreact.

Edith tugged playfully on a strand of her hair, and Sarah glanced up at the older woman's reflection in the mirror. The smile Edith gave her was small but filled with warmth. "Your face gives too much away, my dear." Her smile fell away. "Forgive me for reacting so harshly just then. My issue was not with you, and I am sorry if it seemed that way."

"What did I say that upset you?" Sarah asked, baffled. "It wasn't about Damien, was it? Because he's been a complete gentleman." She thought of

187

the way he had held her against him after they'd fallen in the snow, but the truth was, she hadn't exactly minded or made much of an effort to pull away.

She ducked her head to conceal the guilty flush that stole over her cheeks.

"No, no." Edith's voice sounded distracted as she murmured her assurance. "If you trust the young lord, then so do I."

Sarah looked up at the older woman, who diligently worked the tangled strands into compliance. "Then what is it?"

"I simply—" She halted, seeming to struggle for the right words before she schooled her features into the subservient mask Sarah had seen her use around the other lords and ladies. "I was surprised to hear that you would be supping with the royals, is all. But it will be quite an experience for you, I'm sure."

Though Edith tried her best to hide it, Sarah detected the uncertainty and false assurance her words carried. "What's really bothering you?" It couldn't be that Damien had invited her to dinner. That hardly seemed like a reason to cause worry.

Edith pursed her lips. "It's simply that there are quite a few . . . expectations," she answered carefully, "for such an event. It can be intimidating for one so young."

Sarah had discovered that hardly a decade separated them, yet Edith had taken over a mothering role, seeming decades older in both wisdom and experience and temperament. The harshness of this life had aged the woman and lent her a knowing gaze. Though Edith never spoke of it or complained, Sarah suspected she had seen more of the world than she cared to know, judging by the faraway look that occasionally flittered over her pale features when she thought no one was watching.

Edith's ministrations were no longer the practiced and efficient movements of the maid she had been a moment ago, but her fingers combed through the auburn waves like those of a mother comforting her child. Sarah's heart sank in dread.

"Edith," she said warily, watching her friend's face closely when she averted her gaze. "What are you really worried about? You can tell me."

Edith's troubled eyes met hers. Placing her hands on her shoulders, she said, "I am concerned about you going, yes. But my real worry is that they will know who you are—you will no longer be just another faceless guest to them. If you are with Lisandro at that table, you are worth knowing."

Sarah squinted her left eye, still unclear. "So you're worried about me getting on their radar? Why?"

Choosing her words carefully, she replied, "Everyone is aware that the master Cadius can be prone to . . . *dark* moods." Her shiver seemed uncontrollable. "We all fear him and what he will do if we make a mistake, and the guests are no exception—half are indebted to him for reasons unknown, and the other portion are politically ambitious and only remain because a familiarity with the royals can advance their position. If he knows who you are, he *will* be watching you from now on, wherever you go."

Sarah swallowed, recalling Damien's words from earlier. Could Cadius really have spies everywhere?

Edith's expression softened at her look of surprise, though her voice was just as insistent. "And that begs me to caution you to remain silent on religious matters. I've enjoyed hearing you speak freely of God and *Christianity*"—she whispered the word, as though fearful someone might overhear—"but the notion of a single deity threatens the ego of a man like Cadius and his comrades. That sort of talk is just not expected from a lady, especially not a topic so controversial as the Christ."

"I can't lie," Sarah remarked softly. Edith looked put out, and she hurried to add, "You told me that you and your husband raised your son to believe in God. Would you want him to lie about his faith?"

Edith winced, but her pained expression was fleeting. "If it would save his life, yes. And now I am asking you to protect yours. You know what you believe, so what is the harm in denying it if someone asks?" But Sarah was already shaking her head. Edith added quietly, "You told me He sees everything, so why would He punish you for protecting yourself?"

Sarah took a deep breath, thinking of a way to explain. "It's not that I fear a reprimand from Him, but God is as much a part of my life as breathing—He's the reason I'm alive. I can't . . . *deny* Him. It would be like denying myself. Does that make sense?"

Edith nodded slowly, and Sarah went on. "I promise to not provoke, but if someone asks me outright, I'm going to tell them about God just like I have with you."

"And if it was a matter of life and death, would you still speak up?"

Sarah winced. She wanted to say, "Yes, in a heartbeat." But she hesitated.

"I don't know," she admitted honestly. "But I hope I would have the courage to stand by Him when He's done the same for me all these years. You wouldn't bury the crown jewels in the pumpkin patch when you could wear them for all to see, would you?"

Edith shook her head, looking a little dumbfounded. "No, I suppose not." She watched Sarah's face closely, seeming to spot something in her eyes that wasn't there before. She smiled faintly in bemusement. "My lady, you have given me much to think on. I must admit that though your conviction astounds me, I do respect you for it." Sighing, she added, "So have it your way."

Her eyes turned haunted once more. "But I know first-hand what can

189

happen if you make a mistake. Don't give Cadius any reason to doubt your loyalty. Understand?"

Sarah nodded mutely. Her stomach had become a total mass of knots during Edith's cautioning. She felt more concerned and less self-assured than ever. But she was also touched that Edith cared enough to warn her beforehand, especially since she ran the risk of being overheard revealing such secrets.

Spinning around in her chair, Sarah grabbed the woman's hands in both her own and squeezed them gently. "I will be careful. I promise."

Edith bobbed her head in acknowledgement. She released Sarah's hands and turned to retrieve the gown before she could see the emotion pooling in her gaze. "I can have a tray brought up for you, if you get hungry," she said over her shoulder.

"I can wait for dinner, thanks." Sarah pretended not to notice that it took her a rather long time to smooth the dress out before bringing it to her; she didn't want to embarrass Edith after all she had done for her.

The dress slipped over Sarah's hair with ease, and Edith put a few last-minute touches on her cosmetics—some pink-toned powders made from dried berries and flowers—before placing a sudden vice-like grip on her shoulders. "Whatever you do," she whispered, her voice wavering with emotion, "do not let him see that you fear him."

Her first encounter with Cadius was sounding more ominous by the minute.

Sarah tried to swallow her fear, but the lump that dropped to her stomach only made her feel sick. "How am I supposed to act, then?"

Edith tucked an errant curl behind Sarah's ear—the haunted look had yet to leave her eyes. "Just stay invisible. It is better if he doesn't dwell on you for too long."

Sarah watched her expression closely. Then, because she couldn't take not knowing what had stooped her friend's shoulders so suddenly, she asked hesitantly, "You sound like you speak from experience."

Edith did not turn away or try to change the subject, as she had expected. She stared Sarah in the eye, and a single tear slipped over her lid and made its way down her pale cheek. She gave a pained smile that quivered at the corners. "Some ghosts are best left forgotten."

****

Sarah jiggled her leg anxiously, her apprehension increasing with each second that passed without Damien knocking on her door. She had thought she was too nervous to eat, but when one hour passed and then two, she was so famished that she devoured the contents of the tray Edith had brought in earlier. "In case you change your mind," she had said. Sarah didn't think

190

she was referring to simply snacking before dinner.

The sun had set hours ago. Maybe she had heard wrong and supper wasn't until later. And there was a definite possibility that interrogating Cadius in front of a room full of people was a complete mistake, and sitting here was only making her question her decision.

Jumping off her bed in one lurching movement, Sarah practically jogged to her door and threw it open. She would go mad if she stayed in this room another moment. Closing her door as gently as her nervous fingers would allow, her slippers padded across the hall, and she paused as a servant moved around the corner and out of sight before knocking on Damien's door with a shaking hand.

Her foot tapped impatiently on the colorful rug as she waited for him to open the door. She pursed her lips and knocked again, harder, when he neglected to answer. The door creaked open under the weight of her fist, and she froze.

No sound came from within. Maybe he had already gone to supper and forgotten to close the door on his way out. If that were the case, he had also forgotten to fetch her, which she didn't think he would.

Sarah pushed the door open a few more inches and leaned in slowly, her eyes scanning the dark room as she gripped the doorframe. The low-burning fire cast eerie shadows over the enormous room, but it offered little light. "Damien?" she whispered, as if in fear of disturbing the unnerving dark of the strange room. There was no answer. She took a step inside as her eyes adjusted and then said more loudly, "Are you in here?"

Silence.

"Guess not," she muttered and began backing through the doorway. A breathy shudder from the other side of the room caused her to jump as her eyes flew to the settee and the crumpled form convulsing there.

She gasped when the man muttered her name in confusion. "Ohmygosh, Damien!" She flew across the room and dropped down beside him. Tremors racked his body, and she could tell he was trying hard to contain them. A sheen of sweat glistened on his brow, and his face was devoid of color. Sarah felt instant panic when he looked up at her with glazed, feverish eyes that didn't seem to place her. "What happened?" Fear caused her voice to tremble.

He gave her a wavering grin that she assumed was meant to reassure her, but it looked more like a grimace. "You caught me at a poor time, my lady." Now he really winced, and Sarah involuntarily mimicked the gesture. He choked past gritted teeth, "But I seem to be the one with the poor . . . timing."

"Damien, what *happened*?" she asked again. Her eyes scanned the room, as though the answer were hidden in the rumpled sheets. It looked like he had fallen from bed and barely made it to the small couch before the tremors became too much for him.

He looked up at her with a look she could only assume was his brave face, but his shivering body undermined the effort. "It's nothing. Truly." He gave her an imploring look. "Sarah, please—I don't wish you to worry, and I can see you already are. Forgive me for—" His brow tightened and his eyes closed in pain as a severe tremor moved over his body, too powerful for him to control. He gripped his stomach, as if to quell the vibrations racking his frame.

Sarah watched in horror as the shaking increased. She had no idea what to do to alleviate seizures, or if she needed to hold him still so he couldn't hurt himself. Indecisive, she could only stare, horror-struck and frozen in wide-eyed panic. When she could no longer stand watching his pain in helpless silence, she rose to call out for someone, but his arm snaked out and caught her hand. His hold was desperate, unbreakable.

"Don't go," he rasped, breathless from his episode. Sarah was about to argue that he needed help she couldn't provide, but the convulsions had lessened with his vice-like grip on her arm. He was only shivering now, though Sarah feared it might start again at any moment. It seemed to help to have something to hold onto, though, and Damien's eyes were lucid as he stared up at her, his look beseeching. Torn, she bit her lip and knelt before him again and squeezed his hand with hers.

"I'm not going anywhere." Though she was sure she would have no feeling in that hand tomorrow if he continued to hold on like she was his lifeline.

Damien's body visibly relaxed with her words, and his eyes drifted closed. He looked so vulnerable and tired, and she reached out to brush wet strands of hair from his brow. Her thumb idly stroked the creases on his forehead to smooth them out. It wasn't until the tension on his brow lessened and his body sank heavily into the cushions that she realized what she was doing.

Sarah swallowed and pulled her hand back. His grip on her other hand tightened possessively as his eyes opened to meet hers. In the semi-darkness, the color of his eyes was nearly impossible to make out, but the vulnerability in them was perfectly clear. The firelight caused the gold flecks to stand out against the darkness of his gaze, reminding Sarah of fireflies in a hollow cavern. A girl could get lost in those haunting eyes, Sarah thought, and she already felt the invitation to lose herself in their fathomless depths.

"Don't stop," he whispered hoarsely. He sounded exhausted. How long had he been here, alone and terrified and fighting against his own body? She instinctively squeezed his hand and felt a quick pulse in return. Damien's eyes closed with the reassurance that she would be nearby, and his body sank gratefully into the couch again.

Sarah's thumb rubbed back and forth across his knuckles to lull him to sleep, silently praying that he wouldn't have another episode. As she watched his weary face, she wondered if they truly were seizures. Edith had said that Cadius was capable of great evil. Had he done this? Sarah felt a renewed hatred for the faceless man swell within her chest, which was quickly overshadowed by the fear that someone had tried to kill Damien.

Her grip on his hand tightened, and he opened one eye. Her voice dropped with urgency as she leaned in. "Damien, did you say anything about what I told you during our ride? Anything at all? It's important."

Both eyes were open now and clouded with confusion. He shook his head. "Of course not. You'll recall that *I* am the one who told *you* to remain quiet."

"I didn't say anything, either. But think back—did you mention it to anyone?"

He appeared clueless and struggled to prop himself up. Sarah placed her free hand on his chest to keep him down, and he was too spent to put up a fight. "What are you talking about?"

She glanced back at the open door and jumped up before he could protest. Closing it, she hurried back to him and retrieved his hand once more. Her voice dropped to a low whisper, even though the door was closed. "I think you may have been poisoned."

Now he really looked confused. "Wha—?"

"Is there any way that Cadius could have figured out what we talked about? Could we have been followed?"

Damien was already shaking his head, albeit weakly. This time she didn't fight him when he propped himself up on a wobbly elbow. "Sarah, no. He did not do this."

"Then how do you explain what just happened to you?"

"A drunken father," he answered quietly.

Sarah glanced up at him sharply. "What?"

Damien's lips parted to expel a heavy breath. He lowered himself again, his eyes suddenly taking great interest in the tapestry on the wall above him. "Shortly after Mother's death . . ." His voice faded, and he swallowed before he could continue. "I knew he was in a rage when he returned from the tavern that night, and I hid Isabella in the stable until he could sober-up. But without my mother or sister at hand, I was all the remained for the dispensation of my father's pent-up wrath."

He paused. His voice was softer when he spoke. "It was the final straw, and I decided in that instant to take Isabella away from him. But then my father—he slipped and fell down the staircase, making the decision for us when he broke his neck. Isabella and I left when I was well enough to travel." His story finished, Damien met her eyes, and she saw that the past clouded his gaze.

For a man to murder his wife in a rage was bad enough, but to beat his own son and inflict this level of damage was unthinkable.

Sarah's throat felt unnaturally tight with compassion for the wounded man before her and disgust for the father who had raised him. She was horrified at the brief satisfaction she felt over his being dead and swallowed ashamedly. "And that's when this started? The seizures?"

His expression was heavy and burdened. "Yes. I lapsed into an episode before he had finished. Perhaps it saved my life." He chuckled mirthlessly at the irony. His gaze lowered to the smaller hand clenched in his own, and he placed their entwined hands on his chest. Sarah watched his movements and when she looked up, his gaze was trained on the ceiling, thoughtful.

"For years I questioned if this was God's doing—my just punishment for being the horrible, unwanted child my father told me I was." His throat worked in a convulsive swallow. "But now I realize that the world simply deals the hands that it does, and we cannot protest. Some days cause me to question if there truly is an Almighty, as Mother believed."

Damien's eyes widened when they met her teary gaze, and he struggled to rise. "Oh, Sarah, forgive me. I did not wish to upset you."

She shook her head, wanting to tell him to sit back down before he had another seizure, but her throat was clogged with unshed tears. She sniffed. "It's not that—" She stopped, unable to finish. Overcome with the imagery of a young, damaged boy lovingly caring for his sister, Sarah suddenly wanted very much to fix him and wipe away the past. She was supposed to be guarding her heart, but Damien and his aching loneliness had subdued her defenses. No matter what she wanted to believe, he was already in her heart.

She stared at the back of the hand that had yet to release her own. "I'm so sorry," she whispered. The words didn't seem to be enough, but they were all she had.

He lifted her chin with a gentle finger and kept it there even after she met his eyes. They were soft and warm. "Thank you for listening. You are the only person in my new life that I've told of this." Sarah started, surprised. Propping himself up against the back of the couch, Damien grinned weakly, but it was genuine. He pulled her up to sit beside him. She shifted to face him, and he brought her hand to his lips. The carefully manicured scruff on his chin brushed her hand, and Sarah felt something shoot down to her toes. "And thank you for caring." Damien's breath brushed her knuckles.

"Of course," she rasped past a suddenly dry throat.

Damien leaned his head against the wall and closed his eyes, clearly spent. But he still clutched her hand to his chest like she might disappear while he slept. His lips parted as he began to fade, and Sarah allowed herself a moment to study him in the soft light.

A thin line of dark scruff ran along his jawline and then reached up to touch his full lower lip. A matching set of dense lashes fanned out over usually olive-toned skin on either side of the narrow, perfectly sculpted nose that spoke of his high breeding. The boyish dent in his right cheek, where a dimple had permanently left its mark, and the smile lines on either side of his mouth contrasted with the ever-present crease on his forehead and the squint-marks at the corner of his eyes.

His strong features were definitely refined and handsome, she couldn't deny it. But while these things had certainly drawn her in when they'd first met and only grown on her since, it was becoming increasingly apparent to her, as she watched him rest in childlike trust that she would watch over him, that it had been the vulnerability and pain she had seen behind the self-confident swagger that had intrigued her.

Sarah was caught up in her thoughts and didn't realize that her patient had one eye trained on her, a cheeky glimmer in his gaze. "Something you find interesting?"

And then there were moments when her compassion ended with a roll of her eyes when his self-assuredness leaked through. How could the man elicit so many different emotions from her in one sitting?

Sure her face showed her internal struggle, Sarah tried to recover without inflating his ego further. "Actually, I was just thinking that you looked a little sickly and tired." His grin only broadened, and she knew she hadn't convinced him. Softening her tone, she urged, "You need to rest."

Damien tugged her a little closer and draped one arm heavily about her shoulders, forcing her to lean against him as the weight of it pulled her down. He grinned defiantly down at her. "Actually, I'm quite comfortable where I am. You look lovely tonight, by the way."

Sarah pushed against him so he could see her reprimanding look. "Be serious. You looked ready to drop a minute ago, and I don't think I can carry you to your bed if you fall asleep."

Weariness entered his gaze when he looked at the few feet between the bed and the small couch. "I think this spot is perfect. Besides, the worst is over."

Sarah suddenly understood why his arm felt so heavy across her shoulders; he clearly did not have the strength to brave the minute distance.

Gnawing on her lower lip as she stared at the bed in thoughtful silence, she finally rose on cramped legs, grimacing at the needles that that shot through her numb feet as the blood returned to them. She snagged a pillow and the ornate quilt from the mattress and lugged them back to him, half-carrying, half-dragging the monstrosity behind her.

"You could sleep here, if you want to," she said delicately, conscious of his manly pride and the fact that her urging him into bed like a fretting mother might insult said manhood. Especially if he couldn't make the journey in the first place. "It's probably better not to move around so much, anyway."

Damien looked relieved that she had taken the decision away from him and nodded eagerly. "Yes, the nurse is always right." She grinned indulgently and pretended she didn't catch his tight-lipped grimace as he lowered himself to his side. Sarah slipped the pillow beneath his head and watched it sink heavily into the downy-soft feathers. She started to heft the blanket over him, but his hand snaked out and caught her wrist.

"You have done enough, Sarah," he said. "It must be getting late."

She wasn't quite ready to leave him alone, and she would have more peace of mind watching him here than she would fretting over his condition from her own room. "I don't mind staying a little longer—just until you get settled."

Damien frowned, and she could tell he was about to argue with her. Though she couldn't help wondering if a part of him wanted her to stay. "You should not—"

"How long were you like this tonight?" she asked abruptly.

He stared up at her, hesitating. "Not too long." His answer was careful—to spare her feelings, she knew.

Sarah bit her lip, troubled. She should have known that something was wrong when he didn't come for her and then gone to find him. Maybe she could have done more if she had discovered him earlier, or at the very least been there for him. She gently slipped her arm from his grasp and arranged the blanket over him.

"I'm sorry I didn't come sooner," she murmured. When she slanted him a glance through her hair, she caught his lips curving in a contented smile.

He said with a low voice, "It has been quite some time since I was taken care of so well." Damien's eyes were alight with warmth even as his lids drooped to half-mast. He took her hand again before she could pull away, tired eyes searching her face. "You could have done nothing more if you had been here sooner. Believe me."

"But I could have at least *been* here," she countered.

He smiled, a little bit of the old, playful Damien returning. "I admit that I feel far more at peace with you near. But I suppose if you feel that way, then by all means, my lady, stay with me until the sun sets fire to the darkness."

Sarah bit her lip to keep from grinning, his teasing manner automatically dismissing any underlying implications. "I'll stay until you fall asleep." She sat down on the floor and folded her legs Indian-style.

His smile remained on his face a moment longer before it ebbed. He propped himself up on his elbows, brow furrowed in concern. "I didn't

196

think this through properly, and I cannot request that you to stay."

"What?"

"A man should never ask a lady to take the ground, and it wouldn't be proper to have you remain unchaperoned. I would hate to tarnish your reputation."

He looked so genuinely torn up about it that Sarah couldn't suppress her grin. "That's sweet of you to think of that, but I'm not that worried. Besides, I'm pretty sneaky, so no one will see me leave."

"But—"

"*Sleep*, Damien," she urged. He watched her another second before lowering himself once more, his eyes closing in fatigue.

"I am a weak example for my entire sex," he muttered, half asleep already.

Sarah chuckled softly. His lips tipped almost imperceptibly in a grin before it faded as he succumbed to his exhaustion.

She leaned against the front of the settee, pressing her back to his bent knees, angled so he could fit on the small couch. She wondered if the contact was meant to comfort him in his sleep, or if it was to reassure her of his presence. Either way, in the silence of the room, she couldn't ignore the fact that there was something in Damien that pulled her to him.

Yes, he was attractive, self-confident, and ridiculously charming, the kind of man that got under your skin whether you wanted him to or not by being so irritatingly endearing. But beneath the layers of confidence and charm, there was also sadness that Sarah wanted to wipe away. Maybe God had brought her into Damien's life so she could draw him to the Lord. She had failed to do just that where Will was concerned, but this might be her second chance. Convenient that she only seemed to remember to mention God and faith when the man she wished to save was unconscious.

Sighing, Sarah rose and went to the fire, dumping the contents of the pitcher beside the hearth onto the dying embers. The orange-yellow glow quickly went out with a prolonged hiss as the water sloshed over the logs.

She slipped out of Damien's room, with a final glance at her sleeping patient, into the empty hall. Closing her own door with a muted *click*, she quickly readied for bed and slipped under the quilts. Her body tense with concern, she forced it to relax and prayed for peace and safety for Damien while he slept. Then she tried to close her mind for the night, but it refused to shut down completely, and she remained awake as her mind raced to put all of the missing pieces together.

Yet no matter how hard she tried to fill in the blanks, there were just too many unanswered questions that left huge chunks in her theories. She wasn't any good at solving these things alone.

Sarah smiled to herself in the dark room, reminded that she would never be entirely alone. She whispered a quick prayer for wisdom and decided that tomorrow she would see if there was a way to get a message to Karen. But it was a comfort to know she had at least one friend out there, and for now, she chose to remember that Someone was always with her.

~Chapter 25~

Will closed the door with more force than he'd intended. Though the dull *smack* as wood met wood was perfectly satisfying, it did nothing to lessen the dark cloud hovering over his current mood. Yes, he had been in the right when he decided to let her go, he was sure, but that did not mean that he was pleased about it. He hadn't even gone back to tell Robert that he was leaving for the day, but had come straight home.

Irritated, he stomped his heavy leather boots on the entry floor, knowing he would have to clean up the mess later but needing to act irrational for one *blasted* moment. Shrugging off his coat as he kicked his boots into a corner, he tossed the garment carelessly onto the rocking chair, setting it in a hazardous motion and nearly toppling it.

The chair had been his uncle's house warming gift to him, and, craftsman that he was, Thomas had spent weeks carving ornate designs into the arms and legs of the chair, all things that reminded him of his nephew, he'd told him—the leaves and trees of the forest, tangled vines, animals of the wood, and a bow loaded with a single arrow in the center of the oak headrest; the string was pulled back, always at the ready.

Will frowned. He would hate to break something that his uncle had put so much thought and effort into in one childishly hotheaded moment. But he felt too worked up to go over and still the rocking chair.

He crouched before the hearth, starting a fire with little effort. It would take hardly any time for the heat to permeate the sparse one-room cabin he and his uncle had built when Will decided it was time for him to be a man. At the present, he felt more like a petulant child than the grown businessman that he was.

Sighing, he rose, walking to the chest in the corner of the "bedroom." He gingerly removed the patchwork quilt his mother had made and given to her older brother, Thomas. When Will's parents died, his uncle had given it to him, saying that he needed it more than he did.

199

As with every other time he touched the fabric, he allowed himself a few seconds for the memories to surface as he reverently held the quilt. But when the pain returned with those fond memories, as it always did, he quickly folded and placed it on his bed and out of sight, tamping the remembrances down with it.

With only a brief hesitation, Will knelt and hefted the chest lid open, the rusty old hinges groaning in protest. He pulled out the stack of trousers and shirts and set them on the floor. His breath caught in his chest as he stared at the past, out of sight but never completely forgotten.

The thick woolen cloak had been carefully folded, and atop it laid his precious bow. He had placed them at the very bottom of the cedar chest beside his quiver—stocked full of unused arrows—in the event that someone went searching through his possessions. Will reached inside and pulled out his trusty bow, which his father had helped him make when he was yet too small for the weapon. So many memories. . . .

But he had made a vow, had he not? As much as he wished to don his cloak once more and be *useful*, he was no longer benefitting Serimone as vigilante for the people. With Captain Quinn back on the royal guard, the riffraff on the streets were quickly being purged, and the Shadow was becoming more and more obsolete. And the vendetta that had caused him to create his alter ego was a moot point now, what with Gabriel being nearly nonexistent.

Sarah's words about him being needed came back to haunt him, and he thoughtfully plucked the string of the bow. It had felt good to be needed.

His head snapped up at the sound of cracking branches and an animal's high-pitched squeal, shattering the perfect stillness of the forest outside. He quickly stashed his bow back in the chest and closed the lid in one familiar movement before silently making his way to the tightly shuttered window—the only one cut into the side of the small house. Listening for any further sound from outside, his body tensed as he unlatched the shutter and cracked it open before pulling it wide. A badger that had no business being out of its hole this time of year scurried away through the cascade of powder falling from a low branch. The animal must have been seeking high shelter and fallen from its unstable perch.

Will re-latched the window as his pulse slowed. He was being jumpy, out of practice after so many months in reclusive hiding. He glanced back at the chest and frowned. But he did need to be more careful.

Opening the lid again, he placed everything back inside before covering it with the beautiful quilt. It was a life he had buried long ago, and along with it, his belief that he could make a difference. Experience had taught him that the past was best left in the past, however much he wished to resurrect it.

****

Sarah watched as Edith dutifully shoveled the ashes from the fireplace. She munched on her apple, feeling idle even though the older woman had scoffed at the idea of them working side-by-side, the lady and the maid.

"I don't see why I can't just help a *little*."

Still gripping the small scoop, Edith cocked her head so that Sarah could see the streak of ash on her cheek and the smudge on the tip of her nose, as if she had face-planted in the pile she was scooping. Sarah was going to bring it to her attention when the older woman quirked an amused brow. "Is this the face of a lady?" she asked wryly.

Sarah grinned and took a cloth napkin from the tray, holding it out to her. "Yes, it is the face of a lady, but you still might need this."

Edith smiled in return, though she declined. She said, "It would just be a waste to clean up now," and went back to scraping the ashes into a pile.

Leaning against the hearth, Sarah watched as the sky gave way to dusk through the small crack in the window. She felt nothing but gratitude for their friendship and knew that Edith was on the same page—today she seemed brighter and happier.

"What does the good lord have in store for you today?"

Sarah blinked, surprised. Then she realized that Edith was referring to Damien, not *the* Lord. That was a little easier to answer; she was still trying to sort out what God's plan for her was, exactly. "I don't think that we have any set ideas for today. I haven't even seen him yet." That fact had worried her, and she had walked past his door four times since the morning, listening for any sounds of movement. She thought he might have awakened early and gone out until she spotted a servant tiptoeing into his room with his lunch tray and leaving quietly a moment later. Though she wanted to give him space after his ordeal last night, she was still tempted to check on him.

"Oh?" Edith leaned back on her heels and studied her. "It seemed that the both of you were getting rather close, so I assumed he would have engaged you for the evening." She paused. "Neither of you attended supper."

Sarah swallowed, feeling caught. Did she know something about last night? But her face was merely curious, and there wasn't a note of suspicion in her gaze.

Sarah breathed a little easier. She shrugged. "He wasn't feeling well, so we decided to reschedule for another night."

Nodding, the older woman rose from her cramped position and clapped her palms together, sending a cascade of pale ash onto the floor. She pulled a well-worn handkerchief from her apron pocket and went about dusting her face and hands, though it only served to smudge the gray color over her skin.

Edith held her arm up for her inspection and chuckled. "I will certainly be needing a thorough scrubbing before traipsing about the castle. I'll be doing more harm than good in this state!"

Smiling, Sarah remarked, "You're in an awfully good mood this morning."

Glancing around, Edith leaned in. Sarah had never seen her eyes so bright or her face so radiant, coming from within. She took the younger girl's hands in her own. "We can't talk here—someone might overhear. But, oh, Sarah, I have such good news."

Sarah gave her hands a quick squeeze, watching her face with curiosity. "Well, what is it?"

"Later. It was simply something you said yesterday. I was up all night thinking about it!"

Her eyes were so bright that Sarah had to laugh. "You can't even give me a hint? What if—?"

A woman's scream rent the air a heartbeat before a cacophony of objects clattering over stone echoed downstairs.

Edith and Sarah shared a worried look before bolting from the room. Running to the stairs with identical strides, they leaned over the short length of banister and saw a young servant girl on her knees the level below. She was weeping, wooden bowls and utensils strewn about from when she had dropped the tray in her fall. A single arrow lay broken a foot from the wall, having shattered when it connected with the hard stone. Sarah suddenly understood the girl's distress: It had only missed her by a few inches.

A commotion sounded on the lower level above the girl's cries, and a menagerie of workers and servants converged in the large room to investigate and offer help. Some questioned the distressed servant, while others began collecting the things she had dropped or offered her words of comfort.

"We should do something." Edith began moving toward the stairs, but Sarah stood frozen, chilled by the girl's shrieks and weeping; she sounded terrified. But what had frightened her? A better question would be who had tried to warn her off with that shot?

The shadows shifted in a familiar way, and the back of Sarah's mind registered what was going to emerge before she was able to make out the cloaked figure crouched in the darkest corner below the stairs. While everyone was occupied with seeing to the girl's needs, the Shadow rose slowly and then dashed up the staircase, taking the steps two at a time. His hasty retreat had drawn the attention of the staff below—a woman cried out, a few servants called for him to stop, while the rest stared in disbelief at their first glimpse of the elusive vigilante.

Edith gasped and jumped out of the way as he came barreling up the

202

stairs, green cloak flying madly behind him like a cape, bow drawn, hood pulled low to mask his features. What was Will doing? Sarah hadn't thought he would be this careless, nor would he shoot at an innocent girl, even if it had simply been to warn her off.

She jogged a few steps after him down the hall, ignoring Edith's protests behind her. "Will, stop!" He kept running and did not acknowledge her hiss. Her steps momentarily faltered as she realized her mistake in calling him by name if someone overheard. People were clamoring up the staircase, shouting.

Suddenly, he turned on her, bow raised, an arrow resting against the frame as he pulled the string back with a quivering hand. Maybe she had been wrong in assuming that he had intended to miss the servant girl. Sarah felt a knot of dread form in her stomach when she realized that this man was *not* Will.

Another warning shout filled the hall from behind, startling both of them. The Shadow's hand jerked, releasing the string. Instinct kicked in and caused Sarah to dive mid-run just as the arrow sailed overhead. She glanced up from her flattened position on the rug, hands burning from catching herself on the rough fabric.

Though his face was cloaked in shadows, his body language—arm held out stiffly as if still clutching the string he'd released, fingers trembling—told her that he was frozen in shock. Then he turned and ran from the shouts and cries of alarm.

Sarah kept her eyes focused on him as she rose on shaky legs and took off in his wake, unwilling to lose sight of his back. Accosting her and impersonating Will had just made this personal. Now she was ticked.

Adrenaline pumped her arms and kept her legs moving, eating up the distance between them as his heavy disguise weighed him down. If she could keep close to his tail, he wouldn't have enough time to load and draw his bow before she was upon him.

"Stop!" she called. Not that he was going to halt and give himself up to the girl chasing him, but she wasn't working logically anymore.

The Shadow moved down the long corridor and ducked into one of the rooms. Sarah followed him as fast as her tired legs allowed and saw his cloak disappear into the connecting room. She managed to keep up with him for another room and saw him dart off to the left in the hall ahead, but the maze of corridors and rooms that he seemed to have memorized had her completely disoriented. By the time she reached the hallway, he had already disappeared.

Starting off down the left section of the corridor, she skidded to a stop at the faint echo of a table overturning behind her. Whipping her head around, she spotted a door slamming down the opposite direction. She was sure he had come down this way and silently cursed the passages he seemed to know so well.

Sucking in a deep breath, Sarah broke off at a dead run, following the muffled sound of his retreat. She threw herself into the room and ran in the direction she thought the noises came from, side burning. She found herself in a completely unadorned corridor that she assumed was at the back of the castle. How far had they gone? She whipped her head around in both directions and spotted him at the right end of the passage. The intruder stopped abruptly, throwing open a narrow door and launching himself inside. The door slammed closed behind him and was jarred open again.

Sarah skidded to a stop in front of the opening, gasping. The tight spiral staircase was shrouded in shadows that evolved into total darkness. No sounds came from within, save a dull and haunting whistle that she hoped was the wind and not the false Shadow taunting her from below. Frozen in indecision, her mind conjured up images of what the darkness held, and they were plenty disturbing to keep her from following. But he *had* gone down there, and each moment she spent thinking about it was another minute lost.

Hurried footsteps brought her head around, and she saw Terrance, the man who'd hired her, running unsteadily down the hall. "I tried to keep up. Did you lose him?" he gasped, leaning on his knees as he fought for breath.

Sarah frowned, knowing that she probably had by now. "I'm afraid so. He went this way," she said, pointing down the stairs and hoping he didn't urge her to follow.

Terrance called the man a vile name that caused her eyes to widen. She was even more surprised when he hurried back in the direction he had come. "Quickly!" he called behind him. Sarah jogged to keep up, her legs starting to feel like Jell-O. But if the man knew of a shortcut to wherever the false Shadow had disappeared, then she could push past the cramp in her side to find answers.

She was confused when he led her back to the main staircase where the majority of the indoor staff had congregated.

"Move!" Terrance shouted, elbowing people out of the way to make room for the both of them.

Sarah's knees nearly gave out at the image before her. A hand covered her mouth as she gasped, freezing in horror before her legs quivered and she dropped to her knees beside the crumpled form.

Edith lay in a puddle of blood, face devoid of color, hands stained with a mixture of her own blood and the ash she hadn't yet rubbed off. Her mouth worked when she saw her, causing Sarah's eyes to fill with tears. She choked on a sob, her hand hovering beside the arrow protruding from the prostrate woman's abdomen, knowing that removing it would only make things worse.

Some sense returning to her, Sarah pressed shaking hands around the stem of the arrow, wondering why no one had thought to stanch the flow of blood that had already created a murky red puddle on Edith's uniform.

"Get help!" Sarah screamed in a frantic voice. A few onlookers scattered, though most remained with forlorn or pitying expressions. She turned back to Edith, whose eyes, pooling with tears, were focused on her. "You're going to be fine," Sarah choked out. There was too much blood! "The doctor's coming." Then she remembered that the physician was in prison. Would there be a replacement?

She tentatively put more pressure on the wound, feeling sick when sticky liquid bubbled up from beneath her palms. Oh, God!

She whispered her reassurances in a quavering voice. "Help's coming." Her stomach roiled in panic and revulsion at the sight of so much blood. A skinned knee usually made her insides quiver, and the sight of thick red liquid flowing over her knuckles was enough to make her pass out. Pressing her lips into a tight line, she tasted the acidic tang of her own blood in her mouth. Edith needed her; she would *not* panic.

Edith shook her head weakly, as if she knew the outcome. But Sarah refused to believe there was nothing they could do to save her. *God, please!* She realized that she had whispered it aloud, and the desperate plea seemed to encompass the intuition of all present, no matter how much they might wish to believe otherwise.

With waning strength, Edith reached up to touch her tear-stained cheek. "I understand . . . now," she rasped, throat working convulsively with the effort to speak. Sarah tried to quiet her, telling her to save her strength for when the doctor arrived. But whatever it was seemed too important to let it go unsaid. "I . . . wanted . . . to tell you."

Sarah shook her head, confused by her mutterings. "I don't know what you're talking about." She knew she sounded frantic, but she couldn't help it with the light fading in Edith's eyes and the flow of blood beneath her fingers slowing on its own.

The hand of the dying woman dropped from Sarah's face. Her chest rose less frequently, and her eyes began to droop. Sarah's own widened in alarm. "No! Edith? Edith, stay with me! What about your boy, your husband? They need you."

Edith released a sigh and met her eyes one final time, the corner of her mouth tipping almost imperceptibly. The look on her gray face was a mixture of joy and sadness. Sarah would never forget her face in that moment, nor the look of longing that burned feverishly in her eyes. "I *am* going . . . to them."

Confused, Sarah's searched her face for the answer, and fresh tears pooled in her eyes when she realized her meaning. She tried to control her sobs. "Oh, Edith. Why didn't you tell me?" Now Sarah understood the haunted, faraway look in her eyes all those times. How had they died? Edith had mentioned that she'd suffered at Cadius' hand when he doubted her loyalty. Was it possible that the death of her loved ones had been the consequence she had alluded to?

By the time Sarah blinked to clear her vision, Edith's head had tipped to the side, eyes once bright with life staring dully at the wall. The small smile was frozen in place, now a sick parody of angelic joy on her lifeless face.

Sarah started, becoming aware that blood no longer pooled beneath her hands. She shook her head, unwilling to believe that Edith was gone, and pressed harder on the wound, as if she could replace the blood lost. "No. No, no, no, no!" She knew she sounded hysterical, but it wasn't really her anymore, just a young girl weeping over a friend. The girl's lips quivered as rivulets of sorrow and pain and guilt ran down her cheeks unchecked. No one tried to pull her from the body.

Sarah's throat constricted as she realized that she had just referred to her friend as "the body." But looking at Edith's pale face now, there was no denying that there was no life, no soul left in this vessel: She was already gone.

Desperate, Sarah started screaming for help, though she knew it was useless. "Get someone, get the doctor! Edith, please. Please come back!" Nothing. No light returned to her eyes.

Pulling her quivering, bloodstained hands back, Sarah tentatively touched Edith's cheek with shaking fingers. Her skin was cold. When she pulled back, she realized that she'd left a smudge of blood on Edith's alabaster cheek.

Choking on a horrified sob, she held the back of her wrist against her lips to keep herself from screaming as she stumbled away. In the back of her mind, she registered the sounds of sobbing, her own horror and sorrow mingling with that of the others in a terrible song of agony that she imagined would forever haunt her dreams.

Now that there was room, some of the men moved in to hover over Edith's body, discussing what arrangements needed to be made in hushed tones.

Sarah shook her head, blocking them out. "I'm sorry," she whispered brokenly, eyes trained on Edith's still form, though her friend could no longer hear her. If she had listened to Edith and hadn't chased him, hadn't ducked . . . Sarah swallowed, backing toward the staircase and cradling her bloodstained hands against her chest.

"Sarah? I heard screaming." She turned to find Damien staring at the terrible scene. He looked tired and had dressed in a haphazard fashion, shirt un-tucked and half-buttoned, his usually perfect hair tousled and sticking up on one side. His cheek was still creased from his pillow, and the mark curved as his bleary eyes widened when he caught sight of Edith's gray

206

face. "Is that . . .?"

Sarah blinked at his horrified expression. He'd heard screaming? Had that been her, or had she imagined that?

When he saw the state she was in, his eyes registered alarm and he gripped her arm as he took in the blood dripping from her fingers. "What happened? Were you hurt?"

She had never heard him sound so angry, or as close to angry as the sweet man could be, but Sarah had no idea how to answer the protective concern in his eyes. Her mouth moved as she worked up an answer, but all she managed was a strangled sound. Wordlessly, she was enveloped in his warm embrace, arms wrapping around her. Sarah couldn't remember ever being held so tightly, as though she would disappear if he let go.

Shaking, she held her bloody palms between them, sure she was ruining his pristine white shirt. But Damien hardly seemed to mind as he stroked the back of her head, crooning softly into her hair, unintelligible words that reached her aching heart. His tenderness and the comfort she felt from him was too much in that moment, and Sarah felt something crack inside of her—internal walls pressing in until she could no longer draw breath in Damien's tight embrace. She was suffocating!

She had to get away from here, from the stench of blood and sorrow that clung to her hair, her skin. She struggled free, though Damien grabbed her wrist to stop her, face twisting in concern. The front of his shirt was smeared with Edith's blood.

With a final glance at what remained of the woman who had taken her under her wing, Sarah did the only thing she could do in that moment.

She broke away from Damien, ignoring his calls, and ran like death was chasing her. And in a sad way, it was.

~Chapter 26~

She stumbled blindly through the dark forest, wind stinging her cheeks where the trails of tears and blood had dried. Dusk had quickly turned to night in the woods, and whatever modicum light remained was obscured by the heavy canopy of trees and gnarled branches, eclipsing the woods in near-darkness. Sparse moonlight found its way into the open spaces, giving the snowcapped trees a ghostly glow.

Sarah swatted branches out of her path, sending a powdery shower of snow behind her retreating form. Thorns and fallen twigs grabbed at the hem of her dress, and she yanked her skirt free, ripping the fabric. She stood, huffing in place.

Before, she had been focused on getting out of the castle and away from the reality of death. But now that the initial panic and hysteria had lessened some, her head began to clear in the cold night air. Was she lost? Nothing looked familiar in this disorienting darkness, and she spun around, eyes nervously sweeping the forest. From this distance, the tallest towers of the castle could still be seen through the sparse breaks in the branches.

Wrapping her arms around herself, she shivered as the adrenaline from her run ebbed. Her dress did nothing to stave off the freezing temperatures in the dense forest that received little warmth from the sun. The foolishness of her actions was not lost on her, but she couldn't spend another moment there, with the smell of her friend's death lingering. She had used some snow to rub as much of Edith's blood from her hands as she could, but it wasn't enough.

Sniffing back her tears, Sarah shuffled onward with no real destination in mind, but the pain in her chest lessened the further she got from the castle looming just over her shoulder. If she kept sight of it, she could find her way back. Not that she wanted to.

Something cracked dully, echoing through the woods. Instinctively, she jumped behind a gnarled pine, breathing heavily as she strained her ears for any noise past the rapid thumping of her own pulse. The sound came again a moment later, and then again, evenly timed, a swift *thwack*. Slowly, Sarah pushed away from the tree and took a few tentative steps up the hill toward the sound of an axe slicing through wood. But civilization meant possible shelter . . .

She continued on hesitantly, nerves shot, jumping each time the axe came down, until the forest was abruptly behind her and she reached the top of the rise. She took in the outline of the small cabin, the thin cloud of smoke puffing up from the chimney, and the dark form beside the house. A piece of wood was tossed onto the growing pile stacked against the side of the small home.

When the man turned to place another log on the chopping block, his face was illuminated by the lantern's glow. Sarah let out the breath she had been holding, wondering if she had meant to come here all along. Maybe she hadn't consciously gone this way, but she knew that even after everything, this was where she needed to be. Maybe Someone else had thought that, too.

Her teeth had begun to chatter, and she pulled her arms tighter to warm herself, pushing her forearms painfully into her stomach. Still, she was hesitant to approach him in the dark while he wielded that axe. Not that he would ever use it on her, but she felt too anxious and jittery to think rationally.

Will glanced up abruptly, examining the line of the forest as if sensing her presence. He squinted past the small circle of light into the darkness. "Who's there?" he called. His grip seemed to tighten on his weapon.

Swallowing, Sarah stepped out of the shadows slowly, giving him plenty of space until he could see that she was just a girl. She bit the inside of her cheek as the shaking intensified—fear and exhaustion were taking their toll on her nerves. She choked back tears at the comforting sound of his voice, but couldn't help wondering if she should have come at all after their disagreement.

Stopping outside the circle of light, she contemplated bolting for the forest again and then immediately shook her head, her mind feeling heavy and muddled. "I'm sorry, I shouldn't have come."

"Sarah," he breathed in surprise, taking a step forward at the quavering note in her voice. "Are you all right?"

Her arms pulled tighter, protecting herself from the cold and the images that pressed in. "Um, I just—there was—" How could she explain what had happened? Why had she thought he would want to hear any of it? She unconsciously retreated a step in her insecurity.

Will laid the axe on top of the stack of wood and shot her a wry glance. "I won't use it, if that's your concern." He grabbed the lantern from the woodpile and held it up to better see her. His indigo eyes widened as he took in her appearance. He seemed momentarily frozen and then was instantly before her, concern etched into every line of his face. "What happened? Are you hurt?"

Damien's exact words, yet coming from Will they felt different somehow. Tears clogged her throat, and it pained her to speak. "It's not my blood." Her voice wavered, and she bit her lip to keep the tears in check.

Without another word, Will whipped off his cloak and threw it over her shoulders, and she clutched it with brittle fingers. Picking up the lantern from the ground, he put a hand to her back and ushered her inside. The warmth of the small cabin nearly made her sigh with relief.

Setting the lantern down, he took her ice-cold hands in his own. He frowned, but when his eyes met hers, they were bright with worry as they searched her face. She waited for the questions and reprimands, but he surprised her by silently leading her to the fire. Sarah sat heavily on the floor, her legs quivering when her weight was off them. Will went to the bed and snagged the heavy knitted quilt, removing the cloak and draping the blanket around her. She wanted to thank him, but the words stuck in her throat.

He left only long enough to truck in a pail of snow. Then he removed the pot of delicious smelling stew that hung over the flames using the hook suspended beside the fireplace. He hung the snow-filled pail from the rod jetting out over the flames and left it to melt.

They were both silent as she stared unseeing at the flames, though out of the corner of her eye, she caught the worried glances he sent her way every few seconds. With blood marking her face and hands as she shivered uncontrollably, she must look like a frightened escapee from a mental hospital. But he made no comment.

Pulling the pail from the fire, Will knelt before her and dipped a cloth in the water. He grasped her chin and gently wiped the smeared blood from her face. Sarah watched him as he worked, the part of her that wasn't numb slightly awed by the fact that he was taking care of her like this after everything that had passed between them. What would the townsfolk say if they could see the large, quiet blacksmith with calloused hands caring for her with such tenderness? His face was concentrated on his task, but the way the muscle in his cheek twitched made her wonder if he, too, wasn't totally unaffected by their nearness.

Will dropped his soft hold on her face and draped the cloth over the side of the pail, and Sarah wondered at the disappointment she felt, which turned to a spark of surprise when he took her small hands in his own, placing them in the warm water. It felt like needles on her freezing skin, and she sucked in a breath as slivers of pain shot through her hands.

"Shhh," he murmured, stroking her wrist with his thumb. Her skin adjusted to the temperature, and she began to relax under Will's

210

surprisingly gentle touch. His work-roughed hands were strong and comforting as he used soft strokes to wipe the crusted blood from her hands and wrists. That same muscle in his cheek spasmed under his skin as he clenched his jaw.

"I . . . can do it," Sarah managed in a wavering voice. He didn't need to take care of her, and his feather-light touch only served to remind her of what she had pushed away.

He drew one of her hands from the water, examining her palm as if he had never seen a human hand before. "You don't always have to be strong, you know," he said softly. A finger traced the cuts she hadn't realized she'd received in the forest. For a few minutes, her blood had mingled with Edith's on her hands. The thought saddened her.

Will's fingers stilled, inquisitive eyes meeting hers. "What happened? You're half-frozen and covered in blood. You can hardly expect me to remain ignorant." His eyes narrowed, darkening to a near-black color she recognized. "Did someone do this to you?"

Though she had never really doubted that he cared for her, Sarah felt a faint thrill at the fact that he hadn't written her off. Then reality pressed in.

Throat tightening, she whispered in a small, shaky voice, "My friend at the castle, Edith, was murdered tonight."

His eyes widened with surprise and sadness. "What happened?" He gave her hand a gentle pulse with his own. His tenderness was more than she could handle, especially when she had no right to it.

She rushed on breathlessly, tears spilling freely over her lids, some of her words choked out by sobs. "We were just there together. I should have listened and gone back. I shouldn't have followed him! She would be alive if I hadn't gone after him." She pulled her hand from his gentle hold and buried her face in her knees, sobbing. She felt like an idiot for acting so hysterical in front of him, but she couldn't stop the pain from spilling over. There had been so much blood.

A second later, she heard Will shift positions. His arm wrapped around her shoulders, and he pulled her against his side. Sarah tried to shove him away with weak arms, but he held her firmly, seeming to know what she needed before she did. Of course he did; he had experienced this kind of grief when his parents died, and he did not need an inconsolable imp crying on his shoulder.

But Sarah collapsed into his embrace, anyway, sobbing into the safety of his shoulder. Sorrow came out of her in waves, and when she thought she had no more tears to cry, she glanced down at her torn hem, which reminded her of what she had been running from. Then the tears started afresh. Eventually, the sobbing lessened, and she was left shivering and silent in his embrace.

Will pressed his lips to her hair, and she imagined that his eyes were closed tightly in remembrance of his own pain. "It does get easier," he murmured.

She nodded mechanically. Tears spent, her head returned to her, and her face heated when she thought of how she had thrown herself into his arms. "Sorry," she whispered, pulling back, too ashamed of her actions to meet his gaze.

He released her, albeit reluctantly. "You have nothing to feel sorry about." His voice was low and soothing.

Guilty sorrow tightened her chest. She looked up at him. He was watching her closely, eyes searching her face. "But it's my fault," she whispered brokenly.

His expression softened with empathy. "How could it be your fault?"

Biting her lip, she whispered, "Because the arrow was meant for me."

Sarah knew she wasn't making sense, but she felt too shell-shocked to make much sense of anything, especially when she was still trying to piece together what had happened.

A large hand came up to cup her cheek, gently turning her head to face him. Will's eyes were bright with the fire that burned just below the surface. Jaw tight, he said, "Who tried to harm you?"

She hesitated, knowing her next words would come as a blow to him. "It was the Shadow. He tried to shoot me."

He pulled back as if she had slapped him. Disbelief etched his features. "*What?*"

Swallowing, she hurried on. "Edith and I heard one of the servants screaming downstairs, and I saw the Shadow"—she stumbled over the name—"running up the stairs. Edith called out for me to stop." She pulled the quilt tighter about her, staring at the ground in shame. "I thought it was you and followed, and then he turned on me with his bow and I knew it was someone else. I chased him for a while, but I lost him. Then your friend, Terrance, found me and brought me back to Edith." Her voice had dropped as the story went on, and it was barely audible when she whispered, "I'd avoided the arrow, but it hit her instead."

When she looked up, Will's expression was mostly blank. The only things that gave him away were the twitching muscle in his cheek and the way his chest rose and fell rapidly. "So this man impersonated me and tried to kill you, but shot your friend instead?" Now he looked torn between hugging her to his chest and ramming his tightened fist into the unknown man's nose.

"I don't think he meant to hurt me, though," Sarah amended, then immediately questioned why she was defending the man who had murdered Edith.

Maybe because he had appeared as frightened and surprised as she.

Will looked disbelieving in her theory, but it seemed clearer to her now.

She scooted closer to him, as if her nearness might convince him. "No, honestly. I couldn't see his face, but he was shaking so badly that I think he was startled into releasing the arrow. He didn't intend to harm anyone."

Will rose abruptly and strode to the fireplace, flexing his hand as though to exorcise the desire to use it. He picked up two flat bowls from the hearth and ladled the thick stew into them. He sat down again, so close that their shoulders touched. Shaking his head, he muttered, "Intentional or not, the fool should never have done something so stupid." He handed her one of the bowls. "It's still warm, and you need to eat something."

With her emotions raging like a confused three-ring circus, Sarah hadn't the least bit of appetite until the stew was before her. Her stomach tightened in hunger at the homey smells that reached her tear-clogged nose, and she gladly accepted the bowl. "I didn't know you could cook."

He shrugged. "Nothing too extravagant—just some venison stew."

"Did you hunt it yourself?" The way Will's gaze flickered to her feet in avoidance told her he had. *Impressive,* she thought. Sarah took another appreciative sniff before savoring a spoonful of deer meat, potatoes, and turnips. She nearly sighed as she swallowed, the tangy warmth heating her insides. She cocked her head curiously to the side. "I didn't know you were a closet gourmet. What else can you make?"

He appeared thoughtful. "Well, I can make stew . . . and stew." She smiled faintly at his attempt at humor, and they lapsed into silence as they ate.

Sarah put her empty bowl aside. "More?" he asked, still working on his own supper.

She shook her head. "No, thanks. I haven't eaten anything that amazing in a while, though." She thought she detected a faint flush creep over his neck, but he ducked his head before she could be sure.

She didn't want to make him uncomfortable by watching him eat, and her mind wandered back to the troubling scene with Edith when she had nothing to focus on, so she let her eyes rove over his one-room home. It was sparsely decorated but neatly kept, and the homey sights and smells eased some of the tension from her body. The comforting presence at her side made it easy to let her guard down, and she realized that she had always felt that way around him.

Thinking back to her encounter with the false Shadow, she swallowed hard, debating whether or not to come clean. *Nothing may ever come of it,* she reasoned, then immediately felt awful for thinking of putting her own feelings before his safety. "Will?"

He glanced up, his expression open.

She swallowed again. It was his life on the line, not hers. "I told you that I thought the Shadow was you at first?" He nodded, brows pulling together, as though sensing where this was headed. Sarah hunched her shoulders, wanting to stop her incessant shivering. "I used your name when I called out to him."

Will's expression was frozen on his face, but his eyes shifted as he thought it over. After a solid minute of silence, he angled his body toward hers. He didn't look upset, just cautious. "Was he the only one who heard you?"

She nodded. "I think so. But I should have thought it through. I'm so sorry. You trusted me with your secret, and I might have blown it for you."

Dark hair fell over his forehead as he shook his head. "No, you were startled. I don't blame you for that in the least. If he even heard you, I doubt it would implicate me in any way—there are at least two other Williams in town, and one who lives in seclusion at the forest's edge. The hermit would most likely be the first they would consider for questioning."

Sarah's eyes widened. "Consider for ques—Will, that sounds serious. Why are you not mad?"

He rubbed the back of his neck. "I am, but at myself. You should never have been in that position—you never would have followed him if you hadn't thought it was me." He shook his head in consternation—at himself, she realized. "I should never have burdened you with my secret."

A hysterical laugh bubbled up from her middle and escaped her lips. He looked startled, and she wiped her eyes. Her nerves and emotions were completely shot, and she wasn't quite sure what the tears were for. "That's funny that you should feel like a burden, since you just took care of a girl who looks like she's been hunting for weeks in the forest." She nodded, rubbing her dry and swollen eyes with the corner of the blanket as she yawned. Granny used to say that if a guy saw her at her worst and didn't run, then he was a keeper. Well, she was officially at her worst, and he didn't appear eager to lace-up his sneakers.

Noticing her fatigue, Will said, "You should sleep."

The thought of going back to the castle and walking past the spot where Edith's blood had stained the floor was highly unappealing. "Can I stay here a little longer?"

He appeared aghast, and she wondered what she had said wrong. "I would never let you walk back in the cold at this hour." He shook his head at the absurd idea and then nodded in the direction of his bed. "No, you can sleep here."

"Oh," she said softly. ". . . But where will you sleep?"

He pulled at the loose collar of his shirt, appearing entirely uncomfortable. Sarah would have laughed if she hadn't felt that same awkward awareness she saw in his face. "The floor, by the fire," he answered simply. Then he met her gaze, eyes a little wider than before. "I never would have asked you—I mean, I realize that it might seem—" He

214

stopped, completely at a loss for words.

Too tired to argue or tell him that it was his discomfort that brought on her own, Sarah rose on unsteady legs and shuffled to the bed. She heard him jump to his feet behind her and watched, amused, as he threw the bedcovers aside so quickly that he nearly ripped the neat tuck-job from the wall.

Murmuring her thanks, she set the quilt on the chest in the corner and slipped gratefully into the bed. It wasn't downy-soft like her bed at the castle, but it was heaven to her exhausted limbs. Will tucked the covers up to her chin, hand hesitating near her face.

Looking up at him, she couldn't form the words, nor did she know just what she was trying to say—apologize, thank him?

He hesitantly moved the hand that had seemed frozen on the blanket up to her cheek, gently stroking away the errant tear that tumbled over her lower lid. Her throat constricted at the tender gesture.

Sarah squeezed her eyes closed, wanting to be strong, to not be a burden, but she felt weak and scared. She opened her eyes. "Will?"

"Hmm?" He murmured, tearing his eyes away from the idle strokes of his thumb to meet her bleary gaze. The change in his expression let her know that he already sensed what she was going to ask, and he dropped his hand.

"Will you stay with me?" She couldn't believe the words had actually escaped her lips and felt ridiculous for asking, like some kind of fragile girl who was trying to pull a fast one. But at that moment she *did* feel fragile, and she kept picturing Edith lying there on that bloodstained rug. She wasn't sure she could ever sleep again, no matter how heavy her lids felt.

Will released a breath, looking reluctant. "I'm not sure that's—"

"Please? Just until I fall asleep." *If I can.*

He searched her face, seeming to sense the brokenness in her gaze. Then he nodded, the smallest of acknowledgements, and grabbed the quilt before crawling hesitantly onto the bed. Sarah turned onto her side to face away from him as the bed shifted under his weight. He sat against the wall at the head of the bed, close enough that his arm grazed her back in the small space. She felt awkward knowing how close he was and wondered if she should have just asked him to sit on the floor and hold her hand—her parents would blow a gasket if they saw her now—but despite her discomfort, Sarah already felt more reassured by his nearness.

"Thank you," she whispered, eyes closing as he settled in beside her, the evening's events weighing heavily upon her. She was almost asleep when she realized he was no longer touching her. She stirred anxiously, too tired to raise her lids. "Will?"

"I'm here," he assured her.

She sighed, relaxing once more. She was practically incoherent by the time she murmured, "That's all I needed to know."

~Chapter 27~

Will watched the steady rise and fall of her back as she drifted off, knowing the exact moment when her breathing evened in sleep. She didn't stir, and he knew he should make his bed on the floor. But he was unable—or unwilling—to move. So he sat there, forearms resting on his raised knees, watching her profile for any indication that she was troubled in her sleep.

Although their relationship had experienced its share of ups and downs, it had given him a spark of hope when she had come—she still trusted *him*!—making Will think that perhaps he hadn't burned every bridge with his stubbornness. And it had felt so natural to take care of and comfort her, the ease of which had frightened him some. He was not used to successful relationships, and if he were being truthful, he wasn't familiar with relationships *period*. The fact that he felt so comfortable around her still amazed him, but it was also a tad disturbing.

It was new and at times tenuous, and he still wasn't sure how to handle it, exactly. But for the first time in his life, Will was determined to make it work—this delicate relationship was too precious to let it go without a fight.

Knowing he was breaking every law of convention by remaining there, he shifted forward to leave, and his movements caused Sarah to stir uneasily in her sleep. He froze, not wanting to wake her from the momentary respite she had found in unconsciousness. Restless, she muttered a few unintelligible syllables and moved her face into the folded blanket he used as a pillow. He winced at the soft sigh she released. It was a sorrowful sound, of which he was sadly familiar.

He had recognized in her wide, panicked eyes the fear and sadness he had experienced after his parents' murders. When he had watched her curl into herself as she wept, Will had felt as though he were gazing upon the wounded lad he once was, recalling the way he put everyone at arm's length so that he might vent his grief in solitude. He knew now that doing so had

216

only made the burden of grief heavier upon his shoulders with no one to suffer it with him, and he had pulled Sarah into his arms when he could no longer stand the thought of her suffering that same sorrow alone.

After a moment of warring within himself, her whimpers became too much for him to bear, and Will quietly slipped down behind her. He pulled the spare quilt over his waist and mirrored the curve of her body beneath the blanket, maintaining a fair two-inches of space between them, though he wanted to touch her shoulder to take the burden he knew rested there and carry it for her. Unlike his self-imposed solitude, she would not have to be alone in her suffering.

"Shh. I'm here," he murmured, brushing the hair back from her face. Her brow was furrowed, and he felt tension radiating from her body. He hesitantly draped an awkward arm over her waist. Even if she wasn't aware of his presence, he needed to let her know that he was here for her.

Sarah muttered something that he didn't catch, but she seemed to have calmed some, and the thrashing ceased as she drifted off again.

He wondered at the last time he had felt this close to someone, even if she *was* asleep. Telling himself that he would only stay another moment, Will rested his head against the mattress and relaxed the tension in his body. When several minutes passed, he told himself to pull away and move to the floor.

But what if she has another nightmare? he countered, unconsciously tightening the protective arm around her. No, he would stay until he was sure she would be all right—five minutes more, he assured his conscience as he closed his eyes and buried his face in the soft waves of her hair, breathing in her scent. He had never been this close to her before, and she smelled wonderful.

"Not a minute more," he muttered. Pulling her closer, he continued murmuring assurances into her hair as he fell asleep.

****

Sarah stirred, resisting consciousness like the plague, though the reason for her swollen lids had already triggered memories of yesterday afternoon. Although the heaviness had lessened a great deal during her sleep, her chest still constricted at the reminder that Edith was gone, though she was too exhausted and dried-up to cry.

Squeezing her eyes closed against the images, she recalled the feel of Edith's hand in her own and tried to focus on that last bit of warmth on her friend's skin. Sarah wasn't sure how she was going to wander the castle again, where everything would remind her of Edith.

Moving to roll onto her back, Sarah felt the mattress shift behind her. The arm she hadn't realized was draped over her waist tightened, and she froze, stifling a shriek of alarm. Prying her heavy and resistant lids open with difficulty, she blinked the grit from her eyes and did a quick survey of her dark surroundings. That's right—she hadn't slept in the castle.

Her eyes widened in realization.

Oh. My. Sweet. Goodness. She turned her head stiffly in the limited space and was just able to make out Will's profile, since his face was buried in her hair. She could feel the steady rise and fall of his chest through the blankets that separated them, his warm, even breaths brushing the skin at the back of her neck.

Her gaze wandered the room desperately, looking for something to help her get out of this situation without waking him—there was no point in both of them being mortified, and her cheeks were already flaming enough for two. But aside from throwing his arm off and having to explain *that* to him, there was nothing to do but wake him.

Sighing, Sarah angled her head toward him and tried not to think about the closeness of his face, which was far too perfect for such an early hour. "Uh, Will?" He didn't stir, and she held her breath and tried nudging him with one of her trapped arms. He snorted, and she bit back a sudden giggle that instantly died in her stomach when he snuggled closer, planting his face in the curve of her neck.

Sarah grimaced. It would have been one of those romantic moments in the movies if she didn't feel so claustrophobic when she thought of the embarrassment he would feel in a few moments. She groaned and looked heavenward. *Really?*

Feeling a tad panicky and trapped, she put a little more elbow into her next jab. Will started, his body jerking in sleep before he settled back to bury his face against the side of her throat, murmuring nonsense into her hair. His arm tightened around her waist, pulling her closer as his lips brushed the tender spot of skin just below her ear.

Releasing a yelp of surprise, Sarah whipped her head back around and shrank into the mattress.

"Wha—?" Will stopped muttering abruptly, his body going board-stiff, and she knew he was awake. Unable to close her wide eyes, she bit her lip and hid her face in the mattress. She tried to cover her quick movements by pretending to stir in her sleep, hoping he wouldn't see through her poor acting.

Will peeled his face from her neck, slowly, and his arm unraveled itself from around her waist with painful slowness. She couldn't be sure, but she thought he held his breath as he crawled with practiced stealth off the bed. He opened the lid of the chest, quietly riffling around inside for a moment before cursing under his breath. Sarah managed to resist the urge to peek at the contents and see what had him so ruffled, and then the lid closed almost noiselessly.

At the sound of shuffling feet, Sarah squeezed her eyes closed and planted her fists beneath her chin, sucking in a breath. Unable to resist, she snuck a glance between her tangled curls and saw his distorted figure collecting his boots and cloak. She thought he might have shot a glance her way before exiting his small home.

He seemed to have bought her little Sleeping Beauty act.

Releasing a breath, Sarah shoved her hair away from her face and flopped onto her back, chest rising and falling as she gratefully dragged air into her deprived lungs. The wood-paneled ceiling didn't provide very interesting distraction, and she quickly became aware of the cool temperature in the cabin without Will's warmth at her back. She hadn't meant for him to stay the *entire* night and knew he must have fallen asleep by accident, judging by his reaction this morning. But when had he gotten so *close*?

She closed her eyes and groaned, mortified at the thought of his presence while she slept. She knew she talked in her sleep, and Sarah nervously racked her brain for any recollection of last night's dreams. All she came up with was a vague memory of dark sadness that did not feel quite so indistinct now that she was awake.

Letting her eyes absently wander the room that was Will's home, her logical side questioned what had been going through her head when she asked him to stay with her. Obviously, she had been emotionally compromised last night, but she had yet again put both of their reputations at risk by spending the night at a bachelor's house, especially after the rumors that had been spread about them during her first visit to Serimone.

But the longer she thought about it, the less she cared for those gossips' opinions of them. Will wouldn't give their quick judgments a second thought, so why should she? She knew that staying here had not been the wisest choice, but next to Karen, he was the only person that she really trusted, and she would *not* have made it back to the castle in her distraught state. Looking back on the previous evening, Sarah realized how much of a comfort Will's presence had been to her. If she had been alone after Edith's death, she was sure she would have fallen apart . . . more than she had.

The thought of her deceased friend caused Sarah's throat to burn with unshed tears. Swallowing thickly, she sat up, raising her knees to rest her cheek against them as she hugged the blankets around herself.

Through the miniscule gap in the shuttered window, she could see that early dawn was just beginning to take the edge off the darkness. She fought a wave of sudden grief at the way everything went on as always. It wasn't as though she expected life to stop when Edith's ended, but how could the world continue on its usual course in the wake of such a tragedy? It didn't seem right that everyone could go on so unaffected, oblivious to her death or presence in the world, having made it brighter for those who knew her. Sarah felt a pang of sadness for the people who would never know what an amazing woman and friend she had been.

A cold blast of air swept into the room through the open door. Will tapped his boots against the doorframe to banish the excess snow and glanced up, catching her eye. He smiled hesitantly, his gaze wary, either due to what happened last night or where he had awakened this morning. "You're up." His voice was still gravelly from sleep and dark circles lined his eyes, though they were already bright and alert.

Sarah straightened quickly, not wanting to appear quite so pathetic in her cowed position, though she knew she must look awful with her swollen eyes and the bird's nest that was her hair. She tried to subtly force the strands into some semblance of order but knew it was futile without a comb. Or a weed whacker.

Deciding it was useless to fight nature, Sarah let her arms drop. How did the women in movies wake up confident and gorgeous? She could barely keep her puffy eyes open and was fairly certain she had drooled sometime in the night. Subtly, she wiped the corner of her mouth on her shoulder, wondering if she should pinch some color into her cheeks when he turned the other way.

Just the thought made her feel ridiculous.

Even when he appeared tired, Will had a commanding presence that filled the room and demanded everyone's attention, and the dark shadows on his cheeks made him look more ruggedly handsome than usual. *That's fair*, she thought wryly.

Feigning a chill, she hiked the blankets up a little higher to cover her embarrassment. Oh, well. She had just bared her heart to the man last night and he had yet to run, so maybe a little drool wasn't such a turn-off.

The silence stretched on. "Morning," she whispered in a small voice.

Will closed the door with his foot and dropped his load of wood to dry by the fireplace. Straightening, he rubbed the scruff on his jaw, watching her. Sarah flushed under his inscrutable gaze and averted her eyes. "Are you feeling better?"

She nodded and forced herself to meet his gaze. She owed him that much. "Thanks to you. And, um, sorry about last night. I've never really fallen apart like that before." She managed a chuckle that sounded nervous even to her own ears.

Tilting his head to the side, Will studied her expression. "I hardly did anything."

Rubbing the corner of one bleary eye to wipe away some of the stain from last night's tears, she sighed wearily. "You did more than you know." The tenderness that entered his expression at her words caused her chest to tighten.

220

"I was glad you felt you could come to me." He took a few steps closer to the bed, though his gaze was still wary.

Testing his reaction, Sarah asked, "Even if you had to sleep on the floor?"

He hesitated. "I've slept in worse places." Safe answer.

Before she could think of a reply, he asked her if she was ready for some breakfast. Never one to pass up the opportunity to tease, and because it was easier than focusing on the painful memories of yesterday, her lips tipped in humor. "Stew?"

Will's own mouth quirked. "What else?"

Shaking her head, her smile faded. "That sounds delicious, but I don't think I'm quite up to eating before the sun rises. And I should be getting back," she added regretfully, more than a little uneasy over leaving this small zone of comfort.

He looked reluctant as he nodded and turned toward the door, though he didn't move from the spot. Cocking his head over his shoulder, Sarah caught the boyish shyness and excitement that she so rarely was allowed to see. "There's something I would like to show you first."

She worried her lower lip, contemplating, and then she gave an assenting bob of her head. Rubbing the back of his neck, Will clarified, "It's outside."

"Oh. I'm not sure I'm dressed for that." Peeling the covers back, she pretended not to notice the spare blanket he had used, nor the indentation where his body had been.

Will averted his eyes as she adjusted her skirt to cover her legs. He went to the cedar chest and extracted a black cloak and an extra pair of boots, throwing some leather gloves on top of the stack. He held them out to her in offering. "They are a little big, I know, but we won't be going far."

Curious, Sarah donned the cloak and sat on the bed while she laced up the over-sized boots. She stood and took a few wobbly steps, knowing she must look like a lumbering zombie. Still feeling a little embarrassed over her tirade last night, despite his assurances, she grinned up at him in an attempt to smooth the tense atmosphere in the cabin. "You've got big feet, Taylor."

He shrugged, though there was relieved humor in his indigo eyes. "They've served me well."

"Scaling walls?" She was no longer teasing, just genuinely interested.

"Yes," he answered honestly.

Curling her toes in the ample space, Sarah eyed him. "Because you got into my room rather easily."

His lips tipped. "That was hardly the first time I've snuck into the castle, as you well know."

Before she could get caught up in the easy banter she was rarely used to between them, she asked, "Didn't you want to show me something?"

Nodding, Will led her from the house and around the back, trudging slowly through the snow to give her a cleared place to step. It was difficult to see his footsteps with the pines and gnarled forest trees preventing the early morning light from brightening the path.

Keeping her eyes focused on his footsteps, Sarah lifted her knees high as she clomped through the snow behind him, sometimes having to jump to reach the path his footsteps had cleared when the snow became too thick. Eyes focused on the next patch of compressed snow, she missed the fact that her companion had stopped and launched herself right into his back, nearly toppling them both.

Will regained his balance and spun around to right her. "Steady." Face heating, she looked up at his amused expression.

"Why did you stop?" She looked around. There wasn't anything there.

In answer, he pointed a finger toward the sky. Sarah followed the line and glanced up at the enormous beech tree, which was a huge mass of low, reaching branches and gnarled limbs stretching far overhead.

He turned to her, his face partially shrouded in the early dawn light. "How are you at climbing?"

She hesitated. "Not nearly as good as you. Is it up there—whatever you want to show me?"

"Do you think you will be able to climb in those boots?"

Hugging herself to stave off the morning chill, she shot a wary glance up the massive length of trunk and was reminded of all the trees she and Lilly had climbed together. Granted, those trees were much, much smaller, but it couldn't be that different. Releasing a breath, she said, "I guess we'll find out."

Will helped her onto the first branch and then pointed out the knobs in the ancient trunk, showing her how to jam the toe of her boot in to give her a little leverage until the next available branch. It was slow going at first as Sarah tried to awkwardly get a foothold with her feet slipping around inside her boots as they navigated the tangled limbs. But Will stayed beside her and showed her how to lean against the branches to relieve some of the strain from her arm muscles. "You'll tire quickly if you carry your weight all the way," he warned.

Biting her lip in concentration, she watched his feet and mimicked his confident movements. Sometimes her glove would slip or a boot would become trapped in a jagged notch, but after a few minutes of gracelessly plugging along behind Will, she began to feel more confident and found herself enjoying the thrill of climbing so high.

When Will glanced over at her to see how she was fairing, she motioned him ahead. "You know where we're going—you lead."

With a nod, he took off, his movements becoming quicker and more precise as he ascended. Mesmerized by his lithe movements, Sarah paused to watch, sometimes losing sight of him as he ducked through the patches of fresh sunlight that snuck between the limbs. Her stomach constricted at the sight of him so in his element. This was where he belonged, in the forest where he experienced the kind of freedom on which he seemed to thrive. Suburban Oklahoma could never satiate that need for independence.

The thought surprised her. Though she hadn't even been aware that she was considering it, after seeing him like this, Sarah knew she could never ask him to give up this kind of freedom and leave Serimone behind. It wouldn't be fair to him.

But despite the ache building in her chest, she felt a soft, reluctant smile tug at the corner of her mouth as she watched him swing from branch to branch. The difference between this carefree Tarzan and the reserved Will to whom she had first been introduced was amazing. Her smile spread: The man was in love with this land.

Will chose that moment to glance down at her, as if just now realizing how far ahead he had climbed, and caught her smile. His mouth curved in a knowing way, and he began to descend with strides a tad more boastful than before.

Caught staring, Sarah tried to look nonchalant, resting her back against the branch behind her like she had been taking a break and just *happened* to look up at that moment.

He slipped gracefully down and landed on the limb opposite. "I thought you were behind me," he commented, grinning coyly. He gripped the branch above both their heads with one hand, lazily swinging his body toward her and away, coming close enough that Sarah could touch him with little effort.

Folding her arms across her chest, she pretended to ignore his playfulness and turned her eyes to the spot where he had been. "I saw a squirrel and thought it might give you rabies." She shrugged, feigning disinterest, though he wasn't so easily fooled.

Will's low chuckle brought her head around. He used his momentum to swing himself onto the limb closest to her, sending a shower of white into the air. He ducked to grip the branch above her head, boxing her in as he leaned forward. Though he didn't appear to realize how close he was, Sarah was *very* aware of his nearness and sucked in a breath. His eyes were brighter and more alive than she had ever seen them as they searched her face, his chest rising and falling from his climb. "Rabies?" he asked, confused humor lacing his question.

"It's—" She swallowed, her eyes inadvertently drawn to the rapid pulse just below his ruddy cheeks. "You know what—never mind."

He didn't seem to be aware that the carefree grin still graced his lips.

Pulling back, Will ducked under the branch again. "It isn't far," he said. When she hesitated, he reached a hand out to her, puffs of air escaping his lips in little white clouds that faded in the air between them. "I'll stay with you."

Gnawing on her lower lip, Sarah took his hand and they began to climb together, side by side.

~Chapter 28~

When Sarah's weary muscles felt ready to give, her guide stopped. Leaning against the branch behind her, she tried to steady her breathing.

Brushing the powdery snow from the massive, waist-high branch, Will hoisted himself up and got situated before offering her a hand. The perch came up to her chin, and she knew she wouldn't be able to manage it gracefully. Gripping his hand, she launched herself upward and landed on her stomach with an "*Oof!*" Auburn hair flew over the width of the limb, and she tossed her head back in time to catch his expression of amused surprise before he wiped it from his face. "You were supposed to wait for me." He used his hold to help her into a sitting position.

Sarah grimaced sheepishly, resisting the urge to rub her bruised abdomen. "I get that now."

He did a fair job of hiding his grin as he shuffled toward the middle of their perch. "Come on."

Shooting a nervous glance at the itty-bitty patch of visible ground far below, she slowly pushed herself onto her knees and followed him. "Can this thing hold the both of us? I mean, will it snap and send us plummeting to an unfortunate death?" Her sarcasm didn't mask her genuine trepidation.

Having reached his destination on the outermost part of the tree, Will reclined against the knotted limb behind him. "I suppose we'll find out," he said, using her words against her with a teasing smile.

She ignored his remark and crawled determinedly down the length of the branch, biting back her fear as she entered a narrow clearing where the pines and gnarled limbs disappeared on all sides.

Sarah sucked in a breath, understanding why he had wanted to show this to her. "Wow," she breathed, plopping down beside him, her anxiety melting away in place of awe. Her shoulder brushed his as she leaned back to survey the view, reassured by the wall of tangled branches at her back. "This is . . ."

"Incredible, isn't it?" She looked up at him and nodded, eliciting a soft smile from him with her look of amazement.

Sarah turned her gaze back to the sight before them, blinking against the light. They were perched in one of the tallest trees in all of Serimone, it seemed, and they had a perfect view of the rising sun from their vantage point. It cast a bright orange glow through the trees, and golden light reflected off the high stone towers of the castle. From this distance, it didn't look so dark and haunting, and she could almost pretend in the early morning glow that it wasn't a prison at all but a fairy tale castle. . . . Almost.

No matter where she drew her gaze, the whole land looked bright and alive—sunlight was reflected wherever she looked, bouncing off the snow below and making the ground look like it had been sprinkled with glitter, sparkling like a carpet of diamonds strewn about the forest floor.

"The world looks better from up here, doesn't it?" Will commented softly, breaking into her intense fascination with the view. "Safer."

She nodded mutely, gently kicking her feet back and forth in the vast expanse before them. "Is this your thinking place, then?"

"In a way."

They lapsed into silence again, and Sarah found herself studying him. He looked so at peace, the lines of his face softening in the early morning light. Strangely moved by the sight, she turned her gaze away, back to the rising sun, and was suddenly struck by the realization that yesterday had been Edith's last sunrise.

Her shoulders sank as reality pressed in. Rubbing her hands together in her lap, she asked in a small voice, "Does it ever get easier?"

He angled his head toward her, his eyes filled with compassion. "In some ways. After a time, you don't dwell on it every moment, don't feel as though you're suffocating with grief. But then one day you realize you have reached the night and haven't wanted to give up." He inhaled a wavering breath. "Then you fight guilt, because it seems that you should dwell on the life that once was. But what you're really holding onto is what will never be."

Sarah sniffed back unwelcome tears at his soft words. If anyone had a reason to mourn, it was he. "She was a good friend to me, but I knew her so little that I don't feel I have any right to mourn." She groaned at her selfishness and pain, leaning forward to bury her face in her hands—she could still feel Edith's blood spilling through her fingertips.

Disgusted at the memory and her inability to do anything, her head rolled from side to side in her hands. "I didn't even know her family was dead, and it's all my fault that she is, too. I couldn't stop the blood."

A hand touched her shoulder. "Look at me," he commanded softly.

Too ashamed to meet his eyes, she muttered a disgruntled "What?" through her fingers. He gently peeled her hands from her face and pulled

226

them toward him. Sarah looked up at him reluctantly and released a shuddering breath as she tried to keep from crying again; he had dealt with enough of her emotions for one lifetime.

"What you experienced was traumatic—give yourself time to heal," he said. "And don't blame yourself for something that was out of your hands. We can't go back and change the past, and it will only eat at your soul to dwell on what might have been."

She sighed. How right he was. Even with the ability to travel through time, she couldn't go back and save Edith. "Is that why you come up here?" she asked. "To remind yourself that life goes on—the sun will still rise?"

He nodded and released her, leaning back again. "After my parents, I used to sneak out of my uncle's house before dawn and come here. At first it was to remind myself of them and relive the pain of my loss. But then over time, this view became a symbol of . . . healing, I suppose. That was the reason why I built my home here—so that I could come to this sanctuary whenever I needed to clear my head.

"Sometimes" he went on thoughtfully, "it feels as though your healing and happiness betray their memory, and you have to fight remorse. But however cruel or tragic it might seem for life to move on, it's the natural order of things and the way my parents would want it to be. And whenever I come up here"—he inhaled deeply, seeming to savor the crisp morning air—"it's as though my soul is being reawakened. I feel alive and new, like the world is full of possibilities." He looked suddenly embarrassed. "But that sounds nonsensical."

"Who would you be?" Sarah asked suddenly, reclining beside him. Feeling the unexplainable need to be close to someone, she impulsively scooted nearer, attempting subtlety until she bumped her shoulder into his arm. But he didn't seem to mind when he glanced down—in fact, she thought he might have smiled a little.

"What do you mean?" he asked.

"I mean that if you had the chance to do it all over, be anybody in the world from that sunrise"—she pointed out to the panoramic view before them, then hiked her thumb in the opposite direction—"to that sunset, who would you be for a day?"

He let his head fall back against the raised branch and stared up at the brightening sky through the limbs above them. "My father," Will answered without hesitation.

She blinked, moved by his answer. "Really? I bet you're a lot like him."

Sitting up abruptly, he angled his body to face her. His eyes were filled with childlike excitement. "We were alike, in a way. We both *craved* adventure. My father used to tell me of his grand escapades when he was my age. He fought bandits and once stole a pirate ship in the dead of night, fending off the entire crew with a single sword and knife." He did a few harmless parries and jabs in the air, reenacting the legendary fight for her.

Sarah giggled at his antics, knowing he was probably putting on a bit of a show to lift her spirits. He held up one finger. "He even discovered where that cad who captained the ship had buried over a decade's worth of loot."

Her eyes bulged. "He uncovered buried treasure?"

"Yes, but he gave it to the people of the island on which he found it, saying that this stolen treasure had no owner and so should belong to them."

Sarah leaned back, wondering how much of these stories had been embellished for his son's entertainment. But then again, maybe they were all true. Like father, like son.

She smiled at both Will and his father's adventurous spirits. Sitting up, she asked, "But, wait, did your dad stop seeking out adventure? What happened?"

She didn't understand the slow grin that started over Will's mouth. "When he was about my age, Father discovered a posting for a rather handsome reward. It seemed that some precious cargo had been taken by a band of rogues traveling from the Holy Land. Treasure-hunter that my father was, he went in search of them on horseback. He found their caravan up on a hillside, quickly trying to make a getaway with their prize."

"Did he catch them?"

Will grinned proudly but didn't spoil the ending. "My father was fast. He rode up beside the caravan, unseated the driver, and then threw himself inside of the careening transport as it flew across the valley, managing to disarm the men inside and extricate them from the caravan in seconds. Then he steered the horses a safe distance away before stopping to peek at the cargo."

She waited for him to finish the story, which sounded as though he had it memorized by heart. His father's tale, told on countless nights, had clearly imprinted on his boy's memory. "Well, what was it?" she asked impatiently when he remained silent.

His animated story-telling manner melted away, and Will stared thoughtfully at the tree bark under his hand. He shifted so that his back touched the short wall of branches behind them. "They had taken my mother to sell her in their country. She had thought it was all over until my father came riding up on his horse." He gave Sarah a lopsided grin. "She said she thought Father was some beautiful, pale-skinned savage with dark hair flowing in the wind come to save her." He chuckled at the description only a girl could appreciate.

Sarah smiled along with him. "And were they married after that?"

"Yes. Father refused the reward money her parents offered and asked for her hand instead. Then he settled down and built the shop I now own."

228

A smile of remembrance graced his mouth. "Every night that he regaled me with the tale, Father ended by saying that he gave up his nomadic wandering the day he discover my mother. 'My restlessness drove me to seek out adventure and the treasures therein,'" Will intoned in a deep voice, mimicking his father. He hesitated, and his gaze on her face warmed, voice softening as he recited the words.

"'But when I found her, I knew that my restless spirit could not be satiated by the fleeting excitement I'd pursued on my voyages. My goal, I realized, had always been to find something to give my soul rest: She was the treasure I'd sought all along, and I needn't search any further.'"

Sarah smiled a little wistfully, though her insides had warmed at the sincerity in his voice, as if he weren't simply reciting his father's words but meant them for *her*. "That's all so romantic. Your father sounds like an amazing man."

"He was." Will leaned in and stretched his arm out toward the golden horizon, pointing off to the right of the castle. "Do you see that stream and how the rough portion seems to disappear?"

Squinting, Sarah pretended not to feel how close he was and tried to focus on the line of his finger. "Is that a waterfall?" she asked after a moment of searching.

He nodded, watching her face while she looked for it. "Glenborough Falls. The stream goes underground for several miles north. *And*," he added, pointing off in that direction, "perfectly opposite the falls, if you look hard enough, you'll see the stream reemerge in the distance and then vanish between those hills. Directly past that point, just over the rise, there is a little village in the valley behind. Do you see it?"

Her eyes were still scanning for the correct hill, but then she spotted a little grouping of tiny specs in a small valley, barely discernible from this distance. "What is that place?" she asked, meeting his gaze.

Will smiled. "It's Locksley Village, where I grew up. Just beyond is Sherwood Forest, which works as a barrier between Locksley and Ridlan, though . . ."

Her mind was already wandering. *It can't be—there's no way. It's impossible.* But what were the odds? It was the right era for the legend, and he had lived in a village with the same name. She had even referred to him as Robin Hood when she first discovered the Shadow. Could they really be one in the same?

But that could only mean Karen's theory that Serimone was somehow created by the portal was seriously flawed. She had gone into great detail about the consequences of changing the past, especially the outcome of significant events and the course of prominent figures. If this was, indeed, the past, then they could really be muddling things up right now.

At the idea that her presence was completely unwelcome in this time,

Sarah's mind took off trying to recreate events here without her presence: She would never have been able to help Karen, nor met the Jones family, and she would never have met Will. But if she hadn't been here, Edith might still be alive.

Sarah selfishly didn't know what she would do differently if given the chance. But she knew what the right thing to do was after they proved Cadius' guilt: She would walk away and try not to look back. It would be best for Will if she didn't meddle with history, and she knew that, someday, it would be best for her too.

She leaned her head against his shoulder in the middle of his story, closing her eyes against the painful decision she had just made. But she chose to enjoy this moment for all it was worth. Because somewhere deep down inside of her, in the place that she never liked to stare at too hard, she knew that now was all they had. Anything more was simply a fantasy. She would allow herself to enjoy these last fleeting moments in a world that she had grown to love with the man she had fallen for.

It suddenly felt like she was being cheated of the greatest blessing she had ever been given, and the strings attached to this gift were about to snap. She wouldn't think about the time when they would say goodbye and she would leave him one final time.

Her eyes dropped to the ground below, and she squinted at a small patch of yellow and white. It was hard to make out against the snow, but . . . Sarah blinked. Wild daisies! Briefly, she wondered if Will had dropped that flower the other day, though she knew he hadn't come by. . . . Her heart sank when she realized that he might have seen her and Damien together.

"You seem troubled," Will murmured. She realized he had stopped talking some time ago.

"Do you ever wish you could travel?" she asked abruptly.

Nodding, his voice became far away. "My father traveled the whole world and saw places that I've never even read about in the books he gave me—I've only ever explored the world through his stories as a boy. This is the closest I've come to escaping, and I can still see my childhood home from here." His look turned hopeful. "Perhaps someday I can show Locksley to you. I believe you would like it."

Sarah leaned back. "Why not?" she asked, surprising herself. But now that the words were out of her mouth, she knew where they were going, crazy and impulsive as they might be. But after losing Edith in such a horrific way, she couldn't bear the thought of saying goodbye to anyone else right now.

His brow furrowed. "What do you mean?"

"Let's leave this place," she whispered, feeling a panicked tightening in her stomach as she said the words, but it was too late to take them back. Escape was the only answer, though she didn't want to acknowledge *what*

230

she was running from. Death, failure, loss—she couldn't face any of that right now.

Sarah continued breathlessly, "We'll got to Locksley and you can show me where you grew up—let's have our *own* adventures. Just there and back, though," she amended quickly, knowing she could never abandon her family, but she was desperate to get away from this place and the harsh memories it held for a few days. She was teetering on the edge of a precipice, but if taking a step back meant leaving everyone behind, then she was tempted to jump if it prolonged the inevitable.

But was she ready to leap?

Will stared at her like she'd gone mad. And maybe she had. "We can't possibly."

She felt her shoulders sink. "So you don't want to run away with me?"

"It's not that I don't *want* to," he said, sounding frustrated and a little desperate. He raked a hand through his hair, sending it every which-way. "But not like this, Sarah—not like this. I can't—"

She held up a hand, already feeling more than a little ridiculous. She could tell he was going to refuse, but she couldn't hear the words; it was her last chance at temporary freedom, and she didn't feel like her heart could heal if she stayed. "Don't answer now. I'll be at that brook you took me to at sunset tonight. If you come, then we'll leave. And if not"—she choked back her cringe at the thought—"then I'll have my answer. Please, Will, I'm suffocating here, and I know you want to get away, too."

Releasing a tight breath, he rubbed the back of his neck in agitation. His expression was torn. "All right. I will meet you tonight no matter what." He tipped her chin with his finger, forcing her to meet his penetrating gaze. "But you must ask yourself if this is truly the future you want—you can't always come back from a choice."

She swallowed, already second-guessing her rash decision but hating the alternative more. "Okay."

Shaking his head, Will told her that they should get her back before people started to panic. They climbed down the tree in silence, the mood between them severely dampened as Sarah's words weighed heavily on both their minds.

"Thanks," she murmured as he helped her onto the ground. His hands stayed on her waist, and she looked up at him, confused.

His face was earnest as he leaned closer. "Always remember that you are so much stronger than you believe and more capable than you think possible." His lips curved in a bittersweet smile as he shook his head. "You might not realize it yet, but you don't need me anymore—my work has been finished for some time."

Sarah watched his face closely. "What are you talking about?"

"I used to believe that my life was only worth something if it was lost saving someone or if I spent every moment immersed in adventure." He grazed her cheek with his fingertip. "But you showed me that life isn't about that at all."

"What is it about, then?" she asked, feeling small and lost.

Tucking a strand of hair behind her ear, he gave a promising smile. "Perhaps I'll tell you someday."

Sarah thought about what awaited her back at the castle and the warmth she was leaving here. "Do I have to go back?" Her lids drooped sadly, and he surprised her by pulling her into his arms and holding her tight against his chest, though he made no reply. "I wish things were different," she whispered. She didn't bother to specify—there were too many things she wished she could change.

"It will all work itself out in the end. You'll see."

She nodded mutely. But even as he held her close and told her everything was going to be all right, she couldn't shake the feeling that a storm was coming, and if they couldn't fight it together, it was going to tear them apart.

~Chapter 29~

Closing her eyes did not help. It momentarily blocked out the image of the castle rising up to meet the sky as she neared, but even with her eyes closed, Sarah acutely felt the oppression of the place grow with each step that brought her closer. She opened her eyes, slowing her pace as she came to the back gate, wanting so much to rush in and pack her things, but dreading the moment when she would step inside yet again. She felt inexplicable trepidation over entering the place, fearing that she would somehow become trapped the instant the door closed behind her, leaving her at the mercy of the cruel man she was investigating.

Knowing she would continue to invent these crazed notions as long as she put off the inevitable, Sarah squared her jaw and wrapped Will's cloak tighter around her as she hurried along. He had firmly "requested" that he be her escort through the forest, but she had insisted that she was only going back to tie up loose ends before tonight. And she did not want *anything* distracting him from making a decision.

Sarah walked through the snowy clearing at the backside of the castle, avoiding eye contact with the guard stationed in the watchtower. Though she looked disheveled, he must have noticed her elegant gown depicting her status as a lady, because he let her pass without a word. Sarah released a pent-up breath.

Instead of using the back entrance, she wandered around the side, moving under the archways between the wood gate and the castle walls. Back when Will had shown her around town, the incredible architecture of the flying buttresses had been visible to all, and now they were hidden behind the protective gate, nearly obscured from an outsider's view. *What a waste,* she thought sadly.

She kicked her boots—Will's boots—against the doorframe to the servants' entrance to knock off bits of snow and dirt. She paused for the briefest moment with her hand poised on the knob. Knowing she would only overthink things the longer she hesitated, Sarah shoved the door open and stumbled inside.

She sucked in a staggering breath. The air felt heavy after coming from the freshness of the forest, and she felt something recoil inside of her at the smell permeating the hall. It was so indistinct that she knew it shouldn't repulse her, but there was something about it that made her cringe and raised the hairs on the back of her neck. She was reminded of the times her parents had talked to her and Lilly about spiritual forces that could inhabit places, as well as people.

Before, she had thought it was her imagination overreacting whenever she experienced such a negative response to the castle, but standing in that hall made her sure of the presence of a dark, oppressive spirit that had domain over this place. What sort of evil had Cadius unwittingly let into the castle by allowing the blackness inside of him to thrive? It had probably rotted him from the inside out and had nothing left to do but escape into the castle walls, infecting the rest of the place with that repressive spirit.

Sarah couldn't wait to get out of there.

Closing the door soundly behind her, she fairly jogged out of the dark corridor and up the staircase, momentarily forgetting where she was headed. When she reached the top of the stairs, she froze instinctively, her body remembering the awfulness of last night before her head registered why she was stopping.

She swallowed and forced her eyes to look at the spot where Edith's body had lain. She expected some sign of the horror she had seen— splattered blood, strips of torn fabric lying about—but the floor had been thoroughly scrubbed, and the soiled rug had been removed and replaced with one of dark blue. There was no evidence of what had transpired hours before.

Sarah walked toward the spot in a daze, eyes searching for some symbol that Edith had been there, but of course, there was nothing. Crouching down on the floor, she touched the fabric of the rug, wondering where they had taken the body. It wasn't that she wanted to see it and be forced to remember her friend as a ghost, but she wanted to know that they were treating her with respect.

A sound down the hall caused her to turn that way, and her eyes caught sight of a yellowed piece of fabric lying just behind the doorway. Sarah walked over to the room and bent down to scoop it up, turning it over to examine it. She bit her lip, tears filling her eyes when she noticed the small red *E* hand-embroidered onto the corner of the handkerchief. It still bore the marks of the ash Edith had wiped from her hands.

She sniffed back her sorrow. Edith must have dropped it yesterday when they had run from the room at the maid's cries. Impulsively, she stuffed the worn piece of fabric into her sleeve.

234

"My lady?"

Sarah quickly wiped a thumb under her eyes and looked over at Terrance, who stood on the top step, gripping the banister as if unsure whether or not he should take another step.

"They cleaned up quickly." Her voice cracked, and she cleared her throat.

Moving with more poise than someone his age should possess, Terrance came to stand before her. He looked as drained as she felt. "We couldn't leave her here," he whispered. "The smell, and all."

Sarah nodded despondently, rubbing the pad of her thumb to expel nervous energy. "I know. But what did they do with her? Do you know? Is she already . . .?" She couldn't quite bring herself to say the word *buried*.

With only a brief hesitation, he answered slowly, "Most bodies are taken outside of the city gates for burial. It prevents animals from coming inside. And, yes, we already took care of the arrangements."

Her shoulders slumped. "Outside the gates?" She wasn't sure what she had expected, but she had wanted to be able to say goodbye one last time and pay her respects. How was she supposed to find her before she left?

Terrance leaned forward, and she resisted the urge to pull back at his sudden proximity. He looked around nervously, but they were alone. "Normally the guards take care of this sort of thing when it occurs inside the walls, but I've seen the place where they dump deceased servants." He shivered. "A large unmarked grave out in the darkest part of Thornwood. . . . I didn't want that for her. Myself and a few of the other servants took the body before the guards could get ahold of her and put her to rest last night."

"You did?" Sarah perked up some at the thought that Edith's body hadn't been discarded on top of a pile of faceless corpses. "Where is she?"

"Deep in the rose garden. She loved the flowers." He smiled, seeming to lose himself in a bittersweet memory for a moment before shaking himself back to the present. He gave her a reassuring nod. "We made sure it was a proper burial for a proper lady." Sarah smiled at that.

Terrance tipped his head to the side. "Would you, erm, like to visit her? Pay your respects?" At her eager nod, he added, "It isn't marked, really, since we can't give the guards a clue of what we've done. But there was a rosebush that had been planted earlier this year, so it's fairly small—just three branches that all appear to be growing straight up, twirling around each other. We knew how much she had loved that little sprite, and so we uprooted it and moved it to where she rests. You'll know which tree it is."

Sarah swallowed back the tightness in her throat. "That's really beautiful. She would have loved it."

The older man seemed to get misty-eyed. "She was fond of you, I know. You can go see her anytime you like."

"I can't thank you enough for what you did for her."

235

"I've been looking everywhere for you!" Sarah jerked and spun around. Terrance slipped away silently just as Damien strode up to her, stopping a few inches away and looking so relieved that he wanted to embrace her. His eyes searched her face worriedly. "After what happened, I wondered if the vigilante had somehow taken you captive."

Sarah shook her head weakly, feeling drained. "No, I wasn't kidnapped. I just needed to get away to clear my head. I—" She bit her quivering lip.

Nodding, his fingers brushed her hand tentatively. At the way her eyes filled with tears, Damien didn't hesitate to pull her into an embrace. She almost wrapped her arms around him before thinking to curl her hands into fists, which she planted between their two bodies, using them as a shield against him and the comfort she found in his arms. She didn't want any reasons to back out of her plan to leave with Will, and just seeing Damien instantly caused her to doubt if what she was doing was right. But she couldn't stay here anymore, that much she knew.

Sarah pulled away, sniffing back her insecurity and putting a defensive wall between them. She couldn't look Damien in the eye. If she did, she was sure her resolve would crumble. "Sorry." She gave a mirthless laugh. "I seem to be falling apart."

"No apologies." He placed a hand on her shoulder, and she met his warm gaze. "I can only imagine . . ." He shook his head, appearing upset. "I'm sorry I didn't—that I wasn't—"

"It wouldn't have gone differently," she answered truthfully, sensing his guilt over not having been there.

"Perhaps it would have," he murmured, almost to himself, as he rubbed his arm.

Sarah suddenly remembered that she had bolted yesterday before she could tend to his wound. She had been too emotional to think straight last night. "Did you get someone to take care of your arm?" she asked, motioning to his shirtsleeve.

"Hmm? Oh, yes. And this morning, as well." He smiled, obviously touched that she had remembered. Cocking his head to the side, his expression became pinched with sympathy. "I understand why you weren't able to do it, so don't feel badly. Please."

Sarah took a deep breath and let it out. "I'll try." Though it was difficult when she remembered that she was going to leave him at the hands of some other, more qualified nurse. She barely contained her wince at the thought of one of the young maids touching him, laughing and whispering intimate secrets with Damien—

Sarah blinked and swallowed hard, feeling shaken for more reasons than she could count at the moment. When had he become more than a patient, than a friend, to her? The evolution of their platonic relationship-turned-friendship had been quick, but she hadn't expected her feelings for Damien to grow any further. It came as a surprise to realize that their "friendship" was dangerously close to becoming something else entirely, and she'd chosen to ignore the obvious signs for some time now.

It would be for the best if she put some distance between them, she decided. So why did the thought cause her so much pain?

Damien pasted on a bright expression, but she could tell it was forced for her benefit. "Are you in need of distraction? We have yet to attend supper together, so perhaps tonight is just the time to do it."

"Yeah. Yeah, okay." Sarah felt a stab of guilt at the way his face lit up. What would he think when he came for her and found her room empty?

It didn't matter anyway. She would be long gone by then.

****

She cinched the opening of the sack she'd had one of the servants bring to her an hour ago. It had sent a pang through her chest when the young girl, who was not Edith, came to her room.

Her hands shook as she finished closing her makeshift bag, and she gripped the fabric to stop their nervous shaking. Was she making a terrible mistake? She had never been very good at being impulsive, and this was about as reckless an idea as they came. She was planning on running away with a man—one she trusted, yes, but how well did she really know him? Was it only because he had shown her comfort, and in her desperation she had clung to that one fleeting hope?

"We'll be back in a few days," she assured herself in the empty room, though the anxiety roiling in her stomach made her question her decision. Was she only following through with her thoughtless plan because she was afraid to back out?

Terrified of what she might find if she dwelt on it for too long, Sarah quickly slung the heavy-laden sack over her shoulder. Then she threw on a cloak to cover her baggage, realizing that the lump made her look like a hunchback. Oh, well. It wasn't like they could actually stop her, could they?

She hiked her load higher on her shoulder. All she had stuffed into the bag was a spare dress, a pair of slippers for when she no longer needed Will's boots for tromping through the forest, and a few random articles from around the room that she thought might be useful. She wore the watch on her wrist, knowing they wouldn't have need of it but also realizing that she couldn't leave it behind.

Moving across the room, her eyes caught a flash of red. The rose sat on her bedside table, untouched for days, and had only just now begun to wither. But it was still beautiful, the dying promise of perfection.

Sarah swallowed hard, pushing aside all thoughts of Damien as she poked her head out the cracked door into the empty hallway. She had sent her new maid on a fabricated errand to keep her away from this corridor, and it looked like she had yet to return. Giving her room one final, longing sweep of her eyes, her gaze landed on the flower again, as though magnetized. Damien would be here within the hour to discover her vacated room, and she hoped he wouldn't take her leaving as abandonment.

Before she had a second to doubt herself, she dragged her eyes away from the gift and moved out into the hall, closing the door silently behind her and trying to leave her regret and uncertainty back behind that sealed door.

She slipped down the stairs, setting each heavy boot down gently to make as little noise as possible. Her boot squeaked against one of the steps, and Sarah winced at the noise. Discarding any notion of stealth, she moved hastily along the stairwell, keeping her head down as she passed the kitchen on her way to the servants' entrance. She slipped out the door, escaping into the open air and breathing deeply.

"Freedom," she whispered. She meant to say it with conviction, but it sounded like she was trying to remind herself of what she was searching for and had yet to find.

Walking along the wall closest to the forest's edge, her steps slowed as she neared the sleeping rose patch, which was only a bunch of twigs sticking up from the snowy ground at the present. But she had no trouble spotting the bush she was looking for among the other tangled vines and branches.

Picking her way carefully through the thorny garden, she knelt heavily on the upturned earth that had been disturbed for Edith's final resting place, dropping her load carelessly at her side. She felt tears prick her vision as she stared at the small rosebush—no more than a foot tall—that Terrance had lovingly transplanted to mark the grave. It was nothing more than a tangle of vertical branches, all reaching heavenward as they twined around one another in a thorny dance. But to Sarah it was a beautiful symbol of hope. Edith would have been pleased.

She lost track of time as she sat there, the snow soaking through her skirt and chilling her knees. She desperately wanted to say something, even though Edith couldn't hear her, but she needed that closure, needed to assure herself that she wasn't abandoning her friend by running away.

Then what are you doing? Sarah winced at the disdainful voice inside her head.

To distract herself, she rubbed an icy chunk of snow between her thumb and forefinger. "You'd have liked Will," she whispered aloud, the barest of smiles gracing her lips. Dropping the dirty clod, she focused her eyes on the disturbed ground, wanting to explain, to justify her actions, yet knowing that her words fell on deaf ears. "I'm going to leave, and I don't

238

think I'll be coming back here."

Her next breath was shaky and choked with tears. "So I guess this is goodbye. But you don't have to worry about me. Will is always caring for me, and I have God." *Although I haven't really talked to Him much, as of late,* she thought ashamedly, realizing she hadn't once sought His council in all of her planning. Sarah abruptly realized that she hadn't asked Him because she was afraid His answer might differ from hers. But it wasn't like she was going *against* His will, exactly.

Retreating is your *answer,* her inner voice reminded.

Sarah released a heavy sigh. "I just don't know what I'm doing anymore. I feel anxious and trapped, but I don't know what I'm running from or to." She knew she was babbling and swiped her thumb under the corner of her eye to catch her falling tears. Her voice wavered. "What happened to you really shook me. You took me in and were my first friend in the castle, and I couldn't do anything—"

She turned her head away, biting back her lip to hide her sob. That was when she remembered the handkerchief she had brought with her. She reached into her sleeve and brought out the ratty piece of fabric, clutching it possessively in her fist.

Sarah went on, her voice soft. "You said you had news to share, and I never got to hear it. I wish I could say something to make it right, to make up for leaving you." Her shoulders drooped in a sigh. "I know it doesn't really matter anymore, but I can't seem to do anything right and wish I could fix this. Seeing you like—" Sarah shook her head, trying to cast the image aside. "It just made death seem too real. I don't know, maybe that's what I'm running from."

You can't outrun death. She could almost hear Edith's voice in the wind, and she turned her head toward the forest, foolishly scanning the trees for her familiar face. But, of course, there was no one.

Sarah rose on shaky legs, feeling an intense desire to run from this place and never look back. With tears pouring unchecked down her cheeks, she gave Edith's final resting place a wavering smile. "I hope your boy is beside the angels to greet you. Don't forget about me," she whispered, laying the handkerchief carefully over one of the thorny branches marking the grave. The square of fabric flapped gently in the breeze.

She picked her sack off the ground and gingerly made her way through the slumbering rose bushes. Keeping her eyes focused on the woods, she walked with determined strides into the trees. She was so intent on not looking behind her that she tripped over an exposed root and nearly toppled over. The saying about not being able to see the forest for the trees came to mind, and her steps faltered. But she had thought this through and saw everything clearly. There was nothing to doubt, she reasoned, trying to bolster her courage as she picked up her pace. She was doing the right thing.

And when she began to question in her insecurity, she ran, trying to escape the doubts that followed at her heels.

****

Night was approaching fast. Will planted a fist against his mouth as he stared at the flames, thinking in silence, though his mind was already made up. He could not take Sarah away from her family; she would never forgive herself for leaving them. It was why he had remained in Serimone after his parents' deaths, because he knew he would forever question if the people and his uncle needed him. And there was also the matter of taking responsibility for an unwed woman, and he could never afford for the two of them to marry if he left his livelihood behind. . . . Not that she had mentioned marriage, only a temporary respite.

Will chastised himself for thinking—*wanting* to believe—that more was there than what she had asked of him. The situation was hardly permanent, and she needed a friend and protection on her brief journey, nothing more. It would be completely unwise, foolish even, for them to escape together. No matter that he was tempted.

Against his better judgment, he allowed himself to consider last night, the way she had allowed him to touch and hold and comfort her without a second thought. He had never felt as protective of her as when she was asleep, with her vulnerability and hurt evident in every line of her face. No feeling could compare to that of holding her in his arms, with her fully trusting that he would keep her safe. And when it had been just the two of them as they shared the sunrise, it felt like nothing stood in their way—no obstacles to stop him from admitting his feelings and asking her to be his for eternity, to wake up in his arms for the remainder of theirs.

Groaning, he shoved his fingers back through his hair and rose to his feet. The sun was close to setting, and he was only putting off disappointing her. Whipping on his cloak in agitation, he glanced back at the fire and decided that he wouldn't put it out; he would be back soon, anyway.

He slammed the door behind him, upsetting a patch of snow on the roof. It slipped over the side and landed on the ground in a heavy heap. Frowning, Will stomped through the forest, making his way to the small brook at which they were supposed to rendezvous. He half hoped that Sarah would not be there, because then there would be no need for him to give her an answer he was sure would be displeasing.

An owl hooted somewhere nearby, and he halted in his tracks. There was something not quite right about the sound, and he found himself straining his ears when he heard it again. Turning in the direction he thought the false hoot came from, he caught a flash of green dart behind one of the snowcapped trees. His first instinct was to assume it was an animal of some kind, but it had been too tall for that.

Taking a cautious step, Will could just make out the slight fluttering of a cloak in the breeze. He held his breath. Sarah had said that there was someone impersonating the Shadow. Was it possible this was he?

His suspicions were confirmed when the imposter stepped out from behind the tree, fully revealing himself. The man was dressed in brown leather pants, lace-up boots, and the Shadow's signature green cloak with the hood drawn over his features. He even had the gall to wear a pack of arrows and hold a bow, as if he knew how to use it.

They stared each other down. Will calculated how many steps it would take before he could reach out and strangle the man who was tampering with his sacred identity, who had nearly killed Sarah and taken the life of her friend.

He had just estimated the distance between them when the man skipped backwards a step and then bolted into the forest, challenging him to follow. Will took off after him, running in the opposite direction of his and Sarah's meeting place. He would meet her later after he dealt with this filth.

He followed close at the imposter's heels, but he couldn't seem to overpower him. What the man lacked in speed he made up for in agility as he slipped through small gaps between the trees and darted under short limbs that Will had to avoid. He was beginning to think it was a fruitless pursuit when his ears picked up the rumbling sound of Glenborough Falls in the distance. Now with a new goal in mind, he charged after his target, planning to force him into the water and, if need be, over the falls.

The roaring grew louder, and Will knew they were almost upon the water. But then the man suddenly released the bow and removed the quiver from his back, dropping it to the ground as he ran.

Confused but knowing an opportunity when he saw it, Will bent and snatched them from the ground, barely breaking stride. Slinging the pack over his shoulder, he set the arrow in a movement as familiar as breathing and broke through the trees to find the hooded man sloshing through the shallow water.

"Halt!" Will yelled, raising the bow as he splashed into the freezing ankle-deep water after him. "I have you in my sights!" The man jerked to a stop, turning around slowly to face him. Will squinted into the near darkness. "Now remove the hood."

The man ignored his command and advanced on him slowly, hands raised in surrender. There was something familiar about the way he walked. . . . Will drew the string back, letting him know he meant business. "I said stop!" The imposter obeyed, though still he did not reveal his identity. "The hood," he growled, angling the bow.

The man reached up and flipped his hood back without hesitation.

241

"You wouldn't shoot a woman, would you, darling?"

He felt Jade's cocky grin across the feet that separated them and ground his teeth in irritation. Lowering the weapon, he glowered at her. "You're the one who has been masquerading as the Shadow? You murdered someone, Jade! This isn't one of your little games."

She sauntered toward him, her eyes narrowing in that catlike way that let him know she was pleased with herself. "I've never killed anyone, William." Pressing a hand to her heart in a move meant to distract him, she cocked her head to the side and turned her lips down in a pout. "It hurts that you think I could do such a thing."

"Well, then what is this?" He shook the bow in front of her face. "I could have killed you!"

"I had to get your attention *somehow*." Jade flipped her braid over her shoulder. Shooting him a seductive smile, she placed a hand on his shoulder and leaned toward his ear. He tightened his grip on the bow, but didn't give her the satisfaction of pulling away.

"I was not the one who killed that woman, and you know that," she whispered, her mouth brushing his ear. Will pursed his lips and thought he heard one of his knuckles pop. "But I know who did."

That caught his attention.

Gripping her shoulders, he pushed her back to see her face. "You know who broke into the castle?"

She grinned coyly and ran a finger playfully down his chest. "I know a lot of things."

He grabbed her wrists and held them tight, though she didn't pull away. "Cut the charade," he said sternly, giving her a little shake to knock some sense into her. "Now who killed that woman?"

Her voice turned husky, a habit she couldn't seem to break. "And what will you do for me if I tell you?"

Will released her abruptly and took a step back, suddenly disgusted with this woman he had once called a friend. "Good God, Jade, what is wrong with you? You can be so exasperating!"

The façade chipped away for a moment, and he could see his words had hurt before the indifferent mask veiled her features once more. "Aren't you curious?" Her voice had lost its purposefully alluring tone.

Though he was terribly curious, he knew that Jade would never divulge the secret; she loved them too much to lose one so intriguing. Will turned around without another word, tromping back through the shallow water.

"I know your secret, too," she blurted loudly to be heard over the falls. He hesitated, and she cried out a little desperately, "How else would I know that you would follow me in this costume?"

Swallowing tightly, he turned back to her, feigning ignorance, though

242

his heart was beating wildly in his chest. "What are you talking about? I have no secrets."

Jade straightened the front of her shirt, tucking it back into her pants where it had come loose. She smoothed her braid, a nervous movement meant to regain her composure. "I recently discovered your alter-ego, and I must say that I'm surprised I hadn't thought of it before. You had me fooled along with everyone else."

Dropping the guise, he sloshed over to her. "Who else knows?" She grinned, lording it over him. He leaned down and enunciated each word. "Who. Else. Knows?"

A delicate brow arched in defiance.

"Who did you *tell,* Jade?"

"I'm not the one you should concern yourself with!" she snapped. Blinking, she seemed to realize how harsh her tone had been, and her expression turned suddenly sad. She retreated a few steps. "You foolishly trusted her with your secret, but *I* won't tell a soul, William, if that's what concerns you—I promise. I shall remain silent if you just answer one question."

He narrowed his eyes suspiciously, wondering how she knew about Sarah's awareness of his secret. Jade was still backing toward the falls, and his eyes widened as he realized her intent. "Jade stop!"

She did. Tilting her head to the side, she watched him intently from the knee-deep water. The cold didn't seem to affect her. "Why not me? Just answer me that. She doesn't deserve you, you know," she added quietly.

Will took a few tentative steps toward her, eyes darting to the frothing water that spilled over the falls. She would never survive that drop. "Come back from the edge and I'll discuss this with you."

"And that shall garner your attention?" Shaking her head, Jade stepped onto a large rock that jetted out over the edge of the water. She didn't possess the nerve, did she? Will swallowed.

"You never wanted me," she went on. "I see now that deceiving that girl could never bring you into my arms." Her face looked tormented. "Just say my name. My *real* name—the name you gave me when we were children, when I wished to forget my past."

Will was suddenly aware of how deep her obsession for him went and searched his mind for a solution to get the both of them out of this alive. He took a few more steps, having to pick up his knees as the water deepened. He kept his eyes focused on hers as he sloshed along, and his thighs went numb. "Don't do this. Please."

A lone tear spilled down her cheek. "Why not? I spend my life being used and controlled by men and receive nothing in return. What do I have here but emptiness and loss—of my home, my parents, of your affection?"

Seeing she refused to be talked down, Will suddenly raised the bow in a last-ditch effort. "Get down from there or I'll shoot." He realized that it was foolish to threaten to kill someone on the brink of suicide, but it was all he could think of.

"You won't shoot me." She seemed so certain of it, and he knew it was true; he couldn't do it.

He tossed the bow down, and it swirled in the frothing water and then dropped over the falls. He kept his eyes focused on Jade as he advanced cautiously, trying not to startle her as he rose up on the rock before her. The sun had set, and it was difficult to make out her features in the pale moonlight. "You're right. I can't shoot you."

She wrapped her arms around his middle, startling him. Jade sighed, pressing her body hard against his own, as though he would evaporate if she lessened her hold. "It feels so good to be in your arms." She paused, arms freezing. "But I can never really have you, can I?"

Will hesitated, barely returning her embrace. He knew he couldn't lie to her, even under such dire circumstances. "I'm sorry, no. But that doesn't mean I don't want you in my life. You deserve more than this."

She released him, and he caught a flash of teeth as she smiled sadly. "Thank you for that. I will always love you, William, and your secret is safe with me." Something in her eyes shifted, and his own widened in alarm as he realized she was done speaking. Then she took a step back, and her body tumbled over the falls.

"Marian!" he cried thoughtlessly, lunging for her. His breath was forced from his lungs as he landed on the rock, hard, but he managed to grab ahold of her slick wrist before he lost her completely.

Will grunted, struggling to hang on as the falls pulled at her from below. "Hold on," he yelled, reaching down with his other hand. His stomach slipped over the rock, and he caught sight of her face. She looked vaguely frightened, yet her mind seemed intent on something other than their plight.

"Say my name again," she cried.

He ground his teeth, trying to get a better grip on her. His chest slowly inched over the edge of the slick rock, further over the churning water far below.

"Say it!" Jade screamed desperately when he remained silent. She seemed more concerned in hearing him affirm her existence than she was in helping him pull her to safety.

Muscles straining, he managed through clenched teeth, "Don't let go, Marian!" The words were lost in the roar of the water, but she smiled anyway, knowing he had said what she wanted to hear. Will felt her hand relax, no longer returning his hold.

He arched his back as he struggled to hold on, trying to turn his body to take some of the strain off his arms, but his sudden weight shift caused

244

his body to jerk across the wet surface of the rock. Eyes widening, his free hand searched frantically for some handhold as Jade's weight pulled him over the edge.

His hand slipped over an exposed tree root, and he made a desperate grab for it. Their bodies jerked to a stop as he closed his fingers around the end of the root, and their weight nearly yanked it from the sodden earth. Groaning in pain, he tightened his hold around Jade's wrist. He knew that there was no air in the spray of the falls where her body dangled, but he couldn't let her go.

"Hold on!" he yelled. But she had already gone limp. *Just hold on*, he told himself, closing his lids tightly as he focused on doing just that. His fingers had gone numb, and they loosened against his will, slipping from around the exposed root. He closed his eyes and his last thought as they both fell toward the rocks at the base of Glenborough Falls was that he would get his wish: He would die attempting to save someone.

~Chapter 30~

Tapping her foot anxiously, Sarah stared off into the darkening forest. "Come on, come on," she muttered, stomach knotting anxiously. But the sun had set, and there was still no sign of Will. He had said he would come, whatever news he had for her, but maybe he had changed his mind.

Sarah shivered as a cold mist from the brook blew her way, soaking through the cloak and chilling her to the bone. She'd been waiting for what must have been close to an hour, and she was starving and half-frozen. The time spent waiting had allowed her to think—and overthink—and when Will had neglected to make an appearance, she had felt conflicting emotions. She was partly disappointed that he wasn't willing to do something like this for her, but that displeasure felt more like relief the longer she stood there.

Had she been out of her *mind* to propose that they run away together to Locksley? She had never suggested something so rash and felt ashamed for even thinking up such a ridiculous plan. Crazy girls ran away with boys they hardly knew, *not* Sarah—good ol', logical Sarah. If Janice could see her now, acting as brazen as she, Sarah was sure she'd grab a bowl of popcorn to munch on while she watched the drama unfold.

With time to reflect the longer she spent away from the castle, the place where Edith had been murdered, she began to see the reasons for her recklessness with more clarity. And she felt more ridiculous and impulsive because of it. Yes, she had panicked when she'd witnessed Edith's murder—even now she had to close her eyes when she thought of it—and that panic had only escalated when she considered how she would have to leave Karen and the Joneses for good someday. And when she imagined she might lose Will, the person who had offered her comfort after the tragedy and to whom she had clung in her time of need . . .

From a psychological perspective, it made sense, her holding tightly to the beacon that had helped her through a traumatic experience. But, while understandable, it didn't excuse the selfishness of her actions.

Her shoulders bowed under the weight of what she had almost done to both their lives. She had felt a little slighted when Will never made an appearance, but she was starting to think that it was for the best: She could never leave her family like this, disappearing with a man they had never met in a different era, with no mention of where she was going—her parents would have an aneurism! Not to mention Lilly. How could she have considered abandoning her young sister for longer than necessary, prolonging her return to go on an adventure? And the entire purpose of her being here was to track down the king's murderer, something she hadn't put any effort into recently.

She never should have entertained thoughts of running away to Locksley Village, however brief the trip might have been. As much as she wanted to keep Will in her life, she knew that he could never come back to her world if this place really was based in the past, which was looking more like the truth each day. What if his presence was somehow tied to the future? She would never know whose lives she might be tampering with, all so she could have the best of both worlds without sacrificing anything.

Sending one final, searching glance over the dark forest, Sarah sighed. "Guess I have my answer," she said aloud. But it was for the best, she reminded herself, pushing aside her disappointment. She still had a chance to make things right.

Ashamed of what she had been about to do, she stiffened her resolve and her spine, making the decision to leave behind any notion of running away with her tail between her legs. Feeling the gentle pull of her conscience, she turned and walked back toward the castle, hoping she wasn't too late for supper.

****

"I'm sorry I delayed you," Sarah apologized, trying to level her breathing as Damien closed his bedroom door. She had rushed upstairs, thrown her cloak and sack aside, and with the help of her new maid, changed into a gown that she'd hardly glanced at. She'd hastily run a comb through her tangled locks to smooth out the snarls the wind had whipped her hair into and then rushed to Damien's room, hoping he hadn't already left. He was just exiting his room as Sarah hurried down the hall.

Looking relieved to see her, he offered his arm to her, waiting for her to accept the proffered limb before escorting her down the stairs. "I must admit that I was a little concerned when I found your room empty," he remarked. "I thought you might have gone down without me."

Sarah curled her half-frozen toes inside her slippers, wanting desperately to soak her chilled limbs in a hot bath. But now that she was thinking clearly, she saw what a perfect opportunity tonight was—one she did not want to miss, though she almost had in her recklessness. She could warm up after supper, Sarah promised herself.

"I went to say goodbye to my friend," she supplied, careful not to give away too much of Edith's whereabouts. She didn't want to get Terrance and the others in trouble after all they had done, though she was fairly certain that Damien would think it as noble as she. "I must have lost track of the time."

"Is that why you're so cold?" Damien rubbed his hand over her knuckles to warm them and brought them to his lips, breathing against her fingers. Whispers of air tickled her skin, and she swallowed as some warmth returned to her hands. And, embarrassingly, the rest of her.

Grinning, he commented, "Your color has returned."

"It's warm in here," Sarah responded weakly, dropping her eyes when he placed her hand back on his arm, though he slid his palm over her fingers to keep them warm as they walked. It was thoughtful, but Sarah felt tense as he guided her through a high archway that opened into a wide, well-lit corridor.

Raising her eyes in interest, Sarah noticed that there were several open archways on either side of them that led into dark rooms. But she was far more interested in the padlocked doors that were scattered throughout the passage.

"Is that the only reason your cheeks are flushed?" Damien asked, feigning innocence even as that roguish grin slid across his lips.

"What's behind those doors?" She wasn't intentionally ignoring his question but was more than happy to redirect the conversation to her own curiosity.

"I can't be sure, really," he answered, easily going along with the topic change. "Unused rooms, perhaps?"

"That are chained?" she countered doubtfully.

They entered a darkened portion of the corridor where the torchlight was weak. Unable to see his expression, she felt Damien shrug. "I suppose this old place has its share of secrets, though sadly many mysteries remain unsolved."

"Hmm," Sarah muttered in displeasure. She was beginning to feel the same way. *But tonight could be a turning point,* she reminded herself. A spark of nervous energy shot through her middle.

They emerged into the torchlight once more, and she spotted a set of large double-doors at the end of the hall manned by a guard on either side. Damien stopped before the armed guards dressed in ornamental clothing.

"Damien Lisandro and guest," he said to the men.

Sarah wasn't sure how she felt about being "and guest," but it wasn't like these men would recognize her name—Damien had to introduce himself, and he had attended supper several times already.

The guards nodded in unison.

"Are you ready?" She pulled her gaze away from the hulking doors and nodded at Damien mutely. Up until now, Cadius had only been a name to her, a murderous ghost that she had been hunting for weeks. And now she was a stranger about to meet the man who had been able to end his own brother's life, and possibly more lives than that.

For a brief moment, she wondered if it was best to let sleeping giants lie. But the guards had already reached out to open the doors for them, and she forced herself to take a deep breath as Damien guided her into the lion's den.

Sarah blinked against the light that flooded the enormous dining room. Torches were mounted all along the walls, and standing torches had been brought in to offer the three long, rectangular tables plenty of heat and light. Large wooden chandeliers hung above each table, and the three tiers of candles managed to banish any remaining shadows in the room.

Drawing her gaze across the large dining hall, Sarah tried to take it all in: The clacking of utensils against wooden plates and trays, the dull scraping of tankards being moved around the table, and hushed conversation filling the air with a jumble of sounds.

Only two of the tables were occupied, and sparsely at that—it didn't seem as though there were too many guests staying at the castle, as of late—but the attendees present were clearly wealthy, judging by the men's elegant vests and ridiculous puffery, and the women's incredible gowns and disdainful expressions. No one took any notice of Sarah or her companion as the guards closed the door quietly behind them.

"Shall we introduce you?" Damien asked near her ear.

She shot him a quizzical look. "To who?"

"The royals, of course." He nudged her into the room with a gentle hand at her back.

Sarah barely managed to restrain herself from running a hand through her hair. Was her dress suitable for such a formal supper? She doubted it, since she had selected it blindly from her wardrobe. She couldn't keep her gaze from wandering self-consciously around the room, and she caught the curious and occasionally loathing gazes of a few ladies when they finally noticed her, and more specifically, her companion. Apparently, Spaniards were as hot a commodity here as they were back home, and she felt a spark of pride that she was the one on his arm tonight.

Tearing her eyes away from the contemptuous looks she was receiving, Sarah focused her attention at the end of the table, where she knew Damien was leading her. She searched the faces there anxiously, wondering if Cadius would stick out as the evil mastermind she envisioned. They stopped just to the side of the three chairs at the end of the table, and, heart hammering wildly, she followed Damien's example as he quickly bowed, curtsying as gracefully as she could manage.

"Your grace," he said to the ground. She hadn't managed a good look at the prince and was tempted to sneak a peek at the young man they were bowing before. But her companion had yet to rise, and it was a little difficult to subtly get a good look at him from her submissive position. Her knees were beginning to shake nervously as the seconds ticked by, and she nearly let a sigh of relief escape when the prince told them both to rise.

"I was wondering when we might see you again, Lisandro," he commented, lifting his goblet in greeting before bringing it to his lips for a long drink. The prince set it back on the table, his dark gray eyes turning on her as he rested his hands on the arms of his large, throne-like chair.

Curling hair the same color as the dark wood table framed a young, angular face and straight nose, and he tucked one of the chin-length strands behind his ear, revealing chiseled cheekbones and freckles along the left side of a smooth face. Karen had once mentioned that he was somewhere in his early twenties, but his slight frame and boyish features made him look like a polished youth playing in his father's clothes. But it was the frown lines between his brows that aged his smooth skin, and the eyes that considered her were a dull, stormy color. Sarah wondered if they had always been so dead or if his father's recent passing had been the thing to sap the life from them.

Damien took her hand in his own, giving it a reassuring squeeze. "This is Lady Sarah. She has been acting as my nurse for several days." His voice had turned formal as he addressed the prince, but he smiled sincerely at her, and she felt her toes curl in pleasure at the admiration glittering in his espresso eyes. "But I fear she is grossly overqualified."

"And how are you faring, Lisandro?" Sarah pulled her eyes from his hypnotic gaze and glanced down at the woman sitting on the prince's left. Damien immediately took her hand and bowed over it.

"Forgive me, milady, for not acknowledging you sooner," he amended, eyes suddenly bright with obvious fondness for the woman. "But I am quite well, I thank you."

The woman, who Sarah assumed was the queen, smiled and gently urged Damien to his feet. "I am glad of it. Now"—she turned her eyes on Sarah, and her lips softened—"you must introduce me to your lovely companion."

Damien smiled encouragingly at her, and she took a step toward the queen, feeling completely out of her element. She managed to bend her quivering knees into a curtsy. "My lady," she said softly, looking up into brown eyes that were the same oval-shape as the prince's, though they contained more life and warmth than his.

The skin at the corners of Queen Meredith's eyes crinkled when she gave her a close-lipped smile. "I heard of the way you came to this man's rescue, child. It was quite remarkable."

Sarah felt her cheeks heat and dipped her head. She tried to match the queen's smooth speech. "Thank you. But I really didn't do much."

"You must sit with us." She flicked a delicate hand, and magically the bodies on the bench seat slid down, making space for the two of them.

Sarah blinked and only moved when Damien took her hand and helped her onto the space closest to the queen's chair. He slid in beside her and, seeming to sense her discomfort, sat close enough that his shoulder brushed hers, reminding her that he was there should she need his support. She shot him an appreciative look before turning her attention back to the petite woman on her right.

"Where are you from, child?" the queen asked. Her thick red-brown hair had been piled on her head in a series of intricate braids and curls, and it seemed an unconscious movement when she patted the underside of the arrangement, as if to ensure it was still perfectly intact.

"What makes you say I'm not from around here?" Sarah asked distractedly as her eyes scanned the faces around the table. She met a pair of gray eyes assessing her from the prince's other side, and a chill shot down her spine. It was no wonder she had neglected to notice him before—mostly grayed brown hair tied back from a thin, weathered face, narrow, stormy gray eyes, a close-cropped salt-and-pepper beard over an angular jaw. He was almost like a ghost, and Sarah would have passed him up had it not been for the piercing eyes staring back at her, waiting for her reply. Every instinct told her this was Cadius, and her pulse kicked into overdrive.

"I am familiar with every lady and courtier in the province," the queen was saying. Sarah swallowed hard and forced her gaze away from his icy scrutiny. The woman had lifted her goblet and was smiling sassily. "My powers of deduction are far more keen than some might believe." She took a delicate drink, her movements slow and practiced.

Sarah tried to follow her example and lifted the fresh goblet a servant had placed before her, trying to buy herself time. She smelled the pungent scent of wine as she brought it close to her nose and grimaced. Feeling several pairs of eyes on her, she pursed her lips and barely tipped her glass with a shaky hand before placing it on the table. She licked her lips and tried not to cringe at the bitter taste.

Knowing that several ears were listening in, she forced a smile she hoped appeared sincere and answered vaguely, "No, I'm from a very small and uninteresting province quite a ways from here."

"Well, I am sure that lord Lisandro was quite pleased you came when you did." Queen Meredith smiled fondly at him, and Sarah could tell that she wasn't the only one he had charmed.

A platter of roasted chicken and potatoes was set before her, and Sarah looked up to thank the servant. She recognized her as one of the girls who had given her such a dirty look when she had become a "lady." She quickly ducked her head, not wanting to give the girl further reason to hate her when she realized the former maid-turned-lady was already dining with the royal family.

But she needn't worry; the girl kept her head bowed as she moved past her, only raising her eyes to set a platter in front of Damien, but he was distracted with watching Cadius—she was sure it was him now—with a suspicious gaze as the older man continued to stare at Sarah. The servant girl ducked her head again and moved quickly to a corner of the room, where she gazed submissively at the ground.

Sarah pretended she didn't notice his unwavering stare as she took a small bite of her food. It looked delicious, but the taste was lost on her; she was too occupied with trying to think of something to say that might get Cadius to incriminate himself, aside from coming right out and accusing him of murder in front of a room of guests. All that came to mind to get the conversation turned in that direction was, "I was so sorry to hear about your husband." She directed her condolences to the queen and hoped the man across from them overheard.

Queen Meredith smiled graciously, though it looked plastic, like she had perfected it before a mirror. "Yes, it is a great loss to his people." Her words, like her smile, were clearly rehearsed, though all her practice couldn't hide the tears she blinked back.

"My brother's death shook the land, milady." Cadius' sudden words surprised her, and she turned to him almost against her will. He leaned forward, placing a weathered hand on the table. Sarah wanted to look away from his penetrating gray eyes, but it was as though the intensity of his unearthly stare demanded her attention, and all she could manage was to shift uneasily in her seat. "But this country *will* rise again, under the rule of another leader."

A few of the men raised their glasses in salute to the prince. The queen smiled encouragingly at her son, who pulled his lifeless stare from the bottom of his empty goblet to give her a faint smile of acknowledgement. Sarah noted the way the queen's face tightened with concern. The candlelight caught the silver streaks at her temples, making her look older than her forty-odd years. *It looks like the prince isn't the only one to be aged by the king's death,* Sarah thought sadly.

With all eyes on him, the prince sat a little straighter, looking more dignified than he had all evening. "I will do my utmost to rule with as much honor, fire, and compassion as my father before me," he said for the benefit of the table's occupants. A chorus of "Here, here" went up around the room, and people raised their goblets and tankards in respectful salute to the deceased king and the one who would take his place on the throne when the mourning period had passed.

Their side of the table lapsed into silence as they all enjoyed their meal, though Sarah's gaze constantly wandered to the faces around her: Cadius was rolling his goblet between his frail hands, listening disinterestedly to the man next to him as he prattled on about the tumultuous security of a nearby province, though Sarah couldn't catch most of the hushed conversation. And the prince had gone back to staring into his goblet, though he attempted to look more involved when his mother shot him a worried, pleading look. Family dysfunction at its finest.

Sarah leaned in and whispered to Damien, "Is it always this lively?"

He grimaced. "Occasionally, I can engage the prince in talk of politics, but, yes, I'm afraid it is often this quiet." He took her hand under the table and gave her one of those smiles that made her feel like the only person in the room. "But tonight is far more interesting." His thumb traced idle circles over the scar on her hand, and she had to consciously close her mouth, which had slowly drifted open in surprise.

Clearing her throat, she forced her attention to the real reason she had come and turned to the queen, trying to ignore Damien's finger as it stroked her skin. Almost under her breath, so as to not be overheard by those across the table, she said, "It was such a shock when I discovered the king had passed. Did it surprise you, as well?" She knew she was probing at a sensitive subject and didn't want to offend the newly widowed woman, but she couldn't think of another segue into a discussion of the king's death. Her justifications didn't make it seem any less insensitive, though.

The queen shook her head gently, a pained look crossing her practiced expression of serenity. "It was quite prolonged, I'm afraid. I only wish for my husband's sake that it had been sudden." Her face was a mask of queenly composure once more, but she had wrinkled her skirt severely as she knotted clumps of the fabric in her fists. Sarah felt a stirring of compassion for the woman. It would be exhausting to be such a public figure, having to act a certain way and hide her true feelings all of the time in the wake of her husband's death. Had she been able to mourn privately?

Driven by sympathy, Sarah lightly touched the queen's trembling hand, though she wasn't sure if it was appropriate to touch royalty. The woman appeared surprised, but she didn't look disturbed or upset, so Sarah gave her hand a gentle pat. "I'm so sorry." It seemed the only thing she could say, but she meant it.

Queen Meredith gave her hand a quick squeeze of gratitude. She sniffed back tears, and her smile was wobbly. "Thank you, child."

Sarah pulled back, thinking carefully on her next words before speaking. "I didn't arrive until after he had passed," she said slowly, with the right amount of curiosity in her tone. She felt Damien give her palm a warning squeeze, having forgotten he still held her other hand. Swallowing back the niggling guilt, she hedged, "But if you don't mind my asking, how, exactly, did it happen?"

"Of course I do not mind." The woman stiffened her spine, and it looked like it was meant to give her courage, though Sarah heard the underlying waver in her voice. "It feels strange to speak of it, since his passing is common knowledge here. But several months past, after supper one evening, the king became ill. The physician tried everything—medicine, experimental herbs. We became so desperate that he even tried leeches." Sarah bit back a grimace, and the queen angled her chin into the air. The candles situated on the chandelier reflected off the tears glittering in her eyes. "But nothing produced results, and my husband—well, he never recovered, as you well know."

"And it didn't seem odd to you?" The words were out of her mouth before she could take them back. Damien let go of her hand and murmured her name at his plate, cautioning her. She was reminded of their conversation in the woods, his warning that she not tell anyone about her theory that the king had been murdered. But now she had another reason to solve the king's murder, besides bringing Cadius to justice: She wanted the queen to have the answers to the questions Sarah saw behind her haunted brown eyes.

"How do you mean 'odd'?" the queen asked, her gaze flickering to her son momentarily, but his glazed expression was on his advisor seated beside him. The queen leaned toward her younger guest almost involuntarily.

Heedless of Damien's warning, Sarah said quietly, "I have heard a little of what's gone on for the past few months, and it just seemed strange how it all happened. A mystery illness claims the life of a perfectly healthy king? It just seemed peculiar."

The queen was shaking her head distractedly. "When the illness progressed, I was hardly allowed to see him, but nothing seemed unusual the times that I went to him. It is hardly uncommon for someone to become unexpectedly ill in this climate."

Sarah lowered her voice an octave. "And the fact that you were kept from him didn't strike you as suspicious?"

"The physician feared contagion," the older woman murmured, though she sounded less sure. Sarah, noticing her chance, took advantage of the woman's momentary suspicion, though she tried to keep the eagerness out of her voice.

"Were you able to see him at all after awhile?"

"In the latter months, I had to force my way into the room or have one of the servants smuggle me in." Her throat worked. "But the illness ravaged his body quickly toward the end, and Josiah was nearly incoherent the times I did manage to visit."

Sarah was about to throw another question at her when she saw the

254

tears pricking the queen's vision, and she felt a stab of remorse. Was she really so intent on solving this thing that she couldn't see, or was too wrapped up to care, that her inquiries were upsetting the widow, a woman who clearly had a heart for her people? The woman's husband had died, leaving her the kingdom to manage until her son took over—that same son who was drowning his sorrows in drink and who looked as drained and lifeless as his dead father.

Looking the queen in the eyes, Sarah whispered, "I'm sorry for prying."

Shaking her head lightly, the queen sniffed and offered her a tiny smile. "No apologies. It's common knowledge that I continued to make visits to my husband against the physician's counsel and that of the king's advisor. Since I came into this life over two decades past, I have been instructed and primped and prepared, but I still struggle with cowing to certain rules and conventions."

Sarah cocked her head curiously and shifted a little in her seat to better face her. "I thought you would have been raised to be a queen since you were born."

She grinned a little. "You truly are not from here. It was my elder sister, not I, who was raised to take over the throne. You see, Ridlan, the province where we lived, desired to make an alliance with Serimone, and my sister was the one coached from birth to rule."

"She was supposed to marry the king?" Sarah asked incredulously.

Meredith nodded in the affirmative. "Alexis and the king were married on her sixteenth birthday and remained that way for many years until she died, shortly after Adrian was born."

Sarah stared unseeing at her full plate, processing this surprising bit of information. She shot a quick glance at the prince before turning her gaze to the lady beside her. "How did she die?"

"She caught an illness when Adrian was very young." Her gaze seemed far away, and her voice softened in remembrance. "There was nothing to be done, even with her determination and fiery spirit."

The pieces clicked together in Sarah's mind. "And then you married the king to keep the alliance intact?" She tried to keep her tone curious, but her mind was racing.

Meredith nodded slowly. "Almost immediately." A faint smile curved her painted lips. "We were very different at first—I, a young woman not yet twenty who wanted to experience life, and the king, a ruler only a little younger than my own father, who already had a son and was mourning the loss of my sister."

"Sounds like a match made in heaven," Sarah remarked in quiet humor.

The queen gave a light laugh, covering her mouth delicately with her pale hand. "It was a rocky start, yes, but we soon fell in love, and I raised Adrian as my own."

"You must miss Alexis," Sarah said softly, surprised when the queen gave a delicate laugh.

"Yes, but I like to imagine that she continues to stir up trouble like always." Her eyes softened. "And fond remembrance of her is never far from my thoughts. I still have a box of Alexis's old things stored in her former bedchambers, though I have never allowed myself to look inside," she admitted.

Sarah felt eyes on them, and she glanced up to find both the prince and Cadius watching them.

"I hope my sister-in-law is not boring you with an accounting of Serimone's history," Cadius said with a pinched smile that Sarah imagined was laced with condescension. She suspected he had been handsome in his younger years, but his features had hardened through the decades and made him appear cold and intimidating.

The queen shifted uneasily beneath his gaze, and then she quickly straightened her back, taking on a mask of indifference. "No, brother, we were—"

"Discussing the way she and the king met," Sarah jumped in. She leaned forward, hoping the accusation wasn't apparent in her eyes as she watched Cadius for his reaction to her next words. She feigned innocent curiosity, though her temple was throbbing at the anxiety coursing through her veins. "I was also asking her about the circumstances surrounding the king's death. It struck me as odd the way he died." She could almost heard Damien swallow beside her as his body tensed.

Cadius steepled his fingers, resting his hands on the table as he leaned, almost imperceptibly, toward her. She sensed the movement was meant to intimidate her, and she had to force herself not to pull back instinctively or reveal the sudden spark of trepidation she felt. "My brother's passing was very difficult for us all," he said, his voice smooth and diplomatic. "Why would a foreigner show such interest in his death?"

"Inquisition is woman's greatest virtue," the prince threw in, his words heavy. He smiled lazily at Sarah, and she wondered if anyone else had noticed that he'd had a little too much wine.

Sarah swallowed convulsively when she looked back at Cadius, barely maintaining eye contact with his piercing gaze. "I guess I'm just naturally curious." Her voice squeaked on the end. She tried to shrug innocently, a dumb smile on her lips as she backed down. Her pulse thumped rapidly as Cadius' calculated gaze weighed the truth of her statement. It appeared he thought curiosity more a fault than a virtue.

Her smile faded, and she shrank back a little. "I'm sorry. I didn't mean to upset anyone."

256

"What an inquisitive companion you've found in your company," Cadius observed, his thin lips barely curving in a smile of amusement as he swung his stormy eyes to Damien. There was something dangerous in his gaze, and his smile reeked of court-trained charm. "How *delightful* to discover one so free with her thoughts?" His lowly spoken compliment came out sounding more like a question. A test, Sarah realized. She looked up at Damien, gut twisting.

"Yes." He smiled at her, but it looked strained. When he turned back to Cadius, his eyes changed, flickering with an emotion Sarah couldn't decipher. "She is very smart, as well."

Cadius leaned back against his chair, looking faintly pleased, though his eyes remained narrowed. He raised his glass and said lowly, "How fortunate for the pair of you."

~Chapter 31~

The rest of the evening dragged on painfully. Sarah picked at her plate, but her appetite was lost. The prince had excused himself an hour ago after Cadius whispered a few brief words to him. She could only assume he had told his nephew to leave the public eye before anyone else noticed that their future king was drowning his torment in drink. The queen was a gem and kept Sarah engaged in conversation throughout the meal, though it was apparent that she was in need of distraction as much as Sarah.

Damien offered little conversation, appearing distracted for most of the evening. His eyes occasionally flickered to Cadius, who made a point of avoiding his gaze and remained otherwise occupied by discussing politics with the man beside him.

Sarah felt bad about ruining the perfect evening Damien had imagined, but she'd had to take advantage of her first and possibly only encounter with Cadius.

For all the good it had done.

Her suspicions were increased after speaking with him—the way he never referred to the king by his title and seemed immediately defensive and suspicious—but all she had were her instincts and conjectures. *What did you expect, Matthews? For a cold-hearted murderer to confess his crime to a freshman?* She realized the absurdity of it now, but she had done all she could to get a rise from him. Aside from asking him outright if he had killed his brother, what else could she have done?

Her shoulders sagged in disappointment. She had failed yet again.

At last, Damien rose and gave his excuses to the queen and Cadius, dipping his head to each of them in turn. Sarah nearly jumped from her seat in her eagerness to be away from the gray-haired man's cold eyes.

Knowing it was expected, she curtsied to the queen. "It was a pleasure, my lady."

Meredith smiled with genuine warmth. "The pleasure is all mine." She lowered her voice. "And you have my gratitude for the offer of your company this evening. Perhaps we can take a stroll about the castle during the week." Sarah nodded. The queen looked like she wanted to say more, but then her eyes flickered to Cadius and quickly away. Her mouth closed.

"I am certain we will meet again, milady." The words came out smoothly. Sarah's throat constricted as she turned to acknowledge the man. Cadius stared back at her, the corner of his mouth tightened in what she imagined was supposed to be a congenial smile, but she thought she detected an underlying threat. Maybe she was being paranoid, looking for ghosts where there were none.

With a quick nod, Sarah allowed herself to be escorted from the room. The doors closed behind them, but Damien didn't slow until they were well into the corridor. He pulled her suddenly into a darkened room, and she gasped. He gripped her upper arms, and she could barely make out the shake of his head in the faint light that managed to lessen the total darkness of the room.

"I told you to drop this," Damien said, his voice a harsh whisper.

"I just—"

"And what do you do?" he went on as though she hadn't spoken. "You confront the man you're accusing of murder, and murder of the *king*. That isn't just a hanging offense, Sarah. A man can be strung up and left on a cross for days for committing such a crime against the kingdom." Damien made a sound in his throat and released her. She heard him stride across the room and lost sight of him before he paced back.

"What were you thinking?" he whispered. He no longer sounded angry, but rather distraught with worry.

"I'm—I'm sorry." Sarah swallowed guiltily, wanting to explain her actions. "It was the only way I could think of to catch his reaction. What should I have done?"

He shook his head slowly, and then a hand came up to gently stroke her cheek. "I've lost so much, and I can't . . ." His voice faded.

Sarah knew that if a near stranger had pulled her into an abandoned room and was touching her as Damien was, she would have started screaming and clawing her way out of there. But the truth was Damien was not like other men, and she felt safe with him.

And the rest of the truth was that the feel of his fingers on her skin had her rooted to the spot.

Her lower lip drooped in surprise. "I didn't mean to upset you," she whispered, voice quavering. Her windpipe didn't seem to be working properly.

Damien exhaled. His thumb ran over her cheekbone. "I know," he murmured. "But you don't understand these people like I do. Politics, money, position—it changes you, makes you paranoid. If a suspicious

259

person feels threatened, they can become like a cornered animal, and an animal in the midst of panic can only react instinctively. They *attack*, Sarah; it's all they know to do."

She hadn't realized it would upset him so much, though if she was being honest, she hadn't given his feelings a second thought.

Shoulders sagging, she whispered, "I'm sorry." She seemed to be saying that a lot today. "My intent was to find the truth."

"At the cost of your life?"

Sarah searched the darkness for his face, but the light from the hall didn't reach this corner of the room. "You seem certain that my life's in danger."

"Men like my father—" He seemed to struggled for words. "I've seen how a man driven by lust—for power or otherwise—reacts when he feels vulnerable, when those things he holds most dear are in danger. I don't want you to end up like that."

"What? A man driven by lust?" she asked, defensively striving for humor. But her knees were shaking at what he implied.

Damien's hand retracted from her cheek. "A victim," he answered grimly.

She swallowed, knowing he sensed real danger. She knew his paranoia was well-founded, if the cold looks Cadius had given her during supper were any indication.

"I will be more careful," she promised. "I can't drop this completely, but you have my word that I will avoid confrontation with Cadius at all costs. I'll keep out of his hair."

She heard him sigh. "I have a feeling that's all I'm going to get from you. Perhaps I'd be disappointed if you acquiesced so easily." He sounded vaguely amused. Reaching out, he took her arm and guided her from the room. She blinked against the torchlight and saw a man hurrying down the hall toward them.

"Timmons," Damien greeted, though his voice was tinged with wariness.

The thin man's gaze shifted nervously between the two of them. "May I speak with you, my lord?"

"Sarah," Damien began slowly.

Sensing the newcomer's urgency, she shook her head. "Don't worry about it. I can get to my room just fine."

Damien lifted her hand and quickly kissed the back of it. She felt a little thrill shoot up her arm. "Thank you. I shall look forward to seeing you tomorrow."

She smiled at the two men and then made her way down the corridor alone. She heard the shuffling of boots behind her and glanced back just as Damien and the mystery man stepped into one of the side rooms.

260

"What news?" Damien's whisper echoed off the stone walls and reached her ears. She forced her feet to keep moving, but she froze in place at the man's words.

"Two bodies were discovered in the river about an hour ago, sir— washed up on the bank 20 meters apart. A man and a woman."

Damien cursed. "Do they suspect foul play?"

Sarah realized she was still eavesdropping, but she felt rooted to the spot. Two more people were dead? It couldn't be connected . . . could it? Pressing her back against the wall, she strained her ears to hear the man's faint response.

"I didn't get a good look at the bodies because the guards were on patrol and discovered them quick enough. But from what I saw, it looked like a tumble over the falls was what killed them, but it's too hard to be sure at this point." The man hesitated. "I thought you should be the first to know, sir."

Something in Timmons' voice seemed to strike a nerve in Damien. "Have they identified the man?"

"As I said, I didn't get a good look before the patrol took the bodies back here for identification. They want *you* to identify the man for them, sir."

"And the woman?" Damien asked, sounding eager and wary.

"Can't say for sure," came the mumbled reply. "But I'm almost positive the girl was one of them tramps down on Bowler Street. Looks like the two lovers took a fatal fall." Their voices dropped to low murmurs, and Sarah only managed to catch snippets of their hushed conversation.

Her mind wandered distractedly. Something the man had said caught her attention, but she couldn't put her finger on it. Was Timmons an informant? Sarah had watched enough shows to know that it was common for informants and spies to apprise their masters of seedy events. But why the rush to let Damien know about a woman and a man falling over a waterfall? She wondered if it was the same waterfall Will had shown her earlier.

Will.

Her breathing turned shallow. Will had promised that he would meet her at the brook no matter what he decided, and she knew he was good on his word. The sincerity in his eyes had told her that nothing could have kept him from coming, but he hadn't shown. What if he hadn't been able to?

Sarah closed her eyes and leaned the back of her head against the cold stone. Her knees threatened to give. Had he been with Jade? What had happened that led to both of them going over? Her mind raced so fast it began to ache, and she pinched the bridge of her nose, telling herself it was just conjecture—Will was not *dead*. He couldn't be.

"I want you to take me to them." Damien's voice startled her, and from the sound of it, they were headed her way.

"Yes, my lord." Timmons' boots scuffled across the floor as they hurried down the corridor.

Picking up her skirt, Sarah dashed down the hall with light feet and dove into a deep alcove she nearly missed in her haste. Holding her breath, she watched as they walked quickly past her and down the corridor opposite. Their frames flickered in and out as they moved from torchlight to shadows, growing smaller the farther they went. Sarah told herself to breathe evenly and stay put, though she was itching to make a break for the stairs. A faint clanking sound echoed down her way, and she knew one of them was searching for a key. After a moment, the door opened, revealing muted light from within, and both men slipped inside, quietly closing the door behind them.

Sarah counted to ten and then bolted up the stairs. A few servants were milling about on the landing, and she quickly slowed her steps, ducking her head as she forced her quivering legs to take the stairs two at a time. She hurried down the hall and then up the next flight, breaking into a run when she spotted her room. Throwing the door open, she dove inside, sliding down the door when her legs could no longer support her.

Breathing heavily, she closed her eyes and splayed her legs out. She was jumping to conclusions. There was no reason for the band that tightened around her chest, making it difficult to breathe. Will was still alive. Edith had just died, and there was no chance that he would suffer the same fate within twenty-four hours. It just wasn't possible.

But she couldn't ignore the aching suspicion in her gut. And what was Damien mixed up in? Receiving information like that could be innocent enough, but instinct told her that he knew more than she had heard. Why would he need to identify the victims?

Her eyes snapped open in decision. She had to see those bodies. Not tonight, because Damien and the patrol would be there with the fresh corpses and there was no reason for her to be caught snooping around. But tomorrow she would find out which room they had stashed the bodies in, and until that time, she would choose to believe that Will was still alive.

It isn't him, she told herself, her body shaking uncontrollably. But she had to know, and the only way to do so was to find those bodies.

~Chapter 32~

After a fitful night, Sarah started awake to find three servant girls rifling through her wardrobe and throwing open the shuttered windows to let in the late morning light. She recognized two of the girls and knew they held low opinions of her, one of which had served her supper the previous evening. What were they doing in her room without her permission?

Clutching the blankets to her chest, Sarah sat up quickly, shrinking back from the sudden light. "What are you *doing*?" she asked, disoriented and alarmed.

The youngest by the window, who appeared no older than her sister Lilly, shot a shy glance in her direction before ducking her head submissively. She shuffled quietly past the others and went to the desk, carefully lifting the lid of the small jewelry chest and staring at the contents with rapt attention.

The girl who had served in the dining hall last night stopped with her hands on a gown, glancing over at Sarah. Her expression was mostly devoid of emotion, but her lips were pinched in a tell-tell way. "We were ordered to prepare you for the masquerade ball this evening, miss." Sarah could tell that the formality cost her.

Scratching the base of her scull in confusion, she asked, "At this hour? The ball isn't until tonight." She and Edith had discussed preparations, but Sarah had barely given a thought to attending the affair.

The other servant girl lifted the breakfast tray from the floor and placed it on the bedside table. She shot Sarah a look that was laced with barely masked resentment. "Beatrice and I decided that it will take all day to prepare you." The statement was presented as though all the women would be receiving the same full-time assistance, but Sarah sensed the underlying hint that she would need *extra* help.

Blowing a calming breath out through her nose, Sarah said, "Can we do this later? I have things I want to do this morning."

Both servants frowned, but it was Beatrice who gave a tight nod and motioned for the others to follow her. She noticed the small blond reaching into the chest and barked, "Sevrine! We're leaving."

The girl started and ripped her hand from the box. Her gaze darted nervously to Sarah and then back to the eldest of the group. She said something in a small voice that Sarah recognized as French, though she had no idea what she was saying. Beatrice leaned over and harshly whispered a reprimand as she pulled her from the room.

Flopping onto her back, Sarah threw her arms over her eyes to block out the light, trying to savor a few more minutes of sleep before preparations for the masque began. She wondered what tonight would have in store for her, since her first ball at the castle had been both romantic and tragic.

Her eyes snapped open when she remembered why her night had been so rough. Throwing the covers aside, she quickly ate a few bites of the bread, eggs, and sausage on the tray and dressed hastily in a green ensemble, her anxious stomach complaining over her meager breakfast. Clumsy fingers fumbled to cinch the bodice ties, and she only had the patience for a quick tug at the end. Slipping on a pair of flats, she skipped out into the chaos of the hall.

It was a bustle of activity, with the majority of the staff working on the finishing touches for the ball. Sarah tried her best to stay out of the way as she hurried down the hall past servants hanging decorations, filling vases with colorful perennials and foliage, and draping the stone banister with gold fabrics and woven strands of juniper branches.

Sarah jumped onto the staircase to get out of the path of two young boys who were quickly rolling up the rugs to be replaced with more festive red and gold carpets. An older man reprimanded them for nearly plowing her over, but they had already run off on their next errand.

As she made her way cautiously down the stairs, Sarah realized that she hadn't seen any of the guests in the sea of people she'd just come through, nor were there any found below in the foyer—only the male servants were working in this area, hanging lanterns and mounting extra torches for the night. The female staff must have been assisting the ladies at the castle as they readied for the ball. Sarah reminded herself that she shouldn't feel *too* insulted that the girls had thought she needed all day.

She pretended to admire the decorations, casting her gaze over the room and the men working there. One of the lanterns they were attempting to mount refused to stay in place and kept falling off the wall, nearly knocking one of the workers on the head. It seemed to be creating enough of a distraction that she felt safe to slip quietly down the corridor unnoticed. Damien and Timmons had come down this way just after the man mentioned the bodies, so they must have been down there. She prayed they hadn't buried the bodies already, and she *really* hoped she could figure out which room it had been.

Sarah shivered when she realized that she was racing to uncover corpses.

It took her eyes a moment to adjust as she snuck down the dark, unlit corridor. She walked back and forth across the hall, quietly testing each door to see if any had been left open or had a weak spot. Seven doors and two splinters later, no such luck.

She ignored a few more doors that were chained—no way she was getting past that defense—and then froze at the sound of shuffling boots. She shot a worried look over her shoulder, but there was no one in the hall with her. Turning her gaze forward, she saw that a little bit down the hall a door on her right was cracked open, spilling a thin line of cool, muted light onto the stone floor.

Sarah slid her hand along the ice-cold wall and tiptoed silently. As she edged closer, she noticed a faint mist seeping through the crack in the door, creeping out into the hall only to vanish in the dark patches. She heard the sound of shuffling feet again and was close enough to tell that they were coming from within the room.

Hesitating just outside the door, she mustered up her courage and moved closer, upsetting the fine mist and sending it scattering in all directions. She couldn't see anyone through the crack, so she slowly edged the door open an inch, listening. There was a faint scratching sound, like that of a quill being dragged across parchment, but nothing else. Then she pushed the door in another fraction, tilting her head to get a better look at the room. Her blood froze in her veins.

Two forms lay on the floor, each covered in a white sheet that clung to their wet frames like a second skin. Steam rolled off their cold bodies in waves, hovering over the floor in a thin fog. The room was warm but filled with a cold, hazy light that the flaming torches couldn't seem to banish.

Sarah shivered as the mist wrapped around her ankles, trying to escape past her as she stared, transfixed on the two lifeless forms. Though their faces were covered, the height and build of both were clearly discernible beneath the clinging sheets: one a delicately built woman, and the other a tall man.

She clapped a hand over her mouth, vaguely aware that all sounds coming from inside had stopped. Her wide eyes stared, unblinking, at the man's form. She searched his covered body for some sign that it wasn't Will; a mangled hand, fewer inches on his height, even an extra toe discernible through the fabric—anything to prove that he was still alive and wasn't lying there in that room. But it was too hard to tell with her vision blurring and her stomach sinking. Shouldn't she have felt something, though, if he had been killed? But maybe that was the dread she now felt catching up with her.

A shadow jerked to a sudden stop in her line of vision, and she blinked in surprise. Damien looked just as shocked to see her, but he quickly placed a finger to his lips with the hand holding a sealed letter. He walked out of sight. "Take care of this as soon as possible," she heard him say lowly to whoever was inside the room. Then he was back with empty hands, closing the door and locking it securely.

Sarah retreated until her back hit the wall, eyes fixed on the door. She felt hands on her shoulders and turned her wide gaze on Damien. "Who were those people?" Her voice wavered.

He moved her away from the room and into a dimly lit alcove. It was a tight fit, but right now Sarah was grateful for the isolated space in case she had another meltdown.

"You should not have seen that so soon after your friend." He sounded frustrated with himself.

"Who are they?" she whispered hoarsely, body starting to shake with the panic coursing through her veins and the cold stone pressing against her back. She needed him to say it, to deny what she feared to be true.

Damien searched her face worriedly, then blew out a capitulating breath. "It came to my attention last night that two people had gone over Glenborough Falls. It appears they died from the tumble or froze to death in the river, though we can't be certain at this point."

Sarah's throat worked as she tried to choke back a lump of dread. "They were found near Glendale Forest?"

Looking confused, he answered, "Yes, they border one another. Why?"

"Why did they come to you?" she asked instead of answering him, her voice hollow and foreign to her own ears.

"Unfortunately, I'm a magistrate of sorts and have the privilege of sorting this mess out." He scrubbed an agitated hand over his jaw and the line of scruff, which had lost its perfectly manicured edge and was outlined by the shadows creeping over his cheeks. "I appreciate being appraised of the goings on, but there are some things of which a man wishes to be ignorant. Part of my duty is to alert the victims' families, as well, which is why I *cannot* reveal their identities before I speak with them."

That could take days! Sarah racked her brain for a way to convince him to tell her, but was the finality of knowing any better? According to Damien, knowledge had its price. But not knowing was making her sick, and it wouldn't bring Will back either way.

She managed to force her constricted vocal chords to form the words, "Did you recognize them?"

Damien frowned, his mouth tipping in a tight, grim line. "Yes, but that is all I can say." He closed his eyes when he noticed her shaking. "Oh,

266

Sarah," he murmured, wavering only a brief instant before pulling her into his arms.

Mechanically, she reached around him, clenching a handful of his shirt and trying to breathe normally. She had let Edith down, and she refused to believe that there wasn't *something* she could have done to save her.

Then the voice of self-blame reminded her that she hadn't been there for Will, either, and whispered things that conjured up images of him lying broken on the rocks, calling out for help, for *her*, until his body stilled. The people she knew and cared for here were all dying, and she was powerless to do anything.

She pressed her palm flat against Damien's back, unconsciously assuring herself that he was still there and that she hadn't lost him yet.

"You're all right." The sound of his low voice brought her back to the present, and she realized that she was shaking again. She bit her lip, feeling ridiculous but too emotionally shaken to stop.

Damien sighed and pressed the side of his jaw to her temple, his hold tightening around her as he began rocking her gently. "Calm yourself," he murmured, the corner of his mouth barely fluttering against her skin. She didn't know what to make of the strange tangle of emotions coursing through her. She tried to relax, focusing on the soothing sound of his voice and his words and felt some of the tension leave her shoulders.

"I know how awful it is—to see someone you care for lose their life in that way. It brands you and makes you fear the shadows." Sarah stilled, knowing he was referring to his mother's death.

Sensing he had her attention, he pulled back just enough to see her eyes, the stubble along his jaw lightly brushing her cheek when he shifted. She watched him intently, doubtful but hoping that his words would somehow make it hurt less.

His hands slid down to her waist. "But know that you are safe with me. I won't let anyone touch you." The sparse lighting in their little nook cast his deep-set eyes in shadows. But the shattered bits of light that did manage to touch his face caught the flecks of gold, making them shine in the darkness. She could see the sincerity there and knew that he was making a promise to protect her.

But who had been there for Will? People were sticking up for her, protecting her left and right, and she couldn't return the favor.

"Your arm," she said, realizing that she was clutching his injured bicep.

"It isn't bothering me just now." He said it like it wouldn't matter even if it were.

She removed her hands from his arms just the same, feeling embarrassed for clinging to him like that. "Should we change your bandages?" she asked, a little desperately. She needed to do something to get her mind off things—the memory of Edith and the constant questioning of whether or not Will was gone. It was only driving her mad to stand here with nothing to do but listen to her conflicting thoughts.

Damien sighed and released her waist, sensing her agitation. "This unfortunate business will take several hours more, I'm afraid. I don't think there will be enough time before the party, as much as I was looking forward to your 'gentle' treatments today." He tried to take on a teasing tone, but it fell flat.

"Are you sure you'll be okay until tomorrow?" she asked, her hands flexing anxiously at her side. "It could get infected."

"It will be just fine," he said in a low, reassuring voice. "But I have to finish this first."

Sarah nodded. "Okay. Then I should get some more salve for tomorrow." She knew the leather medicine sack Charles had given her was somewhere in her room, still half full. But she needed to immerse herself in distraction to take her mind off of the waiting and *wondering*. She hoped focusing on a task would abate the sickening knot in her stomach, and she couldn't think clearly right now with Damien standing so close.

She could tell that he sensed the lie in her words, but he also seemed to be aware of her need to keep busy. He offered a half-smile, the corners of his eyes tinged with sadness and deep empathy. "Why don't you do that?"

They shuffled out of their hideaway. "Until tonight, then." He shot her a promising smile as he unlocked the door, and Sarah quickly turned away before she again saw the contents of the room.

She wandered the castle, trying to recall the directions she had been given days ago to find the professor's lab. She kept her head down and made several wrong turns as she wandered aimlessly. Numbness crept over her mind, which was a relief, in part, though it made her thoughts feel muddled as she meandered through the maze of doorways and corridors. She couldn't get a clear grasp on anything and had to consciously focus her thoughts on just making it to her destination, which was made even more difficult by the fact that she hadn't thought to bring a candle with her.

The staircase she was descending ended abruptly. She glanced down each of the halls and tried to recall which direction she was supposed to go. *Straight ahead, right?* she asked herself, hoping it might trigger a memory.

The sound of someone's muffled cough echoed down the corridor to her right, and she knew the dungeons were down that way, reminding her that Charles was in the passageway directly in front. She took a few steps that way and jerked to a halt, staring into the darkness that she knew led to the cells.

The physician was in there. How many opportunities would she have to talk to the man who had treated the king during his illness? Out of everyone, he had to know something or have been a part of the plot itself.

268

With a final look down the lighted corridor that led to the professor, Sarah quickly turned before she lost her courage and started off toward the dungeons.

~Chapter 33~

Navigating the dark passageway was difficult, and Sarah kept a hand on the wall as she shuffled with careful steps into the blackness. Her fingers slid over a slimy stone, and she jerked her hand back, stifling a shriek of disgust as she scrubbed her palm down her skirt to remove the goo. Spotting a small, flickering light up ahead, she quickened her pace and tried not to dwell on the possibilities of what she might have touched.

As she drew nearer, the light began to take shape and was joined by several others. Though sparse in number, torches were mounted along the passageway; they gave off enough light that Sarah didn't have to concentrate so hard on her footing, but she knew this also made it easier for guards to spot her sneaking around. With this in mind, she kept close to the wall, careful not to brush up against any suspicious substances.

She saw the split in the passage and could just make out the faint outline of the cells up ahead. Crouching at the fork, she peered down each of the corridors, recalling that Damien had ordered for the physician to be kept isolated. If they wanted to keep him sequestered, they would have put him somewhere remote, but where could he be?

When Karen had been imprisoned, Will had snuck Sarah down here. It was hard to be sure with the disorienting darkness, but she was almost positive that the two of them had come through one of these passages. She tried to remember if they had passed any secluded cells, but it seemed so long ago now. It felt like her mind was adjusting to time here, and it really did feel as though four months had passed since that day.

Hoping to jog her memory, she swept her eyes over her surroundings, but everything was shrouded in shadows and difficult to make out. Not seeing any guards, Sarah stepped out into the center divide, hoping to get a better look at her options. The faint sound of jangling keys suddenly reached her ears from behind, growing louder. Alarm spread through her when she realized that someone was headed her way.

She immediately ducked into the darkest passage on her left, trying to get her breathing level, and moved quickly away from the approaching guard. Her foot caught on a loose stone, and it skidded across the floor. Sarah winced at the slight sound. It hadn't been loud enough for the guard to hear, but she didn't want to draw the prisoners' attentions, either. The last time she and Will had been here, they had caused a stir among the captives, who pleaded loudly with them for help. She couldn't risk them alerting the guard to her presence, however inadvertent it might be.

Moving down the line of cells with quieter steps, she looked at the occupants for the first time. All of the prisoners here were men, both young and old. Thankfully, most of them had slept through her noisy misstep, lying in the corner of their cells, their arms wrapped around their filthy clothes to warm themselves. A few of the younger men appeared otherwise engaged with staring off into space, though one boy was quietly rolling a small round stone back and forth across the floor between his hands. The sound had probably covered her stumble earlier.

Holding her breath as the scent of their filth reached her nostrils, she lengthened her strides. A wall appeared suddenly before her, forcing her to go right or left. Each narrow hall led to the door of a cell, but only the one on the left was locked and had a lit torch mounted just outside the door. That had to be it!

Her heart thumped noisily in her chest as she crept down the passage and neared the bars of the cell. She caught a faint, unintelligible murmur coming from the inside and swallowed. A lone figure was hunched over in the back corner, facing away from her. He was talking to himself, etching words into the stone floor with a jagged rock. Shadows hovered in the corners of the twelve-by-twelve foot room, making it nearly impossible to distinguish the crudely scratched writing on the walls. But although some of the markings had been gouged deeply into the stone or were freshly etched onto the walls, Sarah could make out enough to see that it was one word repeated over and over, covering the walls and just now starting to take over the miniscule floor space, clearly defining a madman's obsession.

Someone's been busy, she thought, disturbed over the unreadable markings.

Sarah reached up to wrap her fingers around the bars and then thought better of it, folding her arms around her middle. The man appeared engaged, but she couldn't just wait around until a guard spotted her and dragged her away. She hoped being friends with Damien had given her a certain amount of immunity, and she was not going to miss this opportunity because she felt awkward about interrupting a one-sided conversation. She cleared her throat loudly, then shot an anxious look over her shoulder.

The man flipped his free hand in the air in a dismissive gesture, but he didn't turn her way. "My thanks," he commented sarcastically, scratching at the ground.

Sarah blinked, surprised. He'd barely acknowledged her. She shook her head, though he couldn't see the gesture. "I'm not a servant." Her words echoed off the arched ceiling, and she grimaced.

The physician's head whipped around, and he was off his knees in a flash. She heard the rock clatter to the floor, but he didn't stoop to retrieve it. His eyes were wide as he wrung his hands in front of him. He didn't seem to know what to make of her presence. "P-Pardon me, miss," he stuttered. His voice was soft, but hoarse from disuse. "A mute has been servicing me here—that is why I replied so informally."

She was taken aback by his alert gaze and the clarity of his tone. She realized that despite his odd mutterings and obsessive writing, he sounded completely lucid.

Sarah was already shaking her head in dismissal. "Don't worry." His shocked gaze remained fixed on her, and she shifted her weight to her other leg as she considered what to say. After half a minute of total silence, she whispered, "I'm Sarah."

The name didn't seem to ring any bells with him. Ten seconds ticked by before he seemed to collect himself. He stepped toward the bars, keeping a respectable distance between them. "Malcolm Devlin, miss. I am—" He cleared his throat and pulled himself up to his full five-and-a-half-feet. "I *was* the physician to the royal family."

He was so dirty and thin, making him appear smaller and older than she knew him to be. Sarah wished she had thought to bring something for him—water, food, an extra blanket—though this had not been her original destination.

"That's why I wanted to speak with you." She jumped at the segue, the words running together in such a rush that she hoped he understood. "I'm not supposed to be here, but you were the one who treated the king before he died, correct?"

The physician's face became suddenly suspicious. "Yes," he replied slowly, shuffling backward a fraction of an inch. "It's common knowledge."

Sarah gripped the bars, pressing her face as close as she dared. "Did anything about his sickness strike you as unusual?"

He was already shaking his head, retreating to the back wall. His dark eyes were wide with fright. "No, no. It was a potentially contagious infection—quite typical." He pointed down the passage. "You need to leave."

"I'm not here to threaten you. I just want the truth." Her eyes searched his nervous face; he didn't look like he wanted to talk, and she knew she would have to goad him. Knowing he wasn't in a position to cause her harm, she threw caution to the wind and gave up all pretense of curiosity. "You must have known something was wrong. Did they pay you to keep the secret? Or did you poison the king yourself?"

She didn't think it was possible, but his eyes rounded even more. "I would never—they didn't—" The physician seemed at a loss as his lips worked silently. "It was an infection. . . ." His voice faded, and he bit his lip, gaze riveted to the ground.

Sarah softened her tone. "If you didn't do it, then who did?"

He seemed to debate whether or not to trust her. Then he moved forward, grabbing the bars below her hands. She pulled back a few inches to put some distance between them as Malcolm fidgeted in place, his gaze darting about nervously.

"Who, Mr. Devlin?" she prodded, then thought to add, "You can trust me."

"I am telling you the truth when I say that I cannot be certain." His answer was careful and gave away nothing.

"But you suspect someone." It was written all over his face and in the anxious way his gaze shifted around his cell and the empty hallway.

Malcolm waved his head from side to side. "A few of us have our suspicions," he answered slowly. His eyes snapped to hers suddenly, all at once alert and intense. "His disease was unnatural, miss. The progression of it . . . I spent months treating him, and nothing about the illness aligned with what I've learned. I tried everything, but because of my lack of knowledge, I could not treat him. I suspect it was untreatable." The regret in his eyes was clear in the muted torchlight.

She remembered Will thwarting an attempt on the king's life once, overturning a goblet of poisoned wine. Obviously, it had not been the only attempt.

Sarah's pulse picked up in excitement, and she asked the one question that she hoped would receive a straight answer. "Do you think it's possible that a poison could have done that to him? Over such a long period of time?"

He studied the ceiling, as though the answer were hidden there. "Yes, it's quite possible, if administered in low doses over time." He expelled a sigh, and Sarah tried not to be so obvious about holding her own breath. "I consulted the lord Cadius on the matter after the first month, but he recommended that I continue on with the treatment I was administering and not mention the idea of a toxin to anyone. Since he was the king's advisor, I was required to obey."

Gripping the bars a little tighter with her slick palms, Sarah swallowed back her eager questions; the man was clearly lost in the past, brows drawn in regret.

"I should have known." Malcolm's words were so quiet she almost missed them. His bleary gaze was fixed on the wall just over her shoulder.

Sarah angled her head to better see his face. "What should you have known?"

When he did meet her eyes, his lips turned up in a bleak, humorless smile. "Even you suspect the same man we all do." She noticed that he never mentioned Cadius by name. The man was like a ghost that haunted them all.

"If I had acted on my doubts, I might have been able to stop him." Whatever color life underground hadn't yet sapped from his skin drained from Malcolm's face in that moment. "And now I am here because I'm the last piece of the puzzle."

Sarah pressed closer to the bars, shaking her head. "You're in here because you *attacked* Damien," she reminded, feeling instantly defensive of her friend.

"No," he whispered hoarsely. "I remain because they want me out of the way."

That much made sense, but she still didn't understand why he had fought with Damien and said as much to him. His hands covered hers in an instant. Startled, Sarah tried to pull free, but his grip was intense, frail fingers clinging desperately to her and pinning her hands around the bars. The scraped metal grated her palms. "It wasn't as it seemed. You need to go back to the room—"

Sarah's head whipped in the direction of the hall. She heard the same rattling of keys from earlier and knew the guard was coming back this way. She turned to Malcolm. "I have to go." She tried to slip her hands free, but his grip only tightened.

"You must come back soon, my lady." His eyes burned with desperation. Sarah said she would, but he must have sensed her half-hearted agreement. He pressed his face against the bars. "I'm the only thing keeping them from getting away with this," he whispered, trying to make her understand. He emphasized his next words, eyes burning feverishly with desperation and fear. "*I. Won't. Have. Long.*"

She nodded, knowing the guilty party wouldn't allow such a small player in the game to foil their plan. "I promise. I'll come back soon."

He let her slip free, and her eyes scanned his cell one final time before escaping down the corridor. She hid around the corner of the other secluded cell across the hall, waiting in the dark for the guard to pass before dashing up the stairs. As she ran, her adrenaline kicked in, clearing her mind. Pieces of the word Malcolm had been scratching into the floor suddenly took shape in her mind. Not a word, but a name.

Lisandro.

But maybe she had read it wrong, or the light could have played tricks on her eyes, giving the illusion that the crude markings were all one word. She shook her head at that. Damien's name had been written all over the cell and from so many different angles; it would be nearly impossible to

274

mistakenly read *every* one of them. But then why Malcolm's obsession with the name Lisandro? Was it a guilty conscience fixating on the man he had wronged? Did he wish for retribution against Damien for commanding that he be put in here, or was it something more?

Her mind became occupied with trying to tie in this latest confusing piece of the puzzle and decide if it held any relevance to the greater mystery, or if the carvings in the cell truly *were* the obsessive ramblings of a madman. Sarah glanced around, realizing that she had gone the wrong way, and started to panic until she saw the cracked door at the top of the stairs, spilling a modicum of light onto the first few steps at the top of the narrow staircase. As long as it led up and away from the dungeons below, then she could find her way from there.

Dragging a hand over the wall to keep her balance on the short, high steps, she moved quickly toward the top, feeling more on-edge by the minute as she neared the sliver of light. She stepped on something small and hard, pinning it to the ground as her other foot became entangled on the rest of it. Sarah fell hard against the stairs before she could correct her footing, and she heard the object clatter against the stones, landing noisily a few steps down.

With a start, she jumped up from her flattened position and lurched over the few remaining steps. She burst through the door, mindless of anyone on the other side. Panting, she stared into the darkness below, unable to make out anything. Her initial panic began to subside in the light of the hall, and she felt silly for overreacting.

Sarah sent a self-conscious glance over the empty hall, unable to push aside the feeling that she had been here before. Racking her memory for the answer, she realized that this had been the passage the false Shadow had escaped into. This just *happened* to be the staircase she mistakenly stumbled upon? Karen would call it providence.

Slipping a low-burning torch from its perch, Sarah slowly picked her way down the stairs. Her narrowed eyes scanned the stones, searching. The light caught on an object further down, causing it to glitter faintly in the darkness. She squinted but couldn't make it out. Holding the torch far in front of her, she made her way down the steps.

Torchlight bounced off the object, reflecting golden light as she neared, and it began to take shape. Brow twisting in confusion at what she saw, Sarah stooped to grab the gold chain and held it up to the light. It wasn't the fob that gave her pause, since she had seen some men at the castle wear the short chain on their clothes in a decorative fashion. It was the heavy round object on the *other* end that put her mind into overdrive.

"How on earth . . .?" she whispered in confusion. Was that even possible? She spent a minute examining the round object to make sense of what she was seeing and then pressed the knob at the top. The mechanism sprung open, and she gasped aloud at what it revealed. She shook her head, unbelieving, as her eyes scanned the contents.

A memory she had previously thought insignificant suddenly resurfaced, momentarily blinding her to all else—a man fiddling with the chain in his pocket. Seemingly a harmless gesture to relieve nervous energy, but to Sarah it meant answers . . . and more questions.

She forgot her reasons for questioning why Damien's name was all over the physician's cell, her quest to bring Cadius to justice, and why she was even here. The sudden onslaught of total confusion and surprise momentarily overshadowed the disparaging feeling of Will's death as a barrage of emotions roiled within her—surprise, bewilderment, anger, despair, rage, disappointment, betrayal. They flooded through her at once, clouding her vision and making her blood pump until a rushing sound filled her ears. Sarah shook her head. She didn't know what to make of any of this, but she was going to do something about it.

Folding the chain in the palm of her hand, she formed a fist around the ice-cold object. She made her way back up the staircase, closing the door and slipping the torch back into its perch. With purposeful strides, she moved through the hall and down the stairs, facing the ground to avoid eye contact with the servants milling about the foyer. Once outside, each step became more determined than the last. Sarah vaguely felt the bite of crisp wind against her face and realized she hadn't brought a coat. Then she tightened her shaky grip around the chain and suddenly forgot all about the cold.

She moved down the street, teeth clenching when she spotted the person she sought. They stepped into the building, and she hurried after the fraud, stopping just inside the doorway. Her chest rose and fell rapidly with her inward struggle for control.

At last, she was able to speak. "Why did you do it?" No beating around the bush, just a question she wasn't sure she even wanted an answer to.

Robert dropped the heavy sacks on the ground with a *thud* and looked up at her in surprise. His face relaxed into a smile. "Taylor isn't here." Then his expression tightened when he caught the look on her face. "Everything all right?" he asked cautiously, clearly sensing that she was barely holding back her rage.

"*Why?*" she demanded. Angry tears burned the back of her throat but she wouldn't let Edith's killer see her cry.

He thrust his chin out, eyebrows rising in genuine confusion. "Why . . .?"

She reached behind her and jerked the door closed. Robert appeared nervous now and retreated a step when she advanced. "Why did you kill Edith?" she ground out.

276

His crystal-clear eyes widened. "Wha—Hey, now, you've got the wrong idea."

She let the object dangle from the chain and held it up for his inspection, feeling brief satisfaction over his shocked expression. "Really? Because you left this behind after you shot her." Her whole body was shaking, and she clenched her hands at her sides, feeling the disk bounce against her thigh. She pinned Robert with a glare. "Now what's a humble blacksmith's assistant doing with a nineteenth century pocket watch?"

~Chapter 34~

Some of the color had drained from Robert's usually tan features. His eyes were riveted to the watch, and he looked torn between snatching it from her grasp and denying her accusation that it belonged to him. Finally, he said, "It isn't what you think."

Sarah scoffed, the sound coming out choked. She swallowed back her tears. "First answer me why you killed Edith."

He took a step toward her. "I *swear* I didn't touch that woman."

"I saw you!" She shrugged out of his grasp when he reached for her, looking desperate to explain. Sarah shook her head, groaning at the sight of him and planting her fists against her tightly closed lids. "Will *trusted* you." And now he might be dead, too.

She swallowed back her tears and faced Edith's murderer. Robert's face was a mask of pain and indecision. "How could you do it?" she whispered accusingly.

He shook his head. His eyes were wide with innocence. "I didn't. You have to believe me." He reached a hand out again, but she jerked back.

"Don't touch me!" she shrieked, voice breaking.

He held up his hands in compliance, obviously surprised at her outburst. His clear eyes pleaded with her to understand. "Fine. But I'm not the one who shot her."

"Don't lie to me. You were there."

"Yes, I was." He reached slowly into his shirt, as if afraid of what she might do if he startled her again. He produced a letter, the seal having been slit open, and held it out to her.

Sarah eyed him suspiciously before snatching the missive from his grasp with her free hand. But she didn't read it, only held it up in accusation. "What is this?"

He sucked in a breath. "This was hand-delivered to me three days ago with a pouch of silver coins. Well, it was placed on my front stoop, actually.

278

It's a request that I pose as the Shadow, find my way into one of the upstairs rooms, and run when the time was right." He shrugged, his expression ashamed. "That was it. And, yes, you chased me into that passage, but I only ran because I heard someone coming. I didn't know it was you, and I *definitely* didn't find out about what happened to your friend until just this morning."

Sarah tried to process this, to find the lie in his words. But there was genuine innocence and regret in his gaze. "Who gave it to you?" she asked.

Shaking his head, he answered, "Like I said, it was left outside my door. But I did see a man stumbling away." Robert pursed his lips at her eager expression. "No, I didn't see his face. I assumed he was nobody, but thinking back, he had the posture of a guard, I'm sure of it. Even though he *was* loaded from the tavern at the time," he added.

"And you didn't think that something about this deal might have been underhanded?" she asked, disbelieving. "A drunk guard delivering you money and a mysterious command to commit a felony?"

Robert looked suddenly sheepish. "The thought crossed my mind. But this man—this legend—was my hero growing up. I shadow him as a friend and coworker, and then I was suddenly given the opportunity to know what it's like to *be* him. So, yeah, I was blinded by a childhood fantasy. When I saw where he hid his bow and cloak . . ." His eyes searched her face, looking pained. "You'll never know how sorry I am that I didn't just throw that money and the letter into the river."

Sarah was momentarily taken aback that he had discovered Will's secret, but Will had said so himself that it was only a matter of time. She stared at the floor, feeling unshed tears burn the back of her nose over Robert's regret and her own. Why hadn't she realized that there had been two intruders before? They had come from different rooms and passages and gone in opposite directions, throwing her off. She had let it go before, assuming there were secret passageways she hadn't known about.

Slipping a finger beneath the sticky, cracked seal, Sarah unfolded the letter. It was just a small, unsigned note written in elegant script, detailing the date and instructions that Robert had just revealed. She carefully refolded the letter—the evidence—and let her gaze rest on the seal a moment longer. It looked familiar. Edith had once told her that most noble families had their crest pressed into the seals they traveled with. Maybe if she searched the castle, she would be able to find the owner of that seal and get one step closer to finding Edith's killer.

Looking up, she met Robert's tortured gaze. "Do you know who the other man was?"

"I wish I did."

Sarah released a small breath at his genuine remorse. "I believe you." His shoulders drooped in relief, and she could tell it meant a lot to him.

279

"But you're returning his bow the first chance you get."

Robert nodded eagerly, and she sighed. "So I guess that brings us to this." She held the watch out to him, and he accepted it with a look of gratitude. He stared at it for a long moment.

"It was my great-grandfather's," he said at last, his voice faraway. The heirloom clearly meant very much. "I thought I'd lost this."

"I think the glass may have cracked in the fall," she said regretfully. "Sorry."

Robert hesitated, and then slipped the watch into his pocket, careful to hide the chain from view. "Thank you for bringing it back to me."

She had expected him to pop it open then and there to assess the damage to something so precious. Then she remembered the picture inside and knew he didn't want her to see it. From what she gathered so far, he was as caught up in this mess as she. "How do you know Karen?"

Robert's eyes snapped to her face in surprise.

She scratched her ear. "Uh, yeah, I saw the picture. I didn't mean to snoop, but I was trying to figure out what it was, and it sort of popped open." She watched his expression carefully. "But you can understand my confusion at finding a color photograph of the two of you tucked inside a timepiece. . . . Is that how you got here? You came with Karen?"

A grin of comprehension spread over his lips, though it wasn't as bright as usual. "I thought you didn't blend in with the crowd too well." Sarah's shoulders slumped. Yet another reminder that she didn't belong. "I wasn't sure how to approach it, though. Once I tried to 'tactfully' ask a woman if she was different and believed in the unbelievable. Turned out she was just modern and from out of town."

Sarah felt her lips twitch in amusement. "You realize that seems a little creepy."

"I do now, and trust me, I've kept my distance from foreign women since then." Robert rubbed a hand over his jaw, as though nursing an invisible wound. "Had a nasty right hook for such a pretty thing."

Mirth fading, Sarah asked, "Have you spoken with Karen recently?" He winced and shook his head, surprising her. "But if there are other"—she sent a look over the empty room and lowered her voice—"*time travelers* running around in the same place, don't you think you should keep in contact with them as much as possible?"

He sighed. "That photo you saw? It was taken on a Santa Barbara beach two years ago, just before I proposed."

Sarah couldn't wipe the slack-jawed expression from her face, completely forgetting her previous question. "You two were engaged?" she asked in disbelief.

His chuckle was without humor. "No. I asked, and she declined. We were just kids then," he went on quietly. His eyes stared through her, distant with remembrance. "I grew up in Santa Barbara and worked myself to death one summer so that I could go to Cambridge to advance my knowledge of European history. That's where I met Charles, and he and I hit it off. He would show me pictures of Karen, saying she was a fiery child with just as much heart for science as he had, but I never met her until she broke into the youth meeting I was attending." He smiled at the memory, and Sarah openly gaped at him. *He* was the boy Karen had told her about?

"I was so curious that I asked Little Karen to stay." Robert chuckled and slanted her a look. "She'd clock me if she heard me call her that, but she was such a fiery little sprite back then."

Sarah felt her own lips curve and arched a brow. "Back then?" He grinned back. Shaking her head, she remarked, "So I guess you got pretty close after that."

Looking suddenly far away, he answered, "We were inseparable after that night. I was given over to the foster care system when I was a baby, and maybe the fact that we were both orphans bonded us quickly. But, I don't know; I've never had that kind of connection with anyone. I just always felt safe with her."

Remembering her quick trust and friendship with Karen, Sarah smiled faintly. "She has that affect on people. So then what happened?"

"Charles had mentioned his failed experiments in the past, and I offered my assistance." Robert grinned wryly. "I'm basically hopeless when it comes to science, but I'm a fast learner and helped in any way I could, offering my knowledge of history. Then I started working with the two of them and fell in love with Karen." His smile faded along with his voice.

Sarah watched his face, seeing the regret etched into the lines by his eyes that she had failed to notice before. "And then she rejected you," she filled in.

The grin returned, aimed at his own foolishness. "I ambushed a girl barely seventeen and asked her to consider spending forever with me—there was no ring, no plan. Just a blind, cocky boy and his feelings pleading with her to say yes. And this was before I asked her how she felt about me." He chuckled. "All or nothing, I guess."

He started fiddling with the watch in his pocket. "She said she had feelings for me but wasn't ready to settle down before she experienced life for herself." Robert's face became a mask of shame. "I told her if that was the way she felt, then I couldn't work with them any more; it would just be too hard. She stormed off the beach, and I didn't go after her."

"You let her leave?" Sarah asked, surprised that he had given up so easily.

Robert grinned at her perception. "A week later I realized that I should have gone after her and shown her that I was willing to wait and be at her side during her adventures. Because I was." His Adam's apple bobbed in a convulsive swallow. "But we had the working prototype for the watches up by this time, and when I found out that she escaped to this place, I followed her to tell her she was worth waiting for."

"That's romantic," Sarah said with a smile, forgetting that there must have been more to the story.

Face drawn, it didn't appear that Robert shared her opinion. "Well, when I arrived and discovered where she was staying, I went there and saw her outside alone. I was desperate to fix things, but I couldn't go to her; she was almost too beautiful to touch, so I stayed in the trees." His eyes were glazed in remembrance.

Sarah could almost picture his floppy, sun-bleached hair poking out from behind the trunk of an oak, tan face drawn in suffering. It was romantic when the hero in films watched his maiden secretly, and they always ended up together in the end. *So what happened?* she wondered to herself.

As if in answer to her unspoken question, Robert, still lost in his daydream, admitted quietly, "I hesitated and lost my chance: A man came to her, and they talked easily and seemed to care for each other. I knew by the way she looked at him that she was already in love with someone else." He shot her a self-deprecating grin. "That's when I found out first-hand about the inconsistency between our times."

Grimacing at his painful tale, she offered, "I'm really sorry." And she was. His story was heartbreaking, but he looked accepting of Karen's decision, though it was obvious it still pained him to speak of it. "What did you say when you saw her again?"

Robert shrugged. "What could I say? She was in love with him and staying with a caring family." He smiled wryly. "I decided to be a gentleman and to do the right thing. I walked away, refusing to interfere with their relationship or see her again. Then I performed a few odd jobs in Ridlan for a little over a year until I came here."

Sarah waved a hand, wanting him to retrace his steps. "Wait, so you've been here ever since she broke your heart and she doesn't even know it? It's been *years*. Why did you stay?!"

He looked amused at her outburst. "Because this is my home now. I've always felt that I was born in the wrong time, and since I had nothing left to go back to—" He shrugged, at a loss for words. "Anyway, I misplaced my watch and—"

"You *lost* it? Where?"

"Back in Ridlan, shortly after I arrived." Robert took a step toward her, holding his hands up in defense. "Don't worry. Like I told you, it was an old prototype and had numerous issues, so there's no way it's lasted this long, even if someone in this century *could* find a way to get it to work. And there is no way they could."

282

Sarah's shoulders stooped a little in relief. "Oh, okay."

Robert cringed. "You won't tell the boss, will you? I'd hate to have my hero, well, hate me." He rubbed the back of his neck, and Sarah wondered if he had picked up the uncomfortable habit from Will.

She swallowed. "You said earlier that Will isn't here?" That familiar sensation of dread crept into her stomach.

"Yeah. He took off last night to meet someone"—he grinned knowingly—"which I assumed was you. I haven't seen him since. I snuck back into his house this morning to return the items I'd . . . 'borrowed,' but the house was empty. Why?"

Sarah hesitated. Could she really burden him with something she wasn't even sure of herself?

Edging closer, Robert said warily, "You know something."

She bit her lip, then told him of the two bodies that had been found at the bottom of the falls and of her suspicions that one might have been Will.

Her eyes had filled with tears by the end of her story, and Sarah bit the inside of her cheek hard to keep them at bay. "I don't know what else to think."

Robert looked like he'd seen a ghost and backed up a few steps so he could lean against the wall. He shook his head in disbelief. "But he isn't supposed to die like this. I thought it would be incredible to shadow him, to follow in the footsteps of a legend." His eyes met hers, and she saw the same fear she felt reflected in his gaze. "You don't think that this is our fault, do you? Because we've messed with the past?"

She had wondered the same thing, but couldn't bring herself to believe it. "Karen said that they really can't be sure this is the past," she said dully, her argument sounding weak; she was only repeating what she'd been told, and she didn't even believe it anymore. "We can't jump to conclusions."

Raking a hand up through her hair, Sarah huffed as she realized the hour was getting late. "I have to go. But, please," she added, swallowing. "If you hear from him, please come find me."

Robert tried to smile hopefully, but his eyes swam with doubt. "He'll come back. I'm sure of it. He's indestructible."

She gave a half-hearted shake of her head, chest tightening. "Will doesn't need to be indestructible—I just need him to be alive."

****

Sarah hurried alongside the castle, chaffing her arms against the chill in her bones. The poorly veiled worry on Robert's face let her know she wasn't being overly sensitive or jumping to conclusions, which left her feeling weighed down with concern. She tried telling herself it wasn't true, but then where *was* he?

A faint acrid scent reached her nose, and her mind registered the smell as her eyes scanned the tree line. Her feet became rooted to the spot at the sight of the doe, hind legs bound together, dangling upside down from a bare limb. Sarah's stomach clenched at the sight of the blood—no longer pouring from its gaping throat—that had leeched out into the pristine snow, staining a large circle of earth beneath the dead animal's nose.

"A shame, is it not?"

Sarah's body stiffened. That was a voice she had hoped never again to hear. Stifling a shiver, she turned her head from the gruesome scene and met Cadius' chilling gaze. In the gray daylight, his eyes appeared even more stormy and unearthly.

"I'm sorry?" She sounded breathless.

One leather-gloved finger flicked in the direction of the forest, toward the maimed deer. "It's a pity having to end something so lovely."

Sarah's skin crawled at his unwavering stare. Her mind ran rampant, as did her pulse, reminding her that this man may have killed his own brother. And here she was, alone with a murderer with the stench of blood clinging to the air. She told herself to be calm and tried to remember that he wasn't out to get her. Yet.

Not wanting to look into his eyes or at the dead creature, she focused her gaze on a distant tree just past the doe. "Dinner?" she managed to ask nonchalantly.

"It is now." Cadius took a step forward, and his elbow nearly brushed hers. Chest clenching with the effort not to shrink away, she bit the inside of her cheek, knowing that revealing her fear would only give him reason to suspect. "You see," he went on conversationally, "it was caught nibbling the garden, snooping where it shouldn't be."

Sarah felt a pang of anxiety shoot through her, though she told herself she was being jumpy. "It's awfully small. Could it really do much damage?"

For some reason, his eyes sparked to life, and he seemed to take pleasure in her words. "On the contrary," he drawled in his low, cultured voice, "if left unchecked, a creature so seemingly harmless can destroy many months of harvesting."

Cadius smiled indulgently at her, and then his eyes focused on something over her head. She turned and saw Damien speaking with one of the livery boys, his back to them. Gray eyes were again fixed on the animal when she looked back at Cadius.

"Even worse is the knowledge that she has been spotted in the forest with a large buck in weeks past, and he would do great devastation," he intoned.

Her hands balled into fists at her sides, toes curling as a chill caught her spine. Sarah sensed an underlying meaning to his words and resisted the

284

urge to glance back at Damien. Swallowing, she asked, barely above a whisper, "How is that?"

Cadius stroked his short beard. "Usually, the deer tend to keep to the thicket—more foliage and the like—but this doe discovered a way into the garden and seemed to take a liking to the ease of the meal. Naturally, the buck followed." His hand dropped to his side, and his beard twitched in dark humor. Voice amused, he added, "And like any male, he would continue to risk exposure to please her. We cannot have that."

Sarah felt some of the color drain from her face. Her neck tingled with the instinctive desire to see if Damien had spotted them yet, and she forced her eyes to the sagging body of the doe to keep from being so obvious. Now she was sure Cadius was threatening not only her, but Damien too. He had been right when he told her to not mess with a man in power. And Sarah had practically thrown the king's death in Cadius' face last night! She had been too overt in her questioning, and now he was suspicious. His conversational nonchalance as he watched her with the same poorly masked, cold intensity as he did the doe had her pulse jumping.

Swallowing her fear, she replied, "Why not just build a trap as a warning? I'm sure it would back off. It seems like a waste to kill it." It felt strange to pretend they were still speaking of the animal, but if she could convince Cadius that she wasn't a threat . . .

"On the contrary, it is far more useful dead than it is alive."

A knot of dread formed in her middle. "Because you can use it for food," she managed past a tight throat.

His cold eyes met hers, and she thought his thin lips might have curved, like a cat having caught a mouse. "Because it is no longer a nuisance, and the smell of its blood will serve as a warning to the buck." He sighed, as if greatly troubled, murmuring, "If only it had been a little wiser and kept out of the garden. Such a shame."

His words dropped into Sarah's gut with a dull *thud*, and her jaw spasmed in panic when he picked up her hand with his ice-cold glove and dipped his head over it, pausing mid-bow. "What an interesting mark," he murmured, eyes on her scar. His short lashes twitched as something caught his eye to the left, and Sarah turned wide, frightened eyes on Damien.

He had just spotted them, and his own gaze registered alarm as he froze for a split second. The stable boy was still speaking with him, but without any excuses, Damien moved toward Sarah with his concerned gaze flickering between her and the older man. Cadius released her hand with painful slowness, and Sarah nearly sighed aloud.

Damien pasted on a smile, and she couldn't ever remember seeing it look so cracked. "I should escort you inside, my lady, before the hour becomes too late." His voice was strained, and his eyes were worried, looking like they wanted to drag over her features to make sure she was all right.

Sarah couldn't even manage to nod in agreement as he took her arm. Cadius looked pointedly at him before turning his smile on her, and that tight pulling of his lips into a thin light made her skin crawl. "I look forward to the time when we meet again, milady." Then Damien was dragging her back into the castle, his face ashen.

Sarah swallowed at the man's tone, what she felt was a mixture of twisted pleasure and menace, though she hoped she was reading into it. But no matter how she imagined it, it seemed that Cadius truly was looking forward to watching her suffer.

~*Chapter 35*~

Golden light spilled across the floor from the open window as the girls readied her for the ball, and Sarah shivered in the cool air. A chill had settled in her bones after her disturbing encounter with Cadius, and she couldn't shake the feeling that she was being watched.

Thank you, God, for Damien coming when he did. He seemed to save her from trauma often, as of late, and she couldn't be more grateful that he had arrived when he did.

She felt her skin crawl when she remembered the way Cadius' stormy eyes had watched her as he spoke of the doe serving as a warning. Would he punish Damien, too, if he decided to make an example of her? Sarah still felt his arms around her as he pulled her inside, away from Cadius and his threats. No admonishments, no assurances. He just held her, as if he needed to be assured of her presence as much as she needed his comfort. She couldn't bear the thought of him being punished for her brashness, something that Will had encouraged her to keep in check while she was at the castle.

Her shoulders sagged as she thought of Will. Even in the wake of her unsettling afternoon, the reminder of him was always just under the surface, accompanying every thought. When little Sevrine had gone to close the window as evening faded, Sarah asked that it be left open. The sun was falling quickly as night approached, bringing with it a cold breeze that made her feel awake and refreshed, though it did cause her to shiver every now and then. But she welcomed the cool against her skin after forty-eight hours of ups and downs; if she could feel, then it meant she was still alive. And if she was alive, then maybe there was a chance that Will was, too.

Wishful thinking, she thought before she could stop herself.

Closing her eyes, she pretended that the tense silence in the room was filled with Leah and her mother's chatter. They were giggling and laughing as they helped her into her ball gown, which wasn't wrapped around her like a vice—no corset-like structure constricted her breathing. And for a moment, she allowed herself to imagine the way Will had guided her across the dance floor and smiled at her for the first time—

The servant girl gave the ties a swift yank to cinch the back of her dress. Sarah gasped and grabbed hold of the closest bed support to keep from being pulled backward. "Does it have to be . . . so tight?" She pressed a hand to her ribs where the fabric was stretched taut.

"Yes." Beatrice was laying jewelry selections out on the desk and spoke without really acknowledging her. Sarah wasn't so sure she believed the girl.

She had asked the name of the younger sibling, Jenna, in an effort to get off on the right foot and maybe even make things more amiable between them. No such luck, but now she did know that Beatrice was the evil older sister and Jenna was just quiet, though she seemed to resent Sarah as much as her elder sibling did. Out of the entire castle staff, she had to get stuck with these two.

Then there was Sevrine. The little curly-haired angel stood by the window, hands clenched obediently in front of her, as she watched with rapt attention as Jenna cinched the back of the dress. Candles were scattered about the room in preparation for nightfall, and the light cast a golden halo over the French girl's bouncing curls. She caught Sarah watching her and ducked her head shyly. Sevrine didn't speak much English and rarely said more than a simple "Yes" or "No," and sometimes all they received was a nod. Sarah wanted to draw the girl out of her shell, but didn't know how.

Now that she was strapped into the dress and felt more like a slab of tightly wrapped salami than a girl headed off to a grand masquerade, Jenna guided her over to the desk to start weighing her down with accessories. Beatrice selected a loud, jewel-crusted number from the table and clasped it behind Sarah's neck. She grimaced as the weight of the oversized, jeweled layers fell against her chest. The thing was enormous!

She glanced up and saw that Sevrine had fixed the necklace with a grimace of displeasure. Feeling eyes on her, the little girl met Sarah's gaze. With both sisters behind her fussing over securing the gaudy thing, Sarah discreetly pointed at it and quickly stuck her tongue out, pantomiming gagging. Sevrine started and quickly averted her eyes, though a small smile began to make its way over her lips.

Grinning, Sarah asked, "Is there something, uh, *smaller*?"

She could almost feel their looks of displeasure. Beatrice spoke first. "I'm sure we could find something that better suits you." It didn't sound like a compliment.

Together they removed the clasp, and Sarah gently replaced it on the table. "I can find something myself." They didn't seem pleased about her decision, but Sevrine had edged a little closer to see what she would pick.

Sarah perused the selections laid out before her, but they all looked as garish as the first. Then she sifted through the chest and eventually found something she liked enough to pull out for a better look. She held it up for Sevrine. "Do you like it?"

The little girl inched closer and then timidly nodded her consent. The neckline was made up of several layers of thin gold chains that twisted into an intricate knot at the base of her throat, and a cascade of golden chains and small turquoise jewels spilled from the knot. It was elegant but wouldn't weigh her down like the other had.

Sarah smiled. "Should I?"

Sevrine's large eyes surveyed the dressing table, and she poked her nose out as something caught her eye. Small fingers pointed at the table. "That one."

Her gaze landed on Will's necklace. She had removed it last night when she went to bed, and in her haste to find his body, she had forgotten to put it on again.

Swallowing, Sarah laid the golden necklace on the table and hesitantly picked up the pendant. Forcing her tight lips into a small smile, she asked, "This?"

Sevrine nodded her head emphatically, encouraging her to try it on.

Neck muscles tightening, Sarah reached behind her and did the clasp with shaking fingers. The lightweight pendant fell against her chest, its delicate bulk so familiar that she nearly sighed aloud. It wasn't extravagant or eye-catching like the others, but wearing it made her feel whole.

"Beautiful," Sevrine whispered in heavily accented English. She was smiling up at her angelically, and Sarah felt her dead heart flip.

"I think it's perfect," she agreed, returning the girl's smile. Sarah tried to avoid the other maids' looks of displeasure as they adjusted the skirt of her royal purple dress. The scooped neckline hung off her shoulders and was a little more daring than she would have picked out for herself, but she had to admit that it was spectacular with the small white scroll detailing against the darker fabric.

They applied some cosmetics to her face and lips, which was energy wasted, as most of her face would be covered the entire night. Sarah fingered the mask she would wear as the girls put unnecessary effort into dolling her up. Her finger lazily followed the sparkling white-gray swirls that had been painted onto the ivory mask, moving to trace the row of tiny silver beads that outlined its delicate face and trailed along the pointed edges that would reach her temples. It was lovely, and she was grateful that she could hide her feelings behind it tonight.

Beatrice lifted the mask up over her eyes, and Sarah took a deep breath as the maid tied the silken ribbon behind her head. "You are presentable," she declared in a monotone voice, taking a step back.

289

"Thanks," Sarah said, sounding more sarcastic than she'd intended as she wiggled her nose, trying to get used to the light weight of the mask, though it fit her like a second skin. Before she left, she shot a secretive wink to the little angel and received a genuine smile from Sevrine in return.

Downstairs, it was a bustle of activity. Guests were pouring through the front door into the great hall, keeping the doormen constantly occupied and servants busy as they darted to and fro, collecting cloaks and furs and then depositing them in a small room before rushing back for the next drove of guests to throw their coats at them.

There were a few families, obviously well to-do, but most of the new arrivals appeared to be noble couples. Though from the looks of things, some of these "unions" were just for show: No one wanted to attend a ball solo, and it seemed anyone would do, no matter that their unconcealed dislike of one another—visible even beneath their elaborate masks covered in beads and feathers—destroyed any illusion of happiness.

Realizing she was just standing at the top of the stairs, Sarah gripped the banister to steady herself and forced her feet to move, her heeled shoes making the trip slow and difficult. As she neared the landing, she suddenly became aware of the way her eyes scanned the masks below, searching for one face in particular. She couldn't stop herself from imagining the way Will's face would light up when he saw her descending toward him, his smile pulling slowly across his lips. It only made it hurt more when she returned to reality and couldn't spot him anywhere in the small crowd gathered in the hall.

Of course he isn't here, she reminded herself bleakly as she followed the other guests into the noisy ballroom. She knew there was a chance that she might never see him again, but her eyes seemed to have a mind of their own, searching the gathering of guests and nobles the instant she stepped inside the great room. Her fingers brushed the circular pendant, as though the mere touch could conjure him from the shadows.

She was one of the tallest women there in her heels, but she still stood on tiptoe to better see over the heads of the other attendees, her hope-filled gaze moving swiftly from guest to guest even as she reprimanded herself for thinking that he might be present. A servant offered her a goblet from the tray he held, but Sarah barely noticed him as she lowered herself onto her heels, deflated. He wasn't there. She had allowed herself to hope before, let herself think that there might be a chance he was still alive, but now . . .

"You look ravishing tonight." She jumped at the words spoken close to her ear, stupidly allowing herself to believe that it had been Will's voice. Heart catching in her throat, she turned around slowly, not wanting to destroy the illusion.

Damien smiled appreciatively as he took in her appearance, and Sarah felt her neck warm beneath her hair. He had carefully re-sculpted the line of hair along his jaw and had dressed for the occasion, reminding her of the polished man she had first met, though the two-sided mask—painted green on one side and white on the other—hinted at the mischievous nature she knew was there.

Grinning unapologetically, he lifted the disguise from his eyes and set it on top of his head. "Did I surprise you?"

Swallowing her disappointment, Sarah offered him a wavering smile. They were nearly at eye level with the height advantage of her heels, and his eyes were sparkling, more alive than they'd been earlier. "I thought you were someone else."

"Who were you expecting?" Damien was still smiling and appeared oblivious to the way he controlled the room, specifically the women around them. Despite the golden eyes that lent him a cheeky edge in this austere crowd and the fact that he preferred his unique scruff to the thick beards noblemen commonly wore, he clearly belonged here with these people—he worked the crowd without even trying.

Sarah shook her head. "No one." She tried to convince herself of this truth, but it felt like a betrayal to be here without Will. Unable to resist, she asked, "How did everything go this afternoon? I didn't get to ask you, you know, *earlier.*"

Some of the joy left his eyes, revealing the weariness it had masked. "As well as can be expected." He leaned in closer and lowered his voice, the chatter of the crowd nearly drowning out his words. "I ordered that the bodies be moved tonight, using the ball as a distraction. We don't need any of the guests thinking that we keep spare corpses lying about he castle." Shaking his head, Damien added, "It never gets easier."

"I'm sorry," she said. And she was, for so many reasons.

Straightening, Damien gave her a faint smile. "As am I." He hesitated, then tipped his head to the side inquisitively. Eyes softening, he whispered, "How are you?"

She knew what he was referring to, and Sarah felt the first stirrings of warmth in her stomach since yesterday. She ducked her head, uncharacteristically bashful. "Better, thanks to you. You really rescued me earlier."

He looked suddenly uncomfortable. "Did he . . . insult you in any way?" They had been interrupted by Sarah's scuttling maids nearly the instant he pulled her inside the castle, and they hadn't had a chance to discuss Cadius and his storyboard threats.

Rubbing her thumb over the palm Cadius had touched, she wondered how much to tell Damien. Then she sighed, knowing it wasn't fair to keep secrets when they involved him. Lowering her voice, she answered, "He was just talking, although it was really creepy how he explained why they killed that deer, like it was all her fault. But it was like he was implying

291

something else entirely."

"What do you mean?" But his wary expression said he already knew.

Sarah swallowed, trying to mask how uncomfortable she had been, but a shiver snaked up her spine when she remembered the cold look in Cadius' eyes. "When he talked about how the animal should have been smarter, I'm almost positive he wasn't referring to it at all."

Body stiffening, Damien filled in, "He was warning you off."

She nodded grimly. "I don't know why he suspects me." She stopped, remembering what Damien had said about Cadius having eyes everywhere. Her shoulders stooped. "No, I guess I do, since you told me not to mess with him." She swallowed, hating to admit she had involved Damien when all he had done was try to protect her.

"Then what?" he prodded, sensing more.

Through the slits in her mask, her eyes shifted warily over the closest guests, and she leaned in. "I think Cadius was threatening you too." His brows lifted, and she felt a tad embarrassed admitting the rest of her story. "He kept talking about how the buck she was with would follow her anywhere, and that he would either be caught and killed because of the doe, or her body would warn him to stay away."

Damien's hands had turned to fists at his sides, and a vein was pulsing on his neck. She wanted to say that maybe Cadius wasn't serious, or perhaps she had read into the whole unsettling diatribe. But the look in his eyes, the icy, calculated way he spoke, told her he meant every word and would follow through if she didn't back off.

"I didn't think I tipped him off last night," she rushed on. "And I didn't mean to involve you. If I could go back, I'd shut up and—"

He took her hand, brows knitting in a grimace. "Sarah, stop." She bit her lip to keep from rambling more apologies. His voice was diplomatic, but he looked troubled. "I can protect myself. I only wish that—that I could *do* something."

Despite the seriousness of their conversation, Sarah felt her lips pull gently at his protective side coming out. "You've done so much already."

He appeared surprised, and then the tension in his shoulders eased. "It's possible he was only trying to scare you, but I'll do my utmost to keep you out of his snare. But let us forget it this evening; we could both do with a distraction."

Sarah nodded eagerly, and his gaze roved over their surroundings. "I so hate these things. It is nothing but politics and appearing as though you belong. It's such a—"

"A lie?" she filled in when he faltered.

"Exactly." His eyes lit with an idea. Raising his brow in challenge, Damien slipped his mask back in place and held out his elbow, shooting her a cheeky grin. "May I accompany the lady for a dance?"

292

She wanted to accept, to follow him into the center of the room and lose herself in the dance, but she hesitated. Although she and Will had only danced together once, Sarah wasn't sure she could try to revive that feeling with someone else. If she started making new memories, she felt it would somehow betray Will's memory and the picture of him that night. She feared she had already lost him, and she didn't think it was right to replace those special moments.

Then she caught the nervous expectancy on Damien's face and knew he would be thoroughly disappointed if she turned him down. She couldn't explain to him what was eating at her, and it wouldn't be fair if she wandered around like a zombie for the rest of the night, acting like he was intentionally trying to replace Will.

Sarah reminded herself that Damien wasn't attempting to erase anything, but was trying to make new memories with her. He was here and he was a friend, and she wasn't going to be the reason that tonight turned out to be a drag for him.

Taking his arm, she finally pulled a smile, which Damien took as a yes. He escorted her away from the bulk of bodies and toward the center of the room, where a few couples were dancing to the sounds of the lyre and flute and stringed instruments. Damien grabbed her hand and stepped away from her, holding her at arm's length. He walked around her, his face serious and his posture regal, forcing her to spin in a slow circle.

This elicited a genuine laugh of surprise from her. She knew he could be mischievous and a bit of a jokester, but she had only seen his playful side when they were alone. Maybe he sensed that she needed cheering up, because her laughter only seemed to encourage him.

Damien kept his expression serious and stared past her as he pulled her in, placing his hand on the small of her back. Holding her close, he swished their bodies from side to side with quick, jerky movements, twirling them in a tight circle that was a far cry from the practiced movements of the other dancers. Somehow he managed to look graceful and in control when he did it, but Sarah was sure she looked like an awkward, long-legged chicken stumbling along on the dance floor with the regal lord. She tried to stiffen her shoulders, but Damien was so comically stoic that her chest shook with the effort to silence her laughter and kept her from gaining any semblance of control over where she was thrown.

"Please, my lady, you're interfering with my focus," Damien chided in an exasperated tone. He was all seriousness, his eyes fixed on something over her head as he pumped their joined hands up and down. It was a surprise that neither of their masks went flying off into the crowd, though Damien's now sat askew on his nose.

Sarah bit her lip but couldn't cover the laugh that she choked on, finding it difficult to believe that he didn't realize how ridiculous they

293

appeared. The corner of his mouth twitched, hinting that he did, indeed, realize how absurd they must look. But somehow he still managed to keep the superior expression on his face.

For a moment she contemplated dipping *him* to turn the tables, but she wasn't sure she could manage it. Instead, she asked in a husky voice, "Where did you learn to dance so magnificently, my lord?" and wiggled her eyebrows in rapid succession. Damien glanced down long enough to catch her look, and his stoic mask cracked as he laughed.

"Pardon me?" They stopped and turned toward the young man who had addressed Damien. The woman he had been dancing with earlier was presently being whisked off by another partner, and it seemed this young man wasn't quite ready to leave the dance floor.

Sarah shot her own partner a questioning glance, feeling uncertain about dancing with a masked stranger. But Damien nodded to her, catching sight of someone across the room. "Why don't you keep dancing? I see someone I need to speak with before they depart." He met her eyes, searching. Discreetly, he asked, "Do you mind?"

She shook her head because she didn't know what else to say and tried not to watch as he moved away from the dancers, straightening the mask on his face. She forced a congenial smile for her new partner and mechanically accepted his hand, allowing herself to be twirled about the room. Racking her brain for some form of small talk, Sarah realized that he hadn't attempted to strike up a conversation, either, and he didn't look interested in doing so.

Sarah bit her lip and focused on a distant spot across the room, counting the seconds until the dance ended. Her wandering sight hitched each time it caught on Damien standing near the wall with an older man and his wife. He tried to look engaged in the man's ramblings and enthusiastic gestures, but Sarah could see that between the holes in his mask, Damien's eyes roved disinterestedly over the room, as if in search of escape.

His gaze caught on her as she craned her neck to see around her partner. Damien's mouth tipped in a tight-lipped grin before he sobered and turned back to his companions, nodding his head over something he clearly had not heard.

Sarah grinned to herself, knowing that neither one of them really wanted to be here. Since her silent partner's eyes were elsewhere, she allowed her gaze to sweep over the room again, taking in the tables along every wall heavy-laden with trays of delicacies and goblets filled to the brim with honeyed mead and wine. Clippings of spruce and red ribbons decorated the tables and were draped here and there around the room, she noticed as her sight moved to take in the guests.

Conversing with a small group of noblewomen near the dance floor stood the queen, looking regal in her burgundy gown with her hair piled

294

elegantly at the back of her head. The heavily-plumed mask that covered her eyes was fastened to a delicate stem that the queen clutched in her hand. When she found Sarah's gaze, her face brightened, and she lowered her mask to smile warmly at Sarah before her partner spun her around.

Her steps faltered when she caught stormy gray eyes watching her. Standing at Prince Adrian's side, Cadius stared back at her from the crowd, his steely gaze narrowing almost imperceptibly when he realized he'd caught her attention. Sarah returned his steady gaze, which was easy to do considering he wore no mask, though her stare was uneasy over the cold look in his eyes. His disturbing, magnetizing gaze made her feel rooted to the ground even as her partner guided her round and round the dance floor. Though he looked faintly amused, the expression on Cadius' face chilled her.

Lips tipping mockingly, his face a veil of amusement at the same time his eyes relayed his cold disdain of her, Cadius raised his goblet in salute before he turned back to the conversation between the prince and the men around them. Sarah wasn't sure if she was supposed to read into the gesture or not, but the silent near-encounter left her feeling shaken and intimidated. Perhaps that had been his intent all along.

The weight of her partner's arms left her for a brief moment as he spun her freely, and Sarah nearly lost her balance at the surprising move. But his hands quickly settled on her waist to steady her, pulling her close. "Do you mind if I cut in?"

She glanced up sharply, ready to question his friendliness, and felt her heart stop for several beats before restarting in overdrive.

Her former partner's disgruntled face was somewhere in the crowd, but he soon faded from her line of sight. Sarah stared up in utter shock at the man holding her, feeling like she was seeing a ghost. This wasn't right—why was he dancing with her? Her knees buckled under the weight of her surprise, and she had to grip his sleeves to keep from collapsing. His hold on her waist tightened to keep her upright.

"Easy," Will murmured, pulling her against him.

She shook her head in a daze. "What are—You can't—" Her eyes darted nervously about the enormous room, scanning the faces for any sign of recognition, but not one seemed to have noticed Will's sudden presence or the fact that he was underdressed in his boots and crisp white shirt. He'd had plenty of practice in disappearing, and he seemed to take advantage of that skill now.

Swallowing, she turned back to him and managed to croak, "I thought you were dead."

His expression was grim. "I did, too." Blue eyes roved her face. Even beneath his simple black mask, he looked tired, his features appearing paler than usual against the dark shadow of stubble on his cheeks. There was a nick on his temple that hadn't been there before.

Will shook his head abruptly, setting that stubborn lock of hair in motion across his forehead. Bending down so that his lips brushed her ear when he spoke, he whispered, "Follow me when it's safe." Then he was gone, disappearing into the crowd.

Sarah staggered in the absence of his steadying arms. She rooted her feet to the ground so she could keep track of him, a full head taller than most, as he moved lithely through the throng of guests. He stopped just outside the dark passage, one she remembered well from the last ball they had attended together. His gaze met hers meaningfully before he ducked inside.

The air was suddenly suffocating in the wake of her shock over seeing Will again. Had his arms really been around her a moment ago? Was he truly alive? The dancers twirled around her unmoving form, and her stillness was drawing the attention of a few nearby. Had they seen him, too? But even if they hadn't, she knew he'd been there.

Sarah blinked. He was *alive!*

She looked over her shoulder at Damien, whose back was to her at that moment as he conversed with a small group of gentlemen. Slowly breathing out the numbers until she reached ten, she told her feet to move and followed Will's ghost.

~Chapter 36~

Though two torches were lit further down the hall on the right, it was mostly dark just inside the archway. Sarah struggled to make out any movement in the darkness, but she could barely discern the wall a few feet in front of her face.

Light shifted in the stairwell on the right, drawing her attention. She knew that the passage leading down would eventually dead end in the dungeons, but she forgot all this when Will stepped out into the muted light. She made her way over in a daze, and he took her hands when she was close and pulled her down onto the steps, hiding them from view.

Before she could process his solid hold, and very *real* presence, he had her in his arms and was holding her like he wouldn't let go. Sarah hugged him back, mechanically at first as she tried to get past her initial shock, and then she tightened her grip, closing her eyes as she clung to the back of his shirt. Her mind seemed to have purged itself of all tangible thoughts to make way for the realization that he wasn't dead.

Despite the mask in her way, she buried her face in his chest and smiled as he held her in a way she had thought would never again be possible. She'd never been so happy to be proven wrong.

Her smile faded when she thought about how she had almost lost him. "You didn't come," she mumbled against his shirt, the words muffled. But Will seemed to understand as he stroked the hair back from her face. She pressed her cheek to his chest and sighed. "When Damien said that two bodies were discovered in the river, I assumed the worst."

Will's hold tightened, and he rested his chin on top of her head. "I went to see Robert earlier, and he told me what you'd discussed. I came straight away. I'm sorry I wasn't here, that I put you through all of this."

She pulled back to see him, loosening his hold, though he didn't drop his arms completely. He must have discarded his mask in the hall, because it was nowhere to be seen. "I don't care about that. It's probably a good thing you didn't show, because the more time I had to think about it, the more I realized that it was a stupid plan. I was just running away because I couldn't find another solution." Shaking her head, Sarah gave a short, mirthless laugh. "But that wouldn't solve anything, and you were right—I see now that I *would* have regretted it. And I'm sorry I tried to drag you into it. That wasn't fair."

Removing one hand from around her waist, Will reached up to tuck a strand of hair behind her ear. "I would do anything for you if I thought it was right." Shadows played across his face, and a sliver of light sliced across his dark eyes, reflecting off the circle of lighter blue around the edges of the iris that she had never noticed before. He must have known the light was on him, but he made no effort to conceal his emotions, which were bright and palpable in his intense indigo gaze.

Hesitantly, Will reached up and loosened the ribbons at the back of her head, and with careful fingers, he slowly slid the mask up and settled it on her hair. He smiled into her eyes. "That's better."

Sarah choked out a laugh past the sudden tears that filled her throat. She swallowed hard, not wanting to cry during their reunion, even if it was in sheer relief. Blinking, she said, "But you're here now, and I'm so relieved that it wasn't you who went over the falls." Realizing how callous that sounded, she winced, remembering that two people were still dead. She wanted to say more, but overwhelming emotions tightened her chest and it was all she could do to keep from succumbing to the tears.

"But I did," he whispered, surprising her.

Sarah leaned back another inch, breaking his hold. Her eyes landed on the cut near his hairline. "But it couldn't have been you; I saw the bodies. There's no way—" She gaped at him. "Wait, were you *faking*? Because I swear, if you made me go through all that and you were still alive, I'll kill you again myself."

Shaking his head, he answered, "No, it wasn't me. I mean, I went over the falls, but—" Will scrubbed a hand over his jaw, the fresh stubble quietly rasping.

He sucked in a breath. "I was coming to meet you when I realized that someone was following me, posing as the Shadow. After what you told me about the imposter in the castle, I knew I couldn't let him go."

Sarah's eyes widened in surprise and alarm. She had to clench her teeth together to keep from speaking as she waited for him to go on. He was staring at the wall over her shoulder, as though watching the scene play out before him. "I chased him to the falls to confront him, but it was Jade who revealed herself."

Sarah was completely baffled. And angry. "So she's the one who broke in? *She* killed Edith?"

He shook his head. "I assumed the same thing, but it wasn't her; she was protecting someone, but I couldn't get her to say who. We argued, and Jade started to back up . . . She slipped," he said finally, avoiding Sarah's eyes. His throat worked as he swallowed. "I managed to grab her arm, but then we both went over. When I broke the surface, I searched for her in the water, but the river was so dark and cold. . . . I couldn't find her." His voice faded with regret, eyes searching hers uncertainly—perhaps for a sign that it wasn't his fault and everything would be all right. Sarah realized she had tried to find the same security in him, and for the first time she wondered if they were looking in the wrong places.

Will cleared his throat and continued. "I managed to swim to the rocks just before I passed out. When I came to, there were patrol guards everywhere, and a man's body had washed up nearby. I overheard one of the patrolmen say that they had found a woman's body, and I knew they would continue searching." He looked away, eyes glistening. "I had to get out of there, and somehow I made it to my uncle's house. I've been there recuperating since."

Sarah wrapped her arms around his neck, standing on tiptoe so she could rest her cheek against his shoulder. She whispered, "I don't know what else to say except that I'm so sorry." For the fact he had nearly died and gone through that traumatic ordeal, that Jade was dead—though she was hardly as broken up about that as she knew she ought to be and felt a stab of remorse for her callousness. And she was sorry that he would live with the unrealistic guilt of being unable to find her. She was sorry for everything.

He returned her hold with a strangling grip of his own. After a long moment of silence, she pulled back, realization dawning. "If the woman was Jade, then who was the man who washed up?"

Frowning, Will said, "I don't believe you met him, but his name was John." She didn't recognize the name until he added, "He worked for Dunlivey back when he controlled the guard."

Sarah's eyes widened in shock. Images of a young, meek man sitting beside Gabriel that first day she had been dropped into the forest flooded her mind. "I do remember him." Her words seemed to take Will by surprise. "That day when you and I first met when the guards were chasing me? He was there—he was with Gabriel." She paused thoughtfully. "Do you think it's possible that he was involved in whatever went on with the king's death?"

His brows drew together. "How do you mean?"

Sarah felt her defenses come down for the first time in days, knowing she could say what was on her mind with him. "It just seems kind of odd that everyone's being eliminated in one way or another right now, and that's the only common theme that I can think of. I mean, the physician's stuck in prison because he believes Cadius killed his brother, though he won't really say it, and now John winds up dead—"

"Who told you the royal physician is suspicious?" Will cut in, sounding at once doubtful and curious.

". . . Uh, he did."

His brows shot up at that. "You spoke with him? When?"

Sarah hesitated. He wouldn't like her answer, but she knew she had to speak truthfully. "This morning," she said, drawing out her vowels like speaking slowly might somehow confuse or distract him.

Eyes widening, Will asked in disbelief, "In the *dungeons*?"

She winced, knowing at the time that it hadn't been the smartest choice to go down there alone. "Yes." She held up her hands in defense, sensing his overly protective side surfacing. "But before you freak out, let me just say that I was already down there to see the alchemist and just wanted to ask the physician why he stabbed Damien. I knew it was dangerous at the time, especially since Malcolm is obviously on someone's radar, but I wasn't sure if I would get another chance to talk with him."

Okay, that was a weak argument, she thought with a frown. She tried to amend it by saying, "But at least now we know that even the doctor who worked on the king thought that his health had been tampered with, so that's something."

Will was shaking his head at the ground, looking like he didn't know what to do with her. "I know your meeting was fruitful, but you keep putting yourself in harm's way. How am I supposed to protect you?" he murmured, almost to himself.

"I had to do it myself, because you weren't there," she reminded him gently. His eyes met hers, softening. It used to ruffle her feathers the instant he started babying her, which she later realized was really just her overly sensitive view of him keeping her from harm. She was beginning to learn to not take offense so easily when he became protective. Losing as many people as he had in his life, Sarah understood why he wanted to keep those he care for out of trouble, though sometimes it *was* a little unreasonable and overbearing.

Will released a pent-up breath, his lips softening into a smile that was tinged with pain around the corners of his mouth. "Sometimes I forget how strong and independent you are. You are incredibly brave."

Now that was a silly idea! Sarah thought about all the times she had run thoughtlessly into a passage and then cowered in the darkness. She said on a laugh, "Foolhardy is more like it. You're the one who fearlessly scales the castle walls and slays dragons. *You're* the brave hero in the story."

Will shook his head. "I'm not as brave as I seem—I'm constantly afraid of losing the people in my life." He fingered one of her curls idly, and his eyes met hers in question. "Does my fear make me a hero?"

One of her favorite quotes by Ralph Waldo Emerson popped into her head, and she recited it aloud, grinning at how apt it was. "'A hero is no braver than an ordinary man, but he is braver five minutes longer.'"

He smiled at the words and then looked suddenly thoughtful. "I used to think that heroism was in man's nature, that in every man there is a little goodness and heroic bravery. But I've seen enough of the world to wonder if that's true." He grinned sardonically. "And sometimes I fear my powers are not enough to make a hero of me."

Taking his hand, Sarah gave his work-calloused palm a gentle squeeze. "It's free will." She had his attention now. "It isn't the power a hero is given, but the path he chooses to take that really defines him. Heroes are born when an ordinary man makes one of himself by his will to fight. And you've fought for justice for years."

Will smiled down at her, an expression of amazement on his face. She could tell the words had impacted him, but he didn't add anything. Maybe he didn't need to.

Suddenly, a portion of her conversation with Malcolm returned to her, and Sarah swallowed. "Now that you're here," she began, "maybe you can help me investigate the room where the physician attacked Damien." She could tell that was the last thing he had expected her to say. "It's just that when I spoke with Malcolm, he said that something was amiss and that we should go back. I thought it might be worth checking out."

Will considered this and then nodded. "It might be too conspicuous tonight with so many guests in attendance. What about tomorrow?"

"Perfect!" She smiled to herself. The team was back together again. "When should we meet? And where should we meet?"

"I'll find you."

"Are you sure you can find me? It's a big castle. Maybe your sleuthing skills are getting rusty," she teased, slightly amazed that they were bantering again.

Will's lips curved in an incredibly tender smile. "I will always find you." Her mouth went dry, and she didn't know what to say to that. She wasn't used to him expressing his feelings so openly, and she *definitely* wasn't sure how to handle him looking at her like that. Maybe it was his brush with death that made him realize he didn't want to hold back anymore.

"Damien's probably wondering where I am," she choked out hurriedly. It was the first thing that popped into her head, and she hadn't even meant to speak it aloud. And like all word vomit, it was messy and awkward and completely the wrong thing to say to break the silence.

Will straightened, his back touching the wall. "I saw you with the Spaniard, saw how the two of you reacted together. You care for one another."

Eyes widening, Sarah asked, "When we were dancing? We were just having some fun; it was nothing."

"No, I went to see you a few days ago." This was news to her. She said as much.

Shaking his head, a little bit of the old, guarded Will returned, shutting down some of the brightness in his eyes. "I thought you might like one of the wild daisies growing near my home, but when I arrived at the castle, I found the two of you jesting in the snow." A muscle in his jaw quivered, and he laughed hollowly to cover his embarrassment—at finding them lying together on the ground or because he felt foolish for coming, she didn't know. "I didn't want to interrupt, so I left."

Sarah remembered the broken flower she had found, looking like it had been trampled. She grimaced, having nearly forgotten about the daisies she had seen from her perch in the tree near Will's house. Was that truly just yesterday? In the past forty-eight hours, Edith had been murdered, Sarah had discovered another time traveler residing in Serimone, and, for whatever reason, someone had wanted to sneak into the castle as the Shadow and had paid Robert to be the distraction. And now Will was back from the dead.

She swallowed, trying to focus on what he had just said instead of throwing her arms around his neck like she really wanted. Right now he needed to talk, and she didn't want to let him walk out of here until she set him straight.

"You didn't have to leave," she said softly, trying to catch his eyes. He had sounded so nonchalant before, but the way he was avoiding her gaze was telling. Sarah placed her hand on his arm, and he didn't shrug it away. "Damien and I were just goofing off. He knew that I was upset, and so we went to blow off some steam."

He met her eyes, one brow lifting knowingly. She cringed, realizing how the common phrase in her world had probably sounded to him.

"We were having a snowball fight and tripped over each other—that's all. What you saw was totally innocent."

"I never saw you pull away." Will's voice was even, inflectionless, though the tightness in his jaw hinted at jealous emotions.

She pulled her hand back, surprised. Then she became peeved as a part of her reminded herself that he had never actually declared his intentions or feelings for her, giving him no right to be jealous.

But she saw it—every time he looked at her, there was no denying he felt what she did.

Sarah took a breath and said as mildly as she could manage, "Well, if you hadn't overreacted and run off so quickly, you would have seen that I *did* get up and that nothing else happened."

He shook his head, sidestepping toward the exit. Sarah felt the chasm he was placing between them widen. His voice was tinged with misery

302

when he spoke, though she could tell he tried to mask it. "There was something happening, even if you were blind to it at the time."

"That's ridiculous!" The absurdity of it nearly made her laugh, then her smile faded as she thought of the times she had been close to Damien—the look in his eyes or the way he touched her. Had she ever reciprocated his attentions? She had tried to convince herself that they were just friends, but she would be lying to say that there had never been anything between them, that she had never held her breath at his nearness or sighed in relief when he came to her rescue.

Will retreated another step, trying to nod convincingly. His tone was businesslike. "But Lisandro seems well set-off and . . . *pleasant.*" He grimaced as though the word tasted foul on his tongue. "Don't let me hold you back from realizing that you could be happy with him." Each word came out sounding mechanical and rehearsed, but they still managed to shake her.

"You can't be serious," Sarah stammered. He was off his rocker if he was encouraging her to pursue Damien romantically. "Did that trip over the falls knock you on the head? Because I already told you that—"

"*I'm no good for you!*" he burst, startling her. His calm façade slipped, revealing the pain and uncertainty in his eyes as they searched hers. "Can you not see that?"

She blinked in surprise at his sudden change in emotion. "Why are you trying to turn me away from you?" she demanded brokenly.

A hand reached up, as if to stroke her cheek, and then it twitched and dropped limply to his side. Will shook his head at the ground, and his voice was strained. "Coming here was a mistake. Please excuse me." Then he spun around and disappeared from her sight as if he couldn't escape fast enough.

Sarah stood there, reeling, too shocked to call out for him as she stumbled back against the wall for support. She closed her eyes, feeling rejected and confused. *What just happened?*

Then she realized that she hadn't heard the sound of Will's retreat. She opened her eyes again, feeling a spark of hope. A calloused hand was holding onto the edge of the stone opening, knuckles white with strain.

Holding her breath, she tipped her head to see out. Will stood in the hall, facing away from her, the length of his arm stretched out as he gripped the wall. He swore faintly. "What am I doing?" she heard him murmur. "I came here to fight." She was suddenly reminded of what Karen had said about fighting for relationships that mattered.

Sarah swallowed, uncertain but knowing she couldn't let him walk away like this. She wasn't going to lose him again without a fight.

"Will," she whispered, then stopped. What was there to say? But his back tensed when she spoke, and she knew he'd already heard.

"I seem to be indecisive," he said lowly. He tried to lend his words a dry lilt, but his voice was tense. With a tight grip still on the stone, he turned slowly, the lines on his face looking strained in the muted light.

Finally, he released his hold and took a tentative step toward her, though she wasn't sure he was aware of the movement. "I should walk away," he said softly, eyes fixed on her face.

Sarah wrapped her arms around herself. "Then why don't you?" It wasn't a challenge: she needed to know.

Lips curving faintly, he moved another foot so he was standing before her. She pressed her back against the stones so she could look up at him as his face softened. He reached up, hand shaking as he touched her cheek. "How am I supposed to tell myself to walk away when I'm staring at the woman I love?" he whispered, almost to himself.

Sarah's mouth hung open in astonishment. Had he really meant that? She was too shocked to ask as her pulse thrummed painfully at his words, spoken so close to her own face.

His lips parted a fraction of an inch, his head seeming to dip unbeknownst to him. She sucked in a breath through her teeth. The sound seemed to pull him from whatever trance he'd been in, and he shook his head, though he didn't pull away. Eyes pained and face a veil of resigned anguish, Will tucked his chin to his chest. The action put a modicum of distance between them, but he seemed unable to pull back completely.

"But he can give you the things that I cannot offer you—your life would be better because of him," he reasoned, though he looked sick at the thought of Damien sharing a life with her. His voice turned quiet, thoughtful. "When I saw you together, I told myself that I had to walk away and give you a chance at a better life. It would be selfish of me to wish for anything else, especially when it would sacrifice your happiness." He shoved shaking fingers back through his hair, his lips curving into a wry grimace.

"And believe me, I've tried desperately to convince myself of that—to forget about you." Will's eyes searched hers tenderly, though the tortured look had yet to leave his gaze altogether. Sarah's mouth parted in complete bafflement, absorbing every word he spoke. He cleared his throat uncomfortably, and she knew it couldn't be easy for him to express his feelings so intimately. Yet it made it all the more romantic that he was willing to do it for *her*.

He seemed to bolster the courage to continue, and she held her breath. "But each time I started to feel that I was getting somewhere—that it was, indeed, possible to move forward alone—you would come into my life."

At her look of surprise, Will smiled faintly and answered her unspoken question. "The day we met—I was intrigued, but then I got to know you and became concerned."

Eyes widening, she whispered, "Why?"

He let the tips of his fingers graze the back of her scarred, trembling hand. The feathery-light touch sent her pulse racing. Sarah feared he might hear it, but she found she couldn't concentrate on that fact for very long.

"Because I knew you could break me down." He met her eyes. "Every time I managed to get you off my mind, you were suddenly there. When we were trapped inside my shop during the storm, and you looked so vulnerable that I was tempted to hold you"—Sarah's eyes widened in surprise as he continued—"at the autumn ball, in the forest when you weren't even aware it was me—everywhere I looked, you were there." That faint grin returned. "And I found myself seeking you out when you weren't near.

"And then four months later, when I managed to spend an entire day convincing myself that I had at last released your memory and that I could move on, as I was sure you had, our worlds collided—quite literally." He grinned at the memory of them running into each other the day she came back. But his humor faded as quickly as it came. "And then right as I walked away again, convincing myself that I was doing what was best for you, I found you outside my home, having run to me for comfort. You made it hard to let go, but nearly dying made me realize that I didn't want to simply let you go. That I *couldn't* let you go," he quickly amended, throat working.

"Why are you telling me this?" Sarah asked, shaking her head in confusion. Her chest seized at his closeness, heart flitting in uncertainty. He had come back from the dead and admitted he loved her in the matter of minutes. Her head was spinning, and her own rapidly fluttering emotions weren't helping to clear her thinking.

Will smiled painfully and cupped the side of her face, almost reluctantly. Even before he spoke, she could tell from the look in his eyes that he had just needed to touch her one final time. She froze. "Because I am selfishly holding you back from the life you deserve."

She started to protest and was silenced when he brushed his thumb gently over her bottom lip. She could only imagine how wide her eyes had become as his hand remained on her cheek.

"I know you care for me—I see it in your eyes—but how long will that suffice?" His gaze turned away. "What happens when you wake up one morning and realize that you needed something more? Lisandro can offer you everything." Will pursed his lips, trying to hide his torment over speaking those words as he met her eyes once more. "I can offer you my love and pledge my troth to you, but we both would be fooling ourselves if we thought that you'd have a better life with me. I will never ask you to make such a sacrifice. And I think, in time, you'll realize what I do: Lisandro *is* the wiser choice."

Shocked, Sarah could only stare at his pained face, wanting to tell him that she loved him, longing to say the words and relieve the tension between his brows. She had strong feelings for him—now more than ever in light of all that had happened and been said—but she had only known him for a few weeks, whereas he had lived with the memory of her for months. She had spent most of her time with him guarding her heart by reminding herself that she couldn't stay here.

It would be so easy to love him—she already felt the beginnings of the emotion brewing inside her pounding heart—but could she ever allow herself to truly love him? Wasn't that selfish of *her?* He was willing to give her up completely so she could have a better roof over her head. She looked in his eyes and knew that he would walk away if she were the one to ask, no matter how it hurt him. But she also knew right then that she didn't want him to go.

Swallowing, speaking the words as they came to her, she said softly, "The relationships that work aren't built on things or status, because those can all be taken away. They succeed because they're founded on love and commitment."

He appeared surprised by her answer, and then that conflicted look returned. "I know it seems enough for now, but what happens when your feelings fade?"

Her throat burned with unshed tears. "Do you really think you're so unlovable, Will?"

He looked dismayed that he had upset her and heaved a breath, eyes dipping in shame. Then his brow furrowed as something caught his attention, and Sarah saw him swallow thickly. The hand cupping her face moved lightly down her neck, sending a shiver over her spine and causing her eyes to widen. She was about to shrink back in surprise when she became aware that his search had stopped at her collarbone, his knuckles hovering over her skin.

She held her breath, and Will's expression turned pained as he cautiously hooked his index finger under the chain around her neck, almost like he was afraid to touch it. But when the delicate links brushed her skin, she suddenly remembered the pendant she wore.

Face softening, Sarah watched his throat work as he carefully lifted the chain. His jaw tightened, fingers sliding down the length of it until he held the pendant in his palm between them.

"You kept it," he breathed. When he looked up to meet her eyes, his were glistening with tears.

Sarah braced herself, expecting the sight of the necklace he'd given her to make his decision to leave so much more difficult.

His expression flickered between pain and amazement. But then a heart-stopping smile curved Will's lips, the troubled look leaving his handsome features altogether. "All this time," he whispered, then gave a quiet, choking laugh of elation. He looked astonished as his eyes searched her face. "All this time, you haven't forgotten."

She shook her head, tears pricking her own eyes. How long had it been since he'd felt worthwhile, like he was something to be cherished? Her heart ached at the idea that he had assumed she'd forgotten about him, that he had thought he was unworthy of the love she longed to give him.

"You're impossible to leave behind, Will," she croaked, wiping the corner of her eye. He smiled into her gaze. She went on, being careful with her words. "Yes, Damien is a nice man, and I'm pretty sure he's loaded." He winced, and she softened her tone, gently laying her hand on his chest. "But you're the one in my heart, and nothing on this earth could replace you, especially not something as fleeting as social standing or money."

She searched his eyes, needing him to understand, and she fully comprehended the truth of her own words as she spoke. "When it comes to the two of you, I *choose* you, no matter what may come of it."

The corner of his mouth twitched, but then the soft smile faded from his lips. His Adam's apple bobbed in a convulsive swallow as his hand slid up to cup the side of her neck again with trembling fingers. When his head dipped, Sarah felt the pulse in his fingers throbbing against her own at the base of her throat. She froze, knowing he was going to kiss her and feeling unprepared as all tangible thoughts dropped out of her mind.

Will paused when his face was a breath away. Eyes focused on her mouth, he whispered hoarsely, "Would you mind very much—might I—" His mental functions seemed as hindered as hers, and he appeared unable to finish his question. He waited for her permission in tense silence. She managed to nod, watching as his lids lowered until they were nearly closed.

He pressed his lips softly to hers, his eyes seeming to drift closed on their own accord the moment they touched. The feathery brush of Will's stubble against her skin sent a shiver through her. She stood stock-still, terrified to move and break this moment as she tried to memorize everything about her first kiss. But she found that her mind couldn't stay focused as Will's thumb twitched over the erratic pulse thumping under her jaw, and her lids fluttered closed.

Sarah pressed her other palm against his chest, imagining that she could feel his heart beating in sync with hers. His fingers tightened around the back of her neck, and he shifted his head to the side, pulling her closer. Toes curling, Sarah tipped her own head back and unconsciously parted her lips.

Will broke the kiss abruptly, his breaths coming shallow and quick. For a moment she thought she had done something wrong and quickly dropped her hands as her face warmed. But then she felt the way his fingers on her neck trembled and glanced up to meet his glazed look. He appeared as affected as she felt, and Sarah realized that he might have felt the need to break the kiss, because from his expression, it certainly didn't appear that he'd *wanted* to.

She felt appreciation for his sense of mind when she'd had none, but she couldn't hide her disappointment that it had to end. Will seemed to sense that.

Sucking in a wobbly breath, he forcefully tipped his lips into a wry grin. "Sorry," he said huskily. Seeming embarrassed at his transparency, he cleared his throat, reluctantly pulling his hand back and fidgeting in place. His gaze shifted shyly from her face to the floor, though it always returned to search her expression in uncertainty. It all seemed so new to him.

Sarah felt her fluttery stomach sink as she breathed, "Jade was lying, wasn't she?" But the answer was already clearly spelled out by his shy embarrassment.

He nodded, his look turning to one of regret. "I wanted to tell you. That was one of the reasons why I came to you that day—I wanted to tell you the truth. And then again in the tree, but the timing seemed wrong." Will sighed. "I was upset that you thought I would compromise my morals like that, let alone betray you in such a way. I was going to let you talk it out and then set the record straight, but by the time I realized that my silence was only affirming your beliefs and hurting you, I was too late to stop you." He looked suddenly shame-faced. "It was childish."

"I jumped to conclusions," Sarah apologized, voice soft. "I should never have believed Jade so quickly." After a pause, she grinned ruefully. "Since we were both in the wrong, does that mean we can start fresh?"

Will's gaze landed on the circular pendant, and she knew he wasn't seeing just a silver tree, but a promise. He smiled softly, meeting her gaze. "A new beginning."

~Chapter 37~

They left their quiet corner shortly after that, and Sarah sensed it had something to do with their kiss. She wasn't concerned about Will's intentions toward her, but he seemed determined to act the gentleman. She smiled, knowing he'd never been anything but.

Side by side, they walked down the hall, their knuckles brushing on occasion. Sarah glanced over at him the second time it happened and caught him smiling faintly at the ground.

They walked into the ballroom and stood just outside the doorway, both feeling reluctant to join the others. Sarah looked up and met Will's gaze. Neither seemed to know what to say, and she couldn't hide her shy, awkward smile, which only caused Will's eyes to darken.

"We never finished our dance," he said lowly. Sarah felt a thrill straight down to her toes. Nodding, she took his hand; she needed no further encouragement.

Will pulled her close, drawing them in small, tight circles. They didn't join the others but stayed at the edge of the gathering, making it all seem that much more intimate. Not that Sarah would have noticed them, anyway.

Eyes constantly on her face, Will moved them to the sound of the stringed instruments, the gentle hand pressed against her back effortlessly guiding her. Sarah fought for something to say, but for the first time, she realized that she didn't need to break the silence to feel comfortable. She felt like she was floating as his strong arms held her up, spinning her in circles and helping her sway to the music. Neither wore a mask, and Will's contentedness and the adoration burning in his eyes was palpable, and she didn't bother to veil her own emotions. She couldn't remember a time when they had both been so honest with each other.

A reminder of reality diminished the spark of naïve hope she was clinging to, but it wasn't snuffed out completely. A thousand years separated the two of them, and she knew it was complete foolishness for her to allow herself to believe that this could work out like the fairy tale romance she wished it to be. She would be lying to herself if she thought that one dance wouldn't change a thing, that it wouldn't draw them closer or make it harder for her to go home.

Time seemed to hang over her head, a constant reminder that followed her wherever she went, telling her that her duration here could only last for so long. But then there was always the question of whether now was all they had. Sarah knew that if she walked away, she would always look back on this moment, this opportunity to be close to him, and regret never taking the chance to hope.

She refused to be afraid to fall anymore.

She shuffled closer to him, and Will smiled down at her, making her heart skip. She realized that they were slowing just before they came to a halt.

"Sarah," he whispered. His eyes searched her face.

She swallowed. "Yes?"

His head dipped slowly, angling to better see her eyes as toe-curling warmth flooded his own.

"There you are!" Sarah jolted, feeling the arm around her waist slide away. Turning, she spotted Damien striding through the crowd toward them, mask in place. She half expected Will to slink into the shadows, but to his credit he stood his ground.

"That took far longer than I—" Damien slowed his steps when he finally noticed Will standing beside her. "Good evening," he said, smiling in a friendly manner.

Sarah blinked, eyes flitting nervously between the two. Then she thought to introduce them. "Oh, uh, Damien, this is Will Taylor."

"Will?" A spark of recognition lit Damien's eyes, and he looked pleased. She wondered how he would have heard that name until he clarified, "The blacksmith?"

"Yes," Will answered. It was all he offered.

Damien smiled, unaffected by Will's aloofness. "It's a pleasure to make your acquaintance. And thank you for keeping Lady Sarah company." He turned his hundred-watt smile on her. "But do you mind if I steal her away for a dance?"

Sarah wasn't sure how to answer, so she glanced up anxiously at Will, taking her cue from him. A muscle in his jaw twitched, and she thought his nostrils might have flared once. But then he nodded his head. Turning his back on Damien, he took her hand and bent down to plant a warm, lingering kiss on the back of it. He straightened, mouthing the word *tomorrow* before releasing her and moving into the crowd.

Mechanically, she allowed herself to be led onto the dance floor by Damien, her eyes scanned the gathering distractedly. Her companion held her close and spun her about the room, but her gaze continued to sweep the crowd. Her heart skipped when she spotted Will watching them. Damien chose that moment to lean down and whisper something unintelligible against her ear. She blinked, and Will slipped out the exit.

For the next few hours, Sarah and Damien danced and talked, which was only interrupted when he introduced her to some of the other lords and ladies before guiding her back to the dance floor. He was so easy-going and talkative that Sarah found herself smiling and laughing on occasion, though she quickly became distracted. She tried to pay attention to what he was saying and lose herself in the party, but her heart and mind were elsewhere.

****

It was late when he escorted her back to her room, and Sarah was exhausted, and not just from hours of dancing. The emotions of the day bowed her shoulders, and she knew she hadn't been very good company toward the end of the night. But she kept thinking of Will, wondering what he was doing and what he had thought when he saw her and Damien dancing. And then she remembered their kiss and the way he'd held her, and her brain became suddenly useless.

"You've been awfully quiet," Damien observed as they walked down the hallway. She glanced over at him, feeling terrible for stringing him along with her poor company all evening. But he didn't look upset, only vaguely amused and curious.

"Sorry if I seemed . . . distracted." She anxiously rubbed the ivory ribbon between her fingers, watching her mask sway back and forth by her knees as she searched for a way to excuse her moodiness.

They stopped outside her door. Cocking his head, Damien's eyes swept her features. "Something troubles you." She nodded reluctantly, then stopped herself. How did he always manage to subdue her defenses? Brows raised, he waited for her to open up if she wished.

Now that the door to this conversation was open, Sarah couldn't just slam it in his face—not when his expression was so open and he was willing to listen. But could she really admit that she was still recovering from Will's assumed death and his declaration of love tonight?

No, not to Damien. Although she knew that their relationship would always remain in the "friend zone," it was becoming increasingly clear to her that he desired something more, and she was having a difficult time keeping her own emotions out of the mix. She would never dangle Will in front of him like that.

When she remained silent in her tortured musings, Damien leaned down to catch her eye, his own swimming with concern. "Is it Cadius?" he whispered—no one ever seemed comfortable speaking the name aloud—

and Sarah considered taking the easy out. But then she shook her head. Surprisingly, all thoughts of his threats had fled her mind when Will whisked her away. "Do you miss your family, then?"

Sarah started, surprised at how accurate he was in pinning down her emotions from earlier. She nodded, glad for the topic change when she remembered what today was. She answered honestly, "Where I come from, this day of the year is called Christmas. It's a big holiday that we celebrate all month long and where family and friends get together." There was far more to the celebration than that, but she wasn't sure he would understand.

She heaved a breath, suddenly aching for Lilly and her parents. "I've never spent a single holiday apart from them," she admitted.

The back of Damien's fingertips brushed her cheek. "I'm sorry." She nodded, knowing his concern was genuine. She expected him to draw back, but he simply stood there. His gaze turned nervous and confused as he stared at the thumb grazing her pulse, which picked up embarrassingly as his stare lengthened.

"I should go inside," Sarah whispered, though she couldn't seem to remember how to move her legs, since all of the blood seemed to be flooding her neck. The warmth that spread over her skin made her all the more aware of the cool chain of Will's pendant. Had she remembered to tuck it back inside her dress? But the intent way Damien stared at the base of her throat made her think that he wouldn't have noticed the necklace if it glowed in the dark.

Damien was nodding distractedly, she realized, and then his mind seemed to return to him. He smiled faintly. "Yes. Yes, of course." But his hand didn't move.

Sarah cleared her throat. "Goodnight, then."

"Goodnight, my lady," he whispered, hesitating, and Sarah's pulse kicked into overdrive. Slowly, he ducked his head to kiss her goodnight, his two-faced mask watching her from atop his head. Sarah's eyes widened, body stiffening in surprise before she thought to turn her head. His kiss landed on her flaming cheek, just brushing the corner of her mouth, and she gritted her teeth at the instinctive desire to angle her head toward him.

Damien pulled back, looking vaguely disappointed, but he quickly masked it with a slight grin.

"That was forward," he said softly, retreating a step. He looked so embarrassed that Sarah wanted to say no, it hadn't been forward. But when she thought of what might happen if she didn't dissuade him, or what her response would be if he tried to kiss her again, her tongue went dry. It was clear that her evasion of his kiss had wounded him, but she couldn't return his startling display of affection with the feel of Will's lips fresh on her mind. It wouldn't be fair to either of them, and it was difficult enough to keep her head straight with the confusing tangle of emotions warring within her.

"I'll see you tomorrow." Damien's tone was questioning and hopeful.

"Yeah," Sarah whispered. She opened her door and forced a smile for him. "I'll see you tomorrow."

~Chapter 38~

An emotional tailspin, that's what this was.

Sarah frowned up at the ceiling, arms and legs splayed restlessly beneath the covers. The sun had come up hours ago, but she stayed in bed, ruefully musing over last night. She couldn't make heads or tails of what she was feeling, or rather she couldn't feel any singular emotion for more than five seconds at a time.

One instant she felt elated that she and Will had sorted things out and drawn closer to defining their relationship. Then she was reminded of Damien and the way he had tried to kiss her, and *especially* the fact that she had shied away when she didn't exactly want to, and she suddenly felt ill.

It had gone back and forth like this since she woke at sunrise—first giddy anticipation when she relived her kiss with Will, followed by immediate remorse over feeling whatever she had at times with Damien; excitement over knowing how Will cared for her, depression at not being able to fully return Damien's feelings; a thrill at a shared kiss, a pang of regret over stringing Damien along, however unintentional. Then it turned into trepidation as she thought about some of the moments she had shared with the Spaniard and her confusing feelings at those times, comparing them with her feelings for Will. And so it went until Sarah's head felt like it might explode from her tangled emotions.

Now she was vacillating between telling Damien that they could never be more than friends, and slinking into a dark hole to wait until he relocated to another continent and forgot all about her before she decided to emerge. The latter half might be the coward's way out, but it sounded less painful. For the both of them.

"Agh!" With a groan of frustration, Sarah chucked her covers aside and launched herself out of bed. She immediately grimaced as her feet hit the half-frozen floor and quickly shuffled to her slippers, throwing on a robe for good measure.

Sarah plopped down in her desk chair, muttering something about how growing up stunk; it was so much easier when her parents made decisions for her—that would certainly take the pressure off.

She stared at the blank papers lying on her desk until she was sure they would burst into flames, wondering what she could do to occupy her mind until Will came. A twinge of anticipation warmed her stomach at the thought, and she tried to focus on that excited emotion rather than the thousand or so others vying for attention in her mind.

Tapping the fingers of one hand on the wood, Sarah planted her chin on her knuckles with a huff. She knew she was stalling, but she didn't yet have the heart—or the nerve—to leave her room and risk encountering Damien. Avoidance was definitely the gutless choice, but it gave her time to think.

"Not like I haven't done enough of that already today," she muttered under her breath. Her bored gaze wandered over the sparse desk, landing on the seal. She picked it up, rolling it absentmindedly between her palms as she stared at the wall. Her hands froze mid-roll, and she stared at the design, stained around the edges by repeated dips into the purple-dyed wax. There was something about the design, something terribly familiar. . . .

She sat stock-straight. Dropping the seal onto the table with a clatter, she ripped the drawers open until she found the letter Robert had given to her. She picked up the seal again with shaking fingers, holding it up to the envelope. They were identical!

Her mind worked frantically to piece it together. Had someone broken into her room to frame her? Or had the previous occupants sealed the letter before she came? She briefly toyed with the idea that maybe these seals weren't as unique as she'd originally thought and wondered if there might be a match somewhere else in the castle.

Frowning, she realized that they weren't a perfect match, but the design with the raised eagle and the stars behind looked so similar that she squinted to ensure they weren't the same.

Rubbing her temple with the hand that still clutched the missive, Sarah knew she would get nowhere with her questions if she couldn't find some real answers. The only person she could discuss things with was in a guarded cage, and before she could second-guess herself, she dropped the letter back into its hiding place for safekeeping and slammed the drawer closed. Leaving the seal behind on the desk, she jumped up and threw on a heavy dress to keep herself warm in the dungeons.

She bustled toward the stairs, eyes focused on her feet, fully intending to make it there and back before Will arrived, whenever that might be. At the bottom, she glanced cautiously over her shoulder and balked at the sight of Damien walking down the staircase with the man she had seen him with the other night, Timmons.

Of all the luck! she silently cursed.

Sarah froze for a solid breath before dashing across the landing and into the shadows of the long corridor under the staircase. Crouched at the lip of the entrance, she held her breath and listened to the sound of the men's footfall overhead. They stopped at the base of the stairs, voices lowered.

"Of course I understood the urgency of it," Damien was saying, his voice echoing off the unfurnished walls and carrying easily to her strained ears. "But I hardly had the opportunity, and now I'm forced to clean up this mess. . . ."

His voice faded. What were they talking about? Sarah leaned forward a fraction of an inch to hear the man's murmured reply. "It's been taken care of. No need to concern yourself, my lord."

"I was not concerned," Damien muttered under his breath, sounding perturbed. There was another exchange that was too low for her to hear and then they dispersed. Their footfalls faded until Sarah was sure the coast was clear. She suddenly became aware of how ridiculous she must look, huddled in the near darkness to avoid the handsomest lord in the castle.

She sighed.

"This looks cozy."

Sarah started, swallowing a shriek as she lost her balance and tumbled onto her rear. Damien looked more than a little bemused at finding her like this, though the corners of his mouth tipped in humor. Offering her a hand, he tugged her to her feet. She was suddenly very grateful for the darkness that hid the embarrassed flush on her cheeks.

"Thanks," she murmured.

"I was coming to find you. Do you have a moment?" His sudden question took her by surprise, which turned to trepidation when she caught the nervous edge to his words.

"I was sort of on my way out," she hedged slowly.

He seemed disappointed, but he nodded. "Yes. Yes, of course. It's simply that—" He faltered, rubbing his palms together nervously. Clearing his throat, he said, "I hope that last night—I was wondering if that was out of line?"

Sarah hoped the semi-darkness hid her cringe. She had been trying to avoid this. "It surprised me, is all," she answered tactfully, praying he would leave it at that.

But he took a step closer, his eyes searching her face, unsure. His hand rose to her cheek, faltering an inch from her skin before he seemed to gain the courage to brush a tendril back. *Oh, Lord,* Sarah thought, chagrined. *Not again.*

"I think by now you must know how I feel about you," Damien said softly. His words were hardly louder than a breath, but she heard them

316

clearly in the tense silence surrounding them. He shifted, and his expression was lost to the shadows. His words were stilted, unrehearsed. That made it all the worse when he poured his heart out to her. "I don't expect you to feel the same way," he murmured, stroking her cheek.

"Damien—"

"No, please, don't speak. I fear that if I can't give voice to the feelings I spent all night pondering, then this pain in my chest may be my end." Sarah closed her mouth obediently, though she wasn't sure if it would be more merciful to stop him from speaking altogether.

His thumb sent a trail of fire along her jaw where it brushed her skin. She hated that she still responded to his touch and closed her eyes, trying to block it out. But his words, spoken with such tenderness, tore at her. "You are as pure and white as snow, my lady."

Her eyes jerked open in bafflement.

Damien went on thoughtfully, "I didn't realize it until the day we played that game in the snow. When we fell and you smiled down at me, there was a shower of powder falling down around us, behind you. I could see the resemblance clearly then: you make everything clean."

His hand dropped from her cheek only to take her hands in his, holding tight when he felt her resist. "I've never been a fool to fall so quickly, but, my lady, I believe I am falling in love with you."

She sucked in a sharp breath, his earnestness making this all the more difficult. Two professions of love in less than twenty-four hours should have thrilled her, but she only felt a sickening guilt in her middle.

Closing her eyes, Sarah shook her head, sure he could feel the frantic movement even if he wasn't able to see it. "You don't mean that," she whispered.

Damien's voice was smooth and tender, like dark honey dripping off a warm spoon. She had no choice but to open her eyes, searching the dark for the expression she imagined from his soft voice. "But I do. I care deeply for this lady before me, who makes me want to be a better man." He pulled her close, then, and she was too shell-shocked and guilt ridden to resist. Folding her in his arms, he buried his face in her neck.

Sarah felt a traitorous shiver race down her spine when he expelled a slow, shaky breath against her skin. She clenched her teeth, hoping he hadn't felt the tremor. How could she capitulate so easily to his tenderness? Would he never cease to break down her defenses and confuse her thoughts?

Telling and then *forcing* her hands to move, she pressed gently against his chest. He didn't fight her, but she could tell he was reluctant from the way his jaw trailed against hers as he slowly pulled back, his stubble rasping against her skin. His hands lingered on her hips for a moment longer than necessary, and then he sighed, dropping his hold.

"You know I care about you, Damien," she began, grimacing at how cliché her words sounded, scripted right out of the "Let's just be friends" handbook. She consciously steered clear of the "It's not you, it's me" part of the speech, not wanting to hurt him any more than she had to.

She heard him suck in a breath. "But not in that way," Damien finished.

"No," she answered regretfully, then flinched. Why did that feel like a partial falsehood? She knew she felt *something* for him and didn't want to cause him hurt; she found herself wishing that she could give him the love he wanted in return. But her heart belonged to another, and it would be a lie to pretend any longer.

Reaching out, she gently brushed her fingertips against his arm. It was an unconscious attempt to console him, but she feared the light touch might have only hurt him more. Pulling her hand back, she whispered, "I wish I could give you what you want."

He was quiet for a long time, and Sarah was starting to feel awkward—more so than before—standing there in silence. Finally, he said in a voice stronger than she had been expecting and laced with determination, "I'm a patient man. When I wish to be," he added, and she heard a grin in his voice.

She stifled a groan of frustration. Maybe she should have just come right out and said it, plain and simple. "It's probably just a passing infatuation," she reasoned. "You deserve a woman who can love you and stay in Serimone. I won't be around much longer. Then where would we be? Even if I felt that way," she was quick to add. "And I'm easy to get over."

But Damien was already shaking his head. He took her hands again and gave them a promising squeeze. "You can't know what I feel," he admonished gently. She ducked her head, ashamed that she had unwittingly demeaned his affection. Damien hooked a finger under her chin, lifting it, and she was surprised at the fervent note his words carried. "But I promise you this: I will do everything in my power to win you and show you that my feelings are true, though the decision will be yours alone."

Sarah sighed. "You're not going to let this go, are you?"

"No," he answered firmly, a smile back in his voice. The man was persistent, she'd give him that. And he was also entirely vexing.

"You'll just be wasting your time," she insisted, trying to sway him, fearing what might occur if he continued to persist.

"We shall see." Damien's answer was full of confidence.

Shaking her head at his certainty, she heaved another sigh. This conversation couldn't have backfired more, and reasoning with him was going to get her nowhere. "I guess I'd better be going, then."

"Yes. I have some pressing matters to discuss with the future king, as well."

That triggered the memory of seeing Damien with that man on the stairs, and she hedged, "What were you and Timmons discussing earlier."

"Oh, he was informing me that the physician is set to hang. He was moved to a cell situated in the tower at dawn to await the remainder of his sentence." Damien had answered without inflection, as though he were discussing tedious business matters.

Sarah felt her blood go cold. How was she supposed to find him now? He was the last evidence against Cadius! "When?" she whispered, throat closing. "When is the execution?"

"Tomorrow at sunset." He hadn't noticed her internal plight.

Tomorrow! Could she and Will find, release the physician, and get him to testify against Cadius in a day? Her mind worked furiously to conjure up some sort of working plan, but she was too shaken to think properly. She tried to sound normal and managed to croak, "You must be glad for this."

Damien grunted and rubbed his bicep absentmindedly, massaging his wound. It must have been bothering him, but she wasn't sure she was in the state of mind to tend to it properly. "I don't want a murderer loose on the streets," he said after a pause, his voice thoughtful. "But I have never brought myself to take part in a hanging. It all seems so . . . undignified and final, like losing ones life to a pack of wild dogs. No man deserves such a dishonor."

Relieved to hear him speak of the man who had attacked him with compassion rather than the animosity she would have understood, Sarah nodded in agreement. Fighting the nausea clawing at her throat, she whispered, "I really need to go. Please excuse me."

He stepped back so she could pass. "Of course. But, Sarah." She halted mid-stride, unable to ignore him when he called her name. He dipped his head so they were at eye level, and she could only see the flecks of gold dancing in the darkness. "I meant what I said. You are worth waiting for."

"I-I need some time to think," she stammered. The outline of his head bobbed.

"I will be here when you get back."

She hurried past him and back up the stairs, praying Will would come soon and afraid of what might happen if he didn't.

****

The morning passed and then the noon meal with no sign of him. Sarah kept to the east halls to avoid running into Damien, wandering the empty corridors aimlessly as she gnawed on her nearly nonexistent thumbnail. Something was going down soon, she reasoned, if they were in such a hurry to silence Malcolm. But what?

She stopped dead in her tracks. Was the prince's coronation coming up soon? Could that be it? Sarah hadn't heard any talk of it, but Serimone couldn't go on without a king forever. Was Cadius making a move for the throne and eliminating all loose ends? That made sense, but what would that mean for the prince and the queen? Sarah doubted they would give up the throne without a fight. Didn't that mean they were just more obstacles in his way?

Voices carried to her, startling her from her thoughts. Two manservants were heading her way, engaged in quiet conversation. Sarah's eyes instinctively flew to the nearest open doorway, and she quickly darted inside before either man spotted her, hiding behind the door. It was a bit excessive, but she was so used to sneaking around that she was starting to become jumpy and paranoid. And with a killer like Cadius on the loose, she had every right to be.

She sent a cursory glance over the room as the men passed by—the furnishings looked oddly familiar—then her gaze landed on the closed doorway near the hearth and she instantly knew where she was. Sarah moved across the room with light steps, listening at the door before cracking it just enough for her to squeeze through the opening.

The room looked exactly as it had the day the physician stabbed Damien, though the stained rug had been thoroughly cleaned. She acknowledged the fact that coming here was more than likely a dead end, but with Malcolm set to hang tomorrow and with no way to reach out to him, this was the best she could do. She hoped he had left something behind in the scuffle, some clue that could help both of them now.

Ensuring that both doors were closed, she found that the one leading to the hallway was locked from the outside, which worried her. Sarah got down on her hands and knees and started searching the carpet, under the sofa, rubbing her hands over the cushions—she even tipped an empty vase upside down at one point, all to no avail.

"What are you looking for?"

She spun toward the owner of the voice before its familiarity registered, clutching the oversized vase to her chest like it was a lifeline. Will was crouched on the windowsill, holding the drapes aside, the corner of his mouth tipping in amusement.

A bubble of relief escaped her lips in a breathy laugh. She set the delicate pot back on its perch and shot him a self-conscious grin. "I'm not exactly sure." She watched as he stepped onto the long bench, his eyes on her. They both appeared a little awkward as she crossed the room to him, her steps hesitant. She wasn't sure if she was supposed to hug him, give him a sweet peck on the lips, or if she should initiate a high-five.

Thankfully, Will made the decision for her. When she was close enough to touch, he reached out to brush her cheek with the back of his knuckles. His soft smile sent a thrill through her. "Afternoon," he whispered.

All she could manage was a weak, "Uh-huh." Blessedly, she didn't have enough sense of mind to feel embarrassed at the moment.

His hand moved to the back of her neck, thumb brushing the skin under her ear. Sarah stood stock-still. "You know," he murmured thoughtfully, smiling, "I missed you this morning."

Her lips seemed to have a mind of their own as they tipped. "Did you, now?"

Closing his eyes, he chuckled, tugging her in for a hug. They stayed like that for a full minute, neither voicing their feelings, but both seemed to already sense what the other was thinking. His arms enveloped her, holding her gently against his solid chest. It made her feel small and safe and protected.

Sarah felt her smile grow as she tightened her hold on his waist. She could get used to this.

Will buried his nose in her hair and inhaled. "You smell nice." She felt her heart race. "Like—" He pulled his head back abruptly, still holding her. "Do you smell that?"

When he shifted his gaze, Sarah tried to subtly sniff her hair. She knew she hadn't had a shower in a while, but it wasn't like she'd been running a marathon in Arizona. She took another whiff. Maybe it was more of a mood killer than she'd realized.

Will's arms dropped from around her, and she immediately missed their warmth. He took a breath, eyes searching the room. "What on earth . . .?" His voice drifted off. He bent down, running his thumb over the splintered corner of the bench. Then he slipped his fingers under the lip and hoisted the lid up. She heard his gasp, though his back was blocking her view of the chest.

"What is it?" She moved to look over his shoulder.

"No, Sarah—stay back!"

But he was too late. Her hand flew up to cover her mouth, stifling the scream that pressed against her palms. Though his face was gray and he already reeked of decay, it only took half a heartbeat for her to recognize Gabriel Dunlivey's face.

~Chapter 39~

Sarah wanted to stumble backward, to fall onto the sofa and release the scream clawing its way up her throat as she stared at his face, still contorted in the fear and rage he had felt at the moment of his death. But her throat had closed, and she appeared rooted to the floor, having no choice but to stare at Gabriel's twisted and hollow features, his gaping mouth. Even after Will had closed the lid, hiding the man's oversized body from view, she stared at the wood, picturing his gray face and sunken eyes staring back at her. She didn't even realize that Will was holding her, moving her away from the chest.

"They just stuffed him in there," she whispered, shaking her head frantically to dispel the horrific image. When that didn't work, she buried her face in Will's shirt, clutching the fabric with desperate fingers.

He stroked the back of her head, trying to soothe her. But his body was tense, and she knew the sight had upset him, as well. "He can't hurt you." His arms tightened when the tremors racked her body, and he buried his face in her hair. Sarah had a feeling that he was drawing comfort from her presence as much as she was seeking it in his, and it suddenly dawned on her why he was so upset.

"Your parents," she whispered against his chest. He had vowed to avenge their deaths by bringing down their murderer, but it appeared someone else had already taken that into their own hands.

Will hesitated for a second too long for her to believe his words. "It doesn't matter anymore. Someone got to him first."

They were by the window cattycorner to Gabriel's makeshift coffin. Sarah turned her head, needing to breathe the fresh air. Although she hadn't picked up the scent of his decomposing body for more than a few seconds, she could still smell it, burrowing into her senses until the cloying stench was nearly overwhelming. "But why?" She barely managed to choke the words past her trembling lips, staring out at the rooftops of the village with wide, unfocused eyes.

"I-I don't know." But it sounded like he wished he did.

The latch clicked as someone turned a key in the lock outside. Sarah pulled her head back in time to see the door open slowly, her rapid pulse sensing the danger before she did. But Will was quicker than she, and he had both of them behind the drape by the time the door opened wide enough to admit two hunched forms. That was all she saw before Will pulled the covering back into place, steadying the fabric with his hand.

There was hardly space enough for two, even with their backs pressed flat against the stones, and Sarah tucked herself into the corner to give Will more room. But he slid along the wall, matching her retreat, until the right side of his body half covered hers. His back rose and fell against her shoulder in rapid movements, and she knew he was alarmed by their presence. She swallowed.

Eyes wide with fear, Sarah frantically scanned the drape for the shifting forms she imagined would appear, but she couldn't make out a thing as the men entered the room and closed the door. She heard their light steps as they moved across the floor toward them, and she shrank a little deeper into the corner, feeling Will stiffen beside her.

"It's in here?" one of them asked lowly.

"The body was stashed for safekeeping," the other replied. His voice triggered a memory, but it took her a moment to place his features. She wondered if Damien knew of this, or if Timmons was going behind his back, doing someone else's dirty work. Sarah wasn't sure how medieval alliances worked, but she had the sense that he wasn't as loyal to Damien as he should be.

"Here?" the first man asked. Sarah heard the lid of the chest tap the wall quietly. Something *thunked* against the wood, a hollow sound. The man grunted. "Help me with this, will you?"

They hefted Gabriel's body from the chest, groaning and grunting as they did. Sarah grimaced at the *thump* Grabriel's body made when it was dropped carelessly on the floor. Will shifted, moving the curtains just enough to see what was going on. But she squeezed her eyes tight, not wanting to glimpse the corpse again.

"What about the blood?"

"We'll take care of it later."

She heard the two shuffling around, toying with some kind of fabric—burlap?—and then she thought they might have rolled Gabriel's body over.

A sudden breeze caught the drape, circling around her and Will and catching in a bubble against the fabric. Her eyes widened in alarm as the edge of the drape curled and fanned, forming to the wind's movement. Will pressed closer to her, trying to keep from being spotted and to shield her body from view, though she knew the effort would be for naught if he was discovered.

But the men kept working quietly over Gabriel's body, none the wiser. The breeze died down, the drape settling into place—there was never a pause in the twosome's work that hinted at them having spotted the concealed trespassers, and Will exhaled beside her.

"Our window's closing," Timmons whispered. "We need to get him to the tunnels now. Everything is already set." The men groaned again, and it sounded like they were sliding the body across the floor. Sarah hadn't realized that she was holding her breath until the hall door closed behind them and she released it in a gusty sigh.

Will's muscles seemed to move one at a time as he leaned out to see if they had really gone. Panicked, she reached for his arm, clutching his bicep. He looked at her and caught the slight shake of her head, eyes wide.

Pressing a finger to his lips, he gave her a reassuring nod before leaning his head out. "They're gone," he breathed, barely above a whisper—he was still on-edge, even in the grave robbers' absence.

Then he took her hand, gently coaxing her from their hiding place. Sarah moved slowly, her tense muscles unfurling painfully as the blood returned in a rush to her legs. She was half expecting the two men to hear their breathing and come back to investigate, but the room was empty. The lid of the chest was closed again, and there was no sign that either man had been there.

Will released her to open the chest, swearing softly under his breath at the vacant depths.

"They stole his body," Sarah whispered in shock and confusion. She met his pinched gaze. "We can't just let them get away with him. What should we do?"

His eyes focused on the door, and he frowned, expression grim. "Follow."

****

It didn't take her as long as she'd expected to convince Will to take her along. Though she suspected that it was in part because he knew she would persist: The two men had more of an edge on them each moment that they wasted arguing.

They were only a few minutes behind Gabriel's body, and Will's keen eyes quickly picked up the drag marks left in his wake; scattered stones, upset dust, and a crooked chair—all leading them downward into dimly lit passages.

Sarah was sure they had lost their trail, but it wasn't long before Will heard the familiar scratching and grunting sounds again and quickened his pace, urging her on with him. They spotted the men as they passed under a

324

torch a ways down the long corridor, and Sarah caught a flash of the bulky sack encasing Gabriel's body before it disappeared around a corner. Seeing them made her feel too eager, and Will had to gently tug her back to slow her steps to match his.

He leaned down and whispered in her ear, "We have them, but we need to remain unseen." She nodded in agreement, tamping down the desire to sprint after them.

They came to the same crossroads the men had taken, and she could feel Will's tension build as his hand tightened around hers. "What are they doing down here?" he whispered. His pace became clipped, and she wondered at his sudden edginess.

"What's wrong?" she asked under her breath. The tunnel was void of life ahead of them, and she wondered if they'd made a wrong turn.

"They're going outside," he returned lowly. He sounded confused. "I assumed they would want to examine the body, but it looks as though they're going to dispose of it, instead."

A burial. Of course. They wanted to destroy the evidence, but evidence of *what?* And who'd had Gabriel murdered?

Sarah swallowed, sickened.

The floor began to slope upward, the ceiling shrinking until even Sarah had to duck her head to avoid the stones. They had no choice but to walk shoulder to shoulder as the passage narrowed, not that it mattered, since Sarah was already pressed against his side. But then the tunnel dead-ended abruptly. She was about to ask him where they should go next when Will released her hand to grip the thin rope dangling against the left wall. Then he reached up to shove open the overhead door, flooding the passage with light and blinding them both after their prolonged trip through the darkness.

Will was able to stretch himself to his full height through the opening, and he used the rope to soundlessly set the square of wood on the ground above. In the afternoon light, Sarah could see the trees overhead and the moss that had grown over the secret entrance.

Hoisting himself from the small opening, Will crouched on the ground, eyes shifting over their surroundings. Sarah held up her hands, and her feet dangled in the air as he pulled her out of the hole. She naturally landed in a crouch beside him, and he didn't release her hand as he tensely examined the trees.

"We must be near the lake," he muttered to himself.

"But where are they?" she panted quietly, still wary of the unseen presence lurking in the woods. The frigid air blew her hair back from her shoulders, instantly chilling her face and neck.

"Let's find out." Will helped her to her feet, though they both kept low as they moved slowly through the trees, where the closely tangled limbs caused the sun to be all but shrouded from view. It must have been midday, but she could tell from the placement of the shadows that dusk was not far off. So soon? Surely they would lose the two men in the dark.

Her eyes scanned the snowcapped trees and the bit of the horizon that she could make out along the ridges and hills. She narrowed her gaze, fixing it on a point above the next rise. "Is that smoke?"

Will looked just as baffled. He pointed out the toboggan-sized drag marks leading up the slope, and they stepped from the path they were following to move quietly up the incline, which was slow going—Sarah's shoes kept losing traction on the slick, icy snow, and Will repeatedly paused to help her find her footing. Eventually, she found that it was easiest to plant her fingers in the snow and use the point of her feet to hoist herself up a foot at a time, which saved them precious seconds.

As they reached the crest of the rise, Sarah saw that the smoke was extremely thick here, moving in their direction in gusts of choking heat. She tried not to wheeze and focused on taking shallow breaths.

A flash of color and muted voices drew her attention to the small clearing. The men had their backs to them not twenty feet away, and the body sack laid at their feet, now doused with a thick, greasy black film. A smoky bed of fire burned hotly a few feet away, the flames reaching high and sending out plumes of charcoal-colored smoke that stained the pristine snow a dull gray.

Will caught her attention and mouthed the word *there,* pointing to a large boulder a few feet to her left. She nodded, and they shuffled that way, planting themselves behind the rock for cover. He leaned out to watch the men, and Sarah scooted into the small space between the boulder and his chest, craning her neck to see.

"One, two, *three!*" Timmons cried. Together, the men tossed Gabriel's inert form onto the pyre.

Sarah gasped in horror, but the sound was covered by the fire's hungry crackling as it leapt over the body, quickly consuming the thin casing surrounding it. The flames reached high, dancing dangerously close to the limbs above when the final chords of the sack snapped. Gabriel's gray features were visible for the brief instant that the fire subsided. Then it burst suddenly, finding new strength as it consumed his body, snapping wildly.

Unable to look away from the sickening scene playing out before her, Sarah could only watch with gaping eyes as Gabriel's body disappeared from view, replaced by a shifting wall of orange and gold. She wouldn't have been able to move at all if not for Will's hands on her shoulders, gently but firmly pulling her back from the macabre sight. He folded her into his arm, leaning his side against the boulder for support. They would risk drawing attention to themselves if they ran, so the two were temporarily trapped.

326

Sarah closed her eyes so tightly that spots danced behind her lids, resembling the flames that presently consumed Gabriel's corpse.

Her eyelids snapped open wide, and she clutched Will's shirt to keep her hands from trembling. She had wished bad thoughts on the evil man for all that he had done to Will and to Karen, but did he deserve a second death as awful as *this*?

Will pressed his lips against the side of her head to keep from being heard. "Close your eyes; it will be over soon. Close your eyes," he urged more insistently when her lids remained glued open in horror. Sarah tried to comply, forcing her eyes to close and burying her face in his shoulder when they refused.

It will be over soon, he'd promised. *Oh, God, let it be over soon.*

Something soft and delicate brushed her cheek, and she thought it might have been Will's breathing. But then the miniscule sensation appeared on her exposed knuckles. Was it snowing?

Will hunched over her, his arms tightening around her shoulders. She instinctively leaned back to see what was landing on her, but the hand at the base of her skull held tight, which only made her push harder in panic. What was he protecting her from?

She jerked back enough to see the snowfall. No, not snowflakes. Ash, from the fire. Dark, discolored ash falling from the sky. It speckled Will's dark hair and clung to the back of his sleeves and shoulders. Some of the ash landed on his cheek, and he wiped at it in revulsion. She watched a few lazy flakes fall from the trail of smoke overhead, the smoke coming from Gabriel's body. . . .

Sarah shrieked without thought, swatting at the dusting of ash that had collected on her head since she'd pulled back from Will's embrace. She imagined the gray color of the ash matched the pallor Gabriel's skin had held. And it was all over her!

Will grabbed her hands, shushing her, trying to calm her. She realized her mistake and bit her lip, tasting blood as she tensed.

The men in the clearing had gone silent, the only sound the dull crackle and hiss of the fire as it consumed what was left of its fuel.

"Did you hear that?" one of them whispered. She couldn't tell which one; her heart was beating too loudly, though she heard perfectly the sound of a dagger being drawn from its sheath. Their feet crunched over the snow, moving toward the boulder.

Sarah looked to Will, searching his face for the answer. *Fight or flight?* her mind screamed. He was staring at the boulder, chest rising and falling quickly, and she knew what he wanted. But then his gaze landed on her face, and his jaw tightened.

Will jerked his head down the hill, and she knew he planned to run. Pulling her head close, he breathed into her ear, "Can you make it?"

She nodded. That seemed the only confirmation he needed. Taking her hand, he waited only until she had her feet planted before hurrying her down the hill. It was harder this trip, and Sarah slid more than anything. Stopping to face her as he helped her over a rough patch, Will spotted them coming around the boulder. Then he gripped her arm and took off down the hill, practically holding her upright as they both slid and stumbled downward.

The men shouted for them to halt when they had them in their sights, tripping down the hill after them. But Sarah and Will had reached the bottom well before their pursuers, and they took off along the path of the ditch, panting and gasping for breath.

Sarah could hear the men shouting commands to each other, telling the other to move or watch his step. Then another voice, one she didn't recognize, calling out to them, "You there! Stop!"

Sarah shot a quick look over her shoulder, barely catching sight of the man mounted on his horse as he galloped after the estranged foursome. The look on the two grave robbers' faces was pure alarm as they sliced through the trees, abandoning their pursuit to cut a new path through the woods.

"Guard. Don't stop!" Will panted, dragging her along with him. She wanted to tell him that a guard could help, but then she saw how this must look from the man's perspective—four people running from the scene of a flaming corpse. They probably looked as guilty as the men who'd done the deed.

Will's hand slipped from her arm, needing to pump both arms at his sides to keep moving. He was breathing hard and barely managed to gasp, "The lake! We'll lose him in the trees." She followed him, choking on frozen clouds of air that pained her lungs when she swallowed.

The two baddies were long gone by now, but the sound of pounding hooves and the guard's shouts of warning were still clear. Dodging in and out of the thicket, she followed Will into a dense copse of trees, feet pounding over the snow. They ran until Sarah thought she would collapse and it was only pure adrenaline that kept her moving.

Will slowed behind her, and she looked over her shoulder in alarm. But he was striding backward, watching the trees behind them. She suddenly realized that they could no longer hear the guard's pursuit and jogged a few yards more into the shadowed clearing, almost unable to stop her wobbly legs from running. Her feet slipped on the icy snow and she slowed, gripping her aching side, choking and gasping for breath. Had they lost the guard in the trees? He'd surely be on foot now if he wanted to follow through the thicket, which would buy them time.

The clouds shifted, and a small sliver of waning sunlight broke through the thick tangle of limbs nearby. Reaching up to shield her eyes from the light coming off the snow beneath her feet, Sarah called out, "Did

328

we lose him?" Then she went into a coughing fit, doubling over to catch her breath.

Will turned to her, mid-nod. He froze in alarm, wide eyes dropping to the reflective ground she stood on. A single crack echoed through the forest, startling her. Was that a rifle shot?

Waving his arms, Will motioned for her to come back to him. She had never seen him so terrified, and his fear was contagious, rooting her to the spot. "Sarah, no!" he shouted, running toward her.

Her mouth opened in confusion, and then it hit her. The lake! Her body reacted before she could think, and Sarah lurched forward a step, knowing she had to reach the other side. She froze at the deadening *crack* that filled her ears, realizing her mistake too late.

The ice she had thought was solid ground splintered and shattered beneath her weight. She shrieked as her right foot slipped through the sheet of frost that was too thin to hold her weight. Needles of pain shot up her leg as it slid into the freezing water, and icy fingers below seemed to grab hold of her foot, pulling her further down. She planted her hands on the ice and tried to jerk herself free, but her frantic movements only caused the surrounding ice to crack and splinter further.

Sarah froze, panic slicing through her as she realized that there was no way out—her thrashing was only forcing her deeper into the water. Her eyes snapped to Will in desperation, but he was still running toward her, toward the shattering lake, and she knew he would never make it in time. She locked onto his panicked gaze, screaming out his name just as the fragile sheet of glass shattered beneath her weight, plunging her into the dark, icy abyss.

~Chapter 40~

"Will!" Her frightened cry tore through him, ringing in his ears and landing in his stomach with a sickening *thud* of finality. He knew he was too late even as he forced his legs to move faster.

"No!" he yelled when her head disappeared from view, heedless of their pursuers as his shout echoed across the snowcapped hills.

His heart stopped for several beats until she reemerged, choking and gasping and slapping the surface of the water in desperation. "Hold on!" His shout was breathless from terror and exertion. He cried out to her again even after her head went under and it was only the tips of her fingers flailing for a handhold before they vanished, as well. Her dress was pulling her under!

Will felt paralyzed by fear even as his stride lengthened. His feet hit the powdered ice, and he slid several feet, not slowing until the ground began to shudder beneath his feet, threatening to break. And even then he quickly dropped onto his stomach, scuttling across the ice as fast as he could to the hole she had left behind. He gripped the edge of the pit, feeling the shards of ice bite into his palms as he hoisted himself closer. The opening was too small; it wasn't possible that she had slipped through there.

"Oh, God," he whispered in dread. The water was too cold—the edges of the hole were already reforming, sealing her in.

Thinking fast, he slammed his fist into the paper-thin sheet of ice closing over the gap, ripping at the edges until the opening widened. He scanned the water, hoping for a glimpse of her, a limb to grab hold of. But it was too dark, and he had no idea how far she had drifted. His worried gaze traveled over the length of the shining lake, wondering if she might be trapped under a different sheet of ice, fading.

The water stirred gently, lapping against the sides of the crude hole. He whipped his head back and thought he saw a shadow move in the depths. Without pausing, Will drove his hand into the water. The frozen

330

lake stung his skin, and an uncomfortable tingling laced up his arm. What must it be like for her to be completely submerged?

He grimaced, plunging his arm deeper. His fingertips brushed something, quickening his pulse. Will struggled to reach for her, driving his shoulder into the water until his cheek was pressed against the ice.

He could feel her drift past him, unmoving. *NO!* In a panic, he plunged his head into the water before he could suck in a breath, gripping the edge of the hole with one hand. The fabric of her dress slipped through his fingers, and he clutched at the hold for dear life, his lungs feeling ready to burst. It was a struggle to get his head above water, and when his mouth broke the surface, Will sucked in air like it was his first breath in days. Then he dragged her up, releasing the dress fabric to grab her arms so that he could tug her inert body onto the ice. Groaning, he dragged them both away from the hole and onto solid ground.

Huddled beneath a low embankment, he held her in his arms, shaking her, trying to expel the water from her lungs. Will chafed her back, hoping to see some sign of life. "Please, open your eyes," he rasped. But her face was so pale, so still, her lips a sickening shade of blue: she wasn't coming back.

The rubbing motions became more frantic with each passing second that life refused to return to her body. He jostled her to upset the water she had taken in, but to no avail. He touched her ice-cold skin, rubbing his palm across her cheek, trying to stroke warmth back into her face. What else could he do? He was worthless in medical matters—he needed Uncle Thomas!

The cold air blew around them, and a rime was already starting to form on her wet hair. Will pushed it back from her cheeks, trying to brush away some of the water crystals from the damp strands.

His voice was choked, teeth chattering when he whispered, "I cannot lose you." He watched her chest for some sign of movement, but it never rose. Had he already lost her? "No. No, no, *NO!*" he cried at the thought.

Desperate, Will pressed his lips to hers. He pulled back, searching her lifeless face. Nothing. "I will *not* let you go!" He clutched her to him, willing life back into her frozen body as he smothered her mouth with his own. But never once did he feel her chest rise. It had been foolish to think that she would respond to his kiss, that it would bring her back from the grave.

Destroyed and angry, he released a heavy breath into her barely parted lips.

Sarah choked, a gurgle deep in her throat.

Will lurched back in time for her to turn her head and expel the water from her lungs. She retched weakly even when her lungs were empty, and then she gasped for air, choking in startled breaths. Will rubbed her back,

331

choking back his own emotions and the desire to crush her in his arms.

"What happened?" she gasped at last, staring up at him with a glazed expression.

He shook his head, not fully comprehending himself. "I-I don't know. I thought you were gone." He swallowed, but he couldn't prevent the tears from filling his eyes. They froze on his lashes, and he shivered as the wind found the damp hair clinging to his neck. "I kissed you, and suddenly you came back to me."

Sarah gave him a wobbly grin, her pale lips pulling into an expression of mock-chagrin. "You g-gave me CPR, and I missed it?"

He laughed in utter relief. Then he crushed her in his arms, clinging to her, feeling the dampness from her own clothes soak the rest of him. Let it. All that mattered right then was that she was back in his arms, alive and well.

Will's panic faded, replaced by an onslaught of sudden, intense relief. "I thought I'd lost you," he rasped.

The corner of her mouth twitched, hinting at the barest of smiles. "But you found me." The words sparked an ember in his chest that smoldered there, filling his freezing body with warmth, cracking the glass walls surrounding his heart until they shattered into a million pieces at her feet. Staring into her eyes, Will drank in the sight of her until he could stand the distance no longer.

He leaned down and pressed his lips to hers, harder than he had intended, every ounce of pent-up fear and elation pouring out in this moment. The sudden floodtide of emotion made him feel light-headed, and he kissed her in the way he had wanted to last night, forgetting every courting convention ingrained in him since childhood.

Sarah shuddered in surprise, and then she clung to him, seeming to fully comprehend that she had just evaded death. Making a low, desperate sound in the back of his throat, he slid his hand to the side of her neck, pulling her closer. Her pulse was beating faster than a frightened rabbit's, threatening to break through her skin. Beating for him, he realized.

The ember burst into a flame, each rapid beat of his own heart spreading fire into every limb. Will kissed her in reckless, joyful abandon as the flames enveloped them both. His skin thawed, prickling with life as each nerve ending succumbed to the fire. He couldn't recall ever feeling so alive as when she returned his kiss, hungering for the life she might have lost. Tears pressed between their cheeks, but who had shed them, he couldn't say.

When the fire threatened to burn the forest around them, he pulled back abruptly, breathing hard. Sarah's chest was rising and falling rapidly as she sucked in air, her breaths matching his own. Unable to break away completely, Will pressed his lips to her temple and released a shuddering gust of air. "I'm never letting you out of my sight," he growled against her skin.

He could remain like this for an eternity, holding her in his arms and mirroring each beat of her heart. But then reality came crashing down, too quickly for his liking. He noticed now that her entire being was racked with severe trembling and frowned.

Will forced himself to peel away from her. "We need to get you warm," he said hoarsely.

Her nod was shaky, lips parting. Eyes wide in the wake of their kiss, she whispered, "'K-kay."

He stood, kicking himself for being so irresponsible and thoughtless when he needed to get her to safety. However, he couldn't deny that he would rather spend the afternoon in the snow with her—if she weren't at risk of freezing to death already.

He was stretching his hand out to help her up when the sound reached his ears: Hooves, trotting lightly through the snow. He felt Sarah's hand brush his, but he motioned her back. "Stay down."

The guard came into view then, and Will turned his head to see another approaching from the opposite side. He ducked quickly behind their low covering, watching Sarah with a concerned gaze.

Eyes closed, she shivered uncontrollably. The blood that had returned to her lips during their kiss faded, and her heart-shaped mouth started to turn blue again. Her clothes were soaked through completely, and lying in the snow was not helping matters. But she was in no condition to outrun the guards.

Will pulled her into his lap so she was out of the snow, wrapping his arms around her to shield her from the wind. It was not enough, and he knew she wouldn't make it much longer if he did not get her dry.

"I lost them." Will thought the voice came from the left, from the man who had chased them into the woods earlier. "What'd you find?"

"Turns out it wasn't just a fire." The second man's tone was bleak. "Found a smoldering corpse back there. The flames were still going, but I put enough snow on it to get most of it out. It appears someone was trying to cover up a murder."

"Any notion of the victim's identity?"

Will held his breath, hunching further over Sarah when the men neared, trying to hide their heads from view. His chest constricted in pain as her teeth chattered audibly. Not daring to murmur assurances to her like he wished, he instead brushed his thumb back and forth across her trembling lips, trying to quiet her.

"Not much left to identify, sir."

The first guard sighed. "Well, I've lost the trail. I didn't catch any faces, but there were four of them—three male and one female.

Although"—his voice turned thoughtful—"I really only saw him from the back, but the one running with the woman reminded me of that blacksmith in town."

Will sucked in a sharp breath. He thought Sarah's body stiffened before the trembling overcame her once more. He gritted his teeth, knowing there was nothing he could do for her at the moment. It was the waiting that was killing him, the inability to do anything for her with the knowledge that their only chance was to wait the men out.

"Taylor?" The second guard sounded surprised and doubtful. "You don't honestly believe he was involved."

"I have my doubts, but it might be worth looking into tomorrow." The man's disgruntled exhale was audible. "You might as well show me what you've found."

One of the horses nickered uneasily, probably sensing Will and Sarah's anxiety, and then it snuffed loudly as its rider turned the animal down the path.

Will risked a look, stretching his neck until he could see both guards' backs as they moved back toward Gabriel's body—what was left of it, that is.

He shifted, getting up to move, but Sarah grasped at his shirt, her frozen fingers stiff. "C-can still h-hear them," she croaked.

He understood her concern, but he felt too antsy to wait any longer. She needed warmth and safety, and he felt that it couldn't come soon enough. "They have their backs to us now," he said lowly, shooting a wary glance at the guards to ensure this was true. "If we're quiet, we can make a run for it."

"B-but—"

"We've wasted enough time," he whispered, pulling her to her feet. She tottered a few steps and then stumbled to the ground. Will wrapped his arms around her waist and kept her close to his side, carrying most of her weight as they staggered through the snow together. They were both shaking uncontrollably now, and Will kept his jaw clenched in an effort to conceal his shivering.

His eyes scanned the whitewashed landscape—a tangle of trees and limbs, a sloping embankment—no sign of warmth or shelter. Then he spotted the crest of the hill rising in the east and felt a spark of hope. He cut off to the left, going around it when he realized they would never make it over, his legs moving faster with renewed purpose.

"Almost there," he mumbled, keeping his eyes focused directly ahead. Sarah never bothered to answer; she was so quiet now, except for the sound of her chattering teeth. She stumbled and went practically limp against his side. With a grunt, he hefted her into his arms, staggering under the added weight. "Almost . . ." His voice faded with the promise.

334

Will saw the faint shadow of brown amidst the snow and forced his legs to move. The barn was closest, but they had a fire going in the house. He stumbled that way, so intent on his purpose that he wouldn't have noticed her if she hadn't gasped audibly. Will turned toward the redhead.

"Sarah!" she cried, aghast. Karen Ashmore ran a few steps toward them and then whipped around and jogged back to the barn, holding the door open. "Quick!"

Gritting his teeth, he moved Karen's way. A gust of wind had Will's neck breaking out in gooseflesh, and the petite redhead gripped the door harder to keep it from slamming closed.

"She fell through . . . the ice," he gasped as he stumbled inside, shifting Sarah's weight in his arms. Karen quickly closed the door, and the warmth of the barn had him sagging in exhaustion. "She was under for a long time."

Karen hurried over with a thick quilt slung over her arm. "You can put her down now." Will realized that she was speaking to him and jerked his eyes to her face. The redhead was grinning up at him in compassionate understanding. He nodded, realizing that he was still clinging to Sarah even now that the immediate danger had passed. Uncurling his aching muscles, he slowly placed her feet on the ground, and his arm was the only thing holding her upright.

Karen directed her attention to the woman trembling against his side and winced as she took in her condition. "Come on, let's get you into some dry clothes," she murmured soothingly, easily taking control of the situation as she wrapped her arm around Sarah's shoulders and gently tugged her away. When Will's hold seemed unflinching, the redhead shot him an encouraging look. "I'll take care of her."

She held the blanket out to him, and he slowly relinquished his grip. Karen immediately sagged as Sarah's full weight leaned against her. With the lack of her presence, Will's body felt offset, and he staggered to the side where her form had been. The redhead was already moving to the other side of the barn with Sarah safely tucked against her side, whispering words of comfort to her as they moved slowly along.

Unable to stand any longer, Will sank onto a large haystack just behind him, body sagging in relief. Stripping off his sopping coat, he rubbed his head and face with the warm, scratchy fabric of the blanket, trying to be rid of as much water and frost as possible. Wrapping the thick fabric around himself, he allowed his head to fall back against the wall, feeling his eyes close against his will. Now that there was nothing to occupy his thoughts and keep him moving, exhaustion overcame him as the immediate danger passed and his body at last registered that they were safe.

Several minutes passed before the redhead reemerged from somewhere in the barn's depths. Sarah was slumped against the young woman's side, face devoid of its typical color as she trembled. Her hair had been tousled, and the soaked gown was nowhere to be seen; she was dressed now in a garment of gray wool that looked enviously warm and cozy. Where had she found that? Will vaguely recalled opening his eyes momentarily to find the redhead rifling through a trunk, but he had been too wearied to keep his lids open for long.

He forced himself to sit upright, pressing his back against the wall for support. "How is she?"

"Dry now, at least." Karen shuffled over, her eyes trained on her charge's slow footsteps to ensure that she wasn't moving too quickly. "I need to run up to the house to get some hot water ready," she was saying to Sarah, whose lids were already at half-mast. Then she looked up at Will, nodding her head at the blanket. "Wrap that around the both of you to share warmth."

He quickly obeyed, opening the quilt as Karen shifted her weight, softly coaxing Sarah into letting go. He was momentarily taken aback when the redhead plopped Sarah directly in his lap, but he quickly recovered, turning her shivering body so that she fit snugly in the small space.

"I'm t-tired, Karen," she whispered, teeth chattering loudly. Will thought they could both use a little rest and nearly closed his eyes at the delectable notion of sleep. But when he glanced up for Karen's approval, she shot him a worried look as she pulled the blanket around to cover them both.

"I know, honey," she said soothingly, brushing Sarah's hair back from her temples. "You can sleep later. But right now you gotta stay awake for me." Will suddenly understood her apprehension: If she fell asleep at this point, would she ever reawake?

Sarah mumbled something incoherent into his chest, causing both he and Karen to exchange concerned glances.

"Give me five minutes to get some water heating. I don't want her out in the snow before we can get her warm inside," she said to him, her worried eyes flickering to Sarah's face. "Do *not* let her fall asleep. Slap her if you have to."

"Heard that," came the muffled complaint.

Some of the tension eased from Karen's young features, though the worry clung to the corners of her eyes. "Glad to see you haven't lost your sense of humor or sense of hearing." She straightened to her petite height and shot Will a piercing look. *Five minutes* she mouthed, and he nodded. Then she left in a flash, the wind slamming the door closed.

Will hugged Sarah to his chest, rocking her softly as he ticked off the seconds. After two minutes, he realized that it was completely silent in the barn. He angled his neck to see her face and her closed lids. Jostling her gently, he called her name and felt his heart begin beating once more when her eyes fluttered open partway. He released a breath of sheer relief through his nostrils. "Your friend said you need to keep awake."

"Just wanna s-sleep," she slurred, sounding near tears as she burrowed under the warmth the blanket provided.

Will closed his eyes, agonizing over the wounded note in her voice. "I know, love," he whispered, throat constricting. Reaching blindly for her hand, he realized how cold she still was when he found it. How long now? Perhaps three minutes? Even in his exhausted state, he felt so anxious to be moving that it was all he could do to remain seated.

Folding his arms tight about her frame, he felt her shoulder press harder against his chest and became aware of how small and fragile she felt in his arms. And though the constant shivering had lessened some, sporadic, uncontrollable tremors shook her body. Each time it happened, he grimaced, mentally counting off the remaining seconds until he could take her inside. The wait was unbearable.

"You're strong," he whispered to her, needing to hear the words aloud himself.

When he felt they had waited long enough, Will pulled the blanket from about his shoulders, doing a balancing act so he could wrap it around her to stave off the cold air outside. He shifted her body in his arms and rose on shaky legs, cradling her against his chest. Once outside in the frosted air, he didn't bother closing the door behind them but made his way directly to the house.

Dusk had quickly turned into a cold night. He focused his mind on the thought of a warm fire and a roof and not on the steady chattering of his teeth or the fact that Sarah's shivering once again persisted.

The snow was deeper out here, away from town where people plowed and shoveled the streets to make for easier navigation. Will's aching legs sank deeply into one particularly large mound, and it took most of his strength to pull himself free without toppling over. He tried to angle his body so that his back blocked most of the wind, but he knew that even with the added warmth of the blanket, his slow progress through the snow wasn't helping Sarah's condition.

The front door slammed closed, and Seth bounded off the small porch, taking off toward them at a clipped pace. His expression belied his shock over finding both of them in this state, and Will gritted his teeth, struggling to stay upright.

Seth stopped at his side, reaching for Sarah. "Let me take—"

"I have her," Will barked, then immediately regretted it when Seth blinked in surprise. He was exhausted, cold to the bone, and fighting feelings of incompetence, but that was no reason to snap at his old friend. "Seth, I'm sorry."

He shook his head, and Will could tell that he had already dismissed the offense. With a wary glance at the distance between them and the house, he felt his tired body sag. Knowing he was wasting precious seconds in indecision, Will stuffed his pride and shifted his bundle, wincing at the cramp in his shoulder. The instant Sarah was out of his arms he missed her warmth, but Seth was practically jogging back to his home, making better time than he would have, and Will struggled to take up the rear.

A small woman was standing in the doorway, worrying a towel between her hands. It had been years since Will had seen Seth's mother, and he was sorry that it was under such upsetting circumstances that they should meet again.

"Hurry, darling, hurry!" Ruth Jones urged her son, flapping her towel in the air before running inside and leaving the door open for them.

The two shadowed forms disappeared inside, and a few moments later, Will lurched in after them. He barely maintained his balance when he forced his body to cease movement. Someone closed the door behind him, but he couldn't have said who.

The house was already in chaos, the main room packed to capacity. He barely recognized Joshua, as the boy had matured considerably in the years it took to move into adulthood. He stood at the base of the stairs with his hands planted firmly on his sister's shoulders, holding her back. Leah had grown several inches since he'd last seen her, and her face looked more like that of a young woman and not the freckle-faced child Will had known last. Or perhaps it was the grim, tight-lipped expressions they both wore that matured their faces.

Seth stood to the side against the wall with his father, but Karen and Ruth had immediately set to work, placing their charge on the floor as near to the fire as they dared, and went about chaffing her skin with warm towels. The younger woman was rubbing Sarah's hair dry, and Ruth held her quaking feet over a bowl of steaming water, pouring small handfuls of the warm liquid over her skin to acclimate her before she submerged her feet completely. Sarah hissed in surprise, and the older woman shushed her gently, whispering soothing words that only the three women could hear.

Will heard someone come up beside him, but he refused to avert his gaze. A thick quilt was placed about his shoulders, and a hand remained behind after it was settled. "Relax, they've got her now."

Will realized that he was clenching his fists at his sides and tried to release the tension in his shoulders.

"You look ready to drop," Seth observed. "Why don't you get some rest?"

A quick headshake was the only response he received. Will blinked, trying to keep his eyes open. If he sat down now, he wasn't sure he would be able to get back up ever again.

A moment of silence. "I understand," Seth said, so quietly it was almost a whisper. Will's attention snapped to him, but the other man was watching the women with the same tight-lipped expression of concern that Will felt on his own face. His heart sank, seeing in his old friend's features the look of worry that only came with deep love.

"I left the door open," Will said, suddenly remembering. Should he go back to the barn? His legs quaked, protesting the very thought of movement.

"Got it." Seth clapped him on the shoulder in the familiar way he used to do when they were friends.

With Seth gone, his father seemed to think it was a good idea to give the women room to work. "All right, you two. Time to move out." The large man folded his arms across his chest and hiked his chin up the stairs. Both children looked upset to be left out, but little Leah looked crestfallen.

She broke away from her brother and crouched beside Sarah, throwing her arms around her. "Get better," Will heard her say. He felt his throat close and blinked rapidly. It took several soft words from her mother before Leah broke away. Sarah managed to give her a wobbly smile. "I'm too stubborn not to," she assured, voice weak. Will caught the tears Leah quickly wiped from her cheeks before she joined her brother again.

The middle of the Joneses' herd smiled encouragingly at Sarah when her glazed eyes met his gaze. "You'll be all right." Josh sounded so much like his brother when he said it, though Seth would have been more convincing about it. With a tug on her arm, he managed to get Leah moving, and she gave Sarah a half-hearted wave before she disappeared upstairs after her brother.

Samuel Jones leaned down to say something to his wife, and she nodded. He came and joined Will. "You know as well as we do that she's a fighter." He gave him a pat on the shoulder. "And she's in good hands."

Will tensed when the older man wrapped his arms around him in a quick, fatherly embrace, and the band around his chest tightened as he remembered what it felt like to be part of this family.

Samuel clapped him on the back and released him, grinning with a fondness that Will thought would have faded through the years. "Don't be a stranger this time, son."

"I won't," he barely managed.

The head of the Jones house moved to the stairs, appearing completely at ease and at peace. But Will caught the way his eyes tightened in concern and compassion when his gaze flickered to Sarah.

It took a few more minutes of pained silence before Seth came back, rubbing a hand over his head to dispel the melting flakes. "It's snowing again," he said, cupping his hands over his mouth and blowing to warm them.

He came to stand with Will again, and it was silent for a minute before he commented, "Karen told Mother what happened, but I didn't catch all of it. You both fell into the lake by the west rise?"

Will released a gusty breath, raking both shaking hands back through his hair. "Just her. She went out onto the ice without realizing it, and by the time she did, it was too late." He couldn't contain his cringe at the memory.

Out of the corner of his eye, he saw Seth shake his head in disbelief. "But how'd you get so wet?" Will remained silent. "You went in after her, didn't you?"

He risked a glance at the other man. Seth started to grin slowly, that lopsided smile he remembered from boyhood. He nudged Will. "So when did you become a hero? Did I miss something?"

"It was the only thing I could do," Will murmured, feeling slightly embarrassed at the gentle tease, though he hadn't realized how much he had missed the easy camaraderie between he and Seth, even if his jesting was simply to cheer Will up.

"But, honestly," Seth added, losing his teasing edge. "You must be freezing, as well. And Karen said that you carried her all the way out here. If you don't sit down and get warm soon, you'll have Sarah worried when she realizes that she's the reason your stubborn hide caught its death."

Will's first instinct was to glare, but that desire quickly faded when he saw his old friend watching him with concern. He nodded reluctantly, tensing as he walked across the room to the far wall, trying to keep from stumbling. He noticed that Seth shadowed him—presumably to make sure he did not fall.

With a grimace, Will braced his back against the wall nearest the fire, sliding down until he was on the floor. He stretched his legs out, feeling his quivering muscles slowly settle until his whole body slumped in complete exhaustion. It had sapped the last of his strength to keep up with Seth on their way to the house, and sheer worry and adrenaline had been keeping him upright before. Now all of that faded, leaving his body drained and sagging against the wall for support. Sarah had her back to him as the two women continued to work warmth into her body, but it looked like her shaking had lessened.

Seth sat down next to him. He hiked one knee up to prop his elbow on and shot him a crooked grin. "You look like death warmed over."

"Thanks," Will muttered good-naturedly. The blanket dipped on his shoulder, and he tried to lift one of his hands to right it and found that it took too much effort to manage such a small task. "I can't make a fist."

Seth looked surprised, and then he actually chuckled when he saw Will's twitching fingers. He jerked the blanket back into place with a grin. "You've had quite the day." At that, they both turned their heads to watch the patient with her nurses in silence.

Ruth Jones moved to warm the bowl of water again. Though they were only four feet away, neither man was included in their small, huddled group.

Yet Seth remained at Will's side.

His heart warmed at the reminder of the friendship he'd once had, and Will closed his eyes against the exhausted burn behind his eyes, allowing his head to fall back.

"I've missed this," Seth said quietly in that thoughtful, straightforward way of his. Will's head lolled to the side to stare at him.

"What?"

"Our friendship. We fell apart for reasons neither of us can recall. It's foolishness to keep pretending that we can't rectify what was broken."

Will sighed. "I was thinking the same thing."

"So shall we forget the past and be friends? Or at the very least amiable acquaintances?" Seth was grinning easily, but it was obviously important to him.

"Friends it is." Seth's grin spread at his response, and Will settled his head against the wall, closing his eyes. He was surprised at the smile he felt pulling the corner of his mouth as he murmured, "But I remember why we parted ways."

"Really?" Seth sounded surprised.

"You smell like a goat," he muttered on a yawn. Seth's silent chuckle shook the wall at his back.

Will was half asleep by the time the young redhead crouched down before them. Her furrowed brow had left a crease above her nose. "The extra mattress upstairs, can you fetch it?" she asked Seth. "It will be easy to keep by the fire, and I want to get her settled before I head out for the night."

"There's no way you're going back out there." Will's lids opened a little wider at the spark in Seth's voice. He looked unflinching, narrowing his eyes a little at Karen. Will wondered at the exchange, and then he realized that he was peering into a looking glass, glimpsing his own protective response to Sarah. *Ahh,* he thought in comprehension.

Karen's emerald eyes narrowed to slits, defiant, but Seth's gaze remained steady. She sighed. "Fine, I'll stay with Leah tonight. But Sarah gets the mattress," she said, jabbing a finger into his chest. He looked pleased to have won and gladly hopped to his feet, taking the stairs two at a time. She watched him go, shaking her head.

Karen's lips were pinched when she turned, but she nodded reassuringly. "She's fine," she whispered. "I figured since you both need to keep warm right now, we could leave her with you by the fire. Your body heat's better than anything right now, and then you can put her on the bed when she falls asleep. Just keep her awake for a little longer to be safe, if you can." She eyed his drooping lids and bit her lip. "Or maybe I should—"

Shifting positions so he was sitting upright, Will shook his head, blinking the sand from his eyes. "I'm exhausted, but my brain isn't quite ready to let me sleep. I can keep us both awake, you needn't worry." He winced at the slur in his last words.

Karen hesitated, then nodded slowly. "If either of you needs anything, I'll be in the second door on the right. Seth's room is the one across the hall."

He nodded, trying to focus his fuzzy head. But she didn't move. Biting her lip, she whispered, "On her back, there are a few fresh scars, small ones—was that during the fire?"

Will inhaled sharply, having nearly forgotten the gashes that had covered her back, the same ones he had cleaned and tended to for days as he wondered if she would pull through. When he had seen the full extent of Allan's work, he had never hated a man so much. Except, of course, for Gabriel Dunlivey.

Nodding, he answered in a strained voice, "When he dragged her through the forest."

Karen grimaced, clearly troubled by his answer. "Oh." She started to rise, and he caught her hand quickly in his own.

"I-I wanted to say thank you. For all you did tonight."

Her smile was genuine. "You're the one who got her here." Expression softening, she cocked her head, studying him for a moment before stating, "I guess we were both trying to take care of the girl we love."

~Chapter 41~

Karen slipped out of his grasp, since he was too startled at his transparency to release it himself. Pleased with her discernment, she skipped lightly across the room to take over for Mrs. Jones. Karen plopped down beside Sarah and wrapped an arm around her waist. The two friends leaned on each other, speaking in hushed tones. Sarah even released a choked laugh at one point, and some of the tension left Will's body.

He felt a presence nearby and focused his weary gaze on a smiling Ruth Jones. He struggled to rise, and she waved him back with a rapid swat of her hand. "Don't bother with that, dear. I know you must be exhausted, but I simply wanted to say that it's a delight to see your face back in our home."

Will swallowed, remembering that with this family, it had never been a house but always a home—even for him. "Thank you."

The bouncy, middle-aged woman leaned down to plant a motherly kiss on both his flaming cheeks. Then she flitted off, kissing the tops of each young woman's head before moving out of the room to join her husband upstairs.

Will caught Karen's expression of pretend shock, and she angled her body so he could catch Sarah's grin. The redhead's gasp was delayed until Mrs. Jones was out of earshot. "You move on fast," she said in a stage whisper, then huffed. "Holiday's are going to be a little awkward between the fam now."

Gaping at her in surprise, he heard Sarah's soft snort. But his shock quickly faded, and Will felt a grin of his own twitch his lips. He didn't envy Seth the handful he would have in this quick-witted woman, but he had a feeling that his friend was up to the challenge.

His grin spread. And Karen had no idea how mule-headed Seth could be when he set his mind to it. But he was also one of the kindest men Will had ever known, and he doubted that her opinion would be any different.

Will turned his gaze to find Karen stroking Sarah's hair, speaking soothingly to her. Yes, the gentle-giant and this fiery-sweet redhead would make quite the pair.

Karen was helping her charge to her feet. "You know," she grunted, "it's hard carrying tall people, and it doesn't help that you're built in all the right places, either." Sarah rolled her eyes, smiling groggily. Will couldn't help envisioning how her soft curves had filled out her gown at the masque rather nicely, and he ducked his head to hide a grin. He would be the *last* to complain, he could guarantee it.

When he collected himself and glanced up, Karen was shooting him a look that let him know he'd been caught. "Nothing to add, Will?" she asked innocently, though her eyes glinted with devilish amusement. She saved him the trouble of fabricating a reason for his sudden mirth. "Can you scooch closer to the fire?"

Too achy to stand, he scooted along the floor, and she lowered Sarah next to him on the side closest to the flames. Gently snatching the blanket away from her, Karen said lowly to Will, "Keep your blanket wrapped around the both of you—like I said before, your body warmth is better than the extra layers. And then when she falls asleep, wrap her up in this." She hesitated, then grinned as if something had just occurred to her. "Still not deaf, Sarah?"

"Nope," she muttered softly, smiling to herself with her eyes closed.

"Sorry. Didn't mean to talk over you."

Will inched closer, feeling awkward with Karen watching his every move. Then he hesitantly wrapped his arm around Sarah, drawing her against his side. She was hardly shivering now, and he tucked her securely under his arm, wrapping the blanket around the both of them.

Seth appeared at the bottom of the stairs, a thin mattress tucked under one arm. He placed it on the floor near the fireplace and came to join them. One of his ruddy brows lifted when he caught Sarah and Will's closeness. "How cozy," he observed, then turned his crooked grin on Karen. "I should have thought about faking a slip through the ice—"

A hard jab in his ribcage was her response. "We'll let you two get some rest in peace," Karen said, shooting Seth a warning look as she dropped the extra blanket on the bed. He grinned unrepentantly, rubbing his offended side.

Looking all at once stern, he admonished, "Don't get any ideas, young man."

"Good*night,* Seth," Sarah said firmly, startling them all.

The farm boy chuckled. "I suppose we can trust you, then." Will felt his neck heat at being left alone, though the others seemed completely at ease—even Sarah, who was snuggling sleepily into his side, totally unaware of how many laws of convention he was breaking. It was one thing to be

344

alone with her in his home—*entirely* another thing, he thought ruefully—but it felt different to know that others might be watching his moves. Not that there were any moves to be made. He quickly amended his train of thought before his embarrassment showed on his face.

With a reassuring smile at Will, Seth followed Karen up the stairs. His whispered question echoed into the main room: "Why do we never cuddle?" He grunted in pain, and then Karen's harsh whisper faded until the only sound in the room was that of the crackling fire and Sarah's faint breathing.

"Feeling better?" Will asked her softly when his silent chuckles had subsided.

Sarah sighed. "I can feel my toes again, so that's a plus." She wiggled around, turning her body so she could snuggle closer to him. He held his breath until she settled into his side, her head resting against his chest. It felt so natural to have her next to him, safely tucked under one arm. He already felt warmer because of it.

"Comfortable? Would you like me to move you to the bed now?" he asked, momentarily forgetting Karen's instructions to keep her awake. Sarah was sitting on the portion of the large quilt that was bunched on the floor, but perhaps she wanted more padding.

"I'm fine right here." He resisted a smile at her sigh of contentment. Her breathing evened, while his refused to slow. How could his mind continue to function so quickly when his body begged for sleep?

Resting the side of his head against the wall, he watched the flames dance in the fireplace to distract himself from her nearness and remain alert. He was suddenly reminded of the blaze back in the forest and recalled the way the flames had lapped hungrily at Gabriel's corpse.

Facial muscles tightening in a grimace, Will whispered, "Are you all right? After what happened earlier?"

This time Sarah shifted uneasily, and he immediately regretted upsetting her. "What *did* happen? Do you know how he died?" Her voice faded on the last word.

He wanted to spare her as much detail as possible, but he knew she would only persist. "I didn't see a wound at first, but the bottom of the chest in which he was . . . *stored* was covered in dried blood. I can only assume it was a head injury for there to be so much."

"He bled out," she whispered, a note of horror in her voice.

Will nodded gravely. "Yes, I believe so. That's why he looked as he did. And as to why those men were ordered to dispense of the body in such a secretive manner—" He sighed. "Well, that I cannot begin to comprehend."

"I don't understand any of it." Her voice was so quiet he had to strain to hear. She was silent for a long minute, and he wondered if she had fallen asleep until she whispered, "I'm sorry he's gone, but maybe you can move on now."

There was a hint of hope in her voice, and he took a second before answering carefully, "He received his justice."

She heard what he wasn't saying. "But you wish you could have been the one to deal it out."

"Unfortunately, yes." He thought her previous words over. "Perhaps I *can* move on, but I can't help but begrudge the fact that the choice was taken from me. Does that make sense?"

She nodded against his chest. He felt her fingers brush his free hand weakly, though he wasn't sure whom she was trying to comfort. He turned his wrist to wrap her small hand in his, and her thumb rubbed his knuckles gently and then went still. "What happened to your palm?"

"Hmm?" he murmured, eyes closed in utter contentment.

Sarah moved his hand out of the blanket and held it up to the flames for inspection. Her quiet gasp filled the space, and he opened his eyes. The skin of his palm was shredded, blood crusted in the thin gashes crisscrossing over his skin. He was just as surprised as she, but now that he knew how it looked, he was aware of a similar aching sensation in the hand around her shoulder.

"What happened?" she asked again.

"I must have scraped them on the ice."

She looked up at him, confused. She didn't seem to realize that she was still cradling his upturned palm in her hand.

Will explained, "After you fell in, the water was so cold that the opening began to freeze over again. I had to chip away some of the ice." He stifled a yawn and blinked. The adrenaline was fading faster than he'd led Karen to believe, and it was a struggle to keep his eyes open.

He could tell without looking at Sarah that her silence was thoughtful.

"I didn't get to thank you for saving me earlier," she began softly. "Karen said that you must have gone in after me because you were all wet." He felt her shift and glanced down to find her staring up at him, the awed expression on her delicate features turning his stomach. "That was really brave."

He swallowed, unable to remove his gaze even when he felt his neck heat. "I wasn't going to lose you."

"You're always saving me." She smiled lazily up at him and then rested her head back against his chest. A finger delicately swept over the rapid pulse thumping in his wrist, grazing the thin line of risen flesh on the soft part of his skin. "And what about this scar?" she mumbled.

Will's body tensed before he could catch himself, and she sensed the subtle shift in his mood. Scooting back, she propped her head against the wall and stared up at him with half-lidded eyes, weary brow drawn in question.

346

He forced a half-smile. "You are tired. We can speak of it later." Though he truly hoped she would forget it altogether.

Sarah struggled into a sitting position, and he knew her stubbornly inquisitive side was overweighing her exhaustion. "What happened?"

With a sigh, Will's body slumped a little as he stared at the ceiling. "It isn't a happy story."

She didn't push him, and he wondered how to begin.

Dragging in a breath for courage, he whispered, "I went through a very . . . dark time in the months following my parents' deaths."

"Dark time?" Her tired voice carried traces of hesitation.

How else to say it? "The life of an orphan taking over his father's successful business held too many expectations I could not live up to." Will's chest swelled with a pained breath at the memories that came unbidden. "I wished to join my parents and attempted to end my life." He grimaced at how straightforward his answer sounded, but there was no way to polish the story of how low he had fallen. He didn't believe he would ever cease regretting his decision.

Sarah's wide, shock-filled eyes made him close his own in painful shame. "How?" Her voice was hardly a breath.

"By rather . . . messy means." Her fingers stroked the scar on his wrist again, and the soft intake of breath let him know she understood. "Suffice it to say I was unsuccessful, thanks to my uncle."

Sarah drew out the silence, absorbing this, and then she pressed her head against his chest again. "Good," she commented firmly. "I'm glad there's one thing you can't do perfectly."

His smile was faint, and then his heart rate quickened as he contemplated what he might say next. "I have always wondered," he began slowly, drawing the words out, "if my failure was because I lacked the conviction to follow through, or perhaps I was afraid of death and wasn't aware of it." Her eyes flicked up sharply to meet his, filled with a hope he couldn't account for. He inhaled a breath and caught the faint, crisp scent of the lake clinging to her hair.

The fire and the intimate mood it created loosened his tongue, brewing in him the desire to reveal everything to her. It all came spilling out, then, those secret thoughts he had taken captive over the years. But here with her now, with the firelight and the reminder that death had almost claimed her hours before, it only seemed natural to come clean. And Will desperately needed someone to understand, and he sensed that, out of everyone, she would.

Swallowing thickly, he whispered, "Since that day, I have prayed that my loneliness may spur me into finding something to live for—someone great enough to die for. The Shadow emerged from that desire, culminated with my thirst for justice. I felt the need to do *something* with my life."

347

His lips curved, an action that lately seemed to occur on his behalf without thought or force. "But that rainy day in the stable caused me to think that perhaps there was a greater reason that I had been unable to end my life on my darkest day." Will's arm tightened around her. "And now . . . well, perhaps I held on for this moment without even realizing it."

Sarah was quiet again. He let her have the silence, feeling an edge of nervousness as her pause stretched into minutes. He had bared his soul as best he could, and whether she accepted that or not was entirely her decision.

"For a quiet man, you're pretty good with your words," she murmured. The back of her fingers brushed over the length of his hand, stroking over his scraped palm and fingers and then back again. The mechanical motions seemed to soothe her. "Does it still hurt?" her voice was barely above a whisper. She was fading quickly, and he knew he would be soon to follow.

Will closed his eyes, not too far gone to smile to himself. His answer was truthful. "Not anymore, love."

****

Someone was inside his house.

Will's heart rate was up before his eyes snapped open. It took him a moment to blink away the sand and even longer before he got his bearings. Though it was too dark to see clearly and only a faint, deep-blue slice of light cut through the gap in the shutters, he saw enough to remember that he was not in his house at all. The fire had died sometime in the night and only an occasional hiss or crackle popped faintly from the inactive pile of ash and wood.

Shifting to relieve the numbness in his backside, he realized what his chin had been resting on. Sarah's limp arm was slung over his waist, her head tucked securely against his chest. Even in sleep, he had not loosened his hold on her, and pinpricks shot over his shoulder after so many hours clutching her to him.

With a grimace, he rotated his shoulder, careful not to disturb her. But she was sound asleep, breathing heavily.

Will suddenly recalled the sound that had woken him and let his gaze wander the room, feeling more alert. A shadow moved from the kitchen and into the main room. He made out the sturdy build and stock of red hair and relaxed his position.

Sneaking by on his way out the door, Seth looked over at them, and Will caught a flash of teeth in the darkness as the man grinned. He took in the sleeping woman. "Saddle sore?" he whispered.

Stretching out his legs, Will resisted a groan as the blood returned to his limbs. Sarah's hand twitched against his stomach in her sleep, and then he reminded himself that a sore backside wasn't quite so bad. He thought about sending Seth on to his morning work so he could get another hour of rest, but he was too alert to fall asleep again.

With a finger at Sarah's head, Will nodded toward the pallet in the corner. Soreness aside, he felt far better than he had last night, but all his strength had yet to return to him. Seth understood and crouched down, gently taking the sleeping woman into his arms. Forcing aside the unnecessary pang under his ribs as Seth cradled her against his chest, Will rose, using the wall for support as the blood rushed from his head down to his feet to offer assistance.

Laying Sarah down on the pallet, Seth retreated a step and allowed Will to lay the blanket over her. He couldn't resist stroking back the tendrils that had fallen over her face, which had regained some of its color. Crouched beside the mattress, his mind wandered to the previous day, summarizing what they had discussed. She had said the physician was going to be executed this day.

Her lips were parted, breathing deeply in oblivion. She looked so innocent and peaceful as she slept. Though she hadn't yet realized, Will knew that if she was the last person to openly suspect Cadius' involvement in the king's death—and many others—then she was in immediate danger. That was, if he couldn't save the only other witness.

Standing, he took Seth aside. Keeping his voice low, he said, "I need to go."

"You've hardly had a full night's rest," Seth protested quietly. "And how will she take your leaving at dawn without a word?"

"It's because of Sarah that I need to go." At Seth's confused frown, he explained, "She is involved in something, and I have to intervene to protect her. It's difficult to explain just now, but I give you my word that I will when it's safe."

Seth looked unsure. "You realize both she and Karen will pummel me when they discover that I let you run off headlong into danger."

Will frowned, knowing he was right. "Then don't tell her why I left, just that I had to do something and it couldn't wait."

"That's hardly vague," Seth replied sardonically.

"Please, just do this for me. I can't wait any longer. I know she'll be upset when she wakes, but tell her I will be back and that I'm sorry I had to leave."

Seth was silent for some time, mulling this over. Twice his eyes darted to Sarah's sleeping form, and Will could almost see his train of thought: If she was awake, Will would not have the heart to leave.

But then Seth released a heavy breath. "Fine. But come back in one piece." He stooped down by the fire and came back to Will, handing his coat over. "Found this in the barn last night and had Mother dry it out for you. And take one of the mares; I can pick her up from your stable later."

Gratefully, Will accepted the coat, slipping it on quickly. "Thank you." He clapped Seth's shoulder. "Don't let her walk home alone. And keep her safe while I'm gone, will you?"

Seth's face was serious when he looked at Sarah lying there. "Of course. You know I care for her, too."

"That's why I'm coming back," Will replied dryly.

The bewildered expression on Seth's face quickly turned into an amused smile that crinkled the corners of his eyes. "No worries there, friend."

Will thought of the redhead and recalled his friend's interaction with her last night, and he knew there was nothing to concern him. Will nodded and turned to leave.

"And try to stay out of trouble if you ever want to see me alive again."

Feeling humor twitching his mouth, Will said, "When have I ever sought out danger?"

Seth's gentle chuckle followed him out the door.

~Chapter 42~

Frosted air bit against his face and hands as he galloped across the cobbled streets, pushing the mare harder with the intent of completing his task before the sun rose; the animal's hooves pounded against the stones in a rhythmic clicking sound that wouldn't long go unnoticed. The town was still immersed in darkness and shadows, but he didn't have much time before light revealed his unwanted presence. A hurried trip to his cabin for rope and his bow had taken longer than he liked, and he had no time for stealth now. He tried to push away the disturbing realization that someone had snuck back into his home and returned the stolen weapon and cloak.

Slowing his mount's pace abruptly, Will slipped from the saddle in a fluid motion before the horse had jerked to a halt. He wrapped the reins around the hitching post in front of the livery; he would put her inside later for Seth to find.

Four guards were posted at the front gate, and more to the side. *A bit excessive,* Will thought warily.

He moved through the streets at a clipped pace, half-crouched to avoid being spotted if any early-risers or shopkeepers happened upon his path. Picking his way down a side street, the passage opened and he immediately spotted his vantage point on the wall surrounding the castle. The execution yard was on the other side; they would have taken the physician from the tower last night and kept him nearby for easy retrieval.

Hoping memory served him correctly, Will narrowed his eyes at the balistraria—the long and tight arrow slit on the upper portion of the wall, just below the crenellations. He raised his arm, aiming his bow and releasing the chord in a practiced movement that felt as familiar to him as breathing. The arrow sliced into the long and slender notch in the stone, slipping through to the other side.

Will stepped on the end of the rope to stop it from uncoiling entirely, tugging on it until the arrow caught. Though his muscles had not yet fully recovered, he concentrated on scaling to the top and found the familiar pull and strain beneath his skin focused his mind. With his feet planted against the wall for support, he climbed quickly and landed in a crouch on the other side. No guard. *Convenient.*

Hoping the length of rope dangling against the outside wall would not be discovered, he moved quickly along the walk toward the stairs. Instinctively, his eyes roved the courtyard and the top of the wall. His steps faltered, and he was instantly filled with suspicious dread.

At the highest point of the wall, the upper portion of the gallows reached out like an extended arm over the courtyard. The noose hanging from it was stretched tight around the opening of the sack draped over the man's head, hiding his face from view as his body swayed in the gentle breeze. He was positioned high enough that the limp body was above the shadows of the courtyard, swaying in the barest light of morning.

Without edging forward, Will could perfectly make out the man's slight build, his once noble clothing soiled from the dungeons.

He was too late.

Will's eyes roved the body out of habit, searching for some sign of life, a twitch of the foot or movement of any kind. He felt a sinking in his gut when he acknowledged that it was useless: The physician had been effectively silenced.

But how could that be? His execution was scheduled for this evening. The only reason for moving the time of the hanging in secret was if they were concerned of interference from the townsfolk, or if they wished to draw as little attention to the application of justice as possible.

Will's hand balled into a fist around his bow. Of course. It all made sense now—the secrecy, Gabriel's death, destroying the evidence in the woods. It had been clear to him before that they were tying up every stray end in this little charade, whether a viable threat or not, but they were also trying to remain reticent while silently eliminating key players. It was clandestine deeds like this and the utter lack of respect for life that concerned Will.

Whoever was involved was desperate and willing to do anything to keep their baleful character immersed in shadows.

A terrible thought struck him, and Will felt his worst fears swaying from the noose along with the dead man. Now that the physician was no longer a threat, how long would it be until the guilty party focused their attention elsewhere? Did they already suspect Sarah? He prayed that wasn't the case. However, the murderer would not remain ignorant of her suspicions for long, if he was not already certain of her quest, and she was in grave danger if she was the last remaining soul to speak out against him.

Suddenly, the absence of a guard on the wall made sense: with the deed done, he was more than likely assisting the other guards in preparing for retrieval of the body.

As if on cue, three guards entered the courtyard, one pushing a flat cart before him. Will dove into a low crouch, listening to their heavy boots clomp over the stones. He held his breath as one set of boots moved up the stairs, each footfall echoing faintly through the stone wall to reach his ears.

The guard appeared at the top of the stairs, and Will shrank back, his senses on high-alert. He breathed a little easier when the man moved away from him along the wall to reach the physician's body. Bracing himself, the guard detached the length of rope from around a weight that sat at his feet. With a grunt, he allowed an inch of the rope to slip through his fingers at a time.

From his vantage point, Will watched with a twisted stomach as the body jerked downward, the rope slithering around the wooden posts that made up the execution stand.

"So what do you make of last evening?" Will recognized the voice coming from below and dared to raise his eyes above the ledge. Two guards stood with the cart in the courtyard, keeping close to the wall as the body was painstakingly lowered to them.

"Strangest thing I've ever encountered," came the reply. Will hadn't seen much of their faces the night before, but he instantly placed the voices as belonging to the guards who had discovered Gabriel's body in the woods. "I haven't yet inquired about Taylor. Thought it best to do that later, though I'm still not sure. . . ." His voice faded with doubt. Will's pulse quickened.

"I understand your hesitation about his guilt, but I'll go along. Never can be too careful, not with all this secrecy going on."

One head bobbed in the semi-darkness. His voice lowered, and Will strained to catch his words, spoken grimly. "Seems a lot of things are happening in secret lately."

The physician's body reached them, and they hefted it into the cart with a dull *thunk*. They loosened the noose from around his neck, and one of them motioned for the guard above to drag the rope back up.

"Best not to ask questions unless you want to end up like him," the other guard muttered as they wheeled the body away.

The remaining man was pulling the noose back up to the top, and Will took the break in his attention to slip across the walkway and throw himself over the outside ledge. He slid down the rope, ignoring the burn against his raw palms, and dropped onto the ground. Feeling a knot of dread in his stomach, he ignored the tell-tell rope and arrow still trapped in the wall. He left them behind as he ran for home, pumping his legs to beat the sun as it rose over the eastern hills and forcing himself to acknowledge the fact that Sarah wasn't the only one in trouble.

They were both in their sights now, but Will fully intended to keep her out of the crosshairs.

****

Sarah roused from sleep. Narrowing her eyes tiredly, she squinted against the shaft of soft light that fell perfectly over her face. The way it caused her head to ache, it might as well have been a spotlight shined directly into her eyes.

She rolled onto her side, flipping the blanket over her head to shield herself from the light. The quick movement reminded her how sore and stiff her body felt, but it was nothing compared to last night. And though the silent fire had clearly died hours before, she no longer carried that bone-deep cold. She felt almost normal, aside from her aching head and muscles.

Shifting more carefully this time, she snuggled deeper under the covers and caught the faint scent of evergreen and wood smoke. *Will.* He'd been with her when she fell asleep—she remembered that much from her foggy recollection of last night. When Sarah focused, she vaguely recalled someone moving her from the floor to the pallet beneath her, but after that, there was nothing.

A shuffling noise sounded from nearby, and Sarah poked her head out into the chilly air to find someone crouched before the fireplace. It took her a second to place the back of Seth's head.

He turned at the sound of her rustling. "Sorry to wake you," he whispered. "I thought I'd warm the place up before you woke. You look better, though." Sarah felt so groggy and disheveled that she wondered how bad she had appeared last night.

"I feel better," she croaked. She struggled into a sitting position and wrapped the blanket around herself, snuggling deeper into the warmth. It felt a little strange to wake up with Seth there—maybe it was embarrassment over having a man see her so unkempt in the morning—but he appeared unbothered by her appearance. She relaxed, supposing that growing up in such small quarters with women had somewhat desensitized him.

Clearing her throat, she whispered, "Is everybody up yet?"

Seth ducked his head to light the fire, blowing gently on the budding flame. "Karen and Leah are still asleep, but Father and Josh are out tending the animals already, and Mother's in the kitchen doing her best to keep quiet." He grinned back at her.

Now that she was aware of Mrs. Jones's presence, Sarah made out the faint clang and scrap of pots and utensils every now and then.

Craning her neck to glance around, she winced at the pain in her head. Probably mild dehydration—ironic, considering she'd half-drowned yesterday. "Where did Will go?"

Seth hesitated. Setting the remaining kindling on the larger log, he sat

354

on the ground facing her. "I saw him this morning. He said there was something important that he needed to do and was sorry he left so early." Seth gave her a sympathetic grimace. "That's all I really know. I'm sorry."

She was a little wounded at first that he'd left without saying anything, but then she realized that he had probably wanted to let her rest. Resisting the urge to shake her head, she settled for saying, "It's all right. If he took off, it was for good reason."

A grin started to crawl over his lips.

"What're you thinking?" Sarah asked suspiciously.

He shook his head, still smiling. "Nothing. Just that you and Will work rather well together."

Ducking her head, she admitted quietly, "I hope that's true." Now more than ever, she desperately wanted it to work out between them, but it always came back to the question of if she could leave home and her family for him. She was only eighteen, and although she sensed she was on her way, Sarah wasn't even sure if she knew what loving someone looked like.

It wasn't just the matter of moving to Florida and visiting for holidays: if she chose to stay here someday, an idea she couldn't even fathom at this point, it would mean never seeing her family again. And she couldn't disturb the rift between times, breaking it to have Will come home with her. As much as the thought tempted her, she knew there could be massive consequences to such a selfish decision.

Sarah rubbed her gritty eyes in annoyance. She used to think being able to travel through time would solve all her problems, and now it was turning out to be the source of most of them. Hopping through time had become more of a nuisance than anything, and she felt more uncertain and indecisive than ever before.

"Sarah?" She looked up sharply, half-forgetting that Seth was still there. He looked concerned, his face open.

She huffed a breath, wrapping the blanket tighter around herself. Though the fire was starting to grow, she felt colder inside, somehow. "You like Karen, don't you?"

Seth appeared startled by her straightforward question, and then his face broke out in a self-deprecating grin. "I guess I wasn't trying that hard to hide it. But I would be grateful if you kept this between the two of us. I'd like to be the first to tell her."

Nodding, Sarah fell into silence, wondering why she had even asked in the first place. She felt Seth's curious gaze on her. "What's on your mind?"

She bit her lip, thinking. "Would you do anything for Karen?" she whispered, watching the flames danced elegantly in the fireplace.

"Yes," he answered without hesitation. Sarah grinned at his quick, assured remark, but her smile faded.

"But could you leave your family, all that you've ever known, for her?" She planted her chin on her upraised knees, angling her head to see his face.

Seth's gaze was focused on the floor, brow drawn in an intensely thoughtful expression she had never seen on his face. "I think," he began slowly, "that there comes a time when every man needs to leave home and find his own way. I suppose that's when his life really begins." He grinned suddenly. "Whether or not that entails chasing after a lady or two is entirely up to him."

Unable to hide her grin, Sarah rolled her eyes. "C'mon, be serious."

Smile fading, he said earnestly, "Yes, I would do anything for her."

Sarah nodded once. "Good."

"*But*," he said, seeming to sense her loaded questions, "you and Will have to make your own decisions. I know my old friend well enough to see that he would follow you to the ends of the earth and back, if you required it."

"I'd never ask him to do that," she whispered with a grimace. Seth didn't know his words had hit the nail right on the head.

He gave her a soft smile. "You wouldn't have to."

She sighed. "You have an answer for everything, don't you?"

"Yes, I do."

Grinning, she added, "And I'm glad you finally realized how amazing Karen is." She didn't need to add how relieved she was that Seth was no longer interested in her.

Flexing his arms in a gesture that reminded Sarah of the preening peacocks at the zoo, Seth said in a macho voice, "It never would have worked out between us anyway, darling. You're too high maintenance with all the constant saving and requirement of bravery, and whatnot." He flicked his hands in the air in a dismissive gesture.

Sarah gaped at him and then let out a hoarse laugh. "I seem to get myself into a few scrapes now and then, but it's nothing a good friend with great advice can't fix."

He chuckled along with her. Lowering his voice, he said, "You can return the favor of my sage wisdom by convincing Karen she's in love with me." Though the words were spoken in jest, Sarah heard the underlying uncertainty in his voice.

She hid her grin in the folds of fabric, tucking away the secret she held. How could he not see that her job was already done for her?

~Chapter 43~

Breakfast was an interesting affair. It consisted of one hovering mother, two watchful-eyed redheads who barricaded Sarah on either side, and three Jones men who repeatedly reprimanded the lady of the house whenever she inquired after Sarah's health or volunteered to cut her breakfast into manageable bites, which was quite often.

Sarah could no longer hide her grin. Each time Mr. Jones kindly reminded his wife that her patient was doing just fine and was perfectly capable of slicing sausage with her own hands, she shot a look at Seth, and he had to clear his throat when he looked on the verge of laughter. Ruth Jones swatted her husband's arm once when he suggested that Sarah could feed herself just fine, and Samuel raised his hands, surrendering with a good-humored grin.

Sometimes when Sarah looked up, she caught Seth shooting a secret gaze at Karen more than once, though that girl appeared completely oblivious to his poorly disguised attention. Josh and Sarah shared a grin and then went back to their meals.

"Next time you must come back under better circumstances," Mrs. Jones said as they bade her farewell, wrapping Sarah in a tight, motherly embrace. Smiling, Sarah hugged her back. She pushed away all questioning thoughts about whether this would be the last time she saw these friendly faces, these people who had welcomed her into their family without question.

"I won't be going anywhere near the water for a while, trust me," Sarah said emphatically, laughing a little.

There were hugs all around from the women, and Leah beamed up at her, though they were nearly at eye level now. She would look even more like a woman the next time Sarah saw her. If she came back, that is.

"Now are you sure you won't be needing another cloak?" Ruth Jones ambled onto the porch after her, worrying the front of her skirt with her hands.

Chuckling, Mr. Jones pulled her against his side and bent down to whisper in her ear. She swatted at his midsection, but she was masking a grin of her own.

The two brothers were leading the horses out of the barn after hitching them to the wagon. Karen had volunteered to drive Sarah back into town, and Seth had insisted on coming along.

Warmed by the love she felt surrounding her on the porch, Sarah forced back tears and jogged down the steps after Karen, waving back to them. Concealed chunks of frost that floated in the light mist clung to her skin and hair, melting into her clothes. She shivered, grateful that Mrs. Jones had insisted on her borrowing the heaviest cloak they owned.

Josh smiled at her as she approached. "You always seem to cause quite the stir when you drop by."

Sarah laughed breathlessly, surprised to feel so winded after her brief jog. She hoped it wouldn't take very long to regain her strength. "Yeah, sorry about that."

He shrugged one shoulder. "Don't be. Nothing interesting ever happens around this town." Sarah ducked her head to hide her expression as he helped her into the wagon. He couldn't be further off base.

Seth kept the two girls engaged as they drove into town, and Sarah was disappointed when the rutted path turned to smooth cobblestones, the castle gates looming before them. She motioned Seth ahead, and the wagon rolled along the side of the wall. He pulled the horses to a halt at the servants' entrance, frowning.

"You sure you want to go in here?" he asked.

She shrugged. "I know my way around this end of the castle. *And* I don't want to deal with the guards." She didn't add why, and neither he nor Karen asked.

Hopping down from the seat, Sarah wished she could speak with her friend privately, but there would be time for that later. Smiling up at her companions, she said, "Thanks, guys." For all they had done, she wanted to add. But their answering smiles let her know they sensed her unspoken words.

"Always." Karen waved to her as they drove off. Watching the backs of their heads shrink into small dots down the street, Sarah felt an unwelcome pang in her middle. It seemed so easy for some.

She thought of Karen's concern over her barrenness and immediately reprimanded her self-pitying train of thought. Moving slowly up the stairs on quivering legs, she reminded herself that many inward struggles went unseen by others. The greatest demons one could fight were their own, and Sarah told herself that she wasn't alone in that struggle.

When she reached the top of the stairs, her heart was beating rapidly.

"Almost dying really does a number," she muttered. A maid scrubbing the base of the banister glanced up in question, and Sarah smiled apologetically.

Suddenly needing company, she ran to her room and changed into a vibrant red velvet gown that looked soft and warm. Damien had mentioned once that he liked red.

Sarah shook her head at the random thought and hastily laced up the front of the dress and the boots she still wore, which Mrs. Jones had thought to dry by the fire last night. And then she quickly crossed the hall and knocked on Damien's door. She hoped his arm hadn't gotten infected in her neglect, knowing she certainly wouldn't be receiving any awards of merit in the nursing field. But she still had some poultice in her room somewhere. . .
.

She knocked again, more firmly this time, expecting to hear him rustling around inside. The door creaked open at her insistence. She froze, imagining the last time Damien had left his door unlocked, when she'd found him half-conscious in the midst of his seizures.

Pulse thumping with worry, Sarah stepped inside, hoping she was overreacting, and was vaguely relieved to find the room empty. She closed the door behind her, deciding to wait until he returned from his errand.

She wandered the room for a minute to keep her mind occupied but felt like she was snooping. Planting herself at his desk, she drummed her fingers on the tabletop, eyes roving disinterestedly over the lists and half-written notes scattered over the surface. Minutes passed, but there was no sign of him. Sarah scratched idly at a few stray drops of candlewax on the surface of the wood as her eyes roved the lists and business letters he had carefully penned in his elegant script. Had he gone out searching for her?

"Five more minutes," she assured herself aloud. After that, she would inquire after his whereabouts and see if she could find him. *But what if Will comes looking for you?* she asked herself. He had disappeared without notice, and she had no idea what he'd gone out to do.

Sarah snatched one of the seals from the desk, moving it anxiously between her palms and then rolling it between the fingers of one hand. The back of her mind caught on something, and her hand stilled.

Bringing the heavy object closer to her eyes, she admired the intricacies of the design. Her gaze narrowed in thought, and she returned the seal to its place and picked up the one beside it. The designs were identical. She couldn't put her finger on why she was so interested in them; it was just that the slopes and curves pressed into the metal looked so familiar. . . .

Mind working furiously, she tried to recall the exact details of the design on Robert's letter, but so many of the seals were similar—her own had nearly been a match—and she couldn't be sure without comparing the two side-by-side.

What was she thinking? It wouldn't matter even if they *were* an exact match. Damien hadn't written that letter, she was sure of it.

The door opened suddenly, and her heart lurched painfully in her chest. Sarah spun around, instinctively hiding the seal behind her back. She gave Damien a smile that said she was glad to see him, but it wobbled nervously at the corners.

Damien's eyes widened in surprise for half a second before they softened. "I was wondering where you'd gone off to."

She nearly choked on her anxiety over being snuck up on. "I t-thought we should work on your arm." She stumbled over the words, letting them out in a breathless rush.

Frowning, he moved over to her. "Are you all right?"

She nodded. Her eyes were too wide, and she made an effort to look at ease. "Just cold."

He rubbed his hands over her stiff arms, smiling. "Better?"

Some of Sarah's anxiety faded at the warmth in his eyes. She must be crazy to think that he had any part in the schemes going on around the castle. His presence subdued her suspicion, and she felt herself relaxing. Now she was holding the seal behind her skirt in embarrassment. "Much better. Thanks." She walked over to the door, moving her hand so the stolen object was out of his sight. "I'll get everything and be right back."

He smiled. "Then here I will be."

Hurrying across the hall, she closed her bedroom door and stared at the seal in her hands. It was stupid to take it with her, but she had been afraid to admit that, though fleeting, she'd suspected a folly on his part.

Unable to fight her curiosity any longer, she sifted through her things. She would disprove her unfounded doubts once and for all.

She found the missive at the bottom of the desk drawer but couldn't bring herself to reach for it. She knew why she hesitated—what if they matched?—though the idea that Damien was involved was ridiculous.

Quickly, before she could talk herself out of it, Sarah snatched up the letter and flipped it over with clumsy fingers. Her breath caught. *It can't be,* she thought, shaking her head in skepticism. She wouldn't have believed her eyes if she hadn't held the seal next to the depression in the red wax. But there was no doubt that it was the same design as Damien's seal. She recalled the drops of candlewax on the table in his room.

Red candlewax.

But that proved nothing. Ten or twenty other guests could have sealed this missive with red wax. To prove correct her intuition about Damien, her eyes scanned the depressions in the wax, searching for some inconsistency that would alleviate her growing anxiety.

At the bottom right corner, there was a shallow notch where the eagle's tail feather should have been, as if that portion of the seal had not been properly cut out. Sarah's eyes flew to the corresponding corner of the seal, searching for the spot where—

"*No.*" The word was just a breath from her lips, all at once disbelieving and comprehending.

On that section of the eagle's tail, where the feather should have been sunken like the rest, sat one that was slightly raised by the glob of red wax lodged in the crevice.

"It's a mistake," she whispered, eyes wide. But she was holding the proof in her hands.

Unwilling to believe, Sarah wrenched the letter open, eyes scanning the instructions with a sinking feeling. It was written in a matching looping scroll with the same hitch on the a's as the partially written letters on Damien's desk.

Sarah's heart thumped wrathfully in her chest even as she shook her head in denial, trying to be reasonable; she was being paranoid. She knew after all the trouble with Will that she couldn't jump to conclusions at the slightest test of her confidence. Surely Damien had a good reason for writing the letter asking Robert to pose as the Shadow.

But, of course, that would mean he'd had a hand in Edith's murder.

Her quiet intake of breath echoed in the silent room. Suddenly, it felt as if the air had been stolen from the space, and an unseen force had a fist around her ribcage, suffocating her. She dropped the seal onto the table as if it had burned her.

The seal on Jade's secret missive. She recalled it in her mind now and knew it was an exact match to this letter. Dread filled her. Sarah couldn't breathe as the horrific realization crashed in on her, and she gripped the edge of the desk for support.

Damien said he had business at the livery that day, but neither Will nor Robert mentioned seeing him. Damien had written letters to both Jade and Robert, and one—perhaps both—led to Edith dying.

Sensing she was missing an important link from that night, Sarah racked her brain to remember every blurry detail. She recalled seeing the Shadow, running after him, his hesitation to shoot at her and then surprise when he did. Almost as if he hadn't meant to, almost like he didn't *want* to hurt her.

But Damien had come from his room, she countered. It couldn't have been him.

Sarah closed her eyes to envision that moment when he'd run to her, and her lids snapped open in a panic. He hadn't come half-dressed from his own room, where she had assumed he'd been sleeping in late; he had run from the opposite end of the castle.

But that didn't make sense . . . unless, of course, he had simply waited in the shadows for her and Terrance to leave before he followed them. He would've had plenty of time to discard his disguise in a passageway and wait them out. If he timed his appearance right, they would be none the wiser—they *had* been fooled by his game, Sarah corrected.

The pieces fell into place then, fueling the anxiety building within her chest as the accusations and memories flashed through her mind: the matching seals, the secrecy, Damien's insistence that she drop her investigation, lying about where he was going, disappearing for hours on end. It all made sense.

Sarah had wondered if his aversion to Cadius at dinner was because he was trying to protect her and keep her from stirring the water. But she saw now that it had been subservience and fear that had cowed him at the table. Damien was probably working for Cadius! Even as she wanted to deny it, she couldn't ignore the clarity of this fact.

What she didn't understand, accident or not, was why he had killed *Edith*. What purpose had it served to masquerade as the Shadow? How could a man she had trusted so implicitly lie to her and comfort her when he had been the reason for her grief?

Sarah felt a sharp jab of disgusted betrayal behind her ribs, followed quickly by a pang of fear as a memory assaulted her, leaving her breathless. She recalled the raspy sound of the man's familiar voice, one that she now realized had not belonged to the physician at all. Though she hadn't seen it, she could hear the scuffle in the back of her mind, the solid *thunk*, the sound of creaking hinges. Then Edith burst into the room, and Damien was leaning on the chest—for support, Sarah had assumed. Now she realized with increasing dread that they had nearly caught him in the act of stashing Gabriel's dead body.

She could hardly bring herself to acknowledge the horrifying evidence that Damien had killed Dunlivey and Edith. The man who had laughed with her in the snow and made her feel special—that man did not exist. It was all a lie. The Damien Lisandro she knew was a deceiving murderer.

And she had played right into his hands, believing the lie because she wanted it to be true. How had she been such a fool? She had been deceived, yes, but she had been fool enough to let herself be led into the charade in the first place.

Sarah was suddenly very aware that a murderer twice over had been living across the hall from her. A shiver snaked over her spine at the thought that she had been living mere feet from Edith's killer. And then, unbidden, she remembered the way Damien made her smile, how he'd held her so tenderly, like she was something precious, and the way that he, shaking and frightened as the tremors overcame his body, had asked her to stay with him. How could that frightened boy be the same monster she envisioned? She couldn't even compare the two.

She wanted to deny it, to deny all of it—the fact that he had written the letter, her suspicions that he was a cold-blooded killer, and her growing dread that he was involved with Cadius. The only proof she had was the letter he had sealed, and she doubted that would hold up against someone with his connections. She could never get him to confess, even if she had the courage to confront him. What else was there?

The physician.

His face came to the forefront of her mind, startling her in its clarity. He was the only one who knew the truth, who could confirm her suspicions.

With this in mind, Sarah set off for the tower that held the prisoner she sought.

~Chapter 44~

Damien's door was cracked, and she snuck past his room with a thumping pulse before breaking out into a dead run. The textured paper of the letter brushed against her wrist; she had stuffed the envelope up her sleeve for safekeeping in case Damien discovered her, but she was alone in the hall.

It was eerily quiet as she raced up the steps, skirts hiked, her ragged breaths echoing between the walls of the tight staircase. Nearly fifty steps later, Sarah gasped for breath at the top as she got her bearings. The long corridor that stretched off to the right was immersed in shadows, and she couldn't make out the end as the passage faded into inky blackness. But it was the vacant cell that concerned her.

She stumbled forward, needing to be sure and unwilling to believe he wasn't here. The door was open, a single key lodged in the lock and the rest dangling from the ring against the bars. She stepped into the cell with hesitant steps. A bird flapped its wings somewhere outside the tiny window high on the left wall—too far up for anyone to see outside, but she suspected the window's only purpose was to fill a dead man with the maddening possibility of a glimpse of the sky before he was executed.

Sarah shivered.

But Malcolm wasn't there. *Maybe he's in another tower*, she reasoned, even as she felt her heart sink. The thought was weak and formed out of desperation as the walls of the cramped cell pressed in on her. Her eyes searched the space, hoping the physician had left a clue behind. Then she froze, realizing that the sound of the bird's chirps had been eclipsed by the hurried shuffle of boots on the staircase behind her.

She spun. Damien rounded the corner to the top, immediately catching her wide-eyed, fearful expression. His own face was pained, and he held up his hands as if trying to calm a frightened animal. In one hand was the seal she had dropped on her desk, and with frightening clarity, she realized he'd been in her room. He *knew!*

The envelope crinkled inside her sleeve as she fisted her hands. Sarah swallowed, fear coiling in her stomach. She retreated into the cell, though every instinct in her cried out for open spaces.

"Please, let me explain." Damien's voice was soft, but distress tainted his words. He took another step toward her into the cell, moving slowly.

She jerked back and hit her shoulder on the wall, planting herself in the corner of the cell, as though it would prevent him from reaching her. "D-don't come near me."

He winced at her fear and distrust. Still, he advanced. "It isn't what you think."

"Where's the physician?" she demanded shakily. She tried to mask her fear, but she was quickly losing control over her emotions. She felt betrayed and angry and sorrowful over the fact that this man still had some amount of control over her: She *wanted* to believe him. That was the only reason she hadn't run from him screaming—to hear him out—though it was also due, in part, to the fact that he blocked her way.

Damien hesitated, eyes crinkling in pain. He stopped close enough to touch her, stuffing the seal in his pocket, though he didn't reach out. It would only make things worse for her, and it pained Sarah to know that he could still read her so well and cared enough to respect her wishes. "The physician was hanged before dawn. I did not order the execution to be moved."

"But you followed orders and passed along the message." She saw the answer in his espresso eyes before he nodded regretfully. Realization hit her like a battering ram. She now knew it had been Dunlivey that Damien had fought with, but why had she not considered the physician's innocence in light of this? "Malcolm didn't even attack you, did he? Why frame an innocent man?"

Damien's eyes were so sorrowful it broke her heart. She tried to harden herself against him, to tamp down the sympathy she felt at the regret in his gaze.

"Because it was convenient," he whispered, mouth tipping ruefully. "I was ordered to *dismiss* him, and the opportunity seemed to present itself perfectly." The way he grimaced over the word caused Sarah to think that he hadn't been commanded to "dismiss" him at all.

A thought struck her, turning her stomach. "Lisandro was written all over his cell," she breathed in accusation. "You must have seen that he'd etched it into the stone at some point. It wasn't out of obsessive retribution, was it? He was sending a warning!" All along he was trying to point out that he was innocent, and Sarah had assumed the physician was crazy. She had done nothing to get him out, and now he was dead.

"I never intended for it to end this way." Damien reached out to touch

365

her cheek, as if to offer comfort. She imagined it was the same hand that had ended Gabriel's life.

Swatting it away, Sarah glared at him, feeling bolder by the minute as her indignation overshadowed her fear and common sense. "You're a murderer, and you expect me to believe this dribble?"

He froze, shocked at her outburst. She drove the knife in deeper, though her hands were trembling. "I know you killed Dunlivey. I saw his body where you hid it and witnessed your cronies light him up in the forest. Were you the one who had the evidence destroyed, or was that someone else's doing, too? Cadius, perhaps?" In the back of her mind, Sarah was aware that it was entirely unwise to taunt a murderer, but she was beyond holding back.

Damien looked as though his legs wouldn't hold him. He shook his head in shock. "How did you—?" His head swiveled as he shot a glance down the corridor. Lowering his voice, he whispered desperately, "I'm no murderer."

"Oh, right."

His hand flew around her arm in a flash, eyes on fire with the need for her to understand. Sarah winced at his grip. "Honestly! His contract was terminated, and he wouldn't go peaceably. Dunlivey drew a knife, and when we struggled, he lost his balance and caught his head on the corner of the chest. I panicked and hid his body inside and had just wiped the blood off the edge when you came in." Sarah recalled Will's finger grazing the splintered corner of the wood and allowed herself to wonder if there might be some truth to his claim.

Narrowing her eyes at how easily he could sway her, Sarah asked, "And did you stab yourself to make it look like you were the victim?"

Damien shook his head so vehemently it displaced his perfectly arranged locks. "He must have nicked me as he went down. I didn't even realize he'd stabbed me, I was so frightened at what I had done."

She didn't want to believe him, but the panicked sincerity in his eyes made her wonder. "If you were so worried about being found out, then why did it take you so long to get rid of him?"

Fidgeting anxiously, his grip on her arm tightened. She hid her wince with a steadfast glare. "I tried, several times, to dispose of the body, but there was always someone nearby. So I locked the door from the outside and hoped no one would discover him in the meantime."

He said it like his actions were warranted, like they made sense. Sarah swallowed. Maybe in his mind they did.

"Do you at least regret killing him?" she asked, slightly exasperated. Some part of her wanted to see the old Damien, the one she had started to fall for.

His sigh was heavy. "I won't lie to you," he whispered. Throat working convulsively, he answered, "No, I don't entirely regret it." She blinked in surprise at his candor, and by the way he rushed on to explain, she knew her disappointment was palpable. "I didn't want to, but he would have killed her if I hadn't gotten to him first."

His hand slid up her arm to cradle her cheek, eyes filled with torment and regret. She wondered who he was protecting when his voice softened and he leaned closer, as if to brush his lips to hers. Eyes warm, he whispered, "But I am no murderer, Sarah. I'd never hurt you. And if I have any unwarranted sins, surely your goodness will wipe them clean."

He was insane! Alarmed at her desire to believe him, added to her rising anxiety as he leaned in, Sarah lost it.

She slapped him so hard the clap echoed through the corridor like a crack of thunder. Damien reeled, losing his grip on her as he slammed into the wall. She saw her chance and bolted around him, running for the door and grabbing hold of it. With a terrible, stridulous sound as it scraped the stones, she slammed the door closed behind her. The force dislodged the key from the lock, and the ring clattered to the floor, skittering a few feet away.

Sarah watched its progress with a panicked gaze and ran to snatch it off the floor, wasting precious seconds she didn't have. Damien was already on his feet by the time she fumbled to shove a key into the lock. It jammed inside, and she wrenched it free, groping for the next one, her panic increasing with each rapid pulse of her heart. Which one was it?

Her palms were slick, hands trembling uncontrollably. She tried two more, praying she hadn't gone too fast and missed the right one. Her anxiety grew and, though she knew she had to focus, she couldn't help glancing up. She let out a startled gasp as Damien charged for the door.

She inserted the key into the lock, rattling the others against the bars. It stuck. Panicked, Sarah jerked it to the right and ripped the key from the hole just as Damien's hand shot out for her. With a cry of alarm, she lurched back, losing her balance. He reached through the bars, gripping her forearm so tightly that she nearly cried out as his hold forced her against the cell.

"Let me go!" she shrieked, trying to wrench free. But he was too frantic to release her, eyes wild with fright as he pressed his face against the bars, like some feral animal that found itself in a trap.

"Sarah, please don't do this," he pleaded, face so near to her own. "This is bigger than either of us."

Knowing she couldn't let him escape, she chucked the keys behind her to keep them from his reach. Damien watched them slide toward the stairs, but he quickly turned his attention back to her. "You must understand that so much of what I've done was to keep you safe. You're in danger."

"And what about Cadius? Did *he* have me moved so you could keep tabs on me?"

His silence was answer enough, and Sarah glared at him. He was quick to add, "But I only followed through because I wanted to watch out for you: keeping you close meant ensuring your safety, and I was never going to inform him of your dealings. I turned his confidence around to *protect* you."

"Oh, so now you're worried about me?" she retorted bitterly. "You tried to shoot me!"

His eyes softened along with his grip. "I was never going to. I've always cared about you, and I have done so much to keep you safe. I would never hurt you," he said again.

Sarah wrenched free of his grasp, eyes blazing. "You killed Edith! And you *held* me after, like you were an innocent." He winced, but didn't deny it; she could tell he was tired of lying to her.

Tears of agonized disgust filled her eyes. "You've already hurt me, Damien, you're just too selfish to see it." She couldn't keep her voice from quavering.

His expression was tormented as his eyes closed. *Good.* At that moment, she wanted to hurt him.

"Do you have any idea," he whispered faintly, "how it tore at me to know I had taken the life of an innocent—someone you cared for? And I could never ask for forgiveness without admitting my guilt. I would have to carry that alone." Damien opened his eyes, and they bore into hers, searching for some sign of trust. "But I told you it was an accident. Surely you must believe me when I say that no one was supposed to get hurt."

Sarah glared at him. "Everything I *believed* about you is a lie. You betrayed my trust, manipulated me, and pretended to be my friend. Any amount of faith I ever had in you was buried in the ground right along with Edith."

Why was she still standing there? She should leave him and never look back. But she stayed rooted to the spot, needing to know *why* he had been there, why it had happened the way it did. She couldn't walk away with so many unanswered questions. "What was the whole point of the ruse with Robert, anyway? Why single him out?"

He hesitated, dipping his head in defeat until his hair fell through the bars. "His interest in the vigilante was one of the deciding factors, but I cannot say more than that; it's too dangerous." She scoffed.

Damien pressed closer to the barrier, as though he could slip through to the other side and convince her of his innocence. His words came out sounding choked. "I want you to know," he said, "I *need* you to know that what I feel for you is not a lie. So please believe me when I say that it is too dangerous to tell you, that you will be in greater peril if I reveal my reasons. Everything I've done is to protect you, and I will not undo that and risk your safety."

368

His tone was so earnest, but how could she trust him? Brokenly, she asked, "And I'm supposed to believe all this? You've only caused me hurt."

"I saved your life!" Damien cried out suddenly, gripping the bars. His words were filled with frustration over the fact that he was getting nowhere with her. Face awash in misery and defeat, he said more quietly, "I've been protecting you for months and would never dream of turning my back on you now. Isn't that worth something?"

He was speaking nonsense. "What are you talking about, saving my life?" Sarah demanded in confusion.

He seemed to sense her interest and grasped hold of the tiny straw held out to him. "I have kept Cadius off your trail and have lied to many in order to keep you safe. I told you that people have died over less than you know." He hesitated, and the silence was heavy, the intensity of his gaze spearing her to the ground. She saw in his dark eyes a deep desire to convince her that he was not quite the monster she imagined him to be.

She felt a flicker of sympathy toward the man in the cell as she wondered if this would be the final picture anyone had of the great Lord Damien Lisandro—that of a man trapped in a cage by his own lies and poorly placed loyalties.

Sarah's heart felt sick at the thought that he might never see the sun again. As much as she wanted to hate him, and a part of her implicitly did, she only felt a deep, hollow of sadness inside when she recalled the man who had smiled and laughed in the snow with her, the boyish, inexperienced joy he had expressed over a concept as simple as having *fun*.

Then she remembered his serious gaze, much like it was now, as he had warned her off Cadius in the darkened corridor after dinner with the royals. His concern had been genuine then, as she suspected it was now.

She clenched her fists against the building ache, desperately wishing this broken killer before her and the kind friend she'd known weren't the same person. "Please," Sarah whispered, a part of her needing to know his answer but dreading it just the same. "Can you tell me how the sweet, self-deprecating man who made me laugh at the ball when I felt out of place could work for such a monster?"

His dark eyes were filled with sorrow and regret, conveying a thousand unspoken words, pleading for her understanding. But all he said was, "Someday you'll understand."

The two sides warring within made her feel split in half, torn over what to feel and who to believe. Her shoulders sagged under the weight of her inward struggle, and she squeezed her eyes closed against the building ache.

"You know I would never hurt you." Damien's quiet words were spoken with assurance as he witnessed her fight. Gently, like he truly didn't want to upset her but had to make her understand, he whispered, "Have you

369

ever stopped to wonder why you got away that day?"

Sarah finally opened her eyes, giving him a quizzical look. "What day?"

"The fire. Who do you think he worked for?"

Uncomprehending, she began to shake her head and then froze, mouth parting in utter astonishment. "The fire . . . Allan. You killed him," she breathed, eyes wide. Damien winced and gave a minute nod. Stunned, her eyes searched his face. "You helped us get away. Why?"

He opened his mouth to say more, but it snapped closed as they both turned at the sound of approaching footsteps down the corridor. Wide-eyed, Sarah faced him again. His knuckles were white with strain around the bars.

"I can't let them catch on to me," he whispered regretfully, eyes edged with pain. "But I promise you—I give you my word that I will do everything in my power to earn back your trust."

Biting her lip, Sarah lingered in indecision as some of the angry fight left her. He must have sensed her struggle, because he nodded once, encouraging her to go.

Lips tipping in sadness, he murmured, "I shall give you a head start, darling. For old time's sake." His voice cracked.

Sarah understood now: He was coming after her.

Heart in her throat, she spun on her heels and took off for the stairs, snatching the keys off the ground in a last minute decision, hoping to buy time. *Just keep moving,* she told herself as she slipped the ring around her wrist. If she didn't look back—

"Sarah!" Damien's harsh whisper sounded on the verge of panic. She instinctively spun around on the top step, nearly out of sight around the corner, and forced herself to meet his gaze. Even from a distance she could see that he was breathing hard.

"What?" she whispered harshly. Her eyes flickered nervously down the hall as the footsteps grew louder. Surely whoever was patrolling would have heard his call.

Eyes searching her face, Damien shook his head slowly. The incredibly tender and accepting smile that graced his lips caused tears to burn her throat. "Nothing. Just memorizing."

Sarah allowed herself one final, lingering glance, feeling the ache in her chest grow until she couldn't breathe properly. When she could bear the sorrowful sight of him no longer, she dashed down the stairs, choking on a sob marred by fear and sadness. She almost ran smack into Sevrine as she rounded the corner of the staircase, breezing past the startled little girl with no explanation as to why she looked such a fright.

But Damien held his word, and Sarah was halfway down the next set of stairs before she heard him cry out to the guard for help.

~Chapter 45~

Sarah had never run so fast in her life. The staff stared as she blew past, eyes wide, skirts flying about her as she dashed down the stairs and toward the main door. A footman was stationed there and, with a look of surprise, ripped the door open, barely managing a startled "Good day, my lady" before she ran past him and through the gate to Will's shop.

She remembered calling out his name as the pseudo Shadow ran from her, and then Damien's reaction when she introduced the two men at the ball—the look of recognition in his eyes when she'd used Will's name: Damien knew his secret, and it was all her fault.

Driven by fear, her legs ate up the distance to the livery. A golden-brown mare was stomping her front hoof on the ground, tossing her mane in agitation. Sarah skidded to a sudden halt at the sight of the two guards loitering in the alley next to the shop. It wouldn't have been so suspicious if they didn't "subtly" patrol around the perimeter of the building every five seconds.

Were they waiting for her? She amended her paranoid train of thought. Will, then? But why? Whatever the reason, Sarah knew he was too smart to show up at his shop with a couple of goons waiting for him.

She spun on her heels and ducked into the nearest street, making a beeline for the forest. She must have looked like a frightened red hen in her dress as she flew across the pure white snow into the forest, swatting branches from her path. Her skirt caught several times, but she didn't take the time to untangle it; she just ripped it free and kept running, fear and waning time pressing down on her chest and making it difficult to breathe.

Will's house came into view over the rise an instant before she saw him crouched near the woodpile on the side. He was slipping something into his boot and glanced up as she approached. She must have appeared a terrible fright for him to look so instantly panicked.

He shot to his feet. "What—?"

"Damien," she gasped, grabbing his arm for support. Her words came out in a rush, a series of hysterical chokes and gasps. "He killed Edith. He posed as the Shadow and killed her. And the physician and Gabriel! And he might have even killed John, too." Her legs threatened to give way. She knew she sounded crazy, and most of what she said was hardly intelligible, anyway, but she felt a swelling of warmth in her spasming chest as Will's brow furrowed in seriousness. He believed her!

Gripping her shoulders, he looked her over with burning eyes. "Did he hurt you?"

Sarah shook her head vehemently, though she knew her dismissal wasn't wholly honest. "I found out," she gasped, "that he killed Gabriel and framed the physician, and he set the whole thing up at the castle with the Shadow. I have a letter he wrote to prove it." She almost added Robert's involvement, but she couldn't bring him into this; it would only seem like one more betrayal to Will if he found out another worker of his had been disloyal. If Robert wanted to come clean, that was his business.

Gripping her burning side, Sarah added in abrupt sentences, "I locked him in the tower, but he'll get out soon. The physician wasn't there, and guards are spying on your shop." She sucked in large gulps of air, filling her starved lungs.

Will scowled. "I assumed as much about the physician and was just coming to tell you not to go by the livery." He sighed. "Last night I realized Mr. Devlin was the last piece of evidence, and I left this morning to free him, but he had already been hanged by the time I arrived."

That's why he'd left. Sarah nodded jerkily, too winded to speak just then.

"So the Spaniard murdered them both?" he clarified, grounding out the words. "He should have been the one to hang."

"But Edith and Gabriel were accidents." She tucked her chin, wondering why she was attempting to justify Damien's actions. Will's brows rose at the way she jumped to his defense, and she felt the need to add, "He saved both of us the day of the fire."

Will's whole body stiffened at her quiet words. "What?"

"He took Allan out to keep him from escaping and reaching his superiors. I hate to admit it, but he may have kept us from further harm."

"We don't know that." His jaw was set in a stubborn line.

"Think about it," she urged. "Whoever hired Allan wanted to know the Shadow's identity and to have both of us dead. If he'd had the chance to tell them who you were and what we were trying to uncover, they wouldn't have stopped coming after us just because Allan failed the first time."

A muscle in Will's jaw twitched, and he scrubbed a hand over the shadows growing there. He looked agitated. "So I owe my life to a murderer? What a paradox."

372

She sighed at his annoyance, knowing it must be difficult to realize a man he despised so implicitly might have saved his life.

"No. I don't know." Sarah swallowed, hating to dump everything on him at once, but there was no way to sugarcoat the next part of her message. She cringed as she admitted, "And, Will, he knows your secret." Thanks to *her*, that is.

His eyes snapped to attention, the mockery fading. "What?" he breathed.

Nodding reluctantly, she confessed, "I think for some time now. Remember, I used your name when I thought the Shadow was you at the castle?"

Will's lids closed, the lines on his forehead appearing more defined. The half-moon scar over his eye curved upward as his brows furrowed. "So he knows. And if my identity is revealed, a murder is tacked onto my reputation." He sounded resigned.

Sarah hadn't considered how Edith's death would be pinned on the real Shadow, and she couldn't bear the thought of what might happen to Will if he were wrongly accused of her murder. "I don't know what he'll do with the secret, but he's kept it for several days already, so maybe . . ." Her voice faded. Damien was an enigma to her now, and she could no longer judge what he would and would not do.

She whispered, "I don't think it will be long before he speaks with the guards at your shop and puts two-and-two together. He'll know I'm here. I'm sorry."

Will placed his hands on her arms. "No regrets, remember? I knew this day would come. I'm simply glad you're safe." He released a breath. "I will figure something out. In the meantime, let's get you warmed up inside; it's freezing out here."

Sarah nodded and let him guide her around the house. Her head spun with all the information flying around up there, and she tried to remember what she had actually shared with him. She cringed as she added, "And, Will, I think Jade was involved somehow."

His eyes snapped to her face in shocked denial, and she nodded reluctantly. "I saw a letter she got a few days ago, and it was closed with the same seal Damien used on the note I have."

"I just can't believe it." Will frowned severely. "I wonder if the Spaniard convinced her to jump so that her and John's bodies would be discovered together."

"I don't really think—" Sarah froze mid-step as they rounded the house.

Three horses appeared from the trees, Damien leading the troupe. Will slowly drew her behind him, holding an arm out to shield her from sight, as if the riders hadn't already spotted her. But Damien's eyes had locked on hers the moment she looked up.

"How odd to have so much company today," Will said sardonically. Mockery fading, his voice hardened. "What do you want, Spaniard?"

Damien's eyes stayed fixed on her, returning her wide-eyed gaze. His answer was written all over his handsome, tortured features before he opened his mouth. "I've come for Sarah," he said softly, resolutely. His quiet confidence was unnerving.

Sarah shrank back, seeing how his eyes flickered in pain at the slight movement of distrust. He searched her face, his own trying to convey some hidden message she didn't comprehend. Was he searching for understanding or sympathy in her features?

Will's entire back stiffened at the admission. "Did you ever think to ask what she wants?"

Finally, Damien broke eye contact with her, turning a hard-edged gaze on Will. The determination and assuredness, like he knew he was going to get exactly what he wanted, made the hairs on the back of Sarah's neck stand at attention.

"And she wants *you*?" he asked, looking Will up and down. She saw Will's fist clench into a tight ball, knuckles turning pure white. One of Damien's brows rose condescendingly. "A poor blacksmith? No, she's coming with me."

Will snorted in derision. But his hand clamped around Sarah's wrist possessively, sensing the other man's seriousness. "Like hell," he ground out.

Sarah almost nodded in agreement. There was no way she was going with Damien, but she felt too frightened to voice her objections. Her nervous gaze flickered to the two men flanking Damien. She wasn't surprised to see Timmons at his side, but it took her a moment to place the man on his left, and even then it was only because she recognized him in uniform.

She swallowed hard as she recalled seeing him about the castle. Even some of the guards were under Damien's payroll, it seemed.

The barest of smiles pulled at the corner of Damien's mouth, reminding her of a cat who had its prey trapped in a corner. And she and Will were the mice. "I can't exactly allow Sarah to go; she knows too much."

"Then why don't you just kill us on the spot? It's not as if you haven't done so before." Though Will's question was spoken out of curiosity, it came out sounding more like an invitation. Sarah winced. *Don't test him, Will,* she thought.

A flicker of pain crossed Damien's tan face, but it was quickly replaced by a scowl. His horse shifted under him, and he tightened his hold on the reins. "Whatever happens to you is none of my concern, but the lady

374

comes with me."

"I'll tell you where you can put your ideas." Will took a step forward, but Sarah latched onto his arm.

"If I come with you, will you let him go?" she cried out, terrified of the fight she felt brewing between the two men. Whatever the outcome, she knew there would be a loss.

Will turned, staring at her as if she had sprouted horns. He shook his head and lowered his voice, though she knew the others could hear him in the oppressive quiet of the forest. "In his eyes, I'm dead, anyway."

"Promise you won't hurt him, Damien," she called out as a last-ditch effort. He had said he would never lie to her, and she prayed that was true.

"My hands will do him no harm," Damien returned, shoulders lifting confidently.

Will scoffed. "Ask him about his cronies," he said under his breath.

"What about them?" She motioned to his men, feeling a little bubble of desperate hope building inside her. But his continued silence and the stoic look on Damien's face—which cracked only for a moment to reveal the pain written on his features—squashed every ounce of hope.

"That's what I thought," Will muttered. Louder, he asked, "So, shall I end up like John and take a swim over the falls, or will you simply jam by corpse into a chest? Because it appears you're too much of a coward to fight me in an even match."

Damien's eyes flared in outrage. He threw his leg over the horse's rump, dropping to the ground and taking a step toward them. "Do not test me, blacksmith. I came to take Sarah, and that is what I will do." His eyes narrowed in annoyance. "I have a sense I should speak slower, because you don't appear to comprehend that I have the upper hand. Though if it eases your conscience, I vow she will come to no harm in my presence."

"Your promise means nothing," Will spat. "She'll be your prisoner and personal toy, and you expect me to step aside at your *word*? As it stands, I can do something before I'm too far underground to make a difference."

Sarah balked at his heroism and the rather blatant slap in the face he'd directed at Damien.

Watching the threesome out of the corner of his eye, Will turned his head toward her so they couldn't read his lips. Lowly, he murmured, "I want you to go inside and throw the bolt down on the door." His eyes burned with the need for her to do exactly as he said. "Whatever happens, don't come out unless I tell you. *Please.*" Gently, he pried her stiff fingers from his arm and stepped forward to fight.

"Will, no!" Sarah whispered frantically, afraid the others might overhear and suspect his intentions. She reached for him, but he'd already moved from her grasp. A perfect flake landed on the tip of her nose, melting against her warm skin. *Perfect,* she thought disgruntledly. Snow wouldn't help this situation.

Damien's eyes flickered up to the clouds and then landed on Sarah, his look meaningful. She dropped her gaze, knowing his thoughts were on that day in the snow. She glanced up when she caught movement as he pulled a dagger from its sheath on his belt, the long sword at his side left untouched. He grinned mockingly at Will, splaying his fingers. "I suppose I over prepared."

"You'll need it," she heard Will growl.

Timmons and the guard, silent like sentinels, started to move from their mounts to offer assistance, but they froze. Sarah heard it too: barking dogs and shouts.

Will and Damien glared at each other from a distance, and it was obvious neither appreciated the interruption. Then they broke off in opposite directions, and Sarah nearly sagged with relief that the fight was over before it had begun.

Will ran for her and grabbed her hand. "Dogs!" he shouted. Guiding her to the back of the house, Sarah spotted his black stallion waiting in the snow, expelling clouds of air through its nostrils. Will's bow and quiver of arrows were strapped to the side of the saddle, as if he'd prepared for this.

Launching himself into the saddle, he held a hand down for her.

"What?" Sarah shrieked. She shot a look over her shoulder, knowing that Damien and his lackeys were probably already mounted. Would they follow to duke it out elsewhere or try to outrun whatever had spooked the men?

Will stuck his hand farther out, insistent. "Trust me," he said. He always had to pull that one.

Gritting her teeth, she grasped his hand, stuffing her startled cry as he pulled her up behind him. He barely waited until her arms wrapped tightly around his middle before heeling the stallion in the sides.

"Heeyah!" he urged. The animal, which seemed edgy in its idleness, launched forward so quickly that Sarah's head would have snapped back if she didn't have her forehead pressed against Will's back; the stallion seemed as eager to be moving as the man guiding it.

She gritted her teeth and squeezed her eyes closed as they plowed through the snow at frightening speeds. The wind whistled in Sarah's ears, though Will's body blocked most of the blast. One of the newcomers shouted in the distance behind them, announcing himself as a royal guard over the fading sound of the dogs' yips and barks of excitement.

Sarah pulled back, staring at the back of Will's head to keep her eyes off the blurring landscape. "Go back! They're guards."

"We can't stop."

"But they'll help," she returned, itching to look over her shoulder but too afraid to see the world blur. "We can tell them about Damien."

"Dogs mean a search party," he said loudly, as though this should make sense to her. "They're here to investigate me, not help. I won't leave you alone; the Spaniard has more power than you give him credit for. If I'm gone, he'll get exactly what he wants."

Sarah saw with sinking hope that he was right. Even if Will were found innocent, he was the only thing keeping Damien from her right now, and if he was out of the picture for even a moment—

She shuddered, unwilling to finish the thought. Though running only made them look guilty, she knew they couldn't go back. So she closed her eyes and prayed they could stop soon.

The stallion sped forward, legs pumping in long, rhythmic strides in time with the hoof beats pounding against the wet earth. Sarah felt it dodge trees and fallen limbs with surprising agility and speed for such a large beast, carrying them farther from the sounds of the search party until all Sarah heard was the rushing in her ears and the snorts from the horse's muzzle.

After a few minutes of tightly closing her lids with the feel of the world flashing by on both sides, she could no longer resist. She pried her lids open, forcing herself to look around. Her breath caught.

Snowcapped trees blurred together in a hazy white landscape, the purity of it broken only by sporadic flashes of brown and evergreen. The animal's head was pumping up and down, its ebony mane flapping wildly behind its long, elegant neck. It released a heavy snuff each time its head lurched forward, clouds of mist emitting from its flaring nostrils. The horse was moving so fast and lithely that it felt as though its hooves never touched the ground, giving the illusion that they were flying over the earth.

At first it was terrifying to feel so out of control, but then Sarah felt a sudden breathless laugh escape her as she was filled with euphoria. The immediate danger behind them seemed to recede into the back of her mind, and she only felt the freeness of this moment, wondering if they would soon take flight. She could see why Will loved it so much.

"Are you all right?" Will called, angling his chin toward her while keeping his eyes on the tangled path before them.

"It's exhilarating!" The excitement of conquering her fears and the irony of doing so as they raced dangerously through the forest was too much to contain. She laughed again, tempted to throw her arms wide and pretend that she was, indeed, flying through the trees.

Will placed a hand over the ones she had tightly knotted around his middle. She felt his smile and closed her eyes, tilting her head back. Snowflakes fell on her lids and nose, feeling like microscopic kisses over her skin. Sarah savored the sensation of gliding over the ground, the world flying by at her sides, her hair blowing wildly behind her. Freedom in the purest sense.

The illusion was shattered when Will slowed his animal, and she opened her eyes reluctantly, wondering why they had stopped. She suddenly realized how hard the stallion was breathing—saliva foamed from the bit in its mouth and beads of sweat glistened on its neck—and knew they had pushed it to its limit.

"This is as far as he can go," Will said. "They'll keep to their mounts for a time, and hopefully we can lose them on foot where the horses can't travel." He threw his leg over the animal's neck and dropped to the ground. He wrapped his hands around her waist and lowered her until she hovered just above the ground. Feet dangling midair, Sarah looked up at him in question.

He grinned suddenly, unrepentantly, wrapping his arms around her waist and pulling her against him, his hold keeping her off the ground. "Your cheeks are flushed. Riding suits you."

Sarah chuckled a little nervously, feeling heat creep up her neck as she thought about her appearance. She didn't even want to imagine what her hair looked like. "I must look like a wild, wind-lashed banshee."

His grin widened and turned wicked. Eyes darkening, he murmured, "Wildness suits you."

Bits of snow fell on her flaming cheek, melting instantly and sliding down the neck of her dress, which was hardly suited for the outdoors. She shivered. "Uh, can you put me down now?" she squeaked.

Will buried his face against her neck, releasing a breath. "I think we've lost them for now," he answered slowly. She felt his grin spread against her skin.

"Please *put me down*," she insisted, frowning to hide her own mirth. The ride must have knocked a screw loose in both of them—or maybe it was relief that they had momentarily escaped Damien's grasp and that of the search party.

Will pulled back, feigning innocence. "You should have said so before." He set her down, though with purposeful slowness that had her biting her lip to hide her grin.

When he released her, he grabbed his bow and arrows from the saddle and slipped them over his back. Then he smacked the rump of the animal. It let out a disgruntled shriek and took off, disappearing into the forest, a blur of black amidst the white.

"What did you do that for?" Sarah asked.

"He'll find his way back home, and hopefully his presence will distract Lisandro and his troupe, if they come across him." Will took her hand and planted a warm kiss on the back of it. "Are you afraid of horses still?" he asked her knuckles.

His question and kiss took her by surprise, and she bit her lip for a

378

moment. "No," she whispered breathlessly. She didn't bother to pretend that it was the ride that had winded her.

When he looked up, his eyes were warm. He smiled softly. Eyes roving her features, he murmured reassuringly, "You needn't fear—I could never have left you behind. He cannot have you."

Sarah swallowed and stepped into his arms. They immediately closed around her, surrounding her with warmth and protection. "You don't ever have to leave me behind."

He rested his chin on the top of her head. A breath shuddered through his chest. "Good. Because I'm never letting you go."

She couldn't help smiling. The snow fell in earnest now, a delicate shower of white that softened the world around them, cushioning the sound of hooves.

She jerked back. "Is it your horse?" The nervous knot in her stomach told her that was too hopeful.

"They're onto our trail." Will grabbed her hand, and she didn't need any further encouragement to follow.

Limbs and branches slapped at her arms, catching on the hem of her red dress. Sarah was breathing heavily as they continued to run through the woods. Her adrenaline was spent after every mad dash and fright she'd had in the last few hours, and she still felt weak from her spill yesterday. She stumbled and would have fallen had it not been for Will's strong, steady arms that caught her around the waist. When she regained her balance, he dragged her along behind him, but she tugged on his hand to get him to stop.

He looked back at her, his dark eyes filled with urgency. "They're coming. We have to get to higher ground before they catch us." He tried to pull her forward with a tug on her hand, but she shook her head quickly. Just the thought of running again made her tired legs ache.

"I can't go on like this," she gasped, gripping the cramp in her side with her free arm. They were both breathing heavily, but Sarah felt like her lungs were about to burst.

Will stared intently at her for a long moment and seemed to realize that her strength was truly spent. He nodded his head once and released her, turning around to face the direction of the newcomers the same instant that he slipped the bow over his head. Sarah realized his intent with fresh alarm.

She gripped his forearm tightly, glancing at the unarmed weapon in his hand before turning her gaze to his determined face. She couldn't remember ever seeing him so resolute . . . or resigned.

The noises of approach grew more distinct as they closed the distance between them and their prey. Which group was it? The sound of thundering hooves reverberated through the forest, seeming to echo one word over and over in her head: Doom.

"No, Will," she pleaded urgently, "There are too many of them for you to fight." He didn't look at her, but stared straight ahead, anticipating the moment the riders caught up to them. Sarah's hand tightened into a vice-grip on his arm. Still he did not look at her.

"You can make it," she urged. This got his attention.

His head snapped around in her direction, and he stared at her with a look akin to betrayal. She glanced nervously in the direction the sounds of pursuit were coming from. "I couldn't make it in time, even if I had the strength," she said, trying to make him see reason. "I can hide in the forest where he won't find me. What matters is that you can still alert the castle of Damien's betrayal. But you have to go *now*." She reach into her sleeve and thrust the letter into his free hand, trying to close his stiff fingers. He wouldn't take it.

Will's grip on his bow tightened noticeably as he stood firm. "No, Sarah. As long as he lives, he will come for you. I will not run away from this or my duty to protect you. Here is where I stand, and it will end here." He barely managed a grin, and she could tell it was for her benefit. "I pledged you my troth, remember?"

Sarah stared at him, knowing his mind was made up. A minute shaft of sunlight reflected through the gray clouds, streaming through the trees and catching on the shining, polished surface of the wooden bow. He looked so strong and sure as he stood there, his eyes blazing with intensity, snowflakes falling on his dark hair. Her determined protector, who was willing to trade his life for hers. She had always imagined that it would be so romantic to have a hero who would lay his life down for her in a moment of passionate sacrifice, just like the stories had always romanticized.

But in that moment, Sarah realized with painful clarity that the stories left out the important fact that where there was sacrifice, there was also great loss. She would give up all the beautiful sacrifice of this moment if they could both just make it out alive. Though her heart warmed at the romantic gesture, the cost of it was too great for her to allow.

The engraved metal band set around the center of the bow's curved handle caught the sun, reflecting gray light as flakes of snow melted on the surface. The droplets splattered on the ground below in silent succession, marring the pristine surface of the snowy earth. To Sarah, it seemed like the symbol of Will's impending death.

"But what if he kills you?" she said, her voice choked with emotion. It was almost too horrible a thought to voice, but she had to make him see reason.

Will's eyes softened at her words and seemed to caress her face rather than stare at it, like he was trying to remember every detail. He lifted his free arm and fingered a lock of hair that rested against her collarbone, gazing at the silken curl with a look of longing and wonder. His knuckles

380

brushed against her skin, sending a tingle down her spine.

"Your hair is soft," he murmured, his words sounding low and husky. Her heart sped up at the look in his eyes. His hand moved to the back of her neck, his fingers tangling themselves in her hair with painful slowness.

Sarah held her breath as he pulled her toward him and leaned down to press his lips to hers. That kiss in the dark passageway had been gentle, sweet, unhurried, and uncomplicated, and their second kiss had been one of joyful abandon. But this embrace was full of heartache and longing, its bittersweet beauty almost too painful to endure.

Will brought the arm wielding the bow around to encircle her waist, and his hold on her tightened, making her feel safe and protected in his strength. His lips were warm and hard against hers, almost desperate, and Sarah realized with fresh alarm that he was saying farewell. Nothing she could say would change his mind.

The knowledge tightened her throat, and she held on to him urgently, ignoring the wrinkled letter in her hands as she knotted them behind his head. She returned his kiss with as much desperation, trying to convince him to run with her. If he didn't, she was sure this was the last moment they would ever share together.

Sarah focused on his warmth and tender touch, savoring the love and need she felt coming off him in waves. Was it possible to feel such all-consuming elation even as the poignant chasm of misery grew inside her chest, threatening to swallow her whole? How was it possible to feel so torn?

Will broke the kiss, pulling back slowly. He let his forehead rest against hers, and Sarah gripped the front of his shirt, terrified to open her eyes and face reality as she tried to hold on to the memory of this moment.

"Just in case," he whispered. The breath he exhaled was soft against her face, and Sarah forced herself to open her eyes. She caught his tightly closed lids, so close to her own, as his fingers slid over her throat and under the chain.

Opening his lids to half-mast, he let his nose brush hers as he pulled back a few inches, dragging the pendant into view. His hands slid down the chain and formed a fist around the necklace, tugging her closer again. "This was a promise," he whispered, voice hitching. He didn't expand on his words, but she understood what was left unsaid: He would not abandon her.

Will's hand moved from her neck to the side of her face. Brushing his thumb slowly back and forth over her cheekbone, he seemed in no hurry even as the riders drew near. The tender gesture and the warmth in his eyes caused her own to fill, and he gently brushed a lone tear from her cheek.

"Please," she whispered shakily.

"No one can take what isn't theirs, love. Faith and love can only be stolen if one chooses to let them go." He pulled back, lips softening. "My life was once my own, but now it belongs only to you. He can't take that from either of us."

Her throat was too full of unshed tears to speak. She wanted to tell him that his life belonged to God, not her—if only there were more time for that conversation. But as it stood, they first needed to survive this situation.

Sarah's grip on his shirt tightened. "Then let's just run. We can hide in the forest and alert the castle later, after they've gone."

"Here is where I stand," he said again, his voice softer but somehow more passionate and determined than before. "This is where I fight for you."

Sarah blinked at his unyielding resolve. "You really do love me," she breathed, amazed. He had said the words before, but in the back of her mind, she had thought it somewhat impossible that he could truly love her. But seeing the words written all over his face as he professed his commitment to protect her removed any remaining doubt.

Will's eyes stayed locked on hers for another long moment before he turned his gaze to the dark silhouette making its way through the trees. His mouth hardened into a grim line.

"To the death."

~Chapter 46~

Will pulled an arrow from his pack and set it in one fluid motion just as Damien's horse came bounding through the trees. The animal shuffled uneasily, panting hard, each breath nearly a shriek as it fought for air. Damien appeared just as winded, cheeks flushed from the cold and his own rage. He was alone.

Sarah hurriedly stuffed the crumpled letter into her sleeve for safekeeping before he spotted it.

Launching himself from his dazed horse, Damien strode toward them and drew his sword. But Will's bow was up in a flash, fingers gripping the string as he pointed an arrow right at his chest. Damien halted in place, glaring at the man who had him pinned to the spot.

"Please, take another step," Will encouraged lowly, drawing the strong chord back until the frame of the bow bent, resembling a diamond-shape. The notion of Damien being shot shouldn't have felt like such a predicament to Sarah, since she had been tempted to strangle him when she became aware of his true character. He was a murderer, after all, and so he deserved to die.

Didn't he?

It should have been cut-and-dry, but the idea of taking part in doling out his justice made Sarah's stomach clench. Even worse was the thought of Will being the one to claim his life.

She touched her fingers to the back of Will's hand, the one gripping the handle of the weapon. "No," she whispered, hoping he would understand her moral dilemma.

Will looked down at her, perplexed, though she could tell he was watching Damien out of the corner of his eye. "What do you mean, *no*? Even though Dunlivey and Allan got what was coming to them, he still killed your friend. Why are you protecting him?" He looked wary of her answer, dark eyes slightly wounded.

"I'm not protecting him." Her words were full of quiet strength, and she knew he comprehended her meaning.

Will's eyes softened, lips tipping wryly. "You fear too much for a soul that cannot be saved."

She shook her head and found her thoughts resting on Damien for the barest of seconds before settling on the man before her. "Every soul can be saved. All I want is to live long enough to convince you of that fact."

Will's grip seemed to tighten on the string. "That *is* what I'm trying to do: keep us alive."

"Would you like to speak up?" Damien called out in agitation, taking a step forward.

Will raised the bow at the movement, drawing his brows together in an expression that said he was not to be messed with. "Don't," he growled.

But Damien didn't heed the warning and took another step, closing the gap. "Why keep up the heroic charade? She doesn't want you to kill me, so you won't."

"Do not tempt me, Spaniard," Will muttered.

Damien grinned arrogantly, toying with him as he edged closer. "Does it concern you that she wants me unharmed, that she cares for me? Because it should."

An arrow sailed past Damien's head and *thunked* into the tree over his shoulder, burrowing into the bark before Sarah even realized the string had been released. It vibrated inches from Will's poised fingers before settling into place. "Care to test me again?"

Sarah could only gape at his incredible talent. She had never actually seen Will fire his bow before and was breathless over his speed and accuracy with the weapon. He'd hardly moved when he released the string, almost as if it melded through his fingers and snapped forward on its own. Awed, Sarah stared at the arrow protruding from the bark of the tree well over twenty yards away and marveled at Will's ability to come so close to his target. Then she shifted her gaze and realized he hadn't missed.

Stunned, Damien touched his fingers to his face and pulled them back, stained with blood dribbling from the small slice across his cheekbone. He glowered at Will. "You will pay for that."

Will loaded the bow again, though he held it relaxed in front of him. "You're hardly in a position to make idle threats." The words seemed like they should be accompanied by the cocky grin of one with the upper hand, yet Will's face was all seriousness, his tone low and threatening.

Damien looked to her, and his spiteful expression softened. It was like night and day from when he had stared Will down. Eyes searching her face, he said quietly, entreatingly, "I never wanted it to end this way. You showed me what freedom truly is, and I know it's hardly fair to ask you to sacrifice yours. But I can't let you turn me in; I've worked too hard to get where I am."

Sarah thought about telling him that she would go with him, wondering if it might buy some time. But then what? And he knew her too well to buy into the falsehood. It would never work.

Sighing, she said, "Please, just let us go."

"And if I do, you won't say a word?" He sounded almost bitter, and she didn't bother to answer. His sarcasm faded, replaced by a deep sadness etched into his features. "I don't have a choice."

"Everything is a choice," she whispered, but he was close enough now that he heard. Placing her hand over Will's, touching rather than restraining him, she hoped the message was clear. "And I've made mine."

Will seemed to stand a little taller, chest swelling as he sucked in a breath. She snuck a glance up at him and caught the faint curve of his lips before looking back at Damien. Her eyes softened with pity at the torment she saw in his gaze as he stared at their joined hands. And there he stood, alone in the cold. Her heart ached for him.

Lowering her voice in sympathy, Sarah said, "But you're making the wrong choice, Damien. It won't solve anything."

"I never had you, did I?" he asked suddenly, as though she hadn't spoken. He looked up to meet her gaze, his mouth drawn in an aggrieved line.

Swallowing the lump in her throat, Sarah shook her head and whispered brokenly, "I'm sorry." After all he'd done, she still cared for him, and those dejected, puppy dog eyes broke her heart. She knew she'd never see the gold flecks dance with joy in his gaze ever again. Some part of her badly wanted to give him a head start before she turned the guards onto his scent, but then she would be letting a murderer run free. Closing her eyes, she released a shuddering breath.

Oftentimes, the right choice was the most difficult one to make.

"If I could take it all back," Damien whispered. She looked up to see him advancing, watching her intently. Will's hand tightened on his weapon, though he didn't raise it. Damien spoke to her as though it were just the two of them. "If I could turn back time, I would change my past. The future could be different for us."

Sarah's head tilted sadly to the side as she studied him, a lost man clinging to the one thing that gave him hope. But he was looking in the wrong place. Her voice was soft. "Turning back time wouldn't help—trust me. You're only hurting yourself. Please, just go." Her voice hitched with pleading.

His steps faltered, and he winced as if she had slapped him. "Sarah—"

Will raised his weapon. "She said to shove off, Spaniard."

Damien's eyes flared, but Sarah's gaze was drawn to the east as the sound of barks and sharp whistles became suddenly distinct. She nearly groaned. The search was back on.

Will broke eye contact with his target for one millisecond as his ears picked up the sound, but it was enough.

Charging, sword at the ready, Damien's legs ate up the distance between them as he aimed for Will, taking advantage of their momentary attention shift. Sarah's reflexes were too slow.

"Down!" Will cried, shoving her away from him. She stumbled, falling to her knees in the snow. He may have just saved her life, but the action cost Will valuable time.

Even with lightning speed as he righted the arrow, Will was too slow in raising the bow to get off a proper shot. The arrow discharged, hitting the ground at Damien's feet as he advanced, slicing his sword toward his adversary's chest.

"No!" Sarah shrieked, eyes wide.

Will's quick reflexes brought his weapon up to deflect the blow, and the gleaming metal blade connected with the thick, sturdy band protecting the wood. The weapons clanged as they connected, both men grunting. Will kicked Damien in the stomach to put some distance between them, and Sarah realized with sickening alarm that an unarmed bow was hardly a match for a sword.

Oh, God, protect him. She breathed the prayer in her head, and it became like a chant in the back of her mind as she watched the fight with breathless apprehension.

Will's kick had been strong, giving him enough time to throw an arrow into place and launch it in Damien's direction as he stumbled to right himself. Damien immediately dropped into a roll, and the arrow shot over his head, landing somewhere in the snow.

Damien lurched to his feet, eyes shining with purpose and focus. The feral, hotheaded way he had first attacked had quickly been replaced by his training. Now, he was focused and confident, no longer controlled by his emotions or impulsive ideas. The calculated way they studied each other, circling, as if sorting out their opponent's weaknesses, was almost more unnerving that the actual fight, stretching Sarah's nerves taut until she had to bite her knuckles to keep from crying out. She couldn't stop either of them at this point.

Will shifted positions and backed up a step, drawing the fight away from Sarah. Then the men came at each other in the same instant, metal clashing against metal. Will held his hands wide on the bow to keep them from the path of the blade, grunting as each man fought for an advantage.

In a flash, Damien slipped his sword down the wood, slicing Will's knuckles and catching him off-guard as he used the momentum of his weapon as leverage to wrench the bow from Will's grasp. The carved instrument flew through the air several feet before landing quietly in the snow. Sarah considered retrieving it, but didn't know how without running directly through the melee.

With one swift stroke, Damien flicked his sword in the air, stopping Sarah's heart. Will lurched back in time to avoid the devastating blow that would have caught him across the side. But unarmed and unable to deflect the attack, the tip of the blade ripped a long seam in his shirt. Sarah thought it had only caught his clothing, but a thin trail of blood began to ooze from the long gash stretching across the length of his chest. Red quickly stained the white fabric of his torn shirt, saturating the frayed edges until droplets of blood escaped, splattering on the ground and marring the perfect white at their feet.

Grimacing, Will took a step back toward a copse of trees, but the keen look in his eyes belied the retreat. Damien's next blow was cocky and wide, though just as fierce as the others. Ducking, Will rolled to the side, and the sword connected with the thick tree. In a fluid motion, he rolled into a crouch, retrieving the knife concealed in his boot and holding it at the ready as he waited for the attack.

But Damien was still fighting with the sword, trying to dislodge it from the unrelenting trunk of the tree. Will came at him then, and the Spaniard abandoned his weapon, diving to the side to avoid the slice of Will's short blade.

The sound of the approaching search was entirely clear now, and Sarah realized with a surge of fright that they were nearly upon them. "This is madness!" she yelled, trying to get their attention.

Damien had a knife of his own in hand suddenly, and he stared Will down. A dog howled loudly, as though it had caught a fresh scent, and the keening sound raised the hairs on Sarah's arms.

Damien looked at her then, breaking concentration to shoot her a penetrating, searching look before he shot off into the forest opposite the approaching party. Will looked like he was tempted to follow, fists clenching and unclenching as his bloodied chest heaved. The bleeding had slowed, but his heart was pumping too rapidly directly beneath the wound for it to stop altogether, even in the cold. Could he run? At this point, she wasn't sure if it would matter.

A sharp whistle cut through the woods, a shrill musical note followed by a succession of unclear companions. Will's whole body stiffened as he listened intently to the call as it was repeated.

His face cleared, and he speared Sarah with a promising glance. "I have to end this," he said hurriedly. Then he dashed off the same way Damien had gone, snatching his bow from the snow as he ran.

Sarah gasped in shock. "Will, don't!"

"He knows too much," he called over his shoulder.

She gaped after him as the shouts and thrashing in the woods behind her grew louder. She spun around to face the unknown as Will disappeared into the forest, leaving her there to face-off alone as the guards descended on her.

****

Breathing hard from the fight and the loss of blood, Will scrambled through the forest, dodging trees and leaping over the brush. Lisandro had gotten a head start, but Will knew these woods better than any spoiled lord. Besides, he had his knife and bow for a long-distance shot, so he needn't be too close.

His thoughts momentarily steered him back to Sarah, and he hoped she would forgive him for pursuing Lisandro. But he couldn't allow him to live.

Movement in his peripheral vision caused him to jerk his head to the right in time to deflect the knife as a body rammed into him from the side. Will grunted, the movement jarring his chest, and he lost his grip on the bow as it went flying into the woods. He felt the ground beneath him for second before he leapt to his feet. *Never let your adversary catch you unawares,* Uncle Thomas said when they'd trained.

Will grimaced. Driven by wounded pride, he had been too hotheaded to pay attention to his surroundings, or he might have seen the foreign little cheat lying in wait. The man watched him with those beady, murky-brown eyes.

Flipping the knife, Will caught the handle so that his elbow pointed out with the blade. *Let them strike first, but then strike fast and smart.* The words echoed in his mind. Thomas had cautioned him, especially when he would fight with more passion or avidity than proficiency, to wait out his opponent and sift out his greatest weakness.

Unfortunately, the Spaniard appeared to be assessing him in the same deliberate manner. But Will planned to prod him into taking the first lunge.

Pulling the soiled fabric away from his chest in a pointed manner, Will grinned tauntingly. "I assumed you would have better aim. My mistake."

Lisandro shot him a cocky smile of his own, as if he knew something Will did not. The expression was unnerving, though Will didn't show it. "I might have attacked out of rage at first, but do you believe killing you in front of the lady would endear her to me?" Damien clicked his tongue in consternation. "Of course not. That's why I was hoping you would follow." He held his dagger before him, blade out. "Shall we?"

How had he not seen that the Spaniard was luring him away? Shaking his head over being outplayed, Will narrowed his eyes. "I'm here, aren't I?"

The Spaniard took the invitation and lunged forward, knife flashing in a half-hearted movement. He was just testing Will and his ability, and he let him. Even with Will's added height and strength, the Spaniard's agility made them evenly matched.

With this in mind, Will used his wit rather than brute strength. He allowed some close calls, pretending he was weakening as he barely ducked to avoid the blade lashing out over his head. He toyed with Lisandro, playing the fool while he waited for the man's confidence to grow into arrogance before letting him have it.

Will's bulky fist flew through the air, catching the Spaniard unawares and hooking him in the jaw in a blur of movement. Lisandro's head snapped to the right from the blow, and a trail of blood had already begun to trickle from his left nostril when he turned back to face him, eyes ablaze. Now that he knew he'd been played, he would only lash out, and Will knew he could no longer act the fool, but needed to strike fast and try to keep his wits about him.

He threw another right-hook aimed at his temple that Lisandro dodged, but Will didn't let him off that easy. He poured every ounce of his waning strength into the next succession of punches, some simply working as a distraction until he could get a better angle. The Spaniard staggered as two consecutive blows connected with his ribs and jaw, sending him off balance and giving Will a moment to catch his breath as he advanced.

He felt a fist ram into his gut with such sudden ferocity that he nearly doubled over. His opponent took advantage of the break in his attacks and landed a hard fist to his right temple, and the next one caught Will across the jaw. Dodging the succeeding fist, Will landed a serious blow that sent the Spaniard reeling. He slammed the butt of his dagger into the man's shoulder, staggering him, though something held him back from using the blade.

Sarah.

With his momentary lapse in his attention, he didn't see Lisandro's movement until his leg shot out, catching him in the back of the knees. Grunting, he landed on his back, the wind coming out of him in a rush.

Lisandro swiped the back of his hand across his mouth, smearing the blood spilling from his split lip and painting his mouth in a red grimace. He leaned over him, wielding his knife as a drop of blood fell from his nose.

Will managed a grin and winced at the pain in his lip as he struggled into a sitting position. His right eye was already swelling and he felt blood drying on his brow, but he could see well enough to fight. "You should have someone look at that."

A slow, snake-like smile crept over the Spaniard's bloodied mouth. "I plan on collecting my caretaker when I finish with you. Her ministrations were quite *pleasing* before." His eyes darkened roguishly. "Her avidity in her work—"

Will lunged up and grabbed the serpent by his shirtfront, using his legs to launch him overhead. The Spaniard landed on his back, blinking in shock. Will was over him in an instant.

Pinning his armed hand to the ground, Will grabbed him by the throat with his other hand, tempted to choke the life from him as he gave his head a good shake. "You will *never* speak of her that way! She is a hundred times the human being you will *ever* be," he spat.

With a swift jerk, Lisandro upset his captor's balance and, like the snake he was, somehow managed to wriggle free. Abandoning his weapon in the snow, he ran a few feet before Will caught up to him, grabbing him by the arm and throwing him into a tree in his fury. He pinned him against the rough bark with a forearm to his throat, cutting off his air supply. Lisandro coughed and sputtered, and Will loosened his hold enough so that the man could breathe. As much as he wanted to kill him, he knew he would regret it.

Spitting a wad of saliva and blood onto the snow, the Spaniard managed, "Did it pain you to see her laughing with me? *Enjoying* me?" Will ground his teeth at the false implications he gave the word, knowing the man was toying with him, goading him into losing his head. At that moment, Will didn't think he would regret twisting the man's neck. He unconsciously leaned more weight on his elbow and was satisfied as Lisandro's eyes bulged like a croaking frog.

The Spaniard went on it a choked whisper, his grin twisted. "I saw you that day. Did you notice . . . how she didn't get up after we fell?"

Will remembered well their tangled limbs as she lay against him in the snow.

Pressing the pointed tip of his dagger—which *he* had not been so foolish to abandon—against the man's thumping pulse, Will leaned in close to emphasize his threat. "Understand this, Spaniard: You are finished here. You will be hanged on the same execution stand you sent an innocent man to."

"Taking your secret with me," he retorted. Will's eyes flickered in surprise. The man was scowling. "For Sarah—if I hope to earn her trust back when next we meet."

Will was about to remind him that she would never come to visit him in the dungeons when he caught the faint sound of thrashing branches. Grounding his teeth in annoyed resignation, he stood firm, keeping the traitor in place. Neither of them would get away this time.

Lisandro's eyes flickered with sudden realization. He grasped at Will's forearms with both hands, tone pleading. "My intent was never to hurt her—I've only kept her from their sight. Did she tell you I saved your life? That should be worth something to a man of honor."

Will narrowed his eyes in disgust. "You've tried to take it enough times. But, yes, she did tell me. I suppose that's why I'll let them take you to the gallows in one piece."

~Chapter 47~

Will fixed his eyes straight ahead, keeping his lips closed. Explanations would get him nowhere at this point, and he would never give them the satisfaction of pleading his innocence. So he waited in silence as the guard shoved him along through the forest. Lisandro was surprisingly silent, his face bruised and bloodied.

They must not have thought them much of a threat, since only two sentinels had been sent to prod them back to the rest of the search party. Will assumed that running—and also being discovered holding a knife to the throat of a well-known lord—had only aggravated the situation, warranting the fetters tying his hands securely in front of him. Lisandro was also bound, though Will suspected the guards were only trying to avoid the duo stirring up more trouble on the short trek.

Will stiffened as they neared the party, but he cleared his face of any emotion that would betray his disquiet over his unknown fate. He could see six—no, seven guards up ahead through the trees, and three of them restrained hunting dogs with ropes. The animals paced in agitation before their masters as far as the ropes around their necks would allow. Several horses pranced nearby, seeming as uneasy as the dogs.

Gripping his shoulder, the guard kicked the back of Will's legs, and he stumbled to his bruised knees, gritting his teeth. The uniformed man tossed Will's knife and the bow he'd collected onto the snow a safe distance away, toward his superiors. "Found the runaways," he informed, releasing Will and taking a step back.

Though he felt his strength waning at the loss of blood and the aftermath of the fight, Will managed to keep his head upright and kept his gaze fixed steadily on the man he assumed was in charge, judging by his ornamental vestment. He clasped his hands into fists, wrists straining against the ropes binding them as the man assessed him.

Two of the guards' faces broke out in expressions of surprise as they were shoved apart. Sarah's face was a mask of utter relief as she forced her way past them, but a hand clapped over her mouth when she saw the full extent of his appearance.

Will cringed, causing shooting pain to lace over his jaw. He didn't want her to see him like this, bloodied and battered and—no, not beaten, but it was a rather dismal thing to await his undeserved fate.

Sarah ran forward a few steps before Thomas caught her arm, holding her back. Will's shoulders sank a little in gratitude. It wouldn't help matters if she intervened on his behalf, and he tried to get her attention with a faint shake of his head even as his heart leapt in his chest at the fact that she was unharmed.

Sarah looked up at Thomas, confusion and hurt swelling in her eyes when he, too, shook his head. She turned back to Will, watching him with her nervous, wide-blue gaze.

The man in the captain's uniform addressed him. "You fled from His Majesty's guards as they were coming to apprehend you at your home as a suspect in a murder investigation. Why?" He didn't sound accusatory, but vaguely amused and curious.

Will frowned, choosing his answer carefully. "Sir, how was I to know they were the royal guard coming to apprehend me?"

The captain smirked at his vague answer. "Fair enough. But you continued to run after they had announced themselves, as well. Care to explain?"

Will answered honestly; he had nothing to hide and hoped they would come to that realization. "I was protecting the lady, sir."

Grinning wryly, the man said, "The Lady Fair—of course. But she was hardly a suspect, so why drag her along?"

"I told you, sir, that I feared for her safety." He tried to sound as compliant as possible.

The man nodded, as though he understood. His face turned suddenly serious, voice lapsing into a gruff tone. "And what is the lord's part in all this?" He jerked his head toward Lisandro, who was being held upright by the guard who had brought him out. His eyes were closed, head bowed toward the ground in exhaustion, wearing an expression of capitulation.

Will worded his answer carefully, unsure how much of Lisandro's dealings was safe to reveal. How many more men did the Spaniard have under his control? "We discovered a discrepancy in the man's character," he replied slowly. "That was my reason for not turning myself over, sir. I feared that if left unchaperoned, the lady might come to great peril." He swallowed, wondering if the man thought he had fabricated the tale.

"Go on," the captain encouraged, quirking a brow. He appeared solely in control of the situation, and Will no longer believed that Lisandro, whose entire being was cowed in submission, held any power over him.

"There is a letter," Will added, emboldened by the hope that the captain wasn't an associate of the Spaniard's. "It instructs the recipient to moonlight as the hooded vigilante, providing a distraction and scapegoat while the lord wandered the castle posed as the same figure."

"And who was the recipient?"

Will thought Sarah's face paled some at the question, but he answered honestly, "That I do not know, sir. But the man you see before you was the one to kill that woman." At the guard's raised brow of skepticism, he went on. "Lisandro used his own insignia to seal the letter that sealed her fate. You can search his room for the match."

The man reached into his pocket and produced the item in question. "I think you mean this seal." Will's brow furrowed in confusion, which seemed to amuse the man. "Yes, the letter is in my possession, as well, and I have found them to be an exact match. Is there another offense you would like to address?"

"Against myself or the lord?" Will asked cautiously.

With a shrug, the captain said, "Either."

Kneeling a little straighter, he said, "I would refute the offense made against myself that I took part in the death of Gabriel Dunlivey. Yes, I discovered his body and witnessed those two men destroy the evidence—"

"We followed them into the forest together," Sarah threw in suddenly. Her chin was set in that stubborn line that would have been adorable if it weren't so vexing. If he could not clear his own name, Will did not want her dragged through the mud with him.

"But she saw nothing," he tried to amend. Sarah took a step forward, held back only by Thomas's firm grip.

"We *both* witnessed it and ran afterward."

Will closed his eyes. Her loyalty was touching, but it wasn't helping matters. The captain casually rested a hand on the handle of his sheathed sword, and Sarah bit her lip, shrinking back.

"Yes, sir, we ran," Will said. "But only because we were fleeing the guilty party."

The man tugged on the wrist of his leather glove disinterestedly. "Yes, the lady informed us that one of the men was here today. We apprehended the other man—a guard named Lewis."

Frowning at the perfidy, the captain continued, "And he immediately threw his master to the wolves, so to speak. It appears he has been under Lisandro's employ for some time and said that he was the one to deliver the missive to a certain address, along with a pouch of coins."

Will quirked a brow. "If you had just discovered the identity of the imposter, why question me?"

"He claims that he was sent to a residence he had never seen before and instructed to leave the missive and payment on the doorstep, so he saw no one." The man appeared rather disgruntled by this fact. "Lisandro's orders were verbal, so there are no written directions to the residence that we can detain. In any case, the letter was delivered in the dark, and the man admits that he was too far in his cups that day to recognize the place in full light. But he's lucid enough now to speak against his employer."

Will's eyes flickered in question to Sarah, who was nodding eagerly. He looked back to the man. "And what of the other—the one who helped to cover up Dunlivey's murder?"

Frowning, the captain answered, "Timmons fell on his sword before we could apprehend his guilty hide." He closed the distance between them, drawing his own sword. Will managed not to wince as he dramatically—to scare the life from him, he was sure—used the blade to cut through his ties.

Rubbing his raw wrists, Will rose tentatively to his feet. He nearly toppled over. "Are you releasing me, sir?"

The man smirked, one dark brown brow lifting in humor. "Terribly sorry for all the questions, Young Taylor, but I had to verify the lady's story. It was quite a lot to take in, though I've had my suspicions of the lord since I returned to the guard." He chuckled and stuck out his hand. Will shook it in a daze. "My name is James T. Quinn."

Captain Quinn. His uncle had spoken of him in admiration often throughout the years, and Will felt momentarily tongue-tied to meet the man in the flesh, though that could also be from the fact that he had bitten his tongue in the skirmish.

Quinn was older than he had originally thought, with gray marring the temples of his dark brown hair and copious smile creases lining his eyes and mouth. But he was fit, his body and strong hands announcing his capabilities and years of service directing the guard.

"Will Taylor," he offered, though it appeared Quinn already knew of him, and gave the man's hand a quick pump of admiration. "I thank you for releasing me, sir, but I must ask why you sent out such a large search party in the first place? I assumed one or two would be sent to retrieve me."

Quinn grinned slowly. "So you *were* aware that someone was coming?"

Will felt properly chastened and grimaced. "Can you blame an innocent man for running?"

The older man chuckled. "I suppose not. But you'll have to discuss the other matter with Greene. He's the one who let us on to Lisandro."

At that, Sarah broke away from a smiling Thomas and ran to him, slamming into Will's open arms. He staggered under the added weight, and she managed to unclasp her arms from around his neck as he fell to his knees.

She gasped. "Oh my gosh, Will! I'm so sorry. Did I hurt you?"

Sitting back on his heels, he could only shake his head as his blurred vision returned to normal.

"Will," she whispered worriedly, delicately touching a fingertip to his swollen eye. "What did he do to you?"

He grimaced at her touch and managed to turn it into a pathetic half-smile. "You should see the other man."

Sarah shot the Spaniard a wary glance, her first look at him since they'd arrived. She winced at his appearance, and Lisandro caught her eye as the guard gave him a shove.

"Sarah," the Spaniard said quietly. Will imagined his eyes conveyed the final, longing look of a dead man with regrets.

Sarah quickly looked away as he was carted off, and Will could tell the sight pained her. "You didn't kill him," she breathed, putting a hand over the gash on his chest. She looked so relieved that he felt infinitely reassured in his decision to spare the man's insignificant existence.

Lifting his bruised and bloody knuckles, Will touched her cheek. "I couldn't."

Thomas joined them, smiling—at his nephew's display of affection, Will knew. He doubtless assumed he'd never see the day. "I suppose I didn't need to provide assistance," Thomas said, nodding to his battered knuckles. "You had things squared away before we arrived."

"Why did you come?" Will asked, utterly baffled.

Sarah shifted, crouching in the snow to face him. Her expression turned suddenly excited. "My little maid, Sevrine, was hiding in my room and noticed how upset I was, so she followed me to the tower. She didn't hear my entire conversation with Damien, but when she saw me running down the stairs and Damien running after, she was worried and was heading back to my room to wait for me when she ran into your uncle."

Thomas nodded, grinning at her enthusiasm. "I was coming to collect the captain and saw the poor little thing all affright on her way through the hall."

"She doesn't speak great English, but she understands it pretty well," Sarah made sure to add, as though this fact were infinitely important.

Thomas's lips twitched in humor as he and Will shared an amused glance. "Yes, but I caught enough to worry, and she led me to Sarah's vacant room."

"But she'd found the seal," Sarah muttered, scowling as she spread the fabric of Will's shirt to better see the wound. Ever the nurse.

He grinned, capturing her wrist. "Go on," he urged.

Eyes bright, Sarah said, "Well, thankfully, Thomas is good enough at charades to figure out that she was hiding in my room and then followed me to the tower. Right, Thomas?" He nodded in confirmation. "I guess the seal fell out of Damien's pocket when he chased after me, and she picked it up and then later gave it to your uncle."

"I didn't know what to make of her ramblings," he admitted, shrugging one shoulder. "Then when I left the room, I saw that Lisandro's door stood ajar. Call it intuition"—he and Sarah shared a secret grin over this—"but something didn't sit right, so I went inside and discovered the matching seal. I mentioned it to Quinn, and he said it had just been reported that the Spaniard and two other men had taken horses from the stables in rather a hurry. With my suspicion and Quinn's own questions about Lisandro, we set out to find Sarah." He grinned. "Thus, the dogs."

She laughed breathlessly. "Thanks for keeping them leashed."

Quinn's boots crunched over the snow as he strode toward them. "It seems everything is squared away, for the most part. The guilty party is being escorted back to the castle as we speak, along with the man we apprehended for further questioning."

"Do you believe the charges will stick?" Will asked, gingerly working his jaw from side to side.

"Most of them, though for a man with his connections, Dunlivey's murder will be a mite difficult to pin."

Will's shoulders sank a little at that. He at least wanted the man who got to Dunlivey first to *pay* for beating him to it.

Sarah's head snapped up, eyes alive with sudden revelation. "Damien said that he wiped Gabriel's blood off the chest when he fell, and he could still have the handkerchief or cloth that he used to clean up in his room. I know it's a long shot, but he might not have thought to destroy it."

Quinn looked interested and surprised. "It 'tis a stretch, but worth a look." He dipped his head and smiled. "It's been a pleasure to work with such a young sleuth."

Sarah flushed. "Thank you, sir, but it was a lot of teamwork." She shared a smile with Will.

Quinn ducked his head in gratitude at Will and then snapped his fingers, calling for his men to move out.

Nodding his head toward his horse, Thomas said, "Come on, son. Let's get you to my cabin and have someone take a look at you."

Will grinned meaningfully at Sarah, causing her to blush to the roots of her hair. "I plan to."

~Chapter 48~

Will was too weak to put up much of a fight when Thomas insisted he ride his horse for the short trek. His silence during the ride to Thomas's house had Sarah biting her lip in worry as she walked beside the horse. When he had come back from his tussle with Damien, her heart had nearly stopped at the sight of his battered face and bloody clothes.

The instant they arrived, Thomas sent Will into the back room to change out of his soiled shirt, and he emerged minutes later wearing a fresh gray tunic. Sarah hurriedly sat Will down in a chair she scooted near the fire and enlisted Thomas's help in warming a pail of snow over the flames. Focusing her mind on a task kept her thoughts from wandering to her own guilt and the unnerving look on Damien's face as they carted him off. She had expected an expression of betrayal, some sign that he loathed her for turning against him, but the look in his eyes had been one of promise: He wasn't giving up.

She shivered now as she had then at the thought of what that might mean.

Both men seemed to sense her need to keep her hands and mind busy, and Will didn't protest as she fussed over his wounds. Her mind was so focused that it was several minutes later, when she was removing the pail of water from the fire, before she realized that the small cabin was completely silent except for the shuffling of her own feet.

She glanced at Will in surprise. "Where's Thomas?"

Will's cracked lip curved wryly. "He departed shortly after we arrived to oversee Lisandro's official arrest. You didn't notice?"

"Oh." Sarah frowned. "He left us unchaperoned?"

He shrugged one shoulder and then grimaced. "Thomas trusts us."

Drawing her brows together in worry over his poorly concealed discomfort, Sarah quickly carted the pail over to him and wrung out the cloth. Will winced as she cleaned up the bruise over his eye with rough movements. Caught up in the task to keep her mind occupied, she had forgotten to be gentle and forced herself to take her time. He had enough bruises already for her to start adding to them with her carelessness.

Gentling her touch, Sarah barely dabbed at the cut on his brow to wipe away the blood. She shook her head at the extent of his injuries and muttered, "I can't believe you went after him."

Will's dark eyes softened, reflecting in their depths the light of the flames. "If I had let him go, we would forever be running from him and his influence. You were the last thing standing between himself and a clean slate, and I knew he would never stop chasing after you."

Pursing her lips together, Sarah decided not to tell him that a clean slate wasn't the only reason Damien would continue to pursue her, although his reasons still had her somewhat confused. She knew his feelings for her were genuine, but to what extent, she couldn't say. At first she had thought that Damien might be falling in love with her, but now she wasn't sure if what he felt was actual affection for her, or if it was belief that his sins would be cleansed in her presence. Maybe it was a little of both.

Will reached up to touch her trembling hand. "What are you thinking?"

She sighed out, "I'm tired of unknowingly being a pawn." She gently removed his hand and placed it in his lap. "And don't strain your shoulder," she admonished quietly, recalling how it had hung limply at his side when the guards carted him back.

She tried to grin, and it wobbled at the edges. "It's been an interesting day, hasn't it? Flee a criminal, go on the lam, solve a series of cold cases, send a man to the gallows." Sarah looked down quickly, realizing what she had just said. The full impact of Damien's fate weighed down on her, causing her chest to spasm in pain at the thought of him heading to the execution stand. Because of *her*.

She could feel Will's eyes on her but couldn't bring herself to meet his gaze as she took her time soaking the cloth.

"He's a murderer, Sarah," he reminded gently.

She sighed, shoulders sinking. "I know. I just—I guess I wish he wasn't, is all." She expelled another breath and reached up to wipe his lip, then thought better of touching his mouth and handed Will the wet cloth.

"He was a good friend to me," she said softly as he dragged the fabric carelessly over his mouth, his eyes focused intently on her. "Even if it was under pretense at times," she thought to add. "I guess it's just hard to see someone you once considered a friend put in prison and sent to the gallows because of something you did."

"No, that was his choice, not yours," Will said firmly. "His choices led him to where he is. You only did what was right." He tipped his head to catch her eye. "You may have saved other lives by turning him in."

Sarah nodded meekly, knowing in her heart that he was right but unable to shake the guilt and betrayal she still felt mounting inside of her. She whispered slowly, the words forming in her mind nearly at the same instant she spoke them, "How can you disdain someone and regret ever having met them with your whole being, and then at the same time care for and want a better fate for them? You want *them* to be a better person."

Angling her head, she met Will's gaze, her own searching for understanding. "Does that make sense?"

He dropped the cloth from his mouth, smiling faintly, though it looked more like he was wincing in pain. "Yes, though I can't see how you could feel that way about that conceited Spaniard."

Flinching at his words, she said, "You didn't know him like I did. His father murdered Damien's mother in front of his eyes and beat him and his sister. And then Isabella died a few years after they ran away from home."

Sarah turned her gaze to the fire to hide her shimmering eyes. Even after everything that had happened today, she wanted to believe that the Damien she'd laughed and smiled with was still in there somewhere. The wounded man that she had offered comfort to and instantly jumped in to defend when his character was threatened—he wasn't the same man who had claimed Edith's life.

Shaking her head at her own tangled train of thought, Sarah said slowly, as though just coming to the realization herself, "In a way I understood him and his actions, strange as it sounds." She looked back at Will to find his pinched gaze trained on her, hanging on her every word with curios apprehension. "What he did was wrong, and he'll pay for that. But a part of me sees a little boy who grew up the only way he knew how: Alone."

She exhaled a heavy breath. "I see now that all the wealth and social standing he attained through his allegiance with Cadius was to fill the void in his life, at whatever cost."

"Sounds selfish," Will observed matter-of-factly.

"Sounds lonely," she murmured. Sarah took the cloth from his hands and went back to dabbing at his brow, caressing his bruised lid with the corner of her thumb. "I just can't believe he had me so fooled. I feel like such an idiot for believing his lies, though I think it was some of the half-truths mixed in that kept me from questioning him."

With a sudden mirthless laugh, Sarah dropped the soiled rag into the bucket and stared at the ground, shoulders sagging. "I guess I did question him, but I never let myself see who he truly was—maybe I already knew somehow and didn't want to be disappointed."

"People only see what they are prepared to see," Will remarked softly. "And you weren't wholly wrong about him." It sounded like the admission pained him. She met his earnest gaze. "He never hurt you, Sarah, and it's obvious that his interest in you lies in more than your involvement in the investigation. Perhaps you provided the friendship and fulfillment he had been unable to find in his life."

Sarah watched him, heart swelling with gratitude even as she was hesitant to believe his words. "Maybe."

Her lips turned down as she stared at Will's face. She had thought removing some of the blood would make his injuries look less severe, but his eye was still purple-green, his mouth and brow split from repeated blows, and whenever he blinked, his right eyelid barely moved, sagging practically closed on its own. The two men had fought and she'd nearly lost Will because of it.

Tears of exhaustion filled her eyes, and she suddenly felt like kicking Damien for hurting him and slapping Will across the face for taking off without her.

"Why did you leave me behind?" she asked suddenly, her emotions spinning out of control, fear and anger and sadness whipping into one tangled mass of emotion. "Were you just going to leave me behind to take the rap?"

His eyes widened in surprise. "You didn't actually believe . . . Oh, Sarah." He raised his hand to touch her face, but she jerked back from his reach.

She had only wondered at the possibility for a second, but the feeling of abandonment still caused her chest to ache, even in light of the comfort he had just provided. "How was I supposed to know that? You just took off and I didn't know what to do, and I wasn't sure you'd come back." Her words came out sounding jumbled and choked, and she felt a sob building as every emotion from the last twenty-four hours came crashing down on her at once. She felt on the verge of hysteria and pressed her palms against her eyes to hold the tears at bay.

"But I'm fine—"

She jerked her hands away. "You can't *see* yourself!" Her voice rose on the last word, spilling out on the tail end of a distraught laugh. Eyes filling, she barely managed in a choked whisper, "I thought I'd never see you again."

Will's face twisted in pain. This time when he pulled her into his arms, she didn't fight him. She crawled into his lap, and his kindness and sympathy were her undoing. She collapsed against him, letting him hold her as she cried, anguished sobs racking her body.

"I heard my uncle's whistle that he uses when we hunt and knew that he would vouch for you," he whispered apologetically. "It was my only chance to stop Lisandro, but I'm sorry I left you."

Sarah shook her head against his chest and then recalled the gash over his heart. "Y-your wound," she stammered, pushing away weakly.

400

He tightened his hold, drawing her head back to his chest and cradling it there in his large hand. "The bleeding has ceased, and I'll have Thomas look at it later. But for now, it's fine."

Sniffing, Sarah shifted her head to his shoulder and released a shuddering breath. She trembled in his arms, feeling comforted by his warmth at the same time that she wanted to push away and cry in solitude.

Will kissed the top of her head and stroked his fingers soothingly through her hair. "I'm sorry you feel guilty, love, but the Spaniard doesn't deserve your sympathy. He made his bed, and now he has to lie in it."

Picturing Damien's face brought on a slew of other images, all connected to him, and she experienced afresh the emotions she'd felt in each instance—her anguish as she hunched over Edith's body after Damien shot her, the childlike joy she had felt that day in the snow with him, her concern over Damien as he fought the seizures his father's cruelty had caused.

Then she recalled her inner warmth in the instances of his compassion, and the constant reminder of the heart-shattering pain she had felt upon discovering his betrayal. And she was faced with her desire, one she felt even now, to justify the desperation of a broken, unloved boy searching for his place in the world.

Sarah squeezed her eyes tight, desiring oblivion as the onslaught of emotions left her feeling drained and teary-eyed. It seemed that it was all connected to Damien, even her search for the king's killer. Everything led back to him.

She bit back tears of grief and compassion and anger. "He just wanted for someone to care," she whispered brokenly, her voice hitching on a sob. "To love him."

Though Will's hand never faltered as it stroked her hair, she felt his body stiffen. "And do you?" His words were so soft that she barely heard them. Then again, maybe he hadn't meant to speak the question aloud in the first place.

Body shaking, she let the tears fall in earnest, silent drops of anguish coursing down her cheeks. Unable to bury the regret, she buried her face into his chest instead. "No," she fairly moaned. "I c-care about him, but I couldn't—I wanted to . . . make him feel loved, but . . ." She felt the tension leave Will's body at her answer, and she realized he had been dreading a different response.

Recalling her reaction to Damien the instances where he cornered her or was near in a dark passageway, Sarah closed her eyes. She was suddenly overwhelmed with relief that she had never examined her confused feelings for him or given in to the instinctual desire to return his attentions. But her grief-stricken half reasoned that if she had been a little more attentive and showed him that she did, indeed, care, then maybe Damien . . . Sarah shook her head, knowing it was foolishness.

"I couldn't fix him," she managed regretfully. Turning him in had been the right thing to do, but she couldn't shake the feeling that if they'd had more time, she could have made him see that he *was* loved; he was just looking in the wrong place, to a girl who could never give him her whole heart, even if she wanted to in order to save him.

Will rested his chin atop her head, taking her hand in his own and stroking the back of it with his thumb. His knuckles were bruised and covered in crusted blood where Damien's sword has slashed them open. Maybe some of it was Damien's blood. "You aren't being fair on yourself. What if he doesn't *want* to be fixed?"

She paused to consider this. But everything about Damien had cried out for someone to save him. Why had she not tried harder? She should have been more compassionate, showing him God's love instead of simply trying to distract him from past trauma.

A finger hooked under her chin, and Will lifted it to meet her eyes. When he saw her tear-streaked face, his own tightened in sympathy. "I know what you're thinking, and this is *not your fault*." He stressed each word to drive his point home. "If he doesn't want to be saved, there is nothing you could have done differently to change that. Every man chooses his own course and the consequences that come along with it."

"But maybe if I was different, I could have helped him," Sarah countered thoughtfully, almost to herself. Then she frowned. Where had that come from?

But he shook his head, displacing that lock of hair. "Love, how many times must I tell you to never change who you are? You don't need to remake herself, but make the most of the person God created you to be." He smiled softly into her eyes. "Which is a fairly spectacular and compassionate woman with the heart of a lion."

Wow. His beautiful words filled her heart to the brink and caused her eyes to water with the overflow. Sarah sniffed loudly and winced, feeling anything but lion-like in that moment, cheeks stinging from the salty trail of dried tears.

She stared up at him quizzically. "Will, how can you deny God in your own life, but still admit that He has a hand in mine?"

He ducked his head. Lips tipping dolefully at their hands clasped together in her lap, he murmured, "Because He removed His hand long ago."

Sarah's chin quivered at his acceptance, as though things had to remain this way. "You can't still think that, can you? What about all the good you've done? You don't think God's used that?"

Will looked up at her under the hair that had fallen over his eyes, which were filled with childhood pain that had never faded. "My identity was wiped clean when my parents died, and I had to start afresh. All I had was a false persona, someone I created with total control. But in reality, I am only a blacksmith—that is my lot. I have no purpose in the world, but the Shadow does." He shook his head and added quietly, "And he doesn't even exist."

Brushing the hair from his forehead, Sarah dropped her hand to his bruised cheek. Her eyes burned into his with her need for him to understand. "No." Her voice was soft but firm. "The real hero is the man behind the mask, the one who risks his life for strangers without the accolades or acknowledgements. You were the man who jumped in to help me in my search when you barely knew my name, and it's you who continues to protect me when I fall into trouble. Not an identity-less vigilante, but you."

Sarah rubbed her thumb gingerly over the yellow-green bruise, and Will placed a hand over hers, closing his eyes. "God has so much more in store for you, Will," she whispered, her voice cracking. Her next words were spoken with such conviction that he opened his eyes, boring into hers. "He made you for a great purpose—I can feel it. But you're the one who has to accept that."

Will looked like he so desperately wanted to believe her but was afraid to put any stock in her words. She felt a spark of hope. But he was a man who had survived alone for so long by protecting his heart, and she watched Will decathect, retreating into that familiar shell of self-preservation and withdrawing his feelings to avoid potential hurt.

"Sarah," he said slowly, and with a sinking heart, she sensed his answer. "We've had this conversation before, and I know my answer will only upset you."

Sighing, Sarah rested her head against his shoulder and whispered, "I just want you to know you're loved by Him. I care about you too much to remain silent like I did with Damien." She wrapped her arms tightly around him. "I'm not giving up on you."

"I didn't imagine you would." He sounded like he was smiling.

Will held her for a while longer before Thomas came back in, stomping his boots on the entry floor. Sarah jumped and tried to struggle out of his lap, but Will held her tight even when she jabbed her elbow into his ribs in her attempt to free herself. She had just hastily swiped the back of her hand over her cheeks when Thomas turned, and she felt her face flame at how this must look.

"We were just, uh—" She tried to subtly pry Will's hands from around her waist, but he had pinned her against him, his hold unrelenting for such a battered man. She shot him a stern glare, but he avoided her gaze, the corner of his mouth twitching.

Thomas's serious expression melted into a grin when he caught their embrace. "It's a pleasure to have you conscious in my home this time around, Miss Matthews. I believe it's been lacking a woman's touch."

Feeling a chuckle rattling inside Will's chest, her face heated anew.

"Everything go all right?" he asked his uncle, saving her the trouble of stumbling through a reply.

All signs of mirth left Thomas's face as he removed his gloves. "With the one man's testimony—Lewis—we assumed it would be rather simple to convict Lisandro of the murders." He pinched the bridge of his nose. "However, it appears that he took extreme caution in staying away from the scene of the crime for the most part. He instead sent the men under his employ to do his bidding, and they went to fulfill orders that were verbal and undocumented. So now we have an 'innocent' man with power locked away in solitary confinement in the tower."

Sarah shook her head. "But what about the bloody cloth or the letter I gave the captain? It's in his handwriting, and it's obvious he sealed it."

"Lisandro must have destroyed the cloth he used to wipe Dunlivey's blood away, because we were unable to locate it. And as for the letter, all we have are a few lines asking a man whose identity we cannot prove to dress a certain way. And who's to say that someone didn't pilfer the seal to draw suspicion to the Spaniard? From the Law's perspective, it's all speculation." Thomas looked genuinely aggrieved by this fact.

Sarah's shoulders sank. "So we have nothing?"

"Not exactly," Thomas said slowly. His hesitation caused Will's body to stiffen.

Shaking her head, she said, "I don't understand."

Thomas edged closer, his expression pinched. "You told me that you recognized the voice of Gabriel Dunlivey and that Lisandro admitted his guilt to you right out. There's no written evidence depicting that particular murder, so from where I stand, it will be your testimony that locks him away for good."

Sarah gaped at him. *She* had to send Damien to the gallows—*again?* She bowed her head as the weight of his conviction fell heavily upon her once more. "Spectacular."

Will's arms tightened about her waist. "There has to be some other way."

But Thomas was already shaking his head. He watched Sarah with keen eyes, sensing her distress. "If we could get him to confess outright, I wouldn't be here to ask you to do this. But Lisandro hasn't said a word since we apprehended him." His brow furrowed, as though he disliked his own thoughts.

"What?" Will asked lowly.

Heaving a breath, Thomas said to Sarah, "He hasn't spoken—except to ask to see you, that is. Alone."

"What?!" Sarah couldn't believe Damien was still using her, even from behind bars. She shook her head, eyes wide as she struggled to rise. Will didn't fight her this time, and she shot to her feet in surprised outrage. "N-no!"

Thomas nodded. "I knew you would feel that way, but you seem to hold some kind of power over him. Right now, you are the only leverage we have over the criminal."

"She isn't leverage." Will rose and placed his hands on her shoulders. The familiar weight offered her some comfort. "And both sides need to stop treating her as though she is a bargaining chip."

Thomas shook his head. "Will," he said tiredly. Then he turned his gaze to Sarah. "If there were any other options, I would never ask this of you. You know I wouldn't have come if we hadn't exhausted every other option we can think of. But the choice is, ultimately, yours." His earnest gaze bore into hers, and she knew he truly would accept her answer either way.

Sarah bit her lip, staring at her red skirt. "He'll talk to me," she mused aloud, knowing it was true. Damien wouldn't have asked for her otherwise. She looked up at Thomas, praying for her courage to be bolstered to do what she knew was right. "Maybe I can trick him into confessing. I know Cadius was the one pulling the strings all along, though Damien never admitted it outright. But maybe since there's nothing left for him, I can convince him to turn Cadius in. Will a verbal statement against him be enough to convict Cadius of the crimes?"

Thomas pursed his lips, thoughtful. "It would be a step in the right direction, but if Lisandro has any physical evidence that we can confiscate, that would be preferable. If he identifies Cadius as the mastermind, I can more than likely sway the guard from a death sentence and get it reduced to life in solitary confinement."

"Death or a life sentence," Sarah muttered dryly. Sucking in a resolute breath, she said, "Okay. I can try."

"I'll go."

Her head jerked around, eyes widening at Will's firm resolve. "No way! Damien's completely off his rocker if he thinks he can manipulate either of us into going."

"Yet you are." His brow rose in challenge.

"Because *I* am going of my own free will to trick *him*," she corrected, then winced over her choice of words. It wasn't necessarily trickery, but Sarah knew she would do what needed to be done in order to get the truth from him.

"Do you honestly think you can get him to confess?" She turned, but Thomas wasn't looking at her. He actually appeared to be considering Will's offer. They were both insane!

Will hesitated, then nodded resolutely at his uncle. "Yes, I do." Then he turned his gaze on her, all at once probing and searching for her support. "I am not going to stand by and give him the opportunity to get you alone. It could all be part of some diabolical scheme to steal you away."

She bit her lip, wanting to refute the fact that Damien could be diabolical. But as they unraveled his presence in these schemes, Sarah realized that she had misjudged his capabilities. As much as she had been dreading seeing Damien again, she was terrified of what might happen if Will did. She didn't think both men would survive another encounter.

"What can you possibly say to get him to confess?" she asked at last.

Will gave her shoulders a quick squeeze. "The truth. Hopefully, he still recognizes what that looks like."

~Chapter 49~

Though his wound had stopped bleeding long ago and was hardly life threatening, when Thomas volunteered to patch it up before he left, Will readily agreed. Let the Spaniard have a few hours of silence where he imagined his bleak, and possibly brief, future.

Thomas escorted him to the back room and ordered him to remove his shirt. The gash was long and nasty looking, but Will didn't think the blade had gone overly deep. That was, at least, until his uncle set about scraping and cleaning and pressing the skin together to force it to heal properly.

Will's face paled during his uncle's probing, and he felt beads of perspiration collecting at his temples. Already, he was tempted to tell Thomas that the wound wasn't a bother and just to leave it alone. He felt ill, and the man had yet to pull a single stitch.

"Most of it will mend on its own, but you'll need a few threads. Here, drink this, son." Thomas handed him a small vial, and Will accepted it gratefully, swigging back the contents. He grimaced as the unpleasant spirits burned down his throat, and he hoped it would do the trick.

Giving the alcohol a few minutes to enter his system, Thomas went about swabbing a thin anodyne liquid—made up of a combination of healing herbs—over Will's brow to ensure the cut didn't become infected. The older man's face was professional and intent as he swiped the same goopy substance over the gash on Will's chest, years of practice in medicine having lent him accuracy and confidence whenever he was called to heal.

Gritting his teeth, Will allowed his uncle to go to work sewing the deepest portion of the wound closed. The once-physician was quick and precise with each tug and pull of his thick needle, but Will still felt his stomach roil at the sensation of thread slipping through his skin and had to close his eyes against the desire to be sick. He felt blood pool around the edges of the prodded wound, though his uncle's competence kept the overflow to a minimum.

Thomas snipped the thread and set his needle aside. "Try to keep it as dry as possible," he cautioned, then shot his nephew a look. His gaze was entirely perceptive, always seeing everything. Lips tipping in sympathy, he added, "I'll tell her you're dressing. Take your time." Will nodded in gratitude, and the older man closed the door behind him.

He released a pent-up breath, shoulders sagging as he slumped over in relief. The sickening pain during his uncle's ministrations had faded to a dull ache, though leaning over in the chair sent all the blood straight to the wound, causing it to throb uncomfortably.

With a grimace, he rose, gingerly rotating the shoulder the Spaniard's blade had caught to test its mobility. The wound felt worse after his uncle's prodding, and the ache in his shoulder along with the sensation of freshly mended skin pulled tight was enough to keep him from lifting his arm over his head. But he would live, though he'd have a nasty scar to tell of his escapades.

Will shrugged the tunic back over his head, and his chest muscles constricted with the movement, tugging on the stitches. He gritted his teeth as he struggled to slip his arms through the shirtsleeves. It took him a moment to catch his breath before he could rejoin the others with a schooled expression, though he was sure his stiff gate and the sweat around his brow would telegraph his discomfort.

Sarah was leaning against the wall with her arms folded across her chest, gnawing on her thumbnail. When she looked up, she broke away from the wall and was quickly at his side.

Jaw tightening, he fought a wave of dizziness as she gently moved his poor arm over her shoulders for support. Her grimace let him know that he was doing a poor job of concealing the pain.

"Sorry," she whispered, slowly putting his arm back down. She eyed him with pursed lips. "Maybe you shouldn't go."

"I believe I'll rally the horses." Thomas shot his nephew a meaningful look before exiting through the front door.

Will turned to her, summoning a smirk. "Surely by now you must know that it will take more than a scratch to keep me down." He felt the cut on his lip stretch, which hardly helped his case.

Worrying her lip, Sarah nodded slowly. "Okay," she whispered, and he could tell she was reluctant to let him go. "If you feel it's something you need to do, then I won't stop you."

His heart swelled painfully in his chest. Her trust and faith in him, her acceptance of the duty he felt to protect her—even when she seemed set against it—caused warmth to flood his entire being.

Unable to resist, Will leaned down, gently brushing his lips against her cheek. When he pulled back, Sarah stared up at him in glassy-eyed surprise, mouth slightly agape.

"Sorry," he said, though his grin undermined his apology. "Sometimes I'm reminded of just how much I love you and can't help myself." Will hesitated when she continued to stare. "But I can stop."

Sarah was nodding, dazed, and then she shook her head quickly. He grinned at her vehemence, and her cheeks turned pink. However, she said nothing in reply, nor did he expect her to say those three words he longed to hear. It had been the truth when he'd said he would patiently wait for her to come to the same conclusion he had . . . Or not.

A muscle in Will's chest twisted painfully at the thought that she might never feel the same way for him, but he would accept it if things came to that. He would have to.

"Why don't you stay here for now?" he said, knowing his uncle wouldn't mind. And he didn't want her to go back to the castle unsupervised, even with Lisandro behind bars.

But Sarah looked uncertain. "I don't want to be a burden."

Chuckling, Will said, "Don't worry. My uncle will more than likely put you to work while we're away." That wasn't true, but he knew it would make her feel better to be of use.

She nodded, agreeing to stay. With a quick, crushing hug that sent pain through his wound but that he wouldn't give up for anything, Sarah whispered, "And, Will?"

"Mmm?" He felt a breath shudder through her and rested his chin on the top of her head.

"Let him know that the easiest thing and the right thing don't always look the same." She pulled back, brows furrowing and rising in sadness as she held her tears at bay. She added in a small voice, "And, please, tell him I know there's some good inside of him, even if he doesn't think so anymore. I have a feeling he's got at least one good deed left in him, and I hope that's turning over Cadius."

"I'll do my best to convince him of that," Will answered.

She dipped her head, nodding once. "I'll see you soon, then, okay?"

He gave her a tender smile that held the promise of his return. Snatching up the cloak tossed over the back of a chair, he stepped outside. Snow continued to fall, covering the ground in a fresh layer of untouched powder. His uncle was stroking the nose of his only horse, murmuring incoherently to the gray animal. It tossed its head contentedly beside the horse Thomas had ridden from the castle, which was ornamented in a gilded saddle and the purple-and-gold sash of the royal guard.

When he looked over, Will held up the garment. "Do you mind if I borrow this?"

Thomas shook his head and guided the horse over. "You'll need it in this cold, though I believe this should clear up fairly soon." He shot a discerning look up at the gray clouds releasing a shower of cottony fluff over their small world.

Will tied the cloak about his shoulders as he went around to mount the darker animal and was reminded of his own horse; he would have to check on the stallion after this business was settled, and also return the Joneses' mare to their home, if Seth hadn't collected her already.

"Will?" He glanced at his uncle over the horse's back. "Either I am entirely daft or things have changed between you and Sarah."

He didn't understand the older man's serious gaze. Will had thought he'd be pleased. "Yes, they have. But what you entered upon was entirely innocent," he felt the need to add.

Thomas nodded. "I sensed that. But, son, I must encourage you to be careful with her."

Will's brow turned down in a scowl of displeasure and confusion. "I don't believe anyone has ever suspected me of being care*less,* Uncle."

"I know, I know," Thomas said quickly to cool his nephew's temper before it arose. "It's plain to see that you care for her and will do your utmost to keep her safe from outside harm, but what about from yourself?"

Will had a sardonic reply at the ready, but he hesitated when the other man's meaning sank in. "I won't force her feelings, and I would certainly never put her in a . . . *compromising* situation, if that is what you're implying."

"It's not your intentions that concern me, son. I know you would never mar her reputation." The stormy bay shook its head, nickering softly. Thomas placed a hand on its neck to quiet the animal and stared at his nephew with a pained expression. "But you might not have to twist her arm as hard as you think to turn her affection your way."

Will frowned. "What are you saying?"

Thomas sighed, seeming to search for the right words. "Think about the situation from her perspective: You are a young, strong, and handsome man who rescues her from danger and constantly professes his love for her in deed and word." He raised a brow, as though his point were quite obvious. "That kind of dedication is appealing to women and can convince them of anything, especially in the midst of such romantic and perilous circumstances. She will have no choice but to fall in love."

Will felt his heart quicken in anticipation at the words, but he wondered at his uncle's displeasure. "I don't understand why this concerns you."

After a brief hesitation, Thomas rested his arms on the bay's saddle, leaning closer to Will. "I don't want either of you to find yourselves in a match where you are unequally yoked." Will frowned, wondering what ox had to do with he and Sarah. He said so to his uncle.

"She believes in God with her whole being; it's ingrained into who she is." Thomas smiled sadly. "Even if you didn't mean to draw her away, and

410

even if Sarah wasn't aware, she would slowly drift from her faith, either to please you or because it became easier to forget than to fight. You would both wake up one day and realize she had lost her identity."

His smile faded, the typical lines of mirth around his eyes softening. He looked away, but not before Will saw the ancient ache in his eyes. "You know what happened to me, and I don't want that kind of future for either of you."

Knowing the older man wasn't attacking his lack of spirituality but offering sage advice from his own experience, Will removed the edge from his tone. "I would never ask Sarah to give that up simply because I don't share her faith. It's a part of who she is."

Thomas nodded slowly, looking aggrieved. Will didn't understand what he had said to upset him. "I only want what's best for both of you," he commented after a moment's pause. "Just remember what I said."

Will nodded at the man who'd had such a large part in raising him. He respected his uncle more than any other man and would take his words to heart. "I will."

They rode in silence through the snow. His uncle set the pace, keeping his own bay at a mild canter to encourage Will's mount to slow. Will appreciated his thoughtfulness, but he still gritted his teeth against the jarring motion each time the horse planted its front hooves on the ground, and the languid pace was riling his agitation. He wanted to be done with this.

After an eternity of jolts and jerks, they arrived at the castle gates. The guards stationed there quickly opened the way when they recognized Thomas and admitted them into the courtyard, shooting each other speculative glances when they caught Will's appearance.

"Will Taylor is here to speak with the prisoner named Lisandro," Thomas said with authority, nodding in Will's direction. The older man jumped down from his saddle as the guard he had addressed snapped his fingers and motioned one of the guards wandering the yard over to them.

"Escort this man inside," he said to the newcomer, who looked no more than nineteen. "He is here to speak with the prisoner." The young man bobbed his head, snapping his heels together before marching over to Will.

Someone has taken drills a little too seriously, Will thought wryly. As smoothly as possible, he slid his left leg over the saddle and placed his feet on the ground, rather than dropping down. His wound throbbed enough already.

Thomas came over, escorting his horse. He took the reins of Will's former mount. "I can deal with these. You do what you must."

Will thanked his uncle and followed the young guard inside.

Though Will knew the ins and outs of the castle and its surrounding structures, both above and belowground, the guard had insisted on

411

accompanying him to show the way—for his safety, the man had claimed. Will had nearly scoffed aloud. No doubt word of the scuffle between he and Lisandro had already circulated among the guards, and this runt had more than likely been ordered to keep an eye on Will. For his *safety*, of course.

The hall ended suddenly and curved left up a tight, spiral staircase. Knowing exactly where he was, Will stepped in front of his young guide and quickly mounted the steps, hoping to beat his growing apprehension to the top. The stairs ended, and the small cell in the corner—which was usually unoccupied but had held the physician a mere day before—contained one black-and-blue Spaniard.

At the sound of shuffling feet, Lisandro scrambled away from the wall he was leaning against for support—he must have thought himself too good to slide to the floor—and hurried to the bars, one leg dragging almost imperceptibly behind the other. He peered through the bars, gripping them with one hand. The look of expectancy on his battered face quickly turned into one of annoyance as Will moved closer, the guard flanking the stairwell behind him.

The weather-beaten Spaniard grinned dryly. "Why do I even waste my strength on being surprised? I suppose it's too much to hope that she's been delayed? No?" His cocky mirth changed into a sneer. Or grimace—Will couldn't tell which with the way the man's lip and eye were swelling. It caused every expression to look like one of displeasure.

"I should have known you wouldn't allow her to come." No, definitely a sneer, judging by the Spaniard's tone.

Will's heart felt a little warmer just seeing the rogue brought so far down. Then he thought of Sarah's reaction to the sight of Lisandro's arm hanging limp at his side, one eye swollen nearly shut, his tan face marred by cuts and bruises. Will frowned, biting back any taunting remarks he might have felt the need to share.

"I came here on behalf of Sarah," he said diplomatically. "As you can imagine, she was frightened to be alone with you."

He couldn't say for certain, but he thought Lisandro might have winced, though the man quickly recovered, his haughty look returning. "And so you came in her stead to beat the truth from me."

Lisandro leaned his face closer, careful not to brush against the bars. He grinned. "You'll have a time getting me to confess, blacksmith." Then he pulled back, looking entirely pleased with himself.

Will clenched his teeth, sucking in a breath for patience before he opened his mouth, grounding out the words, "I came here to speak with you, which is the last thing in the world that I wanted to do, believe me."

Lisandro's attention appeared piqued for a moment, though his expression remained superior and quickly turned back to one of indifference. "And what pressing affairs could we possibly have to

412

discuss?"

Stepping closer, Will lowered his voice so the guard didn't overhear him. "Your involvement with the king's advisor."

A blink and a minor twitch of his good eye. Otherwise, Lisandro's look remained impassive, if not a little cocky: he knew he had the upper hand. "I haven't the faintest . . ." His eyes widened innocently. Actually, the one widened while the other drooped in amusement.

Will craned his neck, shooting the young guard a look. "Would you give us a moment?"

The guard looked uncertain. "I think I'm supposed to remain stationed here to observe the confession."

He stared him down with a withering glance, and the young man backed down the stairs slowly.

"I'll just be . . . Uh, I'll give you a moment."

"You do that," Will muttered, turning back to the prisoner with the sound of feet hurriedly retreating down the stairwell behind him.

"No more pretense, Spaniard. I'm here because Sarah believes you know something, and for whatever unfathomable reason, she seems to think you're worth keeping alive."

With a mocking, quizzical brow, Lisandro asked, "And how shall I be benefitted if I admit an association with a man I've hardly spoken to?"

Will clenched his fists. "If you turn him over, you won't hang on the gallows and will be transferred to solitary confinement, where we can offer you protection from Cadius." Which was too good for him, Will was tempted to add.

Lisandro scoffed. "Yes, two death sentences to choose between." He tapped a finger against his chin in mock contemplation. "However shall I decide?"

Will wanted to throttle the arrogant man. "Do you have any idea," he ground out, "how difficult this is for me to come here and ask for you to do something that will *save* your wretched hide?"

Sucking in a calming breath, jaw muscle twitching in restraint, he said more mildly through clenched teeth, "Sarah wanted me to encourage you to turn him over to the law to save yourself. Think of Cadius as your final bargaining chip."

The man's throat worked in a swallow, and he looked away. For the first time since he'd come up the stairs, Will saw true fissures in Lisandro's overconfident façade. His eye drooped further, as though the effort of holding it open was too much for the man to maintain as his hand slipped lazily from the cell bar. He appeared all at once to be the weary, defeated man Will had expected to find. The change threw him.

"So she does care," Lisandro whispered to himself, the words breathed out on a barely discernible laugh of triumph. His shoulders bowed, head

413

dipping wearily. "Did she say anything else?" he asked, eyes closed.

Will narrowed his gaze in scrutiny, wondering at his game. The odd thing was, he didn't believe the Spaniard was up to any tricks, which baffled him all the more. Seeing a crack in the man's stubborn resolve, Will took advantage of his weakened defenses.

He said, rather begrudgingly, "I know Sarah cares for you, and she has tried at least twice to convince me that your intentions weren't malicious. I suspect she wants to believe it herself." Lisandro glanced up sharply, a look of hesitant hope in his good eye.

Swallowing, Will said slowly, "I know she doesn't wish to see you hang." He managed not to wince, though the truth of the admission pained him. "As much as she and I disagree on this opinion, I side with her where Cadius' arrest is concerned. The last thing she asked of me was to convince you to turn him over to the law." Now that Will knew the Spaniard's weakness, he decided to play off of it to his benefit.

He lowered his voice, speaking to him man to man, his eyes almost beseeching. "She thinks you will do what's right, because for some reason that God only knows, Sarah wants to believe that there might be some good left in you—she said so herself. Can you truly remain silent and let her down?"

Lisandro's swallow looked painful, and he gripped one of the iron bars for support. Will drove in the final nail. "And she also wanted me to relay that right and easy are seldom the same."

The man's eyes slowly closed as he exhaled, lips curving in a self-deprecating smile. "No one has ever set standards that I should live up to them." Brow puckering, he mused aloud, "Have you ever noticed how small her hands are when you hold them? Yet such immense power. . . ." His voice faded.

Will's nostrils flared at the thought of them holding hands, but he could tell the man was weakening and wisely remained silent, waiting for the right moment to—

"In the bottom left desk drawer of my quarters, there is a secret compartment containing the correspondences between myself and Cadius for the past year." The Spaniard looked up at him then, through a veil of stringy hair. Will couldn't school his look of utter shock before the man caught his expression, though it didn't seem to make a difference that his admission had caught him off-guard.

Lisandro only appeared stoic as he continued in a monotone voice. "Two of the letters dictate my part in the immediate dismissal and removal of Gabriel Dunlivey for services rendered and Malcolm Devlin for unknowingly participating in the charade."

Will's brows rose before he could stop them. Had he heard correctly? The Spaniard watched him through his short lashes, his eyes fixed on Will in tired interest as he awaited his reply. Will squared his jaw. "Which are . . .?"

"Mentioned in previous missives," Lisandro said in resignation. "They are all hand-written and sealed by Cadius himself. I saved every single one as collateral, dating back to—" He stopped abruptly, cringing. Then his shoulders slumped. "I asked her to stop searching, and yet I am the one to admit it outright."

Will held his breath, not daring to move an inch.

The Spaniard shook his head and when he looked at Will, there was genuine fear in his eyes. His voice was hushed. "One letter dates back to a fortnight prior to the king's illness, requesting that I summon a rather sordid alchemist to the castle for a private meeting with Cadius. The man always seemed to be in his cups and needed money desperately. After their discussion, I paid the alchemist handsomely, though I can't say precisely what they spoke of." He shot Will a wry look. "But I think we both suspect what transpired. Cadius was always very smart and was never entirely straightforward about his dealings or what we were doing. But I am no blind fool."

Voice nearly a whispered, he added, "We all suspect the king was poisoned, and if you find the alchemist, you may be able to prove it, if that's even necessary."

Lisandro leaned back, appearing more relaxed now that it was out in the open. "Most of his commands during this event were entirely vague and verbal, so there is only one other missive from that time. In it, Cadius requested that I find pliable men who would do our bidding without any question of morals."

"A scapegoat," Will filled in disdainfully.

Lisandro looked pained by the term, but he nodded in agreement. "Yes. If they wished to convict us, they would also be admitting their own guilt by association, and we would reveal previous instances that were scrubbed from their records. So after Quinn became . . . *ill*"—his emphasis on the word spoke volumes—"we then placed Dunlivey on the guard to take care of matters outside the castle and hired John to take care of matters within."

Will pulled back in surprise, then breathed in realization, "John was sent to administer the poison."

Lisandro's mouth tipped ruefully. "Yes, and his death was not quite the unfortunate accident that you imagined. Both he and Dunlivey had expired contracts and were threatening to expose our dealings."

The corner of his nose twitched in disquiet. "As I told you, I was the one sent to deal with the matters of Gabriel and Mr. Devlin's dismissals, but I had no part in John's death—others were hired to eliminate him. I hadn't even discovered what had been done until that evening when the bodies were found. And what happened to Dunlivey was an accident," he was quick to add.

"And the woman who was found in the water with him?" Will's fists clenched, jaw spasming.

The Spaniard sighed. "An unfortunate accident. I can only assume that she was found with the man and refused to let them bring him to the falls." He grimaced distastefully. "So she went with him. Neither of the men sent to take care of the matter have admitted to there being a woman, but I suspect they're hardly trustworthy."

Will swallowed hard. Jade's death had been reduced to nothing more than a despairing tramp that ended up on the wrong side of the falls. He tried desperately to maintain his calm. "Is that all?"

"One more thing." The man's eyes were suddenly ablaze with a fury that Will had never seen in his dull gaze before. His knuckles whitened around the bar. "Make sure that Cadius burns for everything he's done."

Will narrowed his eyes in suspicion, wondering at the sudden fire in the foreigner's eyes. "Why keep up the lie? Why continue to work for a man you detest? You could have turned him in long ago."

The fight fled him in a rush, leaving the man looking drained and older than his years. "Because without the lie, without his money and support and the position he has provided, I am nothing. This all began so I could get back at my father, so I could outmatch the monster." Voice turning suddenly theatrical, Lisandro intoned in a thick Spanish accent, "'Never trust anyone but yourself; the devil was once an angel.' My father's motto," he supplied drolly.

Lisandro's eyes were tormented with the demons of his past, something Will knew quite a bit about. "But how do you defeat the devil without becoming one?" The Spaniard shook his head. "I don't blame my father, though; I did this to myself. I *chose* this path to reach my goals." His bleak gaze wandered his small cell, and he whispered, "And I must live with the consequences and battle my demons from this gilded cage."

He didn't want to—he desperately did not want to feel pity for this sorry excuse for a man. But he did.

Will frowned at his leniency, and he shook his head at himself, even as he felt a begrudging sense of mercy. Perhaps it was because he knew that this conversation might be the last the man had for some time. "I assumed Sarah was wrong," he admitted slowly. "I believed you to be entirely heartless in your dealings. Apologies." He managed not to cringe as the words escaped his lips.

"Those who are heartless cared too much," Lisandro whispered dolefully. Gaze wandering his cell, he muttered, "I so imagined my journey ending differently."

Will thought about that and mused aloud, "My father used to say that

416

any man who begins a journey of revenge should dig two graves, one for his adversary and one for himself. I suppose there's some truth in that."

Lisandro appeared to consider this. "He was a wise man." Eyes drifting to the high, barred window in the cell, he commented quietly, "You're an orphan—like me in a way." Gaze intent on Will, he asked, "Does it ever get better, or do we simply find a way to live with the pain?"

Will shook his head. He could not believe he was consoling a murderer, the man who had tried to steal Sarah away. Expelling a breath, he said, "I'm not sure if the pain ever goes away entirely. You simply make room for it and learn to live again."

Lisandro nodded, and the corridor lapsed into silence. After nearly a full minute of quiet, he opened his mouth again to suck in a breath. "Tell her . . . Tell her I'm sorry and that I did it all for her."

Watching him closely, Will asked in genuine curiosity, "Why Sarah? Why this fixation on her?"

"Other than the obvious?" Lisandro's almost sly expression melted away, and his eyes bore into Will's in complete seriousness. He whispered, "Because I care for her. And she is different from us—from everyone else in Serimone and Ridlan. She doesn't belong here, and I knew that she could help me escape this place and use her goodness to wipe away all of my iniquities. We could leave together and never look back."

Will had no idea what the man was rambling on about and remained silent. Sensing his desire to leave, the man asked urgently, "Can you relay a message for me?"

Gritting his teeth, Will waited, resisting the urge to turn and go, letting the message die with him. He felt pity on the man, but he was itching to leave this place.

Lisandro stared at the ground with dull eyes. He smiled faintly, lips quivering at the corners. "Let her know that I hope she's right—that there is yet good left inside of me." He met Will's eyes. "And don't worry. Your secret shall remain just so—for her, if she's ever to be mine again."

Will shook his head, almost in pity. "She will never be yours."

Lisandro's gaze swam with pained emotion, and he seemed to recognize the truth in that statement. "Just the same, give this to her." He reached behind him and pulled a small folded piece of parchment from his belt.

Raising a brow, Will asked dryly, "I see your connections haven't failed you, even in prison."

"I asked them to fetch it from my quarters. And a little ink and parchment is the least of their worries." On the contrary, those two things were what landed the man here, but Will didn't point that out. When he didn't take the letter, the Spaniard sighed and shoved it closer. "It's an apology. Be sure she gets it."

Will wasn't sure he wanted Sarah to have any reminder of this man's existence if it caused her pain, but then his shoulders sank when he realized that it wasn't his decision to make. He hesitantly took the letter and stuffed it into his pocket.

Lisandro visibly slumped with relief. "Keep her safe for me."

Will stared back at him and nodded once. "Until my last breath." It was the truth, but they both knew there wasn't much use in making promises to a dead man.

~*Chapter 50*~

Sarah had been a nervous wreck for the first few hours of their absence, but she had found a certain amount of peace by the time Thomas and Will rode up just before sundown. After a crushing hug, Will relayed, as best he could, all that Damien had revealed. Sarah hadn't imagined that he would confess everything so easily, though she felt a powerful sense of relief that his compliance would save his life.

Together, the two men explained that the letters were exactly where Damien had said they would be and were immediately confiscated by the royal guard. After perusing the missives, it was James T. Quinn himself who took Damien's testimony, jotting down every word of the twisted scheme. Then he sent a troupe of guards to seek out the down-and-out alchemist who had concocted the poison. The man, half drunk at the time, had tearfully confessed the entire thing under penalty of death and laid all blame at Cadius' feet.

With both written confessions in hand and a small audience in tow, Quinn confronted Cadius face-to-face, though the stony-faced man admitted nothing. Then the captain took the matter to the young prince, presenting both the mastermind and the evidence before Serimone's future king. Will said that he and his uncle were allowed to stand in during the hearing, since they had both played key roles in gathering proof against Cadius.

"There must have been a strong bond between Cadius and Prince Adrian," Will mused aloud at one point. He described how it had seemed especially painful for the younger man as he hesitantly, and only after a strained nod of encouragement from Cadius, professed his uncle's guilt and sentenced him to the gallows.

He was set to hang the next day.

Sarah sat heavily in a chair when they finished relaying the events. It was over. It was finally over. No crescendo, no dramatic denial: Cadius was found guilty, and justice had been doled out without her witnessing any of it. After all this time and all the accompanying trauma, it was almost anticlimactic to have it end so . . . peaceably. She blinked, feeling the weight lifted from her shoulders, though it was almost too good to believe.

Suddenly, a hole opened up deep inside as the full impact of this realization hit her. Sarah swallowed. It was all over.

"Are you all right?" Will tipped his head to study her face, weariness shadowing his bruised eye and deepening the furrow between his brows.

It would be too difficult to explain what had put the glum look on her face in light of such relieving news. Trying to collect her expression, Sarah managed a weary smile. "Just a little overwhelmed, I guess."

He nodded knowingly. "It's quite a lot to take in."

She managed to keep the despondency from her voice. "Yeah. A lot."

The men decided that keeping Sarah in a house with two bachelors as chaperones wasn't the brightest of ideas, so she and Will set off into the night on his uncle's bay. He dropped her off at the Joneses' and walked her to the front door like a gentleman. She expected—and wanted—him to kiss her goodbye, but instead Will wrapped her in a tender embrace. She snuggled against him, feeling his shoulders bow in exhaustion.

"Until tomorrow, love," he whispered, kissing the top of her head. Then he rode off, a knight on his horse.

Even after the tragedy of the day, Sarah was smiling as she went inside.

It was well after midnight by the time Sarah finished relaying every detail of the past three days to Karen, though that girl's eyes were bright with suspenseful excitement despite the hour. Sarah had earlier provided the Joneses with a watered-down and abbreviated version of the story, shocking them all with her tale. But she saved the especially detailed parts for her friend, who, sensing Sarah was holding back, had insisted that they spend the night in the barn together.

No one protested her declaration when they caught Karen's stern eye and steely resolve. They had known her long enough to tell when her mind was made up, which worked to Sarah's benefit this instance; there were just some things that couldn't be discussed in front of the family.

Wrapped in warm blankets, they huddled together around a lantern in the loft. Sarah smiled to herself. Just like old times.

"The alchemist and Cadius are set to hang tomorrow morning before dawn," she explained, suppressing a yawn. "I think Will said something about them wanting to do it as soon as possible and keep it quiet to contain some of the rumors—give the regime a little time to come up with some way to diffuse the situation, I guess."

Karen gave her a wry look. "Another term for spinning the story. But it makes sense that they wouldn't want word to spread that a diabolical murderer was advising the future king of Serimone." She shook her head in consternation. "But what about the others?"

"Thomas told me that a few conspirators came forward when they heard things going south, popping out of the woodwork because they wanted to make a deal before they were discovered, which was inevitable." With a nonchalant shrug, Sarah added, "Because they had a large hand in it, Damien and the other man the guards captured today will be moved at some point into solitary confinement outside the castle. But with everything else wrapped up so perfectly, I don't think they're in a rush to hassle with it."

Karen was watching her face closely with a pinched expression. "Are you doing okay? I mean, I could tell you really cared for Damien."

She had been trying not to think about that and had thrown herself into the story to keep her mind from her own feelings on the subject. Now that she was finished relaying the events of the day, her shoulders sank, and she sighed heavily. "Yeah, I did."

She forced a sardonic smile at her own ignorance. "I guess you were right all along, though—I can't seem to stay away from wounded puppies. And as much as I wanted him to be a good guy . . ." Her voice drifted off. Sarah bit her lip and glanced away. "He did the right thing in the end, but it hardly makes up for the part he played in all of this and the trouble he's caused."

"So he really tried to frame the Shadow for the murder?" Karen asked in disbelief. She scoffed, eyes flashing in defensive indignation. "What a trick. The Shadow has done nothing but good." She slanted Sarah a look. "That must have come as a shock to find out that it hadn't even been the Shadow, but Damien who had impersonated him."

Sarah looked down at her lap to buy time as she formulated a safe answer. Though Karen felt loyal to the Shadow for rescuing her from prison months ago, she still had no idea that it was Will who had really saved her that day. And Sarah wasn't telling.

At last, she replied carefully, "I knew it wasn't the real Shadow pretty quickly." Karen looked surprised, but Sarah recovered with, "It's like you said; he would never do anything to hurt anyone, so the fact that he tried to shoot me and killed Edith kind of tipped me off."

Wisely, like with her conversation with Will, she had left out her discovery of Robert's part in the charade. She hoped that someday he would be able to come clean with Will, but whatever he decided was his choice. And as much as she was itching to ask Karen about her relationship with Robert, it would be a little difficult to explain how she had discovered their story. She had promised him her silence, so Sarah stuffed her interest and clamped her mouth shut each time she was tempted to break that trust to satiate her own curiosity. And she certainly did not want to risk whatever was happening between Seth and her friend.

Realizing she had been silent for some time and that Karen was waiting for her to elaborate, Sarah added, "Discovering that it had been Damien and finding out his part in everything was a bit of a shock, but somehow everything started to make sense once I knew—his trips into town, not going where he said he was, disappearing for hours on end. And his informant came to him a lot. I overheard them a couple of times and thought they were just taking care of things that a lord had to do."

Sarah frowned, remembering. "But now I realize how much they were covering up. Like the bodies they found at the falls. I'd assumed Damien's concern was because someone was on a killing rampage, but now I see that he was surprised his men had taken care of things so conspicuously and was just covering their sloppy tracks." Shaking her head over her own stupidity, she whispered, "And I kept defending him to myself and others, trying to justify his actions. Maybe I knew he was up to something all along. I don't know."

Karen leaned forward and squeezed her hand. "But it was his testimony that put Cadius away," she reminded quietly. "Maybe he wasn't all bad. What made him change his mind and confess?"

Sarah released a mirthless laugh. "Will told him I wanted him to."

A slow breath whistled out from Karen's lips. "Wow. He really did like you."

That familiar tightening in her chest returned as she thought about Damien, and Sarah admitted quietly, "I turned him in, and he still did what I asked. He just wanted someone to love and believe in him." She grimaced, and Karen's mouth turned down in sympathy. Sarah shook her head at her woeful musings. "But at least that sadist Cadius will go down for killing his own brother."

The redhead perked up a little at that. "Mission solved, huh? Thanks to you." She nudged Sarah playfully.

She tried to smile, but it faltered. "Yeah, mission complete."

Then Karen seemed to understand her reticence, and her green eyes widened in realization. "Oh, Sarah." She wrapped her arms around her in a tight hug. Tears burned Sarah's throat as she held onto her friend. "But you'll come back," Karen said in a choked voice. "It's not like it's over."

"I guess not." She sniffed and pulled back to wipe her eyes. "Do you ever feel like you're living a double life? There are our lives at home, but then we have all our adventures and stand-in families here. Sometimes I feel like it's all pretend."

Karen's eyes roved the loft, a small, sad smile on her lips. "I understand what you mean, but no. I have nothing back there but a date of birth and two gravestones to remember my parents by." Her look turned wistful. "This place is my home and these people are my family. For me, the choice is easy."

The smile faded from her eyes, and her lips pursed. "But it isn't so cut-

and-dry for you, is it?" She sounded like she was musing to herself now. "You have your home family and your friends back here. And Will." She grinned suggestively.

Sarah groaned and flopped onto her back, the straw on the floor cushioning her fall. "Yeah, but I feel like I'm just putting off the inevitable. Where I come from, he's been dead for a millennium. I can hardly go to college in the twenty-first century and marry a blacksmith, time traveling between finals and making supper in a cabin. Talk about long-distance."

At her prolonged silence, Sarah glanced over to catch Karen's raised brow and sassy grin. "Marriage?" She asked slowly. "Something I missed?"

Sarah's eyes bulged, and she covered her face with her hands. "Didn't mean it like that," she muttered against her palms. Lowering her hands, she shot her friend a reproving look. "I was just using that as an example to show how impossible it all is."

Karen's eyes still held a mischievous sparkle. "So he isn't in love with you?"

Sarah opened her mouth to object but waited a split second too long. Green eyes widened enough to put a saucer to shame. "I knew it!" When Sarah didn't join in her excitement, Karen's elation faded into a slow frown. "Oh, I see what you mean."

"Yeah." Sarah released a breath, fluttering pieces of straw near her head. "So the more time I spend with him, the closer we grow. Until, what? I eventually stop coming back to avoid an extra appendage and leave him behind as nothing more than a great memory? That isn't fair to either of us," she whispered, plagued by her dilemma.

"But you aren't quite ready to break it off entirely," Karen observed gently, sounding wise beyond her years.

Cringing as she examined her motives, Sarah asked softly, "Does that make me a terrible person? Wanting to keep it alive for as long as possible and pray for a miracle?"

Karen's smile was gentle, reminding Sarah of her mom when she was getting ready to impart some sage wisdom on one of her distressed daughters. "No. It just means you're human. The obstacles in love are never easy to overcome, but the commitment to fight makes you stronger together." She angled her head to watch Sarah. "I'm not belittling your situation or the fact that you two have a special case, but nothing is impossible with God, Sarah. Never forget that."

It took a moment for Sarah to grin, but it was genuine when it came. "My words coming back to haunt me, I see."

Karen's laugh echoed through the rafters. "Think of it as taking your own brilliant advice."

They lapsed into silence, then, and it was Sarah's sigh that broke into the lulling sound of shuffling hooves and soft nickering. "I've been gone a long time, so I should probably head back soon."

Karen nodded grimly, knowing she meant back to Oklahoma, though it felt like a lifetime ago to Sarah. Jumping between worlds was making it increasingly difficult to keep track of what was *real*, and she found herself selfishly wanting the surreal to follow her home.

Suddenly, Karen's eyes shone brightly, and a shy expression stole over her face. "Do you think a wedding would be a sufficient reason to travel back?"

"I have plenty of reasons to come *back*," Sarah said, readying a list of the friends she had here. Then she sat bolt upright and gasped. "No! He didn't! When? How?" She frowned, her expression suddenly severe. "Tell me he did it right, otherwise I'll kick him in the seat meat and tell him to try again."

Karen laughed at her serious expression. Tears of joy sent her emerald gaze swimming. "This morning." She choked out a laugh and rolled her eyes. "And you know how Seth is."

Sarah cringed. "Oh no—"

Karen quickly shook her head. "No, no. I mean, yes, he tripped twice as we walked through the field to watch the morning sun and stumbled over every word he spoke when he finally got up the courage."

A wistful expression graced her face. Sarah had never seen her more beautiful than in that moment. "But it was perfect. The meaning behind the words, the look in his eyes. . . ."

Sarah's lips had begun to tip in a smile at her friend's words. "You're getting married," she breathed, unable to hide her joyous smile. Her heart ached a little at losing these special moments where it was just the two of them, but that feeling was quickly overshadowed by her excitement for her friend. "Have you two set a date yet?"

"Sometime in late spring." Karen grinned at her, almost sheepishly. "I was hoping I could come and kidnap my maid of honor for the big day."

Sarah felt her heart warm and nodded eagerly. "Of course! Just try to do your best to avoid midterms or finals." She widened her eyes in mock-fear. "Might be a little difficult to explain my absence to my professors. You know, time travel and all."

Karen laughed. "Will do, friend."

Then they hashed out their plans for the future—past and present—in the silence of the barn and fell asleep with smiles on their faces.

****

It was a heavy silence as she and Will strolled through the woods, both of their minds similarly occupied. He had come for her shortly after breakfast, receiving warm greetings from the five Joneses. Seth had pulled him aside for a moment as Sarah slipped on her cloak, and Will was grinning softly when he returned.

Now Sarah bit her lip, indecisive, as her gaze wandered the white canopy of limbs stretching above their heads. The snow had stopped sometime during the night, and the sun was already shining brightly overhead through the fluffy clouds.

"You're awfully quiet," she observed softly to the sky.

"I could say the same about you." She looked over, and Will was watching her intently. Dark circles rimmed his bloodshot eyes, and the bruises on his jaw and around his eye had turned a greenish-yellow color. Stubble lined his cheeks and jaw, shadowing the dark purple bruise she knew marred his chin.

Resisting the urge to scrub her thumb over the barely-there scruff, Sarah swallowed. "Is it over?" She didn't need to elaborate; it was what had them both so silent.

Will sighed, mechanically scrubbing a hand over his jaw like she had wanted to do. He grimaced when he rubbed the bruise and dropped his hand. "Yes. My uncle informed me that Cadius and the alchemist were both executed this morning." He stared at the ground and admitted softly. "Perhaps it was weakness, but I couldn't bring myself to go. Neither could my uncle, though I suppose no one was in attendance, anyway."

At the look of shame on his face, Sarah reached out to place her hand reassuringly on his back. Her chest swelled at the thought that he felt he could share his disgrace with her, that he trusted her enough to reveal something so personal.

His dark eyes registered surprise and pleasure at the easy touch.

"You shouldn't be ashamed that you don't enjoy the sight of death," Sarah encouraged softly. "Valuing life isn't a weakness or a flaw. I think it took courage to not go when your superiors view it as a celebration of justice."

She grimaced at the term and dropped her hand. Although the execution had been more of a private affair, she imagined spectators calling out obscenities and demeaning remarks at hooded men as they walked to the noose. Justified or not, Sarah knew she could never observe such a crude execution of justice, let alone participate in and *relish* something so disturbing.

She shivered at her train of thought and added, "I admire you for standing up for yourself, even when it went against the tide."

Eyes downcast, Will smiled. "Thank you." He slanted her a guarded look. "How are you fairing?"

She knew what he was asking and lowered her gaze. Stepping around a fallen limb, she replied honestly, "I'm learning to deal. I just can't seem to make up my mind whether to feel betrayed or sad or hurt or angry—at him or myself. It's all very confusing." Then she gave him a wry grin. "We girls are very good multi-taskers."

Will didn't make light of the situation. His hand fluttered in the air between them, as if to reach out and offer comfort. Then it relaxed against his side. "I'm sorry."

Dipping her head, she whispered a quick "Thanks."

He inhaled deeply and let it out in a rush. "Sarah, there is something—" He halted and seemed to be fighting within himself. With a grimace of dissatisfaction, he reached into his cloak and produced a small, crumpled piece of paper.

"What is it?"

Will frowned at the malformed parchment and tried to pull the corners straight. "It *was* a missive, but I believe I held it a little too tightly." He met her eyes. "Lisandro asked for me to give it to you."

Her shoulders drooped in surprise, heart sinking as she slowed to a stop. Will watched her reaction. "I thought about not following through with the cad's request because I didn't wish to see that look on your face. But it rightfully belongs to you."

Cautiously, Sarah took the letter with trembling fingers, staring at it in her hands. "What does it say?" she whispered, voice catching.

"I don't know."

Her eyes bore into the thin, wrinkled parchment as though she could decipher the words within. Then she stuffed the letter into the fold of her sleeve.

Will raised a brow. "You aren't going to read it?"

"I'm not sure I'm ready for whatever he had to say," she answered truthfully, then sighed. "I'm not sure I'll ever be ready."

He nodded in understanding, and they began moving slowly through the snow again. Sensing her unease, Will said with more cheer than the topic required, "So, Cadius has been revealed to be the mastermind in orchestrating the king's demise, and every last one of his accomplices has been apprehended. And my parents' murderer is dead." He sounded reconciled to the fact, though Sarah knew he would never be pleased with the result. "It's difficult to believe that it's truly finished."

She watched his face, heart softening at the lost look on his handsome, albeit bruised, features. "Do you think you'll ever be able to prove that Gabriel did it?" She hesitated and then asked softly, "Can you live with *not* knowing?"

Will's brow furrowed in contemplation as he searched his heart. Finally, he sighed. "I honestly can't say. I suppose I must live with it, but I know the desire to prove his guilt and avenge my parents will always be there, just under the surface."

She nodded in understanding. Just because something came to an end didn't mean that the result was satisfactory.

Sarah ducked under a low-hanging branch and teasingly poked him in the arm with her elbow, though her tone was serious when she spoke. "So what will the great Will Taylor do with his time now that the Shadow's vendetta is complete?"

His dark eyes moved from the path ahead and landed on her face. He stopped, and the slow, tender smile lit a spark inside Sarah's chest, warming her cheeks. She didn't think she would ever get used to *that* look from the closed-off Will she'd known.

He touched his fingertips to the back of her stiff hand, a whisper against her skin, and leaned down until he was a breath away. "I have some ideas," he murmured. Then he brushed his lips against hers, a soft caress that caused Sarah's toes to tingle.

Will pulled back, his intent gaze darkening as he grinned. "Somehow, I don't think a little free time will be a bother."

Laughing breathlessly, Sarah turned and continued on down the path. "We need to get you a better hobby," she called playfully over her shoulder.

He caught up to her in a few long strides, and she knew without looking that he was still grinning. "I'm rather fond of my hobby."

She rolled her eyes, though she felt a little spark of pleasure trail up her spine.

They lapsed into comfortable silence, then, the heaviness from earlier lifting after their conversation. Sarah tipped her face to the sky, closing her lids and smiling as the sun washed her face in warmth. She would miss the feel of the sun shining brightly amidst the cool winter wind, the sound of total silence in the woods, the smell of the earth and the evergreens amidst the scent of freshly fallen snow. It would be a change when she returned home to a hot and humid August in Oklahoma, but for now she just wanted to enjoy the feeling of this December moment.

A hand slid into hers, and she blinked, looking over at Will. He smiled knowingly, eyes tender. Her own lips curved upward. She sensed it meant a lot to him that she loved and connected to this land like he did.

Will gave her fingers a gentle pulse. "It makes you feel special, doesn't it?"

"Yeah." For reasons he couldn't understand. She had been marveling at God's amazing creation, but she wasn't sure if he would attribute the sights surrounding them to a God he didn't call his own.

He lifted her hand as they strolled and stared at her palm, as if in great contemplation.

"What?" she asked.

Will shook his head and said softly, "I was just marveling at how small your hands are." At her quizzical look, he smiled and lowered their clasped hands. "Just something I was told."

427

They had been wandering for over an hour by the time they decided to head back to the Joneses'.

"This is nice," Will said as they lazily walked along the snowy path, gently swinging their hands between them. Sarah nodded in agreement, though for her it wasn't enough time. She sighed quietly. *Never enough time.* And she had put it off for long enough.

"I'm going home soon." She cringed at how cavalier she sounded. No segue.

Will looked down at her sharply. "Oh." He swallowed. "Of course. Umm, when were you planning to leave?"

"Tonight," she whispered.

His lips parted ever so slightly in an expression of discontent, but his face remained passive. "So soon," he whispered. Then he nodded slowly as if he understood, and it was obvious to Sarah that he was trying to be accepting. For her.

She dragged in a breath of the crisp air, though it didn't smell quite as perfect as it had before. Maybe she was already losing her connection to this place. The thought saddened her. "I've been gone for awhile and need to head back, but I couldn't leave without saying goodbye this time."

Will halted and used his free hand to finger a strand of her hair, staring at it intently as though it could unlock the key to their separation. "I'm glad you told me." He met her eyes and asked hopefully, "When will you come back?"

That was the difficult part. She swallowed. As if on cue, she caught the faint, joyous shouts drifting on the breeze toward them—Seth and Karen must have shared the big news.

Taking a breath, Sarah hedged, "Well, I'll be coming back for the wedding."

Will looked vaguely amused as he caught wind of the celebration. "Yes, Seth told me—" The lock of hair slipped from his numb fingers. "He said they were considering spring."

Sarah nodded grimly.

"Four or five months," Will whispered, looking pained.

"It's not so bad. We've done it before." Well, he had done it before. She had only made it two weeks. Sarah frowned. She hadn't exactly calculated the time difference into her plan, but she hoped it would only be mere weeks before Karen showed up on her doorstep again.

Will's chest shuddered as he inhaled deeply. "All right. If you must leave for now, then I can't stop you." He shook his head with more fervor than she had expected. "But do not think I am letting go. Perhaps I can travel back with you someday to meet your family."

She smiled at his hopeful words, though it faded quickly as she remembered how impossible that was. "You know, when I come back . . ."

428

Her voice drifted off, eyes searching his face in shy uncertainty. "Where will we stand? We've never really defined"—she motioned between the two of them—"*this.*"

He stopped, looking like the thought had never crossed his mind. Then he smiled softly. "I'd assumed it was obvious." Stepping closer, he said lowly, "Sarah Matthews—Lady Fair—I have some very long-term goals in mind for us, if you'll consider them."

It warmed her insides to know he had given this some thought—a *lot* of thought—and she felt a grin of surprise twitch at the corner of her mouth before she remembered that it wasn't that easy. "We're just so different. Do you really think we can make this work?" Why was she trying to dissuade him?

Because you're too weak to walk away yourself. Sarah winced at her answering thought, knowing it was true. She didn't have the resolve to end things.

Will looked so sure that she held her breath, forgetting all her doubts. He tucked a strand of hair behind her ear. "Yes, I do."

"But how?" she whispered, needing to know his answer.

"Because if you want something enough, you'll fight for it. And our differences are hardly an issue." He grinned. "I'm not sure if you've noticed, but I am entirely adaptable."

Sarah felt the weight on her chest lighten, though it did not disappear altogether. Like Will's past, the uncertainty would always be there, hiding just under the surface. But for now, she chose to hope. "So this isn't the end for us?"

"Of course not, love." he touched her cheek and leaned down, his lips a breath away when he whispered, "I have a feeling this is only the beginning."

~Epilogue~

Damien shuffled slowly down the hall, careful not to overstep the small strides allowed by the chains around his ankles. Armed guards flanked him on either side, and, should he fall behind, he knew they would not hesitate to deliver a few blows to "motivate" him to move faster. So he was careful to watch his steps as they guided him through a low doorway and into the open air.

Pain shot through his throbbing skull at the natural light, and he lifted his fettered hands to shield his eyes from the glaring sunrays. After months spent locked away in the dark dungeons far below the castle, having been moved there from the tower a few days after his imprisonment, the muted sunlight streaming through the cloud cover was blindingly painful.

Someone prodded him from behind when he hesitated, and he moved tentatively down the rough stone steps. His progress was slow and awkward as the short chain barely allowed him to place one foot on the edge of the step and his other foot on the one below. A guard shoved him forward when he moved too slowly, and Damien stumbled, barely maintaining his balance. He turned around to glare at the guard, who stared straight ahead, ignoring him.

Damien turned his eyes back to the ground to watch the last step, a prisoner shuffling behind his captors. The long chain tying together the manacles that bound his hands and ankles dragged across the cobblestone at his feet as he shuffled awkwardly toward the waiting caravan. It looked ominous and final with dark, peeling wood and a small barred window at the back. The old, weathered driver hunched atop it watched their approach, glaring at Damien and gripping the reins a little tighter when they made eye contact.

Damien swallowed hard, keeping his head high while still being mindful of his steps. Never let your adversaries see you cowed—his father had taught him that much.

430

A stony-faced guard broke away from the group to open the back of the caravan, holding the small door open for the prisoner.

Damien flinched at the darkness within. He was in no hurry to enter the vehicle that would transport him out of the city and to a prison where he would live out the remainder of his dismal future in solitary confinement.

But he moved toward the open door mechanically: There was no point in delaying his fate.

The two men at his side grabbed him at the same time to help him into the back of the caravan, since he was unable to lift his feet onto the high step. The ceiling was low, and Damien had to crouch as he turned around, trying not to register surprise as he stared in recognition at the guard who had gripped his hands to help him adjust.

He could feel the outline of cold steel between his palms. The man caught his eyes briefly, and Damien thought he saw a faint nod just before the guard motioned for the door to be closed.

Damien heard the *click* of the latch being secured from the outside in the quiet of the caravan, but he felt no despair over what should have been a sound of finality, marking an end to his free life. He sat down on the short bench seat and didn't bother to glance at the object in his hand. He already knew what it was.

His ticket to freedom.

Sarah and the blacksmith had thought that by imprisoning him, they had put an end to the madness he had found himself caught in the midst of. But they had no idea what they had gotten themselves into. This was bigger than either of them could imagine, and it would not stop because he was behind bars.

In essence, Cadius was the mastermind behind the entire plot—a puppeteer controlling every piece in his debauched puzzle—but they were wrong in assuming everything set in motion years before would suddenly cease once Cadius saw the gallows. Everyone seemed to have overlooked the most vital piece, the person at the center of it all, and the wheels of this plan would continue to turn without Cadius setting them in motion.

Damien knew he was one of an elite few who were aware that everything was already in motion. The cart bumped through town. Through the bars, he caught a few curious stairs from the townsfolk, as well as some fearful glances. They were all ignorant.

His shoulders slumped in exhaustion, but not yet defeat. It would be impossible to stop what was currently happening before their very eyes, even if they didn't yet recognize it. He knew that it was only just beginning, and if Sarah tried to stop it, she would find herself caught in the crossfire.

He stared through the bars at the hazy sky beyond, imagining that she was out there, somewhere. Had they already found her? Had his months of infuriating seclusion made him too late?

431

He ground his teeth in vexation, fetters jangling as he rubbed the mark over his heart—a ghastly T. The symbol had been burned into his skin the second night of his imprisonment. Months had passed and still the mark ached, recalling to mind the feel of the hot iron as it branded him as the traitor he knew himself to be.

He tightened his grip on the key, feeling the rough steel bite into his palm, feeling anger course through him. No, it was far from over.

www.ingramcontent.com/pod-product-compliance
Lightning Source LLC
Chambersburg PA
CBHW030929020726
47498CB00001B/173